Wolf's Blood

Wolf's Blood

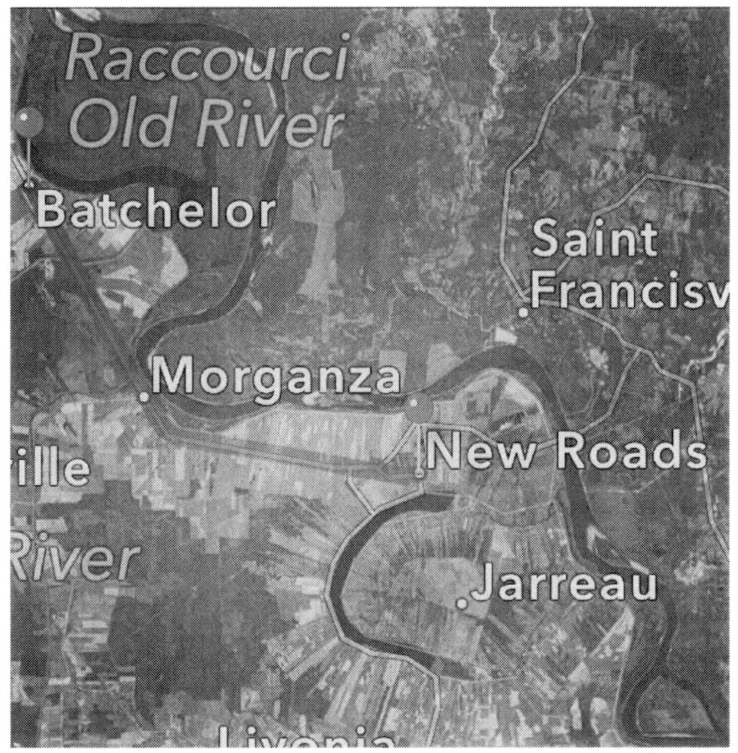

Mikhail Kerrigan

ISBN:	Hardcover	978-1-4990-7329-4
	Softcover	978-1-4990-7330-0
	eBook	978-1-4990-7328-7

This book was printed in the United States of America.

Rev. date: 11/07/2014

To order additional copies of this book, contact:
Xlibris
1-888-795-4274
www.Xlibris.com
Orders@Xlibris.com
553933

Acknowledgments

To Clover, the figment of my imagination,
Without which it would not be possible
My brother Chris, Brian and
Grandma Betty

Prologue

Raccourci Island, LA
1844 A.D.

I

Poison green eyes tore through the mists toward the Malstros' two-story plantation. Set back almost in the middle of Raccourci Island the plantation profited from the Mississippi's erratic nature. They produced a healthy amount of profitable sugarcane, but when the river spills its banks the laborers quickly switch over to rice production. The beast, panting in the hot Louisiana night crept up slowly, careful to not betray its strategic position in the sugar fields. He was keeping crouched down as he moved, almost onto his belly, until there were only several yards left until the end of the sugarcane.

Moonlight cast an eerie glow as the wind blew the Weeping Willows to and fro. Shadows danced along the ground from the blowing branches. The atmosphere was eerily quiet as the Wolf pack stealthily approached. Only the horses, a half mile away in a stable by the laborer's shacks, which were down by the swamps, sensed a preternatural presence and they paced back and forth nervously. A Wolf-thing with green eyes had broken from the pack, a twisted abomination of dire wolf and man mixed together, hunting for livestock. This night was not unlike every other night where he was stepping farther into human domain and killing easy game. Tonight was a different matter altogether, though. The lycanthrope sat on his haunches, hidden in shadow along the edge of the field.

With slits for glowing green eyes, his form was something out of a nightmare. His sleek black withers looked like a shadow in the scenery, and his lupine shape towered over the little goats he stalked every night. But now he pined for something other than food. The smell of a human girl hung thick in the air, and it led in the direction of the house, upstairs. He grunted steam from his nose; his ears were animated, searching for threats anywhere, swiveling at the smallest sounds. He had a short muzzle and thick shoulders, a long body and long legs. The creature's tail stood up in dominance. Her fragrance was emanating from the upstairs of the house and it was intoxicating. This night a different aroma hung in the air somehow. He smelled a mixture of him residing in her now and it emboldened him to come closer than he ever had before.

He zeroed in on the upstairs window. The light of the candles glowing in the room made it easy for him to see in. He focused his eyes toward the human shape. He remembered her even if it was only a silhouette that he was looking at. Candle light flickered and wavered as he watched, he adjusted his eyes to see the girl getting dressed beside her bed. He was suddenly grateful for his exceptional eyesight. Lust-filled thoughts teased him and his self-control began to ebb. A lust fueled heat started in his powerful neck and flowed down to his groin. Just then, for a brief moment, the curtains fluttered open further. A great surge of excitement rushed through the beast as he sat staring wantonly at her in the moonlight. His eyes moved from her soft blonde hair to the delicate ivory radiance of her bare skin. It had been countless years since he last felt that which a man feels for a woman.

The beast tilted its head, and the yearning for her touch began again. He could practically taste her rose scented flesh when a subtle change came to his nose on the wind. Every instinct warned him to be cautious, to be weary of his hiding place. Nevertheless, he inched closer, his lupine form now visible in the moonlight, a wolf with the mind of a man.

Aticus treaded a fine line between sanity and truly going insane. This night, coupled with the sweet fragrance of the girl his right mind turned a left. Damn them, the pack's fear of humans, he thought. They were pitiful things, weak and stupid, no better than their own livestock. Why should any of them fear humans? Most humans no longer even acknowledged his kind anymore. Humans were the prey, abundant and ignorant, his cousin taught him that; but the pack still refused to hunt them. He felt that eating the human's livestock was no better than being a mere dog, begging for scraps. Even now, he could faintly hear nervous whimpering, as his pack crept toward the pens. It was different in the old days. Hunting wild game then, this was plentiful with human existence still in its infancy. But the human population had exploded. As a result, finding wild game unmolested or unprotected to freely hunt, was few and far between, and the forests made way for dwellings and cities.

Aticus tried to stop it, but the fury stirred in him. He felt justified in his carnal hatred towards humankind. After all, they had hunted him first. It was man who hunted down his cousin on his father's side, known as the beast of Ge'vaudan, years ago and killed him. It was man who surrounded Aticus in a field of rye. It was man who set ablaze the fields, hoping to burn him alive like they'd done to so many of his kind already. It was during that horrid plague that man thought, almost rightly so, that night-walking wolves and other such witchcraft was the cause. He grinned, thinking, teeth clenched. It was his only solace some nights that humans were often oblivious to the countless hordes of innocent mortals murdered, caught up in their own bloody hysteria.

The human mob had wanted him to die, had almost succeeded, almost. The flames had begun to lick at his flesh, and the acrid smoke was billowing forth, choking him. Pure instinct and adrenaline took over, and he began to dig furiously. There was no escape from the fire except down into the earth. So he buried himself in the moist soil, digging ever deeper down. He dug for what felt like an eternity. Eventually he lay completely immersed, snug in his own personal grave until the fires finally died down.

He was horribly scarred. It was on almost his entire body and he was still struggling to breathe from the heat that had singed his lungs, his face almost unrecognizable as he lay dying from his injuries. Fire was the one thing besides silver that he couldn't heal normally from. But a chance encounter of another lycanthrope had saved his life. The Wolf Devon or at least that was the name the lycanthrope called his self. He vaguely heard yelps and grunts, though he wasn't sure. The delirium grew and it was hard enough to concentrate. Devon, in wolf form, repositioned himself so that Aticus' head was near his groin then he hiked his leg. Hot salty urine went in to Aticus' mouth making him gag reflexively. Then Devon's stream worked its way to the center of Aticus' severely burned and scarred body. As soon as the wolf was done relieving himself he stepped back and watched his urine as it worked miracles.

Aticus' scars started to harden in a yellowish transparent shell and then cracked and fell away leaving pinkish but healed skin on his chest. In addition, Aticus' labored breathing was better now as he coughed up yellow crystals. In all his years, he thought, if a werewolf has been burned it would be the death of them. He stared in amazement at Devon.

Devon scratched his claws across his forearm until blood steadily flowed. He cupped his hands as the blood trickled into his palms and offered his life force to Aticus who selfishly gulped the blood down, the overspill trickling out over his chin. Devon explained to Aticus in his mind that the canine has a remarkable ability. Two separate breeds mate and their offspring become a wholly new breed all its own. So true of the lycanthrope, but instead of breeding, one kind gives their blood to a separate breed and the blood temporarily gains the abilities of the donor.

Now, almost dying from his wounds, the words of his grandmother made sense to him. As she, So-seti, tutoring him before she got caught and was presumably killed by hunters, had said that only the lucky lycanthropes survive to see the next millennium, long life was a long shot. Evident by the absence of his lycanthrope aunts and uncles that had been hunted and killed when Aticus was young for their constant persistence to enter into human lands and hunt human owned livestock; gorging themselves until the humans were fed up with them.

Devon had given Aticus so much blood and urine the blood had mutated. Aticus could not be engulfed by fire like Devon but he could be immune to a brief flame. He went to the newfound Americas for a fresh start, leaving Devon behind, which made his heart ache a little, shriveled black thing that it was. He knew from the first moment he looked into Devon's eyes that he was an intelligent lycanthrope and he could have learned much from him.

The New World, he hoped would heal his scarred psyche. He would be inconspicuous because the land was still so vast, uncharted and untamed. He was very wrong. Humans from all countries began to come in waves, building houses and churches. The Christians started paranoid inquisitions of their own, separate from the already whispered tales of pagans and other religions, sending his kind into hiding again. For all the horrors bestowed upon him by humans. When he thought about the young girl upstairs he found himself softening up again. After all, this young woman he watched had found him almost naked in the forest once, and instead of running in fright, she was mystified and intrigued. Shaking himself out of the memory, he was horrified to find himself almost at the edge of the front porch. It was almost like his body was on autopilot and Alicia was the programmed destination.

II

Alicia finished writing and closed her diary. She quietly stored it away beneath a loose floorboard under her bed. She hated to be secretive but she feared her father had been snooping around her room of late. Her heart hurt thinking of her father and what he must be thinking about her. As quiet as she'd tried to be, she was almost certain he had heard her leaving a few times as the sun was coming up. Though she thought his nervousness probably had more to do with the unexplained killings of their livestock weekly. She had watched him carry what was left, usually only a bloody pile of bones, to the edge of the woods several times and bury it. He never spoke of it, so she never asked. She had grown paranoid that her father secretly knew about her clandestine gallivants but she could not tell him about Aticus, how could she ever explain her love for him to her father? She couldn't even explain it to herself really. It was a soul deep connection she felt to him.

Deciding that a quick wash would make her feel better, she grabbed the small bottle of perfume from atop her dresser. It was the only reminder she had of her mother, it a reminded her of a warm summer's day laying in fields of flowers so she only used it when she was in dire need of feeling safe and comfortable. She undressed and laid her robe neatly across the four-poster bed, and then she headed toward the washroom where she filled a washbasin and sparingly added drops of the scented oil.

Her blonde hair, still wet, shone silvery in the candlelight and the smell of roses and apricot oils from her bath still hung in the air. She had a striking beauty about her, an hourglass figure, graceful neck, and heart shaped face. She slipped the cotton nightgown over her head, covering her budding breasts and pink nipples, taut from the cool night air. She opened the curtains wider; the reflections of her own face briefly startling her. She laughed at her own nervous reaction while unconsciously rubbing her thumb across her new onyx necklace a gift to her from her secret lover, just as she did every time she was anxious of late. She was ivory skinned and still slightly baby faced, her wide blue eyes gave the impression of surprise and her small cupids bow lips curved up in a smile even when she wasn't happy at all.

She knew it was silly. No one was there in her window and the bedroom door was closed, but she could not shake the feeling of being watched. She turned back to the window, straining her eyes against the darkness, trying to make out the tree line. Then she caught a brief flash of green orbs below. It was a familiar green and reminded her of the man she had so recently found in the forest. A man who was strangely attractive and alluring, he had called himself Aticus. She thought about sneaking out this very night to visit with him in the quiet of the woods. She did not tell her father about him but she found herself thinking about him often during the times when they were apart. She pulled the curtains closed and sat down at her vanity, brushing slowly through her blonde hair; a ritual that soothed her since she was a little girl. She was almost asleep sitting in the chair when she heard a commotion coming from downstairs. She gasped and jumped up as she heard a gunshot echo into the night, her heart racing.

III

Gerome Malstros, a potbellied but otherwise muscular, elderly farmer and retired military man, had short-cropped gray hair, and light brown eyes that sat in a round, reddened face, watched his livestock from the screen of the open door in his living room. Though seemingly calm, he stood at the ready, blunderbuss in hand. The gun he got during his stint in the French militia, funded by a prosperous position in the God's Light Inquisition, a radical fringe unit loosely tied to the Catholic Church, dedicated to eradicating all the "children of the night". Mirtha, his second wife, was fast asleep upstairs, and he knew Alicia was taking a bath, her scented oils wafted down the stairs. The scent of roses reminded him of happier times before his first wife fell ill. Gerome could not sleep because for weeks now something had been picking off his cattle and occasionally one of his bigger goats. He often went to check the chicken coops but recently he had discovered a massacre there at well. He wondered if Mirtha's sudden onset of illness hadn't been from worry over the state of their farm. He was determined that tonight he would see them through till morning without a loss.

The teeth and claw marks told him that it was a big animal, definitely more than one. When he checked for prints, he knew the horrible, yet unbelievable truth. They were wolves and huge wolves at that. He had even seen a six-foot alligator splayed open and half eaten at the edge of the river further in the woods. If this could be believed, and the town was alive with rumors of the half beasts called loup garoux, werewolves. A sneer crossed the man's face. He knew their secret, though there was little a fat old man past his prime could do about it. He paced around the living room, his overalls making a familiar swishing sound. Gerome stoked the fire place once again, adding a few logs. Then he resumed his place beside the screen door again.

"It's gotten bolder," he spit a pocket of chew out into an empty can as he focused in on glowing green eyes across the field. Legend or not, *something* was edging closer and closer to the house.

Close enough now that Gerome could make out the outline of black fur and white fangs as he stood in the doorway. He turned and lifted the lantern off the shelf by the door. He had it lit and before he had time to think about it, was running down the porch steps, as fast as his bloated legs could carry him. What was he doing? He wondered wildly. If he died tonight, who would take care of Mirtha and Alicia? He could not imagine that Alicia would be consolable; she had been so fragile since her mother had passed away, and had never really warmed up to Mirtha, had never considered his second wife anything like a mother. His heart was racing so fast he could see it in the rapid rise and fall of his own chest as he slid to a stop out in the yard, and only a few yards from where the beast sat on its haunches. He could faintly smell the putrid breath of the beast as it panted languidly, almost drooling. He began to second-guess his impulse to come out into the darkness, and tried to catch his breath, to get control of his rage.

"Get off my land!" he screamed at it as if the animal could understand him. Suddenly remembering his weapon, he threw down the lantern and brought up the barrel of his gun and trained it on the dark shape, but the beast sat still in defiance. It even seemed to straighten its posture before it pointedly dropped its eyes from the girl's window and looked into the farmer's own, shining green pools staring back at him above glistening white fangs.

A low, deep guttural growl emanated from its throat. It smelled the anger that seeped out of Gerome's every pore, but it smelled fear that emanated from him as well. It was a musky aroma that he rather liked a lot. The weapon would do little good for the man before sharp fangs could tear soft flesh. It rose up on the balls of its feet now, lengthening, standing erect before this dump of a man, more than six and a half feet tall. It curled back its lips to reveal a mouth full of jagged fangs wet with saliva. Huge muscles rippled beneath its ebony fur. A lupine visage, with vaguely human shaped arms and legs, six inch claws unfurled finishing the image of the beast.

Gerome's eyes widened in shock, he couldn't believe what he was seeing, what he had ever only half believed had just come to life before him. Just a minute before he had been looking at something, albeit freakishly large, that had wolf or animal features. Now this thing was halfway human, or a grotesque mixture of both. Gerome gaped at the huge beastly form as it prepared to lunge at him......and with blinding speed, that had become second nature to him after the days of pirating on the Gulf, Gerome lit the fuse of the gun and aimed. The flash and crack of the blunderbuss discharging startled the wildlife around them.

In one quick horrifying second the beast saw the glimmer of round shiny moons, the images of her Majesty the Queen of France, in the center. At the same instant he realized, horrified, the smart old bastard had filled the blunderbuss with silver coins! Death passed before his eyes, heat and searing pain spun him around as the coins found their mark. The impact knocked him into the mud. A stream of crimson trickled down from the socket where his left eye had been only moments before. The wounded beast convulsed madly, clawing at its face as Gerome watched in silent disbelief, his mouth gaping. The injured beast shifted back into a human like form, except for the left side of its face which was a twisted mass of lupine features without an eye and bits of matted bloodied fur which was pulsating, seemingly no longer under his voluntary control.

The beast went down on human hands and knees, now a pale nude figure of a man with long black stringy hair that hung in clumps about its face. It touched its ear which remained a wolf's ear, twitching and bleeding. Then it touched its nose, a twisted mixture of human and animal. The pain was unbearable. Where the silver met its mark, it was a constant state of flux, trying to transform to wolf or man but failing to commit to either. It then grasped at the gaping hole where its eye had once been rocking itself in anger and howling in pain.

Gerome gave a shout of victory before he caught the glaring red-rimmed eye of the wounded abomination. Glowing with rage, its fangs bared in hatred, cold chills rippled up Gerome's spine as he met its singular gaze.

"Poppa!"

Alicia came running down the stairs from her bedroom, her legs taking her bare feet two steps at a time, but stopping at the cusp of the screen door, horrified by what she saw in the yard. With her dad's forgotten lantern dimly lighting the scene, she saw the man prostrate on the ground before her father.

"What…what have you done?" She shrieked, tears streaming from her wide eyes.

She saw the injured man, her man from the secret outings, saw his naked manhood, powerful biceps, chiseled abdomen, and she could even see the fine hairs that covered his skin. Despite everything, this excited and shamed her. She could not help herself. She found herself unable to look away from him, even despite the intensity of the situation. She could not see the bloodied side of his face. He had his head down low, his hand covering the wound, but she could quite obviously see he was in pain.

The man-thing saw Alicia in the doorway. The fireplace illuminated her face, casting soft shadows on her expression of wonder and horror. She stood shivering in her nightgown. He could see the silhouette of her soft body and the tears that ran from her beautiful, stunned eyes. He felt something tugging at him, pushing its way to the surface, something he had not felt in centuries. He felt humiliation.

Another beast, a larger reddish-brown wolf with golden brown eyes, leapt over the cotton covered ground toward them; fur standing on end, aware that a shot had been fired, running to the black haired man's aid. This beast had almost the exact form of a true wolf, only huge in comparison, and it had short dreadlocks in its fur. Two others, a grey wolf and a fiery red wolf fled when they heard the shot. Treading cautiously, the brown furred beast was weary of drawing too closely to the farmer but clearly concerned for the man. The wolf, Tomas, growled at Gerome who was standing in front of his pack-mate, in frustrated anger. Gerome hoped that the beast before him didn't know his gun was empty and he had spent his shot, and he stood his ground, fearing to turn his back. Now there were two of them and he had only a lantern on the ground with which to defend himself. Cold beads of sweat formed in the lines of his face, a stalemate. It seemed that it could last for an eternity.

"Poppa, what have you done?" Alicia screamed again, and was off the porch now and heading, barefoot, straight towards the wounded man with up-raised hands.

"No don't!" Gerome barked, stepping between his daughter and the wolf thing, never letting his eyes drift away from the wounded thing or the large brown wolf.

Alicia didn't stop but she slowly crept up to the wounded man. She found herself reaching out to comfort the man from the forest, the musk he radiated intoxicating her.

The half man with black hair could not let Alicia see him like this. Embarrassment colored his pale face and Aticus twisted his body away. He sprang up from all fours, and ran off into the cover of the darkness beyond the lantern's light. He could hear Tomas close beside him. Through the weeds and the thickets he ran, morphing into his animal form. Dirt changed to mud as his paws sank into the earth. Further and further they moved until he could feel drops of water on his face. When he could run no further he had stopped at the marsh, almost to the makeshift cabin he called home. He converted back to the broken man as he climbed the steps with the aid of two others, into the stilted cabin long ago abandoned by the help when they moved to the other side of the river one particularly rainy season.

As soon as the old man rushed to comfort his near hysterical daughter, the other beasts that had hidden when the altercation began, leapt from their hiding places behind an old shed and followed their pack mate into the darkness. When Gerome looked back he saw a blood dotted trail where the beast had fled back into the shadows. He would have pursued them, foolishly, had his concern for Alicia not been so urgent. Once he was able to coax and shuffle her back inside, Gerome finally calmed her down a little. He went about making sure all the windows and doors were nailed and bolted securely shut while Alicia sat clutching a blanket around her before the fireplace, sipping gingerly on the tea he had made her. He sat beside her and they both shivered despite the heat.

Gerome went upstairs briefly to check that the commotion had not wakened Mirtha. She lay upon the bed, peaceful in her sickness, sleeping. He could hear the wheeze that she made every time she inhaled. He stood there a moment, listening, and then slowly backed out of the room and shut the door quietly behind himself. Back downstairs and into the living room, Gerome gently touched Alicia's shoulder. She turned and he could see that she looked muddled and drawn, her eyes sunken orbs and moist tears clung to her cheeks; she had regained her usual composure, however.

"Go wake up Victor and the others. Tell them to saddle the horses." He said, knowing that no harm would come to her in the brief walk back to the servant's quarters behind the house. "After that, hurry up and go get dressed."

IV

Aticus was still losing blood, his already pale skin turning a splotchy blue. He stumbled into some clothes, not bothering to button up the shirt he put on, and then went to a trunk in the corner of the room. He threw open the lid so violently that the hinges burst, clattering onto the floor, the lid hitting the wall at an angle. Tearing through the contents until he found what he had been looking for, a French double-barreled flintlock shot gun.

"What do you think you're doing?" Tomas gripped Aticus' forearm and spun him around.

"Someone get me a rag for the bleeding!" Aticus growled, ignoring his friend as if he wasn't there, barking his demands to anyone who would listen.

A gray haired old woman offered him a shirt that he quickly snatched from her hands and ripped up until it fit the upper left side of his face and he wrapped it once around his head and tied it off. After a quick adjustment, Aticus proceeded to fill the double-barreled shotgun with black powder, pack it, and load it. He inspected the gun briefly, pressing down a switch to reveal a razor sharp bayonet. He folded it back into place until he heard the click and then started off; pushing past faces frozen and afraid. He could only imagine how he looked to them right now. He was slightly trembling, whether from blood loss or rage he didn't know.

"Wait!" Tomas barked, pressing his palm into Aticus' chest," At least let me get my clothing on and grab a gun."

Aticus waited impatiently tapping his foot, adjusting and readjusting his makeshift eye patch until Tomas had gotten dressed and was ready to go. Aticus left and Tomas slammed the door behind him and jumped to the ground.

"Let's do this!" Tomas said resolutely, shaking his head, dreadlocks swaying, as if to say he knew this was a bad idea.

With their guns securely slung over their backs they set off, still human, running only slightly awkwardly on all fours back towards the plantation. Ancient lycanthropes, their arms were longer than normal anatomy, proof of their age, with oversized hands. Running like a bear or a horse, both arms and legs synchronized and limbs were alternately stretched out or close to the torso. When their alternating limbs felt traction the hands or feet were respectively propelling forward and the process repeating again and again at break neck speeds.

This ends one way or another tonight, thought Aticus, still woozy from his grievous injury. He was getting dizzier and starting to see double, but it did not hinder him making his way through the swamp and into the forest. Aticus was a man possessed and Tomas could barely keep up with him.

The pair finally arrived to the edge of the clearing, the plantation so tantalizing close now. With his wolf thing eye he could see four servants, two on horseback, standing guard, another one hitching horses and the last one carrying things out of the house while the family hurriedly packed their belongings onto a trailer. He gestured silently for Tomas to circle around. Horses snorted and pawed nervously at the ground as the farmer hefted sacks and boxes, his wife and daughter tossing smaller items and articles of clothing haphazardly alongside them onto the bed of the trailer.

Without taking into consideration this was his only ammo, Aticus fired off a wild shot at the farmer who had taken half his sight. Everyone ducked, looking around wildly, and when no second shot rang out, they continued to load parcels and boxes with renewed frenzy. The two servants, guards on horses, fanned out farther from the family, the horsemen tried to reign in and calm their mounts with soft words and gentle pats. Their eyes searched the darkness blindly. With a single mindedness and complete focus, Aticus zeroed in on Alicia. A howl issued from behind the barn, only a few yards from the family. The horses whinnied and stamped impatiently. Gerome heard Mirtha gasp and then sputter and cough.

Aticus changed forms save for the wounded half of his face, his partially Lupine ears twitching. Tomas tried giving him instructions and warnings, but it was too late, he was on the move. He ran, now a two-legged wolf thing, Aticus first started toward the servant with the double-barreled shotgun. He lunged for his jugular, but the startled man slid sideways, almost falling from his horse and brought up the butt of his gun in time to stave off the strike. A clumsy hit to the head temporarily stunned Aticus, but he quickly came to his senses and put all his weight behind a lunge before the man could pull himself completely upright on his saddle. He knocked him into the dirt and pinned him there, his gun had clattered harmlessly away on the ground.

From atop the other servant's horse his started to take aim but the gun was thrown from his grip as the horse's powerful front legs began to kick blindly, big glassy eyes rolling back in to the horse's head in fear. The man tried to regain his balance, the gun clutched in one hand, the other grabbing for the reigns but it was no use. He headed toward the ground and hit with a bone jarring thud. Aticus seized the moment. Canines sank into soft flesh, his muzzle wet from the crimson-colored life force spurting uncontrollably from the man's shoulder. The man let out a hoarse scream before his eyes began to dim, his free hand scrabbling weakly at the ground.

Rising from a protective crouch over his daughter, Gerome looked up. The large brown wolf was still too far to harm his family but the black wolf with one eye now crept into striking distance to Alicia. The servant on the ground bravely waved a torch trying to scare it off. Frantically Gerome searched for his pouch full of coins, and found them. Just enough for one more shot, he dropped the black powder and silver coins in the blunderbuss and took sight of the black Wolf just as it started to jump up from the servant's corpse.

A shot rang out, Aticus had been hit in the abdomen this time, knocking the wind out of him and sending him flying off the dead man. His belly was on fire. More deadly silver, but luckily it went all the way through and out his back. Aticus frantically looked around for Tomas, who now engaged the servants by the barn who trickled out, attracted by the loud conflict.

The farmer took advantage of the confused situation and scurried over to the team of horses, pushing his daughter up onto one and pulling his wife up behind him on the other. With steadily blurring vision, Aticus saw Alicia slipping away into the night. He saw red. With growing wrath and renewed vigor he stumbled towards the torches which lit the yard, and threw one through the living room window.

Aticus knew he was in trouble, the blood loss made him unsteady and stumbling he fell down onto one knee. A howl tore through the night air, a signal to retreat. He mustered the last of his strength and ran just as the house went up in flames. Mortally wounded but in hybrid form he made his way to the safety of the woods. Looking back, he saw two more servants put out the house fire; two more took off in pursuit of the Brown Wolf in the opposite direction. Safe now, Aticus let out a long, painful breath. He collapsed and felt his wolfs face hit the soft mossy ground. Before the darkness overtook him completely he caught a faint whiff of burnt roses in the air.

V

Absolute anguish could be seen in one cold green eye. Aticus snarled, grinding his canine fangs. He looked down at his feet annoyed by the weight of his custom-made leather boots. He was used to going barefoot so the weight of the shiny leather contraptions seemed ungodly. Such large casings made his feet feel as if he wore iron shackles. Oh well, he thought, a trivial matter when walking upright. It took two years to fully heal from his injuries. However, he had to wear a half hood to cover up his lupine ear, patches of scars, fur, unnatural half dog snout and missing eye. He was truly the stuff of nightmares now.

Aticus' eye squints at the powerful light of the sun. He squirmed uncomfortably but there was little relief as he started to get a headache. Dull at first, then blinding, strong enough that he was barely able to think as it seized him. Two years ago he had taunted the aged farmer and his blunderbuss. Two years ago, he lay in a coma close to death. Two years ago he awoke to find himself out of touch. No longer in control, no longer alpha and it set off a chain of events that ended in an explosion that rocked the sleepy island.

He had trouble thinking and his head was pounding like a jackhammer. He laughed, sanity slipping away from him. An animal looked out through that mortal eye and what he saw was an endless supply of prey. The world was a smorgasbord for him, atop the food chain. He howled like a madman. The thought of every mortal he passed as an entrée on a plate humored him.

It was a bit of a walk on just two legs from the dense forest and down a man-made mud trail to his familiar swamp. Nothing remained of the small cabin he and his fold had once occupied. The burnt remains, what little there was, had returned to the Louisiana muck. He walked briskly across the moist ground stopping only now and again to investigate the sound of something odd beneath his feet, or an unusual smell. He could take a whiff of what was left with his animal nose. Sporadically he picked up the distinct smell of a decaying corpse swallowed now by the Earth.

His wolf brother, he thought to himself, a somber expression coming over him. A few more paces and he would be at the edge of the swamp, the very same swamp that had turned into the site of an earth shaking explosion. Aticus felt the weight of his shoulders as they drooped down at the remembrance of that horrible night. The memories slowly crept into the stronghold of his consciousness in great detail.

He remembered with agonizing pain as Lance, his beloved friend, and Tomas worked tirelessly to uncover him from his would be grave that horrible night. They tried to lift him as gently as possible, carefully propping up his bloody body. Aticus had screamed out in pain, clenching his teeth, as Tomas gingerly slid his arm under his back. It was hypersensitive and the slightest touch sent a new wave of nausea and unbelievable pain through his entire being. They had laid him down in the cabin and covered him up.

His body clung onto the purest instinct of its beastly self for survival. Fever dreams were the only vivid thing to him the first few months as his body attempted to repair itself from the inside out. He dreamt of water from the crystal streams of his youth, in the high steeps of the mighty mountains just north of the Gobi Desert. He slipped in and out of consciousness until his body healed.

In his few conscious moments he remembered his cohorts beside him, rubbing against his body with sadness and covering him with moist healing leaves. He could see the beautiful angelic face of a dark haired woman, Tonya, the breeder of the pack. Her belly swollen with the next litter, as she knelt down beside him and offered her swollen breasts to his greedy, hungry mouth.

So warm, bittersweet milk of nourishment the only thing he could possibly hold down. The milk strengthened and invigorated his body. Three months passed by in this helpless state, there came a new strange voice, Stefan's voice. His calm reassuring voice reminding him that he would be okay, he just had to recover enough so that he could affect the change without it killing his weakened body. As soon as he could do this, he would be healing faster and be able to fend for himself.

Finally, he felt the skin on his face, and though raw, it was healing. He had managed to sit up and he felt movement in his limbs again. He turned his head slowly, the joints popping as they stretched and loosened. Aticus glanced around the room he was in, his eye sight no longer nearly perfect, but slightly cloudy as if he had just risen from sleep. A puzzled expression stretched across his face. Where was he? He had never seen this room before. Instinctively he sniffed the air then he jerked back as the smoke laced air burned through his nostrils. It seared his nose, throat, and lungs.

"You're awake." A slender figure stepped from the shadows of the room," glad you made it."

"I...." Aticus sputtered as he tried to rise up off the bed.

Every muscle in his body seemed to pull to the ripping point; his very bones seemed to ache. He paused for a moment supported by his arms, and then he tried again to stand up right, suppressing a scream inside. He shook his head to clear his vision. It was the gray-haired stranger, Stefan. He studied him intensely. Stefan's blue eyes told the tale, ancient lycanthrope, both physically and spiritually. A nurturer by nature who couldn't help seeking out those who cried out and Aticus' dying yells for help called out to him. He answered his mission to help lost souls. Too much information for Aticus to handle, he collapsed back onto the cot and leaned into the wall.

Stefan had long full gray hair that fell over his wide shoulders. His eyes were wide, with a piercing gaze that seemed to absorb all the light in the room and cast it out in an eerie silver illumination like the Moon itself. High cheekbones gave him a look of distinction and his body was clothed only in a pair of homemade gray cotton pants, which revealed a muscular physique. His core muscles easily visible beneath his tightly stretched skin.

"I'm Stefan," the figure offered, with a glimpse of a smile, "this is your home, protecting your fold, I saved it for you."

"What?" He blinked in confusion and bewilderment. He felt his sight slipping away from him grasping onto the wall to steady his weakened body as he carefully lay back down on the floor.

He closed his eye and slumped onto his back, Stefan's words echoing in his head. Aticus drew in the aroma of apricots and roses. He turned white as a ghost as memories poured through him. He dreamt about Alicia and days gone past when he had two eyes. He dreamt of Stefan too. Long ago, he remembered, Devon had told him of a lycanthrope who answered the pleas of his kind. Fading in and out of a restless sleep, Aticus wondered if he had called out to Stefan through the blinding pain. Had he somehow remembered Devon's words?

He remained in the sanctity of his shack, but now Stefan was leader, it was no longer his fold now. Knowing he was nowhere near to being his old self, more helpless than he had ever been, and that there is safety in numbers. Stefan was a generous host as he had seldom a guest.

"Hey Aticus," Tomas walked in and sat down next to him, putting his hand on his shoulder; "Really good to see you, I thought I lost you."

He flashed a smile, Tomas was a loyal friend. Reddish-brown dreadlocks covered his head, and he had a noble jaw and pointed chin which was always unshaven, his eyes were the same rusty color of his hair.

"When the servants came, I was chased for twenty miles or so until I lost them in the swamp, where their horses could not follow, but by then I had lost your scent as well."

Tomas wrapped his long powerful arms around his oldest friend, and then offered him a drink from his flask. Aticus took a big gulp and handed it back to him, the warm liquid passed down his throat and invigorated him. Blood from a recent kill hung thick in the air. Probably deer, he thought, his senses were not the same since the injury.

"Probably another deer," Sneered Tomas, and took back the flask for another draught.

Aticus was restlessly shifting about, shaking his head left and right. Tomas lifted an eyebrow as if to say, I understand where you are going with this. He unfolded an old blood-crusted piece of cloth from his pocket.

"Here, I thought you'd like to have this." Tomas tossed him something.

It was his modified eye patch he had hastily made that horrid night. Aticus held the blackened cloth in his hand. Tensing up, he eagerly tied it on. Something changed in his eye. The eye was cold as Ice. He clenched up his face, his entire 6 foot five frame tightened, throwing up an evil smile.

"So Stefan is pack leader now?" Aticus knew the answer to that question even as the wheels in his head were turning.

"Yes. When you were injured and howling for help, Stefan responded and you were in this coma for almost two years." He searched for a shiny apple from the fruit bowl in the living room, bit into it; the juices flowed out the corners of his mouth.

So that meant that Aticus had called for Stefan, had probably invited him right in. That meant he owed him his life and much more, it had probably cost him his pack. Aticus remembered Devon's urine streaming over him, the burns and how they tingled and itched as they had begun to heal. Devon told him during one of his more lucid moments about another ancient such as himself who might have helped him as well. Stefan. He remembered sarcastically asking Devon if he and this "Stefan" were God's angels sent to help injured abominations. Devon had chuckled and everything went black again.

"And one of Stefan's rules is that we don't hunt men under any circumstances." continued Tomas, wiping his mouth with the back of his hand, snickering.

Aticus hit the table with his fist, scoffing. Something had changed in him after he had put on his cloth hood, a virtual rebirth. He continued to live under Stefan's conditions, his pointless rules, in the murky swamp hidden by trees. He grew restless cooped up in this stilted shack with the mosquitoes, flies, and vermin. Always having to remain hidden in the shadows from what he considered to be weak hairless creatures. The only way he stayed sane was his loyal friends Tomas, Lance, and Montezu. He knew when the time came he could count on these allies who had been there when he was Alpha, before his injuries, which he still nursed. But about the others he wasn't as sure. Bile grew with every breath. He shook. A cold chill ran down his spine. Touching gently the corners of his narrow lips he traced the scars of his face.

His gaze fell upon Stefan one evening who now sat in the corner, calmly staring off at the clouds, the sun beginning to sink below the horizon, heralding night. Stefan's silver eyes gleamed as he watched the dying light with interest, his turning gray in the darkness.

"We can't just sit here like he wants us to!" Aticus spat out the words, looking around at the others in the room, his gaze falling back upon Stefan in defiance. "We were made to hunt not cower with fear!"

Aticus continued his speech, trying to rally support from those around him. Lance listened with seeming interest but continued to stare out the window of the shack. His brilliant red hair ablaze in the dying light of the sun, fierce blood-Brown eyes gleaming with inspirational anger. Tomas shifted restlessly, he sensed the anger and tension. He knew where it was all going to lead. He weighed the options silently.

If Tomas was uneasy, to the group it didn't show. Aticus had been his friend and pack mate since the day he found Aticus and Lance on the planes hunting a herd of buffalo in what felt like a life time ago. He was slumped lazily between the wall and the floor. Tomas sat bare-chested with just a pair of handmade tan leather human-skin pants on. One outstretched leg rested on the floor the other leg bent toward himself, knee pulled up to his large caramel chest. His high proud cheekbones and golden brown squinting eyes betrayed his Native American origins, when he was angry they darkened to almost black. Smooth hairless skin made it easy for Tomas to paint on the ocher colored markings on his chest, the ritual of a skin Walker. He was a short thin man (though by no means as short as Stefan) as a Wolf it was easy for him to navigate through the thickets. His original fine shiny black hair had slowly turned a coarse brownish red, russet-colored fur, like a lupine.

The strongest among the pack all once Aticus had healed. Born with the parasite that spread through his body, he brought with it an enhanced sense of authority. Stefan stood up and stretched his limbs leisurely, then turned his eyes upon Aticus. Silver eyes full of wisdom appeared in Aticus' blackened soul. Stefan was the smallest of them at about five feet, seven inches, but very muscular for his short frame. Sparse gray hairs covered the length of his body; his thin face had the markings of a true leader, though it held no real measure of his true age.

Aticus' forehead creased with lines of anger. Hostility had emanated strongly from every pore of Aticus' being during his argument. With each passing day Aticus felt himself stronger and Aticus saw strife growing amongst the pack.

The headaches Aticus suffered had been steadily increasing, and were almost unbearable. The majority of the pack had expressed frustration with Aticus and his restlessness. Even Montezu, a white haired, pasty colored albino man, born into a bloodthirsty shape shifting cult south of the border, had agreed with the others. Aticus was slowly dividing the pack. Some supported him as the rightful leader, but most were content with Stefan, the current Alpha male. Montezu did not begrudge Aticus his bid for Alpha, but he knew Stefan was less motivated by raw emotion and certainly less obsessed with vengeance.

Perhaps it had come time for a change though. After all, he had stood with Aticus, Tomas, and Lance to defeat the onslaught of human occupation just North East of the Mexican American border. He had once howled for help when the human mob encroached upon his hunting ground and it was Aticus, Tomas, and Lance that replied, not Stefan. Montezu was always impressed by Aticus' ruthlessness. Montezu went to the live along the borders of Canada for a time every year but he always faithfully came back to Aticus and his pack. He had not expected to find Aticus no longer the Alpha upon his return some years ago.

Montezu shaved the sides of his head, sloughing off luxurious long white hair with his rusting blade, and then burned sigil-like features on his temples, the blood trickling down his pale thick neck, down to his white silk tunic. He was a powerful man his shoulders were round and pronounced and he had wide muscled hips that in his Wolf form translated to a powerful and lethal take down. Born albino, his commanding features and a milk white complexion were odd to his Mesa American birthright of dark, tanned skinned, and almond colored eyed peoples.

Aticus had stopped pacing and his eye fell upon one of the younger men among them. Drake had dark brown hair and eyes, and a sturdy build. Drake seemed preoccupied with his thoughts, unconsciously tapping his foot, arms folded over his muscled chest. He cared little for what Aticus or Stefan had to say. The only surviving child of a litter of six by Tonya, the quarrels over power interested him very little.

Tonya tried to avoid the steady gaze of his one cold eye. After the incident between Aticus and the farmer they no longer hunted all together, but in smaller groups, ranging out much further from their usual areas. Stefan and some of the others had gone out on a hunt. Aticus meant to rally those who remained to his cause, perhaps to surprise Stefan upon his return.

"You fools! We cannot just wait here like this twiddling our thumbs... Humans are feeble little creatures, we don't need to beg for scraps or bow to man's rules," Aticus paused, turning to look over at everyone, "Like HE would have us do."

He snarled impatiently. He tried to point out some of Stefan's weaknesses, tried to interest them in the thrills of vengeance. He pointed to his missing eye and asked them to help him reap the payment for that painful debt the humans owed him.

He examined all his fellow misfits in the room, wondering who would support him in his call for action. His best friend, perhaps Lance had been listening more closely than the others. His red hair practically stood on end with enthusiasm. The setting crimson sun made the freckles on his face and body standout. His jaw was clenched and a red five o'clock shadow hid his pointed chin. He was shirtless with sparse red hairs on his chest a wiry frame, long arms and legs, and large pointed ears that translated to: a Wolf built for speed. In Wolf form he could hear a mouse building his nest 5 miles away, and could easily out distance most of the pack while out tracking. With his long reach he was once also the best at the lance, thus his name sake.

Long ago in England, renowned for his abilities at the tourneys, he was dispatched on a mission to get rid of a troublesome "wolf" with green eyes that was plaguing a small village. But nothing could prepare him for Aticus. The werewolf was on him before he knew what was going on. He was mauled and Aticus was about to finish him when he hesitated. It was something in his eyes or even the scent of his body, but Aticus stopped before the deathblow, making him his prodigy. And try to elude him as Aticus might, he had followed him ever since. Perhaps he would continue to follow him in this bid for Alpha.

No one had made a move to follow his lead. He could almost taste the tension and fear in the air. The pack had all been coddled by Stefan so long and still skittish from the conflict; they all had grown fearful of change, almost docile. So be it, at least no one would stop him. He had a score to settle still. As Aticus turned to leave, the door swung open in front of him. Stefan stood in the doorway, coming from the back room to help put away the night's prize the bare-chested form of Drake. Aticus wondered how long he had stood outside the door, how much he heard.

Stefan met the steady gaze of Aticus. His silver eyes glared at him disapprovingly. Standing less than six feet tall, he tensed up every muscle on his small body. Only barely a fine, grey fur covered his body and face. They faced each other now. Aticus stood staring down his nose in hatred and defiance, his one good eye fixed upon Stefan. Tonya came from behind putting a restraining hand on his shoulder.

"Settle down Aticus, you're still weak your anger will uncontrollably change you." Tonya could not help her growing affection for him now that he grew stronger he exuded an irresistible pheromone and aura about him, but she also had a strong tie to the pack.

When she had been in the midst of puberty Tonya learned how to commune with her wolf spirit, taught by the kindly old medicine woman. Long midnight black hair, smooth tanned skin, and intelligent yellow eyes made it easy for her to be accepted into the pack after the slaughter of her tribe and family. A thousand cavalry had descended upon the Navajo, surprising them, and caught off guard they were quickly dispatched. Teepees were set ablaze. Children cried out for their mothers, most of who were cruelly tortured before being killed. She only survived the onslaught because she was able to transform, hundreds of people looking for natives, a small wolf easily slipped past them and she was safe. She traveled the land on her own, alone until she heard in the distant night a calling to join a young misfit fledging pack.

"Get away from me." Aticus' voice was scratchy and low as he violently shrugged her hand off his shoulder.

Tonya immediately stepped back, and started to cower in fear, floor boards creaked as she slowly retreated, watching, almost whimpering. Aticus' muscles quivered and flexed rhythmically, his body hair growing erect and plentiful.

"Stand down, Aticus, I mean it!" Stefan yelled in a voice that was a calm and steady leader's voice, with no hint of hesitation or fear.

Stefan stepped up the threshold to the shack stepping into the living room, void of all furniture except for a small wooden table directly in the middle of the room. The other pack members peeked out of their rooms to see what all the commotion was about. Aticus, fangs emerging as he willed the transformation, lifted a lantern from a nearby table. Too hasty to aim, he threw the lantern, which crashed against the wall, shattering glass and white-hot flames cascading down the dry-rotted wooden wall, onto the floor boards, and snaking down to Stefan's feet. He instinctively leapt back then jumped out the door into the night. He landed awkwardly in an overgrown bush that surrounded the house.

Following after Stefan, who fled towards the woods, Aticus' face was already contorting from that of a man's, to that of a wolf-like beast.

He shed the few scraps of clothing that he wore, letting the full force of the transformation come over him. The muscles and limbs lengthen, reshaped to suit a lupine's needs.

A collective gasp went through the group. A sudden flash blinded and incapacitated them when the flames spread on the wall and oil lamps suddenly exploded. The flames began to spread further, paint peeling and bubbling off the aged walls. It spread quickly through the living room, like ivy growing unchecked, and blocking the exits like a fiery wall.

Those trapped inside were now panicking, screaming, fire wrapping their bodies like death shrouds. One of the only females, Tonya, still cowered against the wall. The smoke was stinging her eyes and she clutched at her pregnant belly, as if she could somehow keep her unborn litter safe. Her other children were already choking to death across the room, unable to breathe in anything but the kerosene fueled smoke. Drake hunched under the smoke, braving the flames, desperately searching for more of the pack to save from the house. He heard Tonya's coughing gasps and cries as he made his way along the wall, hoping he could still get to her. Tonya and Drake both looked at one another but just then, the heat and flames made another lantern burst upon a shelf, blinding all who were inside making their escape all but impossible.

Stefan knew it would eventually come to this. Aticus was from powerful stock. Since the beginning, when he stepped in as Alpha to fill the void of a near dead Aticus, he knew that Aticus would never listen to reason. If a show of power was what it would take, then by God, that's what he'll get, Stefan thought turning on his heels, sliding in the grass making a stand.

Stefan changed form more slowly. They were now both fairly changed and standing face to face to each other. Teeth bared, Stefan leapt forward without hesitation. His claws going for the beast's black furred throat. Aticus threw him off easily. A small group, a mingling of man and beast, those that had escaped the cabin, gathered around to watch the life or death battle, circling them.

"You're too weak Stefan!" Spittle dripped down his muzzle as he barked. "You're too complacent and you said yourself, you wanted to die my friend, so here is your chance!"

Stefan knew this was true. His reluctance to change shape made him age more normally and his bones began to normalize too. A lycanthrope that changes just every other week has bones like titanium from the shattering and subsequent re-calcification that the bones go through. He was, for all intents and purposes, just like a changeling again and that didn't bode well for him now.

The black and the gray wolves circled each other carefully studying each other, looking for an opening, a weakness. They made a circle in the weeds, flattening them under their malformed feet.

"It's my pack! And the pack needs strong leadership!" Aticus' breathless words were scratchy and snarled, far from human. He seemed to be waiting for a reply.

Stefan stiffened up, realizing that Aticus was trying to distract him as he closed the distance between them across the circle. A quick arc of Aticus' right arm, and claws tore into Stefan's gray furred abdomen. Stefan snarled, quickly sidestepping the second strike, and turned his head so that his powerful jaws sunk in to Aticus' ribs with a sickening crunch. Calculating eyes focused upon the larger black Wolf as Stefan feigned backward, predicting the next strike Aticus would make. The black beast back-peddled, dazed, shaking its head, a fresh claw wound to its side.

It was a lucky hit, Aticus thought, and lunged in for another attack. He hit nothing but empty air as a blur of silver slipped by him. Stefan sprang up behind him, claws raking across his massive back and around his middle. Wisely, Stefan locked his sinewy arms around him, forcing Aticus toward the fire that had spread from the rubble of the cabin, over the ground and onto some nearby sapling trees. Kicking furiously to regain his footing, Aticus sent up burning embers into the night sky. A dead patch of weeds went up in flames as the embers settled on them. A crackling fire was building before Stefan's eyes.

The flames spread wickedly, winding toward the swamp just behind them. A ghastly realization came over Stefan. He remembered that swamps were notorious for producing methane gas, which would normally be acceptable, except that the fires were spreading and there was a low floating cloud sitting directly behind him. Aticus sniffed the air and backed up, then picked up a branch that had fallen and stuck it into the burning weeds. Stefan's keen ears perked up, he knew what was coming next. Before anyone else had realized the danger, Aticus threw the fiery branch with all his might, spittle flying with the branch from his mouth. Now is the time, Aticus thought, to test the gift Devon had given him. The sound of gas igniting was unmistakable. An explosion rocked the earth like a massive quake. The top of the water and the surrounding land lit up in a ball of fire. Flames devoured the dead leaves that lay about, setting the trees and field ablaze within seconds.

Despite the fiery chaos, two forms emerged. Stefan was now engulfed in flames and Aticus as well. They were locked in mortal combat. They rolled on the forest floor among the flames, snarling and tearing at one another. The rest of the spectators tried to flee, monstrous figures running about in pain and confusion as once again flames threatened to engulf them.

Aticus clamped onto the Gray wolf's exposed throat. Simultaneously his claws tore into Stefan's side ripping muscles and tendons, tufts of burnt fur flying up into the air. The heat from the fire was intense and nearly unbearable. The blood spilt from both combatants, painting patches of ground crimson. In the end only one could live. A howl from Stefan, badly burned and bloodied, wafted through the air until it was interrupted by Aticus' claws sinking into his breast plate, cracking it wide open. Stefan let out a wet gurgle as Aticus' arm vanished into his chest. His claws squeezed Stefan's heart and with one violent yank and a spray of blood, released it from his chest.

Aticus viciously gobbled up the falling alpha's still beating heart, blood pouring down his chin. A wave of ecstasy came over him, knocking him on his back and for the first time he could remember, the pounding in his skull had ceased. His eye dilated as the Wolf's blood mutated and coursed through his body like heroin running through his veins. When the wounded beast had finished gobbling up Stefan's pineal gland tears of victory flowed freely from his one good eye.

Aticus shook the memories out from his head and sighed. He retraced that horrid night as he searched for and found his double-barreled flintlock. He flipped the switch with his thumb and smiled as the bayonet flipped out. He sloughed off the dirt and sniffed the barrel of his gun. He could still smell the black powder emanating inside the barrel. Aticus secured the gun to his belt.

One more place to see before he moved to the old Land. He adjusted his gaze to the dilapidated plantation house. He stopped and stood in what he knew had been the very spot where the gun had taken his eye. Yes, it took even more than that from him, he thought. Reliving the moment, the instant he saw the muzzle flash and the gleam of silver just before it struck his face and ripped the organ of sight from his head.

The same old porch he had stood in front of, while he watched his prize slip from his grasp. Slowly Aticus trudged up the steps of the porch to say goodbye. The screen door creaked as it closed, his skull felt like it would explode as he rubbed his temples to alleviate some of the pain. Headaches he had off and on since the silver fragments still embedded into his brain his sight began to get hazy. Aticus slowly took the stairs, stopping immediately at Alicia's room. Sneezing as dust swirled up, he pushed open Alicia's bedroom door. Stopping for a second, unaware that Alicia's diary had been kept just under the floorboards, then opening the windows and stepping onto the small second story balcony. White knuckled hands gripped the porch rails; maybe there would be a hint of her in the balcony, Aticus thought. He sniffed the air around him then drew in a deep breath before crinkling his nose in disgust. Maybe it had been wishful thinking on his part but he could smell no trace of her, not even a hint, and no sign of Alicia whatsoever. He tried to get a hint of roses, like laying in the dew soft lawn as the sun peeked up on a warm spring day. A tear sprang out of his eye, nothing, no hint of her at all.

Arrival

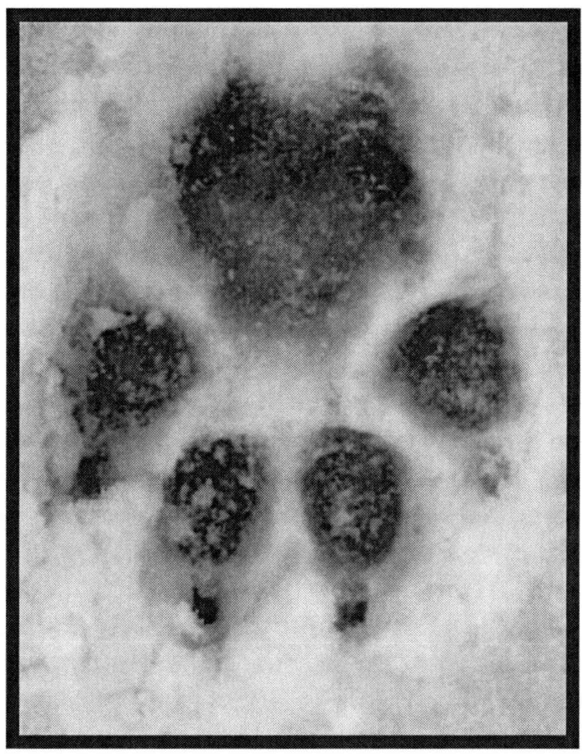

"Each time you breathe in, you take in some of the same air that Socrates breathed out a thousand years ago"

-unknown

1

Present day

New Orleans, near the port authority, Louisiana

Lex Noralon greedily sucked down his fifth cigarette to the butt and smothered it against the rail of the freighter and then flicked it into the waters of the Gulf. He watched the cigarette as it was engulfed by swirling waves. He imagined it was him in the chilly waters, helplessly being dragged down into the murky depths of oblivion. He had a year's worth of growth on his sun-ravaged face and his brown hair hung wild, down to his shoulders, very different from his usual buzz cut hairstyle when he was out of operation and land bound.

A chill ran down his spine as he donned his orange hardhat with a sticker that read, "Heaven didn't want me, and Hell is afraid I'll take over." Lex was hardened by his years on the boat, six months on, then off, his schedule for longer than he cared to count, but even he knew the risks of docking. He had lost many friends to falls into the water because of slick bows, decapitation from frayed steel towropes or just plain inattention. But it did not stop him or detour him from the hazardous work imagining how he would spend a year's worth of pay when he was ashore.

"Let's get it over with." Lex wiped off his hands on his pants, put on his utility gloves, and waved toward the people on the towboat.

Lex's hard earned experience took over his body and he was on autopilot now. Hold the rope taunt, release; Hold it taunt, release, repeat the process until the freighter and the towboat were close together. He saw the tugboat rocked as the freighter and the boat banged together, the sound like nails dragging on a chalkboard, almost done with his job he told himself. Lex signaled for two additional personnel to tie down and attach the tug to his freighter then he was off to set up the load for transport to land.

He walked down the aisles of every storage unit of the football sized freighter painstakingly inspecting then securing the loads one by one; row upon row, aisle upon aisle. He mused at the multicolored cubes stacked up in a row until it towered three stories high like a giant game of Tetris. He feverishly scratched down the units on his clipboard oblivious of the malevolent and antediluvian presence sleeping, feverishly dreaming, in an unlocked and open storage unit.

Weeks ago, Aticus had found himself a comfortable place among the dozen or so storage containers of the Poseidon ocean freighter headed for the Gulf of Mexico. Aticus the Wolf lay down curled up in the fetal position, muzzle touching tail. The rhythmic rocking back and forth by the churning, but by no means forceful, waves of the Pacific Ocean until it lulled him into an uneasy sleep. But sleep meant dreaming... where Alicia would be waiting for him. Beautiful young, straw colored long-haired Alicia, now the mesmerizing phantom of Aticus' dreams.

He had been entertaining the thought that his time on this Earth had expired. He had even so far as trudged out in the form of a man to the unforgiving extreme North, somewhere between Siberia and the frozen seas, to live out his last day on this accursed planet. It had been a long trek, moving at a snail's pace in knee deep snow towards a desolate wasteland, but he had found a perfect place to expire. It had taken months but he made it at last to his birthplace. It had been months of slogging through frigid temperatures and his bones ached. Meaning he could not transform into a wolf again. He laughed to himself a bit when he realized the implications of it all, that he would die humiliated and a man just how he came into this world; a humiliated, puny human infant born amongst wolves. He found a cave to protect himself from the elements and began to live out his last days as a man. After all, he was born a man among wolves; it was only fitting to die as one. Months turned into years, which turned into decades. Now emaciated from lack of food, the only source of water to drink being the falling snow, he had felt his time was near.

As he drifted in and out of consciousness he thought of vampyres, who are cursed to roam the land for eternity. He thought of Lucius and of their many talks. When he infiltrated and began masquerading as a bishop in the Roman Catholic Church. The sermon on Heaven and Hell and the eternal soul had him lost in thought for a time.

"I have no soul," Lucius decided one lonely night when Aticus and Lucius were philosophizing, "that's why I figure I am doomed to walk this earth for eternity. Heaven can't take me; my body is of the earth."

Lucius reveled in his self-pity for a while before ultimately destroying the church itself and every congregate he came across. Enter onto this stage the group called "God's Light" or "Lumière de Dieu" in French,

"Lucem Dei" from the Latin or "La Luce di Dio" in Italian. It was a secret fraternity of extreme monks and holy men of all denominations which were hidden in the shadows of the church itself, hell-bent or depending on your perceptions, salvation bent, on the eradication and extermination of what they considered unclean abominations. It was for those crimes; the murder of the congregation and the burning of the church, that Lucius caught the attention of God's Light and was hunted down and eventually captured just like Aticus' grandmother had been.

Aticus thought if heaven could not accept a body without any soul what are the chances of two souls intermeshed as one, one Wolf and one man, being saved? Was there a second God specifically for his own race? Or was it true what the Baltic cult had once said, that werewolves were the dogs of God himself? They had said "Werewolves are the eyes of God." He didn't know if he believed that or not. He pondered that for a second, as he also pondered the Bible verses. Exodus 22:19 says "anyone who has sexual relations with an animal must be put to death." Leviticus 20:15 says "if a man has sexual relations with an animal, he must be put to death and you must kill the animal." Leviticus 20:16 states "if a woman approaches an animal to have sexual relations with it, kill both the woman and the animal. They must be put to death; their blood will be on their own heads." Deuteronomy 27:21 is "cursed is the man who has sexual relations with any animal."

He had not decided whether or not he even believed in heaven or the pages of the Bible because he had been born from canines, his father was a lycanthrope who impregnated a real Wolf bitch. However, there had to be a reason the lycanthropes had their ritual bonfires when an unlucky werewolf had died, myth and legend had it that when a werewolf or for that matter a person, died not baptized he turned into a vampire forever cursed to roam the lands. He had never seen for himself a dead werewolf pop right out of the ground as a vampire. Aticus patted his lucky flintlock two-barrel loaded with silver slugs, but for that matter there was always beheading or a silver bullet to the brain as a guarantee that the unlucky soul could not return.

He laughed to himself, it would be just his luck, he thought, to come back cursed for eternity when it was eternity he was sick of. The first few months were almost too much for him to bear as the full Moon rose into the sky it took all of his willpower to not shed his human form and bound out on all four legs through the waiting icy night. He figured both shots of silver through the soft palate in his mouth, a sure shot to the cancerous pineal gland, and in his last dying moments he'd press the release that would spring forth the silver garrote, beheading him, and that should do the trick.

Twenty seven days for the parasite occupying his skin cells to die. Some infected smooth muscle cells only live an average of a few days. Infected white blood cells died after thirteen days, red blood cells died after hundred and twenty days, and liver cells died after eighteen months. Twenty full moons came went until Aticus was almost wholly human again and aging at an accelerated rate. Aticus looked upon his reflection in the glass-like ice on the sides of the cave and staring back at him was a decrepit stranger.

First his gaze wandered over his hands; long, thick black nails, now weak and fragile. Aticus could see the blue veins starting at the top of his palms rushing through his extremities, his skin now wrinkled, thin and almost transparent. Mesmerized by his skin and muscle that was once like marble, hard and smooth to the touch, now frail and wrinkled, muscles atrophied. He had been young, virile and muscular and now he shook in disgust mesmerized by his features.

Aticus stared at the body of an old man. He had grown a beard but it wasn't his full shimmering raven black-blue hair, Ice scratched at the thin grey-black stubble that sparsely grew on his face now. It says that man could only survive for seven days without food, but not a lycanthrope. Six years without substance, just the snow to drink from, and although he was emaciated and hallucinating raving mad from hunger he still existed. His face now had skeletal features; cheek bones bulged through delicately brittle and wrinkled flesh. His green eye now dim and murky like the consistency of a cloud covered night sky, sunk in, discolored and blackened. His ribs protruded through his skin. He felt his time finally near but he was too weak to go for his gun, in fact he was too weak to move at all. Must rest, he thought, slumping against the wall and sliding down to the floor at the mouth of the cave. He lay down on the soft snow, he would dream until he drifted off into nothingness… snowflakes raining down on his frame like a soft cotton blanket tucking him in for his eternal rest.

Aticus awoke. His head felt like somebody was scratching nails on a chalkboard over and over again. Somehow slightly rested and renewed now he felt an unknown presence in the cave.

"Aticus!" The voice wasn't coming from anywhere in the cave, he heard it in his mind.

"Aticus!" The voice in his head resonated louder now and hauntingly familiar. "Look at yourself..." Aticus complied; with his wrinkled hands he wiped the frost off from the sides of the mirrored walls.

"You were a proud strong lycanthrope, and oh how I loved you." Alicia's words were tender.

"Look at you, Aticus," he complied again; looking into the improvised mirror and what he saw sickened him inside. He had looked at his image before but never stared at it as intently as he was doing now. "You were a strong, proud lycanthrope I loved you so much." The air in the cave smelt like wildflowers and roses reminding him of Alicia's scent.

Alicia's scent was overpowering as Aticus closed his eye he felt her soft delicate hands rubbing his back then sliding up onto his aching shoulders. Afraid to open his eye lest Alicia's phantom spirit vanish; he softly choked out, "I loved you too."

Alicia slid in between Aticus' arms and his frame resting her head on his chest. Her gold spun radiant hair tickling his whiskers. He opened his eye to peek at his reflection, the anxiety dwindling and vanishing as he looked at the reflection of Alicia, who didn't evaporate. She had not evaporated at all. In fact, Alicia moved closer to Aticus and a sweltering heat filled his entire body. Nude she radiated an ethereal glow. She looked the same as Aticus had remembered; her long blonde silk hair, her flawless milky white complexion despite the fact she had been outdoors in the sugar fields for all of her adolescent life. Aticus could not tear away his gaze from her teardrop, doe eyes, clear as the ocean. He couldn't help himself but to tenderly caress her long slender neck with his giant course hands. To touch her small firm breasts with perfect quarter shaped pink nipples that bared the evidence of the deathly cold of the cave. Aticus couldn't help himself as he felt longing when he felt her toned abdomen with a deep belly button that looked like a question mark. His eye made its way down to curvy hips and the swell of her naked ass. His modest nature and love for Alicia made him quickly skim down past the soft blonde-haired mound between her legs; however, he stopped at her muscular taunt thighs. Thighs that bore evidence of her back breaking work on the plantation. Although her family had enough help that she didn't need to offer to lend a hand.

The nearness of Alicia's body exhilarated him as she opened her soft inviting lips and spoke once more. The way Alicia asked the question so innocently took him aback, "Why did you leave me?"

"I didn't want to leave you, Alicia," Aticus exclaimed defensively, "Your father attacked me! Wounded me! Once I was well enough to come looking for you, you were long gone." And On the verge of shedding a single tear, Aticus struggled to compose himself.

Grief turned to rage as thoughts of some one hundred and seventy years came back to him, hitting home like a sledgehammer in his mind. Raping Aticus' feelings and violating his perception. With shaking hands and gritting teeth he growled, "I told you! I told you humans wouldn't understand!"

A sudden forceful gust of frigid arctic air infiltrated the shelter of the cave that had previously protected them from the worst of the elements. The wind stormed passed both Aticus and the ghost of Alicia reflecting the werewolf's icy temperament. The squall dissipated but the real raging storm began when Aticus opened his mouth and spewed out hateful words that penetrated Alicia like a knife.

"I shouldn't been so foolish to trust you, a furless two-legged human!" Aticus had been unconsciously gripping her shoulders tighter and tighter to keep the rage in but in doing so crimson trickled from Alicia's shoulders as his nails broke through her delicate skin.

His rage gave way to misery, like a river that had grown too strong for its dam; a dam full of stress cracks, that breaks and floods the land, when he looked into her puffy, pain filled eyes. Her big doe like eyes bloodshot and filled with hot tears.

"I… I… am so sorry!" Aticus stuttered, profusely apologizing while gently wiping the tears that had fallen and began to pool on her cheeks.

"No you're right Aticus. You were right all along." Aticus froze, confused by the confession but he let her continue anyway. "When we left, Poppa whisked me away; I was so devastated I was so confused and lonely."

"My poppa made me flee the state but three weeks after the loss of your eye…." Alicia caressed Aticus' missing eye and then fondled his long grey flecked black hair. "I woke up in my old house… I was so confused, I dreamed, dreaming of wolves and of you."

Aticus and the corporal ghost Alicia clung to one another, their foreheads touching as she continued.

"My Poppa was beside himself, he thought I was possessed. He had a mission that grew into an obsession to extinguish all wolves and all your kind that he came across." She sighed then continued.

"He gathered groups of friends and hunters by the hundreds and slaughtered thousands upon thousands before he died of a heart attack. Once Poppa died the true horror began. With Poppa's stability no longer in the picture to keep her in check, my stepmother went off the deep end, she went insane and looked towards me to blame the destruction of her house and the eventual death of her husband to unleash her anger upon. To alleviate the hurt, my stepmother forced me to the Sanitarium.

Aticus felt sick because he knew where this was going. He hugged her tightly, and Alicia invited him in for a long embrace, an embrace that interlaced two lovers into one.

"Alicia I'm..." Aticus tried to say he was sorry but Alicia interrupted him to continue with her story.

"The doctors from the sanitarium locked me away. I was devastated. I worried that the padded walls were all I was going to see for the remainder of my life. However, I somehow escaped and again I was at my father's plantation pining for you, my love. Now the hospital looked for me and I was running from the law. People had trouble understanding me, hell I had trouble understanding myself!" Alicia sighed again and rested her head on Aticus' shoulder.

Aticus cleared his throat, swallowed and began to ask the question he had been dreading to ask since he wrapped his arms around her, "You're not with me anymore are you? Are you a ghost, Alicia? You feel so real I don't wanna ever let you go."

Her head no longer on Aticus' shoulder. She began to smile shyly, the shy smile that melted Aticus heart so many memories ago.

"Oh my darling Aticus…" With both hands Alicia touched his bony cheeks then proceeded to interlock her delicate hands around his broad neck. "I died a long time ago of a broken heart and loneliness. You are dying now and that's why I finally appear before you here in this desolate cave." Proceeding to stretch up the length of his body, to Aticus' ear, she whispered, "but I have a surprise for you darling."

"A surprise… for me?" Aticus asked wonderingly, pressing her body tightly against his own, reluctant to release the ghost of Alicia.

"Yes, a surprise for you in the New World. Go to the New World at the plantation, where we first locked eyes on one another." Despite his renewed vigor holding her tightly to keep her close the ghost of Alicia's body evaporated from beneath his hands he could just make out her transcendent form and his decaying reflection in the ice.

"Don't give up on me Aticus; you have much work to do. Avenge me! Avenge me and all the suffering that I received at human hands! Avenge what could have been of me and you. Go back to where it all began, back to my Poppa's plantation and I'll be waiting for you!"

Alicia floated backwards and began to merge into the icy rocks right before Aticus' eye.

"No!" Aticus frantically reached out for Alicia's quickly fading figure to no avail.

"No!"

"No!"

"Noooooo!" Clawing at the brick like buildup of snow and ice that had developed throughout the centuries until his hair and beard were covered in chips of crusty frost he screeched out again, "No!"

"No!"

His fingernails bloody from the frantic scratching of the mirror like ice he finally fell back onto his knees, he saw only his own reflection through the bloodstained cracked mirror, "No!"

The dirge of sorrow could be heard several miles away. The requiem of loss echoed through the wilderness frightening and stirring up birds that were able to survive the unforgiving terrain took up flight. The audible sounds from Aticus' troubled slumber startled him awake interrupting the yowls of sleep panic.

Groggy but the fog of sleep quickly lifting; Aticus struggled to get off the ground, his biceps and shoulders stiff, sore, and inflamed. He saw black and gray fur mud covered paws where brittle wrinkled hands should be. A steady drip, drip, drip echoed throughout the cavern, the source the wet muddy underbelly of Aticus' wolf. Drenched from muzzle to tail, Aticus the Wolf shook the saturated fur but it still dripped down and pooling in puddles that once were snow as steam choked the cave.

He realized to his surprise the steam came from his own Wolf body. The heat from his transformation, the metamorphosis like a nuclear bomb going off inside the body, making a damp muddy enormous circle in the snow. He must have transformed in his troubled sleep, the anger and anxiety of losing Alicia again had triggered the change.

Looking into a puddle that once was snowfall he didn't even recognize his own lupine visage. What once was his ebony black fur, fur that was luxurious full-bodied, abundant and silky; now thinning at the muzzle and neck and his black fur now dull straw-like and peppered with gray. His only good eye, the eye that wasn't covered by the makeshift bandanna/patch made up entirely of human skin stitched by ligaments made to replace the ragged and torn rag of long ago, now a pale dull and lifeless jade. His shoulder blades piercing through his skin and hackles now white as snow.

The Baltic cult was right, he thought, shaking the last remnants of his lucid dream away. He was the dog of God, a werewolf whose duty it was to keep the dirty, corrupt, polluting ever-expanding humankind in their place! He had a purpose!

The continual consistent pounding in his skull, the constant pressure in his head whenever he woke up for the day each and every day since Alicia's father grievously wounded him, further solidified his resolve. Silver coins, some big, some small, some the width of a fingernail, all of the coins with humankind's delusional men and women of importance throughout the centuries. Silver projectiles lodged into his face dangerously close to his brain were preventing him from healing and more importantly preventing part of his face from transforming back and forth, his visage a grotesque mixture of Wolf and man.

Closing his eye he saw in his mind the French and German monarchs, the faces on the coins, their power just a fantasy, he knew what he must do now. He could not waste away in this dank dark cavern of his. His refusal to transform had wasted him away, accelerating the aging process, until he was a crooked old shell of a man. However HE is the dog of God and had a divine mission to fulfill.

Stiff legged, he slowly crept out of his voluntary crypt and into the frigid openness. He howled once again, a wail that resonated two-hundred miles away. Even when the baying could no longer be heard by human ears it wasn't deterred, the frequency changing. An inaudible pitch heard worldwide only by lycanthrope. Invigorated with a higher purpose he began to walk but his legs still shook. So malnourished and dehydrated, Aticus started to walk but his legs shook and collapsed beneath him. His only hope a wail he sent off throughout the land. Fueled by Alicia's haunting words, he started an agonizing crawl on his belly toward civilization before he fell into unconsciousness.

Nights turned to days then days turned to nights and back again all of them a blurry memory in Aticus' hazy mind. Until a sudden ear shattering sound of blasting horns and whistles assaulted his senses and sharpened his cognizance. The crisp salt air and the steady rocking told him that he was on a ship, probably out on the ocean. Light filtered through the storage compartment casting an eerie shadow on the nude man sitting cross legged with his back against the wall staring at him. Sunlight from cracks and holes in the unit made the fiery red hair radiate from the nude man. Aticus' heart raced as recognition washed over him. It was his pack brother, Lance, who heard his calls and came to his rescue.

Cooped up in silence and still starving, Lance was anxious to get out. Sustained on the bone marrow alone, it had been three weeks now. Saliva pooled beneath Lance's muzzle, the prospect of just one juicy taste of the demolished boar's scraps was almost too much for him to bear, but he had to wait until Aticus awoke. Aticus will be hungry too, and hunger will lead him to mind splitting headaches.

The aroma all about the small container excited him more than his pack brother, food. Lance remained true, loyal, and he found a course to America like the aria had ordered him to. Foregoing his own hunger for his alpha, Lance tossed the Wolf Aticus the much-needed sustenance. Aticus still in his Wolf body hesitantly staggered toward the bloody kill making sure he didn't lose eye contact with his Wolf mate. He knew all too well that his position as alpha leader was conditional at best. He knew Lance had him at a disadvantage. Withered and tired, his dull fur masking wrinkled skin. He worried that any crack in the foundation of leadership and Lance could turn on him. The hungry Aticus growled a stern warning, step back!

"Aaaarooorrggrrrrr." Lance snarled a subtle nuance of changing pitch, high and low treble and bass that human ears could not comprehend but it made Aticus at ease.

With his belly full for the first time, mind at ease, he looked over at Lance who now had transmuted into his Wolf form and was sleeping peacefully with his muzzle resting on his forepaws. Aticus found a comfortably padded place between well chewed hip bones and crates to lie down. He yawned, stretching to get comfortable as he fell asleep a smile on his muzzle, dreaming of Alicia, America, and New Orleans.

Lance put his snout up and sniffed the air around him, tail spontaneously wagging excitedly in response. They had definitely arrived onshore, and confident no one was snooping around the container yet Lance cautiously snuck up to the edge of the still ravenous Alpha Wolf. He gently nuzzled the nape of Aticus' neck, lightly nudging him alert; growling snarl with fangs bared, Aticus slowly opened his eye. Lance retreated, his tail between his legs. The one eyed Wolf still groggy and sluggish. He had recently been dreaming, a beautiful lucid dream that he was reluctant to wake up from, about Alicia, beautiful Alicia welcoming him home. However, a wicked headache consumed him almost immediately. With a series of grunts and growls, Aticus issues his commands to Lance, who dances around the small storage unit panting excitedly, and then pushed his head against the door to slide it open.

Lance's body went still, halfway in and halfway out of the storage, signaling with his raised tail that the coast was clear. They moved stealthily and in unison escaped from the confines of their makeshift cage and onto the deck of the cargo ship.

Lex stood writing down on his clipboard the serial numbers of the waiting storage units destined to go on the Ferry for their ride to the shore. Containers five or six high stacked up together like multicolored Legos. Diligently inspecting each container to assure himself that the contents were not tampered with, once he was confident that the storage unit was neither damaged nor tampered with, he assigned a number for it and moved on to the next row.

"That's weird." Lex muttered glancing up from his clipboard and check marks.

This storage unit door was completely open, he realized. He exchanged his pen and clipboard for a flashlight and walkie-talkie then proceeded cautiously into the dark interior of the open unit. The putrid smell made him pull up short and wretch. The smell of dead and decay was more than Lex could stand but he endured the stench and pushed further into the darkness with just the unsteady beam of his flashlight to lead the way.

"What the..."

His flashlight stopped abruptly over what he thought looked suspiciously like dried blood. He set down the walkie-talkie on a nearby crate and hesitantly touched the crimson crusted blend. He rubbed the reddish black substance between his first finger and his thumb, and then against his better judgment, he tasted it. On his tongue a familiar copper taste, it was blood. He cautiously moved forward checking the floor by each crate until from the corner of his eye he noticed torn up clothes and another red puddle shaped stain. With closer inspection he saw human and large animal bones; he frantically fumbled for his walkie-talkie, checking his dirty overall's pockets, until he realized he had set it down on a crate near the entrance to the unit.

He heard growling emanating from somewhere nearby but he could not pinpoint the source of it. Lex hysterically moved his head back and forth the flashlight following, sending needles of light into the dark spaces around him. He spun around and saw that between him and the exit were livid glowing eyes that shone ominously at him, reflecting the light from his shaking flashlight's beam. For a moment it felt like he was dreaming, after all he was on a ship, which had for months, navigated the Atlantic Ocean. There could not be a wolf stowed away on the ship but the rust colored wolf was there just feet from him all the same.

He used the flashlight like a baton instinctively, striking the Wolf in the muzzle as it crept closer, he a heard a snap as the Wolf yelped and covered its muzzle with its paws. He seized the moment, making a break for the open door but the wolf was on his heels, snapping at his feet, he scrambled to the right near some of the crates and up on top of them. Up on the crates he could see the walkie-talkie just a few feet from him, so frustratingly close to him. He tried to reach for the radio but it may as well been a gap the size of the Grand Canyon, every time he made an attempt to grab for the radio the Wolf snapped at his arm.

Lex prepared to strike out at the brazen Wolf again with his light baton, holding it high over his head but the Wolf stopped advancing suddenly, then incredibly it seemed to smile up at him. He heard a throaty snarl behind and above him. The short hairs on his neck stood up and his heart was pounding as he turned around. Above him in the pyramid of stacked crates, in the gloom, stood a formidable and even more massive raven-black wolf, one eye shining green in the dim light. He was now trapped with wolves above and below him.

The black werewolf tried to transform his paws into hand like claws, it was sluggish and painful. Cooped up for six months the Wolf had been, and now was too weak from hunger to metamorphosis. Lex tried to move but powerful haunches sprang forward, the beast leapt for his throat, knocking him down off the crates. He thought he heard the Wolf speak before powerful jaws crushed his windpipe in one fierce crunch.

"Starrrvving!"

Hot lifeblood spewed out of the man's neck, wetting Ice's muzzle as he gurgled and turned white. Lance, the rust colored wolf, cautiously staggered over to Lex's legs leaving the entrails and heart, in fact all of the prized middle, for his leader. Timidly nibbling on his exposed ankle trickling with blood, his eyes affixed on Aticus, always alert, one sudden movement and Aticus would snap at him. The only sounds that filled the space were the ripping and tearing of flesh and the satisfied growls and snarls of the wolves as they glutted themselves.

Now with full bellies, the two wolves stretched their weary legs and fled their shelter, staying in the shadows until they were at the Stern of the boat. Aticus stretched his back in an arch trying to metamorphosis back into a man. A low raucous yowl left his muzzle, the pain too much for him to endure.

"What in God's stormy hell?" The seaman yelled, his flashlight zeroing in on the two furry stowaways.

A crowd was gathering at the Stern, the dozen or so seamen were not prepared for what stood in front of them, as the two wolves stood their ground. A flash of tooth and nail had the seamen running for their lives. Screams pierced the night as they ripped into arms, legs and bodies. When the dust settled the wounded scuttled for cover, whimpering and crying out pitifully.

Aticus and Lance's mouths were covered in blood from the men on the deck they had dispatched. It would not take long before reinforcements, this time armed, would arrive. The wolves had to jump ship. Aticus could smell the crisp clean air, the Louisiana border; with a grunt and a growl to command Lance they jumped overboard together, splashing down into the muddy Mississippi River.

They paddled upstream against the lazy currents until their paws were able to touch mud-covered ground. Panting from exhaustion the wolves dropped at once onto the solid ground. After a brief rest the wolves trudged along silently through the drone of cicadas and the occasional hoot from a tree owl. Sensing an inherent, ancient, preternatural presence, even alligators, such well-bred killing machines they went unchanged for centuries, cowered out of the wolves' way.

The vicious attacks on the seamen brought about a deadly chain of events. Lance glanced over his shoulder, the terrified screams from the entwined freighter and Ferry momentarily capturing his interest. He paused to turn and watch the ships veer dangerously off course the ships grounded and capsized. Then an explosion rocked the land.

Lance shook muck from his mane and tail. Aticus tried to shake the sludge off his fur as well. He tried transforming back to a man in the glow of the burning river. Muscles rippled and bones cracked but still no change. The pain was unbearable as Aticus tried to metamorphosis again, and again failure. The ride to the New World severely weakening their systems, Aticus and Lance already needed to consume more flesh again. Aticus flung up his muzzle and let out a howl. An aria that only children of the night could hear,

"I am here, come to me, come to me and we will form a new pack. I am here, back in Louisiana, I am here. Find me and a new day will dawn on all of human kind!"

2

David cursed his friends for poaching as the blood from the animal bite on his forearm still dripped onto his mud caked jeans. He needed to go someplace safe so he could get rid of four jackrabbits, two raccoons, one 12-point buck and, more importantly though, the bulk of them had long ago used up their tickets, an albino alligator that they had procured before all hell had broken loose. Dust and debris caked onto the windshield of his new Dakota pickup truck, making it hard to see out of. He pressed the button for the windshield washer fluid but that just made it worse. Dust became a muddy mixture the consistency of sludge, which seized the windshield wipers after smearing a brown mess across his field of vision.

"Damn it!" swearing, he slowed down and punched the dashboard with his fist angrily putting the truck into park.

He left the headlights on to shine weakly into the fields as he leaned toward the glove compartment and opened it revealing his 9 millimeter. Loading his gun he laughed hysterically. This puny thing is not going to stop anything substantial, David thought, let alone the beasts that had attacked them.

The day's events suddenly catching up to him he lowered his head and sobbed. Two of his friends were dead and he hadn't been able to do anything to stop it. With the truck stopped the eerie silence outside hit him like a sledgehammer as he mulled over all the possibilities in his head. Just an animal attack, he told himself, he didn't need to run. But He couldn't handle being caught poaching again. His third offense he faced a real possibility of prison time, leaving his wife, Jill and son, Jack, alone. He opened his red eyes and watched a bush across the clearing beside his truck. As it shook he gripped his 9 millimeter resting on his lap. He thought the beast had found him! He would inevitably be the third victim as he waited for the creature to burst out. The death grip loosened as he breathed a sigh of relief as a large rabbit bound out from under the brush, before disappearing again into the tall green grass.

He promptly realized a sudden change in his eyesight. Not at all daytime but the dead of night and he could suddenly see clearly. The full moon had radiated some light but not enough to explain his sudden clarity as if the noonday sun was high in the sky.

"I have to get to my uncle's." He told himself aloud.

Uncle Steve expected their group after the hunt and he trusted him. His uncle would know what to do next and being in familiar surroundings might relieve his sudden anxiety and obvious hallucinations. After getting out long enough to wipe the windshield with a greasy rag he slumped back into his seat and slammed the door shut.

"What a cluster fuck!" David yelled.

One more nervous glance around and he started the truck throwing gravel into the air as he pushed the gas pedal down, on the road again. Although he had cleaned his cab from top to bottom the peculiar odors coming from inside grew. He fought back the bile coursing up his throat as the aromas around him got stronger still. The smell of Crawfish, alligator with Cajun fixings, red beans and rice that he remembered eating over a month ago, so good he got an order to go. Now, no trace of food anywhere, just the mixture of smells had him nauseated.

He rolled down both windows and put two fingers to his neck to feel for his pulse, outrageously high. He could see the streetlights from the highway just ahead. He could feel his whole body throbbing with each erratic beat of his heart. I'm having a panic attack, he told himself, pulling onto the highway. It was hard to concentrate on the road as he nearly crashed into an oncoming driver who quickly flipped him the finger.

David could swear the hair on his back and neck was growing as he took one hand off the wheel to scratch on his scalp. His frame quivered as the thought of bugs moving back and forth over his body made him gag.

He blazed through a red light as he desperately searched around the cab for his cell phone, but found his half-full bottle of Jim Beam instead; this would make it all better! David downed the spirits, spilling not a drop, until the bottle emptied and his throat burned from the heat.

Two more turns onto another dirt road on route to Steve's house he felt himself driving on autopilot. He felt like insects were crawling around beneath his skin on fire and at the same time itching beyond belief. David tried with both hands to relieve the incessant itch on his backside but he failed utterly. The road curved and he almost hit one of Uncle Steve's neighbor's mailboxes before he righted himself again. Finally past the six dilapidated trailers before his uncle's gravel road. The intermittent streetlights gave way to densely packed Oak and Cyprus trees. His vision seemed to fade in and out. If not for the full moon and floodlights in the driveway David would have missed the place. Somehow Uncle Steve with shotgun and flashlight in hand was waiting for him out front of the cabin in an unincorporated village of Royal Bay.

The cabin looked desolate, abandoned and neglected. The Royal purple paint had long ago faded to pink. The horizontal planks dry rotted and termite infested, missing planks revealed torn insulation. The front windows were all broken, wrapped with aluminum foil to stave off the rain. In the front of the house, once a thriving flower garden now brittle, brown and pedal less, while the Ivy thrived and continued creeping up the walls of the cabin.

Uncle Steve nervously smiled periodically his toothless smile. A true swamp rat he had an unkempt long brown beard and ratty wild braided hair that hung to the small of his back. He had no shirt under dirty oil stained denim overalls.

"David what the hell happened to you!?" Steve yelled, standing back a healthy distance, his shotgun at the ready, he yelled eyeing the empty hitch behind the truck, then unconsciously looked toward the woods as if the boat had just been a pawn in a cruel game of hide and seek, "What happened to my boat?"

David put the truck in park and stumbled out of the vehicle. Steve cautiously laid down his gun and made his way over and put his arm around David's broken body to help keep his knees from buckling. He was worried about his nephew but he was more worried about the boat that hadn't come back with him.

"You had me worried when you called me." Steve said still looking around for his missing boat as if it was simply hiding in the trees, too shy to come out.

"What?" David shrieked. He looked down at the cell phone clutched in his fingertips, he must've found the cell phone when he found the Jim Beam and didn't remember it "I called you?"

Steve looked at David like he was out of his mind.

"Yeah you called me just a few moments ago but it was hard for me to understand you. Your phone must have been breaking up or something."

Steve pulled out his cell phone and put it up to David's ear to let him listen to the last saved message. As he listened to the message he was horrified. For one thing, he didn't remember calling his uncle whatsoever, and for another thing he sounded like a monster. He heard guttural grunts and snarls sprinkled throughout the garbled message.

"I don't even remember calling you." David stated, confused, as a fresh wave of nausea began setting in.

"Man you look white as a ghost, what the hell happened out there? Where the fuck is my boat?" Steve whispered, unconsciously rubbing small circles on David's back with his flashlight.

"Can we go in the house?" David groaned, the perpetual rubbing was helping with his nausea but he was fairly certain he was running a fever now as he wiped at the sweat already beading across his brow. The warm night air suddenly felt suffocating and overly damp.

David welcomed the helping hand from his uncle and they made their way into the cabin, the rust covered screen door creaking shut after them. The familiarity of his Uncle's front room comforted him, the dim lights from the oil burning lanterns, and the Cedar smell from the logs of the walls felt like his youth down in the Bayou. Taxidermy deer, bear, and foxes were strewn throughout the room and along the walls in all directions, wicker chairs and Uncle Steve's homemade bar remained the centerpiece of the entire room. David sat down in the middle of bar, Steve, confident that David was secure on his stool, made his way to the backside of the bar and leaned down to produce a lead crystal decanter full of caramel colored homemade moonshine.

David looked at himself in the mirror across the wall; he didn't recognize what he saw. Bloodshot eyes peered back from a sweaty pale face; a wide nose with flared nostrils sat above a five o'clock shadow gone wild, even his cheeks and forehead appeared to have grown sparse thin hairs under the dust and mud that smeared parts of his face.

Steve tried not to look at David too blatantly as he took two dusty crystal glasses and poured himself a drink, downed it with one gulp, and then poured another drink and slid it across the bar toward David.

"Here, this will help calm your nerves and then you can tell me what happened in the woods..." Steve said, worrying about his missing boat, frowning.

"Don't worry Uncle, your boat is safe," David sighed between shots, "it's at the campsite, the one out beyond the tributary?"

Steve knew this campsite, he took the nephews there when they were younger and that comforted him a little. He poured himself another shot, the seventh one since he brought out the dusty decanter, and then poured David his fifth drink. Steve patted David on the back, his skin was still burning hot but Steve could tell it had gone down at least a little because David's trembling had subsided. In between drinks Steve managed to take David's temperature despite his skin being so hot, his internal temperature was actually normal.

"I'm not worried about the boat," Steve lied, glancing out the window. "What exactly happened out there today though? Is everybody okay?"

David began to break down and sob uncontrollably, "There was an attack.... two people are dead."

David began to recount his long horrifying story in between sobs, while Steve downed another shot and huffed when he realized he had finished off the decanter. David explained that while their group of seven was poaching whatever game was available they came upon what they thought was a feral dog with a missing eye eating the remains of a rabbit trapped in one of their snares. Unsettled and willing to give up the hare to it, the group tried to back track and circle around the huge dog, but then it suddenly appeared on the trail in front of them. One friend in the group, Alex, got off two shots, missing it, before another huge dog came slinking out of the woods, this one a bright reddish copper color with two eyes. When it suddenly lunged he had been quick enough to fire another adrenaline fueled shot that tore a ragged hole through the beast's shoulder, knocking it back with an angry yelp and a splatter of gore.

The black one ran to the red beast's side, and then stood in front of him in a defensive position, teeth bared and snarling angrily. That was when Quinn LeBeau, the twin brother of Lou LeBeau, stepped forward and set his sights on the black dog with one eye, motioning for Alex to step back. Before Quinn had the chance to fire the large black dog-thing lunged up at him, its curved fangs tearing delicate flesh like a steak knife through butter. The enraged green eyed creature seemed to bask in the hot sticky spray from Quinn's now mangled and exposed neck. His mouth gaped open in shock as he dropped to the ground, dead before he ever knew what hit him.

The hunters were all paralyzed with fear, unable to move, when the unthinkable began to happen; the wounded red dog-thing got up, its limbs unsteady as its paws dug divots into the dirt for balance. Its wounds seemed to heal by themselves. The bullet pushed outward in the bloody wound, the gaping crater's edges seeming to pull in tighter as a gleam of the bullet broke the surface. The ravaged gore now made room for smooth healed tissue.

First one, then a second broke free of the undulating flesh and fell with a dull thud to the dirt beneath the animal. Meanwhile, the black furred dog-thing had dragged Quinn several feet away from where he had fallen and hungrily devoured the stomach contents of their fallen friend, and then proceeded to stand up on its hind legs and look unwaveringly back at the shocked group with what seemed to be distain. The dog-thing then looked at its paw, and wincing, the paw slowly morphed into a human-like hand with six-inch long talons. It smiled, its muzzle drooling as it howled triumphantly into the sky, standing there like something out of a nightmare. David glanced up to gauge his Uncle's reaction, half expecting to find him smirking and shaking his head, sure that they had gotten into the wrong kind of mushrooms out there in the woods. He was a little surprised to find Steve ashen faced and troubled looking. Steve swallowed hard and gestured for David to continue his story, clutching the empty glass in both sweaty hands. David leaned back on his stool and could almost picture the guts of his friend, Quinn, strung across the sticky dirt.

The red furred dog taking his orders from the obvious black leader, stood up on its hind legs too, metamorphosed slowly for emphasis into a man with the exception of a large beast's head.

"You guys are in trouble now!" Incoherent garble spewed out from the red wolf-thing's muzzle.

The half-inebriated group of hunters scattered like roaches in a dark room as if a light had suddenly been turned on, tripping over themselves trying to escape the nightmare before them. David went on to explain that group had separated and it was every man for his self. David only looked back for a second when he heard bloodcurdling screams from a silhouette being mauled in the growing darkness but he couldn't make out who it was. He had made it to the campsite and his truck. Turning the key he was relieved to see it started on the first try when broken glass rained down on the back of his neck, he turned to see the black one eyed thing trying to shove its grotesque head through the cab window behind him. David explained how he tried to block the thing from biting his face off and was desperately trying to kick the truck into gear. He heard the gear shift, and as he hit the gas, the beast snapped one last bite and caught his forearm before the force of the truck moving launched him backwards and he slid off the bed of the truck.

His uncle came around the bar to inspect his forearm, bushy gray eyebrows lifting in skepticism. The wound had strangely healed and it looked like it had been healing for a couple of days. David himself amazed he stared at his wound bewildered, the alcohol had kicked in and his nerves are subsiding. Something in the air smelled strangely, putting David off. Steve rattled on but David ignored him now intent on finding the source of the nauseating irritant coming from all around them. Suddenly that was all that he could focus on.

"Now are you sure that is all your blood?" Steve inquired. "It don't seem like you would have been bleeding that badly with them little scratches and tiny puncture wounds" Steve stared at David, suddenly realizing that he wasn't listening.

"What gives? Are you okay?"

David comprehended with an uncanny certainty that the source of the strange smell all around them emanated from Steve himself. Steve smelled like an outsider, putting out pheromones that told David that Steve was different somehow, dangerous. He wasn't like what David was becoming as unseen parasites pulsed, divided and infiltrated inside him. He tried to resist the urge to bite his uncle but instincts took over him, and he and an irrational side of himself took over he had to protect himself from his uncle.

David pushed over the decanter spilling and breaking Steve's precious crystal glasses as he lunged toward Steve's exposed throat, his teeth sunk into flesh stopping only inches from his carotid artery. David's thoughts and emotions were on overdrive he knew exactly what he was doing but could not help himself. War raged in his body an internal conflict in his mind too much for him to bear. He pushed away from his Uncle and flopped to the floor like a fish out of water, in the grips of a full body seizure.

Steve stood motionless for a moment, blood running over his hand as he felt his neck, his heart racing. He reached with bloody hand into the pocket of his overalls he thanked his lucky stars for his only real vice in another wise "off the grid" kind of life, pornography. This required him to put in a Wi-Fi that was now going to save his life and the life of his nephew. He reached and found his disposable prepaid cell phone and dialed 911.

David stopped writhing on the ground as his muscles tensed up the neck and lower back arching, his arms stretched out like a cross. Steve couldn't believe his eyes David's teeth and fingernails seemed to lengthen; his hands scrabbled lightly at the wooden floor, leaving marks in the wood. His mouth hung open as if his teeth were too big for it and his tongue lolled to the side.

David's eyes suddenly sprang open, he roared, "Hungry!"

Steve jumped back, still holding his neck, as David began to get up from the floor. David didn't give his bloody uncle a second glance as he headed out the door for the forest. Full of wildlife, it was like a smorgasbord for his ravenous hunger. Steve putting pressure on his wound with one hand and on the phone with the 911 operator with the other, without a second thought hurriedly rushed to his nephew's aid.

When Steve stumbled to the truck and to David's side he dropped the cell phone and gagged at the site of his nephew gorging on dead uncooked animal flesh. The sirens from the ambulance interrupted David's feast; instinctively howling at the loud shrill cacophony. The deafening sound and alternating lights from the ambulance arriving was too much for David to tolerate and he fell on his head hard, for the second seizure of the night. The ambulance swung into the drive and paramedics ran towards his writhing body.

"Before his seizure he was hallucinating." Steve explained to the paramedics, trying not to trip over his words in his panicked haste.

He had to explain that David had a fever and seizures and he had howled like a Wolf. Two of the paramedics, seeing the blood down the front of him, checked him over. The other paramedic, a trainee named Cody, sat by David, patiently waiting for his seizure to be over. Cody slid a cushion under his head and set his emergency bag on the ground. As the seizing began to lessen he pulled out his stethoscope, blood pressure monitor and other odds and ends. Finally lying still, he checked David's pulse and put the blood pressure cuff around his arm.

"Where did the blood come from?" The paramedic tending to his neck asked Steve.

"What do you mean?" Steve scoffed.

The paramedic intently and thoroughly wiped at his neck with a gloved hand, clearing away the blood with a moist alcohol wipe looking for a wound but found none.

"Sir, the blood on your neck is not yours, except for your jagged scar, you're perfectly fine." The paramedic stated.

Steve gingerly reached up to where he had been bitten, and ran his fingers across the puncture wounds which moments before had been bleeding profusely, only to find raised lines and pink bumps where they had been. He stood there confused for a moment, as the paramedics turned to check on David.

Assured that Steve did not need dire assistance the paramedics were off to assist Cody. When they rounded the trainee, one of the guys sucked in a breath. Cody had a tongue depressor down David's throat so he could get a better view of his mouth, a gloved hand checking David's lips and gums.

"Don't do that Cody!" The paramedic exclaimed. "He could have a seizure again."

Before the paramedics warning could register in his mind, the unconscious man woke up and growling bit down on Cody's thumb. He yanked his hand out quickly but it was too late, the latex barrier of Cody's glove had been ripped open, the skin was exposed. As Cody stumbled back to assess the damage David jumped to his feet and ran toward his Uncle.

"Quick, grab me six units of Alprazolam." The second paramedic ordered to the first paramedic, who was already on the radio to headquarters.

The paramedic thought the Alprazolam would ease David's seizure symptoms and it would also calm him down, sedating him. Despite being the size of a professional football player the paramedic had trouble restraining him. The paramedic scowled; incensed that the situation had even gotten so out of hand due to Cody's bumbling. The paramedic glanced around to see Cody sitting in the dirt still inspecting his hand and was relieved when Steve stepped in to help hold David. He wrapped his arm around his crazy nephew's abdomen and the other arm rubbed his shoulder trying to speak soothingly to him.

David's nose scrunched up as he breathed in Steve's aroma and stopped struggling. Pleased, Steve's scent had changed, smelling just like him now. The lull in the madness was more than the paramedic needed to inject the Alprazolam and sedative into David's arm, instantly sedating him. Collectively, everyone breathed a sigh of relief as David started to go slack. The three paramedics secured David on the gurney, stuck an IV into his arm, and threw the latch on the wheels to keep the gurney from moving.

"I tried to warn you to not stick your fingers into the patient's mouth," the blonde-haired, middle-aged paramedic smiled, "if he is epileptic, well… you know the rest. Have your thumb checked out; know a human mouth has more bacteria than a toilet."

"Yeah thanks." Cody grimaced, "I don't think he drew blood though." He assured them while he wiped his hands with disinfectant.

As Cody spoke he didn't notice the pink streaks forming in the foamy hand wash and he quickly dried his hands off, just his luck! First night out while training to become EMT, and he screwed up everything! He would've have kicked himself if not for the fact the feeling strangely anxious and figured the burning in his thumb was enough of a punishment.

"Don't beat yourself up too badly tonight, Cody, just rest." The linebacker sized paramedic said, patting him on the back. "It is a full moon out tonight, everybody is a little crazy and out of sorts."

The ambulance driver loaded David into the ambulance bed while the dusty blonde haired linebacker headed back to Steve to get any medical history about David. He could smell the alcohol emanating from Steve's mouth as he talked and knew the other guy in the ambulance had been drinking as well. He asked about illicit drugs being done, a flat denial, but he wondered if the toxicology screen would come back clean. Inwardly he shook his head and decided that these guys brought this on themselves. After getting a quick report written up, the ambulance took off down the dirt road leaving Steve heading back inside alone.

The backlight from the computer put off an eerie glow as Steve searched the web for something specific. It wasn't the usual pornography that he was searching for tonight, unlike every other night, it was something different. He didn't hit his usual websites, full of buxom blondes wearing only fur or guns, but instead looked up a history of lycanthropy.

Steve's gums hurt a growing pressure in his jaws more than he could stand. He ground his teeth back and forth and white porcelain powder flaked over his computer desk like a miniature white-topped mountain. He read a couple of paragraphs, clicking on another link, and then finally went back to the first. He rubbed his eyes, strained from reading, and then caught the reflection of himself on the monitor. He had a new fresh full set of teeth, but ground and to the point of being fang-like in appearance. His familiar usual reflection had all but vanished; all his life he had felt the call of the wild, had been hot headed and instinctual preferring to live off the land. The parasites found a good host with Steve, as he looked at the canine like man staring back at him; he wasn't afraid, but almost pleasantly surprised.

3

The moon reigned high and enormous in the Louisiana night sky, a full moon, first of three technical phases. Nathan Bordeaux arrived at the strip mall, cold sweat dripped from Nathan's forehead as he wiped at it with his shirt sleeve. Dizzy, bleeding and it was getting hard for him to see the road now, but the florescent lights of the 24-hour drugstore in Royal Bay glowed brightly, to his relief he arrived at his destination.

He put the truck in park and left it running as he got out and staggered across the parking lot towards the store. He rummaged through several thoughts in his head as he entered through the automatic sliding doors.

What was that monstrosity? He wondered. I shot that beast center mass, or did I? What was it? A large dog? A boar? But it had stood up! What if it was some kind of Sasquatch? No. This is real life, he told himself. It was probably a deformed bear or something. Wracking his brain he thought, did I leave anything to tie me to the scene of my dead friends? After all, though, *he* hadn't been the one to kill them; they were all out there poaching illegally. Why do I feel so shitty? Was it rabies?

No, rabies would not have manifested itself so quickly; it would take days to get sick. Maybe I'm just extremely anxious, he reasoned. That would explain most of my symptoms, right? After all, the bite on him didn't happen that long ago. What he did know was three of them were dead for sure, and there had been seven in the group, six? No there were eight in their group, wasn't there? He wasn't sure now, unsure about everything else too, as a headache began clawing its way into his head. He stumbled into the pharmacy stopping at the counter and leaned onto it, cradling his head in his shaking hands.

"Good evening, what can I help you with tonight?" The overworked clerk yawned, her eyes never looking up from the romance novel she held on her lap, never looked up to notice his unusual posture. He looked like a question mark in appearance as if Quasimodo had burst out of the silver screen.

"Neosporin, a shit load of ibuprofen and some acetaminophen," He said hoarsely to himself.

The clerk just pointed to the first aid aisle without saying a word. He muttered some curses under his breath then pulled out a shopping cart for added stability before setting off.

Moving in and out of consciousness now as he wheeled around and, with the help of the cart and his hands holding onto shelves, he slowly moved down the aisle. Shaking as he picked up some bandages and tried to straighten his back, feeling like his head was about to implode. His vision blurred and then cleared as he shuffled down the aisle, snarling to himself.

He hesitantly stopped by the sunglasses display to look at his reflection in the mirror; he didn't even recognize what he saw looking back at him. His once bold blue eyes were puffy slits, the whites bloodshot. His well styled shoulder length brown hair matted and unkempt, once plump youthful cheeks now looked white and taunt. His dry cracked lips parted to reveal receding gums and blood trickled from the corner of his mouth. He gasped and staggered back, trying not to black out.

"Son, are you okay?" A concerned elderly man, stopping his work stocking the shelves asked, coming over to help.

He reached a hand out to steady Nathan. His half-closed eyes widened immediately, as he registered the closeness of the old man. The stockman started to ask him again if he was alright, but seeing Nathan's fierce gaze, he let his words trail off and dropped his hand to his side. In the flickering bright lights, it appeared that Nathan's eyes were glowing, and he coughed and let out a warning snarl. The old man eyed him as he backed up another step and concern quickly dissolved into open disgust.

"You stupid drunk, pay for your stuff and get outta this store!" The gray haired old man spat, then grabbed a nearby broom and readied it as if it was a weapon.

Nathan paid him little attention. His body was on autopilot as he staggered once again up to the counter. The woman reading looked up at him for the first time. Taken aback by his disheveled and ghastly appearance she gasped, putting her hand over her chest. She shook it off, got back into her professional, albeit lax, manner, and checked him out with a forced smile. She and the gray haired old man whispered nervously to each other as Nathan staggered out the door with his bag.

The dark calm of the parking lot outside comforted his throbbing headache, dulling it a little, and his eyes began to open wider and focus. A fog had lifted from his mind. Confused, Nathan looked at his watch. He didn't know how he had gotten on the sidewalk outside. Last thing he remembered was looking at the mirror inside the drugstore. He glanced down at the bag in his hand.

Almost to his vehicle when the flashing lights and wailing sirens of an ambulance shrieked by on the highway, disorienting him, until he stumbled further out into the parking lot putting him directly in the path of an oncoming car.

Rubber transferred onto the asphalt permanently as the driver stomped on the break, tires shrieking. The bumper was about to smash Nathan's knees, but he miraculously leapt out of the way.

Nathan twirled around and rested both hands on the side of the hood. The driver flew out of the driver's door uttering obscenities. He did not hear the boy's grousing, however; too busy watching his cuticles recede, bleed and grow. Nathan could not believe what he was seeing. Time seemed to slow down while he considered this new symptom. Are they growing? No, impossible, he thought. A wave of nausea ran through him, knocking him down to his knees. He rested the side of his head on a hot tire and then violently vomited, proceeding to black out.

"What the fuck, man?" Bobby the driver looked down at his vomit spattered shoes and kicked Nathan in the side where he lay unresponsive.

His friend watching from inside the safety of the car could not believe his eyes as Nathan sprang up like a lunatic and scratched at his friend. Nathan's bloody fingernails mixed with the boy's own blood as Bobby clutched his hurt arm to his chest and held onto the open car door. The other kid leaned over the center console to yell to his injured friend.

"Hey Bobby, get your ass in the car! Something's wrong with this guy, he's on fuckin PCP or something." The passenger, Terry, yelled as his friend cried out in anger and pain.

Nathan's body reeled around to meet the sudden sound of Bobby's friend, Terry's voice, from the passenger seat. With his back turned to him, Bobby seized the opportunity and quickly made a break for the driver's seat. Pulling his door shut hastily he dug in his pockets, searching for his keys.

"Let's get out of here man, this guy must be tweaking and we don't wanna die for a soda pop, Terry." Bobby said as he started to put the key into the ignition blood dripping onto the steering wheel.

Startled they both jumped when Nathan hopped up on the passenger side of the car door, and lunged for Terry's hand hanging out the open window. He snagged Terry's fingers with his bloodied mouth and clamped down with a death grip. Punching out with his free fist, Terry hit Nathan in the face and yanked his injured hand back as a frenzied Nathan reeled back in pain and surprise from the blow.

"Go man! Go! Let's get the fuck outta here!" Terry squealed, holding his bloody fingers in his lap, covering them with his good hand. Bobby did not have to be told twice, he put it in drive and hit the gas, his arm aching and stinging still. He didn't slow down until they were to the far end of the deserted parking lot, and he pulled out his cell phone and punched in 911, barely having the nerve to check his rearview mirror. He almost expected to see the nut job in the back seat of his car. Nathan Bordeaux was just a shadow in the distance now.

Nathan came to from a dream-like state again; confusion setting in, but curiously… his head was not hurting anymore. His colored vision unexpectedly turned a spectrum of black and white, surprising him. He could no longer see in color but the world looked unexpectedly crisper and brighter to him. In the distance, he could hear sirens blaring coming closer and closer to him. Background noises seemed louder and clearer to him now too, he thought as he blacked out again, and his body instinctively fled.

Nathan ran from alley to alley on all fours, in his teeth he still clutched the purchases from the pharmacy in the plastic bag with drops of vomit and blood on it. He ran toward a residential area brimming with unsuspecting people snuggled up in their homes.

"Hey, Dad!" Chance yelled out for his father as he noticed a strange man from out the window in his bedroom. "There's somebody in our backyard."

Chance ran through the hallway yelling, "Dad, Dad, Dad!"

Watching the pay-per-view boxing match which Gene Francis had been waiting all day for, he barely paid attention to his child, Chance, when he vied for his dad's attention. Chance shook his dad's arm, spilling beer in the process.

"What, buddy?" He tried to divide his attention between the fight and his son. The fight was winning, as the man in the black striped shorts knocked out the man in the white shorts with three more rounds still to go.

"There is a man in the alley, I saw him under the streetlight, and I think he's in the backyard now." He turned his father's head to his get him to look towards the window.

"What?" He was up off the couch, peering out the kitchen window when he saw a figure in the darkness. "Hey buddy, got your bat with you?" He edged closer to the back screen door to get a better view.

Chance ran into his room and came back with bat in hand, and handed it to his father. "Are you going out there?"

"Yes, stay inside please." He said while peering out the mesh of the back screen door.

He readied the bat, holding it like a sword, and slowly opened the door as he motioned for Chance to stay put.

"Be careful, Dad." Chance whispered, impulsively clutching his sleeve.

He motioned for Chance to be quiet as he stood still, cocking his head slightly, listening for any sounds of movement. It took a moment or two before Gene's eyes adjusted to the darkness outside, and he slowly crept a little further out the door, glancing back to be sure his son stayed in the house. He cringed as the grass and leaves rustled with every footfall, until he finally made it to the tool shed. There were no signs of an intruder anywhere; confidence building he strolled out into the alley.

A sudden growl erupted from behind him, causing him to twirl around, and standing before him a thing that just barely resembled a human man. He was bleeding out of his ears, his eyes sunken and black, glowing from the dim streetlight above him. His nose looked stretched and flattened, with yellow mucus streaming out from both nostrils. His mouth and lips were grotesquely elongated, as if someone had stretched them downward. He was breathing rapidly; spittle had pooled at the corners of his mouth and dripped down the front of his two sizes too small camouflage shirt.

Nathan's ribs were visible under his shirt since his chest was heaving and larger than an average human's and he had an unusually extended and exposed abdomen with thin fine hair all over it. Gene's eyes trailed down to the thing's waist. The button on Nathan's camouflage cargo pants had popped off and Gene could see his quadriceps pushing tightly at the seams of his pants. His obscenely small pants exposed his engorged calves and his boots were torn to the sole, leaving Nathan's toes exposed. Gene blew out the breath he had been unconsciously holding when he heard his son's panicked call.

"Dad?" Chance had strolled outside, halfway from the safety of the family's house, halfway to this deformed lunatic, and yelled into the darkness.

Gene spun around to his son, one hand still gripping the bat; Gene flapped his other arm frantically to keep Chance from coming any closer. When he turned around again he was suddenly face to face with the thing, staring into wet gleaming eyes. He almost felt sorry for this thing; his eyes were so full of pain and confusion. There they stood eye to eye, both of them motionless. Nathan relaxed his bulging shoulders, drooping and seeming to shrink a little, and for a moment something inexplicably human could be seen in its eyes.

A few miles away, an ambulance screamed into the night and Nathan's mild demeanor altered drastically, grinding human teeth were snarling again as he stretched and twisted around his neck until it gave an audible "pop". Gene could see the lunatic's distended neck and a racing pulse that he could almost hear throbbing. Gene, torn between subduing this crazy man now and keeping his boy from harm, frozen still, called out to Chance in desperation.

"Chance, get in the house now!" Gene raised his bat in a readied stance.

He had no time to react, in a split second Nathan jumped toward him; the weight of the madman toppled him to the ground, the bat clattering away from his reach. He beat Nathan on his back with his fists as hard as he could, but to no avail, as sharp teeth found his wrist before he could land another blow. Gene cried out in pain as Nathan bit into flesh. He wrenched his head around as the pain began to register; hoping that his son had ran inside. He saw Chance standing stock still, his mouth hung open in helpless horror. Gene tried to shift, but he did not prevail, completely pinned to the ground under the crazy man.

"Daaad!" Chance cried pitifully.

Gene was getting light headed now; his strength leaving him as his blood soaked into the gravel and dirt. He didn't know it, but he was incredibly lucky as the tearing teeth had missed an artery; two centimeters over and he would have bled to death. Suddenly the weight pushing him down lifted as Nathan hopped up. Gene struggled to sit up, to find the madman, to protect his son. He struggled to his unsteady feet but the darkness overcame him, crashing into him like a wave, he collapsed.

The lunatic sprinted down the alley, again looking for a dark safe place to hide. He came upon a homeless man huddled in a torn coat, clutching a bottle of gin. The conflict ensued again until he fled off into the night again, he ran until he came upon a nursing home on the corner of a quiet and dark street. The yard was serene and poorly lit. He scaled easily over a privacy fence, tired and scared, and found the perfect hiding place in the L-shaped brick building. No one would notice him here, he thought, as he nestled into the dark nook with the wall to his back. Although still in pain, he felt secure enough to drift off to sleep. As dawn approached he dreamed of a wolf.

4

Col. Miller was a highly decorated officer of the US Marine Corps. He proudly wore his medals of valor on his military jacket. A courageous man, a stubborn man, and a homeless and drug addicted man. His once handsome visage concealed by a graying, dirt covered, wild bush of a beard. Col. Miller's military hairstyle had long ago got away from him, his once brown hair graying with age and now hanging down past his shoulders in scraggly knots. His once intense, caring gray-brown eyes now beaten down and defeated from years of living on the streets; his cheeks were sunken in, gums red and swollen, and jaw line sagging from his missing set of dentures, filling his face with deep lines, sunken in from malnutrition.

He cursed under his breath at the dried blood and torn collar of his once pristine camouflage uniform. Col. Miller would refuse to eat if his uniform had been tarnished and he only had enough coins to go to the Laundromat to clean the filth away. Homeless or not, he considered himself a proud patriot and any blemish on his fatigues was not acceptable in his eyes. He inspected the wound he had just received. At first he had cursed himself for not going to the emergency room, but now he could not believe his eyes, the bite mark had already healed itself. Little relief to him as he had been dreaming about a warm bed and hot food, assuming if he made it to the E.R. today they didn't just bandage him up and send him back out the door.

Col. Miller's hands were shaky as he downed with one gulp what was left of his half-pint of grain alcohol, warming him on the inside. Stomach growling with hunger as he walked the shadowy brick structured alleyway of Royal Bay's business district, staggering toward his clandestine destination. He silently cursed the maniac he had followed down the alley last night. He had been too tired to walk all the way back to camp, and he hoped to beg a few dollars for bus fare off a guy who ran past. The guy had turned and leaned into him, trying to bite his face off; Miller shoved him away, but not before the guy had nipped his neck. What a freak!

"Can you give me a nickel?" There was barely concealed desperation in Col. Miller's voice.

The crack dealer said nothing as he motioned by hand the universal sign "show me the money". Col. Miller did just that, wads of cash crumpled and wet in his dirty hands. He had gotten the bills panhandling. Courtesy of the masses so wracked with guilt from the shadowy homeless veterans. Most had served their country but they were often damaged physically or psychologically past the point of being a productive citizen. A few silver coins or dollar bills helped to relieve their guilt while they looked the other way.

"Not my business, man," the crack dealer observed as he handed Col. Miller a nickel's worth of crack, eyeing him up and down, "but I got mad props for you, you're a decorated soldier you shouldn't be poisoning your body this way."

Col. Miller laughed to himself, only outwardly nodding in acknowledgement of the statement made by the crack dealer named Maurice. Ironic, he said he respected him but always sold him the crack anyways. After several days without a meal and starving, freebasing cocaine made the pain of hunger and cold go way for a while, the bliss and numbness made the whole world go away as well. Shaking in anticipation he searched for his lighter.

When the transaction had been made Col. Miller had the poison in his pipe. He closed his eyes as he inhaled waiting for the bite of hunger to fade, but it would not disappear, and in fact every inhalation made the hunger seem worse.

"Whoa man!" Maurice was slack-jawed and dumbstruck as looked into Miller's glowing eyes.

Col. Miller's eyes narrowed as a new, unfamiliar and painful pressure grew in his mouth. The pressure in his jaws unbearable he opened his mouth to alleviate the pain, but drool spilled out onto the pavement. Maurice stood absolutely still, still gripping dollar bills in his hand. He could not believe his eyes; the former toothless Col. Miller now had a mouth full of canine fangs. He took a step back, his eyes fixed on Miller's mouth.

"What the hell?" Maurice demanded.

Col. Miller pictured half his face sliding off, hitting the alley floor with a wet smack. He wondered if this was what a "bad trip" was like, he'd never felt like this before, he had always felt better after a hit or two.

Maurice slowly backed up, trying to make small, quiet movements, but it was too late. The glint of his sunglasses hit Miller's eyes, making them glow brighter, and he lunged at Maurice. Maurice turned and as he tried to run, he stumbled and fell, sliding into the dingy brick wall on one side of the alley. He threw his hands up in defense, trembling, his eyes closed automatically. His heart still pounding, he peeked between his fingers at the decorated veteran gone deranged.

Col. Miller stood still as a statue, over Maurice with a full set of over-sized, bloodied, ivory fangs huffing loudly. Amazed at Col. Miller's seeming transformation, he had always had a wild beard that made him look like a Wolf man, and his visage now was still that of a human's face with the exception of the glowing eyes and pointy teeth. Maurice instinctively reached for the gun he kept in his jacket but Col. Miller's supernaturally strong arms pinned him down to the ground and powerful hands gripped his wrists, pushing him into the dirt, he cringed with pain as his palms turned white, the blood flow in his veins interrupted.

Maurice tilted his head back and began laughing hysterically between grunts of discomfort, his gold plated teeth visible. He thought he would die by a bullet; some other gang member who wanted his corner, or by some hero cop who quickly cried "self-defense", but not this kind of surreal situation. The Col. snarled, and Maurice cringed as a shower of hot spittle rained down on his face.

"Man!" In a last ditch effort to save himself Maurice pleaded for his life. "Man, it's me, Maurice, I'm your main man, and we go back, don't do me like this please...."

The Col.'s head moved back and forth inquisitively and for a brief moment something in his rage filled, beastly eyes became human again. Col. Miller released Maurice's wrists.

"M...auu...rrr...i...ce!" Col. Miller's inflamed mouth struggling to form speech.

Maurice could still see fangs glinting above him as he lay helpless on the ground, gently rubbing the feeling back into his tingling wrists. He started to sit up when Col. Miller suddenly struck out at his left shoulder. Searing pain went through his entire body as canine teeth scraped across his collarbone.

Maurice's life flashed before his eyes, he resigned himself to the fact that these were the last moment of his ill-gotten life. Eyes swollen and puffy as he cried like a baby, he could feel and smell his urine as it was evacuating his body. He was gasping for breath, unable to even scream, as Col. Miller's body pushed down on his rib cage.

"Mauriccce." Col. Miller rumbled... breath putrid and hot against his face.

Maurice kept his eyes closed, his body shaking in fear for what was to come as he struggled to breathe. Suddenly he was able to suck in a breath as Col. Miller's weight lifted off his chest. He sucked the precious air into his lungs in gasps as he watched Col. Miller run off on all fours, out into the streets of Royal Bay, his entire body shaking, Maurice blacked out.

The wild bearded lunatic, called Miller ran stealthily down boulevards, straying away from Streetlights. His body moving on instinct headed home to familiar aromas. As if in a dream, nightmare or an out of body experience he watched his body run to the relative safety of Royal Bay and his homeless encampment. He could see clearly the barrel fires and the makeshift tents which were still half a mile away, the full moon's light guiding him with its glow.

Half a dozen men and women warmed themselves idly by a barrel fire; they were dressed in layers upon layers of filth caked clothing, unaware of the danger coming their way. An obese man, his head covered by a dirty black sock hat, was warming chicken soup in a can suspended over the fire, while the others anxiously waited for a chance at their one and only meal for the day.

"Colonel, is that you?" The woman with long, straw-dry brown hair called into the gloom beyond the fire.

Col. Miller watched as his body lurched onward, as if he was a marionette controlled by invisible strings, moved by an unknown master. He recognized the woman who was jogging up to him, concern etched across her sun burnt face; Nancy, a 30-something-year-old teacher, she had recently been laid off from her school and lost her home in the process. Nevertheless, the beast was in control of his body, fueled by instinct and an all-consuming hunger out of his control.

"Colonel Miller, what is wrong, are you hurt?" She reached out her hand to him as he turned towards the full moon light.

Panic filled her, tangled and matted brown hair falling around her whitened face as she looked down, but she had not yet registered what happened. Blood jetted from the four now missing digits on her left hand. She stared at her mangled hand, her eyes widening to comical proportions, pain not yet registering in her mind. She looked back up to the fiend that stood before her. She had no time to react as Col. Miller seized her forearm with his powerful grip, yanking her closer and fangs punctured her skin, chewing through her elbow in violent crunching bites until her lower arm was ripped free from her body. Gnawed, loose skin flapped in the wind. An arterial spray of blood painted her vision red as she began to fall back, the shocked teacher dead before she could utter more than a strangled cry, she hit the ground.

Col. Miller saw the shocked and horrified faces around him, able to remember and name some of them in his head before he blacked out and his infected body, driven by instincts and primal urges, completely took over. One by one, the persons fell to the beast's unquenchable rage and hunger. When all was said and done, the bodies littered the ground all around him, blood pooled at his feet, and finally the fog lifted from his mind.

"What the hell, guys?" Sgt. Alexander yelled.

Sgt. Adam Alexander heard the commotion and emerged from his makeshift tent. He leaned forward in the wheelchair and wheeled off to see what was going on. Only 27 years old; another veteran in the US military deployed in Afghanistan before an IED permanently took him out of action and claimed one arm and both legs. He wore a prosthetic arm that attached to the stub of his right shoulder; the doctors had done nothing about his missing legs, a mishap in his insurances, so he was wheelchair bound for the rest of his life.

The aroma of barbecue assaulted Adam Alexander's senses, his gut twisting in knots from starvation, mouth salivating in anticipation. He wheeled himself with one hand faster than seemingly possible, afraid the barbecue he had smelled would be running out before he arrived. He was almost smiling when he turned the corner and his chair bumped into a detached and mutilated human leg. He looked up, seeing bodies and parts strewn haphazardly about. Sgt. Alexander's hand hurt from the pressure of the wheelchair's wheel as it had skidded to a stop. He convulsed and vomited after taking in the site that lay before him. Wiping his mouth, he turned his head, hearing a sound near the edge of where the light from the barrel fire barely reached.

Col. Miller sat on his haunches, greedily consuming what look like a large order of ribs. Alexander froze; still in the dark shadow of an overpass, he hoped that Col. Miller did not see him. Thick clouds of smoke blew across in front of him, smelling of charred flesh, obscuring his view momentarily. His heart was pounding so hard he thought that alone might betray his position. Slowly he wheeled back, edging closer to some of the makeshift tents, hoping to find refuge from Col. Miller's view. Nevertheless, Col. Miller stopped his consumption of the dripping human flesh just as quickly and niffed at the air around him as the wind changed, zeroing in on another living target, Adam Alexander. Never in his life had Adam felt the term "sitting duck" been more relevant.

Adam tried to turn his wheelchair, to escape, too slow, the cumbersome wheels catching on the rough ground. Col. Miller was on him in an instant, knocking him and the wheelchair over onto the ground with a clatter. Adam looked desperately into Col. Miller's vacant eyes as they looked up at each other, their faces only inches away, but the person that used to be Col. Miller was there no more. Years of military training, instinct and the will to live made Adam fight back. With his one good arm, he pushed Col. Miller back and with his elbow, hit him in the throat, knocking him down in a heap.

"Hey Miller, you off your fucking rocker or something?" Adam screamed as he dragged his wheelchair in the dirt between him and Col. Miller, clutching it like a shield.

Col. Miller, not deterred by Sgt. Alexander's barricade, reached out and stretched his muscular limbs over the chair, found Sgt. Alexander's throat easily and began squeezing, blocking off his airway. With a last ditch effort, Alexander struggled to take in another mouthful of air and shouted in a scratchy voice.

"A-ten-hut!"

The crushing pressure that he felt diminished slightly and he drew in another precious breath. After a moment's hesitation, Sgt. Alexander saw a flicker of recognition come into Col. Miller's eyes, and the Col. slowly let go of his stranglehold on the Sgt.'s bruised neck. With the exception of a full set of canine fangs and gleaming eyes, Col. Miller looked, for all intents and purposes, entirely human again.

Miller wiped sticky blood from his mouth with the back of his hand as recognition of the disabled man on the ground come flooding back to him. It was Sgt. Adam Alexander, essentially a brother in arms who the Colonel had always looked up to, and had even come to love. He fought the beast inside as he stepped back from Alexander, grabbing his wheel chair and up righting it for Adam and wheeling the chair toward him.

"What's happening to me?" Col. Miller growled.

As he tried to speak the pain and distortion of his jaws from the newly formed fangs made talking almost impossible to him, a distorted slurring garble was all that the Sgt. heard. However, the pain and confusion in the Colonel's eyes were more than enough to convey what he had meant to say, as he helped the Sgt. onto his chair. Then he recoiled stopping a few feet away, a miserable moan escaping his drooling mouth.

"Hold on, Miller, wait…." Adam put his one good arm out and put his hand up in a gesture for him to stop. "We'll figure out what's happening together, all right? Don't run off."

Alexander could almost see the beast compelling Col. Miller in his unnaturally bright eyes. Miller seemed to be fighting some primitive inner impulses that were plaguing him. Adam wheeled closer as the Colonel clawed at the sides of his head, fighting an internal conflict in his mind, then letting out a deafening howl that pierced Alexander's ears.

"Friend!" The Col. struggled to speak, to argue with himself.

Locking eyes with Adam, the Colonel suddenly attacked. He lunged and bit down on his friend's right shoulder, the prosthetic tearing off in the process. As suddenly as the attack had erupted, Col. Miller backed off again, retreating to the shadows but watching Adam with focused curiosity.

"You son of a bitch, you bit me!" Adam cried.

Looking at the gaping hole in his shoulder where the prosthetic arm had been attached only a second ago. Adam leaned forward, suddenly feeling flushed and dizzy as the shock wore off. Nausea wracked his body and his vision began to dim right before he vomited and started shaking. His body skittered on the ground as he seized, toppling out of his chair, foam poured out of his mouth.

Col. Miller watched in unexplained eagerness as Adam's right shoulder sprouted tendrils that snaked out and writhed like live wires. In the middle of these moving vines there formed a gelatinous mass that would shortly become humerus bone. Miller held his breath with exhilaration as the developing arm took shape and then became what appeared to be a fully mature Wolf's arm. It was the same with the lower limbs too; the parasite had a blank canvas to work with, freshly forming a wolf's appendages, complete with hocks and a long slim tail.

Adam wept with confused gratitude he flexed his now fully functioning legs, and began to sprint for the first time since coming home stateside, he ran. He ran directly at Colonel Miller. He hit him with so much force, Miller was knocked off his feet, landing on his back in the blood stained dirt. Adam hugged him, for the first time with two arms. This was followed by a sloppy doglike lick from a still human tongue to Col. Miller's cheeks and face, while whimpering happily.

Adam had quickly decided, while he still did not know what happened to him he would follow Col. Miller to the ends of the Earth if he so ordered it. However, he had a hunger that the usual can of beans or corn mash could never satisfy. His insatiable hunger would have to wait as his newly acute supernatural senses told him that groups of outcasts, runaways and homeless people were making their way along the tracks toward the camp. Sgt. Alexander and Col. Miller looked at each other as they sniffed at the air. They had no reason to speak; just giving a series of grunts was all that it took to agree upon their plan. A primitive sort of telepathy, honed to perfection throughout the millennia by werewolves, cemented their battle plans. The sparse hairs on the back of Adam's neck rose up and he felt alive for the first time since his injury as Col. Miller circled around the back and hid in the bushes waiting for the first group. There would be an ambush, those that died from their injuries would be consumed and the survivors were to be welcomed into Col. Miller's own special military.

5

The glass doors of the hospital slid open and Maurice, his makeshift bandage leaking profusely, stumbled inside. The stale sterile aroma of the waiting room hit him all at once, making him hesitate a little. It was all that he imagined a hospital would be, the overhead florescent lights all on, yet dimmed from years' worth of dust, the smell of disinfectant permeating the air. He stared at the tiles on the floor, dingy yet glimmering. He laughed to himself as the voice of his mother played through his head, "don't worry," she would always say, "the floor is so clean you could eat off it!" Maurice thought it was a good thing he wasn't hungry. Eyes still on the floor, he made his way toward the receptionist at the end of the room.

A cacophony of shrill noises assaulted his senses as he walked. To the left of him a baby cried and swung its tiny fists in the air, to the right a couple yelling at each other at the top of their lungs. His arm was still bleeding and now it burned as he staggered over to the receptionist window where a woman braced herself against a column and sobbed into her sleeve. A ragged and dirty homeless man sat in wait, mumbling as he rocked back and forth. The whole check-in process took only minutes and was relatively painless, but the waiting, Maurice told himself, was the hardest part.

Static and squawk of a policeman's radio startled Maurice out of his thoughts. He instinctively clutched at the illicit drugs in a secret compartment inside his coat. It was just then he came to his senses and looked up, realizing he had stumbled into a hornet's nest! A sea of blue for as far as Maurice could see spread out before him. Cops stood leaning against walls, chatting quietly to each other, writing on clipboards, and sitting with injured convicts.

"Dammit!" Maurice exclaimed, though only in his head, but in his paranoia felt that all of the officers in blue had heard him anyways.

Maybe he was distracted by the screaming baby. Maybe he was distracted by the incessant bickering of the couple in the back of the room. Whatever the case may be he saw them all now… baffled that he had been so oblivious when he first came in. He could see the homeless man in handcuffs, crimson glinting on steel as his blood slowly trickled down from his forearms. A woman that had been sobbing now wiped her wet eyes and runny nose, and then he heard her state to an officer writing on a clipboard that she didn't know what had come over her boyfriend when he attacked her.

He had to get away from here. With an ounce worth of crack on his person, this was the last place he wanted to be besides the police department itself. He stood and slowly crept backwards toward the hospital doors, not daring to make eye contact with the half dozen or so police officers now walking into the waiting room to join the rest. They let the exam room doors clatter shut behind them and they all had a look of grim determination on their faces, all of them Maurice felt were stealing glances suspiciously at him.

An injured man, visibly angry argued with the receptionist his voice getting louder and louder. Until finally a nurse came out and calmly whispered unknown words to the irate man that quieted him. Snapping on her latex gloves the nurse rolled up the man's sleeve preparing to examine the wound he was so upset over.

"Sir…" surprise visible on her face, "You don't seem to be hurt at all, where is the blood coming from?" She studied the glazed look on his face for a moment before looking around for help. Maurice watched fixedly as his back hit the wall by the double doors to freedom.

After looking around for help for a moment, a doctor or even another nurse, she accidently twisted the crazed man's arm as she turned back to him. She didn't see it coming. Foam from his mouth violently spewed out toward her. The nurse, caught off guard, wasn't quick enough to react. Nor did she imagine that the parasites were targeting her intentionally, as the projectile mixture of blood mixed with foamy sputum flew into her mouth making her gag as she reflexively swallowed to get a breath.

"I need security!" the nurse screeched as she doubled over gaging, "anybody!"

Maurice, shocked, watched in horror as all hell broke loose! His back to the exit doors and the commotion quickly escalating, he knew that if he were going to get away this was the opportune moment but he stood watching the surreal scene. In stunned silence, unable to move as several uniformed officers came to the aid of the nurse. The sick lunatic fell out of his chair and down on top of her, she yelled out helplessly, as she fell backwards, the two cops closest to her reaching out as if to catch her. A scuffle ensued as the uniformed men tried to subdue the crazy man, their backs to Maurice as they wrestled him, trying to pull him away from the nurse who was scrambling away on the floor.

The click, click, buzz and the smell of something reminiscent of bumper cars at play told Maurice the officers had just stunned the man. But he pushed up to his feet, as a soft growl intensified to warn the officers to stay back, apparently the shock had not affected him whatsoever. Wide-eyed and scared he couldn't help but watch, Maurice saw the men advance as they used the Taser again. The guy bent forward as if in pain, but when they finally moved in, he violently wrenched past their arms, keeping low and pushing one of the men out of his way as he charged forward. Mace arced after the man as he tried to flee.

Maurice realized in horror that the vacant eyed man had his sights now set on him! At the last minute of his charge, the man inexplicably hesitated, and that gave the cops more than enough time to regroup, circle around and tackle him. Finally subdued, six policemen each held down part of the lunatic, and the other officers stood protectively in a circle around them.

Locked doors to the interior swung open. Two men in white coats, presumably doctors, came running to the aid of the struggling officers. They quickly gave the restrained man a heavy dose of what Maurice assumed was a tranquilizer, maybe anxiety medication or a mixture of both, which they shot into his hip. As the man started to go limp, the doctors turned their attentions to the attacked nurse who was currently shaking and moaning on the floor.

In the other side of the waiting room the reception door swung open, "Maurice Jackson?"

As the scene began to calm down an elderly salt-and-pepper haired, caramel skinned woman with clipboard in hand called out his name. Seemingly unaffected by the melee, she pushed her bifocals back on her bulbous nose and looked around the room, searching for her next patient.

"Maurice Jackson? M. Jackson?" Her loud and monotone yells turned to a piercing annoyance as she called out for a third time, "Maurice Jackson!"

Ignoring the situation just wrapping up before her eyes, the nurse impatiently tapped her pen against the charts and then looked around the room until her eyes found Maurice. She walked up and laid a wrinkled but delicately soft hand on his shoulder and startled him.

"Excuse me, honey, I didn't mean to startle you," Her tone reminding Maurice of an elderly aunt or grandmother, and instantly calming him, "Sweetie is you Maurice Jackson?"

He quickly nodded.

"Great, come with me sweetie and now that I found you in this crazy waiting room you get to go in and wait for the Doctor." The nurse laughed.

Glad to be out of the unusually large police presence and the patients seemingly out of their minds. Maurice followed the woman with the soothing voice as she headed toward the examination rooms, unlocking doors with her ID badge as she walked, clutching his still bleeding wound.

As he walked past the numbered rooms, each with curtains half open he couldn't help but notice the patients who waited there. All of them had vacant, hollow eyes and a lot of them had some form of what looked like a scratch or wound somewhere on an extremity.

"What's wrong with them?" He muttered the question to no one in particular; his eyes were transfixed he staring in at the patients as he walked.

Maurice overheard a female patient with a mousy voice from one exam room muttering, "Huge white wolf... Red eyes, white Wolf, red eyes watching... white Wolf."

The pleasant nurse with the glasses slid open the curtains to exam room five, she answered Maurice's earlier question, "I can't talk about any patient and their injuries, privacy policies and all that, sweetie, but we are uncharacteristically swamped tonight. There must be a rabid boar or even a feral dog out there somewhere, all the injuries·we got comin' in tonight, people torn up and scared to death."

Silence permeated the air, the occasional rustling of curtains or ringing phone being the only sounds. It was a far cry from the noisy and chaotic waiting room. The nurse said nothing for a moment as she finished checking Maurice's vitals and she began nervously talking again, almost to herself.

"Some of the patients complained they were bit by some kind of huge feral dog with brown fur looking like dreadlocks! If you ask me, dreadlocks or matted fur is the same thing!" She smiled and winked as Maurice unconsciously smoothed back his own hair, all in dreadlocks.

"I been workin' at this hospital for the last thirty years and believe you me, I have seen worse than this," The woman gestured out toward the other rooms.

She then began telling the story of the alligator preserve and how over a dozen gators got loose and took off all over the city. She told him about the loss of limbs and the deaths that ensued, a nightmarish bloodbath that lasted over a week until all the beasts were found and killed. He leaned back on his good elbow as she continued talking.

"And then there was Hurricane Katrina! Nothing compares to that." The nurse went silent for a moment, lost in thought as the horrors came flooding back to her, "I survived Katrina; I can surely survive this comparatively mild weekend of crazies!"

"147 over 91, hon." The nurse said as she removed his blood pressure cuff. She said aloud in a compassionate yet clinical tone, "Pulse is 126."

The nurse, named Maggie Futunan, took the bandages off and began to inspect his festering wound until a disruption coming from the nurse's station made them both swivel their heads around simultaneously.

It was the muttering woman from exam room one, arguing with a Doctor. She had grown inpatient and strangely enough, her wounds no longer seemed to warrant an emergency room visit as she showed the confused Doctor.

Her ears not being what they used to be, but her curiosity increasing with age, Nurse Maggie quickly finished her examination of Maurice's open wounds and scurried over to the door to listen more to the quarreling.

Maurice's hearing, however, had always been outstanding. He regarded it as his saving grace on the streets hustling. He had a quicker warning when danger was near. He stayed put on the crinkled paper sheet, swinging his legs to and fro, on the examining room table he could easily hear everything. It was the mousy voiced woman arguing with an orderly. Panicking, she must have made a mistake, the wounds were far less serious and she was desperately looking to the Doctor for confirmation.

She wanted them to sign off on her discharge papers. Before she could say a thing the Doctor interrupted her talking in an almost unintelligible foreign accent. He gestured to her mumbling something about being busy but that there was room on the second floor for her to get a psychological evaluation before the doctor left the room to see if the bed had been readied leaving her to her own devices.

The argument no longer interested Nurse Maggie as she turned from the curtained doorway and proceeded to open Maurice's file. Checking everything over and signing the bottom of the top form, she closed the folder and said, "You would be surprised how often that happens here, people with no insurance come here claiming they're on their deathbed and the next minute they're just fine or there's the people that come in under the influence and are afraid of taking a piss test, so they end up signing out and not getting seen by the doctors."

It had never occurred to him that he might have to submit to a drug test. After all, he came in because he had a massive wound. He didn't come in with gang related gunshot nor was he wheeled into the emergency room for a suspected overdose. Maurice was nervous now and he couldn't seem to make eye contact with the nurse anymore.

"So..." Maurice tried to sound casual and even a little bored, "when do you think I will get to see a Doctor?" He asked, eyeing the door nervously.

Nurse Maggie smiled knowingly as she touched his leg and said, "Don't worry sweetie, I took one look into your dilated, and bloodshot eyes, checked your pulse which is quite high, and I can tell you, we're not going to drug test you."

Maurice felt like the nurse was reading his mind as she commented further, "We need to stitch up your arm first hon, so don't be nervous, and the Doctor will be in real soon to see about it, okay?"

"Okay." Maurice nodded sheepishly.

"Besides, the lab is so backed up testing earlier blood work; I don't even think we'd have the time to check everyone tonight. We were afraid of an outbreak of some sort earlier tonight, but so far all our test results have come back negative. No form of smallpox, anthrax, bubonic plague, a super staph, flesh eating bacteria, or rare fungi has been detected, so that's good. Some cultures could take days or weeks to form but the doctors here are confident we're not looking at a deadly disease that might spread."

The mere mention of anthrax or some form of synthetic nasties made Maurice's hair on his neck stand on end. If this was the starting of a new form of disease, instead of running away from the scene of death and doom, he had fallen face first into Ground Zero.

Maggie left the room to collect and check on more patients, Maurice high on crack cocaine and alone with his thoughts, paced back and forth awaiting the doctor's entrance. Startled when he peeked out the curtains and a petite blonde haired girl stood motionless before him. The one with the mousy voice Maurice guessed. Her eyes were vacant but she seemed to be staring daggers right through him. She sniffed at him, her neck and head moving about in such a way that reminded Maurice of a cautious dog. Shivers coursed down his spine.

Is this actually happening? Maurice thought stepping back into his exam room. Her platinum blonde dirty bangs fell down in her face as she moved ever so slightly, still sniffing toward him. Is she growling at me? Maurice looked down at her thin pierced lips, saw her jaw line reverberating, yes she was! He backed up as far as he could go before he hit the examination bed, making the paper crinkle loudly.

Looking at her more closely, she was a short, stick figured stature of a girl, no more than fourteen or fifteen years old! Maurice with red-faced embarrassment gathered his wits. How could such a girl fray his nerves so badly? Then her head twisted again, as she sniffed the air around him once again. The blonde girl stepped closer to the exam room that held a trapped Maurice. He focused on those eyes. Her vacant, expressionless, almost animalistic eyes fixated on him. She took another step. Maurice frantically searched for any form of makeshift weapon to defend himself from the blonde haired girl but she abruptly stopped in her tracks. Once again she took in the air around him. This time a confused expression appeared upon her face as she crinkled her nose before running off further and hiding in the shadows like a scared stray dog.

From either side of the hallway a loud buzzer blared, signifying the open door to the waiting room. The shrill sounding alarm made Maurice cover his ears in shock his hearing strangely sensitive to the high-pitched sounds. Further aggravating the sharp noise, a policeman burst through the double doors his radio shrill, one hand gripping a gurney with a loose wheel. It wobbled and squeaked at every rotation.

Just behind the first gurney, riding the coattails, another gurney appeared. This one had a man in the midst of a full blown seizure. Two paramedics were impatiently waiting for the gurney with the loose wheel to get out of their way as they each held a hand on the man to keep him from falling off the bed.

In the midst of all of this the blonde girl who had faltered, confused somehow by Maurice's scent, come out of the shadows and managed to slip away through the open door. Maurice slowly stepped out into the hallway not yet aware of the strange blonde girl's exit to survey the scene.

"David Tambo, twenty-six years old, blood pressure is 133 over 50," Cody wiped the sweat from his forehead with his arm and continued, "on arrival he was active and alert then went into a seizure on scene."

The two paramedics grunted as they transferred David from the gurney to a bed. Cody faltered in the transfer for just one second, but that was all it took get the attention of the other linebacker paramedic. After stabilizing David and watching him sleep peacefully for a minute the pair walked out of the room.

"Are you all right man?" The EMT patted Cody's shoulder, "you should really get your hand checked out now, Cody."

"No I feel fine. In fact," Cody said in uncharacteristic excitement, "I feel exhilarated!"

Cody returned the pat on the EMT's shoulder, harder this time, not realizing his own strength had increased. "My pulse is a little high but I had two of those energy drinks that I am addicted to. I feel healthy and strong!"

"It's a scratch; I'll be fine," Cody beamed, pulling off his bandage he flexed his hand and was grinning broadly.

"I'm glad you feel fine but all in all it would make me feel better if you clocked out tonight to get yourself checked out." The paramedic deliberately tried to refrain from eye contact with Cody.

The paramedic had been friends with Cody their entire lives so Cody's dilated eyes and overly dramatic emotions worried him immensely. He knew he wasn't on drugs so he wasn't going to rat out his lifelong friend for this, but the strange scene at Steve's cabin worried him to his core.

"All right friend," Cody slapped his friend's already bruising back. "Maybe when you get off work you can come over."

The paramedic grinned nervously, "Yeah buddy that sounds great."

Cody entered the hallway and looked around to see Maurice curiously looking out of the curtains from his exam room locking eyes. Embarrassed that he had been caught staring; he quickly looked away as Cody headed toward the doors.

Cody stopped midstride. He had a strange feeling suddenly come over him. He felt as if he knew the dreadlocked man that stared at him just across the hall. With one nimble turn with the balls of his feet he walked up to Maurice, looking down into his eyes.

"Do I know you?" Cody asked.

"Me? No man, I don't, you don't know me." Maurice stuttered; he would give his right leg to get out of this situation. He just wanted to get his arm looked at, stitched up and go home.

Cody cocked his head to one side confused and uncertain. He knew he knew him in some way!

Maurice took a step back when Cody stepped forward again. Maurice turned his head from side to side looking for anybody who might have noticed this odd exchange. Maurice had been mistaken about this whole strange interaction. He lived his whole life in the projects and he suspected he would die there too. Any interactions with white men had always been negative and he sure didn't have any white friends! He made up his mind in an instant that if this paramedic came any closer he would knock him out. Maurice felt his fists clench up and his breath quicken.

Cody shook off his thoughts, shrugged and turned toward the door again much to the relief of Maurice. Letting his guard down and taking a deep breath in, relief flooded through his body, then he let it out with a whoosh of air.

As he turned a cold hand touched his shoulder and he felt as if he jumped toward the ceiling.

"Excuse me, are you Maurice?" Voice calm, a reassuring and foreign man asked behind him, the emergency room doctor on call for the night.

"Umm…," Maurice forgot all about his wound, although the wound had steadily bled since arriving at the hospital. "Yes, yes I am."

The Doctor with the short stature and pleasant disposition motioned for Maurice to follow him. He lay down on the paper sheets again while the Doctor proceeded to examine him. Nurse Maggie brought in a sterile tray for the Doctor and smiled encouragingly while the man began the process of sterilizing, anesthetizing and stitching up his bleeding wound.

Unbeknownst to anybody a sleeping David awoke from his drugged slumber. Earlier than the anesthesiologist had estimated, his new metabolism working overtime to clear the combination of drugs from his system at an exponential rate, he sat up. An alert and awake David looked around. Confusion set in and followed by anxiety which quickly turned into rage, the instinct to survive taking over as he lurched forward and quickly jumped up from his bed, attached IVs ripped out of David's body. His logic and reasoning clouded, only the simple brainstem and his primal instinct were functioning now.

David quietly snuck up on his prey, a male orderly oblivious to the danger behind him. Busy amongst piles of paperwork, the orderly felt the hot breath against his neck before turning around. His blood ran cold from the horror that he saw. The orderly was looking at a human, he was sure of that, but this man's form had mutated somehow. As if out of one of HG Lovecraft's nightmares David was a sight to behold. Slumped and dislocated shoulders leading to his elongated arms. He had IV tubes sticking out of his inner elbows leading off to nowhere in particular. It made him look like a squid demon. Black and blue bruises covered him from head to toe.

The orderly's eyes widened focusing in on David's enormous hands elongated stretched and flattened out like silly putty, fingernails grown into daggers. He had no time to scream, lethal daggers thrust into soft eyes blinding him. Then a dagger-like claw plunged into the man's mouth like a human bowling ball. The orderly's last coherent thought before he died, this guy's hands were bigger than his entire head.

With just one hand David hoisted the orderly up off the ground and exerting little effort smashed him against the wall. A cracking sound something akin to an egg splitting open could be heard. An angry growl started from the mutated voice box of the thing that used to be David. He hefted up the mortally injured orderly and smashed his misshapen head against the wall yet again. The head crumpled like a soggy cardboard box getting stepped on. The orderly twitched, prompting David to smash the broken and shattered head into concrete again and again until his twitching legs went still. David discarded the lifeless body to the ground in a heap, like a pile of dirty clothes.

In this strange place he had done away with the threat. Sniffing the air he decided only fifty feet stood between him and freedom. His head swiveled from side to side, cautiously gaging for hidden dangers, ears at alert, sniffing a curious smell. An emergency beacon of sorts, distress pheromones…A compelling sense of duty washed over him.

On all four limbs, a trick made easy by his lengthened arms; he prudently moved past Maurice, the doctor and four other patients asleep in their beds until he made it to the end of the hallway. He could smell the over powering scent of aftershave coming from two men in the exam room. The curtains were closed but he could smell the odor of a third, the origin of the distress pheromones.

Close enough to touch his forehead to the curtain he could now hear the low rumbling growl of a trapped animalistic human being. He felt an overwhelming obligation to help him in some way. Closing his eyes he could sense a sort of sonar that he didn't have before. Both men were on the right side of the bed at the end of the room. The men were facing away from him, one stuffing his mouth with food the other lost in a world of imagination reading an e-book.

First his head, then his whole torso, seemed to materialize like an unholy phantasm through the curtains. The rings of the curtain quickly smashed together like linking magnets. A melody filled the air, rings chiming to an unknown conductor. The curtain ripping off the rings one by one until it fell, covering him in a paisley print shroud. Both of his hands stretched out to find the unsuspecting policemen who had no time to defend their selves.

Both officers reached for their side arms and both the dinner and the book fell to the floor. One man gasped as David's arm hit him with such force as to knock him off his feet. Spinning around his head hit the wall in such a way that his neck popped loudly. A limp and lifeless body crumpled to the floor. Simultaneously David had a hold of the second man's neck taking him up like a rag doll and slamming him down against the floor. The officer's last thought as David's hand steadily tightened around his throat until his windpipe collapsed inward; it had to be the most ridiculous costume he had ever seen, a ghost made up of sheets!

David proceeded to tear the binding curtains to shreds. Breathing heavily David froze for just one moment, worried the commotion had brought on unwanted attention. The hospital intercom squawked, "Code red, room 310 … Code red, room 310." Somewhere in the hall the distinctive hum of an elevator, its doors were opening a moment before closing, then moving on the way up to whoever pressed the button. A telephone rang incessantly at the nurses' station and nobody answered the call.

Confident that he didn't draw any undue attention to himself, David looked over to the source of the distress call. Hand cuffs rattling, the man in the bed immediately sat up. His excitement was short lived; however, when he tried to get up out of the bed, like a rubber band snapping back, he was immediately forced back down on the bed again by his restraints. He was a short man in his mid-50s, with brown scruffy hair and graying stubble on his cleft chin, his brown eyes were glowing red in the ambient light. Nothing about him screamed remarkable, just an average man in a hospital bed. Except the glowing eyes and a blood stained shirt torn open where once a laceration had been, he could have passed for anyone normal.

All David's heightened senses screamed that somehow, in some way he was a blood kin to the man handcuffed to the bed. Instinct compelling him to do something, anything to release him from his bondage, he yanked at the side rails of the hospital bed. The bars did not give. Though most logical thought had gone to the way side, complex thoughts struggled to creep in. He knew somehow that the men with the blue shirts and the shiny badges held the key to his kin's shiny bracelets. Rummaging through the dead men's pockets and eventually finding the key, despite his diminished dexterity he unlocked the hand cuffs, freeing the captive man.

Free from his captors and shackles the grateful man yowled; unintelligible to human ears, but David heard a loud and clear, "thank you!" Instead of running toward the exit the infected man, now free from his shackles, ran toward the stairs into the hospital itself. He had an overwhelming sense that there were others of its kind in the hospital too. In fact he took in all of his extremely enhanced senses, his hearing, taste and now a strange sixth sense told him that there were a lot of people in the hospital that were now brothers and sisters of sorts to him.

David reasoned that he had saved one brother and right now he had no time to see the others. He had to get out in the open crisp night air and run off this amazing energy that had suddenly come upon him. David turned from the corpses on the floor before him and stepped out into the hallway.

6

Nurse Maggie had always admired this doctor's extreme efficiency as she inspected the stitching, the tight crisscross pattern almost exactly uniform even though the wound had been extremely uneven and difficult to suture.

"I give you antibiotics, you take." The Indian accent had been awfully problematic for Maurice to understand, "you see doctor at two weeks."

He didn't understand what he said, but he had nodded yes, anyway.

Somewhere in the hallway Maurice, the doctor, and Nurse Maggie heard a faint thud and then another in short sequence. Nurse Maggie stopped her cleanup to listen more closely. She worried that a patient had fallen and brought down an orderly with him. She heard a faint rustling sound like a boy run stick a chain link fence before abruptly stopping.

"Hold on sweetie," the nurse touched Maurice's shoulder in reassurance, "I have to see if everybody is all right out there, and it won't take but a second."

Maggie stepped into the hallway just in time to see a shocking site. A giant of man or at least a human like figure lumbered out into the hallway. Maggie couldn't help but gag as she beheld the nightmarish scene in front of her. She had seen many deformed and decaying corpses in her rotation in the mortuary. The bodies blue, bruised, bloating and looking more like monsters than humans but it didn't prepare her for this sight. He towered before her, a sickly complexion, ribs to hips abnormally extended, pointed shoulders slumping foreword.

Maggie looked into his face as the creature cantered towards her. She looked into eyes which were more animal than human. His nose, or if you could call it a nose, was flattened, misshapen and elongated. As the thing's cheek bones lifted, tightened and grew, the jaw seemed to pop out of place to make room for the lengthening teeth. She noted the ears before David grasped her throat. Oversized and pointed ears that made David look like an elf from the pits of hell.

A twist and a snap and the compassionate, humorous, hardworking nurse of forty years lay in a heap on the floor, the life fading from her eyes.

The Doctor surprised David when he opened the curtain and gasped. Tightly wound, spring-like calves exploded into action as David jumped through the doorway, knocking the doctor down and taking his breath away in the process.

Maurice lay shaken flabbergasted. He scrambled onto the exam bed, paper sheets tearing in the process. Much to his horror he was now cornered, his back pushed against the wall. He looked on helplessly as David stabbed his fingers into the doctor's throat. Long, sharp and hardened fingernails easily punctured the frail skin. As if the doctors throat were a purse, the snatcher greedily opening up his ill-gotten gain as he splayed open the doctor's neck as if it were a Gucci designer bag. Opening the flesh like the doctor had done to his patients millions of times before. Maneuvering the muscles and tendons until the porcelain white bone appeared. Like sharp knives his hands tore through the veins and arteries. No specialist in this world could ever stitch the shredded mush that survived the lacerations. A warm gore fountain spewed out, ebbed and then spewed out again to the beat of the dying doctor's weakening heartbeat.

Visibly shaken as Maurice stared at the reflective puddle of blood on the floor, thinking it was a good thing that he had been able to get up off the floor. His shoes had cost over five hundred dollars, but he hadn't paid for them. He got them from a desperate man wanting to barter shoes for crack. Staring at his Italian leather shoes with triple stitching, these designer brand shoes were his pride and joy. He buffed them every night. Maurice found himself laughing hysterically when he found one, just one lonely and miniscule spot of blood had fallen on his precious shoes.

His laughing stopped abruptly when he heard low, angry growling. The puddle rippled as David drew closer but Maurice refused to look up at the mutated man. So be it, at this very moment he resigned himself to die. He said a prayer and closed his eyes. David's hot breath could be felt on his neck, and Maurice cringed. His eyes tightened further when he felt the thing's forehead pressed against his own. David's forehead didn't feel like a normal head, instead of hard bone, it felt almost spongy. The flesh pressed against his seemed to rhythmically pulse, as if the skull itself were trying to change its form.

Maurice had to steady himself, and tried to take a deep breath. His frame was tossed off balance from a sudden and powerful tug on his arm. Only sheer determination kept his eyes closed as warm hands gripped Maurice's wrist like a turkey leg. David sniffed at his bandaged collarbone and finally stepped back from Maurice.

Oh Lord this is it! Maurice's blood ran cold when he imagined all the horrible ways to meet his maker. He clenched his teeth as his heart pounded.

Rip!

Warm fluid soaked through his button up shirt and down his legs. Any second now he expected an unendurable pain to seize him. However, the pain never came.

Agony! The pain did not come to Maurice. He did not feel anything, the shock setting in, he reasoned. Then he could smell the unmistakable odor of urine. I've done it, he thought, I pissed myself! The acrid stench filled the air as Maurice's shaking hands moved about to his saturated pants. He was suddenly confident he did not wet himself however, and in fact, the pain had not come to him either! Hesitant, a moment later he began to open just one eye at a time.

Maurice saw for the first time the naked mutant and a sudden realization came flooding over him, I'm not injured, it's not my clothes that were torn! A stream of urine steadily soaked Maurice's pants, bitter dark yellow droplets that ran down over his leather shoes.

"What the...?" Like a horrible accident that you couldn't take your eyes away from, Maurice stared at the blue-black bruised and now naked man. "Did he? He did! I think a wild man somehow marked me!"

This blatant display reminded him of his mongrel dog named "Wolf". Enamored by canines, in his lifetime Maurice had had many dogs, a Siberian husky, two Alaskan Malamutes and his pride and joy, a half Chow and half a Husky mongrel named "Wolf". In the beginning after Maurice had saved him from an uncertain future and "Wolf" came home to stay with him, "Wolf" had sprayed everything in sight. Even going so far as to hiking his leg and spraying Maurice! When he extended his hand to smack "Wolf", Maurice looked into his big fierce eyes and his heart had melted. "Wolf's" eyes revealed respect, loyalty and thankfulness.

One scorching hot July day three men looking for an easy score of drugs almost ended Maurice's life. He had just locked the door to his small apartment heading out for the day when he came face to face with the business end of a gun. "Wolf" sensed something was amiss with his master. The mongrel looked out the window to see Maurice down on the ground. "Wolf" then jumped out the window, shattering the two pane insulated unit almost mortally wounding himself in the process, however, not before also taking out the two surprised muggers.

A tear came to his eye from the memory of that proud day. Now looking into this lunatic's eyes as salty urine soaked through his clothes, permeating his skin and ruining his shoes, he couldn't help but be reminded of Wolf's eyes. The human mutant had eyes that reminded him inexplicably of his beloved pet. He had canine eyes! Canine eyes on what once were human eyes. Maurice took a shaky breath.

David sniffed Maurice's collarbone with his flat misshapen nostrils. Maurice had an unusual aroma that was different than both Nurse Maggie and the scared little Doctor. Maurice cringed again; still afraid he would be attacked like the others. Instead of attacking him, David let loose his arm and with one powerful leap he ran off through the hallway.

Maurice stood wet and alone in the exam room, shaking as the urine turned cold against his skin. He couldn't take his eyes off the Doctor lying on the floor that now had two mouths. One mouth God had given to him at birth, and the other mouth a grotesque vertical sprawling gouge in his neck courtesy of David's claws.

He had a sudden realization enter into his head and ground him on earth once again… Somebody is going to notice these bodies. With the unusually strong police presence in the waiting room, Maurice shook off the thought of David waiting for him just beyond the curtains more afraid of the cold prison cells he made his way to the closest exit.

The hallway made a U-shape back to the emergency room. Maurice reasoned it would be impossible to explain to the police why there were two bodies while he miraculously came out unharmed. The flip side of that coin, though equally unappealing, the entrance doors on the other side always locked by nine o'clock and there would be a good chance that the crazy man was off that way.

He had no chance to think about it when he heard the intercom blare, "Dr. Lewis come to the emergency room, Dr. Lewis come to the emergency room."

Instead of exiting from the emergency/registration room that he came in at he decided to take his chances on the door that had been locked since nine. Quickly stepping over one body then the other Maurice navigated through the corridor. As he passed one particular room he noted the torn curtains and two more bodies of police officers on the floor. The perpetrator of that crime had to have been David also. He quickened his step as he heard doors opening and voices.

A strange realization came over him. Somehow he knew the man that pissed on him had made his escape. No longer in the hospital, Maurice had the strange feeling that the man had already left town somehow. But how could that be, a man that he had never met, never seen before until this bizarre day, and he instinctively knew where he was? Maurice could open his mind and see the man, like an uncanny tracking system, a primitive Lo Jack, if you will. He knew somehow that a second lunatic roamed the halls of the hospital too. In fact, Maurice could feel a few of the patients in the hospital slowly going through a metamorphic change. He knew somehow that it was a metamorphic change and not rabies or a disease taking hold in them. He pondered this for a moment, this newfound ability to "read the touched". Confused and angry noises near to him, spurred him out of thought and he moved on.

As he neared the locked exit doors shards of shattered glass told him that the second lunatic had definitely been through there. The crisp night air smacked his face from the broken and gaping doorway, energizing Maurice. Each step he took made him cringe as he heard the crunch of broken glass he envisioned the glass embedding itself in his once expensive shoes. He breathed in the fresh outside air. It was a refreshing change from the hospital's sterile and stuffy smell. Looking at his fresh stitches a sudden realization came over him. He had been there when all of the murders took place. Beads of sweat formed on his forehead as Maurice tried to reassure himself everything would be fine. He had given the receptionist a phony driver's license with a phony address. And as far as finger prints, well that would be no problem as he had been born without them, a condition called "dermatoglyphia". In fact, his Creole grandmother said he had been born lucky and blessed by the spirits. Is that why he had survived? And how did he not know the things then that he suddenly knew now? Like the fact that the patients that he sensed upstairs were not just sick they were going through a change just like he saw in the blue, bruised, mutant man? And how is that when he opened his mind he could sense him?

Maurice had been on autopilot, lost in thought as he walked and walked. When he finally opened the door to his apartment his loyal mutt "Wolf" was there to greet him.

Bounding around in circles and running about excitedly "Wolf" jumped up on Maurice's chest and jumped off, then hunched down ready to jump up again. Suddenly "Wolf" stopped and instead of jumping he buried his muzzle in Maurice's crotch. He lingered in Maurice's crotch for an awkwardly long amount of time. "Wolf" smelled something peculiar coming from his clothes, coming from his person. He whined and buried his muzzle in the shag carpeting.

Maurice stood still and when his dog looked up again he saw betrayal in his eyes. He couldn't be sure but he thought he heard a whimper as his loyal friend retreated to the safety of the adjoining kitchen area. Maurice strained his eyes to see the shadowy form across the room. "Wolf" and Maurice's eyes met. The glowing yellow eyes of Maurice's companion were filled with unease, is if he did not know Maurice anymore.

The dog whimpered again as he laid his head on his out stretched paws. His whimpers reminded Maurice of the first time he met the mongrel, suspicious and lonely. It was as if "Wolf" suddenly did not recognizing him. Maurice cautiously walked forward and kneeled down, his hands sinking into the dog's lusciously dense fur.

"It's okay boy, it's just me." He said, compassion filling his voice.

Maurice had always treated his dogs more like humans than pets. Even as a boy, Maurice had tried to rescue every flea bitten and mangy stray that he came across. It left his mother pulling her hair out. She agonized over the decision to keep yet another dog, another mouth to feed on a clerk's miserable salary. But she always gave in, even when the low income apartment building had a no pets allowed policy. Maurice's father had died when he was just a toddler and his mother thought the dogs were good companionship for him. "Wolf" had been there when his mother eventually succumbed to emphysema and heart disease. He remembered clutching the dog as he shed tears into its musty fur, comforted by its wet tongue on his hand. This whimpering now reminded Maurice of the un-trusting and scared dog he took home so many years ago and it hurt him somewhere deep inside.

"Don't you recognize me anymore boy?" Maurice lovingly patted "Wolf's" tense brawny shoulders. The dog remained rigid and unmoving, only blinking as it stared down at the kitchen floor. The fur on the dog's back stood up straight and his tail curled up close to his body. "What's wrong with you?"

The pungent aroma of urine hit him all at once making his nose wrinkle as he staggered backward. "Whoa!" His soaked pants clinging to his legs, he tried not to wretch.

Worried about his dog, he had almost forgotten all about his strange encounter at that hospital until now. His eyes began to water as he choked on his own body odor. His despairing mood in a newfound hopes once again. What if the god-awful tang was what had his dog so on edge? A shower and some fresh clothes, definitely a good night's sleep and maybe his dog would be man's best friend once again.

Steam billowed out from the shower as Maurice finished and slid open the glass doors. Taking a deep breath in, exhilaration over taking him, he stepped out of the shower and quickly covered his clean body with a fresh towel. Tying the towel around his waist, he then tossed his precious shoes and all his clothing, now ruined, into the waste receptacle. The smell of urine from the bruised man and his own pungent sweat were now gone. Maybe now that he was clean his dog would be less intimidated and friendlier towards him. Lightly patting his dreadlocks dry with yet another fresh towel he peeked around the corner and snuck a look at the dog that now curled up on the couch.

Maurice's heart sank, "Wolf" laid silent, stoic, and his un-trusting eyes were trained nervously on Maurice's body. Fuck it; it had been an eventful day to say the least and his mind and body were completely exhausted. He flopped on the bed without shutting off the light or having brushed his teeth.

He lay in his bed still but sleep eluded him. Noises that came from the apartment adjacent to him, coupled with the bright bedroom lights had him tossing and turning until he heard a rustling sound at the edge of his bed. His pulse quickened when he heard the familiar jingle from "Wolf's" collar. Frozen in fear and afraid he would spook his dog if he moved an inch, Maurice closed his eyes and listened.

He tried his best to contain a smile but it crept in any ways as the mattress shook. "Wolf" had jumped onto the corner of the bed with Maurice. As nervous as his beloved dog had been, his instincts to protect his beloved master had prevailed. The dog was still startled and perked up with every noise and movement that Maurice made, but with "Wolf" lying near him, Maurice was finally content enough to drift off to sleep.

Maurice drifted off in dreams, but not peaceful or pleasing dreams. One of a Wolf's pack now, everywhere he went his pack followed, continually multiplying in number. Maurice ran until exhausted, he gave up running. He readied himself for whatever the Wolf pack had planned to do to him. Turning around he could see thousands upon thousands of radiant red, yellow, and even blue lupine eyes staring back at him from the darkness that enveloped them. In between the pair of red and yellow eyes one brilliant green eye stood out among the thousands. The form approached him, this one with the luminous green eye until they stood face to face; breathing in each other's breath.

"I'm coming for you Maurice! Get ready!" The form in the darkness howled.

7

Gene's head pounded as he came to. Eyesight blurry, he could not see past his shed. Confused, disoriented, and bloody the fog lifted in his cognizance. Outside at the shed by his the house his heart skipped a beat when he thought of Chance.

Was his boy all right? His boy was outside when the intruder attacked him! Worry about Chance weighed heavily on his mind. He struggled to get to his feet when he saw Chance sitting down Indian style with his head down.

"Chance, oh buddy, are you all right?" He shouted.

With an open palm he smacked his face and shook his head; he had to get it together for his son's sake. He got down on one unsteady knee to get a better look at Chance. On closer inspection Chance's hand was bloody.

"What happened to you?" Worry was evident in his voice, he pointed out somewhere in the vicinity of the alley, "Did that man hurt you?"

Down on his knees he leaned closer, scooping him up in his arms and looked for any more other signs injury. Chance's eyes were vacant and glossy with a confused look on his face.

"You bit me, Dad." Chance said matter-of-factly. "I'm really hungry, Dad."

Chance's face was flush and sweating profusely, hot to the touch when Gene felt his head. Gene's mind was racing to recover some fragment of memory that he had lost. Did he really bite his own flesh and blood? He felt sick to his stomach from the prospect.

"Stop it, Dad." He shooed his hands away, "I feel fine. I'm just starving, please, Dad, I want something to eat."

Guilt washed over Gene then denial set in. He got up off the ground and offered Chance a hand.

"Let's go in and we'll wash your hands off and maybe then your Mom will be back with some food."

Gene surveyed the yard, confident the threat had gone he ushered his son inside. The screen door shut with a thump that startled an already skittish father.

Turning on the faucet steadying his shaky hands on the marble countertop he tried to shake the remaining cobwebs in his head. Suddenly his gut twisting in knots he rested his forehead on the counter as well. No type of virus or disease manifested itself so early he reassured himself.

Water, water, water! He could not get enough life sustaining, thirst quenching water. He couldn't help himself gulping down draught after draught the excess dripping onto his chin and spattering onto his shirt.

Gene sighed as the cold water finally satiated his thirst. He looked back to see his boy running like a madman at full tilt circling the living room. Relief washed over him, the guilt of biting his only son vanishing. Seeing him made him chuckle, jumping about, trinkets floundering on their resting place as the incessant hurdling from couch to coffee table and back again shook the trinkets perilously close to falling to the floor.

Gene couldn't put his finger on it but something subtle had changed in Chance's appearance. Something foreign had invaded his son for sure. Although he had no time to ponder this change as a sudden, incapacitating throb coursed through his intestines twisting them in knots like a damp towel squeezed dry. Wave after wave of nausea hit him like a freight train until he passed out.

Gene came to outside his house. The moon brilliant and bright high in the sky told him several hours had passed. Not since his drinking days when he drank himself senseless, waking up to a missing piece of time he could not recover, had he felt like this. Staggering in circles around the yard for minutes until making his way back inside where Chance stood in the kitchen eager to greet him, desperation and hunger in his eyes.

"Dad," Chance said with a frail meek voice, "My stomach hurts, I'm hungry."

Chance held his stomach standing just inches from his father and the backdoor. Closer to his son now he could see what he thought had been physically wrong with him. His clothes did not fit him anymore. The collar of his shirt looked heavy sliding down to his shoulder. It was a new shirt too; Gene knew it because he bought it for him less than a week ago. Now the shirt looked like an ill-fitting hand me down soaked in sweat from head to toe making the shirt heavier still. Chance had been portly, a languid child. Now it seemed like with every bead of sweat the fat melted away. His son had grown at least 2 inches and he knew this because chance stood eye to eye with him. His eyes were more than dilated he could just make out the blue in a sea of black but was suddenly interrupted from comparing his son's features when his son squalled loudly.

"Dad, did you hear me, I'm really hungry!" Chance said, his stomach growling.

"Hold on a buddy I will get you something to eat," Gene winced.

His gut twisting in knots again from a terrible thirst he decided to go to the faucet once more before finding something substantial for his son to eat. An intoxicating, strange aroma inundated his senses, one of decayed meat. A concentrated smell of garlic, salt, and many Cajun spices made his mouth water. He wondered where the aromas were coming from. He focused further and he zoomed in on the buzzing of the refrigerator. Did he find the source of the aroma just from concentrating? Gene was beside himself.

He looked up in the window at the brilliance of the full moon unfettered by clouds in the night sky. His eyes began dilating then the world went black.

When his mind awakened he noticed a tacky foreign substance on his hands and all over his cheeks spilling over to his chin, neck, and shirt. Frantically he looked around for his son, oh God he thought, did I bite him again? Relief washed over him when he found his son by the open refrigerator.

Chance had a dark red substance all over his mouth too. Gene licked his lips tasting a distinct familiarly sweet substance. It was barbecue! The open refrigerator door confirmed his suspicions. The doors on the refrigerator were off its hinges, shelves off the top posts and catty cornered spilling milk and leftovers onto the floor. Aluminum foil wrappers lay torn open in a heap their content or what was left of the meat stripped to the bone lie in a pile on his shoes.

"Dad, look!" Chance looked at his palms excitedly. "Look I'm rich!" Chance proceeded to hold up his cupped palms so his dad could get a better view.

Holding in his hands is what gene thought to be small bones. Further inspection however left him slack-jawed and stunned. It isn't bones he stared at but teeth. Chance's temporary baby buds had fallen out and permanent teeth complete with root had grown in his mouth. Gene nervously smirked; if the tooth fairy existed he would be rolling in dough!

1, 2, 3… Gene finished counting the top teeth then on to the bottom. His teeth or a facsimile there of were cruder in appearance more canine than human but positioned securely in his gums. Gene stared at Chance's baby teeth still in his grubby barbecue stained hands when he realized that not only did Chance have all his teeth but he counted more! In fact he saw his son mutating right before his eyes.

He saw some of the distinct familiar features that made Chance his memorable son. He had the wide round blue eyes, spread back in his baby face. A high forehead that magnified every expression he made and a fleshy face even though he had lost extreme amount of weight. However the familiarities ended there.

He had blue eyes for sure but the eyes were one of a predator. Chance reminded Gene of teen Wolf or teen Wolf two. In fact he reminded him of many, many B-movie spoofs in which a character is hilariously inflicted with lycanthropy and set out on two legs like a guerrilla or an orangutan. His proboscis had elongated and his lips spreading out and widening until there were no distinguishing lips altogether, just a horrid oral cavity whose distorted disturbing expression one of an eerie smile.

Chance's whole head had become and oval shaped monstrosity not unlike an egg. His pointed ears seemed out of place bursting out of his unkempt wild hair. Chance 11 years old, was nowhere near puberty yet but his chin had become scraggly five o'clock shadow needing a desperate shaving. His hair had grown down his face leaving him with a mutton chop appearance. Chance's jaw and cheekbones shattered turning into a small muzzle.

This would've been time for Gene to run but he stood steadfast. The transmutation of his son should have scared him, however in the depths of his primitive mind he was overjoyed, undergoing a transition phase faster than normal Gene beamed with pride. He couldn't help but instinctively howl when Chance ripped off every shred of his clothing.

He had grown another four inches in a matter of hours. He could see his spine as it was curving. The sacrum and coccyx bones had lengthened bursting out his skin whipping about in a skinless display of excitement. His shoulders were displaced so limbs could function on all four feet.

Unfettered blonde hair became blonde fur traveling to his broadening neck then abruptly stopping on the base of his spine making a V formation, the beginnings of a glorious crest, swaying back and forth like waves in the sea whenever he stirred. His shoulders down to his abdomen still absent of fur but his groin sprouting up blonde fur looking like a loincloth as if an attempt at modesty. Chance had become a semi-hairless lupine creation.

Chance sensed his mother's approach before Gene, scampering off like a scared little rabbit towards the safety of his room. Gene peeked through the blinds as the headlights of his Range Rover rolled up the driveway the glare temporarily blinding him.

Even though they had eaten every scrap in the refrigerator Chance is hungry again. Three rooms back with the door closed Gene could hear Chance's incessant whining and growls.

A neurotic obsessive compulsion washed over him, a primal need to feed his seed. Survival of his kindred a basic need in his primeval consciousness. Hunger gripped him as well, a churning stomach and drooling mouth is evidence of this. A whiff of fresh hot fast food permeated the walls and he breathed the pleasing aroma in.

Gene feared his boy changing; growing at a rapid rate through the esoteric adolescents of sorts he would need more than processed chicken substitute and cold fries. Cheeseburgers, chicken nuggets and fries are not only what Gene and Chance smelled coming through the windows and door. The sweet warm smell of fresh tender meat set their juices a flow.

Chance's door slowly opened as he fixatedly yowled at his father. The silent communication between the two forged their dark strategy. Gene stepped back against the kitchen table. The hybrid Wolf thing that was Chance crept up from the shadows of the hallway toward the living room.

The key slid in to the lock and turned, the door opened; Gene's wife stepped in and looked around, "anybody hungry?"

8

Wolf's Den Tavern

Lou LeBeau made a sigh of relief when he burst through the dense forest into a clearing and found a dirt trail that he recollected; almost to New Roads. He tore at the straps of his motorcycle helmet and threw it on the ground; it bounced along the trail until it disappeared in a tall gathering of weeds. He had been sweating so profusely that the cool night's air was a wonderful relief to him.

His brooding blue eyes were bloodshot with tears. He still could not believe his brother had actually died. He had seen the gory scene with his own eyes, had seen his brother torn to pieces. He had tried to shoot the monstrous thing but to no avail. The mysterious beast just continued mauling his brother. Nevertheless Lou was not the type of person to linger on a horrible situation, even the death of his own brother. He focused on the matter at hand which was him trying to get out of the accursed woods to safety.

Lou instinctively checked his wounded chest, now numb to the touch and strangely, he felt better. His wound only an hour ago was an oozing jagged gaping hole that began to heal, now just a scar with a rosy glow. He felt exhilarated, a teenager and Superman all wrapped up into one as he throttled the motorcycle for more speed, his natural endorphins were on overdrive.

Lou flew down the road at breakneck speeds, glad to be on the flat surface which afforded him the luxury of a smooth ride. Until he came upon the flashing neon green lights of an out-of-the-way hole in the wall bar a strange sensation came over him, compelling him to stop. Lou slowly stepped on the break as he turned into the gravel drive of the Wolf's den Tavern and Tattoo Parlor.

Row after row of Harley-Davidsons and Choppers lined the parking lot. While surveying the impressive lot, Lou suddenly became self-conscious of his own ride and what a beater it was among all these others.

The place itself a rundown, termite infested, two story wood building that seemed to loom over Lou. Up on the balcony patio there stood four greasy haired bikers that noticed him the second he rode up.

"Hey boy!" A blonde bearded, tall and lanky man stopped his conversation with his three friends and turned his attention down to Lou, "Hey boy, I'm talking to you! You better be getting on that shit bike of yours and movin' on!"

Lou ignored the blonde biker's ribbing and made his way to the front entrance even though he could feel the biker's eyes burning holes in him. He was almost out of sight when a volley of beer cans rained down at him. Lou instinctively looked up to the balcony and the bikers.

"Boy I'm not kidding! Be on your way, go in and its hell to pay!" The biker drunkenly warned a beer in his hand.

Directly below them about to head inside when a golden shower came streaming down soaking Lou's hair. Lou was shivering at the thought of what it might be when he realized it felt ice cold, just beer he thought, though only slightly relieved. The biker's raucous laughter floating down to him, something came over him as he pushed the sodden hair out of his face. He tilted his head up, smiled shyly and gave the bikers the bird. The laughter abruptly trailed off.

"You're dead man!" The blonde yelled down to him, signaling his friends, they immediately swung the door open loud music exploding out of it. They disappeared inside; the door slammed which shut with a clang.

He should've been scared out of his wits being by himself in this desolate spot with menacing strangers, but the upcoming conflict only exhilarated him and he felt unmistakably drunk with power like a perpetual PCP trip wrapped up with a steroid chaser. He felt as if there was a powerful Wolf-like being guiding him, a duality that he easily accepted. His senses were on fire with new smells, sounds and his vision crisper than it had ever been, despite the darkness. Lou walked through the dual glass doors confidently and stepped inside the tattoo parlor. Obviously closed for the night the lights were off and the tattoo studio door locked but a sign on the wall said, "Wolf's den Bar... upstairs and to the right."

Lou walked up to inspect the sign but a noise caught his attention. He wheeled around on his heels to survey the scene. In the dark he made out a shadowy figure closing the door to the tattoo parlor. He waited a moment to be sure that there weren't any people waiting to ambush him and then continued quickly up the stairs to Wolf's den.

He went still for a moment; his hand frozen on the doorknob, listening to the rhythmic bass beat of the house band. As he entered the upstairs into the dance room he was blown away by the clean, modern lines of the room in contrast to the rundown exterior.

Halted by a large man putting a hand up, Lou impatiently flashed his I.D. to the bouncer and disappeared into the ruckus of the crowd. His senses were awash with exciting new sounds, colors, and smells that he had never sensed before. He felt alive for the first time as if he had been reborn, listening to music how it was always meant to be.

"Can I get you a drink?" An attractive scantily clad waitress asked him as he walked up to the bar.

"Jack and Coke, more Jack less Coke, please." Lou had to yell so she could hear him over the loud music.

Lou leaned his back against the bar with his elbows resting on the top of it so that he could soak in all the new aromas and sounds bombarding him, loving every minute of it. The musical beat seductive, almost rhythmic in intensity. Lou took his drink from the waitress and handed her crumpled bills, enough to pay for his drink and a generous tip.

The flashing strobe lights had Lou feeling quite strange and disoriented; almost nauseous when the crowd parted. He could see the four bikers from the balcony coming for him. Realizing he would be soon cornered by the angry bikers he scanned the bar for any kind of weapon such as a wine bottle or beer bottle but coming up with nothing.

"I knew we would find you!" One lanky biker spit, in-between taking gulps from his bottle of beer.

Lou could instantly tell from the blonde biker's clothing that he concealed a gun. As the four men circled around him he racked his brain for a way out but it was no good. He began to think he had bit off more than he could chew. Lou looked around for a judicious bouncer or a Good Samaritan in the writhing sea of men and women mingling and gyrating to the music who might be able to defuse the situation, Lou found none.

"Hey guys I don't want any trouble," He said as he turned his back on the four men, as if ignoring them would make them give up and go away. He downed the remainder of his drink in one gulp and lowered his head, "I just want to drink my drink in peace."

Fine invisible hairs began to sprout all over his body, like a comforting blanket. His jaw began to ache and throb as, little known to Lou, new teeth began to sprout in his mouth. He shivered enthralled in ecstasy as the parasite began to take hold of him and induce a metamorphosis, pain mixed with pleasure. Instead of fighting the strange feeling that had come over him he welcomed it and urged it on.

Lou took a deep breath and spun around to face the antagonists who yelled obscenities at his back, fists clenched in anticipation of the coming conflict. The dirty, blonde biker instantly grabbed for his concealed piece, the rest of the group following suit took out brass knuckles and knives. The one biker without a weapon grabbed an unused chair and held it up over his head at the ready. Lou found himself growling involuntarily. Keenly focused as his senses sharpened and he reveled in the sensation, ready to scrap.

"You're so fucking screwed man!" The dirty biker said through his stained, clenched teeth.

The biker stepped up to Lou and pressed the cold barrel of his gun up against Lou's temple. The group watched, grinning, weapons at hand. The two men were standing eye to eye, staring at each other, both seemingly unwilling to back down. Lou could see the blonde man's eyes were bloodshot from one too many drinks… He thought this might work to his advantage.

The biker began yelling something at Lou as he pressed the gun harder into his skin. Lou didn't pay attention, watching the sea of people part behind the bikers, like Moses parting the Red Sea, people automatically moved aside. A blur of motion and the biker who had held the chair held it no more, only harmless shattered pieces remained on the dusty floor. The lead biker still oblivious to the interloper shrieked in Lou's face until the strange man darted forward and with a vice like grip squeezed in between his hand, barrel and trigger of the gun, rendering it inoperable.

"What the shit?" The dirty biker called out as the struggled for control of his weapon.

"Not in my house!" Boomed the unknown man; the shout sending chills down the bikers' spines.

The bikers cowered before the interloper. The two men with knives slunk back into the crowd; the others were in shock, too stunned to move.

"There will be no guns in my establishment boys!" Viddarr, the owner of the bar, loudly commanded.

Viddarr, an impressive sight to behold, even with his frumpy attire, a gray hooded zip up sweatshirt and matching gray sweatpants and his presence unmistakable for the owner of the place. Standing about six foot, four inches, with his forehead concealed by his hood, he still like a granite statue as his brown and crimson flaked animalistic gaze burned holes in the blonde biker's eyes.

"Give me the gun." Viddarr commanded.

The blonde biker, Daxx, begrudgingly handed over his weapon and nodded to what remained of his gang to put away their weapons too. The bikers edged ever closer to their blonde leader as if he could protect them if it came down to blows. Viddarr sensed their uneasiness and seemed to enjoy it. Grinning, he exposed his crooked canine like teeth as he feigned an attack on one of the dirty blonde's minions, watching him cower behind his shivering leader.

"I don't want any trouble in my establishment." Viddarr put a heavy arm around Lou, "if you boys want to go out to the parking lot and settle this outside, you are more than welcome to."

"But for now I'll be confiscating this." Viddarr gestured at the 9 mm.

He examined the 9 mm from muzzle to butt then back again, shaking his head with a smile as he wrenched the gun from Daxx's hand. He took the clip out and checked the chamber, ejected the remaining bullet, which hit the ground with a dull thud. Viddarr gave the dirty biker back his gun minus the clip. The dirty leader hesitantly reached out for his gun, sweat beading on his brow.

"If you use this ill begotten gun on me you're a dead man… you and all your piss ant Mickey Mouse club members." Viddarr spit when he spoke as he put a firm hand on Lou's shoulder.

Lou tried to hide his pain from Viddarr's iron grip but he winced anyway. An agonizing pain as if his shoulder had shattered. Uneasiness crawled up from the pit of Lou's stomach. Something about Viddarr made him want to tuck his tail between his legs and run. He felt like he had gone from the skillet to the fire. However he felt secure in Viddarr's self-declared "safe haven" the Wolf's den, a reprieve against the four men that wanted so badly to beat him into the ground.

"What's your name?" Viddarr turned to Lou, his eyes aglow with the pulsating lights of the club, burned a hole into Lou's soul.

Viddarr turned his back on the lead biker to examine Lou's healing wound. He wrinkled his nose and breathed in Lou's essence, his eyes brightened and a radiant smile crept onto his otherwise grim face. Thrilled that he had just confirmed what he had expected; Lou was definitely going through "the change" and at a rapid rate.

"My name is Lou LeBeau." He said meekly.

Viddarr's posture and demeanor changed quickly, a new rage kindled in his eyes. An overwhelming instinct to protect his kin took over him. His powerful arms seemed to elongate as Viddarr turned around, reaching for the blond biker who had pulled a dagger from his belt. Lou couldn't believe his eyes; Viddarr seemed to transform his limbs at will. Brown hair grew out of them like a dense tidal wave of fur tresses, ebbing and flowing. Lou saw the glint of silver from one of Viddarr's many tribal tattoos as his arms flexed. Massive monstrous like hands reached for the dirty blonde's throat lifting him clear off the ground.

"You hurt Lou in my club or on my land and I will kill each and every one of you slowly!" Viddarr growled, "I promise you that!"

The Brown bearded man, the smallest of the four, tried to tiptoe up from behind and stealthily once again pull his knife out. Viddarr's back to him, He swallowed trying to build up his nerve his Adam's apple bobbed under his scruffy facial hair. He prepared to strike but he hesitated as he tried to steady his shaking hands. Viddarr's ears twitched and appeared to slightly swivel, like a satellite dish moving into position to lock onto a signal.

He didn't even move his head while he repositioned his body casually to defend against the source of the sound. Viddarr quickly and with little effort struck out with his other arm, all while still holding the dirty blonde biker high off the ground. The gleaming dagger fell to the floor as a now talon like palm smashed down onto the bearded man's forearm.

Earsplitting shrieks and cries muffled the sound of the sickening crunch of the bearded man's forearm breaking. Viddarr quickly spun back around with an ease that blew Lou's mind, startling the rest of the bikers and knocking them off balance. He still had a hold a strong grip on Daxx's neck, his hands uselessly clawed at his Viddarr's hand uselessly wheezing. Viddarr tightened his grip and the man's face started to turn purple.

"Get out!" The sound of his booming voice interrupted some of the people trancelike dancing, "You wore out my patience, leave now or I will kill you on the spot."

Patrons craned their heads to see as Viddarr released his hand from the blonde man's throat, dropping him to the floor. The acidic scent of urine wafted in the air, as the blonde man's pants darkened. His friends, instantly compliant, helped him to his feet as they all scuttled to the exit door and down the stairs. Viddarr made eye contact and nodded to one of the burly bouncers who then grabbed a few other bouncers to assure the safety of the other patrons as the rough-and-tumble bikers forcibly made their way outside.

Like a switch that had been flipped, the agitated demeanor and grim expression utterly gone from Viddarr's face. He beamed with excitement as he turned around again to face Lou. Viddarr once more put his arm around Lou's shoulder, almost protectively; Lou noted that his muscled limb had converted back a heavily tattooed human arm again, no dense fur visible. Viddarr called for the bartender's attention with a snap of his fingers. A scantily clad woman eagerly came to his side with a half-gallon of vodka and two shot glasses on a brown serving tray.

The faded, yet ornate label and decorative glassware told Lou the vodka Viddarr had, probably his own private stock, was very old and expensive. She carefully poured two glasses to almost overflowing, all the while her eyes never completely left Viddarr's face, then handed Viddarr the shots. He motioned dismissively to her, that her services would no longer be required, and with visible disappointment in her eyes she left the bottle of alcohol and quickly retreated back into the shadows to the other end of the bar.

"Drink up!" Viddarr smiled as he offered Lou his expensive vodka, then looked down at his dirty sweatpants, "Excuse my grungy appearance I was just out for a run."

Lou accepted the drink but sat secretly confused by the owner of the Wolves den's focused interest in him. Before he could finish his first glass

Viddarr poured him another. Lou began to protest with his palms up and shaking his head but Viddarr was insistent so he reluctantly downed another shot. He gagged while trying to keep down the potent firewater as Viddarr prepared them yet another.

"I don't think I can take another." Lou choked, wiping his mouth as he tried to suppress the bile building up in his throat.

The alcohol had not helped his edginess. He had felt funny to begin with, the strange compulsion to enter this place along with feeling like his skin would burst at any moment when he began to hear, see, smell, and feel things that he couldn't comprehend.

Lou was taken aback by what he saw happen next; Viddarr's eyes began to glow and what were once human eyes now had an unmistakable animal-like appearance. A scowl crept over his thin lips and lines of disappointment creased on his otherwise seamless face. Unknown to Lou, Viddarr was irritated but excited. After all, he had been calling out every hour on the hour for the strong changelings, ever since Aticus' call of arrival, and Lou was the only one so far to heed his call.

"Drink," The alcohol sloshed over his hands as he pushed it across the table towards Lou. "It will help with the assimilation." Viddarr said kindly, no hint of his earlier agitation.

He put his hand on the bar to stabilize his woozy body now drunk and confused more than ever, he thought, assimilation? Head swimming from the alcohol, his brother's recent death and the monsters' attack and here he sat with Viddarr. His strange yet appealing scent that told him in some otherworldly way they were kin.

Viddarr looked into Lou's confused eyes and compassion came over him as he poured Lou another drink. Lou reluctantly knocked back yet another one as if Viddarr was his father and he didn't want to disappoint or displease him.

"Assimilation?" Lou asked aloud in an unsteady voice while Viddarr roughly grabbed his chin and looked into his eyes, checking for signs and changes that only he might recognize.

"Yes, assimilation." Viddarr said, again smiling crookedly as he released Lou's face. "I am so thrilled and delighted that you came to me!"

Viddarr pointed past the inebriated crowd and through the pulsing lights of the dance floor to a door that said "employees only". He didn't say anything, only gave Lou and pat on the back and a gentle nudge that hinted "follow me" as he got up.

Lou staggered from the relative darkness of the bar, onto the dance floor and made his way through the sweating, grinding crowd of people. The sound of the industrial music's beat invigorated him as he forced his way past the men and women, most of them dressed in Gothic, Emo or Biker apparel, all dancing together as one. He abruptly stopped and squinted, rubbing his eyes he now saw what could only be described as black and white hues. He focused his drunken eyes to see further all senses came into play as a 360° kaleidoscope of sight, sound, and smells made his equilibrium feel off kilter.

Lou took a deep breath in and smelled Cyprus trees and unique wild musk that reminded him of his younger years going to the Zoo and seeing bears for the first time, he instantly whipped his head around to search for Viddarr. He saw in color again but his brain started to sense minute intricate aromas as well, culminating in a cacophony of colors the human eye could not process. He took in a deep breath and this time he smelt roses, fresh salts and baby powder. His head involuntarily whipped around and focused in like high-powered binoculars on a well-dressed woman pining for Viddarr's attention. He promptly moved her aside gracefully, staying his course to the metal doors ahead. That's when Lou noticed several women, some with their dates, who stopped what they were doing or saying to stare at Viddarr longingly. A new strong scent made Lou's eyes water and he pinched his nose to block the nauseating smell. He twirled around to find the source of the stench when to his horror he realized he was colorblind once again.

Lou looked over in Viddarr's general direction, he had almost made it off the dance floor and over to the doors but he had been delayed by several women desperate for his attention. Lou saw Viddarr only in black and white when an idea came to him and he took a long deep breath. He could not believe his eyes as color vapors shimmered in the air around him like heat waves dancing off a freshly paved road on a scorching summer day. The aroma of a zoo, specifically the smell of brown bears infiltrated his nostrils and his eyes involuntarily focused in on Viddarr and his long braided brown hair, color coming back to him again.

Disorientation knocked him to the ground as he realized he saw smells! He breathed in and instantly picked up on ash, charcoal, grapes and blueberries. He followed the smells to see a woman that had too much blue eye shadow on. He could smell beeswax, and that reminded him of crayons and getting in trouble with his twin brother because they wrote on the walls and T.V. with them. He also detected the strong scent of cherries as his eyes intently focused on her very red and luscious lips. He breathed in again deeply now noticing tequila, rancid crawfish, and bile and he realized that he stared at a grayish green faced woman that had had way too much to drink. He closed his eyes and cupped his hands over his ears; trying to block out the amplified and hectic noise all around him. But he still heard a distressing conversation. He did not hear through his ears, he realized. The exchange vibrated the sparse fine hairs of his forearm. A source of the vibrations also a clue where the conversation had come from, so he turned to that side.

"I know! She is so wasted!" It came from a shirtless male that smelled like the ocean's salt waters and strong whiskey.

"She is so bombed she's about to pass out standing up!" The man with an overwhelming smell of acne medication said, sounding amused.

Lou timidly opened his eyes and took his hands from his ears when he overheard the whispered conversation with the two men. He focused in on nothing just staring at one of the paneled walls when everything truly came into focus. Sight, smell, hearing and touch all came together to work like one well-oiled machine, instinct taking over and giving him preternatural abilities. He heard loudly and clearly the dark whisperings of two men plotting to attack the unaware and overly inebriated woman slowly crossing the dance floor. Unfocused, yet aware of everything, he heard her labored breathing, noted the noxious smell of bile and whiskey swirling like a whirlpool in her gut and concluded that a violent bout of vomiting was in her near future. As he stared at nothing he envisioned the poor sickly green face of the woman and heard the conversation of the shirtless tan man and his acne scarred fellow plotter. He could clearly see in his mind's eye the red and infected pustules on his pock marked cheeks and could smell the surgical steel piercing in his lip, a smell that reminded him of a hospital room. The entirety of this he took in from the crowded and noisy dance floor in seconds, the bar about 100 feet away, all but invisible in the dim lighting to normal human eyes.

Lou found himself shaking with instinctual rage. It coursed over him as he thought about the helpless and oblivious woman, and found himself letting go of what he considered normal human thoughts. He saw himself, as if floating over himself, but quickly snapped back to reality as a sudden excruciating pain blinded him. On the verge of passing out, his inflamed gums burst like a volcano, white peaks pushing up out of pink soil. Wave after wave of orgasmic ecstasy over took him as the mounting pressure in his gums subsided, revealing bright virgin white enameled molars.

The bones of his third fingers as well as each of his pinkies exploded beneath his skin and became a disgusting gelatinous mixture of calcium fragments. His eyes widened as he watched his fingers lengthen and felt the previously shattered bones begin to harden as if they were concrete setting up in a foundation. Lou felt himself floating over his body again, his mind still there, all rational thought and reasoning foreign to him now just the mind of the Wolf remained.

Viddarr was standing by the employee entrance when he noticed Lou still halfway across the floor shaking, with buckets of sweat pouring down the dance floor and more importantly his steadily glowing eyes shining like beacons amongst the flashing black lights. Viddarr growled under his breath, a faint mutter that the music instantly drowned out, except for Lou's sensitive ears which caught it.

"LeBeau!"

Lou heard Viddarr loud and clear but again, not through his ears but in his mind. Lou cocked his head from left to right, curious, but he didn't move. Viddarr sprang into action, marching back through the crowd he gripped Lou's shoulder so hard it bled, and pushed him back over to the door which he opened with one hand and with the other effortlessly hurled Lou through the opening. Lou felt like a rag doll as both feet lifted up off the floor and he found himself soaring through the open door.

"Sorry but I had to get you out of the crowd before you could wolf out on me!" Viddarr explained.

"Wolf out?" He didn't have the time to ponder the words that Viddarr had said while he found himself on his belly like a snake. As he looked up at Viddarr he suddenly remembered the two scheming men, "But that poor girl..."

Nothing happened at Viddarr's bar that he wasn't aware of. He knew about the inebriated woman and her peril and nodded a reassurance to Lou that something would be done. He opened the door and waved in the direction of the girl and then the two men across the bar. Immediately bouncers from four corners nodded and rushed to the woman's rescue.

After the two men were cordially forced into a dark corridor by the four redshirted bouncers that Lou swore to be some form of giants straight out of a comic book, his racing heart slowed to a tolerable speed.

Viddarr offered a hand to help him up off the tiled floor. Slowly he got up on his feet gasping rubbing his numb hand as Viddarr's powerful grip cut off the circulation to his wrist. He couldn't help but notice all the digits of Viddarr's hand were the same and his black fingernails were unusually long, thicker than humanly possible, cutting into Lou's still human fragile flesh.

Viddarr could tell by Lou's diminishing perspiration and heart rate which a normal rhythm now that he could stop worrying about his haven being wrecked. He had worked his fingers to the bone for the Wolves den tavern when he had finally awoke from his state of suspended animation. A kind of hibernation of sorts, but to Viddarr it was hell.

After all, the tavern was his literal den, a neutral zone, his sanctuary, and his escape from all the realms of what he considered the dirty unchanged. Viddarr had all the carefully considered safety precautions in place so that the newly infected, Viddarr called them changelings, and the parasite itself would mildly lay dormant while they were in his club. Thin copper screening all throughout the ceiling, hidden away in the plaster, the music had a hidden low frequency sound loop that only a canine could hear which forced a calmed state as if they had been force-fed tranquilizers. All the precautions had worked very well for a century… until Lou came.

Viddarr's excitement could not be hidden; Lou had responded almost simultaneously when he howled an aria for all the virgin lycanthropes in the Louisiana area to come to him. And his reaction to the two lowlifes at the bar only proved he was going to be a very strong lycanthrope so he couldn't afford to take any chances, Viddarr locked and secured the doors.

Lou could feel the unknown presence leaving him and he could think clearly again, like a fog had lifted, but strangely the absence of the monstrous presence made him feel empty inside, somehow incomplete. He had felt so strong, powerful. Now with the presence gone he felt weak and helpless. A lone tear dropped onto his cheek.

"Wolf out?" Lou asked again, wiping his face, before rough callused hands violated Lou's mouth unexpectedly, causing him to gag. Viddarr, without regard of objections, opened Lou's mouth as wide as it would go, inspecting the newly formed teeth and smiling to himself.

"The Change is beginning already Lou, which means you're merging with the wolf quicker than I ever seen before." Viddarr explained, stripping off his gray hooded running shirt before looking into Lou's eyes and seeing a hint of the longing and a loss inside Lou's eyes. "Don't shed a tear boy, the Wolf is not gone."

"The wolf?" Lou asked as Viddarr examined Lou's hands, smiling with his crooked teeth exposed, as he did.

"Yes," Viddarr finished his examination walked toward a desk drawer and pulled out a fragile looking perfume bottle wrapped with a sigil pendant, "you have been given a gift."

"Wolf out? What is this about the Wolf and I've been given a gift?" Lou wondered aloud.

He stared intently at Viddarr noting again that he was heavily tattooed with broad round shoulders, a massive chest, a lean long abdomen, slim hips, and had arms that were longer than normal ending in huge hands. Viddarr caressed the perfume bottle as of it was the elixir of life itself, closing his eyes he breathed in deeply its fragrance and held his breath. The minutes ticked by until he finally exhaled and turned to face Lou.

"Yes," Viddarr's animalistic brown eyes staring straight into Lou's soul, "you were attacked by my brothers and one of them bit you. The Wolf's blood is coursing through your veins as we speak, yet you have your wits about you still."

Lou intently mulled over the night's events in his mind as Viddarr closed his eyes, again sucking in his precious fragrance. The more he thought about the attack and subsequent death of his brother by the hands of the monsters, the more his temperature rose. Grief turned to rage and he found himself growling involuntarily. His dilating eyes catching just a glimpse of florescent lighting from the rafters, started to glow as the mechanics of the eye itself began to change, becoming more animalistic in nature.

"THEY *infected* ME!" As his larynx began to metamorphosis his usual human speech turned into garbled grunts, "and *they killed* my brother!"

Viddarr's pride was hard to conceal, he shook with excitement. He had no doubt that Lou was a kindred spirit, genetically compatible and one of those who had the parasite from birth lying dormant, in cryptobiosis. Lou would have gone his entire life with the gift unnoticed inside him. Just minor differences between Lou and a normal human… like his bushy eyebrows, thick hair, unusually toned muscular appearance, thick large hands, and his lust for adventure and the outdoors as a tell. Lou would have never realized his potential unless he had miraculously stumbled upon the well-guarded ritual known by the clans of the lycanthropes themselves to awake the solitary slumbering parasite within him. He must have been born of lycanthropy blood, though extremely diluted; the cocktail of enzymes that were released by the invading parasites awoke it from slumber and the mixture of his parasite and those of Aticus' caused parasites to mutate. This, Viddarr realized, is how Lou's mind held it together throughout the changing when a normal human would have been walking around like a dead eyed drone, a slave to their baser instincts slowly transforming, in two or three Moon cycles and be racked with pain.

Viddarr closed his eyes for the third time and once again savored the sweet smelling perfume. Viddarr truly meant this as he laid a hand on Lou's shoulder to comfort him. "I'm sorry about your brother. He would have made an excellent addition to the pack if exsanguination did not overcome him first."

The combination of the copper screen and a low frequency droning, so low humans were unaware of it, had an instant calming effect on Lou's mood, so by the time Viddarr went to the perfume bottle for the sixth time it peaked his curiosity. He couldn't help but notice Viddarr's odd addiction to the perfume like a crack addict needing his fix.

"What is that?" Lou pointed at the bottle in Viddarr's hand, "some kind of designer drug?" He was beginning to relax now and found a comfortable leather bound chair which he proceeded to flop down into.

Viddarr, lost in thought for a moment, turned to Lou and without warning flung the perfume bottle at his face. No thought, just instinct taking over, Lou's forearm was a blur of motion as he caught the perfume bottle mid-flight before it struck him. Lou's instinct and speed impressed Viddarr who exhaled a breath of relief knowing full well if the perfume bottle had shattered onto the floor it would have been the end of Lou.

"You are very lucky my friend, if you had dropped that I would have torn you to pieces." Viddarr smiled as he said this but Lou knew from his eyes he had not been joking.

Lou brought the bottle up to his nostrils imagining that if he sniffed the unknown substance he would become a green hulking midget, running around in his underwear or something similar, as hallucinations took over his mind. But then, he was already hallucinating wasn't he?

He thought, taking a whiff of the fragrance. He smelled the potpourri of honeysuckle, blooming sunflowers and a hint of blueberries or blackberries, he couldn't tell. It was very sweet and slightly salty.

"It's just perfume!" Lou exclaimed, eyeing the bottle, taken aback a little.

Viddarr snatched the perfume bottle from Lou's hand, visibly offended. "Yes it's just perfume!" He again closed his eyes and returned to his own world as he passed the bottle under his nose.

"You smell only some sweet scents, but I smell so much more." Viddarr explained.

He went on to explain that the scent was from his long lost love. He had gathered her sweat and tears the day that she had died and bottled it up. Carefully adding just enough alcohol and water so it didn't dry out, he had been doing this ever since she took her last breath so many years ago. Then he obtained a magical amulet so when he found the woman with the sweet scent the physical reincarnation of his soulmate the enchantment would force her to remember him.

Lost in memory, he hesitated for a moment, "I could close my eyes and she is there again..."

Viddarr seemed lost in time as he relished the scent one final time before turning and carefully swinging an oil painting outward, revealing a hidden opening. The painting was a portrait, presumably of his lost love which he still pined for; every brushstroke was rendered with precision and care. For a moment Lou thought it looked as life-like as a photograph, it was of a young girl about twenty years old. Her striking light blue eyes seemed to captivate. She had a proud chin, her blonde hair, which framed her face. The brushstrokes of her hair gave her hair life as if being blown by the wind. No signature claiming this brilliant piece of art; however one look at Viddarr admiring the portrait who the true artist had been. He could almost see Viddarr tirelessly working with paints, using just his memory to render such a beautiful likeness.

Viddarr stowed his precious bottle in the hidden alcove and gently pushed the painting back up against the wall. He considered Lou for a moment before continuing.

"Years of practice and you too will be able to smell the distinct aromas and subtle nuances of terror, desire, ire, hate, lust, and longing that sets apart every human individual and singles him out, or be able to... Capture their memory." For the first time Lou could see a truly human side of Viddarr who stood with tears pooling in his eyes. "This is the wolf growing inside of you, do not fight it. You are wolf wearer now. Your spirit wolf grows strong inside of you."

Lou knew Viddarr had been right sending shivers up his spine making his stomach clench in nervous excitement. It had not been a series of bizarre hallucinations after all! The spirit wolf was coursing in his veins and he was reveling in it.

Viddarr turned away from Lou, letting this sink in, swinging his long brownish black braids. The sides of his head had been shaved at one point but now the hair had grown back so the sides stuck out like a lion's mane.

"Forgive me Lou," Viddarr said, touching bushy forehead apologizing, "like I told you, I was out for a run."

With that Viddarr pulled an electric shaver out of one of the drawers of the eloquently detailed desk, plugged it in and proceeded to make quick work of the bushy hair at his temples and around the back of his head. Something told Lou that Viddarr had done this ritual many times as no stray hairs fell to the floor, the clumps made it into the wastebasket he stood over.

He then called Lou over and gestured for him to lean over the hair catching wastebasket. Lou obeyed leaning down and lowering his head. He watched his hair fall in clumps while the clippers buzzed a straight path down the middle of his head. Leaving the sides of his hair intact, giving Lou a "reverse Mohawk". Viddarr's work done he put away the shaver and told Lou he could sit down in the nearest seat.

Lou reached up and felt the strip of naked scalp that ran from the top of his forehead all the way back to the base of his neck. He sank deeper into his seat and looked around for the very first time to really inspect the room. He couldn't help but notice the plush soft brown leather chair which he sat upon. He also noted all of the décor in the room seemed an exquisite quality, ancient looking and obviously expensive. This, Lou thought intuitively, is probably Viddarr's sanctuary.

Lou couldn't sit for long, exhilarating and a little nervous tension had him up and looking out through Viddarr's tinted plate glass window at the night sky. From the second story window he could see the banks of the Mississippi as it slithered past. He also spotted the two men who had been plotting against the inebriated woman, looking around and seemingly in a desperate state of confusion.

Appearing dumbfounded, the man with the overabundance of the scent of acne cream stood still as a statue, the only movement he made was one hand rubbing his chin. The man who had an embarrassingly orange tan stood looking up into the night sky. Lou could swear the orange man had turned around and spotted him. He ducked back a little, leaning away from the window.

"Don't worry," Viddarr said assuring Lou, then quietly putting his hand unexpectedly on Lou's shoulder, almost causing him to jump out of his skin. "They cannot see us, they cannot even see the bar anymore."

Lou raised an eyebrow at this.

He went on to explain, "long ago I saved a troll-born Rune Caster or witch called Yala from certain death at the hands of our mutual enemy, The God's Light. As gratitude she taught me many runes and to cast them. One such rune keeps my domain safe from those that have mischief in their hearts; the trouble makers will not be able to see the bar or anyone within it once they leave."

Lou had so many questions but he finally said just one word asking puzzled, "*Troll-born*?"

"Yes, troll-born, a race of men and women that had certain features that divided the troll-born from the normal human race. Yala was born with a face only a mother could love..." Viddarr paused a moment for affect and then said, "sadly even her own mother did not love her."

"Anyway she taught me a couple of incantations one of them I cast when I built this place years ago. Would you believe that at one time this place was a brothel? I don't begin to understand her incantations and frankly I'm usually suspicious of sorcery and magic." Viddarr looked into Lou's confused eyes. He turned from the window and paced around the room to find a little wooden box.

"But how did that old saying go? Magic is only science, yet to be explained." His eyes lit up as he remembered the location of what he was looking for.

"Look at me going on and on. There'll be time enough to socialize, but right now I've got to get you ready." Viddarr mumbled while he crouched down and opened an ornate cabinet next to his desk and carefully pulled out a small, very old, homemade box.

On all sides of the box was a mixture of Runes and Slavic writing, in a wispy design. Lou moved closer to examine the box further. On the top of the box depicted a full-bodied wolf standing on all four paws encased within the wolf the body of a man.

"War is imminent for humanity. I'm sorry to say I think I sold my soul to the devil when I heeded Aticus' call and agreed to aid him." Viddarr said with a hint of regret in his voice.

He then proceeded to pull out from the box, one by one, what looked like small stainless steel spikes of two different sizes and lay them out in order on his desk. On closer inspection Lou realized the spikes were not made of surgical steel as he might have thought, they had the distinct patina that only came from polished silver.

"In the days of old, my tribe, the Úlfhéðnar, pierced their bodies with silver encrusted bones or wore inscribed silver fired clay of their own designs to distinguish themselves from *the others*." Viddarr reflexively unscrewed the bases from the spikes and then he pulled out a scalpel from inside the box in a practiced manor as if he did this often, "however, gone are the old days of sticks and bones..."

Lou looked at the screws, the scalpel, and the spikes and he saw for the first time, because of his proximity to Viddarr's newly shaved head, that he had his own spikes embedded horizontally in his scalp where his hair had been shaved from his temple. They alternated from big to small, five on each side. Lou's stomach twisted in a sudden realization Viddarr intended to embed these silver spikes in his flesh as well!

"When the battle begins, the silver will distinguish you from among all the others in the growing pack. Where you put the piercing dictates your station, you'll be my Lieutenant. When that time comes, the silver will let the younglings know that if you give orders, they are to obey them without hesitation."

Lou lifted one eyebrow up in confusion and shook his head as if in protest but something about Viddarr's presence forced him to temporarily hesitate. The logical side of his mind should have convinced him to run away from this back alley surgery. He should have yelled out in protest as soon as he realized what was going to happen. An overwhelming sense to obey Viddarr, however, came over him at that moment. It was a feeling that he could not understand, but like a scared but fiercely loyal little pup, Lou consented.

The scalpel pierced Lou's skin. A steady hand cut a straight line about half an inch across, and then stopped. The only way that Viddarr knew the membrane had been penetrated was a small trickle of blood forming along the cut. Then with two gloved fingers, Viddarr lifted up the skin and forcefully inserted the screw between the muscle tissues. Pausing for a second to ensure everything was okay, and Lou was still breathing steadily, he then screwed on the top portion of the spike until it was tight. One down, six more to go, Viddarr worked at a fevered pace embedding the spikes in Lou's skull. He paused only when Lou let out a small gasp as the bases of the spikes were inserted. He could feel through his gloves that Lou was sweating profusely now.

"We use silver just at the base of the skin so when we transform the piercing is not affected by the alteration… Anything made from other than that and it will tear and fall out in our transformation," Viddarr explained working with the skill of a surgeon.

Viddarr implanted the seventh and final painful silver spike in Lou's skull in just enough time to keep Lou from passing out from the excruciating pain, and coaxed him to try to breathe more slowly as he hinted he was finally finished. While Lou leaned forward, Viddarr, beaming with pride, put away his piercing and surgical tools. When he saw that Lou was more composed and relaxed he continued talking to him.

"In the beginning it will be hard to control your impulse to lash out and feed, as the Wolf's blood grows stronger inside you. Remember you are two beings, becoming one. When you become Wolf always remember you're still a man! You are in control of the beast because you *are* the beast. You are a human that can channel the beast do you're bidding, not the other way around and you must always strive to remember that too! Now, I'm off to hunt. Be wary of those four men, the bikers you so successfully pissed off, that will inevitably find you. Good luck." Viddarr stood and opened the office door for them.

Lou's stomach fluttered as he wondered about the men and what they might try to do to him if they found him. He reasoned that they wouldn't dare to touch him while he was in Viddarr's vicinity, but he wondered just how far that protection extended?

Viddarr led him out another emergency exit, bypassing the loud music and frenzied patrons, whom Viddarr told Lou, didn't need to see him leave. Lou chuckled to himself Viddarr explaining that it was "for their own good!" that he avoided them. The pair traveled down a dark dusty secret corridor, then traveling up again until eventually exiting through open the double doors to the fresh night air.

Lou stepped back to watch fixedly as Viddarr tore away his binding pants. The speed with which he transformed, made Lou's eyes hurt, almost too fast for the human eye to perceive, into a hulking dark brown wolf. He looked most like a dire wolf, Lou thought, admiring his luscious, thick fur luminous in the moonlight. Viddarr turned to reveal a short, stout muzzle with lips set in a scowl which revealed white curved and very sharp looking fangs. Fangs he could easily sink into unsuspecting prey. Lou wondered momentarily if the expression on the Wolf's face was meant to be a macabre smile of sorts when watched as the Wolf sped off towards the woods.

Leaves crunched under foot as Lou walked around to the front of the mystically cloaked Wolves den. Just as he rounded the corner, his blood began to boil, hairs all over his body stood on end, and a clarity he had never felt before came over him. He knew for the first time he really did have both the senses of Wolf and the senses of man. His brain was making a mad dash to process the wealth of information and combined them all in a surreal cornucopia of preternatural sound, smell, and imagery but he relished the convoluted chaos all the same! Lou felt rigid, his sinewy physique nearly bursting, virgin nerves merging, intertwining and firing in unison in an explosion of epic proportion, so he didn't even notice the two men sneaking up on either side of him.

Callused and tattooed hands roughly grabbed Lou's upper arms on each side. He took a hit to his abdomen, taking his breath away. One, two, three strikes and he fell to the ground. His shirt wet, sticky and warm, clinging to him. He didn't get hit with a fist. In dreamlike horror he realized he had been stabbed with a knife.

How strange, Lou thought, he didn't even feel any pain. Hadn't someone told Lou when you are stabbed or shot, for a moment you don't feel the pain because you are in shock? The mechanics of the knife; solid, thin and razor-sharp like a surgeon's scalpel cutting into skin and flesh... the patient doesn't feel pain, at least for a little while. That was exactly what happened to Lou as he pressed his palm firmly over his abdomen, trying to suppress the bleeding.

Woozy he stumbled then fell. Milky white fingers turned crimson as the blood oozed out between the gaps. Dime sized splotches slowly turned to nickel, quarter, then silver dollar size until eventually his white checkered shirt was soaked red. Lou could just make out a human shape in the darkness before he closed his eyes, his hand flopping onto the gravel beside his face.

Daxx, the dirty, blonde leader of the biker gang, slipped out from the protection of is gang smiling in triumph as he looked down at Lou. His smug demeanor was hard to conceal when he saw Lou white faced in a heap on the ground, bleeding profusely. His boys had caught the black haired bitch responsible for this whole embarrassing incident. He had to get out his pent-up aggression after the confrontation which had led to Daxx and his gang getting kicked out. At least the night would not be a total waste, he thought to himself.

"Hey Daxx, it didn't seem like the bouncers took us that far, but I have yet to see our bikes anywhere, let alone that fucking bar!" Dirt, the Brown bearded biker was in an all-out, psychotic break, brought on by the dirty bathroom crank, three days of alcoholic indulgence, not to mention the disorienting and strange absence of the bar itself vanishing.

"Don't worry about it Dirt," Daxx squeezed Dirt's cheek and smiled, "at least we found that stupid pussy so he can pay!"

Daxx patted Dirt's back, trying to reassure his fragile mind. In truth, after the bouncers forcefully escorted them outside and into the cold night, he had yet to get his bearings straight either. The trip under the bar to the exit outside seemed relatively short, yet Daxx could not see the lights from the Wolves den anywhere around. Resigning himself to sobering up and waiting till first light, Daxx returned to the task at hand the punishment of Lou's body.

"See!" The underling, the one who had stabbed Lou yelled, "you don't fuck with the Wolf riders!"

The second biker cleared his throat and spat on Lou's face, then proceeded to kick Lou in the ribs with his steel toed boots until he heard a crack.

"Fucking die you bitch!" The other underling spat.

He quickly motioned to Daxx and Daxx handed over his empty gun. He searched in an inside pocket of his leather biker jacket for an extra clip until he was interrupted by an unnerving sound, the origin of which sounded uncomfortably close.

Just beyond the clearing where the trees and brush began to thicken, so even the full moon's light could not penetrate night's eerie darkness, a lone wolf howled. So close to the four bikers and one dying man but still far enough away that they could not pinpoint the source of the sound concealed by shadows and camouflaged by the trees. They glanced nervously around, interrupting the would-be assassination with Lou still lying on the ground.

Lou's weakening heart fluttered then beat faster than before, gaining strength. Somehow, between Lou's bouts of unconsciousness he had managed to hear the distinctive high octave pitch of a proud song, sparking recognition. Though no longer human, a wolf's now, his cognizance recognized Viddarr's voice, he instinctively knew it. An overwhelming instinct of survival progressed through the depths of his broken being.

Viddarr had become his blood brother, his general, in a pack in which he had become a fledgling member. Viddarr had given Lou an order to stand his ground and fight with only his melody. Lou struggled to open his eyes, the lids were stiff as if they were a seldom used door that refused to open, but he managed to open his eyes.

The ocular bundle of nerves almost the biggest bundle of nerves in the human body is the storage pathway to the brain itself. That is why when Lou looked up into the night sky he was instantly captivated by the full moon's glowing presence. His eyes began to dilate as his transformation started.

Lou thought about Viddarr's aria, *stand your ground and fight.* He thought, *do not fight the Wolf inside you, you are two organisms as they become one... stand your ground and fight!*

He was possessed by the parasites, the spirit of the Wolf itself. He felt his spine shatter into millions of pieces, releasing thick molten, magma-like plasma from his groin to the top of his head to the bottom of his toes and then back again. Wave upon wave of bliss made him lose control of his bodily functions and ejaculate in his pants. He staggered, trying to hold back a groan of pleasure. As if he was a marionette, pulled and controlled by an unknown force, Lou instantly got up on shaking knees, then he stood up, obeying Viddarr's command.

When the orgasm subsided there remained a throbbing immeasurable sense of power. Lou could feel a very presence and an instinct unknown to normal men. His bones had reshaped themselves, his gums burst and had emerged fangs, his skull and face both became more than human, the very hairs thicken to fur and scurried in thousands of frantic pathways across his flesh, his heart had ceased its crashing palpitations pumping strong, slow and steady now. His lungs once straining for breath, gulped an unobstructed deeper breath. The scents, sounds, colors and forms which were unknown to normal people burst upon his senses as if for the first time he fully understood the supremacy that the Wolf's Blood parasite could provide. The bikers stood stunned, in disbelief. The man the bikers stabbed three times still lived. He stood for the first time more than human, more than wolf; he had become a virgin lycanthrope and hungered for vengeance.

Daxx and the others looked at Lou, slack-jawed and still in drunken disbelief. An extended nose, cheeks, jaw and enlarged lips cast the illusion of a grotesque smile upon the wolf man's façade. However, the sharp bloody fangs were all too real.

The underling holding the bloody knife did not have time to see Lou's slightly stretched neck or his head arched as if it is a question mark, as he snarled at the man. His ears, hairless yet distinctively lupine-like were high up and framed on his pate in such a way that it complemented his silver studs in the full moon light and juxtaposed the strip of black hair that had just a moments ago been shaved off.

The underling with the knife couldn't help but be transfixed with Lou's haunting eyes. They were glowing, an intense yellow, an effect of the dilation which increased the cones and rods, reconfiguring in the blood of the Wolf's blueprint. Too busy staring at the glowing eyes to see Lou's extended nose with huge, widespread nostrils breathing blistering breath onto his exposed neck or his enlarged jaw as it clamped down on his windpipe.

The armed underling could not count the forty two teeth that pierced his fragile flesh, locking man and beast together in a deadly embrace. Forty two teeth; thirty two human teeth and ten lupine teeth, including carnassial teeth, that made it so his jaws had to expand to make room for them, which meant also the enhanced ability to crush and shred bone. Now, Lou's carnassial teeth shredded the biker's windpipe, destroying the armed underling's spine in the process. Limp hands could not hold the bloody knife any longer and it dropped down onto the ground. The now unarmed underling followed soon thereafter.

In a flash Lou turned to the other underling, the one with the gun in one hand and the fresh clip in another. The man did not have time to dodge the unusually bulky, extended arms; one arm was reaching out to grab his thick throat with while his other made a wide, swift swipe of claws. Before he could load the 9 mm, the biker's arm was filleted like a fish. The biker looked down at his arm with astonishment, seeing his skin peeled back like the rind of an orange, the bones of his wrist visible, his mangled veins and arteries severed and blood pulsing out in an arc with each beat of his terrified heart.

The wounded biker did not have time to see the thick fur sprouting out of Lou's sinewy forearm. The buttons busted off the cuffs of his white shirt that had gotten ridiculously tighter, smaller and shorter which might have looked comical in a different setting. The tops of his matted fur looked like the peaks of a mountain range, the blood that covered his fur looked like black snow.

The petrified group could see the beast-Lou's furry chest, his heart beating feverishly, and his ridiculously small shirt, stretching three times smaller than it had been before, as it ripped open at the buttons, flapping in the wind and exposing the beast's lean taunt abdomen. Lou's expanded hips and swollen thighs made his jeans tear and burst at the seams, looking like tightly worn shorts.

The mortally wounded biker's vision faded in and out so he could not see the thick dark fur in patches all over Lou's tightly wound calves as the beast's feet tore through his boots like wet paper bags, the balls of his feet resting on the dew covered grass now. Forefoot and toes thick and callused but not yet the full pads of a lupine, dug deeply into the earth. The mid-foot and hind-foot upright, the beast was still on its toes even though the ankles had yet to transform into the lupine's signature reversed knee. The pale faced biker did see, however, Lou's two pinky toes as they atrophied and fell to the blood spattered ground, before the biker fell over and closed his eyes forever.

Lou felt himself floating, as if tethered above his own body. He could see the two dead men on the ground in a pool of blood. Daxx was whiter than usual, glassy eyed, and slack-jawed. Dirt was bent down fumbling with something in his boots.

Remember this, Lou ordered himself. A hunger like none he had ever felt before came over him, but he was distracted by the glint of the weapon now in Dirt's hands as he stood up looking triumphant.

The more Lou tried to reason logically and the more he tried to respond on his own actions, the hazier his mind would get. That's when it hit him, what Viddarr had said, *don't fight the beast!*

Lou felt himself letting go, keenly aware of all his heightened senses, all of the sights, smells and sounds. Consciously he was aware of all his cognitive faculties but his extremities were moving on only instincts now, his cerebral sub consciousness in control.

Danger! Lou thought, hunger racked him but the man called Dirt had produced a snub-nosed revolver which had been concealed in his steel toed boots. He had swung the gun around and it was aimed in Lou's direction.

What should I do? But his body had moved before he had a chance to think about what he would do next. Like a bushido master practicing with sword in hand since he was young enough to hold it, he simply reacted without thinking.

Conscious for the entire melee, the beast of Lou was amazed by his power and the lightning quickness of which he was now capable. Lou's body was in fervor, acting in concert beyond his control, Lou watched on in a lucid dream-like state of observance.

Daxx watched helplessly, reduced to the mentality of an infant, as the unfathomable spectacle unfolded. The leader of an ultra-violent gang he had seen his share of vehemence. He had even done the dirty work himself countless times, decapitating and dismembering a disloyal snitch or another rival biker that wandered into his turf. However, this was a fable from his youth, a terrifying nightmare that had come to fruition before his very eyes.

The frenzy of the attack reminded him of a wild dog fighting for scraps. In fact, even though Lou still had features that distinguished him as human…still a "bipod" for all intents and purposes, Lou appeared to be a feral dog. He heard a whirlwind of sounds, of snarling, snapping, and pleading, screaming and growling, as Lou tore into Dirt's wrist. Lou the wolf-man Clamped on and twisted it this way and that until the gun dropped from his bloodied and useless hand.

Daxx strained his eyes to see the blur of carnage called Lou. The wolf-thing gnawed off the loose flesh and snapped Dirt's shoulder. Lou's head twisting back and forth until fangs tore through arteries and bone. Dirt, off balance, fell to the ground leaving him breathless from the beast-Lou's weight on top of him.

The heart beat no more in Dirt's crumpled and broken body. The beast man stood, unaffected by his own severe blood loss from the wounds he had received earlier. Only the whimpering leader, Daxx, remained alive.

"I'm sorry," Daxx apologized trembling, "I humbly bow before you, please don't hurt me!"

He groveled and pleaded, snot dripping from his nose into his dirty beard. Daxx fell to his knees; he, the leader of the great Wolf Riders found himself humbly trembling before the fabled wolf man. The biker's pleas fell on deaf ears, however. Lou's clawed hands tore through Daxx's cheeks, and the Wolf-thing Lou sunk his curved teeth into Daxx's throat. Daxx's heart stopped before he hit the ground. The dirty deed finished, the wolf man collapsed in exhaustion as well.

9

Royal Bay, Louisiana-- 20 miles from New Roads

The brakes squealed, testing the limits of Alex Seller's old, gray Ford F1-50 pickup truck. He did not even wait for the truck to come to a full stop opening the driver's side door and leaping out. He fell to the ground, rolling on the grass until skidding to a stop on his knees.

Alex bolted for the door of his house, shaken and blood spattered, but the blood was not his own. The bright orange safety vest glowing as the pickup truck's one headlight caught him like a spotlight in the night. Visibly shaken the color had gone out of his youthful face his blue eyes sunken in making him appear like he was at death's door. Still several yards from the house when the screen door opened, from the lights inside, a shadowy silhouette wearing a Protestant dress appeared.

"Alex, what's happened?" Alex's wife, Tracy's voice quivered when she saw all the blood.

Alex craned his neck around, to see if he had been followed, stumbling as he did so. Tracy reached down to grab Alex's forearm and helped him up.

She asked the same question again, a nervous tremble to her voice, "what's happened?"

"We were attacked! Two of my friends are dead! "Alex trembled as Tracy helped him up off the ground.

"Monsters, we got attacked by goddamn monsters! David and Nathan were bit but I think they're all right, they got away at least! I'm not injured. We just really need to get in the house!" Alex was still looking at his surroundings nervously until he looked into Tracy's green eyes. She had a calming affect over him, reminding him why he just had to have her as a wife in the first place. She was calm under pressure, she exuded confidence, and her eyes showed it.

"Calm down honey, let's get into the house. I'm sure it's not as bad as it seems and I'm sure there's got to be a logical explanation for what you saw. We can call the police and......"

"We can't call the fucking police; we were out there poaching for Christ's sake, Tracy!"

Tracy held the screen door open with one hand, braced it with her body while helping Alex get up the two steps and inside. Suddenly the screen door violently wrenched open further catching her off balance, she let go of Alex who fell just inside the entrance. She spun around to see what had happened, and what she saw chilled her to the bone.

A talon-like, rust colored, furry hand gripped the screen door, tearing it off its hinges, screws and splintered wood rained onto the ground. Its visage was more beast than man. Pointed wolf-like ears hung back from its elongated skull, short and sparse red hairs covered its short muzzle... seeming too large for its mouth which was filled with a complete set of dagger-like fangs.

Spittle drooled down its thick neck as it talked, "Little pigs, little pigs, let me in!"

Her once confident green eyes now filled with dread and terror when she peered into the Wolf man's eyes, the Devil's eyes, she thought, glowing red eyes. Shaken and still reeling in disbelief time stood still for her as she took in the whole image of the thing. The beast towered over her and had to be over seven feet tall. It had a thick furry chest that came down to V at its wide hips, its arms were elongated and hung at its sides as it panted, looking down at her. It had on odd ill-fitting camouflage pants which were too small and ripped on each side. She realized in horror that this must be the "monster" Alex had been talking about, and he must be wearing one of Alex's friend's pants. Her breath caught in her throat, a scream stuck there, as she looked down and saw that it stood barefoot, on the balls of elongated feet with an ankle that was bent backwards like a reverse knee.

"Tracy, get away from him!" Alex shrieked, managing to get to his feet and yanked Tracy by the waist through the open door, pushing her behind himself. "How did you find me?"

They backed further into the room when the Wolf-thing leapt up the two steps with ease almost filling the doorway. His face reverted to that of an almost normal man, except for canine fangs. He reached up and touched his nose laughing.

"Follow the nose, it always knows! Actually you are the only one that lives on the outskirts of town, Lucky you." The man thing surveyed the situation, confident the two humans were too scared to make a run for it, he made himself at home.

"If you don't mind," he gestured to the loveseat. "I'm waiting for someone, he won't be long."

The man did not wait for an answer, he plopped down onto the loveseat with his legs propped up on one side and crisscrossed. He reached for the remote on the coffee table, and pressed the "power" to turn on the flat screen TV. He glanced once more at his hostages who stood gaping at him, clutching each other fearfully. The living room opened up into a kitchen and he had a clear view of the back door, certain he could retrieve them easily if they tried to run, he turned his attention back to the movements on the screen.

Tracy slowly edged backwards toward the kitchen hoping to get to the cabinets where she was certain a handgun was still hidden. All the while, her eyes were trained on the intruder. It was amazing. He looked just like a normal man now, watching TV, smiling and laughing almost in unison with the T.V. audience. This thing went against all known laws of nature, she thought. All of the red fur had vanished, leaving a normal shirtless and freckled chest visible. Even his hands were mostly normal, he had short black nails and although all the digits were oddly all the same length, they at least were no longer claw-like. As she felt the counter bump up against her back, Tracy heard the interloper yell out, startling her.

"Hey, Tracy, you got a cold beer with my name on it in there anywhere?" He turned his attention towards Alex, "Oh hey I love this movie! It just started, watch it with me, why don't you?" The man paused and then melodramatically smacked a hand to his forehead. "I am so rude! My name is Lance, what's your name?"

"Alex Seller." He said meekly, leaning up against the wall, his eyes shifting nervously to the kitchen where Tracy was quietly opening cabinets. He knew when she had found the revolver, as her shoulders tensed up and she tucked something out of sight in her hands.

Rounding the kitchen counter, Tracy looked at the man and said smugly, "Yeah I think I have something with your name on it right here."

Up on his feet in a flash, but Lance was not fast enough to avoid bullets. Bang! Bang! Blood flooded into his mouth as his left lung collapsed. Tracy had no time for another shot before Lance leaped toward her. His hands were once again like claws, one grabbed at Tracy's wrist and the other clawed at her face.

Lance was transforming quickly now to a rusty colored Dire Wolf, large in appearance, it towered over Tracy's body. All of his features were canine now except for his hands. Huge talon-like hands that had Tracy's head, tiny in comparison, in a vice like grip. The two bullet wounds were already healing from the inside out, pushing the lead slugs from his body until they fell out and bounced off the linoleum floor.

"What the hell is it with this family and shooting me?!" He growled an incomprehensible guttural sound since his voice box mimicked a canine's now.

Plaster cracked as Tracy's head was smashed into the wall with the sickening crack. Her body flew off the floor as she was tossed around like a rag doll and all the while Alex watched in horror, frozen by fear and blinded by the tears in his eyes. He wheezed, unable to release his own terrified screams.

Tracy moaned and as her arms went limp she finally dropped the gun; matted blood stained her once blonde hair. Lance suddenly stopped his onslaught of punishment and converted back into human form, naked now, he released her body, slumping to the floor. Lance knelt down over Tracy's unresponsive form and felt for a pulse.

"Don't worry..." he looked at Alex with a sinister grin, "she's still alive. You know, you and your friends really shouldn't have been hunting out there tonight. There are a lot of dangerous predators out at night. Like me. And you really shouldn't have shot me, you and your bitch!"

Lance reached down and unbuttoned Tracy's Jean dress, stripped it off of her, and then proceeded to put it on. Lance ran a hand along Tracy's bare thigh, admiring her for a moment. Seeing Tracy's prone body, lying still and wearing just her underwear, something inside Alex's head snapped, he now he burned inside with anger and shame. Supposed to be her protector, but she had tried to protect him and now she was seriously injured. Before he realized it, Alex was on his feet.

Lance, who was now wearing Tracy's dress, was on top of him and pushing him down before he got the chance to go for Tracy's discarded gun.

"Do I look like grandmother now?" Lance asked sweetly, smacking Alex with his open hand several times until he was red in the face.

"You're the devil!" Alex spat, struggling uselessly beneath the man's weight.

Lance's head went up and he sniffed the air around them. He put a clawed hand on Alex's shoulder.

"No, but my friend," he pointed over Alex' head toward the front door, "well he is!"

Alex was reluctant to see what stood behind him, but he mustered the courage to turn around. What he saw horrified him. Standing just feet before him looked like a monstrous prehistoric raven-furred dire wolf. It wore a half-shroud over the left side of its face made of a patchwork of tanned human skin, threaded up with human sinew. Alternating spikes, three large, three small, were screwed into its scalp keeping the shroud secure with large brass grommets. The cranium of the monster was unusually large, its brow line thicker and broader than that of a normal Wolf. Its right eye wide and shone a brilliant green and set back in its head further. The Devil's right ear thin and curved outward at the point. At had a longer thin muzzle with a large wet, black and scarred nose. Alex could see abnormally curved fangs within receding gums. Its shoulder blades were pronounced and the thing was carrying a medium leather pouch at his side.

Squinting, Alex saw that in its drooling jaws was a human torso with its entrails dragging behind. Alex gagged, trying to keep in the vomit as he realized it was one of his friends the beast had, but without the head he could not tell which one it was. One boot was gone along with the foot and only cracked and bloodied bone remained. With a nauseating thwack, the beast dropped the bloody body onto the floor and stood up on two legs. The reverse knee of the Wolf lowered gently to the floor becoming a heel, paws turned into four toes with extremely long feet that retracted right before Alex's eyes.

Busy staring at the fiend's feet when Alex began to realize the Wolf face was now altering into a man's façade. The beast man was stunning in a sense that any wild animal was, beautiful in its own primal way. His skin was flawless, pale and iridescent. He had a Cro-Magnon like appearance with a long thin nose and a broad chin and his right ear was set back and slightly pointed. Now receding, he could see six piercings in his lobe. His one eye, something about that eye, Alex thought, was primitive. It was a wild, emerald colored eye. Cheek bones sat high and defined above thin crimson lips and a wide mouth. The bloody fangs receded but his canines were still more pronounced in respect to that of a normal human's.

Lance pushed off of Alex and went towards the kitchen. Gingerly stepping over Tracy's still unconscious body, he made his way to the refrigerator and began riffling around inside, clinking bottles into one another. Alex pushed himself up onto his knees and his attention devoted to the naked man who entered the living room. He got dressed casually, pulling clothes out of the bag that had been around his shoulder. Noticing Alex's stare, he formally introduced himself, his demeanor cold.

"My name is Aticus." Aticus gestured for Alex to have a seat on the couch. It was more of a command than a suggestion which had Alex fearing for his life, and he meekly complied.

Aticus frowned after one glance and a sniff around the room. The living room was quaint, with recently painted walls, buttery in color and spackled with a country living motif the wall bordered with eggshell painted from ceiling to floor. He could smell the aroma of lavender and fresh linens from the candles above the curio cabinet but he could also sense gunpowder and human mixed with lycanthrope blood hanging in the air. He regarded Tracy's prone body and Lance who stood, wearing her dress. Aticus growled, digging through his bag for more clothing and violently threw a man's outfit at Lance's face. Lance promptly stripped out of Tracy's dress and into more appropriate attired.

"The bitch shot me and I didn't have a choice." Lance said, pointing toward Tracy's unconscious and half naked body.

Aticus looked over at Lance, shaking his head in displeasure; he cautiously wandered over to Tracy with only a side way glance at Alex who sat on the couch in the fetal position, rocking himself back and forth with a glazed look in his eyes.

"You're pathetic." Aticus spat in Alex's direction.

He stormed past the petrified man then he knelt down and cradled Tracy's head in his massive hands. He positioned her head on his chest parted her tresses on one side and began licking her injuries with a long, rough tongue. He carefully held her up as he removed the matted blood from her straw colored hair.

Fully dressed now, Lance tossed Tracy's dress on the floor and plopped down on the couch again, sitting uncomfortably close to Alex, putting his arm over his clammy and sweating shoulder, "you know; I'm starting to really think Aticus has a thing for your wife."

He smiled a fang-filled mischievous smile, "Seriously look."

Lance nodded toward the kitchen. Lance leaned back so that Alex had an unobstructed view of Aticus and Tracy. He was delicately stroking her hair and seemed to be gently embracing her, holding her to his chest while he slowly inhaled her fragrance. It was a strong bouquet of lilies, baby powder, with an edge of panic to it, but Aticus sensed something else as well and it thrilled him, the aroma of angry defiance, fury, and a faint smell of luteinizing hormone.

"Mmmmm."

Aticus carefully laid Tracy back onto the cold floor, tracing an invisible line with his nails on her smooth skin, from her hips over to her navel. He began to feel a stirring heat and pressure in his loins. He stared at her face and took a deep breath, knowing he needed to distance himself from her if he was going to be able to restrain himself.

"You have a chance to survive this night, I promise you." He whispered, carefully removing his Flintlock pistol from his bag and holstering it in is belt. Then he removed his bag off his shoulder and placed it like a pillow underneath her head.

Aticus picked Tracy's gun up off the floor then entered the kitchen. He opened the cabinets to find a glass for water. He could feel Alex's eyes on his back as he opened a silverware drawer, quickly finding a steak knife; he went back over to Tracy's still unresponsive body.

"You know Alex, I truly despise you." He looked at Alex with rancor in his green eye.

His arm transmuted again into a wolf's, as it did Aticus sliced the knife vertically into his furry wrist until lifeblood began spewing out into the glass of water. He would not dare show it but he was beaming with pride for Tracy. She was definitely a fighter; she had obviously stepped up fearlessly to defend her den and her cowardly love from an interloper. He rubbed her cheek, gently trying to rouse her seeing her eyes flutter minutely.

"Drink my dear," He said, passing a disapproving glance at Lance who was obliviously indulging himself in human trappings, comfortably watching TV.

He held Tracy's nose until she reflexively opened to catch a breath. Her mouth open he poured the unholy mixture into her throat until the glass emptied and Tracy was coughing and sputtering. The sound of his wife choking and moaning made Alex jump up nervously from the sofa but he stopped short when he felt Lance's hand firmly grip his shoulder.

"He'll kill you where you stand." Lance whispered, tugging at Alex's shirt. "Sit back down and watch this movie with me, it will be over soon." He said, his eyes never straying from the TV.

Lance's statement shook him to the bone and the horrible truth began to set in. They were not going to survive the night, and there was nothing that Alex could do about it. All he had wanted to do was have a couple of beers with his friends, get away from Tracy for a few hours and go hunting. He was not prepared for the nightmare he had stumbled into and now faced, in his own home. He felt sick to his stomach watching Aticus who was sniffing all around Tracy like a dog with a new chew toy, drool dripping out of his mouth.

Tracy's eyes began to open slowly as Aticus breathed in and licked at her naked thighs. Instinctively Tracy tensed up and blindly kicked at Aticus, her knee finding his head and knocking him off balance, he fell away from her. Still disoriented, Tracy scrambled to her feet, her hand clutching at her wounded head. She was stunned to realize the wound was literally healing beneath her fingertips. She felt the skin draw together, leaving only dried flakes of blood on her scalp and in her hair. She reeled backwards, pressing her back up against the kitchen wall, trying to focus her blurred vision.

Aticus should have been livid, he should have seen it coming to begin with, but was not angry instead beaming with pride, a natural fighter. In one quick motion he restrained Tracy's arms and leaned in for a closer look at her head. Her wounds were healing, this much he was sure and not sweating profusely yet, a good thing, he told himself. He pushed his cheek against hers to feel her temperature, careful not to release her arms and risk an attack again. She had a normal temperature, a good thing as well.

"Devil, why are you doing this to us?" Her voice was hoarse, just below above a whisper, but Aticus got the point. He leaned back from her, just enough to have room to react if she went mad again.

"Oh no, my dear, I'm not purposely trying to torture you. Your idiot husband was just in the wrong place at the wrong time..."

"And don't forget his friends shot at us!" Lance interrupted, looking at Alex with malice and annoyance in his eyes.

Alex tried to speak but nothing would come out. Tracy glanced from Lance to Aticus, as if deciding a plan of action. Aticus checked the gun, and confident with what he saw, handed the weapon back to Tracy, handle first.

As soon as she snatched the gun from Aticus' hands, Tracy slid away and leveled the gun at him. "It doesn't hurt you to get shot in the body, huh? Well how do you like it in the head?" She roared, pulling the trigger.

The first shot left him teetering off balance as the bullet struck his forehead, two more and he fell off his feet and on the floor. Lance impulsively responded his fur rippling; his wolf-form flew away from Alex on the couch, heading straight for the gun in Tracy's hand.

Fangs grazed Tracy's hand as a muzzle clamped down onto the gun. A quick shake of Lance's broad and powerful neck and the gun slipped from her hands. The wolf pushed the gun away on the tiled floor then rushed to a prone and still Aticus. The interlopers' attention elsewhere Alex sprung from the couch and dashed to Tracy's side, holding her protectively. She was trembling violently as the rust colored wolf snarled at them. The wolf lowered its belly to the ground, its forearms; wound like springs, claws dug into the floor, and raised its haunches and tensed, ready to pounce.

"Wait!" Aticus moaned, lifting a bloody hand up in protest. The voice was guttural and authoritative, making Lance's Wolf form lower its head and tail and whimper with irritated obedience.

Aticus winced. After all, even after all the years he had to get used to pain being shot in the head still really fucking hurts, he told himself. He unsteadily staggered up from the floor, wobbly legged and light-headed. He felt around on his forehead. Two bullets had stopped cold lodged in his skull. Ice flicked them both out easily. A horrified screech from Tracy halted him suddenly, but then with a fanged smirk he proceeded to dig out the third bullet and toss it away.

"Watch them!" Aticus ordered, Lance obeyed, submissive and ready to please; his scraggly tail held straight up in the air erect. Confident that Lance had the situation under control; Aticus turned his back on Alex and Tracy to rummage around the house.

A clean shiny trail was made where Ice dragged his finger across a dusty book shelf. A glancing vengeful eye took in all the trappings of human society. A wedding picture of a young happy couple particularly angered him. He instantly snatched the picture up and smashed it to tiny sharp shards on the edge of the shelf. He closed his eye as glass rained down onto the shag carpeting. His migraines back now, his skull beating like a bass drum.

"You hapless, fucking naked two legs," Aticus opened his eye, staring daggers at the couple huddled helpless before him. "You humans think you can do no wrong!"

Aticus slowly strolled over to the loveseat and end table, staring at the pretty little trinkets so neatly arranged before him. "You think you're on top, the head of the food chain. You live in a delusional fantasy land and your blanket of denial keeps you warm at night, we and the other's laugh at you!"

The others he had been referring to, other children of the night. He had come upon cousins of the werewolf, vampyres… if ever an equal to the lycanthrope the vampyre was one of them, specters and Shifters. Shifters were another matter altogether, shifters still confounded him. Through the centuries he had seen one or two of these strange men and women and they perplexed him. He knew his affliction physiologically material, the Wolf-essence intertwined with a human soul. He was aware of bundles of nerves firing all at once. He felt his body jerking, contorting, and bending into a new shape. Bones arced and twisted, as if they were the consistency of match sticks snapping. He could feel his skin stretching like a rubber band. Unlike him, the shifters would meditate and through consciousness invade the animals mind to do the shifter's bidding. Or they would summon any animal spirit and put the spirit on as if it were a new suit. Although the human body seemed to transform all just an optical illusion in the mind's eye.

Soon his thought process returned to the unfortunate humans again. What they didn't understand they always feared and as a result the weak human-kind sought to destroy and to annihilate, that is what had happened to Aticus' family.

Aticus strolled to the freshly painted walls, carefully picking up another portrait of Tracy and Alex's wedding day. He sneered at the happy and smiling family consisting of father, mother, grandmother, grandfather, brothers and sisters in Alex's side; then turned his attention to the great grandmother, grandmother, father and mother on Tracy's side of the family.

Aticus thumped the back of his hand against the picture frame hard enough to shatter the small pane of glass. A low guttural growl could be heard from across the room, steadily growing in tempo, until Aticus exploded with rage.

"That is just so sweet!" Aticus spat, waving the picture at them. "Did I ever tell you I had a family once too?" He dropped the ruined picture to the floor and looked Alex in the eyes, raising his eyebrow, and waited for a response.

"Oh, Oh no, I guess." Alex whispered quickly, glanced in Tracy's direction, and then lowered his head again.

Aticus pushed between them, forcing Alex who stumbled back towards the couch away from Tracy. He suddenly flipped the coffee table onto its side to get closer to Tracy. She seemed to be frozen, hypnotized as she stood near Alex, but for all intents and purposes, 1,000,000 miles from him.

Aticus didn't even give Alex a passing glance now, as he inspected Tracy's eyes, seeing something in them that greatly pleased him. He could barely make out the green of her irises; only a small circle was left ringing the darkness of her dilated pupils.

"Yes I had a family, a family of wolves." Aticus snapped, then woofed unintelligibly to his friend, prompting Lance to obey.

Aticus went on to tell the story to his captive audience about his birth. His dad, a nameless lycanthrope impregnated a normal Wolf Bitch. Two months later, Aticus and his litter of brothers and sisters were born.

It wasn't a joyous occasion; the she-wolf had given birth to six pups. Of the six pups only three survived. She had given birth to three stillborn and those that had survived were weak. His brother had gray-black hair and brown eyes, a long bushy tail, and you could tell by his girth that he had not starved in the womb as much as the others. Aticus' sister had long thin snout, blue eyes, and golden luxurious fur but she had been smaller and her white furred belly bore signs of starvation. Her ribs could be seen sticking out of her chest when she rolled around in the grass. The littlest of the canine litter, but she seemed happy-go-lucky, reveling in the night air, in the world, as she ran around blindly in circles, fearlessly dancing and playing.

"That brings me, to me," Aticus said with a sneer, "one of the three that survived, the puny runt. I was born hairless, weak and defenseless, I was born human."

Lance had returned with a glass of water and ice wrapped in a dishrag for Tracy. Trying to lay the ice wrapped rag on her forehead, he was met with resistance. As he reached for her Tracy's snarling curled lip and exposed teeth made Lance hesitate.

Aticus smiled ear to ear as he took the cold rag and glass from Lance's hands and gingerly placed the ice pack on Tracy's forehead; his effort this time met with little resistance.

"There, there my dear," Aticus said to Tracy softly, "are you thirsty?"

Tracy eyed him for a moment and then snatched the glass from Aticus' hand, greedily gulped it down, spilling water all over her bra and down her stomach. Aticus removed the rag from her head and gently caressed Tracy's cheek. She was coming along nicely, Aticus thought, and then he turned to Alex who stared at the floor in a catatonic state of fear and shock.

"Now where were we?" Aticus thought out loud, "Oh yes, I was born human, a puny human."

Aticus glanced over at Lance, who was now sitting on the floor watching television, then continued with his story. He took Tracy's hand and guided her to sit on the couch next to Alex. Robotically, Alex slips to the other side, breathing shallowly.

"A hapless human when I slipped form her loins, but it didn't matter in the She Wolf's eyes, I was her son." Aticus said. "Humans hate what they don't understand. They hate anything different, anything strange, and anything out of the norm. They self-righteously seek out and destroy anything which threatens their delusional idea that they are the superior beings of the world. The delusion of human superiority over animal makes me sick... You know, humans are animals as well!

"It was the animal that cared not what form I took at birth. The she Wolf took care of me. She nourished and protected me and my brother and sister, while our Dad was nowhere to be found." Aticus' lip quivered at the mention of his father.

Aticus didn't seem to care who was listening anymore, going off on a tangent, lost in his own world. "When I first laid eyes upon a human, it was when my mother and brother were killed. We fled for safety to the forest, I, struggling crawl on hands and knees, my sister fleeing on four paws to spur her along."

Aticus' fists shook with rage in remembrance of this. Walking over to the half-eaten torso that still lay in the doorway, the thoughts and memories had his head pounding again as he motioned for Tracy to come to his side.

"The humans sickened me with their senses of entitlement, cutting down trees and clearing forests so they could make more villages... oblivious of the impact on the world and nature." Aticus whispered to no one in specific.

Tracy obeyed Aticus, as if on autopilot she crawled on her knees to him. Aticus tore a chunk of bloody muscle from the torso, throwing it at Tracy who still sat on her knees. Tracy's precipitous reflexes sprang into action and she snatched the meat before it hit the floor.

"My sister and I were left to fend for ourselves and figure out what this gift of transformation meant for us." Aticus said, as the memories of the days gone by possessed him.

Down on bended knee now, Aticus reached to unclasp Tracy's bra, as she tore into the flesh of Alex's dead friend with abandon. He stroked her tangled hair and gently pushed her down, pulling off her panties freeing her for the transformation to come. Alex started to protest, but one dark look from an angry green eye, and Alex sat back down, silent. His stomach clenched with a combination of fear, a nauseating feeling growing as he watched Tracy writhe around on the floor, nude, and the he could hear the gut churning sounds of Tracy's chewing, ripping, snarling, and grinding teeth. Alex finally leaned forward and wretched all over the carpet. He gasped and wiped his mouth as Aticus continued talking, seemingly unaffected by his reaction.

"My brother and mother were gone and I obsessed over my father's absence," he reflected on this for a moment, then continued, "Eventually my sister and I honed our unique abilities. We began to smell others that were just like us."

Aticus glanced down at Tracy and smiled darkly, "That is when I smelt my father's presence!" He paused for a moment, choked up at the memory.

Tracy had devoured all of the bloody flesh and now nestled up to Aticus, wrapping her arms around his hips and resting her head on his leg. As she looked up at him, in her eyes a mixture of admiration, respect, obedience and one of sadness at the story that Aticus told. This pleased Aticus immensely, not only had the Wolf's Blood parasite traveled swiftly and directly into Tracy's core, but her loyalty to the pack leader had met with little resistance, and had taken hold quickly.

"It took only a few months after we discovered the lingering scent of our father to reach him." Aticus said softly, his emotions coming through as he slowly, delicately, and almost lovingly caressed Tracy's bare back, running his hand all the way down to her rounded buttock.

Alex shook his head and closed his eyes, ashamed and angry. Ashamed that not only had he failed to stop these hostile invaders, but he believed that his wife's inevitable rape was near at hand, perhaps only moments away, and he sat scared and powerless to stop it. Alex took a shuddering breath and Aticus spoke again.

Aticus described the scene in almost perfect vivid detail. How bursting out of the underbrush, his sister and he had seen dozens of pikes placed on top of a cliff. Even though he had been born human, Aticus' mind was that of a wolf's...and as such, all his instincts screamed run when he peered up the mount on an ominous scene.

Three corpses, all in different stages of decay, were skewered on the pikes. The salty sea breeze on the cliffs tickled the pair's senses as they searched the smells on the air, the jumble of corpses and their scents, for their father before leaving the safety and concealment at the forest's edge.

Aticus couldn't help but stare at the three men stuck on pikes. A sickening feeling came over him like a weight heavy in his stomach, as if iron weights were weighing him down. Something was horribly wrong here, he could almost taste it. But in her determination, his sister would not be detoured. Ignoring Aticus' warnings she stepped out into the sunlight...

"Ayaa, my sister, named for the sound that she first howled when she had been born," Aticus said, visibly upset, each word sending a fresh ache of pain through his head. "Died that day..."

Aticus rested his forearm on the wall and looked out through the open doorway, with dawn approaching the ground was blanketed by thick undulating, virgin-white fog rolling slowly across the yard towards the highway. Aticus yawned, growing tired, but he knew he had to finish the story for his own sanity.

"I could barely handle the death of my sister!" Aticus suddenly beat his fist against the wall, giving everyone in the room a start. "We were born by wolves, so the passage of time had no meaning to us. We at least had each other before I lost her."

"Then I had nobody." Aticus' story continued, "Sure..."

"I found my grandmother briefly before she slipped through my hands. And my cousin, Sacco from Ge'vaudan before he too was killed leaving me alone to negotiate the ways of the human world on my own again." Aticus sighed, running his hands idly through Tracy's matted hair, gently combing out the tangles.

The only sound in the room for a moment the clapping and laughter of another sitcom starting on Alex and Tracy's flat screen TV. Both Lance and Aticus exchanged glances. A silent communication passed between the two men, prompting Lance to get up and start out the back door, shedding his clothing and transforming into a Wolf as he went. The previous silence in the room now filled with the Wolf Lance's howls.

Now Aticus' attentions once more turned to Tracy. Wiping away tears in his eye, Aticus checked the progress of Tracy's transformation. She had grown six petite pale teats down her torso. Alex's blood boiled as he watched Aticus caress and massage her shoulders, down to her back. She arched toward his touch, and Aticus gently pushed her down, straddling her. Alex's face flushed red with unbridled anger. He could hear Lance outside and he decided that while Aticus' attentions were focused on Tracy, it was the perfect opportunity to move. In a split second he grabbed for the lamp on the table beside him, preparing to jump up and swing at the man who was about to violate his wife.

Before Alex's feet could even touch the ground, Aticus slapped his face. He had moved so quickly all Alex saw was a blur as the huge hand made contact with his jaw, shattering it. Alex was thrown back against the couch, and as Aticus' left hand completed its arc, his right hand reached for the gun in his belt, flipping the switch to the silver dagger and swung it in the direction of Alex's face.

"I thought you might survive the night, however, just look out the window," Aticus said with sneer, "Dawn is now approaching and your time is up!"

Tracy heard the hammer as it clicked back. Despite the instinctive knowledge of a pecking order and compulsive need to be loyal to the Alpha wolf, Aticus, she instinctively moved toward her husband, whipping her head around and baring her teeth, a warning for the aggressor.

"Move, Tracy!" Aticus spat, impatiently waving the antique gun around.

Despite the fact that every cell in Tracy's body told her to be loyal to not question or defy what the Alpha Wolf said, she stood fast, positioning herself between her husband and twisting her head around to block Aticus from taking a head shot at Alex.

"Fuck!" Aticus' fangs involuntarily sprouted from his jaws making the word nearly incomprehensible.

Tracy growled, tensed to strike, until Aticus finally laid his firearm down. Aticus wiped the blood off his mouth. His jaw ached yet again, his biochemistry still unused to the quick, seamless, and usually painless metamorphosis he had previously grown accustomed to throughout the millennium.

Aticus agonized over Tracy's actions. Her loyalty should be absolute to him, the Alpha leader. After all, Aticus exuded powerful pheromones, an intoxicating aroma which was always radiating out, and a subtle supernatural mind control that usually made it impossible to resist him, especially for the really young changelings, the weak-willed or the ingenuous; but not Tracy.

I guess love trumps loyalty, Aticus thought bitterly. After all, it had been love that had set the wheels into motion and sealed his fate of losing an eye and almost losing his life, and it had sent him fleeing to the old country in the process. Ironically, it had been love that had also saved his life when he was on the brink of starvation and it had been love that brought him back to the Americas. Outside, he heard Lance's beautiful melody, inviting other lycanthropes to join the growing pack.

Aticus looked over at the frozen and angry person who used to be a lively Alex then over to Tracy who held her ground protectively. Maybe Tracy's fierce loyalty would turn out to be a good thing, Aticus thought. The Wolf's Blood already flowed and flourished in her veins without resistance. She was exceptionally strong willed and having her husband around may come in handy for controlling her until the transformation is fully realized, Aticus mused.

"There, there," Aticus whispered softly in her ear, "I am a sucker for love. I won't kill your husband."

Aticus inhaled Alex's shaking body and grimaced, from the smell of him the full metamorphosis would be all but futile, more than likely Alex would die in the process, however it would please Tracy and pacify her.

"Tracy, bite him." Aticus commanded and then turned away from Tracy.

His back turned he could not see Tracy as she bit Alex. But he heard his screams and a sickening sound of crunching bone as her teeth bore down into Alex's shoulder. Aticus smiled a smug smile. See, Aticus thought, Alex was finally useful. Tracy had immediately obeyed his order, Aticus again smiled smugly. He saw Tracy snuggling up close to her hysterical husband as blood dried on her chin. He saw Alex was already shivering and sweating profusely and his body had gone rigid. He shook his head in disappointment as he opened the front door to see the sunrise.

10

The crickets made their melodic chirring but they were drowned out by the songs of the sparrows waking for a new day. As the screen door shut at the Seller's place Aticus drew in a deep breath and sighed. Another new day, he had seen hundreds of thousands of them, but he knew somehow this day was different. He had been given a purpose for living again.

Aticus rubbed his cheeks; his cheeks were pulled taunt again, the elasticity of his face returning, not the wrinkly visage from before, even his very bone structure denser. He took in a deep breath, the muscles in his chest engorged and tight, he felt in his prime again; a strong heart now pumping blood throughout his veins.

The howling stopped. Aticus was sure that Lance had by now made it inside to check up on Alex and Tracy, so he began lazily strolling along the property's boundaries. He untied and took off his boots, wiggling his toes against the soft grass.

He looked down at his hands; He mentally made the hairs on his hand sprout up. Soon, hairs were replaced by fur; fingers were lengthening and fingernails growing until they were claws. He turned his paw-like hands, turning them so he could see his palms, the palms thickening to toughened pads. All of this took seconds to occur, but to Aticus it seemed like a lifetime of agonizing, excruciating pain as his body was still not yet used to the experience.

Concentrating, his hands were human hands again. The lines on his hands seemed to have disappeared. His hands were flawless, reminding him of marble or granite and somehow reminding him of his sister, Ayaa, and of the Lucem Dei.

Aticus lay down on the soft grass to soak up the upcoming sun's rays. Yawning, he rubbed at his eyes or the socket that used to be his eye and the one that remained. Fragments of silver had embedded into his socket, forever disrupting his ability to transform or heal. One more centimeter further and the fragments would have hit his pineal gland, preventing any metamorphosis altogether. It would not have killed him, he was an old lycanthrope after all, but it would have aged him greatly. Without the metamorphosis to renew old cells he would not be here today. He had survived the encounter, but the fragments remained securely embedded into his brain, forever changing his biochemistry. Every day, every hour, every second, for all of his life until the day that he dies he could expect excruciating headaches that rocked his foundation. He grimaced as he grasped at his ear or at an ear mangled and deformed with the lobe missing. Angry fangs emerged in his mouth but vanished just as quickly, he was determined to make the most of this new day. Aticus closed his eye daydreaming of Ayaa and of his family.

As a human and mortal when you become older the memories of your childhood quickly fade away, but with a lycanthrope or other immortal, as time wears on many childhood memories become romanticized. As time progressed in the truly ancient, some lycanthrope could even remember a romanticized version of their very birth. The process of metamorphosing from human to Wolf and back again, a process in which the entire body cell by cell tears apart and molds itself back together again and again. Dying and coming to life again as a different being. For the ancient of his kind their whole life, including their birth, would eventually flash before their eyes. As the centuries wear on, more and more memories flashed though the werewolves' minds, more vivid and vibrant than before.

He tried to put away the skeleton key to his dark cobwebbed closet but ultimately could not. Memory after painful memory flooded through his brain as he lay in the Sun. His head throbbing as it always did each and every day.

It was a sunny day not unlike today, however, the bitter cold rolled in from the Siberian forest. A beautiful Raven-black Grey wolf's legs shook at the weight of her swollen pregnant belly. She bayed out at the sky that today would be the day that she would give birth. She walked into the forest on swollen knees just far enough to shelter her from the elements. She found a place secure from the snow by a grouping of rocks and the dense canopy and coverage of Siberian pine where the ground did not see the sun let alone the snow. She eventually found a crevice in the rock formation, and then she lay on her side and whimpered as the contractions grew more frequent and stronger.

Her mate had vanished shorty after they conceived and now she had to give birth alone. Hours turned into a day as the sun rose over the horizon, painting a beautiful mixture of crimson and purple across the sky that man had no hope to ever in his vanity duplicate. Panting, shivering, and nauseous, the exhausted she-wolf bore down. One by one in sixty minute intervals she gave birth to four still born pups.

She had no time to mourn; however, contractions compelled her to push again. A stout blind black wolf, a boy, burst from the safety of her womb resting his unstable limbs on the frozen ground. The she-wolf lovingly licked the remains of the placental membrane off his face.

"Ooow..." The black pup exclaimed, shivering at the sudden shock of cold on his little wet paws.

This time her heart raced in excitement as another one of her young burst out from between her loins. The placental membrane tore from the pup's face revealing a flat wet nose on the scrawny yet lively little female.

"Ayaaaa," the blind pup yowled as she searched, blind and cold, in the dirt for her mother.

Another contraction rocked her again, involuntary muscle contractions told the she-wolf to push one last time. Howling, bitter, icy wind and the warm earth intermingled into a moist white fog as an infant emerged. Tiny at four pounds, three ounces, white as snow and shivering, a baby boy had been born.

Though precious, the baby was a strange sight to behold. Tresses of matted black hair ringed around his crown, skinny with long arms, legs, big hands and feet. He had no umbilical cord so he had no belly button to speak of. His face was obscured by the placental membrane which the she-wolf steadily licked off him. She dare not waste such an easy source of protein, and made sure she got all of it.

The two newborn pups, Oyo and Ayaa, eventually found their way back to their brother and then to their mother's warmth. The membrane had been cleaned from the human baby's face leaving a thin opaque film on his eyes. The film masked the brilliance of his emerald green eyes.

With a heavy heart the she-wolf gathered the stillborn babies to her chest with her paws and lovingly consumed them. One by one stopping for the briefest moment to mourn each one she eventually ate them all, now they were a part of her and merging with her again.

Feeding time, which was evidenced by the two puppies' and the one baby's consistent, exasperating shrieking of their little but endearing mouths. Oyo blindly bullied himself on his mother's swollen and tender teats. Positioning his body in such a manner that only one teat remained. Ayaa finally located the only available teat remaining suckling the live giving sustenance that only a mother could provide.

Aticus searched for his own milk source but came up dry. Ultimately, defeated, Aticus rolled off the feeding trio and flopped to the ground. The baby did not cry as the bitter cold wind smacked his cheeks like sandpaper. The starving baby did not wail but his stomach churned in knots. Out from the mothers warming presence and famished Aticus waved his balled fists in the air and closed his green eyes.

Aticus felt a cold wet nose nuzzling his neck. Ayaa interrupted her feeding to find him. She whimpered at Aticus and gently nudged him toward their mother's warmth. With a little coaxing she persuaded Aticus to try and latch onto the one available teat. However, he was met with snarls of warnings by their brother.

Ayaa snapped to defend her brother Aticus. She angrily jumped for Oyo's throat, toppling him down and off their mother. All of the teats were now free Ayaa wrestled around with Oyo until she heard her human brother safely suckling from their mother. Confident that her human brother got his fill Ayaa stopped tussling Oyo and searched blindly for her mother again. With Ayaa between Aticus and Oyo as a buffer the three finally fed peacefully.

A week or two passed and the pups opened their eyes, all but Aticus; his eyes were strangely already open at birth. Despite the occasional dispute, which Ayaa quickly squashed, the trio were inseparable, especially Aticus and Ayaa. On frigid nights the possibility of freezing to death always imminent because of Aticus' fragile human skin so Ayaa lay beside her brother to keep him warm. They learned to get along and to play together, pretending to hunt together despite Aticus' obvious shortcomings and disadvantages.

Mother Wolf lazed about on the cold ground watching her pups at play. Frolicking about without a care in the world, human occupations did not threaten them, at least for a while. Oyo and Ayaa developed at a normal lupine rates and Aticus' biochemistry was that of a lupine too, despite the human frame he had grown at an accelerated rate. At three feet, four inches, he had outgrown his brother and sister but he still walked on all fours, a consequence of living among wolves. Ayaa and Aticus played a spirited round of hide and seek while Oyo stealthily stalked his oblivious brother.

Aticus found his sister hiding in a hole in a massive hollow tree. He scratched wildly on the bark. His fingernails were not yet strong enough to do any actual damage to the bark of a healthy tree but Aticus' strong fingers managed to tear off the bark of a rotten one, revealing Ayaa.

Ayaa snapped playfully at Aticus' chin with enough force to surprise him who reflexively withdrew, enabling his sister's escape under overgrown brush. Whirling around to go after his sister suddenly the breath flew from his lungs in an audible "whoosh", Oyo had hurtled all his weight at his unsuspecting brother. Aticus could not move. His brother's muscular paws had pinned his human shoulders down.

Oyo had always distrusted Aticus. Oyo and Aticus may have been brothers but secretly he disdained Aticus. After all he was abnormal, an oddity, hairless, tailless and no muzzle to speak of, so Oyo could not understand Aticus and Ayaa's friendship and jealousy began to rear its ugly head. Oyo growled a menacing growl; much different than the frisky growls that were heard every day by Aticus and Ayaa, a growl of warning and a threat of violence.

Oyo's paws pressed down hard on Aticus' shoulders, his claws slicing the skin until blood flowed freely. Oyo's snarling spittle pooled on Aticus' chest. His crooked head, ears back and stiffened tail, told of a looming strike. His jaws clamped down on Aticus' throat before he had a chance to react. Aticus yelped as he futilely tried to escape his brother. Aticus arched his back and wildly kicked with all his might. A dirty foot caught Oyo under the rib cage; another foot caught him in the groin.

Ayaa peeked out from a thicket of overgrown wild berries bushes, full of sharp thorns. The high, shrill distress call from her brother made her suddenly spring into action, howling a response. Her paws hardly touched the muddy frozen ground as she ran to rescue Aticus.

By the time Ayaa got to her brother's side the scene had changed drastically. Aticus had escaped Oyo's paws and gotten his neck out from Oyo's clutches. Oyo, still reeling in pain from the shot to the groin, lay on his side on the snow covered ground. Ayaa seized the opportunity and biting Oyo's back haunch, tried to wrench him away from Aticus. It was no use whatsoever as Oyo kicked his back legs, hitting Ayaa square in the muzzle.

Aticus heard his sister yelp in pain and saw her reel away, whimpering. Ayaa had fought for him tried to protect him often because, no matter how strange he appeared to be he was still family, for her loyalty she was now huddled in pain injured on the ground. Something inside him snapped.

Aticus dug his hands and feet deep into the snow and barreled straight at his brother who was already on his feet bracing for impact. The dueling brothers crashed into one another, the impact startling ravens and with a flapping of wings they flew from their nesting branches. Squawks of warning as the birds flew away, a few black feathers swirling in the wind.

Oyo scratched at Aticus leaving bloody gashes in his back across his naked human skin. Aticus tried to sink his fingers into his brother's neck and shoulders, to rip into him, but his human fingernails were just too short to penetrate his brother's thick fur. They were locked in a deadly embrace, twirling around one another so fast the human eye could not follow.

Oyo the pup fought as a wolf, Aticus the human fought as though he was a wolf too. However, upon two legs the wounded Aticus had the upper hand for a moment. Aticus' large furless hand finally caught Oyo's neck. His paws left the ground and he flailed wildly about trying to catch any piece of Aticus that he could with his snapping fangs.

He growled, snarled, and wailed as he tried to bite and scratch his way out from Aticus' clutches. Aticus yelped as a claw came at his face. Blood streamed into his eyes from the gash on his forehead but Aticus did not relent. Even with the stinging blood blinding him and his body bruised and wounded, his grip did not loosen. His hand tightened on Oyo's throat until he whimpered with his tail between his legs, a sign of surrender.

The mother wolf had secretly been watching as the conflict played out. She had just caught two wild rabbits and ripped them apart, she regurgitated what was left for her children. A series of yips and yowls told the younglings it was now feeding time and any conflict must be suspended.

Ayaa was the first to lick her wounds and wander over to feed. Aticus was exhausted and had lost a significant amount of blood. Only twenty feet away from the life-sustaining nourishment but with his bruised and battered body he may as well have been a mile away. Still gasping for breath and on his back, Oyo had no intentions of eating until he caught his breath. Ayaa finished her share then lapped up a little extra. She slowly strolled over to her two brothers and ignoring Oyo altogether she sat at Aticus' side. She spewed out the mush close enough so that he could eat without moving, movement begat pain. Ayaa's rough tongue licked at Aticus' gashes on his neck, shoulder, and chest until they were clean and had stopped leaking.

Oyo, with his tail still between his legs, slowly and painfully limped over to his mother. He stopped twice to look over his shoulder at Aticus and Ayaa, involuntarily growling in humiliation and jealousy as he watched their unbreakable bond.

Satisfied that Aticus' stomach was now full, Ayaa circled around her brother, scratched the dirt with her claws and lay down next to him. Any slight noise caused her ears to perk up; any movement that Oyo made caused Ayaa to snarl in defense of her human brother. The mother wolf noticed this and smiled a wolf's smile as she lay down on the ground to soak up the sun's rays. At least one of her pups had taken a real shine to the strange furless pup. She had grown fond of, with all his strange quirks and differences, this mix of pup and babe. After all, he had defended the den when unwanted scavengers, though piglets, had invaded it. He had become a true wolf in every sense with the only exception his delicate and fragile skin. She had seen the conflict between the two brothers and her heart said stop it, but however bloody it became, her pups would become stronger for it, so she did nothing but watch. Over now, Aticus was the clear winner of the conflict and had become the strongest of the three, surprising and delighting even mother wolf. Ayaa clearly had grown quite fond of her brother Aticus, so maybe Oyo in time would grow fond of him too, or at least now if another conflict arose she knew Aticus could take care of himself.

Mother-wolf closed her eyes in the sunlight and relaxed, knowing her family could fend for themselves and the first time Aticus would be left in charge. A slight chill wind from the north near the mountains gently flew through her old gray fur as she made herself comfortable then drifted off to sleep on the steadily melting snow.

The weeks went by without incident in the solitude of the forest while winter and the mountains inhibited human encroachment. Then months blew by, like the blink of an eye. Fall, then winter came and passed and the family of wolves and the human child soon enjoyed a pleasant summer, the only worry locating their next meal. Unfortunately, the next meal had been getting harder and harder to find. Game had relocated closer to the creeks and springs as the ice melted in the heat and long days of summer.

The streams and creeks, the life source of the animals, had always also been a godsend for nearby humans. The humans made their huts and villages further into a Wolf territory. But the wolves migrated away during the day, coming back only to hunt at night; oblivious humans went on with their daily lives unaware of the predators.

Aticus looked over his surroundings high up on the hills where his family rested on a grouping of rocks which might be used as a natural camouflage. Mother wolf had led them here enough times to hunt and drink and they were stealthy enough to not worry about being seen. He could hear his mom singing to the mountains, a howl of sadness, and an aria of loss. Almost the equivalent of an adolescent, he could make out select words and phrases which told the story about a chance meeting and an eerie call to her lost beloved. He feared that it was not the scarcity of game that prompted the move closer to humanity, but rather her lost mate.

Aticus tried his best to interpret the miserable melody… She would wait for him every full moon on the edge of a human village singing a song of joy and sudden sadness. Searching for food in an occupied human territory she happened to spy another dire wolf. She saw a potent male with strange captivating eyes, green eyes the color of emeralds. With thick fur, mane-like in appearance black as night, majestic soft down which windswept in the icy breeze. Their attraction instant; and they begot a litter of three.

Heat burned from her loins as the mother wolf remembered the midnight black wolf with the striking green eyes and how they had feverishly coupled. The pregnancy had demanded more food than usual, human's livestock a guaranteed morsel but requiring dangerous raids to do so. With the full moon high up in the night sky they had found a family of sleeping sheep nearby a human habitat and stealthily snuck into it. Termite ridden boards easily gave way to the black wolf's might. The soon to be mother wolf had found a less barbaric and much quieter way to enter into the pen, ducking beneath the loose bottom boards. She had taken the side on which the ground dipped down allowing easier passage for her swollen belly. After some undignified squirming and clawing, she finally made it into the pen. In doing so she had a closer view of the sleeping ewes and plump rams. Her angle where the moon's light was concealed by the thick tall trees she saw vacant open eyes and the beginnings of the faint smell of decay. She looked up to see her mate already several paces in front of her. The sheep were not sleeping, they did not smell right at all, they were dead, and mother wolf froze.

The black wolf, with the wind against his back, missed the distinct smell of decay and was still on course to capture his prey. With his ears laid back, on his belly, he slowly and methodically crept up to the tempting mass of wool. A squeal than another, a yelp of warning fell out her muzzle then she saw movement coming from the corner of her eyes. Coming from the tall trees and the safety of the cover of darkness four men revealed themselves.

It had all been an elaborate trap.

Crimson cloaks blew in the wind; complete with bronze helmets and padded armor. There helms emblazoned with a triangle and in the middle of the pyramid an all-knowing eye decorated in silver. Marking the three corners were silver sigils that the mother will could not comprehend. Two of the men had spears in their hands; the other one had a large net held at the ready which appeared to be comprised of lightweight silver. Her description of the armored men would be forever burned into her memory. Mother wolf had no worry about being seen herself as the men with their strange crest were too busy concentrating on sneaking up on the prize before them.

Just then the beautiful black wolf stopped his inspection of the dead sheep, a noise catching his attention. His curious demeanor soon turned to a convulsive snarl that shrank his green eyes to slits and exposed two sets of fangs as his upper lip had turned completely inside out, drool foaming out of his mouth and dripping onto the dirt. He heard the three men steadily sneaking up to him before he saw them. Yelps of warning formed in the back of her throat.

Then in an instant the black wolf's demeanor changed again as he strained to look at his mate. A shrill howl left his throat stopping mother wolf's attempt to warn her beloved before she had been heard by the three men. She understood the howl.

"Run!"

Her heart hurt at the prospect of leaving him but she obeyed. A healthy wolf would rush in and fight off the attackers with tooth and nail. However, two months pregnant every limb in her body ached in constant agony when she walked far, her paws swelled and the tendons strained. A growl from her belly reminded her she would not be eating tonight but that would be okay because her stomach roiled with queasiness and food was the last thing she wanted right now. She slowly recoiled back to the fence, back into the shadows where she had entered. With her paws digging furiously at the shallow ground she was able to widen the hole enough for her exit. Turning around, she backed under the boards on her belly and back onto the grass, never taking her eyes off her beloved.

The elegant black Wolf spun around to the surprise and horror of the three armed men who up till now thought they were tracking the Wolf in silence. Startled, one of them released his spear prematurely. The blade sunk into the earth just inches from the wolf's shoulder, hitting the ground with enough force to make projectiles out of the small rocks it knocked out of the way. They peppered the wolf's muzzle and stung his cheeks as if bees defending their hive.

Distracted by the first spear the black wolf had no time to react when the second spear hurtled into the air. Slicing easily through fur and skin, displacing shoulder socket and severing nerves, the wolf's crimson life's blood dripped onto the ground followed by a shrill yelp of pain that echoed through the forest, startling wildlife and prompting mother wolf to almost burst from the safety of her concealment beneath a lone thick shrub. What she saw next froze her to the core and confused her primitive wolf's mind.

Silver interfering with the special "magic" that pulsed in his blood made her mate's fur recede, leaving a fragile nude muscle bound limb. The spear had impaled the wolf's shoulder, a special silver cord entwined around the shaft of the spear itself, made the injured arm instantly transform to a human arm, a human arm flapping limply in the crisp wind. Cracking sounds echoed as the ligaments reformed to suit a man's hand, wrist and elbow.

An unkempt wild blonde-haired boy of no more than 12 or 13 years old smirked in triumph as his spear hit its mark. His eyes lit up in pride as he looked up at his father.

"I got him! I got him, father!" Flushed with pride for his younger son but also a little jealous because after all, his own spear had missed, the man slapped his son hard on his back, clanging his armor.

"I am proud of you my boy!" Glom thundered, smiling a toothless smile.

Malstros' hands rested on his knees as he crouched down to catch his breath, he remembered it like yesterday when three strangers had arrived at Babylon's Gate with the proposition for the great King. Glom of the Malstros hillside, known to his people as "the fair", the right hand for Nebuchadnezzar 2; King of Babylon had sat silently, listening, stiff and unwavering at the side of king's throne as the three foreigners spoke in turn. He had scrutinized each of the three men one by one as they spouted off their proposals. Then in their native language he deciphered, they were agents of "The God's Light", agents tracking men and women they considered a threat to humanity.

"The Fair" had grown up nobody's fool and was sure there had to be more to the story than met the eye, however, Nebuchadnezzar 2 was blinded by all the gold and jewels which too often appeased him. He agreed to the proposal: a quarter of his army in retainer and three good men for three years to hunt the foul beasts. A substantial award would be granted for the three men for every head brought back to the "God's Light". Throat dry from thirst, stomach growling in hunger, yes, Malstros remembered like it had been yesterday.

He and his two sons had tracked this monster wolf for three months now, carrying them far from the safety and prosperity of the Euphrates River and the mighty city of Babylon. Now they were far from their home, between the Black Sea and Caspian Sea near the Kazbegi Mountains. Three times now, they had almost caught the wolf rummaging through the refuse in the outskirts of the village in Armenia on a full-moon night but it had slipped away by dawn's light. And once, they had nearly caught the monster as a man as he abruptly stopped at a creek to rest and drink. Naked from head to toe, oblivious of the mercenaries watching, the man had stared in quiet wonder at an adult she-wolf who was thirstily lapping at the clear and fresh water. Until a change in the wind had alerted him to their human presences he had been quite captivated with her. He sniffed the air with his human nose and just like that he was gone in a blur.

The scouts had reported with enthusiasm that the beast had returned to the spot that they had nearly captured him at as a man only months before. Currently lurking in the area, his eldest son came up with the idea to lay out bait and wait until the monster came to them. The exhausting and agonizing waiting had paid off in the end as he imagined how he would spend the reward money offered by the God's Light. Glom stepped back to let his kids do all the hard work. Glom "the fair" Malstros, one of a long line of the much esteemed Malstros family throughout the decades, imagined retiring from military and politics and settling down with the reward money and perhaps a few extra luxuries. The famous hunter stood back unfolding a silver twine net which he quickly tossed to his sons, who together with all their might tossed it over their target with success. The brothers gavc cach other congratulatory looks before they pulled out their swords in unison.

Now the abominable beast with its one human arm stared with its green glowing beastly eyes following their every move. Horror and disgust should have come over the mother wolf as she watched her beloved become a twisted hybrid of wolf paw and bear arm. No revulsion could be seen in her sorrowful eyes, quite the opposite reaction was evident; she had been mesmerized, filled with wonder and amazement. Her mate was special, amazing. She had not seen another like him. Her black wolf was hurt, trapped and there wasn't anything she could do about it. She whimpered in frustrated anguish.

With his one injured limb and tangled by the net, the wolf struggled. The two sons faltered, their swords in hand, suddenly losing their bravado as they stared into the eyes of the abomination snapping and snarling at them. His skin rippled like waves on the ocean, tangled and trapped by the net but still dangerous.

Flooding the wolf's body was something primordial and much too dangerous for humanity... a type of new but antediluvian adrenaline something only the lycanthropes had, something they needed to survive, parasites spitting out an unnatural mixture of new genes and hormones called *The Wolf's Blood.*

The uninjured muscles quiver under his black fur and skin began to undulate and entwine. Bundles of the green eyed wolf's muscles snapped reforming to make it suitable to that of a humanoid; his one good shoulder dislocating as new ligaments began to knit back together again, the ball socket now suitable for a human-like arm. An ancient lycanthropic shifting to suit his needs, seamlessly, effortlessly and instinctually; and that need was sure survival! The hesitation of the two men all he needed to stand up on his human-like legs as his hip bone expanded and contorted to the needs of a biped.

The black wolf had become an amalgamation of wolf and man, more man than wolf except for the head and feet. The feet still remained long, wide, and thick with talon paws that gave it an extraordinary amount of stability. The ankle to the heel functioned as a reverse knee, giving him amazing jumping capabilities. His head still a lupine visage, long muzzled and curved fangs as he continued to snarl at his persecutors. The man-wolf a monstrous site to behold indeed, but the fact remained that even with his intimidating appearance he could not escape entangled and injured by the silver snare.

The two sons slowly approached to finish him off as he let out a deafening howl, hoping his beloved would get the hint and run. Clenching the bloody spear with his one good claw he wrenched with gritted teeth until the shaft shattered into pieces. A fine thread of silver like a spider's web caught the light of the moon. He looked in horror at the shiny webbed thread as it swung toward him, designed to mimic the spider webs in nature, almost impossible to get off the body if you were unlucky enough to stumble upon it. The black Wolf frantically traced the loosely swinging web with just one long, curved nail to the point of origin… the gaping wound in his shoulder. Slowly the wounded wolf pulled the string from his shoulder, inch by painful inch. Like a clown pulling handkerchief after colorful handkerchief from his breast pocket, a never-ending trick but without the abject amusement and applauds.

After all their time tracking the elusive beast the father drank from his wineskin a smile creasing his wrinkled face, pleased how easily the "Wolf" had been captured. His young son would get the lion's share of the bounty he decided, after all, without a direct hit, it would have been a whole different story as to what happened. Last time the "God's Light" set off to find and kill this powerful wolf with the striking green eyes, twenty had set out but only his family had returned.

Glom surveyed the scene he saw that the fence spanned about a hundred yards in all directions disappearing on one side into the woods. From where he stood he could see a gentle hill sloping upward, a simple little hut stood at the top of the hill where his mercenaries patiently waited for their signal to attack. He grew more confident of his impending victory. With his two sons distracting the beast he drew in as deep a breath as he was able for his advanced age and blew on his horn, signaling the mercenaries to begin their attack. With shaking hands that had gotten worse as his unidentified disease progressed, he slid out his silver spear from the hilt on his back and limped to the gate.

The black beast drooled and snarled, smacking away a thrust of the elder boy's sword, sending him off balance. A paw-like hand swiftly latched onto the elder boy's forearm, claws digging into soft skin, involuntarily making him wrench around in pain and entangling him in the net in the process. While the beast chewing through the net that immobilized him. All would be lost with the other arm still limp wounded Wolf would not be able to fend off a second attack save for the fact the cowardly youngest son. Gale the youngest son of Glom moments ago made a hit directly on the shoulder of the beast now stood frozen with fear, his eyes wide and glossy.

"Gale!" Glom shrieked at his cowardly youngest son while stumbling across the field to save his eldest son. "Get in there and fight you cowardly son of a whore!"

The clatter and clang could be heard by the beast as Nebuchadnezzar's small Army filed out one by one, archers drawing their bows, waiting for the order to let the arrows fly. Glom drew another weak breath and signaled the soldiers to light their torches to engulf the arrow tips in flames.

Archers let loose a volley of flaming arrows that sounded like angry hornets and looked like bright comets crossing the sky. One by one, the flaming arrows hit the earth, just one fiery arrow hitting the ground set off a wall of flames 10 feet high.

The archers were blocked off from the scrimmage by the raging fires that quickly spread toward the black Wolf, but they did their job, also blocking off the high hills to which the Wolf might hope to escape. The archers fled from the very same hills but with a long march around and soon they would be able to reinforce Glom again.

She-wolf anxiously whimpered watched helplessly from her lonely shrub. The tar soaked ground ablaze and turned the night sky a hazy hue of red, bringing hell to Earth. Flames, only yards away made the air around her superheated drying her throat and burning her lungs, the smell of her singed fur made her wretch, her stomach turning knots. Mother Wolf's watering eyes squinted, the inferno distorting the molecules in the air bringing shadows dancing to life. Her precious mate had almost torn free of the net and had Gael the eldest son in his grasp. He had hoisted himself up off the ground and like a child's rag doll he swung the man around and around by the forearm, heedless of his agonized screams.

After his father's taunts of cowardice convinced him to aid his older brother, the younger boy thrust his sword but just haphazardly and cautiously, the beast was easily able to fend off advance after advance with his snapping, snarling fangs. The old man Glom, near blinded from the brilliant lights of the fire, finally limped to his sons' assistance. From decades of experience a well-aimed lunge of his spear pierced the belly of the beast; he ruthlessly twisted and then yanked it out. Glom drew back prepared to strike yet again.

Until now any interaction with humanity for the she-wolf had been scarce, fleeting and harmless. The explicit violence perpetrated by the humans to her beloved made her head spin. Mother Wolf gasped; a yelp involuntarily leaving her muzzle, startling her and disrupting fragile branches that might give away her measly shelter. Desperate, her fur standing on end with her whole body tensed, this time mother wolf had to act or her lover would perish.

About to pass out from blood loss and pain, Gael, and the black wolf grasp heavy fluttering eyes noticed from the bush a form he had not seen previously. The lights from the raging fires made the impenetrable shadows flutter revealing another wolf's eyes, aglow posed to strike. Much smaller and looked female, Gael summoned his strength, found his bearings; he desperately tried to call a warning to his younger brother that there was a second Wolf to dispatch.

"Gale," His throat scratchy and dry, ribs pressing in on his lungs, in unbearable pain and struggling to get out just one broken phrase, "there's another…"

The black Wolf with his fierce green eyes turned toward his beloved, awareness hitting him like a ton of bricks, he could clearly see her form in a background of orange illumination where the shadows were banished. She crouched in an "M" shape, chest in the dirt with her ears set back, slits for eyes, fangs bared to expose her curved white canine teeth.

The beautiful black Wolf knew suddenly what he had to do to keep his mate from harm. The Wolf looked at her with compassionate green eyes, rapidly turning into eyes that commanded attention and loyalty. Eyes that said, "I told you to run, don't come for me!"

Simultaneously, before Glom could rear back for another strike, before Gale could summon his nerves, before Gael could warn his family of the other wolf's position and before the she-wolf could creep any closer the black beast grunted, his muscles quivering, hurdled Gael toward his family knocking them down like they were bowling pins, Gael the oversized and awkward ball.

Glom groaned as his back tightened, then snapped, falling on the ground and rolling over on his side. The spear in Glom's hands flew into the weeds uselessly, like quicksand sinking down to its murky depths. Gale slid on his rump, friction ripping the skin from his hands; he too lost his weapon in the process. Regardless, the two men, Gale and Glom, were at least far enough away to see the beast's wild thrashing. Gael, however, had been entangled by the torn net when thrown by the beast and kicked furiously, unable to get his ankles free. The black beast managed to free himself of his snares completely and jumped up in the air on his powerful limbs. He fell upon Gael's helplessly ensnared body, easily pinning him down. Hip cracking like a gun shot, Gael let out a short huff the air forced from his lungs.

The black beast pushed down upon Gael's body, breaking ribs and suffocating him in the process. The beast transformed in an instant, now back to a form more familiar to that of his beloved. He looked like a normal black Wolf, albeit an enormous thing, his ancestry kin to the dire Wolf. The black Wolf's had a thick neck, head, curved fangs and muscular back. The only thing to give him away was a limp bloody human arm, a pasty hand dragging uselessly behind him. Illuminating green eyes found and locked on to his beloved's eyes.

The black beast reacted, but not from instinct, not fear, neither from rage nor the desire for revenge; black beast reacted with cold calculated reasoning; human reasoning. The green-eyed monster sunk his fangs into Gael's throat. No amount of padded armor could protect him from the wolf's long fangs and powerful bite. He swung his neck quick to the right, then a swift left with his powerful muzzle and Gael's skin flipped open like a cheap paperback book, spewing Gael's lifeblood into the air in a red spray. Gael's throat crushed, he could not betray the position of the beast's love.

"No! Nooooo!" Glom shrieked as he groped around for his missing spear.

"Gael... Gael... Gael." Gale whispered frantically under his breath. He had found his dropped sword and now clutched it to his chest with all his might like a long-lost childhood teddy bear.

Dying gasps and gurgles of his elder son ringing in his ears and his other son distracted and too cowardly to move the father desperately flailed about on the tar soaked grass still futilely searching for his weapon. The elder son's skin stretched like melted cheese until it snapped from the wolf's jaws, his long tongue lapping up blood like a water fountain, and soaking his shaggy muzzle. Gael, husband and father of several children including recently a healthy baby boy, "Gull", struggled for his last breath as the light dimmed in his eyes. His hands scrabbling at the wolf's sides weakly, than fell still.

"Ooow!!!" the wounded Wolf wailed into the night. His orders for Mother Wolf were clear; "Do not move". All though she would be visible and exposed in the firelight, any movement would call attention to her position now. She thoughtlessly obeyed his commands and her muscles stiffened.

A roar began to resonate from the wolf's matted, blood spackled chest, soft and quiet at first, then rumbling louder and louder, clearly a warning for the two remaining men not to follow … then he suddenly scuttled off. One paw dug into the moist, blood-soaked soil while his limp human arm followed uselessly.

"Go after him!" Glom yelled desperately between the frantic whistling of his horn, warning the archers of the wolf's escape.

The diversion worked, Gael, the one who had spotted his beloved in the bushes now dead and the two remaining men hobbling downhill toward the ever thickening darkness after him, on the hunt again for the wounded Wolf, the pregnant she wolf now safe from harm. As if on cue, billowing thick, grey clouds finally spewed forth their contents. Cold rain began to fall like angel tears, the skies seeming to cry in sorrow from the violence witnessed here. A sprinkle at first, but then a downpour, while it wasn't enough to quench the raging fires it gave mother wolf a chance for escape if she could make it through the wall of fire and get to higher ground where humans dare not follow. She looked around, her heart pounding, her nose burning from the acidic smoke and saw the muddy puddles forming between the fire and the yelling soldiers.

She lurched forward and rolled in the mud, she rolled from head to swollen belly until it covered her from ears to tail, until she looked like a clay sculpture come to life. She turned her head toward the darkness. She could still smell the soldiers even through the thickening smoke. She then turned her head toward the fire that still raged even through the downpour. Tail between her legs and heavy mud dripping from her entire body, without hesitation, she ran toward the flames.

Mother Wolf's pads burned and began to crack; although her eyes were wet with tears and shut tight they began to shrivel as she traveled through the inferno. Her lungs began to blister and burn, she had made it into the epicenter of the blaze but now began to suffocate, and the lack of air began to disorient her. Now she didn't know where the flames started or ended and it threatened to end her life and the life of her unborn litter. The soft mud began to harden as the moisture began evaporating. Her limbs began to stiffen with every move she made. Her swollen belly began to cramp and her chest began to tighten, her ears began to pop, hiss, and snap, the all-encompassing noises of the flames threatened to consume her very soul. A lone raindrop wet her muzzle then another and yet another until a torrent of wet cooling drops quickened her heart. Mother Wolf opened her dried eyes, the moisture returning to them again; she hardened her resolve to get out from the hell she had been trapped in and trudged forward.

The she-wolf finally made it out of the wall of fire, the flames steadily creeping downhill. The mud covering her body had been hardened by the extreme heat, keeping her fragile body safe from the worst of the flames. Looking like a marble statue, no imperfections anywhere except for scorches from the heat. The mud began to crack, softening from the rain which still poured down on her, cooling her as she ran. She ran until the sudden pangs of pain hit her, she knew her pups were coming, and quickly.

11

Like many times before, Aticus day-dreamed… romanticizing the psalms that his mother once sung. He dreamed of his family again, another memory seared into his brain of Ayaa, Oyo and Mother Wolf… his family, happy and together. Sure the relationship between Oyo and Aticus had been strained at best but they were still family. But he began day-dreamed about pyramids and watchful eyes, an all-knowing eye. The colors Crimson and purple mixing together and he began to get anxious. The wretched "God's Light" found him even in his waking thoughts!

Although the family pack had made their den very close to a human village and every night mother wolf wailed her sad songs, they managed their concealment for months until one warm summer day changed all that. The smell alerted mother wolf even before the noise did, although the troop made no attempt to squash the raucous laughter which inundated their surroundings. They were just three men but their footfalls sounded like a battalion. The pups and Aticus were blissfully unaware of the men approaching, too busy basking in the sun's warming rays, until a series of yowls from mother wolf warned them of an approaching danger.

Quickly, mother wolf had a hold of Oyo by the scruff and flung him as gently as she could into the camouflage of brush. Next mother wolf, with a good hold of Ayaa's scruff tossed her child down the gently sloping hill by the creek, yelping from surprise instead of pain as she hit the water. She had no time to toss Aticus before the soldiers broke through the entanglement of thick vines between the trees.

"I finally found you, bitch!" Gale, son of Glom and brother of the slain Gael, said triumphantly.

The son whose first hunt had been her mate, seasoned now and no longer the scared shaking boy he had been, stood confident with dagger in hand. Two of Gael's sons, Gamell and Googg, still only children themselves began to encircle the mother Wolf.

"I knew it, Gale! I knew this abomination would lead us to her!" Googg said with excitement. "Gale, you were right! There was another one after all!"

Gale felt vindicated; he knew his beloved brother had warned him of another wolf before he died. He had in one of his hands a long, rusty chain and he gave it a quick yank. The chain slithered through the tall grass like a snake, pulling taunt for a moment and then going slack again. The dense trees and overgrown weeds and vines obscured the dark figure shackled to the end of the chain.

"Kill the bitch and be done with it! We'll finally be heading back home. My father is ill and he can't stand being away from home too long." Gale whispered vehemently.

Mother wolf braced herself and began to snarl. She may not have understood their words but their intentions were clear. She exposed pearly white fangs warning the three intruders to stay back. Branches of a nearby bush suddenly exploded to life. Mother Wolf tried to deliberately hide Oyo but he arose from the underbrush. However Oyo's noises and movement were masked by mother wolf's snarls of warnings.

Aticus felt his brother's teeth against his neck. That's it, Aticus thought, Oyo had patiently waited until the opportune moment to strike. Pressure on his neck increasing until it was all he could do to keep from passing out. No control of his body anymore as it was tossed up and now in flight, he landed in the mud face first beside the creek at the bottom of the hill. Dazed, Aticus looked up only to see Googg had rounded on Oyo and thrust his shiny sword into his heart. Aticus sat slack-jawed too stunned to move. How could he have been so stupid, guilt coursing through Aticus' human veins, Oyo was not trying to kill him, but had rushed in and saved his life. Aticus' throat swelled up in sadness as the sword jerked out of his brother's bleeding chest, a quick slice and Oyo's head bounced along the tall grass.

The head tumbled downhill and with a splash came to a stop in the water, tongue sticking out at Aticus. Tearing his eyes from Oyo's decapitated head, Aticus noticed his sister. A muddy mess, Ayaa was only visible when she opened her eyes wide. She stared up the hill, whimpering quietly.

Her stomach churning, the mother wolf retreated back to the edge of the hill and stopped. She knew her two remaining children were down the hill and she wouldn't dare risk exposing them. Mother wolf went on the offensive Snarling and clawing at the three soldiers. She couldn't help but glance down the hill to look for her pups to assure their safety, though. Four blinking eyes stared back at her, comforting her, but that distraction cost her. Googg side-stepped her deadly fangs and thrust a dagger into her ribcage. Mother wolf yelped in pain and he raised his dagger for the death blow.

Before Googg could react, a second wind invigorated the she-wolf; sparks turned into an inferno of desire to live, to escape her tormentors and to ensure her remaining pup's safety. She twisted her ribcage around and the awkward angle of his hand made Googg lose his grasp of the dagger. Mother wolf's shoulders shoving him back and hitting his head on a low hanging Cypress branch. His knees buckled, trying to catch his balance but ultimately falling on his back. Dazed, he searched for his brother and Uncle through the thick fog in his mind. The blow to his head left him confused, his ears ringing and not able to reach for his scabbard before the she-wolf pounced on him.

Gamell, diverted by a cluster of trees, weeds, and falling branches circled around in an attempt to save his brother, Googg. Between clusters of trees there lay a long forgotten fox den. When the stream flooded, leaves and branches inundated the hole in clustered masses. Navigating the refuge made it extremely difficult but Gale managed to pick his way around to the other side in an attempt to save his nephew, still carrying the encumbering chain with him. The confusion had lifted from Googg's mind just in time to see the grotesque snarling teeth and wild eyes of the mother Wolf.

"Gamell, my Brother!" He yelled for help.

Googg repositioned his body the best he could with the weight of the wolf bearing down on him. With fingers outstretched he desperately tried to retrieve his sword. With his body awkwardly positioned, however, moving left him exposed for the next strike. Muscles almost at their breaking point he struggled to get his elbow and forearm between his exposed neck and her deadly snapping teeth. He smelled her putrid breath, which reminded him of the meat market back in Babylon. Googg, almost out of breath, fended off her dangerous muzzle with its wild snapping powerful incisors. One or two strikes came dangerously close to his cheek leaving trickles of drool behind. Mother Wolf swiped and scratched violently at his leather padded armor but it did nothing but score the hardened shell. His legs kicked for traction in an attempt to right himself. Then their desperate eyes met, Googg and mother wolf, locked in a stare that seem like a singularity. He unexpectedly saw through mother Wolf's eyes, and those eyes were not at all the eyes of a cold blooded killer, they were the eyes of a mother that just witnessed the murder of her pup and fought valiantly to protect herself. An indescribable sorrow for the loss made tears spring out from his eyes as he thought of the senselessness of what had already been lost for both of them, so clearly just self-defense and nothing more that had driven the mother Wolf into such frenzy.

The uncle did not hesitate, like last hunt, navigating a series of fallen trees and branches he finally found his nephew. His brother made it none too worse for wear with just minor scratches and bruises, but then mother Wolf had found a weak spot in Googg's armor. Her nails scored the armor and traveled up his shoulder to pierce his unprotected neck. Only two of five nails punctured his flesh but it had been a mortal hit when it shredded his jugular vein.

Googg felt an uncontrollable sensation come over him. One of pissing himself but above his waist, warm and wet every time his heart knocked in his chest. His neck gushed blood, prompting him to release his faulty grip upon mother wolf's muzzle to try to quell the copious amounts of sticky substance. Like sticking a finger in a cracked dam the blood still flowed and his heart still beat his life away. He made a halfhearted attempt to stab at mother wolf but failed, only penetrating the thick fur before he lost his grip. A torrent of scratches made mincemeat of his face, the wolf only stopping when Googg stopped squirming. Googg's brother and Uncle had made it through the obstacles only to find mother wolf facing them head-on.

Pacing quickly from side to side so Gale and Gamell could not get a clear swipe at her, mother wolf's eyes did not dare look away from her attackers. After some hesitation they raised their swords but a sudden snap of her vicious fangs, still dripping with their relative's blood, made both men hesitate. It seemed a stalemate, until Gale shook that massive chain. Something stirred from the shadows and glowing green eyes appeared. The pacing wounded Wolf stopped in her tracks, stunned as the thing moved out of the shadows into the light.

A shackled and humiliated man-beast appeared. It looked like an emaciated Wolf walking on two legs but both the other arms all the way to his shoulders were severed. She stared in horror at the silver stakes protruding from his stumps and noticed the wolf's once luxurious black fur. Gone, in its place were thinning, unhealthy, sparse black patches fur which were greying. The beast locked onto mother Wolf's eyes. Vacant sorrowful green eyes so old and alien yet seemed so familiar. The scent of the horrid thing unmistakable, the scent of her long lost mate, he had finally returned to her.

Aticus and Ayaa saw the unfamiliar wolf man too but the unmistakable pheromones and implicit bond told them that they were laying their eyes on their father for the first time. Angered by the chains that bound his father, Aticus grinds his teeth. He can't help but notice the shiny pyramid and a dazzling jewel eye set upon it adorning the corset that constricted his father's breathing and held him tight like a walking prison. A screeching yelp made Aticus' ears twitch and impulsively glance over at his mother who now howled in pain. Gale seized the opportunity and when mother Wolf had been distracted plunged his sword deep into her chest, piercing a lung. Gamell smiled smugly and with one resolute arc the head of mother Wolf rolled down the hill to join the head of her pup at the creek's edge.

Aticus lay naked in the noonday sun. He tossed and turned with the sun in his face but the warm pleasant day soothed his bare skin. Unpleasant memories plagued him, so much so he could not bring himself to open his eye now. Even with his eyes shut tight the sun at its zenith he could not help but see the Gods Light "eye" under his eyelid. Just thinking about the eye Aticus shut his eye tighter still the unstoppable train of his memory steaming forward.

The surviving siblings slipped from the tightening noose of the God's Light bastards and the villagers alike. It had been three weeks since mother and brother wolf's untimely deaths and they were completely alone, Aticus and Ayaa now had to fend for themselves. But they strived to forget the horrors of that fateful night, and in time they learned to be happy again. Since Aticus' birth he had aged rapidly, the result of the lupine metabolism. Puberty had come swiftly, Aticus tying Ayaa in growth.

Before the tragedy of their brother and mother's death they were inseparable so when the siblings had to collaborate for food the occasional kill of a small boar or two, brought them even closer. Every waking day the bond grew stronger, not a moment went by the pair weren't together. Ayaa even kept him warm at night, sleeping by him so peacefully.

A strange sensation seized him every time he looked into the full Moon, wishing that he could stare at it forever, until thirst overwhelmed him. Lapping up clear, refreshing water cupped in his hands Aticus glanced at Ayaa who watched him with piqued curiosity. She saw in the water's reflection his human hands. Now he stared at her with curiosity as she too dipped her paws into the cold water. Ayaa's physiology finally developing neural pathways of thought; wondering why her paws were so different from Aticus she crooked her head in concentration until she yelped aloud in surprise. One of her paws began to change!

Aticus' eyes widened in amazement at the sight of his sister's changing, as her pads softened and thinned and as the digits of her paws lengthened. Whimpering, not so much in pain but in fear and surprise, Ayaa curled her body into a tight ball until her mutating paw turned fully into that of a human hand. Amazed at the site of the miracle Aticus sat in awe his arm stretching towards her until their hands touched. Ayaa sat up on her haunches as her other paw began the metamorphosis as well. Aticus could still remember his sister's sweet voice.

Her vocal chords began to transform, in an invented twin language Ayaa excitedly yelled, "Ahh...yo."

Ayaa's lupine visage with the long, proud muzzle began to pulse, transforming, shrinking into a gorilla-like nose, transforming still more, until finally becoming a beautiful and innocent human's face. Her big doe eyes were moist with tears of happiness and wonder. Ayaa smiled a human smile and slipped her new hands into Aticus', entwining their fingers. Aticus and his now human sister would stay that way until the next full moon. Eventually, the sibling's roles changed as Aticus made the transition into a Wolf's form.

Aticus grinned when he thought of her and their new found abilities. For three whole days he had run, chased and played as a true wolf but without any family to guide either of them through the trials of lycanthropy spontaneous transformation had been difficult to say the least. Every full moon they would sneak in to an unsuspecting village as wolves and wreak havoc on the villagers. Come daybreak they liked to walk around in human form with stolen clothes to see what damage had been done. Jealousy and pride came over him, even now, when he thought about his sister. She had the privilege to grow up a majestic canine.

A tear ran down his eye remembering pleasant times with his sister. For three days each month they would play together in lupine form due to the moon's phases. Aticus would slip into a lupine shape much earlier than Ayaa. So she would kneel down on one knee next to Aticus' lupine form. She would rub his muzzle in a slow counter clockwise fashion then would rub his soft fur and scratch his lupine ears until the transformation came upon her as well. They would run off together across the land brother and sister. Their mother left them alone in the world, but they had each other.

Everything changed when one hot and windy day they unexpectedly caught a faint and familiar scent. Both Aticus and his sister's heart skipped a beat. They ran on two legs, his sister still unfamiliar with running on two legs anxiously tripping on loose twigs and rocks. The pair negotiated the familiar hills and valleys that they had grown accustomed to until they saw the three crosses up on a nearby hill. Excited running became an uneasy jog as the overpowering rotting stench permeated the air around them. Aticus slid to a stop so abruptly he lost his balance and tumbled onto the ground, only yards away. Ayaa stared up at the crosses with tears in her eyes and a stricken look on her face. Aticus had already prepared himself in his mind for his father's demise but not for the scene that stood before him now. He squeezed his eyes shut tight and could not bring himself to open them until a gasp from his sister startled them open again.

On the far left and far right cross Aticus saw two unknown and decapitated corpses positioned like they had been crucified. The middle cross was set higher and upon it was a headless man's corpse. His arms were severed and someone had cut out his heart and shoved a spike threw his spine and into the wood. The hairs on the back of Aticus neck stood on end. He saw the familiar spikes that were imbedded into the corpse's stumps. Even with the rotting flesh masking the scent he breathed in the unmistakable smell of their father. He had obviously been kept alive for whatever reason until inevitably being brutally slaughtered.

Aticus shooed away a dozen or so flies circling his head and glanced at Ayaa. She had smelled their father first, and now lying on the ground, Ayaa was blubbering hysterically. A cold chill ran down Aticus' spine. Deja-vu consumed his paranoid mind. He found himself on yet another hill. The songs his late mother sang of their disastrous encounter and how she was parted from her mate consuming his mind. Trapped at the top of the hill she had lost sight of her mate. At the top of the hill Aticus had lost his brother and his mother. Now he found himself on the top of the hill with his sister. Suspicion came over him but he couldn't look away from his father's body. His stomach was still bloated and swollen from the gases so that the skin had cracked open in places, weeping fluids onto the ground around him in a circle like a perverted ring of protection gone horribly awry.

This sounds of trampling feet vibrated through the ground. From the sounds, just three men, another of their calling cards of late, the men of "God's Light" were soon to be upon them. Aticus realized this display had been a trap meant to flush out hidden lycanthropes that came to mourn or witness their kin's unspeakable tortures.

"Ayaa!" He warned in their invented language, he had yet to see the hunters, but he knew they were close at hand.

Aticus ran without caution to meet his beloved sister, and as he neared her he tripped a hidden wire. Suddenly the ground gave way beneath him. The only thought running through his head was that he was falling indefinitely, but was glad that Ayaa managed to miss the traps. He found himself without sight as he plummeted toward the ground with a loss of equilibrium that made his head spin. To this day when he thought long and hard about it, he could still remember the dank cold all over his body and the moldy grit on his tongue.

Aticus' forearm put up no resistance to the spike placed firmly in the ground. Eight foot spikes scraped between his chest and up his back as he fell. Alternating spikes meant to maximize damage to any unlucky person to fall in the trap. They would be deadly to any animal on four legs but with Aticus able to walk upright, the damage was greatly minimized. The sudden stop made Aticus' knees buckle then pop, a searing pain radiating all through his legs and up his spine as his feet found Earth and the darkness consumed him. His ears were still keen however; muffled sounds of violence violating his soul.

"One down, one to go!" Someone said with unbridled enthusiasm.

"Get the girl!" Someone with a gruff and mature voice ordered spurring on hurried footfalls of two anxious-to-please men.

Immediately Aticus knew the raspy voice, it was the one who hunted his family and was responsible for leaving them orphans. He found himself frantically assessing the situation. His arm stretched up and out like a twisted salute, joints and bones at their breaking points, but he had to get out of this hole he now found himself in.

He couldn't help but hear from above the shrill scream of Ayaa as she stumbled to the ground, or at least that is what he saw in his mind's eye. His stomach churned, anxiety twisting it in knots until vomiting up his meager dinner of well chewed chunks of rabbit and grass.

"No!" He heard Ayaa's desperate pleas in her broken and alien speech, "No, please don't!"

He heard fabric ripping, the violent and nauseating smack, smack, smack of pounding flesh made Aticus' soul ache imagining all the horrid possibilities that were much worse than death. Something deep in his core snapped that day. He yanked his forearm with all his might against the silver pole but with no success. Then a series of frantic jerks made his arm pulsate with a pain he had not felt since the onset of his first transformation but still the stake did not move. He heard growling resonating through the trap, astonishing him as he realized it was coming from his own throat. Bloody droplets one, two, three then a steady flow ran down from the pole as the wound on his hand deepened.

His wounded body abruptly and involuntarily transformed into a hulking beast, humanoid in appearance, lupine muscles intertwining amid human muscles combining to make the perfect killing machine. He had changed, he would have marveled at this situation, he had never before transformed in between moon cycles but fueled on instinct alone he thought he had to get out of the pit to save his sister. He didn't waste any time but began gnawing on the flesh of his trapped forearm with his extended muzzle. His hand had not transformed as a result of the deadly silver, and it serves him well. Imagining the hand violating his sister he viciously gnawed on his forearm until finally freeing flesh and muscle from bone.

"Brother," Ayaa exclaimed struggling to be free, "help me!"

The commotion and loud commands that could be heard up above him made Aticus crazed. Still stuck in the hole, still impaled, he could not help his sister as he heard steel rendering tender flesh, then shrieks of pain followed by a quick swish and then deafening silence.

The skin on Aticus' forearm had separated from the elbow revealing bare bone and the wound from his forearm had stretched open allowing him to slide his arm up and down. Fangs tore through his exposed bone until sweet marrow emerged. A snap then twist from his powerful neck and Aticus was free! His Loose forearm swung wildly about. Calves wound like springs and nerves like a hairline trigger, he burst out of the hole as remnants of his clothing, now only bloody rags, waved about him like a red flag of vengeance.

Aticus dug his feet firmly into the green grass, preparing for anything except for the scene laid out before him. It made him physically sick. The soldiers were gone; with Ayaa dead and Aticus falling into a trap leaving them to believe he was dead or dying their macabre job had been done. Ayaa's decapitated and lifeless body lay on the ground. Black and blue bruises manifested all over her inner thighs. Blood clotted in the gaping wound in her chest. He could tell right away, her heart had been taken.

Aticus scooped up Ayaa's limp body, holding her closely while sorrowful howls echoed over the hillside. He tried to breathe in her scent for the last time, a mixture of sunflowers and feral musk. He remembered so many times in the bitter cold she had snuggled up to him with her soft, soft fur. Agony seized him over the thought that she was no longer warm. She had died wearing human skin while Aticus now exuded warmth in his lupine fur.

The sounds of howling coming from the hills prompted the three men to split up with two doubling back in Aticus direction. Heartbreaking thoughts had Aticus distracted until he sniffed the nauseating scent of his sister's torturer.

The pair involuntarily gasped and stopped in their tracks at the sight of the beast. All of their information and training had been incorrect, the sun high in the sky, moon nowhere to be seen still they saw a monster in their path. Without any hesitation the one with the nauseating smell tried to draw his sword before Aticus leapt upon him. Delicately balancing Ayaa on his shoulder Aticus grabbed the rapist's head with his clawed hand and smashed his head into a rock, crashing his head against the rock again and again until the skull burst open in a spatter of gore. Blood and brain matter splashed onto the remaining soldier's face. A quick swipe with Aticus' other claw threw the other soldier up into the air and he fell down onto the ground with a solid "smack". The soldier had survived however. Aticus with all his fury forgot his missing hand and forearm being chewed off to escape the hole. He impulsively grasped for his missing forearm and finding a whole arm, complete with hand he let out a sigh of relief… He had forgotten in time even this lost limb would grow back, one of the wonders of lycanthropy.

His memories flashed forward through the decades to his grandmother who had heard his sorrowful howls and had blessedly come to the rescue. She told him about the last of her surviving ancestors, a cousin to him though long lost. He had been genuinely happy to have found a true relative, to learn all that he could about his species, and for the first time in years he had companionship since his sister's death. His grandmother taught him the enigmas of transformation. Longevity was a consequence. So-seti taught him some secrets of the Wolf and laws of man before she too was murdered at the hand of "God's Light". The symbol emblazoned upon their bronze chest plates were forever burned into his memory. There had been so many questions left unanswered. He mourned at the thought of his sister. If grandmother had guided her to transition from wolf to woman or back again would his sister survived? Memories cut through him like sharp daggers thrust into his thoughts.

By the time Devon saved him from certain death, with yet another encounter of angry villagers and "Gods Light" Hunters, the seeds of hatred had been firmly planted and nurtured. His grandmother told him the ways of the lycanthropes and their origins, Devon told him how to tell time and the basics of human behaviors. Before then, telling time seemed so foreign to him, so useless. Now the ability to tell time infuriated and depressed him.

The physical wounds healed quickly but the mental wounds cut deeply and those worms of thoughts burrowed into his brain, festering and spreading. After Devon left for the virgin new world, somewhere in modern-day Canada, leaving him alone again, something in him had just broken. The year of our lord, 1759 ad., Aticus had to come down from the mountains hell bent for vengeance and blood, so much bloodshed.

An abundance of time existed for him and it took him centuries to find an only relative of his. Fueled with a lust for revenge the pairing of him and his insane cousin had been destined by the stars. They made their way through Europe leaving a bloody mess in their wake, killing indiscriminately across the land for decades. His cousin had made a name for himself in the rural villages of France being called the beast of Ge'vaudan. His cousin, Sacco, out for blood and food courtesy of the unwitting town folk, but not Aticus, he knew the continuing bloodshed and tales of werewolves in their midst would flush out everyone participating in "God's Light". The eventual death of his treasured but entirely insane cousin did not detour his own blood lust, killing every offspring from the "God's Light" ministry he could find.

In 1810 A.D., Aticus moved to the Americas tracking that faint but distinct smell, determined to eradicate them all. However, everything changed when he met Alicia.

Alicia.

Alicia, he could still hear her calling his name.

Aticus heard a rustling coming from the bushes, startling him from his daydreams. In the fog of thought things were not as they appeared to be, disorienting him, he rubbed the sleep from his eyes.

"Alicia?" Aticus squinted to see a woman; the sun's rays illuminating her silhouette and making her appear an Angel come to Earth.

"No…" The stranger answered in a familiar voice, her Navajo dialect distinctive.

His senses awakened fully and he could see the beautifully caramelized smooth skin and raven black hair that hung down the length to the small of her back. He breathed in the fragrance of cinnamon and sandalwood. The wind gradually moved her silken hair and light caught her luxurious black hair making it shine in the sun. With her hair swept back her forehead and cheeks now showed the disfiguring burns from the explosion that almost cost her life many years ago. Her yellow eyes burned with the intensity of a noble Navajo princess, eyes full of loyalty, but also distrust.

"Hello Tonya." His surprise evident in the expression on his face, "I'm surprised to see you here!"

"Ah Aticus," Tonya nimbly touched his chest, "you called, and I must obey."

12

God's Light Monastery, California

The Diablo mountain range in the California Coast, along the pacific coast located in the San Francisco Bay area held the clandestine God's Light compound. There were four God's Light compounds held secret to the public at large; the Diablo God's Light compound in California the second biggest in the ministry. High up in the mountains sat the sanctuary a dug-in, gigantic circle in the ground. The rolling hills concealed a village and cathedral with vast boulders and majestic redwood trees. Once in a while the clouds in the sky expose bright rays of sunlight producing a blinding shimmering reflection in the huge eye, which is the Gods Light symbol, high above the cathedral.

God's Light, still alive and well throughout the centuries, converted to Christianity two thousand years ago but they had their origins in Samarian lore. The star meant for the praise of the God, Anatu, and head of the Sumerian pantheon. The star looked so much like an omniscient eye that it made it easy to assimilate with almost any religion. Founded to exterminate the supernatural creatures which were considered a threat to all mankind, but as technology progressed they shifted to the study and research aspect as well.

The sanctuary looked like a handmade menagerie. A makeshift habitat of sorts, a twenty foot wall encircled the outskirts of the dug-in town with wooden cottages encircling the compound. Like the Quakers or the Amish time did not exist with the inhabitants isolated from civilization. The inhabitants of the compound go about their day normally without modern day conveniences. There were no televisions, telephones, radios, cars, or even microwaves in the dwellings. Like a spoke wheel seven circular cobbled streets intersected four more streets which lead to the center of town and a beautiful Gothic cathedral which was shipped to America from Europe brick by brick. All streets widened to meet at the base of the Cathedral.

A small infirmary in case of emergency, a three-part library/apothecary/general store and even a bar graced the outskirts of this quaint city. The laws and rules of the country did not apply inside the tall walls. Simple villagers worked in the shadows of the striking Cathedral, a place for worship and prayer, and each and every one of them employed by God's Light. The Cathedral has concealed, elaborate and high-tech security measures which must be circumvented before the employees are allowed entrance underground. Diablo Mountain provided the perfect place to dig underground in confidence and secrecy. Sprawling and intricate corridors led to the secret activities which were held down below.

Families employed by the God's Light every Wednesday and Sunday came to pray within the Cathedral. Long, oak, cushioned pews graced the sprawling room. Fourteen pews split in two rows to accommodate a red carpeted aisle leading up to the altar. The Altar of Christ stood back and center on the wall and held a concealed corridor leading to an elevator. The trap door was the only way to get in or out of the massive complex. It would be sacrilege if innocent parishioners found out that instead of their own Christian God's eye the massive and elegant eye bolted into the back of the altar had originally been the eye of Anatu, watching the masses.

The only way in or out of the town without a hazardous trek down the mountain, a monthly helicopter that dropped off food and supplies, medical and mundane. The God's Light had been well supplied a week ago yet the sound of helicopter blades whirled early for an extraordinary occupant. Below the helicopter a small trailer, like a ridiculously oversized dog carrier complete with air holes along the sides, hovered, suspended in the air. Fortified chains kept the trailer level just above the ground.

"Chopper came early." Matt, a scientist for four years with the God's Light, commented to James, an advisor and also an employee.

"I'm so excited." James locked his knee on his weak left leg, braced his good right leg and wrapped his right arm around Matt's shoulder for added stability, "Thank you, um, um, uh, uh, Matt. I heard this lycanthrope was um, uh, was captured before the time of Christ. She has survived as long as um, um, um Lucem Dei has uh, existed."

James' heart raced a mile a minute just thinking about glimpsing the legend in the flesh. He had a genetic malformation which had burst in his head many years ago, which left him paralyzed on his left side. A good long time had passed before James could function almost normally. But he still struggled to find and say the words in his injured brain.

"No problem man." Matt hit James playfully on his back hard enough to knock his weak foot and knee off balance, prompting James to clutch his cane tightly for stability.

They both were garbed in white lab coats flowing down to their ankles. Shiny ID badges complete with their photos were clipped to the pockets on their chests. James was level 3 and Matt level 4, the numbers corresponding to the levels in the complex. Friends, they were inseparable since they met four years ago. Similar religious beliefs set them apart from the rest of the God's Light employees. The two stood out from the overbearing, radical, zealot Christians that made up most of the employees here.

The Cathedral's Iron gates fit for a titan begrudgingly groaned open. Byron Atkins, the leader of the North American God's Light chapter, hobbled out. He carefully blotted the sweat off his brow with a handkerchief and began barking orders on his walkie-talkie. The deafening reverberation of the helicopter drew closer as if in response. Shadows were cast over his bald head and artificial grass began to blow. Byron shouted one more order then, signaling with his hand, the trailer started to be lowered.

"Watch out, James." Matt warned, motioning with his hand.

James awkwardly stepped aside as the ground started to rumble. Pebbles sprang to life jumping around and shaking as the cobblestone street leading towards the church vibrated then gave way. Artificial lights shone from the increasing gap, spreading out until revealing an underground room with shadowy figures waiting for their orders below. Matt and Byron signaled the helicopter to adjust left or right as the trailer continued to carefully descend. James strained his neck to see just a glimpse of the sedated and immobilized anomaly.

In a flurry of commotion, employees wearing a mishmash of colorful religious robes came out of the Cathedral to give assistance to Byron and the hovering trailer. With the sun at its apex James could just make out the eyes of an animal before shadows claimed her again.

Matt knew exactly what James was wondering and yelled to be heard over the noise, "From what we deduced her name is So-Sata or So-seti or something like that."

Aticus had been wrong for thousands and thousands of years. He thought his grandmother was dead. Instead, a much crueler fate had come upon So-seti, captured by God's Light for interrogation and torture until her mind was on the brink of madness and collapse.

All eyes were on the helicopter and the trailer-like container as it descended through the slim hollow in the earth. The whoosh of hydraulics began as a ten-ton jack lifted a platform into the air until it met the rust covered trailer. An annoying noise, not unlike fingernails running up the length of a chalkboard, made the assistants cringe.

"I heard she spoke some sort of wild, lupine language full of yaps, snarls and growls and a broken Samaria dialect of sorts. I don't know the specifics or even why she survived as long as she did or what they are keeping her for, but I'm really excited for this opportunity." Matt continued, unconsciously ducking down from the helicopter's whirling blades.

Fumbling around the assistants and careful not to trip on the trailer's narrow gap, James looked closer at the dozen or so dinner plate sized holes in the wall of the container. Although heavily, almost lethally sedated, So-seti's eyes were open and taking in all of her surroundings like a waiting viper. Her wrinkled nose crinkled up, drawing in the entire area's aromas until she zeroed in on James watching her through one of the large holes. Their eyes locked for what felt like an eternity. So-seti's red glowing eyes did not dim with time but sharpened like a laser beam on James' eyes. He felt like all of his life, all of his study of myths, all of his dedication to Lucem Dei, despite obvious mental and physical disabilities, religiously throughout the years had finally come to a head. With a lesser security clearance he had never seen a real-life lycanthrope here in flesh and blood, only in his head as he was stuck in libraries researching the myth.

Just her brilliant eyes, shadowy wrinkled visage and fangs could be seen, prompting James to try to get a closer look at her before the trailer lowered all the way, but in a fierce betrayal his knee suddenly gave out. James grabbed at his cane to steady himself. The cane betrayed him as well and slipped across the loose gravel.

"Watch it buddy!" James suddenly felt Matt's strong, steady hand on his shoulder pulling him back.

"Thank you. I, uh, guess, um, uh, excitement came over me, I guess, uh..." James said as his stomach sank in embarrassment.

His eyes reflexively looked over at Matt while he apologized. Momentarily distracted, James could only see the top of the storage unit now as it descended safely beneath the Earth. Matt gently nudged James' shoulder persuading him to step back. Byron and two others began to detach the helicopter's chains from the trailer.

"I believe they're keeping her alone in level 5." Matt offered confidently, shifting his full six foot six frame while the chains swung loose. The helicopter hovered up slowly then out of sight. "We busted our ass to get the room just like her old one so she doesn't freak out."

Red-faced and sweating Byron caught his breath before again barking instructions in his walkie-talkie for the unseen staff down below. Oblivious of Matt and James, Byron bullied between their shoulders like a football player before climbing the steps of the Cathedral and disappearing into the broad entryway.

"You know, James, this may squash the debate we were having about the origins!" Matt grinned, exposing deep dimples and unusually pearl white and perfect teeth. "Maybe once and for all we can settle our bet."

"Which one um, um of them?" James smirked, "We have so many uh, um, bets." James put his arm around Matt while the separated faux cobble street finally united.

Matt was reminded of the many nights in the park when work was done. Matt would meet James to play chess to blow off some steam. They would vent many problems and come up with solutions to others while they laughed and talked the night away. Many nights James would beat him, game after game, leaving him awestruck as pity came over him thinking of James' lot in life.

Matt had remarkably striking bone structure and bright blue eyes that hadn't changed through eight years of mind numbing study for his doctorate. All throughout his career his colleagues second-guessed and laughed at him because of his youthful, adolescent appearance. With his curly hair, long ears that stuck out, lanky length, and weighing one-hundred and ten pounds soaking wet, most of the others labeled him a freak. Although brilliantly gifted in the mind, Matt had many avenues closed to him, day after day, until he happened upon God's Light.

"Dr. Matthew LaFallette, please come to the office." The walkie-talkie squawked, "Dr. LaFallette, come to the office."

Matt shrugged begrudgingly and rolled his eyes. Matt hated the underground area more after he had been on the mountainside and taken in the scenery, but he had to earn his paycheck. In unison Matt and James silently strolled over to the sidewalk, stopping only at the Cathedral steps. Helping James up the steps, Matt pulled the doors open and walked inside the church.

They saw a guard who sat comfortably, legs crossed while quietly reading beside the entrance, there to guard the elevator. The red iron doors closed behind them with the immediate echoes of their footfalls reverberating in the massive dome of the Cathedral.

After the two men walked in the guard flipped a switch, momentarily blinding them. Strobe lights alternating slow at first then faster and faster startled James. He squinted, struggled to walk, staggering and eventually tripping on his numb left foot. He felt that Halo effect that he had gotten used to since his stroke now coming over him.

"Hey buddy, are you all right?" Matt directed the question at James but he was looking at the security guard accusingly.

Ire in his voice, Matt scolded the innocent security guard, "Turn off the damn strobe lights! James had a stroke and this is going to give him a seizure!"

The strobe lights, which managed to involuntarily transform any lycanthrope in disguise, threatened to give James a full on grand mal seizure. Matt switched off the strobe lights before the guard had a chance to respond, leaving the parishioner dumbstruck. The robed guard took one look at James' limp left arm and a well-used wooden cane. The guard flinched slightly looking at the black paint flaked off the cane where his hands had gripped it for stability over many years.

"Hey, I'm sorry. I'm just doing my job." He said in a monotone voice, quickly sitting down in his seat again, "are you okay?"

"Um, uh, yes I, um, um, guess so." James stuttered, gathering his wits together and taking a long deep breath before he was sure the threat of a seizure had passed.

"New guy didn't know you're disabled." Matt said, once more giving a glaring eye to the guard who wasn't paying attention to the two men, burying himself in his book once more.

Smacking James on his back teasingly he made off to the altar. Tones on a hidden security touchpad sounded almost melodiously as Matt punched in the various numbers that elevated the altar and opened the hidden doors. No floor controls to speak of, just two laser palm controls which were designed to fish out any lycanthrope that successfully snuck past the strobe lights and the sensitive sentinel.

Matt pressed his palms on the glass. A flash of light, a brief pause while the laser ensuring Matt's fingertips were properly spaced out and not all the same length then the elevator doors closed. The elevator made its way down into the depths of the gods light compound. The jerks and vibrations made James involuntarily grip the rail with his good hand any drastic movement made his head spin. The elevator stopped and James opened his eyes. The doors slid open with well-oiled efficiency.

"Back to the salt mines." Matt said sarcastically, hesitating for just a moment before stepping off the elevator.

"Yeah," James laughed, shaking his head, before he stepped off the elevator too.

The elevator doors opened into a sophisticated fully equipped scientific research facility. Security cameras were half-concealed in the ceiling in four corners to diligently watch for any suspicious activity. Lofty, clean, steel walls stretched and exaggerated each and every movement like a fun-house mirror. They were standing in a breathtaking and expansive underground foyer. For all their years working here, Matt and James could not get used to the God's Light lobby and the unnerving silence or the sterile, metallic smell all around them. Even the receptionist, who registered the comings and goings through the one door to the hallway behind her, went about her day silently and blissfully oblivious to those around her, black ear buds piping music into her ears to keep her awake.

Once they registered with the receptionist the friends Split ways Matt went off to answer the boss' call, and James made a B-line straight to where he knew he'd find the mysterious container in the middle of the foyer still on the hydraulic platform in the middle of the room. With Matt and several parishioners in a meeting, presumably a meeting for the new acquisition, and the receptionist off in her own little world, James was left alone to admire their new guest.

James couldn't take his eyes off the container. He stared at it looking back at his own reflection, indefinitely lost in thought. He could see a large pink and white scar clearly visible in the break of his thick, unkempt brown hair that reminded him every day he had survived an aneurysm that could have ended his life. James' features that of an intelligent man, with a high forehead, the lines deepening in thought and frustration. James still had a noticeable droopiness of his left eye and lip. However, the laziness of the left side of his face inhibited any wrinkles there may have been. The right side was a whole different story; wrinkles crisscrossed his eyes and lips like an interstate. His pulse raced in excitement but he did not know why.

James couldn't help himself edging forward and staring at the porthole with his good hand touching the warm steel. Straining his eyes he gradually made out a thin silhouette, the silhouette of a woman. He had to get closer. James could see no movement. He thought about his younger days when he went to a carnival and he won the most colorful goldfish he had ever seen. He took the fish home, poured it into a bowl, and swore that if the fish survive the night he would get all the supplies the fish needed. The goldfish survived. Expensive tank, expensive medicines, expensive accessories were bought and brought home. Only to find the goldfish had died, its colorful belly floating at the top of the glass bowl. James could not stand it anymore. His stomach roiled. He found himself irrational and shaking as he reached for the locked handle as he thought about the precious werewolf and the dead goldfish.

"James! Step away from the cage!" Someone shouted, prompting James to step back awkwardly and look around.

Matt, Byron, and another scientist named Carson stepped out of a nearby hall. James wasn't sure who had yelled the order, but he complied. Byron skipped down the steps with a set of keys secured by a chain on his belt and walked towards the container, his eyes gleaming like he had just spotted a huge present on Christmas morning.

James stepped back as Byron turned the key, a harsh grinding sound echoed throughout the hallway as the bolt slid open. James saw the light from the lobby illuminate a horrid head covered by sickly white hairs and a white sheet covering a skeletal body. Her arms were still strapped down to the cot. No movement could be seen. No movement even when Matt and Carson jostled the stretcher trying to get it out from the container and onto the marble floors.

He imagined his dead goldfish as the corpse-like creature rolled past him. Butterflies churned in his stomach. Whether the corpse reminded him of the brilliant colored dead goldfish of his youth or it justified and vindicated the obsession of his adolescent life he couldn't decide. Her death now would be just like the goldfish and it was truly a tragedy for all his life's work had only recently come in the flesh. Irrational compulsion took over him. He found himself pushing past Byron and right to the stretcher. Impulsively James checked her pulse for signs of life.

"James!" Byron exclaimed, moving quicker than his plump body alluded, roughly jerking James's hand away, "get your hands off of her."

Fresh and unfamiliar aromas, the sudden jarring of the stretcher, the uncomfortable tight restraints, and incredible hunger were just too much for So-seti to bear. She came out of her self-induced and beneficial coma, staring up at James, "Jaamesssssssssss!"

"Jamesssss!" So-seti spat.

Groggy, So-seti could only make out three shadowy figures moving around her, the chain at its limits her skeletal hand gripped Byron's wrist, James' heart skipped a beat, and he stood motionless, she is still alive! The other pseudoscientist turned parishioner inevitably rushed into action.

"Jamesss!" So-seti hissed quietly, her grip tightening as the scientist with his white coat madly looked for a sedative in a drawer inside the container.

"Get her off of me!" Wide-eyed and trembling, Byron looked around for assistance but found James unresponsive and staring at the monstrous wonder.

So-seti could see more clearly now, the sounds around her more distinctive and she zeroed in on James' unique scent. Even in her stupor, strapped to the stretcher, flown in darkness and transported by helicopter an intriguing redolence hung in the air all around her, reminding her of something taken from her a long, long time ago and it encouraged her to strengthen her grip around Byron's forearm.

A swoosh and Byron stumbled back, his arm freed. Carson had found a silver blade amongst the surgical equipment and had severed So-seti's claw. So-seti's decapitated arm flailing about, Byron flinched before remembering her neck securely strapped to the bed too.

A well-rehearsed emergency plan taking place, Carson pulled from his pocket a ten-gauge needle, the preloaded syringe emerging. Concentrated paralytic toxin made from puffer fish, Saxitoxin, in small doses designed for facelifts, this outrageous dose designed for paralyzing a legend.

The plunger descended until So-seti had been given the full dose. So-seti's vision blurred as the toxin flooded through her system. She looks at her decapitated wrist as gravity succeeds in lowering her arm back onto the soft cot. Conversations, some hostile, seem to merge together, infuriating her as she tests her restraints but realizes her body had betrayed her.

"Carson, um, um, um if she wasn't dead before um, um the medicine," Yelling, James could not believe his eyes as he tried to reach for a frail So-seti, but Matt quietly obstructed James' path urging him to be still. He could see the exposed shoulders and So-seti's neck veins expanding, "That much uh, um, uh, Saxitoxin, with her um, um, um obvious health issues, uh, surely her heart will explode!"

"It will just paralyze her, calm down!" Carson argued, annoyed at James and the conversation he rolled his eyes. "It is the preloaded amount prescribed by the Vatican God's Light."

Carson removed the syringe and stepped back, happy with his quick actions and with So-seti, lying as fixed as a statue. Byron, still wide eyed, rubbing his wrist, was annoyed that he let himself be exposed to mortal danger. He prided himself in safety and calculated decisions. Matt gauged his boss' behavior to judge his mood. The mishap did not intimidate him in the least. In fact, Matt watched as his boss crouched down and smiled as he picked up the severed claw-like hand.

"Kathy," Carson calmly and quietly ordered, the receptionist Kathy perked up, closing her gaping mouth and taking the ear buds out of her ears, "go get a specimen bag for this and see if our guest's room is ready yet."

"Yes sir," Without any hesitation Kathy dialed frantically the numbers that connected her downstairs.

She had said his name hadn't she? And in English to boot! James' head whirled, ignoring his associates to stare at her in mute wonder. So-seti's eyes, swollen and glassy, were open; shrewdly taking in everything around her but her head remained still. His heart hurt when he saw the thin, almost transparent sheet that covered So-seti. He noted the circular stain of blood where her hand used to be. He noted her fragile physique with legs that abruptly ended at the knees. If So-seti had been captured a long time ago what horrible tortures she had probably had to endure, James thought. Uncontrolled tears welled up in his eyes and spilled down his flushed cheeks as he stared at her knees.

He looked back to her bony face, startling him when he realized So-seti's eyes were now staring back at him. Her furrowed nose wrinkled, her nostrils flaring as she tried to take in all of James' unusual but enticing scent.

Carson looked towards the C-shaped desk in the middle of the room as an unseen conversation unfolded between Kathy and her well used headpiece. Her bangs took flight with a huff of accomplishment and a swipe of her neatly manicured nails to her forehead and her hand fell back onto the arm of her chair.

"Byron..." A sudden pause and a catch her throat, "The room is ready." Kathy said with professionalism trying to steady her voice, her wide eyes betraying her frayed nerves.

James turned back to So-seti, her striking eyes staring at him suddenly too much for him to take in all at once. He tried to instead focus on the dazzling white marble tiles beneath him, so clean and orderly, he thought. A surreal moment occurring as So-seti's eyes burned into his brain. From this moment forward his life would never be the same.

So-seti whispered, windpipe straining for just one word, "Jaaamesss."

13

Kathy stood up and walked around her desk to hold the frosted glass door open. A scientist named Carson carefully maneuvered the top, and Byron the bottom, of the stretcher bound for the lower levels. Matt futilely lost in conversation while his inattentive friend, James, strained his neck trying to get one last look at So-seti before the doors closed.

So-seti stared up at the florescent lights moving above her, trying to turn her neck but failing, forced to watch the flickering bulbs pass over head one by one. James' strong aroma fading as the stretcher with its faulty wheel headed towards her new home.

Ultimately she stopped fighting to move and succumbed to the paralysis. So-seti closed her eyelids below her furrowed brow and dreamed. A habit she had grown accustomed to, to keep her sane, throughout the centuries. The smell had reminded her of a lonesome and sorrowful howl where late at night in a lonely forest she had found her grandson, Aticus.

She remembered the stormy night, the howls like an emergency beacon getting louder and louder as she drew closer to the source of the sound. She remembered sloshing around, all four paws sticking in the mud until she locked onto him in the dark, unforgiving terrain, crawling on her belly, circumnavigating overgrown grass and weeds until the howling stopped abruptly. She remembered fondly finding her grandson for the very first time hiding between the groves. He had the emerald eyes of her sons, with strikingly familiar features that cemented his origin.

Pity washed over her majestic lupine form. With the exception of his eyes, he was covered with mud and grime from head to toe, the rain soaking his greasy, long black hair and pasting it across his forehead and hanging off his long human nose. His clothing just as grimy, nothing more than a toga of sorts, rags meant to cover him whether as a human or Wolf. So-seti cautiously crept forward, her tail wagging in excitement, but was met with bared human teeth, a feeble warning for trespassers.

"*Do not worry my child.*" So-seti had whispered in his mind in a language far older than Aticus. "*I heard your calls and I am here now.*"

So-seti transformed seamlessly into a mature, stunning woman. She had a taut and flawless physique with full-bodied raven-black hair, which fell delicately to her shoulders. Unmistakable aromas that he had been searching for encouraged Aticus to impulsively jump up and cling to her with all his might, another surviving relative! She would teach him her wisdom and knowledge, long lacking since birth, and help him learn the ways to walk in the worlds of man and wolf.

So-seti's body jostled about as the stretcher lurched suddenly, turning toward the doorway, off balance and threatening to overturn. Byron stopped abruptly so he could slide his card into the card reader. A green light, a beep, and the doors to her new prison opened.

"Welcome to your new home!" Carson slyly smiled, looking directly at So-seti.

So-seti looked around in shock at the clean, modern steel walls. Stainless steel drawers graced the room wall to wall, clean smooth walls with no distinguishing features for distraction, absolutely no clocks anywhere to be seen either. Walking distance about five yards in either direction; Carson hurriedly pushed the I.V. stand somewhere in the corner of the room while Byron pushed the stretcher the rest of the way into the room. Carson ripped open an I.V. kit and began the procedure on So-seti.

"Saline bag," Carson and Byron both mumbled under their breath.

"Silver nitrate," both men said in monotone, robotically going through their motions like they had practiced hundreds of times before.

"... Yeah, before she freaks out in her new change of environment!" Carson nervously mused.

"Like a fish in a clean tank," the director Atkins added.

So-seti did not object to the silver needle with the sterile tubing looping into the I.V. stand violating her armpit. She closed her battered eyes again as Byron hooked up the Saline and Silver solution.

Byron plugged in a multi-parameter monitor then walked it over to the stretcher. He turned his attention to the Anesthesia Gas Monitor, the EKG Machine and last of all, ECG Monitor. The thought of So-seti's body so near made Carson cringe in disgust but he had work to do. Carson taped two leads onto her drooping and wrinkled breasts then two more onto her emaciated and sunken abdomen. They slipped a blood pressure cuff onto the arm. Carson finished the job clipping onto her pinky a pulse/oxygen meter.

"No change." Byron said, looking over her vital signs.

Byron Atkins quickly turned to the monitor, pressing the button that released the silver nitrate into So-seti's veins. She did not even open her eyes in surprise now, conditioned so long. She just tightened her eyelids until the worst of the pain subsided.

Carson had a sick fascination with this, captivated almost instantly by the bulging at the source of the injection site. Her body involuntarily arching as it spread like a crack on a windshield the veins engorging and flowing out from her body until the entire surface of her skin turned pale silver. Carson smiled, almost sadistically, drool forming at the crevices of his lips. Smiling until the silver nitrate bag had all but dried up.

Byron checked her vitals again and said, "One more time."

Her second dose of intravenous silver nitrate well on its way, Byron and Carson quietly finished up securing their prisoner, "I was excited at first, but the very image of her chills me to the bone now." Byron said under his breath, unconsciously wiping his hands on his jacket.

"Don't worry about it, Byron." Carson smacked Byron on the back, "she is a paraplegic, thanks to the silver stakes implanted directly into her bones. She is fucking disabled... just like James." Carson said jubilantly, making his hand go limp and shuffling around comically like a zombie.

Carson's immaturities made Byron turn up his eyebrow and frown, protesting the pathetic display. Byron's judging glare made Carson immediately stop. The work now complete and double checked, Byron motioned to Carson and they headed towards the door.

"Get comfortable," Carson said under his breath as the doors shut, securely locking So-seti inside.

14

Alone in the room, her second dose now dispensed, she had plenty of time to look at her surroundings. Dull, stainless steel counters surrounded her but nothing else was in the room to clutter or contaminate the area. Her last prison cell, of sorts, had been a room constructed completely of wood. A result of which many patterns emerged that filled her imagination to the brim, the passage of time not as unbearable. But her new cell walls were made of steel. No stains or imperfections to stimulate her imagination this time.

She heard the soft and steady beat of her heart on the monitor and nothing else but her breathing. Since the paralysis wore off an hour ago, she had tirelessly tested her bonds. Every appendage had been securely tethered except for her severed hand, which flailed about freely. Her severed hand and the familiar trace aroma surrounding her reminded So-seti of Aticus.

The fanatical howling that Aticus learned and deciphered from his mother's howls, on full-moon nights had been like a beacon when she searched for him and when she found him she vowed to never let her grandson go. So-seti felt sorrow when she thought of Aticus, brought up in this world confused with nobody to tutor him. She taught him to build a hut for protection when the rains came. She remembered teaching him to build a house near to civilization or rather, near to the prey, but not near enough to get noticed. But most importantly she taught him to seamlessly go from Wolf to man and back again without the sway of the full Moon.

So-seti managed a smile, Aticus was an excellent student, and he exceeded her expectations. They would hunt together as wolves sometimes in the daylight with no moon in sight. Come home to their hut with their prize and consume their prey as humans, grandmother and grandson enjoying a meal.

Ironically, it would be her very help, guidance and the construction of their home that brought about unwanted attention from the town folk that would be the beginning of the end for reconciliation. So-seti remembered trying to teach him the spells of her human ancestors;

the very incantations that birthed "wolf's blood". The invocations unknowingly brought about attention from the God's Light. And ultimately she failed her vow when she had been wounded and captured. The beat on the monitor associated with her heart rate increased just thinking about the God's Light. The accursed God's Light! The soft buzz of florescent lights soothed her momentarily to look at her wrinkled hand before the chains pulled taunt.

Two millennium of imprisonment, Lupine and long-lived she didn't take stock in the passage of time, but she knew it had been a very long time since the loss of her grandson. No sun or moon to mark day or night, stuck deep inside the structure, no temperature variations to gauge the seasons. The only marker was the God's Light apparel changing throughout the years, togas turned into lab coats, and sandals turned into modern, shiny shoes. But their sigil, it remained the same, the triangle with the accursed eye in it.

She had time now to think about the catatonic state she had been in. She had suddenly awaked when she heard the whirl of the helicopter blades. When God's Light employees walked by she pretended to still be catatonic but So-seti couldn't help turning her head to look at James and his intoxicating scent. Flying in a helicopter had been miracle enough, let alone the scenery, the wondrous scenery she felt an enormous chasm deep inside her heart. Despite the fact that she had been heavily sedated So-seti had managed to look around and out a large porthole to see unbelievable changes all around her. A few stone dwellings turned to a steel structure and plentiful. Some structures reminded her of the Tower of Babel, reaching vainly for the heavens. She even saw another flying machine high in the sky, sleek and shining white with blue stripes, until it faded into the distance.

Idle thoughts going through her mind about flying machines with fancy white and blue stripes, sturdy steel structures, the familiar aroma throughout the room and the curiously unique smell of James had stayed with her and made her feel alive for the first time in a very long time. She couldn't gauge exactly how much time she had lost but it was a travesty that she had lost time to begin with and she had to do something about it now. She struggled to break her restraints but atrophied muscles and two doses of silver nitrate made it impossible.

Her dusty and dry eyes began to moisten until they were wet with tears. A lump in her throat formed. Small fangs tried to form but quickly receded. She tried to form claws but got nothing but blood for her effort. Five small skeletal fingers emerged from her severed arm like an emerging tooth bud on a baby and just as quickly retreated into the severed muscle thanks to the silver nitrate.

She remembered Aticus' obsessive howl and howled, "Howwl, oww, oww!"

She howled the aria for hours until hoarse from effort and dying of thirst, she relented. Several yards underground and the room made of several inches of soundproofing material before the final steel panel had been painstakingly applied; the howls reached no ears.

15

Byron Atkins rubbed the cold sweat from his shiny, bald head. His obese hands were trembling and he was dizzy again. He stopped what he was doing and opened his desk drawer to find his blood sugar monitor. He had forgotten to eat again; too busy running the day-to-day operations of God's Light.

He found his monitor, placed in the test strips and with a press of a button his index finger began to bleed. His blood sugar was normal, but suddenly his body stiffened as still as the statues that lined the hallways at Gods Light monastery.

"Mm, the smell of sweet, sweet blood." The voice in his head gave him chills and what little hair that he had left crowning his head above his ears stood up as he put on his round rimmed glasses and frantically looked around the room.

"Don't worry, old man," the voice in his head was low and sinister now. The shadow voice a reminder that he wasn't an immortal, unlike the unholy things the group tracks down and tries to kill, *"you're still safe. I'm still in pieces, caged up in the basement down below. I come to you because I have news."*

With an untrained eye it was just another shadow on the corner of the wall, but this shadow pulsated. Now with his glasses on, he could see him, Lucius, the second most powerful Vampyre, a direct descendent from Cain. The scars on his throat and body from the encounter with the powerful vampire and subsequent capture reminded him that if not for Hunter's help he would have died; instead, Hunter trapped Lucius, quite literally like a rat. Hunter had caught Lucius in his rat forms and one by one trapped the rats separately so he could not amalgamate back into a man. Now his shadow was doomed to roam the halls helplessly trapped in the Diablo God's Light compound.

"*There's something going on amongst the lycanthropes. The obsessive howling is making it hard to sleep during the day.*" The shadow of Lucius moved from the corner now to the doorway. Through beady eyes, Byron was watching the shadow like a hawk.

"You don't even sleep, Lucius, you're too powerful! I haven't heard any of this howling that you speak of." Byron regaining more confidence now, his shoulders and spine stood up straight to give an illusion of control.

"Yes, it's true I don't require sleep, although I sleep throughout the day to break up the monotony and the boredom." Lucius sniped.

The shadow of Lucius was still by the doorway and the shadowy arm moved slowly in Byron's direction. A chill made his face freezing cold. "*I hear things a human could not; I don't completely understand their language. The gist of it is there have been three defections and two assassinations and the lycanthropes are all headed to the Gulf of Mexico region, making their way to Louisiana.*"

Byron tapped his unique silver pen, obsessively on his 18th century antique maple desk, lost in thought. He pressed the button for the intercom by the edge of his desk and leaned forward to speak, "James, call Hunter to set up a meeting then come to my office please, report to my office please."

Lucius' shadow form paced back and forth at the doorway seeming to watch.

He got his cell phone out of his breast pocket and dialed. "This is Byron… Secure the private jet, a passenger needs to be transported to Louisiana."

Byron built up his confidence now, instead of the pulsating shadow he concentrated on the busy work he had up on his desk, unaware Lucius' shadow form growing closer. "What is your interest in this, Lucius?"

"*I am always interested in curious movements that may affect…*" Lucius' paused for emphasis, *"My Empire."*

Byron felt goose bumps rising when he heard "my empire" whispered by Lucius, he still considered the Earth as his playground, he thought, but he hid his fear well.

"Sir?"

A knock on the door, a courtesy before the door opened. The pulsating shadow retreated into the corner and dissipated. It was James, reporting the progress on the plane and estimated time of arrival for Hunter.

"Excuse me sir the uh, uh, plane is, um, fueled up and ready to go."

Byron sighed with relief, standing up and straightened his tie. He felt sorry for James, with his weakened left extremities and resulting neuropathy after a genetic malformation had burst in his head, but at the same time James reminded him how good he had it. The diabetes was the only thing he had to deal with and it was manageable; James would be crippled for life, which made him smile inwardly.

"I have to go outside the gates to meet my superiors for an update," He tapped pages of a report until they were even then stapled the reports without even looking James in the eye. "I need you to look after the bitch demon, So-seti. I would delegate a more experienced scientist but…"

James heart raced as Byron continued, "She seems to be mesmerized by you. Maybe she'll be docile and more pliable until she gets used to her surroundings."

Up close something about Byron Atkins always rubbed James the wrong way. His bleach white suit two sizes too small, baldheaded, a snout-like nose, beady eyes, ruddy complexion, always perspiring smelling like stale sweat and faintly of urine. Not to mention his smug demeanor. But he was the boss, James told himself, whenever he walked into a room he just had to grin and bear it.

"Yes sir." He told his boss while tapping his cane on the marble floor. A habit he knew Byron hated but with his disability he knew he could get away with it.

Small victories, he told himself, smiling slyly as he left, awkwardly shutting the door behind him. James slowly hobbled down the hall until he came up to the two armed guards at the exit to the Cathedral. Pausing a moment so they could check his credentials then he hobbled onto the elevator.

Lucius could travel straight down through the soil and rocks several miles underground, the pulsating shadow crept unseen past all the armed guards. The shadow slipped easily beneath the electronically locked doors which So-seti was held behind.

"Aaaaah Luciussss… I know it's you, Lucius, even in your shadow form I can smell the decay." So-seti spoke in a language that only Lucius and she knew.

The pulsating shadow crawled up the wall to get a better look at the once powerful queen lycanthrope. Lucius' shadow enveloped So-seti like a shroud.

"*If vampyres could cry, I'd shed a tear for you, my sweet.*" The shadow stroked So-seti's fragile-skinned, decaying cheek.

"Oh Lucius, what ever happened to us?" So-seti paused for a moment to clear her throat, "we survived for eons just to become lab rats...no pun intended, dear"

So-seti was just a decaying corpse with a faint, erratic pulse now. Gone were the days that the mere mention of her name could strike fear into the most hardened men. Lucius knew her in her prime, so beautiful and so wild. With long, lustrous, black hair, almond shaped sapphire and jade eyes, high proud cheekbones and delicately thin rosy lips. She had an impeccable figure with luscious perky breasts and curvaceous hips fit for childbearing. No man or woman, no king or Empress could resist her in her prime.

Lucius longed to touch her, to soothe and comfort her, but when he tried to touch her, his shadow form went right through to the bone making her shiver. Lucius' shadow form seemed to flow in circles by the cot where So-seti lay. "*I feel pity for you, unlike yourself, So-seti, when the Sun sets I am free to roam the land.*"

So-seti turned to follow the shadow around and around like Lucius operated a laser light pointer, a simple cat toy, which had her turning in circles.

"*In one of my soothing strolls...um, or rather... glides, I heard a distinctive voice.*" Lucius hovers just inches above So-seti's body. "*A haunting and beautiful aria... a Song about tragedy and loss, sung by one of your close offspring...*"

This peaked So-seti's interest, she struggled to sit up on her elbows as far as her chains would allow her to go. She peered with lupine eyes through what she knew to be Lucius' face but would look to others like a dark shadow. Lucius veiled So-seti's form, and cast a ghostly hue over So-seti's wrinkled face. She saw through the shadow the outline of Lucius' form, the glowing pinpricks of his cunning eyes, though Lucius had no body his ruthless form still survives, she mused to herself, this is Lucius' blackened soul!

"Lucius do not tease me, tell me what you know!" So-seti spat, drooling with anticipation.

Pages on clipboards fluttered, the saline fluids swayed, her IV stand rocked back and forth as Lucius' form moved like a black cloud in high winds off of So-seti and away from the stretcher.

"*Your grandchild, Aticus, has survived through the harsh ages,*" Lucius paused for dramatic effect and letting the information sink in, "*he thinks you're dead.*"

Hearing the tragic but potentially exhilarating news of her long lost grandson her pulse rate spontaneously quickened. With every accelerated heartbeat the silver nitrate, liquid poison, running through her bloodstream became more diluted, and she perspired a silver amalgamation of sweat from her forehead.

Her eyes brightened with hope but just as quickly dashed as she hastily looked around at the sound proofed sections lining the room, her neck snapping and popping to the point of malformation until her week spine finally cracking as the base of her skull collapsed back onto the cold stretcher.

Disappointment turned into rage which fueled and began awaking the hidden Wolf, trying to rend out of her thin, brittle, inflexible captive human skin, tearing and bleeding in the weakest spots. So-seti's pale gray skin thickened, her exposed bright blue arteries and veins vanishing, moisture seeping into her flesh hydrating her aged skin and making it more malleable right before Lucius' eyes. So-seti's cryptic skin full of wrinkles that looked like life-size jigsaw puzzles began to get a healthy rosy bronze glow.

Lucius beheld her with admiration, still strong throughout the millennium, shedding her skeletal frame for an ample muscular physique. So-seti still had an elderly look to her appearance from centuries of torture and poison, her legs were still missing, but she had a fire in her eyes now.

"*I have tried reaching out to your grandson, Aticus, to no avail. I have no vocal chords to get my message across.*" So-seti heard Lucius say inside her mind, his only means of speaking.

Telepathy came easy for the ancient sorceress. But to use Telepathy you had to find the target in mind, preferably even be eye to eye with them. If she focused she could open her mind to thoughts elsewhere in the building. Even the powerful could not use telepathy to cross vast distances, especially finding a target as diseased in the mind as Aticus might be. However, the lycanthrope could howl orders over an enormous expanse.

"Hoowww ooow hoowww...Hoowwl!" So-seti cried out until her throat hurt and the room rang with vibrations.

The werewolf howling in the night could be heard by human ears up to eight miles until it reaches ultrasonic frequencies that can be heard by a lycanthrope thousands of miles away. With just four lycanthropes dispersed they could send a message halfway across the globe in an instant.

"*Oh my sweet, So-seti... God's Light chose this hill for its solitude...*" If Lucius had a face it would have been smirking, "*it disrupts all communication, even telepathy, and surely mongrel howling.*"

So-seti could not tell for sure how far down and deep into the mountains she had traveled but she knew for sure that the combination of a soundproofed room and buried deep into the earth left little hope that her grandson would ever hear the important message, that she survived...

A harsh sound startled both So-seti and Lucius. A flashing red warning light appeared on the monitors that governed the IV dosing monitor. A liquid silver solution traveled the length of the tubing into So-seti's veins. As silver solution invaded her heart her muscles and flesh instantly dehydrated. Fresh, bright eyes began to glaze over and darken; the eye sockets blackened and sunk in, like a sinkhole collapsing. With So-seti's moaning much too much to endure, Lucius retreated into the walls leaving her alone with her pain muddled thoughts.

Aftermath

16

Batchelor, LA

Detective Jenkins moaned as he stretched out the kinks in his stiff legs. His muscles felt like bricks every morning but it didn't stop him from running. He put an old gray pair of sweatpants on, and donned the T-shirt from the night before, instinctively buckling on his badge and shoulder holster of thirty-one years. The sun seemed to rise sluggishly, weary of awakening for a new day. Jenkins smiled, checking his watch and adjusting his headband. Looking in the mirror, he rubbed his chin, rubbed at the five o'clock shadow that now grew wildly. The lines under his eyes were getting more prominent and his military style haircut was more silver than brown nowadays. In his younger days he was a handsome man. His once taunt cheeks were starting to droop. Even his blue eyes, once commanding, had dimmed and were showing signs of age. He was getting older in the face but his body endured.

His chest was still huge from his professional playing days and his biceps still stretched beneath his T-shirt. Stopping only to get his side arm, then to put a hunting knife in his sock, a necessity since a routine jog had once almost cost him his legs when a huge alligator thought he was an easy meal and then he was out the door. He looked up at the full moon partnering with the morning sun.

"You know you don't have to run today," a ghost in his head whispered, "your marriage down the crapper, mother is gone. You don't have to impress anyone anymore."

Jenkins tried to ignore the ghost's hurtful venom as he tried to do many times before and grunted, "Well let's get this over with."

His route was like clockwork, every morning it would take him down town, through Main Street, across three blocks to the park, around the makeshift community Lake, and then down the railroad tracks and back to the suburb where he lived. His calves cramped up first, and then his chest filled with fire. Finally his back ached before he stopped for a break.

"Boy I'm out of shape." He huffed, out of breath, hands massaging his legs.

His black 9 mm Glock side arm was sticking out from his shoulder holster as he rested his hands on his hips laboring for breath, sounding like a rusty pump. Then something caught his police trained eyes. A nude man was climbing out of the window of an apartment building nearby, bloodied and disheveled; he fell to the ground with a crunch and a grunt.

"Halt!" Jenkins yelled, still out of breath.

He identified himself as a police officer, and before Jenkins knew what was going on, his hands instinctively drew his gun. The man looked up at him in surprise. His eyes were wild and he was grunting like an animal. They locked eyes for a moment before the bloody man took off on all fours like an animal.

The man wove wildly through the front yard then abruptly slid to a stop startling Detective Jenkins. The blood covered stranger snapped his neck back to look at Jenkins, snarling and foaming at the mouth. Growling a guttural warning to Detective Jenkins who thought he saw razor sharp, curved fangs. The bloodied man sported fingernails like five, six-inch talons as if holding several stilettos. He twirled around and quickly closed the distance between them, and lunged at Jenkins.

"No, don't shoot!" The ghost in Jenkins' head shouted.

Jenkins aimed and fired two in his chest and one into his head. The bloody man fell on the grass, dying where he had fallen. Jenkins kneeled down, eyes widening in bewildered confusion. Upon closer inspection there were no fangs, no claws. The boy looked about eighteen or nineteen years old. As he stood up, his body began to shake and a cold sweat poured over him. A lump welled up in his throat. The boy almost looked like his own son. The color drained from his face. His dead son, the one he accidentally shot dead one night when he snuck in early from college to surprise his parents for their anniversary.

Louisiana P.D. said he had done everything by the book. His son had his hood up still, to shield himself from the cold and his iPod was blaring in his ears. His son was reaching for what he thought at the time was a gun. He identified himself as a police officer … He blamed the long hours of work and the medication that he took to sleep that night that had him in a fog.

"Dad," he had muttered in surprise, the blood pooling in his throat," why?" he had whispered, blood trickling out of the corners of his mouth as he began to collapse.

The memory of that day came flooding back so suddenly it drove him to his knees. He was only running and he had taken his gun out, he wondered why. He didn't even have his cell phone on hand to call the department. He got close enough to assess the situation at hand, but not too close as to contaminate the scene as he planted his hunting knife in the dead boy's hand. Then he jogged over to the nearest house and knocked frantically on the door.

"Oh, that's pitiful!" The ghost of his son Philip spit, "just like your friends, refusing to blood test you…"

Ignoring his son's hurtful jabs he ran towards the closest occupied house. His voice cracked, and he began crying, "Police, open up!"

He waited, impatiently wiping away his tears as the door opened, and an old woman looked out the crack.

"What's going on?" Spoke a grumpy woman, groggy from being woken up. Still in her nightgown, she rubbed sleep from her eyes and tried to focus in on detective Jonathan Jenkins. She was staring at the gun and holster on the disheveled detective nervously, "What's happening?"

"Ma'am I need you to call Captain Rogers," handing the old woman a card." Tell him there is a D.O.A. and an officer involved shooting in your neighborhood."

Jenkins paced back and forth nervously as he waited for his back-up to arrive. He swore his heart was about to explode when he saw the lights and heard the sirens of his brethren approaching. One unmarked police car, two patrol cars, and a white coroner van stopped in the middle of the street. Capt. Thompson Rogers had gotten out of the unmarked car and slowly strolled to Jenkins' side while slowly scrutinizing the scene.

There was clearly a mixture of condescending curiosity in his voice as he was asking, "What happened here?"

Before the divorce, eventual meltdown, and move to seclusion in Batchelor he worked with Captain Rogers, still a master sergeant in the Pointe Coupee Parish Sheriff's Department back in the day. Rogers had responded when Jenkins accidentally shot his son. He couldn't help but wonder if it was happening all over again, a nightmare of split second poor decisions.

"I don't know exactly", Jenkins purposely looked down at the grass trying to avoid the Captain's stare.

"It just happened so quickly." Jenkins went on with his story, how the bloody man crawled out of a window, how he was running on all fours refusing to stop. He took a deep breath, "and his menacing claws, um, he started coming at me with a hunting knife."

Captain Rogers quickly scanned the crime scene. A busted window from the inside out, nude stranger some of the blood crusting up all over his body obviously not his own. Next to the body lay a shiny hunting blade.

"Well the information that you have given seems to check out," He rubbed Jenkins' back to try and comfort him, "It will be alright."

"You did everything by the book..." The ghost of his son sarcastically whispered.

The policeman doubling as paramedics futilely tried to revive the wounded stranger before giving up and calling over the coroner. Dr. Jacobs, the coroner, went through the motions, cause of death obvious three bullet wounds; two to the body one to the head. Then he examined the dead man closer as he stuck a patch thermometer on the chest, taken aback by the results.

"Detective Jenkins, come over here a second," Dr. Jacobs motioned for Jenkins as he got up off the ground with a groan and dusted off the knees of his blue jumpsuit.

"What's up?" Jenkins asked, his hands on his hips, avoiding looking at the dead man now lying beneath the blue sheet.

"How long ago did you say this happened?" Jacobs had the patch thermometer in his gloved hands.

"It's been thirty minutes ago." He estimated, the worry lines creasing his forehead.

"His temperature is one-hundred and three." Dr. Jacobs said looking preoccupied, "obviously sick, but how sick I don't yet know. I haven't seen anything like this before."

The doctor was rubbing his hands together; he didn't know what to do. This was a small town and usually nothing like this ever happened. He wiped the cold sweat from his forehead with the back of his hand. No need to get the CDC involved just yet, he thought, at least not until he was sure what kind of virus or bug it was.

"Is it contagious?" Jenkins asked, eyeing the corpse with repulsion and fear. It would be just his luck, he thought, a shitty end to his miserable existence.

He was no longer in control of the scene. Squad cars blocked the streets off in both directions and uniformed officers strategically roped off with official yellow police tape the yard leading to the house before the crime scene. The neighbors came out in droves, curious from the commotion, and stood in the streets barefoot and still in their robes, sipping their coffee and smoking cigarettes, whispering gossip to one another.

The veins on Jenkins neck throbbed as anger settled over him, he lifted his arms in a flapping motion, stepping up to the growing mob trying to disperse them.

Dr. Jacobs shook his head in silence. He did not want to worry about the safety of the growing audience around him. "Not sure till I get him back to the lab whether or not it's contagious."

Dr. Jacobs motioned at the body. His assistants diligently zipped the corpse up, hoisting it onto a gurney, and rolled it up to the waiting white van. Dr. Jacobs strolled over and put his hand on Jenkins' arm.

"Don't worry, my friend," Dr. Jacobs tried to comfort him, "from the fever I estimate he was probably not in his right mind. There was nothing you could do."

Jenkins wasn't listening, staring at the ghost of his son, his mind off on a tangent of iPods and empty hunting knife sheaths. Two patrol cars went in opposite directions. Jenkins stood alone in the yard with his thoughts, his sweatpants becoming stiff with his drying sweat.

17

Dr. Jacobs had taken his own car separate from the coroner van so he took the scenic route to Pointe Coupee hospital to smell the powerful Mississippi river. He had grown up in the New Road's area so the 16 mile trek had been second nature to him. He arrived at the back entrance of the Pointe Coupee hospital and his coroner office with time to spare. All seemed quiet when he turned off his engine, walked across the lot to the door and anxiously pushed the button for the employee entrance.

Dr. Jacobs pushed the elevator call button for the morgue. A "Bing" sounded and with a creak the doors stubbornly opened. Nurse Danielle Or'Léon just getting off of a grueling third hour shift looked up innocently, her green eyes wide. The site of Dr. Jacobs waiting for the elevator startled her.

"Oh…" Danielle responded, spilling her lunch onto the floor. She had paid for it with a check that would probably bounce better than the spilled food.

"I'm sorry." Dr. Jacobs apologized, instinctively holding the elevator door with one hand and going on his knees to help her salvage what was left of her lunch with the other hand.

"No, no, it's my fault." Apologizing to Dr. Jacobs, red-faced and jittery, "I am just on edge from everything that happened here last night."

Her salad was largely unsalvageable as most of it had spilled from the plastic container upon hitting the floor but Dr. Jacobs managed to save her carrot cake, still wrapped. Her juice had leaked from its broken container, handing her the cake he asked, "What happened last night?"

"Nurse Maggie, Dr. Lewis, and two policemen were murdered," Danielle stepped out from the elevator to finish her conversation, "then to top it all off, several patients went missing and two or three glass doors were vandalized in the process, I'm not sure the number." She informed him, pushing her brown hair out of her face nervously.

Dr. Jacobs still held the elevator doors and Danielle stood frozen. An awkward moment or two passed before Dr. Jacobs asked, "Who would do such a thing?"

"I don't know." Danielle leaned in conspiratorially, "there are rumors circulating around the hospital that with all the carnage a huge animal like a bear or boar ran loose through the halls last night." Nurse Danielle stood silent for a moment contemplating the circumstances, "realistically, I think a crazed man on PCP just got away from the cops!"

Dr. Jacobs couldn't help but recall the nude boy on the lawn shot to death by an officer, whom he knew and trusted, he said softly, almost absent mindedly, "I think you're right, Danielle."

Just thinking about the night's events again made Danielle shiver uncontrollably. It did not help that the temperature in the hospital seemed to be set just above freezing. She loved the idea of a horror story but when it came down to it, she was easily frightened. With a gentle pat on her frigid arm Dr. Jacobs comforted the nurse, until the outdated intercom squawked, startling Danielle out of her skin again.

The wheels in his head were already turning; maybe it was a new designer drug instead of an infectious contagion. A nervous smile broke Dr. Jacobs' stern façade. He continued his forced smile to encourage Danielle. He felt bad for the nurse's skittish demeanor, not unlike a Chihuahua in a thunderstorm, which was speaking truthfully, he had seen her cower during some of the more damaging storms. He had his reservations, although he had awoke to the strange encounter that led to the homicide of a young man who may or may not be racked with a horrible disease, only to hear a more gruesome scene.

"It'll be all right, Danielle," Dr. Jacobs lied; too preoccupied with what he was going to find when he entered his morgue. "Listen," pulling out his Pointe Coupee Hospital employee card to pay for and replace the spilled salad and juice, "I will pay for the lunch I ruined, just come by the morgue to give me back my card when you're finished eating."

The display of chivalry made Danielle blush, but she politely accepted the card knowing she couldn't afford to pay for lunch twice. Dr. Jacobs stepped into the elevator as the doors closed the elevator moving again. The coroner headed toward his office in the basement and the nurse headed back to the cafeteria.

Another moment of uncomfortable silence before the elevator came to a stop and the doors opened to the basement. Danielle Or'Léon nodded a thanks before heading off in the direction of the cafeteria. Dr. Jacobs hesitated for a moment, resting his forehead on the flapping door, bracing his arm onto the entrance wall and feeling the cold steel on his palm. It would be at least four bodies, he thought to himself, two close friends. Just imagining what horrible injuries befell his two friends made him sick with grief.

He managed to convince his legs to move dredging through the hallway. Eventually he stumbled upon his office and hesitantly opened the morgue doors shivering from the extreme cold, the morgue temperature set just above frostbite. A wave of professionalism coursed through him, even though the first site he saw was the corpse of Nurse Maggie as she rested on the icy steel, her dead eyes shaming him because of her nakedness the others still in their black nylon body bags. She was the first of four cadavers that had been moved to the examination table for Dr. Jacobs's skillful findings.

The morgue looked like a square, drab room forever smelling of decaying flesh. Immediately to the left of Dr. Jacobs a surgical table spanning wall-to-wall. Behind him a surgical glove dispenser and dual sinks. One side of the faucet attached to a hose that steadily climbed upwards until it attached to a showerhead and lightweight controllable floodlight in the ceiling center. The floor gradually sloped downward at the center to a large drain, easier to wash the blood and fluids away. On the right of him were two doors with frosted windows that read "Office" and "Storage" respectively. Flickering lights illuminated the office door where another employee shadowed around until the door opened to reveal Dr. Jacobs' assistant, Doug.

"They're all prepped for you, Doctor" His assistant of fifteen years said, rubbing his hands under the faucet, lathering, scrubbing then rinsing away before he managed to successfully turn the faucet off with his elbow. "I figured you wanted to get started on the nurse first, am I right?"

An absurd amount of time passed before, with a shake of his head, Dr. Jacobs answered "yeah." Inconceivably, Nurse Maggie lay dead before him when just days before he had heard her boisterous and obnoxious laugh echo through the hallways.

Immediately they set to work rolling the stretcher around and maneuvering the light until they had an optimal view of the body. First glance told him that her neck was obviously broken, the vertebrae visible and out of place under the bruised skin. In fact, the whole head had been twisted with such force that vertebrae number two had splintered, intertwining between muscles, and had been forced up under the skin, her head permanently twisted to the side.

Dark bruising appearing on her flesh suggesting human hands had twisted her neck. But if that was the case, he scrutinized, it had been outlandishly cartoonish human hands. He looked up at his hands, twirling his own fingers around in comparison, so puny. What had Danielle said? An animal? It would have had to be a very large animal.

"A bear?" Doug Gage offered, shrugging, he seemed to know Dr. Jacobs' train of thought. "Maybe a bear that escaped from the circus?"

Dr. Jacobs chuckled as Doug proceeded to mimic a bear peddling a tricycle, but in his mind the evidence was far off. Offering an alternative Doug said, "Or a Gorilla."

Their joking of circus bears aside, they went to work in silence. They continued in uneasy silence until Doug, who slept with the TV blaring night after night at home just for the background noise, had quite enough of the deafening silence and reached up to the shelf and turned on a dusty radio with a broken antenna. Doug twisted the knob left to right until the music of his liking, an industrial band, shrieked out.

The morgue doors clanged open suddenly and Doug's well-worn shoes took flight towards the doors as Dr. Jacobs' checked his watch then twisted his head looking for the expected delivery.

"Hey now, a phone call or something to know you're headed this way!" Red-faced with embarrassment Doug scolded the technicians as he stepped out of the stretcher's path.

"Your boss knew we were coming." The tech rebuked in unison, wheeling the stretcher past Doug Gage and roughly transporting the delicate cargo into the far corner of the room.

Dr. Jacobs stared at the shiny black body bag; even he had forgotten or at least wanted to erase from his memory the potentially harmless or dangerous contagious pathogen that leeched onto the dead man being wheeled into his morgue. But now he had no choice but to think about the contagious body.

Dr. Jacobs stiffened up, the color draining from his already ashen face, "this patient may be harboring a disease. I hope you took extra precautions."

Greg, the lead employee, avoided being caught up in any argument by quickly slipping away into the office. It was not official until Greg signed all the forms to release the cadaver to the care of Pointe Coupee. In an added bonus frosted windows gave him a barrier between his grumpy coworker, Quentin, and the Doctor.

A part-time employee, Quentin's shift had just started after getting off of the end of a ten hour day at A-line, and he was in no mood to fight today evidenced by the rolling of his eyes, "we were careful! We did everything by the freaking book."

Quentin tossed his latex gloves with revulsion over toward a nearby trash receptacle and glanced at the clock. Knocking on the frosted glass to the office door, He called for Greg, "Hey man, I'll be up in the van don't be long." He didn't wait for an answer before walking toward the exit.

Greg shook his head, and finished up his paperwork. He walked out of the office. While Dr. Jacobs and Doug were distracted still working on Nurse Maggie he silently walked over to the cadaver unzipping the body bag sneaking a peek at his face. Not counting the crime scene in the yard he could not shake the feeling that he had seen that face before.

However, the humanoid man lying in the stretcher looked just as foreign to him as well. Wide set eyes under their closed lids, protuberant and long forehead with the exception of a bullet hole, a flat nose smashed in the middle of his face and a prominent boxer's chin convinced Greg he had probably seen him on Friday night fights. A quiver, a miniscule flutter instantly brought his attention back to the cadaver's face. He could've sworn the flesh stirred before shaking his head and casting the thought off. The radio on Greg's belt began to squawk with new orders for the white van, distracting him. Chalking it up to lack of sleep and his overactive imagination he looked away from the open bag and answered his radio.

"Are you done yet?" Squawked a grumpy and sleep deprived Quentin.

"Well, I'll leave you to it Doc, I better get out there or else Quentin is going to go postal!" Greg said cheerily before pushing out the double doors.

Turning back to their work once more after muttering "thank you", both men thought long and hard about the likelihood of an animal, both coming to the same conclusions, not likely. Down the line they made their notes observing the absence of scratch or claw marks on the body, no fur anywhere in sight.

Dr. Jacobs and Doug painstakingly evaluated the lifeless cadavers. The doc made a Y incision; surgically removed each and every organ and weighed it while Doug recorded it with his digital recorder. One by one they sliced and then stitched up the bodies till they were down to one. Dr. Jacobs glanced at the clock… All the stalling and hesitation had worked, almost lunchtime.

"Doug, you can stop for lunch." Dr. Jacobs smiled, but in his mind he accomplished two things, one was with Doug gone nobody could see the anxiety building up in him while he worked, and two if it was an infectious disease, Doug's exposure to it would be minimal.

"You're the boss." Doug said as he and Dr. Jacobs unzipped and lifted the cadaver onto the cold steel rack before he left for lunch.

First things first, the doctor drew a lot of blood for testing. By the time he finished he had enough, six vials drawn. Then a peculiar sight caught his eye. The face seemed to flatten somehow, like a balloon losing air because of a minuscule pinhole. Shaking off his unpleasant thoughts the doc tried to finish jotting down several silent notes before throwing his clipboard on the stainless steel table.

"I need coffee, strong coffee." Dr. Jacobs blinked three times as if blinking any number of times could stave off his hallucinations. "And I have to get some fresh air." He thought aloud.

Several minutes later a weary Dr. Jacobs struggled through the double doors, trying not to spill two coffees filled to the brim, for Jacobs and his assistant who would be in shortly. Twirling around and setting down the coffee he was surprised to find Danielle standing there splotchy and crying hysterically, mucus streaming out from her red nose as she backed away from his last corpse to be worked on.

"That's, that's," in-between sobs, Danielle proclaimed, "That's Cody!"

"What?"

Dr. Jacobs questioned, whipping around to get a better view and as he did spilling the coffee, earmarked for his assistant because of the extreme amount of cream and sugar, onto the floor. The steaming brew slid considerately towards the drain in the floor and out of sight.

His mouth fell open when he beheld Cody's body. If he had any doubts he had been tricked or it was a goof and somewhere hidden cameras were rolling, when he saw the one bullet hole in the middle of the head all doubts were erased. That's impossible; well it's improbable, the old rusty gears were already turning, Dr. Jacobs in complete disavowal now. Could this corpse really be Cody? How had he not realized that?

Wide-eyed still staring at the paramedic, Dr. Jacobs remarked quietly, "He was horribly bruised or he had a bad allergic reaction."

He was not responding to Danielle but already in full denial mode. He could not shake the lingering doubts that plagued him. It wasn't an allergic reaction at all, was it? Before, the bizarre revelation that the body would become Cody, Dr. Jacobs had been close to him, he could almost see the exaggerated cheekbones. He saw the protracted eyes that could not be explained by bruising or expansion of the skin. Don't forget the jawbone; Dr. Jacobs saw the fighter's chin, almost a Cro-Magnon chin that convinced Dr. Jacobs, Cody, a colleague and friend of his for years had morphed into another person.

"How did this happen?" Danielle meekly asked Dr. Jacobs her tearful eyes looking up at him for answers.

When Cody's ambulance had returned to the hospital and there were no more emergencies to be seen for a while she had joked around with him, confessed her secrets and fears with him. Dare she say she had a developed a crush on him? Now she found Cody's lifeless body resting on the gurney. Her shaking hands involuntarily moving toward Dr. Jacobs' shoulders in finding them her knees began to tremble then collapse. Dr. Jacobs's arms instantly held up her limp body.

He carefully carried the passed out body of Danielle to the office and laid her down on a comfortable couch. The brilliant lights from the hallway crept in to the grayish artificial light from the room like the sea approaching the beach at high tide. Dr. Jacobs turned around to see the doors opening and the figure of Doug Gage emerging. In his fist a bunch of crumpled papers.

"After lunch, some of the labs and the toxicology results were ready from your gunshot victim," Doug Gage carefully rolled and flattened out the crumpled papers he had in his hands setting them down on the desk. He gestured to the half smoothed out papers, "you better have a look at this."

"Is it contagious?" Dr. Jacobs asked without looking up at Doug.

"Most of the labs are not in yet, but I think you should look at this." Doug sat down in a nearby chair breathing labored just like he had run a marathon.

"After the results came back we ran it again with a control patient just to see if the machine was not broken," said Doug forcing the report into Dr. Jacobs's hands, "it was working perfectly."

Scanning the report quickly Dr. Jacobs said, "What drugs did Cody turn up positive for?"

"All of them. He tested positive for all of them." Doug responded, but could tell he was reading the reports for himself.

18

Miles away from the Pointe Coupee Hospital, the Sun still making an arc over the Louisiana horizon and the full Moon was now a distant memory as Gene and his son awoke refreshed and renewed despite the fact they were naked and huddled close together sleeping outside. Chance let out a lazy yawn his arms outstretched, seemingly unaware of the unspeakable acts perpetrated the previous night. Gene stretched as well his muscles sore but engorged and it felt miraculous.

Gene strutted around in his nakedness; the topography was such that a privacy fence between the houses obstructed any peeping toms. A start traveled through him, trying to remember what day it was until he remembered it was only Sunday. Thank goodness he thought. His job as a driver at Metro bus systems would not be in jeopardy. But lightheaded wooziness come over him, as he tried to walk calf muscles were wound up tight like compressed springs and every time he took a step it was as if he was walking on the moon.

Like a binge drinker without the headache his memory was fragmented pieces upon pieces lying on the floor like a hopelessly unfinished puzzle. He tried to recall the night's events until remembering the crazed man foaming at the mouth. He found himself involuntarily rubbing at his wounded arm which miraculously healed. Then a forgotten thought renewed and ran loose through him, a wave of guilt as he remembered biting his son, he hysterically looked around for Chance.

A huge sigh of relief passed through him when he found his son alive and well, naked as a jaybird but safe and uninjured. On a closer examination, though, he had grown taller, definitely more meat on him. Chance's perfectly manicured hair, had grown longer and somehow shaggier, if you didn't know him you wouldn't notice the difference, but his father did.

His son's transformation to beast thing had obviously stopped, hair and fur receded, the arched spine straighten, shoulders popped back into place looking human again. But he observed his son more diligently because even his shoulders, a source of embarrassment for his son, had filled out too, had become rounder. If he squinted his eyes a bit he could even see the striations on the muscles. The arms were a strange sight somehow they stretched beyond normal. Gene marveled at the site.

He was distracted by his son's nose, sniffing the air around him. His ears swiveled like a satellite turning for better reception. He watched his son and was mesmerized by his actions-reminding him of a stray dog as he sniffed for something he himself could not smell.

In truth, though, he was inundated by scents all around him too, sharper hearing too... the whole gambit of senses intertwining together translated to crisper senses. A bird sang somewhere nearby threatening to give him whiplash as his neck quickly lashed around homing in on the

Cardinal midflight. In fact, every neuron exploded, an instinct to give chase grasped him, and it took all of his being to resist the sudden urge.

The cardinal now rested on a nearby branch and it shook his recollection... he saw a bird not of red feathers and full of organs, this cardinal was made of red ceramic, hollow and broken into several jagged pieces lying on his floor. Gene rested his shaky hands on his head as more and more fragments of memory flashed through him. He remembered his oblivious wife as the door opened, her smile ear to ear, her arms labored with hot bags of her husband and son's favorite greasy fast food, exuding tempting aromas. He could recall vivid details of memories, the smells of fast food, a fit of sorts overtaking him when the hunger pangs set in.

Chance's mom awoke to her normal life that morning and she return home only to find a bizarre sort of "twilight zone" or "tales from the dark side" episode in progress. Her son tore through the hallway like a bat out of hell, drool pooling around his jam-packed oversized ragged teeth that dripped off onto the carpeting. His growing nails scratching against the paneling as his misshapen muzzle sniffed out the sustenance. He had shed all the rest of his clothing, but you couldn't tell because bunches of fur in strategic areas more than made up for it.

She gasped, stepping back, arm out stretched as if to protect the food from a ravenous stray dog. He swiped at his mother's unbalanced frame until she staggered back and fell to her hands spilling double cheese burgers onto the floor, the bag bursting and spraying ketchup packets as she landed hard on her buttocks.

Her son reminded her of a wild rabid animal, eyes wild with rage, his face, especially the nose and the mouth somehow misshapen enough to remind her of a cheap Halloween prosthetic. She closed her eyes fearing her crazed son would crush the whole of her body...For a few moments her eyes remained tightly shut. The impact never happened, so she opened one eye at first, and then the other. She saw her son on all fours greedily scarfing down with his mouth the warm spillage. She gripped the paneling with shaking hands whipping her head around expecting to find her husband and his cooler head would prevail and give her some sort of normalcy to grasp. Her husband, Gene, stood pale and still as a statue-his cold dilated eyes staring at the spilled bag on the floor like it contained treasure.

Gene came to, on his knees, food strewn out in all directions on the floor. Unfinished fries still in his mouth. Chance had jumped up on the couch and held his mom tightly, leisurely licking her on the face.

He found his wife wild-eyed with a traumatized look on her face, as if to say help me in some way! The wife submitted to lick after slobbering lick from her grateful but demented son. Her arms outstretched as if to give her son a hug but in Gene's eyes she looked like a person drowning, a last ditch effort her arms out raised until sinking to the depths of the sea. Instead of helping however, he turned his back to her staggering into the kitchen. Demanding hunger rocked him again, his first and only necessity to feed.

The earlier raid on the kitchen left the cabinets and refrigerator bare but it didn't discourage Gene as he ravaged through the remainders of the picked through barbecue. He finished off a speck of bone from the rib until it shone bright white; a sudden realization hit him like an aluminum baseball bat. If he was nowhere near placated then his son, most assuredly, would not be pacified either.

"Hel..." Gene's wife tried to plead but the words could not leave her throat.

Gene heard the distinct sounds of snarling, the warning before the strike then a blood gurgling scream. He felt his heart racing, cold perspiration spreading all over his body. He made his way into the living room one picked-over rib in his left hand and a chicken drum in his right-hand before quickly devouring the chicken drum, bones and all. He suddenly froze, lightheaded then dizzy, now he braced his unoccupied hand on the chair near a desk to give him some stability.

Starving with hunger the fast food had pacified for a moment and Chance had gratefully licked his mother in love and admiration but the infection spread through his veins. Now Gene's wife's had fended off Chance's spontaneous attack. The wife suffered attack after attack by powerful teeth trying to consume tender flesh. Her son's claws trying to grab hold of any bony surface that would give him stability. He clawed at his mother's blouse until suddenly the breast pocket ripped away. The sudden instability of a torn pocket fluttering away had Chance's claws frantically grasping about before smashing through a glass coffee table and hitting roughly onto the floor. Gene's wife unrestrained for the first time ran for her life. She hurdled through the demolished coffee table and her son to get to her purse, which she had dropped beside the door as she had been ambushed.

"Pepper spray," the wife said aloud as she fumbled around in her deep purse pockets, trying to find the key/aerosol combination, "Gene!"

Gene stumbled to his wife's aid as a bizarre, potent rush of adrenaline ran through his entire body the neurons in his muscles firing simultaneously. Finding the pepper spray his wife sprayed the entire contents in her son's direction. Chance protected his face and curled up in the fetal position as the pepper spray fell down on him like rain.

Gene could see the frustration and vulnerability in her demeanor, the pleading for help in his wife's eyes. However, instead of saving his wife he looked around to find Chance's shaking body. He couldn't help himself as he regarded his son's pleading eyes. Gene's heart began to flutter and race, like an engine Tachometer running on red line but the racecar drivers' boot stomping on the petal and burying the needle to go so much faster. He could see his heart beating out of his chest, his cognizance no longer in control and his hands involuntarily seizing up. He could visualize a dazzling white ring that can best be described as an almost transparent halo brightening as it constricted in his mind. He suddenly found himself somehow out-of-body. He could see his wife and his son, his hearing muffled as time seemed to be slowing down. Both were in distress, but somehow he heard the calling of his son like someone shouting in a bullhorn. Every sense he had responding, an overwhelming need to protect his still fragile son from an assault. He heard himself growling as a wide circle of darkness overtook his sight, the circle shrinking until he could see no more.

The darkness had subsided and Gene awoke to find a bloody broken rib bone in his hand; his son's arms clung tight to his buttocks. Chance hugged his father tightly, his stringy, wet hair dripping from the pepper spray, clinging to Gene's bloody stomach. His head swimming, still delirious he tried to get his bearings from the confusion that such a sudden awakening always brings. As if sleepwalking and now unaware of his surroundings and a sizable chunk of time gone he stumbled with shaking knees, wobbly as if he just got off his stationary bike. His son leeching on to his leg he tracked the blood stains on the new laminate flooring until finding his wife. The broken bone fell to the floor as Gene cupped his palms to his mouth in a desperate attempt to keep down the rising bile in his stomach as sudden shock overcame him.

The wife's head turned unnaturally, accusing eyes and unexpected grimace staring up at him. She lay motionless on her back with broken rib bones protruding out of her chest. The amount of blood spreading on the floor he assumed the entire vascular system had been shredded. That would explain the broken rib gene thought in horror. NO it was just a pig bone, wasn't it? He stared at a torn blouse and her pale complexion. The bruising throughout the face and several bite marks throughout her neck and back suggested she put up a hell of a fight, but he didn't remember anything. The strangest thing of all, he felt no remorse as he stared at the broken spine beneath the throat that violated the muscles and the tendons protruding beneath her skin. They were High school sweethearts, married young and had been faithful ever since. But he felt a strange obligation toward his son, his descendant. Somehow he knew this and now the blood flowing through them had a special blood bond. His son had been fighting for his life and he would kill for his safety.

Gene peered down at Chance's eyes, still ravenous, his son drooling at his lifeless mother's body. Determined to do something about Chance's ceaseless starvation he grabbed hold of his wife's body unlocked Chance's tight embrace and quickly headed off toward the kitchen. No thought whatsoever when he selected a carving knife out of the knife block. Last night, fileting his wife like a fish would have sickened him but the fact of the matter was his whole biological makeup had changed. The parasites passing through his system like the speed of light. The infection changing Gene from the inside out starting with the brain, the very thought processes that defined humanity's ideals. Unseen changes in Gene's makeup that would stay with him even if there was no moon in sight; changing his personality as if he had long ignored a case of syphilis that had burrowed into his brain.

He flipped on the dial to medium heat and set a pan on the burner. Opening the refrigerator he emerged with his homemade barbecue sauce in hand. His dead wife no more than a hollow shell now, opportunistic meat bag for his son's survival. He makes short work of her arm and thigh and throwing a slice of each in the skillet. A pleasant bittersweet aroma began to fill the air. Though a taboo, the smell of warming meat on the skillet made Gene's mouth water in anticipation. The noise of pots and pans clanging about piqued the curiosity of the famished and irrational son. He peeped out of the corner and moved his head side to side in curiosity, his new longer hair dancing on his now plump and full shoulders as he crept forward timidly.

"Come here, son." Gene said meekly gesturing to come this way.

The steak turned a tender auburn color and sizzled as Gene slathered barbecue sauce about the whole of it. Then he carefully split the steak into two halves so two starving mouths could devour the juicy steak whole. As hunger racked Gene again he went on with the tedious process of dismembering and removing flesh.

Chance's hungry eyes met his father yet again as a quiet grumbling started in the center of the belly. Now hunger pains racked the both of them. He tossed the brown meat to his boy who promptly caught it in his mouth and swallowed. Gene stared at the other juicy steak then at Chance's still hungry eyes. Gene reluctantly tossed his son the other carved steak meant to satisfy his hunger. Now he would have to carve more of his wife's body up into pieces, but he had come to grips with that as he blacked out.

When he came to again he found himself outside with his son grasping the corpse and his stomach full. A revelation struck him as his hands rubbed his swollen belly, when he yearned for meat he felt himself losing control but when he ate some sort of protein the blackouts subsided. He saw his son chewing on the remnants of a thigh his eyes still animalistic. His wife was reduced to just a skeleton now.

"Z, y, x, w, v…" Human again, his human self, capable of logical thought. Gene said the alphabet backwards. Gene could not help but expose a toothy smile, "1, 2, 3, 4…"

Elation crept in as his brain slowly regained the full ability to reason. No more of his slow intellect, like moving molasses on a freezing day. However he missed the pure animalistic instinct that came from losing his humanity. But the ordinary world, his reality, would never be the same. He relished all of the unique sights, sounds and scents that he could never sense before, as he looked around the garage to find a shovel to bury what remained of his beloved wife.

Chance growled a warning when Gene grabbed hold of the skeleton that had been his wife. Gene encountered some resistance at first then slowly he slid her body across the grass not daring to take his eyes off Chance until his son lost interest and turned away.

Gene went about the tedious digging as if he lost a tolerated family pet, no emotion creeping in. He dug a five foot shallow hole, without breaking a sweat and with one hand threw his wife into the ground as Chance all but forgot the memories of last night, now off playing with a trapped squirrel.

"Where's mom?" Chance asked finally, innocently strolling up to meet his dad while he wiped the barbecue from his mouth. It was now plainly obvious he didn't remember the horrors.

"I don't know." Gene answered, lying, while staring at the fresh grave and the shovel with moist dirt caked on it.

They stood upon the very ground that the mother and wife lie rotting underneath, Gene and Chance put their arms around one another. They knew in their hearts that Jeanette, wife and mother of one, would not be returning home but they were strangely unaffected by this. An instinct older than mankind had come over them. They felt part of a new family, a growing family and they were overjoyed.

19

As the sun made its way leisurely across the sky over Gene and his son he couldn't help but think about the infected people growing exponentially. He could actually sense it in the air around him. Like a blitzkrieg, monsters swiftly made their bloody mark upon Royal Bay. The young, old, weak willed and immune deficient walked around in the day in a dreamlike state on autopilot going through their mundane tasks dreaming about howling wolves, oblivious to their sickness, pliable to Aticus' will. The strong-willed infected had fully changed, the fever had subsided and they were able to dust themselves off, the haze of denial setting in and toil on in their dreary existence.

Nathan found himself disoriented as he awoke and steadied himself. He stumbled to his feet with the help of a window air conditioner. Unsteady, he put his palms on the unit until his dizziness faded. He had blacked out yet again last night and he strained to remember just a fragment of the night's events. He remembered wearing a shirt that had progressively grown too short for him now torn to rags. He remembered stalking through the shadows of the night on all fours. In the alleyway he stalked in the shadows unsuspecting victims to quench his hunger until he tired, coming to rest at the Royal Bay retirement home… among the many blackouts his stomach turned as he recalled attacking two boys in the parking lot.

"What was I going to do with them when I caught them?" Nathan scoffed to himself, "Eat them!"

"What did I do last night?" He asked himself, his head feeling like it was squeezed in a vice.

He was barefoot and dirty as he dusted off his shirt that was stretched out and torn, with his hands. It was hard for him to keep his pants from falling off because the button had burst. He desperately searched for clues on the ground where he had slept finally finding the plastic bag which held an ace bandage, ibuprofen and receipt from the drugstore.

"Well that's a start." He spoke softly. "Maybe I'll find my fuckin' truck."

Nathan stepped out from the shadows and into the sunlight. When He did, he screeched in pain. The sun was so bright it blinded him temporarily. Involuntarily closing his eyes, he blindly searched around for the shade until he found an old tall Cyprus. Slowly opening his eyes to the pain-free murky canopy Nathan beheld a glamorous fresh world for the very first time.

"Wow, did I drop LSD or did I have too much to drink?" He scoffed to himself; of course not!

He put his hand to his forehead to shield out the sun and trudged on. He began smelling sweet sap in the distance, chains rattling from excited dogs all around him, blowing leaves from the trees and noticed the smell of stale trash. The faint smell of motor oil in front of him and the smell of Chinese food wafted through the air behind him told him the geography of the city as if his mind had a GPS system built inside. He had no problems finding his truck.

After he returned home Nathan bounced into his comfy bed but rest eluded him with a frantic knocking. With the toss of his covers he headed out to answer the front door. Nathan grasped the handle opened the screen door to find his weary friend. David's hollow animalistic eyes softened. In an instant an unspoken bond developed from the two infected friends. David made himself at home in the separate garage as they consoled one another.

20

The capsized barge and her murdered crew were swept out to the Gulf of Mexico never to be seen again. As the days, then weeks, progressed the people of Royal Bay marched on with their lives as if the surreal events were just a distant dream. The infected returned to their jobs, back to their families. Royal Bay residents staggered on about their lives as if the strange events never happened.

The full moon's appearance across the sky could be foretold by the flood of news reports featuring Pointe Coupee General Hospital on the

Internet and radio, and marked increase in personnel at the Hospital. This full Moon resulted in the inflicted with the mysterious disease walking out of the Hospital. Since last month's full Moon the hospital had an increase in researchers to uncover the recent rash of violent outbreaks. The hospital called in geneticists to track down the still yet unknown beast. Three weeks' worth of genetic tests had resulted in failure after failure so far. Six tests just yielded only human DNA and two specimens somehow were deemed "contaminated" thought to be a mixture of human and canine. Vehicle after vehicle now pulled into the parking lot and every slot stayed full twenty-four-seven, bursting at the seams to accommodate the employee only area. Personnel had a steady increase since the mauling's from a yet unknown animal. There were whispers about the disappearance of Dr. Jacobs.

At the same time the full moon progressed, in a different neighborhood Col. Miller and Sgt. Adam Alexander, who now had all of his limbs, gathered an Army of the displaced and homeless. They transformed into a Wolf-like state, each one different from the other depending on the physiological anomalies and how long the parasite had progressed as the full moon arose once. For three days they were on the hunt but when the full Moon waned they were human again and the growing packs slumbering in the safety of the overpass homeless encampment.

Meanwhile, Lou clung to Viddarr's coat tails and watched his every movement, learned from him. Bobby and Terry went home to their mother and father, who were separated from one another. The boys headed off to separate schools, one of them at the private Catholic High School of Pointe Coupee, home of the track and field stars, the hornets-the other boy going to school at Livonia High School in Batchelor, LA., though they were apart somehow they knew each other's emotions, at night they dreamed wild lupine dreams.

Steve prowled just short of the marshlands in the rustic area alone, giving rise to the reports of wild boar loose in the Pointe Coupee Parish. Aticus, Lance, Tonya, the youngling Tracy, and a sickly Alex Seller, who was a glorified ghoul running a perilous fever, were overtaking unincorporated rural shacks in a circle like a tightening noose.

As the days progressed the hospital quieted down clearing out patients with a clean bill of health. The CDC acknowledged an infection but gave Pointe Coupee hospital an all-clear. The tests indicated no smallpox, bubonic plague, or even leprosy, so rumors of a rabid animal were more and more likely, but without an animal or body to confirm it they were only rumors.

21

The rain had largely put an end to the raging fires at the Asher house. The fire trucks had little more left to do than put out the stubborn brushfires that had not realized their time was up. As soon as it was safe to move about, police and reporters swarmed the scene.

For several months arsons plagued unincorporated trailers, shacks and houses. Seller's house, the old Lux house, and the Traiteur trailer burned to the foundations. Now the Asher house burning and abandoned. The weeds had grown to the top of the windows and a sea of grass engulfed the rock driveway, long neglected by its owners.

Captain Rogers surveyed the area, pushing his shades down low on his rounded nose. He had hard, stern features that showed little proof of his age. He was a shapely man in his late-30s. His light brown eyes were grim as he surveyed the scene.

"Oh brother," He shook his head in frustration; Captain Rogers already juggled the shooting and bizarre disappearance of the nudist for his friend, detective Jenkins. This latest arson weighed heavy on his shoulders.

He headed toward the charred, badly damaged door. Let me guess, sigils drawn hectically all over the wall. Then there would be one silver slug in the victim's decapitated head. Accelerant poured in a perfect circle all over the body and lit, so inefficient. The marks and sigils upon wall then the ritualized corpse worried Captain Rogers. He suspected that there is more than one suspect in Pointe Coupee Parish. He should have been used to the carnage. Alex Seller and Tracy's disappearance and the arson crime scenes of the Lux family, the children missing and the parents decapitated, all in his parish. However, Captain Rogers knew this and missing family and the victim, Nate Asher; he went to high school with him and recognized the mouth full of gold fillings right away.

Rogers brushed the sheen of sweat from his forehead and prominent chin with a handkerchief from his pocket. Damn the heat, late summer, Deep South on a lonely dead end road the sweltering swamplands in the distance were boiling up hot enough to fry eggs, he could hardly breathe in his bulletproof vest and dark blue uniform but he had a job to do.

He noticed the face of Amy Anderson in the corner of his eye and cringed inwardly. She was a young reporter, rather petite, with fiery red hair, a narrow face and straight nose. Her unique looks set her apart from the other reporters. Amy, lately, had relentlessly followed him to every crime scene. She wasted her talents with writing for a hometown newspaper turned garbage tabloid called *The Eclipse.*

He had joined the Louisiana state police department for the best interests of his wife Susan, because of her failing health, ill from leukemia and his young daughter, Hannah. The pay was outstanding and he got the medical benefits his wife so desperately needed, benefits which his last job had refused him, racking up extreme debt. Irritable and preoccupied with the astronomical medical bills he found a release in a steamy physical affair partly due to the lack of intimacy that his wife could not provide. But he neglected the needs of his young daughter. Thankfully Suzan's chemotherapy and surgery was a complete success, so much so she went into remission, was cancer free, and came home two months early, forcing him back into a sense of normalcy. He even broke off his love affair with the young reporter.

He was certainly in no mood for her constant badgering. Not today. He ducked past a volunteer uniformed fireman as her shrill voice called out his name. He felt a hand on his shoulder, and froze like a deer caught in the headlights. She had him. Grumbling under his breath he turned to face her.

"Captain Rogers." she huffed, nearly out of breath. "There were some questions I wanted to ask you." She flashed him a smile," how about it?" holding her digital recorder up.

Amy often wondered what choices' brought her to this point in her life. She'd always loved to be a writer, but she wanted to be a fiction novelist, not a person that wrote fiction-based news reports for *The Eclipse.* She had even left town for a while to pursue a journalistic career, but she just wasn't happy with the dull facts and specifics. She needed a more creative outlet for her imaginative mind. She stumbled onto *The Eclipse.* It was a well-respected newspaper in its time until the digital age made the printed page a dinosaur, about extinct. Until a shift in their format to sensational news on the net brought it back from the brink. She could come back home and work from her house and just mail in the stories, rarely having to make an actual appearance there herself.

That smile, Captain Rogers thought, got her into more restricted places than he could count, even his heart. He looked up and his eyes flashed hot with anger. The last bit of information he had given to her she'd turned into a fictional tale of man-eating monsters and full moons. In certain circles it had even been suggested that all these recent murders were done by some kind of cult. He despised those who twisted the right of free speech and used it to write such trash; still, seeing her again made his heart skip a beat…

"Captain Thompson Rogers, do you have any new leads on the identities of the savages?" She turned the recorder uncomfortably toward his face.

Capt. Rogers cringed at his horrible first name and Amy Anderson's casual use of it. Her question had not changed since the arsons began. She had almost seemed interested in stopping this assumed cult that had first appeared in the area several months ago. If not for the smut that she wrote, he'd almost believed her to be sincere.

He fixed a blank expression to his face and remained silent, stewing. The answer was obvious, but she still stood at the ready, recorder in hand, and eyes watching him closely. A couple of months had passed and no closer to having a suspect.

Realizing she wasn't going to take the hint, he turned to her. "Miss Anderson." With his professional visage to mask his love for her, eyes vacant, he said in a monotone voice, "No leads." He fumbled for a pair of latex gloves and put his right hand up to signal her to stop.

"This area is a restricted!" He yelled turning and entering the residence.

Immediately inside he choked from the soot, ash, and smoke-filled room. His eyes watered as he caught the acrid smell of urine. A flat screen TV hung, relatively undamaged, on the back wall of the living room. Two couches and a love seat, though smoke damaged and singed, also survived. He scratched his head in confusion. It looked as though The Asher's hadn't moved anywhere. That or they had left everything behind.

The walls were filled with graffiti, arcane images and languages that he didn't understand. Fuck, he thought, it was going to be the same. He made his way down the steadily darkening floorboards leading to the bedroom, knowing what he would find. The corpse was badly burned, so much so it was hard to make out if it was male or female. Its arms were outstretched, appearing to reach out to Rogers. The skeletal remains of the head rested on his hips. He quickly cupped his palm to his mouth in an effort to stop the vomit coming up from his throat. After a brief moment of slow breathing, he was steady enough to take his digital camera from his pocket, to document the crime scene. The beheading, arcane images and a clear view of a gun wound to the head, Déjà vu all over again. A couple of quick flashes with his camera and he then he got on his radio to put in a call for the coroner.

Amy watched as the new coroner brought out a body bag from the blackened structure. Her mouth dropped open slightly as the burnt remains were loaded on the ambulance. Impatiently waiting for the Captain to finish, she reached a shaky hand for her cigarettes and lighter.

Her nerves were steadier now as she exhaled smoke out of her lungs. Flicking her cigarette, she saw something and paused. What was it? She wandered closer was it a large dog or maybe a wolf's paw print. Carefully squishing down the butt of her cigarette, being cautious not to disturb the crime scene, she hunched down to get a closer look. The recent rain made the earth soft, soft enough to preserve tracks. One, two, three, four and five...She fumbled for her cell phone and snapped a picture as Captain Rogers came out the door, surprising her.

"Captain Rogers!" Her voice cracked as she ran to catch up to him.

He reluctantly stopped and sighed, under his breath he said, "Say, Ms. Anderson, what is it I can do for you now?"

She suddenly gotten tongue-tied, she didn't tell him about the animal tracks leading off into the woods. She was briefly entertaining the thought of letting him view the prints but thought better of it. He was looking for men, not their pets. Still, she couldn't shake the felling that the paw prints were involved in some way or another.

She steadied her nerve, "Do you think it's the same suspects?"

Against his own better judgment he answered her. "I'm not supposed to comment on any ongoing case, but your rag doesn't have any readers anyway," she could hear disdain in his voice," yes, it seems to be the same people."

"Look at this." And against her better judgment she showed Capt. Rogers the paw print photos hoping it would grease the wheels of conversation.

He took the cell phone halfheartedly from her hand. He examined the photo then hesitated before finally giving back her phone. He hated to admit it, but the silver bullets, cutting off of heads, archaic symbols... and now dog tracks, he could almost see why she wrote what she wrote in her last article. And he'd die before admitting it, but he thought she had written in an extremely professional manner, in his opinion she wasted her time writing for that rag *The Eclipse*.

Captain Rogers looked out beyond the woods, deep in thought, unaware of watchful eyes staring back at him. "Maybe you're right.... Maybe they're religious fanatics but do me a favor and postpone your next story until I say so." It was more of an order than a request.

Amy had a funny feeling like she was being watched. A white albino wolf fervently stood in the distance and watched as the policeman went about their business unaware of him. Montezu's Wolf form had caught a whiff of the reporter three houses back and instead of meeting up with his pack he observed the reporter. Crouched on his haunches taking in the information in front of him, careful not to wag his tail or switch an ear from flying pests circling around his body.

Montezu's powerful limbs, stout shoulders and immense chest made the prey plentiful and easily available to him through the years even with the drawbacks of his brilliant white fur from muzzle to tail. As soon as Aticus' howling began night after night, his lupine nature took over and so did a fiercely loyal pack mentality. He headed off to the Gulf of Mexico region, tail wagging all the way eager to be socially accepted after years of self-imposed isolation.

A continuing low-pitched aria caught Montezu's attention in the south Texas area between the Mexican and United States border. He had just recently crossed the Louisiana border and entered into Pointe Coupee Parish when he had caught the scent of his blossoming pack but curiosity got the better of him. He had seen three houses now lit like kindling with the strong aroma of an alpha male left behind at the scenes of all. The aria made it quite clear what his duties and obligations were as well as the plans.

The white Wolf shadowed over bushes and overgrown branches jockeying to get the best view of the crime scene across the street. A taxi cab struggled to make its way along a dirt road full of potholes obscuring his view of Captain Rogers and Amy Anderson. The team wrapped up without spotting the brilliant white Wolf hidden in the brush.

22

Raccourci Island, LA

Louisiana, home of the grand, majestic, mysterious New Orleans and the infamous Mardi Gras held every year. However, it was not time for

Mardi Gras. Sarah excitedly peered out the cab window heading north away from the Gulf of Mexico clutching what looked like crumpled old papers in her hand.

The Deep South laid claim to arguably some of the most magnificent plantations in the world, especially Louisiana. Like The Myrtles Plantation in St. Francisville, Louisiana, near Baton Rouge. Listed on the National Register of Historic Places, the plantation is a bed and breakfast now and it offers historical and mystery-filled tours. Or the Butler-Greenwood plantation, established in 1796, the house built in 1810. Most of these places were just a glorified tourist paradise and bed-and-breakfast mecca. In fact dozens of homes dotted Louisiana's landscapes. But little is known about the Gerome plantation. A sprawling estate just past Green Lake in the middle of Raccourci Island concealed by an almost circular river, dozens of swamps, small lakes and Cyprus trees.

Bang! Then a jolt that made her hands find the armrest in the taxi's passenger doors. She thought the suspension would break, the shocks would seize up, or the tires would fall off at any second. She and the car bounced around like a mechanical bull with the setting on high.

"You okay, Madame?"

The taxi driver looked to be in his mid-40s, his cheek bones protruding like they were going to burst out of his caramel colored and wrinkled skin. His black eyes just two slits like coal but vigilant, on the watch for wildlife going astray and wondering onto what passed as a street. A wiry black man with close-cropped, fine black curls on top of his head. As the taxi struggled on she herself was imagining what the African-American taxi driver had originally wanted to do with his life.

"I'm alright, but thank you for asking."

As the taxi headed toward its destination the rocking back and forth on the old makeshift wooden bridge, full of nervous anticipation, Sarah began to feel nauseous. She glanced out her window while clutching a beautiful gem necklace, her family heirloom given to her while just an infant, the only clue to her biological family. It had been tossed around from one foster family to the other but survived. Twisting her necklace unconsciously, a habit she relied on since she was young to soothe her anxiety. Regrettably, there were no sides on the bridge protecting her from the rising water so she closed her eyes and thought pleasant thoughts. It was amazing that she was about to own land now. An unknown benefactor in her biological family, she supposed, had willed her the plantation. She fidgeted with the hem of her dress, staring out the window at the scenery, the trees getting thicker and the roads were getting bumpier the closer she got to her house. Sarah opened up her compact to freshen up a little. She had ivory skin and a baby face; her wide green eyes gave the impression of surprise and her small cupid's bow lips curved up in a smile with long raven-like black hair that completed the visage.

"Roads are gettin' rough," the taxi driver said.

He squinted at her in the rearview mirror. Making conversation because the long drive had been so silent the taxi driver could not stand it anymore. She was beautiful, with a petite nose and pixie ears. He caught himself looking in the mirror a lot at her.

"Yeah," she said in a raspy voice, "and I bet it's just going to be getting even worse."

Distracted, fumbling in her purse, she did not have a clue that the taxi driver took more time staring at her than looking at the road as they lurched and bumped along.

"So," he said with a thick southern drawl, "are you from around these parts?" Noticing she don't talk with a southern accent.

She was taken aback and somewhat offended, "I'm not really from around here." she said sarcastically, "but apparently my ancestors resided here for years."

"No offense Miss, it's just that no one comes back here that doesn't live here." His cheeks reddened with embarrassment.

"None taken," her face softened up a bit. After all, he was just making conversation she realized. He was just being nice.

She had been smart; living on her own she finished high school and got into college, contact with her foster parents had been sporadic at best. She was surprised when she heard a knock on the door. A mysterious lawyer said Sarah was the long-lost relative of the Malstros' plantation, a sprawling Raccourci Island landscape. He had given the deed to her along with his number.

As a struggling college student it came as a blessing of sorts to hear of this windfall. She already had $40,000 in debt from credit card bills. She had to borrow $10,000 just one month ago when her car was repossessed. Almost three months late on her rent now. Mysterious as though it may be, it's like she won the lottery.

"Has nobody been to this place?" She leaned forward to ask him, her hands gripping the back of the passenger seat. The taxi driver was delighted and at the same time nervous at her sudden closeness.

"No ma'am," nervously clearing his throat, "not since I was young I think, that is."

She sat back again, her elbows on her thighs, and touched her index finger to her lips in a quizzical fashion. How profitable is this property? She wondered. She imagined herself self-sufficient and rich enough that she didn't have too ever work again. Property, she thought, was her ticket out of debt.

After what was an uncomfortable silence again, she saw the farmhouse just off the road. It wasn't a farmhouse exactly, she thought, more like a whitewashed mansion gone gray with age straight out of "*Gone with the Wind*". She smiled slyly as she fancied herself Scarlet.

The taxi pulled up and stopped in the driveway, turning grit and dust into the air. Through the haze of dust she stared up in amazement at the house. It was a turn of the last century mansion, complete with ornate pillars spanning the porch, an old wooden swing and doubled doors. Dirty, needing repair, and signs that it suffered a fire were obvious but Sarah fell in love with it anyway.

"Thank you, I am fine from here," Sarah shoved a fist full of dollars, including a generous tip in the taxi driver's hand, "thank you, I have friends coming, and I'll be fine."

From the massive yard Sarah looked in the bay window from outside dark soot was prevalent throughout. What seemed like a century's worth of dust and cobwebs crisscrossed the porch. In the shadows a black widow spun a grasshopper, a snack for later, in-between the columns on the porch. The six columns grayed with age, paint cracking and peeling from neglect, stretched upwards to the second floor's lattice balcony. The columns themselves greatly exaggerated the half octagon concrete structure. Sarah approached cautiously, as if any further she would suddenly wake up, the bubble would pop and the dream would end. She would be back in her cramped roach infested seventh floor apartment. She steadied herself, feeling dizzy from all that was impressed upon her, and took in the sights all around her.

Birds were chirping from a nest in a nearby cypress tree. A warm Southern breeze blew by which reminded Sarah of honeysuckle and wildflowers. She closed her eyes and let the noonday sun warm her face. Being an orphan tossed from foster house to foster house now she could settle down safe and secure. So beautiful she thought, even in its dilapidated form!

She took her shoes off then strolled around lazily so the overgrown grass tickled her calves, a reminder that she was not just dreaming. She stopped in the shade of the large cypress tree before catching her breath and fumbling for the ornate master key. She could see seared planks on the porch that spread out to the doorway and abruptly stopping feet from the upstairs steps. Taking her back in time she imagined gunshots, cannons exploding. Another time to a war fought brother versus brother. Then she stepped on the porch and entered the estate. Sarah hesitated at the scorched foyer before continuing on to the living room.

"Frankly my dear, I don't give a damn!" She says as she excitedly thumbed her Blackberry smart phone to check how far away her friends were yet.

She finished her text then pressed send. Satisfied that her message was received she proceeded to wander around the manor again. She gingerly touched with one fingernail the once impressive and expensive couch, now a former shadow of its once glorious self. The satins and silks had all but fell away revealing the rotting wooden structure. Surprisingly the cushions were still intact and she imagined herself again as Scarlett O'Hara. As Scarlett she could lie down to rest her legs but she caught herself before she had the impulse to flop down. She imagined 100+ years of dust and grime floating through the air.

Just before the entrance to the dining room an old portrait caught her eyes. It was a hand painted portrait. The young woman standing between them really had piqued her interest. Although she had blond hair and soft blue eyes it was a spitting image of Sarah, albeit slightly younger. As if she stared through the mirror of time.

"I'll be damned," Sarah grinned ear to ear, "the old coop wasn't lying, and I am a long-lost relative!"

This time she couldn't help herself. The portrait that hung on the same wall for probably over a hundred years was off and in her hands. She turned it on its back looking for a signature or name, Alicia-1840. Definitely her blood she thought still mesmerized at the eerie similarities as she unconsciously touched her face.

She turned her attention now to the upstairs and the bedrooms. Still holding the portrait she moved slowly and methodically through each room until she came upon a quaint sign that read "Alicia" In block letters on the door.

She stopped suddenly in the middle of what she assumed was Alicia's room, aware for the first time the eerie silence enveloping the house. She instinctively walked forward to the rocker in the middle of the room and sat down. She sighed with relief as the repetitive squeaking sound the chair made broke up the quiet all around her. Her anxiety lessening as she stared at her reflection in the vanity mirror on the wall, imagining herself as Alicia with golden hair. Until the floorboards groaned and creaked, the unexpected noise shot her up to her feet once again.

A cracked board jutted out from the rest of the floor. Sarah moved the rocking chair out of her way and removed the plank loosening three more boards, which Sarah promptly tore away as well. Sarah's eyes widened, for a split second she was sure she saw a gilded book. Yes, she thought, it was definitely a book but now she saw just a boulder hidden underneath the floorboards. A strange place to hide a rock she thought. She stared intently at the rock for a while, until curiosity got the better of her and she hesitantly reached out to feel what looked like a solid object.

"No, I'm sure of it, I saw a book... I'm not crazy." She whispered to herself mustering up the courage to lift the rock.

As soon as she lifted the rock it turned to dust revealing what she was sure she saw in the first place, an expensive looking gilded diary. She hurriedly pressed the diary to her stomach as if pressing it closely might keep the diary from turning to dust just like the strange boulder had. It was peculiar, but she had suffered a lot of bumps during her ride here she giggled to herself.

A horn blared repeatedly from somewhere outside shaking her back to reality. Sarah wiped with one hand the years of dust and grime from the side window where the noise had come from so she could see out, all the while grasping with the other hand the diary with white-knuckled intensity. Her ride and her friends were almost up the drive to the plantation, stirring up dust hitting on the horn all the way. The white van was almost tan from dust and debris as it wobbled through the winding dirt road. The tires bouncing around as the van found pothole after pothole but the driver refused to reduce his break neck speed. Sarah trotted down the stairs and out the door as the van pulled up.

"Hey beautiful," the driver, Tommy, yelled out.

Tommy had his head out the window. He looked like a happy puppy going for his first car ride with his wild long, blond hair waving in the wind with a wide grin on his face. He was obviously happy to see Sarah. Sarah reflexively grimaced, shuffled her feet in the dirt and looked down to the ground.

"Hey." She said meekly.

When she first found out about the inheritance, plantation, and subsequent road trip she had told her close friends, hoping they would tag along so she had a ride back home. The prospects of New Orleans had her roommates excited and they were on board instantly. Unfortunately someone had told her on and off again boyfriend, Tommy, too.

"Great, this will be fun." She muttered softly under her breath as she nodded to her friends Desiree, Roxy, Tina, A.J., Garrett, Jac, and finally Tequila, avoiding eye contact with Tom.

"Yeah, we're in New Orleans, this is going to be a blast!" Tequila yelled out excitedly, oblivious to the fact that Sarah was being sarcastic. She slid the door open and offered Sarah a hand up into the van.

She boarded the Van unaware of a strange eye glinting in the sunlight, one emerald wolf's eye that sparkled in the fading rays. It's shape hidden by raven black fur and shadows. The van was between Sarah and the house, obstructing its view of her, but it was watching the van intensely until it pulled away.

Aticus waited in the shadows until the dust cloud from the van settle and he could no longer see taillights. His wolf-self emerged cautiously from the brush. Still weary from the freighter ride he had to take across the ocean. Travel by airplane wasn't possible. One unlucky lycanthrope learned the hard way a half a century ago when the sudden rise in altitude made him spontaneously change startling every passenger aboard the plane. The wolf sat on his haunches taking it's time transforming back to a man. Like an awful stretch all of Aticus' nerves on overload, the muscles quivered and rippled from paws to shoulders. Paws turned to fur covered claws fur receding and lengthening until they resembled hands. His shoulders stretched back and popped until human arms again. Aticus' muzzle receded revealing a mouth with a twisted funhouse grin. His spine dislocated and popped into place again. The last thing, his tail, which slithered around and receded, and he stood erect with his bare skin shivering until he got used to his nakedness. The whole transformation took less than a split second but still slower than normal, still acclimatizing his form again.

His heart was still racing from the nearness of the plantation, the plantation that he became obsessed with since the loss of his eye and the loss of his love. The plantation he had been dreaming of for months now. He had been dreaming of Alicia who whispered to him in the night, whispering her undying love for him. In his dreams, she whispered that she had come back to the living. That she needed him to come back to the plantation. He had traveled so far because of the dreams. However, a cruel cynical world, crippling headaches from silver poisoning, and more wars had all but hardened him. He couldn't shake his childhood; mother, brother, and sister were all dead. Humans had hunted packs and invaded dens until they were almost extinct so by reflection the lycanthropes were always in hiding and on the run. He was tired of it and thirsty for vengeance, the blood of man. He decided he would wage war on man.

Aticus' ears perked up from the rustling sound coming from just behind him. He didn't turn around. It was Lance; he knew it from the musky scent. Lance, like Aticus, was also wholly human and naked as a jaybird, but you couldn't tell it from looking at him from the caked-on mud that covered him from head to toe.

Lance loved being lycanthrope, and all the benefits that came with being Wolf, splashing around in puddles, chasing snakes and rabbits, feeling the wind through his fur. He had decided long ago Aticus' attack on him and subsequent infection was the best thing to happen to him since he was born and he would gladly follow Aticus to hell and back if he was asked.

Lance slowly strolled up to Aticus, now basking in the heat of the sun on his tall naked frame. Aticus turned to face him and laughed out loud instinctively. Lance was so caked in mud and grime you couldn't even make out his slim features. Only a break in the mud in one or two places could you see his freckled body. Even his red hair was caked gray.

"Chasing a beaver," He shrugged matter-of-factly, "It took me to the edge of the bog before I caught up to him!" He cracked a fanged smile.

"Mark the four corners of the barn. The others should be in the country in a month and I do not want them to be lost. Make it strong. When we are finished here I'm going back to the trailer to wait for Tomas, who just arrived in Louisiana." Aticus instructed.

Aticus was in a completely different world remembering dreams about Alicia but he would not be diverted from his master plan. After he had a good look at the plantation itself he would go back to the trailer. With Tonya and the owner of the trailer, a fledgling called Michael, they were almost done mixing a fabled formula. Before his Grandmother left him she taught the secret ingredients for the mixture called Wolf's Blood.

He did not wait for Lance to respond to the orders he had given him, leaping towards the wild lawn. Running on two legs he clumsily sped toward the house. He didn't even break his stride as he tore through the unlocked door and up the stairs.

In Aticus' lucid dreams he was upstairs with Alicia as she opened the floorboards to reveal her diary, gold inlaid hardback diary. She held Aticus and pressed her lips against his in an impassioned embrace. Then she placed the diary back underneath the floorboards.

His heart fluttered and the sudden stop made him slide across the floor of her room. The fur stood up in excitement, the boards were tossed to the sides and the hiding place was empty, it wasn't just a dream, he thought, Alicia had come home.

Aticus tried to spontaneously transform his arm into a lupine paw, wincing in pain as he did so. He looked at the graying mansion and decided he wanted to seamlessly transform pain free before formal introductions would be made.

Lance transformed into a hybrid Wolf and slowly trudged through the thickets before he found the barn. The dirt trail had spurted grasses and thick ivies. The barn itself safely ensconced in weeping Juniper and willow trees that had grown tall and strong with time.

The barn would serve as a base of operations once Viddarr's Mystic runes had been cast that would conceal the whole of the structure. Lance hiked his leg up and urinated on the fourth and final corner when a howl caught his attention. His ears perked to a low baritone howl, Aticus' crooning giving him more instructions.

The translated orders amounted to, *"Lance follow the van."*

23

The Van left the makeshift driveway and Tommy smiled and remarked, "Boy, I'm sure glad to be leaving that shithole! What do you think that godforsaken place is worth, Sarah?"

Tommy turned toward Sarah who deliberately turned away from him and lowered her head, pretending to fumble for the newfound diary turning page after page. Purposely avoiding Tommy's gaze she said under her breath,

"It is decrepit, I agree with that, I know I was excited about selling the place, but now…"

"I checked the Internet and with the current real estate market in Louisiana, we could make bank if you sold it, Sarah." Tommy informed Sarah.

The creases in his forehead deepened and his wide eyes turned into slits of frustration; intermittently he stared at Sarah trying to get her attention while at the same time trying to watch the road. This infuriated him even further when he noticed she was not paying attention to him but instead reading through the pages of her ancestors' book.

"I don't know, Tommy." She said softly, without even tearing her eyes from the diary she had been reading, "Besides, when I talked to the lawyer things were not finalized yet." She didn't even address the "We" aspect of his comment, unwilling to talk more than she absolutely had to.

Sarah could hear Tommy muttering something under his breath. She pretended Tommy's filthy mouth had been intended for the huge pothole that racked the van but she knew it was intended for her. Bracing her for the back and forth rocking of the vehicle, like an ocean dweller on a stormy sea, her eyes locked onto the pages of one of Alicia's inner thoughts.

She glanced through a sampling a bit of her diary, ***"I found him quite by accident, just bird watching and enjoying one quiet, warm, pleasant day. A start came over me, at this tree line just near to the river's edge. I thought I saw the green glowing eyes and Raven black fur of a huge predator…*** Skipping through pages, ***"…I my eyes shut tight to wait for the inevitable attack…"*** a pothole distracted her.

Sarah skipped through pages until picking yet another place and reading aloud, ***"…I braced myself and began to pray. However, it was not talons or the claws of an animal; I felt his delicate warm human hands upon me…"*** She said to herself, as Roxy touched her shoulder, breaking her concentration.

"Hey Sarah," Roxy said, a half Korean, half Latino mix which made her stick out from the rest of the group but in a good way, always the life of the party and a close confidant of Sarah's. She leaned in and whispered, "I noticed you seemed a little shocked when you saw Tommy. If it helps, I'll room with you when we find a motel, if you want."

Roxy had been a fixture in Sarah's life since freshman year. Sarah closed the book to look towards Roxy's infectious smile. Roxy's slender and short stature, her sleepy blue eyes, round face, caramel complexion and voluptuous rosy lips made Sarah laugh when she crocked her head from side to side with one eyebrow raised in an inquisitive fashion.

The close quarters of the van began to cramp Tequila's legs; she stretched out her legs and put them on the laps of the three passengers sitting next to her. The annoyance gave way to acceptance with her impish smile. She was oblivious to AJ and Garrett's reddening faces as she searched through the pockets of her deliberately low cut jean shorts for her blackberry.

Tommy gave up trying to get Sarah's attention and now he observed the dirt path while intermittently beating the fragile GPS in frustration as he navigated down the unfamiliar road for the third time. He wrinkled his nose at the thickening smoke billowing forth from the back of the van. Once in a while in a straightaway he snuck a peek at Sarah as she stared out the side view window daydreaming and oblivious to him.

"Hey I found a perfect place." Tequila exclaimed, she had been staring at her BlackBerry like a zombie but now she excitedly waved her BlackBerry around trying the group's attention, "look, it is perfect! The rooms all have their own kitchenettes and everything!"

Tequila slid off the vinyl seat and hit Tommy's back playfully to get his attention. Tommy tried his best to ignore her. His response came before he ever even seen the glowing view of Point Breeze Motel. "Yep, yeah, sure, whenever we get out of this damn forsaken maze that place sounds nice, Tequila..." He said just to appease her as he rolled his eyes.

Making a game of annoying Tommy she purposely moved uncomfortably closer to him, putting her right arm on his shoulder and her left arm, with the BlackBerry, purposely in his face until he was forced to acknowledge her presence with an uneasy smile.

"Yeah, yeah I see it Tequila!"

Jac and Garrett, both brothers, had always had an infatuation for Tequila. They were friends with AJ, who was friends with Sarah, who was friends with Tequila. When the chance arose to take a road trip, the three musketeers as they called themselves jumped at the chance. Roxy opened a side window in the rear of the van and lit up a cigarette. The group bellowed out an annoyed protest in unison but Roxy was oblivious.

"Roxy," Desiree silently tried to get her attention. "The van is overcrowded and cramped already, please stop the chain smoking."

Luggage stacked up like a game of Jenga, Tina and Jac, lovers, took up the middle couch seat. They were locked in an intimate embrace oblivious of the quarrels and the group. Roxy and Desiree brought up the rear of the van. Their legs were curled up in a ball so the luggage would fit; their backs resting uncomfortably on either side, their arms resting on the rear tire fenders. Desiree and Roxy coming had been an afterthought, when Sarah found out there were more men than women going with her she frantically tried to find schoolmates to even out the uneven ratio.

The jarring jolt from the progressively deepening potholes quieted the group suddenly. They traveled in irritated silence for the majority of the trip. Sarah stared out absent mindedly at the view of the river to her right. Four left turns and her family estate could be seen in the background once more releasing a collective grumble from the group as they were still hopelessly lost.

Sarah stopped reading for a moment to look out at the scenery. The miles upon miles of greenery and the unique fragrances of honeysuckle, fresh Tributaries, and warm lake waters comforted Sarah's soul and somehow reminding her of her dreams running carefree through the grasses and the weeping Juniper. Unaware of Lance's wolf, visible as a red streak as it hurdled through the weeds and the obstacles on all fours, concealed by the trees, easily keeping pace with its prey, the white Van.

However, a white wolf burst out from the river's edge to stalk the stalker. He had glowing golden eyes, a red sigil tattoo on his muzzle. Virgin white furred abdomen and in contrast to the white fur an obsidian black diamond-shape on his belly. He had stalked tiny elusive pray for millennia. So he easily kept up with the bumbling huge red Wolf with an odor that assaulted his senses.

Weekly obsessive howling sparked Devon's curiosity. He felt a stirring in the air, smelt a new pack emerging. He had searched for three days, feverishly investigating for other signs of hiding places of the growing infected… Track marks, dead carcasses, anything that would tell him how many there were, where, and how large the unknown blasphemous pack had gown, finding trailers, houses and shacks. Now he stealthily tracked the crimson wolf now.

The Lycanthropes were driven to hide out; they were forced to live in the shadows of humanity, driven to the brink of extinction hundreds of years ago. Devon and most of the Lycanthropes were peaceful by nature, driven into hiding, they spent their days frolicking, chasing, hunting small game and napping. With little interaction with man, humankind all but forgot the werewolf, they were found now only in the recesses of the mind and imagination. And that's the way Devon liked it. That is why it worried him so, Aticus emerging from the shadows with his hordes.

The van driving a straight shot on the interstate boredom had gotten the better of the group and they were at each other's throats by the time they finally made it to New Roads. A twenty-two mile trip but the beat-up van had been lost in the back roads and marshes for hours. Finally finding its way back to civilization the van slowly made it past the Pointe Coupee general hospital and onto the Point Breeze Motel and Lakeside Kitchenette Apartments.

Sarah noted four hunters laughing and joking amongst another, seated and stretched out on the end of an open tailgate, waiting for their leader with guns in hand. Gung ho for whatever beast might be terrorizing the neighborhood. Sarah felt a chill come over her and she clutched the old diary closer to her breasts. Guns scared the hell out of her; guns, booze, and paranoia were certainly a dangerous combination.

Chet Vandal, a self-declared swamp rat, had come from Mississippi spillway to Pointe Coupee. He heard somewhere that the Pointe Coupee Perish was offering a bounty for the animal responsible for the growing uneasiness. Finishing his sixth beer before pumping his shotgun he gave an easy glance at Sarah as the group of ragtag college students passed by.

Sarah had no time to think about the potential horrors as the van turned another corner she could see a sign for Point Breeze Motel a few miles away. The van came alive again with excited conversation. The van turned onto a paved road, badly needing repair, snaking past the False River's edge until they were at their destination.

Devon's white wolf form stopped just past the interstate and before human domain, watching the other wolf from behind. Lance stopped and looked in the distance beyond the lake, his superhuman hearing making out every whisper. Now almost human, a wolf-man in appearance with a smashed-down elongated black nose made for an extremely short muzzle-like visage. Red fur completely covered his entire bare body giving him a shadowy appearance. Only the glowing red eyes gave away the stalker's position. To the human eye the tiny groups across the Lake made for a colorful blur, but Lance's eyes were not human. He could hone in on the lake like an Eagle's eye, and turned his attention to Sarah, the target of his master's obsession.

24

Sarah stood out on the sundeck awestruck by the view. For almost two weeks the group muddled around to clean up the Malstros decrepit mansion's façade as her friends gauged a monetary value in doing so, Sarah fell in love with the place. Sarah had just gotten off her cell with her mysterious benefactor. Then she turned to view the apartments. She couldn't help loving the landscape and admired row after row of hotel rooms, one room directly against the other the rooms shared an interior wall. She walked up the steps to a stilted porch and her desired room and walked in. Sarah smiled at the quaint, square-shaped accommodations. Featuring kitchenettes of quality crafted cabinetry and a sunny, comfortable openness, she finally opened the backdoor and come out to the extended decks, and swimming piers. She could see her and her friends staying in relative comfort forever with the benefactor's sizable weekly allowance.

Desiree had walked the length of the beautiful property, just as Sarah opened the room door to come outside.

"It is a lovely place." Desiree said, "Thinking about moving here?" referring to Sarah's inherited property.

Sarah shyly smiled and nodded, confessing, "Yes, I have been thinking about it."

Four adjacent screen doors opened from cabins and Roxy, A.J., Garrett, Tequila and Tommy stepped out in to the adjoining covered deck. Except for Tina and Jac, the love birds, who were sleeping in together oblivious to the group.

As Lance did every day while Aticus dealt with more pressing matters, the red wolf lay concealed, lying on his forearms in mud and thickets, his red colored fur camouflaged against the crimson clay of the river bank, snooping on Sarah and the group. The wind turned, suddenly filling his moist snout with Sarah's intoxicating and seductive scent. He knew the orders were only observe, but the sweet fragrance that Sarah unwittingly gave off was too much for Lance to endure.

Salivating uncontrollably, Lance's curved fangs glinting in the sun, his tongue protruded out of his muzzle in expectation. His massive lupine head turned from side to side all the while eyes fixated tracking his target, Sarah. His paws splashed in the mud and puddles as he locked onto the aroma of the other women. He steadily picked up his pace galloping the five-hundred yards towards where Sarah, Desiree, Roxy, Tequila, Tommy, AJ, and Garrett stood on the porch. The red Wolf progressed no further, fearing that the soft recently mowed and manicured lawn offered him no concealment, and he waited, biding his time until Sarah would be by herself... an opportune time to strike.

Looking out over False River Lake, once a part of the powerful Mississippi, but cut off from the river long ago, the fish were plentiful. AJ gripped one of the fishing poles he had gotten out of the back of the van and remarked, "Well, I'm sure not going to waste this day fixing up real estate when there is plenty of fishin' to be had!"

AJ's lips were thin and his teeth were nicotine stained but his constant boyish smile infectious. His wiry build and shaggy brown hair matched a scruffy complexion. He pretended to be preoccupied by a lure and fishing pole while sneaking a peek at the females of the group as they proceeded to change into their bathing suits. He almost shuddered when Roxy grabbed the neck of her bulky college T-shirt with her hands, lifting up her shirt to reveal a skimpy swimsuit that complemented her caramel colored and flawless skin.

"Sarah come fishing with me. It's a great way to avoid, hum mm, you know..." AJ's voice trailed off to a whisper, "oh, hell, I'll just say it; you can hide from Tommy for a while."

Lance stood on his haunches, forelegs wound tight like a spring, ears perking up on guard as the group of individuals spread out. The women, with the exception of Sarah who borrowed a fishing pole from her friend AJ, scattered off in their separate directions. Tequila and Desiree laid claim to the apartments as Roxy made her way to the lake. The employees and the group could have seen a Crimson colored Wolf, if they were not occupied with the mundane tasks at hand, watching their every movement on the edges of the sparse trees hidden by overgrown weeds. The shimmering lakefront precariously close to the lupine, his paws sunk into the mud up to the ankles. The swiftly moving, heavy silver clouds playing shadow puppets against the trees, masking the wolf's intentions and obscuring his silhouette as he watched.

Roxy happily flung her shoes off in the grass and headed toward the lake. Desiree, Tequila and Garrett failed to notice the sleek-lined Wolf on his belly, motionless watching, biding his time until AJ and Sarah were out of site. Lance's Wolf kept an excruciatingly slow pace. He crept along so slowly that even the birds and squirrels failed to see the imminent danger.

AJ released the hook on his pole releasing the line. Lost in conversation and their eyes trained at the lake they were still oblivious to the predator trailing them. AJ skewered the worm that he had gotten out of a white Styrofoam container he had bought in the office. The worm squirmed on the hook as it was cast into the water.

"Tommy is mad at me, but," she went about baiting her hook then casting her line out too.

"But," A.J. Interrupted, "the South has this old world charm to it, doesn't it?"

Sarah looked over to the red and white floater as it splashed into the clear waters. AJ smiled his boyish carefree grin. The floater rocking to and fro like a sailboat on a rough sea, the first signs that the fish were taking the bait and nibbling had begun.

"Yeah," she confessed, "It's not just that," she answered as she continued, "Even with its imperfections, like for instance there is no running water or electricity and obvious work to get it habitable again..." Sarah abruptly stopped, struggling with her fishing pole and tussling with the encumbered line.

Sarah reeled in the line prematurely the result a gleaming empty copper hook but no fish to show for it. "I told Desiree already because she has family out here in the area and she's my best friend, but nobody else so far... Tommy is going to be furious, but my mind is made up, I want to keep the house."

AJ just silently listened. He had given up fishing since the fourth cast and nothing to show for it. His fishing pole, hook and line sat empty submerged in the water.

"I don't know," Sarah said quietly, "it's just that I founded the place of my biological ancestors, I felt alive for the first time. I heard wonderful music again. So inspiring and I am hesitant to give it all up."

Sarah went on to say that when she stepped into the foyer she was instantly transported back in time. She had found an upright piano. Sarah could envision her ancestor Alicia and she could imagine her hauntingly beautiful voice as she sung. The piano renewed a hidden passion in her, a desire to compose music.

"Well, it's a good thing my lawyer for the estate decried that it would not be eligible to be sold on the market for three months." Sarah flashed him an innocent smile.

AJ broke his longing gaze on Sarah when he saw the bobber move. He quickly wound in the line while comforting Sarah, "that is devious, if you thought about selling the place you had to wait three months so you had the opportunity to change your mind. If you think about it you beat the lawyer to the punch, if it helps you at all!"

Sarah Spontaneously laughed and hugged AJ with one free hand while holding her fishing pole with the other, "I love you! Why did I break up with you again?"

"Because, my dear, I AM a whore." AJ chuckled matter-of-factly. His eyes alive with excitement partially from the sudden warm closeness and sweet fragrance of his ex-girlfriend the other more important part the bigmouth Bass he had finally snagged out of the lake.

Sarah loosened her grip realizing she broke up with AJ for that exact reason. His slim tall figure dressed in varying shades of black. His proud high cheekbones, rugged chin. Always brushing back his dusty dark Brown hair that concealed his pouty brooding blue eyes, the eyes of a poet or struggling artist made it hard for the women to resist him and he made good use of this she realized just a little too late. However, for all his faults and affairs, his honesty and loyalty to who he considered his friends touched on the chivalrous.

"You know I can convince Garrett and some of the others to stay and help for a couple weeks more if you decide to stay and fix the house up."

Sarah smiled; of course AJ is right she thought. She looked at Roxy sunning herself upon a beach towel on the deck. Only a blur in the distance, but Sarah imagined Roxy's hands were resting under her head, red rimmed bug-eyed sunglasses over her closed eyes, oblivious to those around her even when the deck rocked up and down with people.

Roxy may have been a blur to Sarah but not to the red Wolf called Lance, whose eyes zoomed in on Roxy like a sensitive telescope. Lance could even see Roxy's intricate tattoo with its curved lines that complemented her hips that her skimpy bikini revealed until he finally turned his attention back to Sarah who had her back to him.

Lance's ears swiveled honing in on the couple, his forepaws twitched, preparing to strike out and sink his fangs into AJ's unsuspecting jugular and abduct Sarah before she had a chance to react. The eager wolf pounced out from the camouflage of thick brush, shrubbery, vines, and dense prickly ash.

The fern-like leaves rustled a cluster of angelica trees with their extremely low hanging branches parted to reveal pearl white long curved fangs. Lance's lupine tongue whipping back and forth like it had a life of its own. Glowing red eyes locked on AJ still having a conversation with his self. Sarah lost in thought and daydreams of yesteryear. She fantasized about a man who lived in the forest and an unrequited love. Unaware of the large beast that just burst forth threatening their lives.

As Lance's wolf had pounced out of the brush preparing to attack the couple the white wolf burst from the undergrowth and thwarted the imminent attack. The white wolf with its lean strong torso and forepaws transfigured into two well-built human arms in an instant and subdued the red Wolf in a stifling bear hug. It yelped but the strong hands of the wolf man muffled his cries. The white wolf leaned backwards with his hominid-like body. The red wolf tumbled backward, gravity and the weight of the red wolf doing all the work until they hit the unforgiving Earth together with a muffled thud.

AJ heard a swish prompting him to finally turn around to see only swaying branches. The water seeped into the paw prints in the mud. The white wolf-thing deliberately tumbled away from AJ and Sarah as Lance's Wolf scratched and clawed, trying to free itself from the white wolf-hominoid's clutches.

25

Devon tried to discourage an attack on Sarah, AJ, and the unassuming patrons of Point Breeze Motel. The altercation felt as if it raged on for days. The white Wolf-thing and Lance's red Wolf were locking in and out of combat until they were deep in the forest. The white wolf-thing skidded to a stop feeling confident he would not be heard by anybody. He caught Lance's calf and threw the wolf's body like a rag doll into a prickly ash tree. White Wolf-hominoid released his iron grip on Lance's leg, leaving him battered and bruised.

"What are you doing here?!" the white wolf-thing questioned with a mouth full of oversized fangs that made his speech garbled.

The white lupine's skull began altering, red sigils dancing along his undulating cheeks until forming an identifiably human face. The recognizable tang of the unconscious red lupine surprised Devon. He recognized him as Lance, a tall fiery redhead of London, born in the Dark Age, sired from Aticus, Devon's ex-pack mate.

The robins and cardinals chirped and cried their intruder alarms but too late to warn the white haired lycanthrope Devon. Whipping his head around, suddenly the breath from Devon's lungs left him. Leaves floated up into the air and Devon's feet left the Earth as his body tumbled toward the dirt. Two wolves, one with Golden eyes and brown fur with dreadlocks named Tomas and the other Wolf name Montezmu with majestic thick white fur its eyes glowing red, struggled with Devon in concert with one another to restrain him.

"I know you!" Devon mumbled his mouth full of dirt. Dancing shadows filled his chin and cheeks as he transmuted back and forth human to lupine, and then back again struggling to get free.

"I knew that stank had to be Lance," Devon looked at the unconscious red wolf. He breathed in Tomas' strong musty scent, "This must be Tomas, I can tell by your odor!"

Tomas growled a response and tightened his grip against Devon's arm as Montezmu's lupine muzzle bit down on his trapezius tearing a chunk a flesh away. The bacteria that grew in the lycanthrope saliva made the wound heal slowly in another lycanthrope. Three against one, Devon thought. He did not flinch however when Montezmu's fangs bit down on his back again and tore the muscle leaving a deep bleeding wound.

Devon remembered the albino from their brief interactions, "Is that you Montezmu?"

Silence…

Devon had grown weak from blood loss but somehow, he felt it in his bones, He had to lead them further away from the hotel. He twisted his body around to see Montezmu. Devon's calves to his feet changed. Elongating shins snapped like twigs then congealing again to form a lupine-like reverse knee. His newly formed extended paws gave him much-needed stability. He managed to get the upper hand on the two aggressors. Devon swiftly snatched hold of Montezmu by the elbow with a vice-like grip. With one fluid movement he twisted Montezmu's fore-paw lifting him up in an arc at the same time he brought up his knee smashing into Tomas' chest. Tomas yelped as the air rushed out of his lungs cracking the wolf's ribs. Montezmu scratched at Devon's chest one last time as he hit the ground hard. The tables had turned; Tomas' wolf gasped for air and Montezmu had been stunned into submission. Still dizzy he had a fractured forepaw that he nursed, slurping with his tongue. Shifting form into a sleek lined white Wolf built for speed Devon fled deeper into the woods and further from Point Breeze Motel.

The albino Wolf, the brown Wolf, and the red Wolf were all on their paws again. First Montezmu whipped his head around. Howls filled the air. Tomas responded in kind, breathing regularly, albeit painfully. Lastly resonating from Lance a Howl higher in octave, a distress call…

Bursting out of the vines seemingly from nowhere an obsidian Wolf with one glowing green eye tackled Devon's Wolf form. His left paw caught Devon on his fluffy white scruff literally lifting him up off his front paws. Taking advantage of the situation the black Wolf's right paw tore into Devon's forehead.

"Devon?" It was more of a question than statement.

"Devon!" Aticus exclaimed, forcefully turning Devon's lupine head so they saw eye to eye. "Oh Devon, Happy days are here again!"

Memories come flooding through Aticus' disease-ridden brain. A great deal of obligation ran through it too. After all, Devon had befriended the lonely and inexperienced lycanthrope, saving his life in the process. Aticus felt an obligation to Devon for this, he couldn't deny it.

"I'm glad to see you, Devon!" Aticus loosened his grip on Devon's head but not his scruff needing some control.

Devon converted back to a hairless human, with no fur to hang on to Devon dropped to the ground on his knees. His nose cringed at the strange smell permeating through Aticus' body. A mixture of Aticus' familiar musk and a faint scent that sickened, worried, and saddened him. He could whiff the distinct bouquet of his mentor, Stefan, running through Aticus' veins. He choked on the bile flooding up his esophagus.

"Where is Stefan?" Devon asked but in his heart he knew the answer.

Devon slyly watched Tomas as the injured Wolf thing withdrew and went left while Montezmu withdrew and went right, classic flanking maneuver, he thought. Lance cautiously stepped aside from Devon's lethal reach too. With all eyes on Devon he circled around to his blind side.

"Oh, Stefan, Well... he will always be in my thoughts. He's here," Aticus touched his cold, cold heart, "forever in my heart!"

"You killed him!" The ancient Stefan had been defeated. He knew this for a fact when he breathed in Aticus' smell. He silently swore to get revenge as his body stiffened, preparing to strike down Aticus where he stood.

"I loved Stefan but he ... grew weak," Aticus drew a thin lipped smirk with oversized curved fangs on a human face, "just like I love you, Devon!"

The loving but veiled words had not been lost on Devon as he quickly accessed his options. "Why are you so interested in this human group? That's how I found your foul smelling friend overtly preparing to attack those innocent people!"

Aticus inched closer; Devon reflexively drew away when he looked closely at Aticus' appearance. He could not help but see his disfigured face. The ocular cavity had all but been destroyed, his optical nerve had been severed and tiny sharp silver shrapnel had embedded itself in Aticus' sinus cavity and the eye socket that used to hold an animalistic green eye. The result of the silver blast left his skull deformed. Instead of the usually rounded smooth or egg-like shaped oval human cranium the skull with the missing eye actually looked elongated, tetragonal or a plateau half-crown tapering off until a normal hemisphere with the other emerald eye could be seen. The lupine ear on the wounded side stood up higher and further back than normal, a hairless ear with a chunk missing from the bottom. This was his visage when he turned his head from side to side. Before Devon could act Tomas and Montezmu restrained his arms so he could not attack their leader.

"Because you have saved my life I'll strike a one-time bargain with you," Aticus looking up and down, Devon had a sickly ashen appearance about him, no threat to him or his pack, "The group will be safe from harm and as long as they are at Point Breeze no harm will come to them. But step off the apartments and all bets are off!"

"No!" Devon growled his head transforming right in front of Aticus' eyes.

Aticus saw stars in his eyes as Devon head-butted him on the wounded side of his face. Devon wrenched his hands from his captors, transforming them from hands to claws. Devon rushed forward. Frozen, his head exploding; he could not defend himself. Devon rushed in on the stunned Aticus. His paws gripped Aticus' shoulders. He jumped, knee bent, until he thrust newly formed powerful limbs over Aticus' head. No looking back Devon thought as his four legs landed softly on the dirt and leaves. He heard a volley of angry howls fill the forest.

"Do you want us to recapture him, Aticus?" Devon heard someone say off in the distance behind him.

"No," Aticus still had his eyes closed, the pounding in his brain insufferable and stifling his thoughts. "No, in fact, I'll honor my promise. Point Breeze belongs to my long-lost friend Devon. No harm shall come to those who dwell there…," Devon did not hear Aticus' proclamation, already splashing through the riverbank and disappearing into the shadows. "New Roads and Raccourci Island, however, are a different story!"

After Devon successfully evaded his aggressors he realized he was losing blood. Unsteady and dizzy even on four feet he finally settled in the brush near in old weeping willow tree. Plenty of concealment, he told himself, involuntarily dropping to all fours and resting his muzzle on the cold, hard earth. He felt his skin crawl again as his fur receded, revealing undulating skin rising and lowering like a tide. He felt the intense heat that he had grown all too accustomed too, his body temperature elevating as if his body a science beaker and the fluids binding with one another, giving off a thermal reaction.

His massive paws meant for powerful claws, deadly strikes, and nothing more began to transform involuntarily. The blood loss was just too great. Devon's sleepy and heavy eye lids began to droop. Solid lupine bones began to quiver until there were just a gelatinous mass. Shrinking then giving way to a fresh cartilage and bone again more suited for a hominid.

Comfortable and safely hidden by leaves that covered his bloody but scabbing wounds and big fallen branches the thick vast clouds concealing the sun, Devon tried to get some much needed rest. The scratches and bites that he had received would heal in time. Sleep would elude him, though, troubled by the strange aroma permeating through the air. He knew without a doubt Aticus had started a pack, developing an army for what ends he did not know. For centuries they remained hidden to mankind and for good reason as mankind had a track record of killing and destroying things that they fear or don't understand, a peaceful cohabitation in the light of day would be futile! Aticus was diseased;

the silver sickness had run havoc on his brain. He could tell by the silver rings and hazy appearance in his green eye. Devon couldn't help but imagine the silver violating his mind like imaginary worms burrowing in his brain until it was Swiss cheese and felt sympathy for him. However, the sickening aroma permeating his being told him that he had become addicted to his own kind, forbidden blood, lycanthrope-cannibal. What he was doing here was a mystery too. In time, though, sleep trumped his worry and he got some much-needed rest in the folds of moss and leaves and branches that tucked him in like a warm blanket as a crescent moon arced across the sky.

26

Two boys skipped through the woods, a shortcut, while they headed to their respective homes they passed the day away playing tag. Low and droopy branches caught the taller boy, snagging his shirt and slowing him down. The littler one had a marked advantage able to maneuver better. Picking up speed now the little boy laughed turning around to see if his opponent had caught up with him yet. The pair raced over leaves snapped and crunching, startling and waking Devon's injured Wolf who had concealed himself in the decaying refuse.

Devon yawned and stretched, perking up from a dream filled fog, had he been asleep all day? The sun high in the sky told him the answer, yes. A raucous noise right next to his makeshift den engaged his curious nature. He snuck up on the two boys.

"You can't catch me!" the little boy shouted breathlessly.

He did not see the flies buzzing around, the wild mice feasting on the flesh or the snakes feasting on the mice, a whole ecosystem beaming with life because of death. The boy fell directly into the middle of the carnage, his face and body covered in gelatinous body fluids released by the decaying human corpses.

In just four hours the serene woods with peaceful wildlife noises grew into bustling chaos with blue uniformed bodies and yellow crime scene tape since the discovery of the two mauled corpses. The boys that found them stood white faced, wiping away tears from their cheeks and behind the crime scene, the taller one still clutching the cell phone, the screen glowing 911.

Capt. Rogers had just finished getting the boys' statements when he peered over his shoulder to see Amy Anderson. His chin creased in frustration, but he couldn't suppress a smile, "great."

Huffing, Capt. Rogers jogged through the uniformed officers. He let out a groan; knees popping as he bent ducking under the caution tape careful to secure his officer issued 9 mm and his Taser. Straightening up and dusting his uniform off to meet the journalist behind the crime line.

"We've got to stop meeting like this." Amy joked and wiped away her red hair from her green eyes grinning, "No seriously… I missed you, what? It's been over two weeks since I've seen you last."

"It's no laughing matter, Amy." He scolded, his expression all business like. "And no, you were there at the trailer murder/arson only a day ago, what are you doing here?"

"Oh yeah, good times," Amy placed a flirty hand on Capt. Rogers's bicep, "To answer your question I have a police scanner, you know. What's the scene here?"

She was looking over Capt. Rogers shoulder to the half-eaten corpses on the ground her digital recorder in hand. She was casually chewing a Nicorette gum and blatantly ignoring Capt. Rogers disapproving looks.

"Nothing much here of interest to you Amy, animal attack, that's all." Capt. Rogers said trying to appease her curiosity.

"You don't find it curious that huge canine prints were found at each crime scene you have investigated?" Amy was staring at one of those prints as she spoke.

"You know Amy; I'm getting awfully tired of talking to you and I am misrepresented in your joke of a paper. What have you done to sink so low?" He seemed to ask her a variation of the same question every time he saw her.

"Look Mac," she laughed "I told you before… I had a cushy job but the editor and I had creative differences, I quit."

Amy sheepishly smiled "Besides, if this pans out the way I think it's going to this would be my ticket to the big league papers or maybe even a book deal."

Amy put her hand on his shoulder and flashed a kittenish smile. Her flirtatious mannerisms were almost too much for Capt. Rogers to bear but he secretly could not get enough of her flirty repartee, leaving him beaming and feeling younger than his thirty eight-year-old self. When he saw her, he become irritated and irate but after talking to her he felt boyish and nervous as if he was talking to a schoolyard crush.

Amy shoved some photos in to his hands, "I've got pictures at the Sellers, Asher, Traiteur, Lux's homes all of paw prints. Hell, even the hospital..."

Capt. Rogers would die before admitting it, but remembered all their encounters in excruciating detail. In fact, though outwardly he resented Amy's presence he secretly enjoyed their encounters but he felt guilty as if he was continuing an affair in his head even though the affair which had been broken off cooled before his wife grew suspicious.

Capt. Rogers glanced at each and every one of the photographs deliberately before looking into Amy's eyes giving the photographs back, "I think you're way off base with this. You're looking for a legendary Sasquatch, a bigfoot, chupacabra or imaginary vampire angle that is not there."

He could see the energetic, hopeful light drain out of her eyes; it pained him to the bone, "But... At every scene there were huge prints everywhere."

Capt. Rogers interrupted her, "I shouldn't be telling you this but all of our manpower is tied up in the disappearances for several hospital patients and most of the people of Royal Bay. I know, Royal Bay had just a handful of residents but it's really a ghost town now. There is nobody to work in the post office, gas station, or general store even. Personally, I'm going to devote all my attention on the disappearances, to hell with an animal on the loose and the fucking murders, I don't want to be sidetracked by fairytales."

Rogers was no longer looking at Amy's eyes he was looking down at her breasts. She had on a white tank top, a man's "wife beater" he thought and her black bra was visible on her shoulders. He was getting hot but it was not the temperature that made him sweat through his uniform it was Amy's too short to be legal pair of jean shorts. Amy noticed Capt. Rogers noticing her and shyly smiled, she had him where she wanted him.

"But *really* look at my pictures before you pass judgment." Amy said.

"I think the large tracks are the work of an opportunistic scavenger. The smell of an easy meal was too much for it. We're checking leads now about Wolf-dog hybrids escaping from their homes or wolves that got loose from their sanctuary from St. Louis or somewhere else but okay, I will look at your photos more closely." He relented, stopping for a moment. "Where do you live these days? When I get off work I can come by and look at your evidence."

She was already writing down her address and phone number on a spare piece of scrap paper, the delight washing over her as she handed him the address. His face was flush with excitement and guilt, "I'll call you before I come over."

Twigs snapped somewhere in the vicinity whipping Amy's head to the left. She could not help but gasp her hands instinctively covered her mouth. What she saw tested her sensibility and modesty. The conversation meant for Amy's ears fell by the wayside, Capt. Rogers, gesturing with his hands obliviously staring down at the scrap of paper carried on about the lost years as she stared at the as yet undiscovered, unclothed intruder hiding nearby.

Amy strained her eyes to see the mysterious man. Wild close cropped white hair, the style of which reminded her of a Japanese anime styled haircut. His almost animalistic eyes seemed to glint in the sunlight and they locked on to Amy's eyes. He had bright red sigil tattoos running the length of his forehead, cheeks and long wide nose. Reminding Amy of an Iroquois soldier or a Wotan warrior, the painted people known in history for their dyed faces or tattooed visage that struck fear in the hearts of the opposing tribes. She thought of the distinguished former heavyweight champion of the world, his tattooed face made famous. Even with the ominous sigils he had an almost innocent childlike expression to his face. It reminded her of the books of Edgar Rice Burroughs and Tarzan. She smiled at the thought, you Tarzan, I Jane…or uh, Amy.

Amy couldn't understand the phrase; "She went weak in the knees" until she saw Devon and she had to grasp a branch on a nearby tree to steady her shaking knees. Amy looked him up and down to try to gauge how old he was but there were no true markers to speak of. Amy noted his skin and there was a lot of it being naked, smooth and pliable. He had no imperfections on his form save that of four glowing rosy and healing scratch marks that scored from his neck to the bottom of his ribs. She couldn't help but stare at his ribcage, thin fine pitch black hairs upon his well-defined pecks down his powerfully built milky white torso that made a diamond configuration.

She bit her upper lip until she could taste a warm metallic copper fluid, suggesting her teeth had punctured her inner brim. It took all her self-control and restraint to not reach out for the mystery Tarzan but it brought unwanted attention from Capt. Rogers who immediately unlatched his safety holster to his Taser.

Capt. Rogers no longer ogled Amy's figure. He put on his black plastic rimmed glasses to get a better look. He finally noticed the stranger partially concealed by the Cyprus trees, a white haired young man intently staring at the journalist.

"Hey, you," Capt. Rogers completely forgot about the red headed reporter, "Freeze! Get down on your knees, police!" The man turned to flee.

Capt. Rogers instinctively rested his free hand against his Taser running into the woods without backup. The Bald Cypress gave way to weeping willows with branches that looked like an old Confederate soldier's graybeard flowing to the Earth. Using the whip like branches of a willow tree for stability Capt. Rogers muddles through buttonbushes, thicker scrubs and heavier thickets in pursuit of the interloper.

Like a skittish feral animal the white-haired nude suspect leaped, hopped and evaded the Captain. He avoided capture as he traversed the harsh terrain. Out of breath, Capt. Rogers pulled out his nonlethal stun gun and lined up the shot.

The leads and length of conductive wire burst forth and travel several yards in the blink of an eye until they were tangled up in the leaves and branches of a willow tree. A miss, the wires fell harmlessly in the grass; Rogers put his hands on his hips catching his breath. Once caught his breath he run after the subject again. The pair traversed through the weeping willows, Capt. Rogers' sliding on moss and the thick weeds slowing him down in the process.

"Dammit!"

A volley of curses came out of Capt. Rogers's mouth as he inspected the overgrown vines and weeds for foot prints. Only barely visible foot tracks and the broken and disturbed branches on a windless day were visible, the stranger eluding capture.

27

Devon hid for two days before he felt safe enough to come out of hiding. Now he feverishly looked for signs to find the hiding places of the growing infected. He dug up old track marks, dead carcasses and searched houses long abandoned by their owners.

Lost in thought he remembered his last run-in with Aticus and his new pack. Touching the wound gingerly with his hands he could feel scars. Devon feared any disruptions that threatened the human's imaginary dominance and Aticus had been doing just that, disrupting their fragile civilization. He survived more inquisitions than he cared to count. Many of his brethren were lost to Catholic funded torture and slaughter. Many, many more atrocities were perpetrated by the God's Light organization. Many loved ones, friends and pack mates were lost to the horror of fire, acid, and silver blade. Even Aticus almost lost his life because of them, if not for Devon's quick cunning and reflexes.

It was still light outside; the stifling heat had finally broken. Signs that summer had almost come to an end and soon fall would be near. The fragrances of bald cypresses and black oaks mixed with corn and tobacco had gotten powerful. The wild grass, which had grown higher and wilder, assaulted his senses. He couldn't help but think of that reporter, Amy. He thought of her smooth skin and her baby face that looked so innocent but most of all her eyes. Her deep blue eyes were so insightful.

Nearly to the thicket of brush downwind before he could smell anything Devon heard a minute sound coming in his direction. He perked up, excited, wandering just shy a few yards from him the meal his body so desperately craved. He saw a magnificent buck with antlers sprouting off in many different directions, sinewy shoulders, and a huge neck. It had a beautiful rust-blonde colored pelt. Devon's blood began to boil; his eyes dilated and began to glow, the hair on his neck stood erect. Famished and weak, helpless to stop it he felt a change coming on. The buck and a human Devon locked eyes. The buck's feet were frozen in fear. Numbness came over him, nerves firing in succession, he had grown accustomed to as bones broke all over his body to accommodate the coming form. He muttered an indistinguishable sound as his jaw broke on both sides simultaneously. Eyes watered as his skin stretched and tore. Rational thought harder to keep in his head as instincts took over.

Before the buck could move Devon reacted with blinding speed. Claws where there were once hands went straight for its neck. With one strong jump the metamorphosing Devon locked on to his prey. The twisted mass of deer and Wolf-thing fought horn to claw until white fur and fine Brown hair amalgamation fell to the dirt.

Warm blood trickled down to his muzzle; salty coppery sweet sustenance instantly gave him ease. And with the deer's dying breaths he transformed back into his human self. Devon felt guilty as he watched the deer die. Deer's head spinning around like the antlers were too heavy for him. If not for starvation he would've been in more control of his animal self and instincts would have flowed easier. He could have gone for brainstem instead of nicking the jugular. He ate like a glutton and he didn't stop until his stomach seemed about to burst. His belly full, he needed a nap but no use trying to nap now. Hs he brushed his white blood stained hair from his eyes and sat up on his knees.

"Well, might as well," he remarked. Naked, the blood of his kill was getting thick and flaky and he was miles away from any stream for enclosure he knew about. "It is like a good stretch, isn't it?"

With his distinguishing features, pointy ears, fine hair all about his entire chiseled body he stuck out like a sore thumb if anybody happened upon him. He took a deep breath and not like before when he was sick from hunger and blood thirsty he mentally willed his change. Waves like electricity came over him and ran up and down his body from head to toe. It felt like pure ecstasy, being in control. He struck his palm into the dirt and took a big deep breath. The transformation was instantaneous and almost pain free and human thoughts were easier to maintain now that he'd fed.

28

He made a beautiful Wolf thing. He had a long muzzle, fur white in color and soft to touch. He had thick shoulders and short legs. His under belly was black as coal and he had a large chest that streamlined into a small belly. He loved his wolf self and he rolled around in the grass and chased his tail just having fun getting his energy back. Devon reveled in his wolf form so much.

Distracted playing in the grass Devon didn't smell and almost didn't see the man in the tree line. He froze where he stood sizing the man up. The hunter had a luminescent orange hunting vest which made him stick out from the weeds, and he was armed with a shotgun. He staggered around haphazardly with his gun. He had been drinking; this much was obvious, he didn't see Devon yet. Devon weighed his options, he could incapacitate him and flee or lay low in the weeds and hope the hunter didn't see him.

"Hey Chet," another man dressed just the same as the drunken hunter emerged from the forest.

Devon could kick himself for not smelling them. Then it dawned on him, they're hunters, they immersed themselves in animal urine to mask their human scent! Never taking his eyes off the hunters He hunched down on his belly slowly, and then an idea came to him. They had clothing, water, probably beer, and if he was lucky, a truck nearby.

His paws began to lengthen until they converted to hand-like claws with six-inch, razor sharp black nails. Tendons and ligaments contorted until arm like appendages emerged. Devon stretched his muscles and tendons like a spring opening to its limits. He shifted his weight onto his paws and with a deep breath he jumped from the shadows. A rustle of weeds, birds fluttering away obscured by thick shrubbery, a white shadow rushed at the hunters. The blur of white fur had the hunters doing a double take.

"What was that, Chet!?" Brad exclaimed.

The hunter Brad with blond hair and an orange-hunter jacket on twisted around wide-eyed looking at the swaying honeysuckle. He could smell the honey-like essence that the disturbed flowers set off. In the blink of an eye Brad's gun was in splinters, twisted metal and wood particles in his hands. He could swear he felt coarse fur brush his hand that clutched his now mangled rifle.

"Fuck!" Mitchell the drunken belligerent hunter staggered in the direction of honeysuckle staring off at the swooshing vines.

Mitchell swore he saw something in the overgrown brush just to the left of his friend Chet, the third hunter in the trio. Hard to see with inebriated eyes and the thick waist high brush but he thought he saw a shadow of a dog just inches from Chet's boots. Mitchell pointed a shaking hand down at the pine needle covered ground near the bushes as color drained from his face.

Once again Devon exploded out from the bushes superhuman speed propelling him to his target. The hunters stood stunned as the beast-Devon zeroed in on the second gun. Devon saw it all in slow motion but the speed with which the beast moved caused the hunters to get disoriented. A blur of dazzling white fur and in an instant the second gun destroyed like the first with a whirlwind of fangs and talons.

Chet stood wide-eyed, staring at his empty bloodied palms. His mind would not allow him to comprehend what was unfolding before him. His fragile psyche began to crack; it would not allow him to process the doglike thing standing upright like a bear, its huge paws finding the heads of his friends before they had time to react. In one fluid motion the beast picked them up off the ground and smashed their heads together and then flung their limp bodies against a massive oak tree.

Chet could've run when the snow colored monster named Devon stopped and got on all fours again. He could've run when the monster was staring intently at his fallen friends before slowly turning around and gazing at him quizzically. Chet locked eyes with the monster. Incandescent smoldering smoky gray eyes, strange, he thought, they almost seemed like human eyes. Now standing before him he could see the thing, it wasn't a dog at all or bear for that matter. Chet could tell by the lupine skull, it's larger than usual curved fangs, its muzzle and it ears that it was some form of Wolf standing before him.

Standing six feet, five inches and an ex-MMA fighter in his glory years, testosterone and alcohol made him generally a man without fear. However, the closeness of the beast made Chet's world views come crashing down around him. It is impossible! It's a yeti! Fantastical white-haired versions of the Bigfoot or Sasquatch come to life, he thought.

The Wolf-thing's huge white, engorged muscular shoulders looked like a football linebacker's shoulder pads. The beast's neck looked like a healthy juvenile tree trunk with thin, short white furs masking pulsing arteries. Massive but extremely thin and streamlined… a well-oiled hunting and killing machine.

Chet willed himself to run, walk, even move, but he stood immobile. As He looked into the beast's eyes the beast stared into Chet's. The beast straightened his hunch, standing all the way erect at seven feet tall and now Chet stared up at him. Able to get out one hay maker from his glory days in the MMA Chet managed to surprise the beast Devon in the muzzle, bloodying his nose and watering his eyes. But He froze when he looked into Devon's eyes letting out a blabbering nonsensical bellow just as a powerful upward swipe temporarily turned out the lights.

The upward motion had Chet's feet up off the ground and knocking the breath out of him as he hit his back and bruised his buttocks. The other hunters unconscious he'd have to fend for his self, bloody, blind and wounded.

Chet obliviously clawed at the dirt, desperately trying to withdrawal like a crab that had been found hiding under a rock. Stinging sweat and tears forced Chet's eyes shut. He could not see beast but could hear and smell the beast, his musky wild aroma and he could hear a "swoosh" as Devon's claws came over him once more.

29

Devon's wolf held still in the brush, holding his bounty in his clamped jaws scanning the area until finding the truck and searching vigilantly for signs of others until satisfied there were no stragglers. The wolf stood up on hind legs revealing its white form and began to transform into a man. He put on the shirt of one of the hunters wiping as much blood from his hands as possible then slid on a loose pair of jeans and found the keys to the Ford truck. He quickly checked the multitude of keys. Finally finding the right keys he opened the driver's door and slide onto the seat. Sticking the key into the ignition and a flick of the wrist made the engine cough, sputter, and then purr like a kitten.

Devon's stolen truck was almost on the main road now as the dense trees began to thin out and the light began to break through onto a gravel road. Devon could faintly smell the asphalt from the highway in the distance. An overwhelming stench of decay, urine and a strong musky odor that Devon or the lycanthropes could sense had him changing course and locking onto the familiar stench. In the distance Devon could see a dilapidated house, the source of the smell. He pulled over on the side of the road and got out of the truck.

He finally found the Seller's house one source of the many distracting aromas. His head full of memories, deep in thought. In the back of his mind He couldn't shake the fact his friend Stefan had been slain! He remembered the pain and the pleasure he felt the first time the change came over him and how scared and awkward he felt. But along came the strange lycanthrope Stefan to save him and show him the way.

Devon remembered Stefan had smelt his unique odor of rage and fear, bleeding, and had run toward Devon. He had the raw power inside of him but was yet unable to harness and control it. He remembered cowering in the corner, half man, half beast, howling like a wounded dog, crying out in pain. Stefan heard the howls and came to his aid. Stefan sloshed around; his feet died red from the blood. Stefan looked upon a mound of dead Scythians; twenty nomadic warriors, their body parts strewn about like an incomplete jigsaw puzzle with hopelessly lost pieces, a crimson tide of liquid crept out like streams until it disappeared into the ground. The dead Scythians' body stirred almost looking alive as Devon slowly crept out of the macabre hill. Reluctantly, he had slowly crept from the shadows that were covering his grotesque form and into the light.

He had a hairless wolf body with human ears and hands. Hunched, white fur covered, his back in a diamond formation, and his muzzle barely covered in sparse spots with short white hairs. The compassionate lycanthrope kneeled down in thc blood stained dirt and held out his hand and the skittish Devon accepted. He received Stefan's guidance. His body now adjusted to the strain of the change.

He stopped at the Seller's porch now to feel the breeze on his exposed face before continuing into the house, his memories continuing.

Stefan and Devon's hands locked in a protective embrace. His body had been so deformed, a diamond of white fur on his back still quivering, he cocked his huge half-formed head back. Devon then sheepishly laid his head down on Stefan's out stretched palm. He showed him how to control and manipulate the change. He showed him how to suppress rage and to think like a man through the fog of powerful emotion and instinct.

For six full seasons he stayed to teach Devon until a panicky and unsure puny human turned into a confident and brave lycanthrope. He felt a sense of loyalty to Stefan, like a father figure. So in the year our Lord 1846, when peculiar winds finally hit Europe, Devon's stomping ground, he began to feel a sudden sorrow and incredible pain prompting him to travel to the Americas.

30

By the time he had searched every nook and cranny, night had come and gone and an emerging dawn grew warmer. Just the type of weather he loved. His chest hair exposed to the breeze, his legs tingled, and joy surged through him. He breathed the air in deeply as he opened the front screen door and stepped outside onto the porch; the inhabitants of the house long were gone.

Amy Anderson sat in her car watching the stranger through her binoculars. He stood on the porch again, still as a marble statue, staring up at the sun with his eyes closed, almost nude. The rising sun made the shadows dance on the definitions of his muscular frame. Wearing what seemed like an oversized camouflaged hunter's vest and pants that barely stayed up on his hips. She hadn't been able to stop thinking about him since he had emerged from the woods unclothed and Capt. Rogers had chased after him to no avail. The stranger exuded confidence and she couldn't help but be excited and thrilled.

Amy's face began blushing, bringing out her already rosy cheeks and freckles, "Get a hold of yourself Amy, you're a professional."

She couldn't help her eyes moving down the length of his body then staring fixated by the obvious outline of his well-endowed member. "Remember Amy," she said to herself over and over again "he could be the killer and is probably deranged...sane people don't usually hang out naked in the woods at crime scenes."

He had unkempt, long, snow-white hair, sigil-like red tattoos spanning the length of his wrinkle free face and offsetting his wild gray eyes. Devon finally noticed Amy staring at him. His instincts told him to run but he stayed the course, sizing her up. He leaped off the front porch without using the steps and onto the soft green grass without a sound. Amy adjusted her binoculars.

Devon opened the truck door with an angry yank and jumped into the driver's seat, shifted into drive, kicking rocks and dust up as a result. The truck turned and disappeared onto a back road obscured by the Sellers' house. Amy tried to turn around to try to catch up with the truck. The truck had driven off in a cloud of dust, nowhere to be found.

He thought about the obsessive aria, an aria that could be heard by other lycanthropes over three continents, about Alicia's long lost love. Devon stirred from seclusion and from his den in Alaska he traversed through the lower forty-eight states. One Aria in particular told about the Malstros plantation. Devon took advantage of the four-wheel-drive making an unscheduled detour off the crudely paved and potholed roads that gave way to massive amounts of mud as the tires spun, throwing filth and sludge onto the truck's mud flaps and leaving enormous grooves in its wake.

He cautiously but steadily drove through the hollows and back jarring bumps until he arrived at his destination; Raccourci Island. Miles away he could see the expansive yard, overgrown brushes, a rundown and neglected two-story house. Excitement made his foot stomp the pedal all the way into the floor. The cab jumped in response. A jolt then an ear shattering squeal before he found himself clutching the top of the dashboard as the cab shook, teetered, and dropped, the broken frame gashed and shredded the dirt before finally coming to a shuddering stop. A hidden pothole did in the truck's axle. All right, Devon thought, throwing his arms up in frustration. He had to walk the rest of the way.

As Devon thoroughly investigated all four corners of the decrepit house, terrified eyes watched him. Frail, frightened eyes, Tracy's eyes with the absence of Alex; and the dozen or so women and children Aticus had gathered all watched Devon from the relative comfort and safety of the barn window upstairs. Women and children too weak or wracked with pain from multiple alterations to call out for help, much less stagger twenty feet to climb down the ladder and too weak-willed to defy the breeder male, Aticus. They would not be discovered, the troll-born's magic had been successful... the barn had been hidden from prying eyes.

31

Several hours of searching had Devon tired and frustrated. He did not find anything of significance outside either. He found tracks of their comings and goings but nothing else. Defeated, slump-shouldered he set off to find his truck now a glorified junk heap on wheels. The tires were flattened and the wheels were resting horizontally on the rocks. The driveshaft and shocks were completely busted. It was on foot again, but he decided this time he would stay on the dirt roads and highways until he made it back to New Roads.

He couldn't shake the uneasiness and he knew in the pit of his gut what it meant, ultrasonic frequencies were howls of a growing pack. No more procrastination, shaking his thoughts away he headed out on a poorly maintained dirt road. He knew this land in the old world like the back of his hand. He traversed the seven continents before the birth of the industrial revolution. He could smell each and every local game and locate their den, nest, and burrow miles away even with hurricane winds, betraying scents, and the winds at his back. He stopped at a crossroads governed by a bullet ridden stop sign. He had grown to become a powerful lycanthrope, as a cunning lupine he had no need or desire for the trappings of pack life. But there was no denying a stirring in the air. Curiosity had got the better of him. He knew the now-emerging pack had a leader, Aticus. He wanted a peek at the pack's social structure.

Were they benevolent or malevolent in nature? Was it to be run as a republic or is Aticus ruling with an iron fist?

Amy rationalized to herself as she stopped for the fourth time at the bullet ridden stop sign on a barely visible road, all this work would be worth it. She had been out in the general vicinity on the hunt for a white-haired wild-man. Amy all but kicked herself for losing him at the Seller's house in the first place. It would be the last time she circled around the route that led to Sellers' house then a stop at Raccourci Island. She cursed her decision to stay in the car and follow by roadway instead of veering off on a lesser-known shortcut.

Her foot eased off of the break just in time to see the shadowy figure emerging from the forest. Her heart stopped, could it be!? She had finally found him! With a screech of tires Amy's car abruptly stopped.

"Excuse me!" Amy yelled, but her voice broke and then nerves overtook her. Then with a tentative smile, she squeaked, "Are you hurt, or lost, has your car broken down somewhere? Can I interest you in a ride? My name is Amy. I have a motel room. It would give you a chance to shower and nap, you look like you need it." She rambled nervously.

Devon stopped though he did not turn around; thinking about his stolen truck broke down in the middle of the wilderness so painfully close to the Malstros' plantation. The wheels of his mind turning, he considered the invitation. Fresh water, food, company, and a chance to heal his infernal wounds and rest just did not fall in his lap every day, he thought. Besides, there was something about Amy's fragrance and the inquisitive blue eyes that had him enthralled.

"That would be nice… Thank you; I'm Devon by the way." He grinned, before turning around and striding to the waiting car. Amy did not know what to expect when she found the wild-man but his eyes looked wise and civilized.

They traveled silently, each sizing the other one up until they reached Point Breeze Motel parking lot. Amy stepped out onto the porch of Point Breeze Motel smiling as she found the key to her room in the back into her purse.

"Damn", he thought to himself as he self-consciously tried to clean the blood of a recent kill off his chin and face, "Did Amy see all this blood?"

"Well, I got a room but it's only got one bed," Amy hesitated, "so if you stay the night..."

"That is fine; I'll sleep on the floor. It will be a refreshing change from the cold Earth," Devon said this under his breath, Amy heard him however. Despite what he had said Amy imagined he had tents set up to stave off the elements and a sleeping bag perhaps, in the woods somewhere, unaware instead of sleeping bags and tents he had preferred twigs, leaves, and cold, wet grass, "If It doesn't bother you, I mean."

"It is awful kind of you," Devon blushed.

"If you wouldn't mind," Amy said, "I would love to pick your brain a bit about the recent string of arsons in the area."

As Amy unlocked and opened the door to the cabin, Devon thought that staying in the Point Breeze Motel may be a blessing in disguise. Aticus promised no harm would come to those who dwell in the Motel, nevertheless Devon knew the flurry of activity all somehow centered on the group in the white Van. He could watch the group more closely while staying at the motel.

"That is actually why I am out in this area too," Devon surveyed the horizon," I am hunting a dangerous animal and I tracked it to two local parishes."

Somehow satisfied with Devon's answer and not quite ready to pry, Amy walked into the bathroom and turned the shower on, "I am sorry for cutting in line, but I feel icky. When I'm finished the shower is all yours."

"Take your time," Devon nodded as he pulled the curtains halfway open to stare at the beautiful view from the window.

"I have been going to the library every day for some research so I will be out during the day tomorrow," Amy peeked out from the bathroom her unclothed body concealed by the doorway, "but you are welcome to hang out here."

Still full from a small deer and exhausted from healing wounds he reasoned it would be nice to have a place to bed down comfortably without risk of anyone else stumbling upon him. He saw the thick soft blanket on the bed; he couldn't help but smile, it actually would beat leaves and sticks. He could not help but think of Amy as he sat on the bed and got comfortable. Smooth skin, that milky white complexion and shy smile.

Amy casually strolled out from the bathroom drying her shimmering red hair off with a Point Breeze Motel towel, dressed and refreshed. A spontaneous animal magnetism happened right before their eyes; as he gazed at her, holding her in a trance like state. Her gaze fell upon him, he was gorgeous, and there was something different about him. She had fallen in lust with him from the moment they had met.

Devon stood before her now captivated as well. Her long red hair hung down to her shoulders, pink and orange highlights burning like the fires in his soul. Devon breathed in Amy's freshly showered skin that hinted of coconuts. Devon instinctively reached out for her hand leaning in to inhale her freshly washed hair.

"Hold me tight." She told him, her hands caressing his massive defined back.

He had a large chest and broad shoulders that she could rest her head upon. He ran his hands over her body. Strong powerful hands, she thought to herself, while his golden brown eyes seemed to pierce the very secrets of her soul. She felt wild and reckless, throwing caution to the wind.

He held her tightly in his arms. His body was warm, almost searing to her touch, as she rested her hand on his chest. His lips melted her inhibitions as they met and lingered with hers. Lightheaded from his nearness she felt as if her blood boiled. He pressed himself against her lifting her effortlessly from the floor to the bed. Her body ached for his touch but she feared what lay beneath those animalistic eyes that glowed with a golden hue. He ripped her freshly laundered shirt from her back rendering it to pieces with the twitch of a hand. He had large shoulders and a broad chest her hands glided over his body as he gingerly removed the pants she had just gotten on a moment ago. She worked diligently at the buttons of his pants tugging in frustration at them. He helped her along, his camouflage pants falling into a heap. He stepped out of his camouflage pants in a circle on the floor and flung her backwards onto the bed.

His large hands found and fondly held the base of her skull as he leisurely savored her luscious lips. She uttered soft moans as their lips mingled together for what felt like an eternity. Her spine arched in anticipation. Amy felt Devon's engorged member pressed against her smooth thighs. Devon's tongue tasted her salty perky breasts until her rosy hued nipples reared awake. Then his tongue moved down to her navel pausing for a moment while his hands slowly slid down the length of her hips and along her warm sparsely red-haired triangle. Her creamy thighs parted to make way for Devon's head. She inhaled deeply, he smelled like blood, sweat, and pine. She pictured a beautiful but deadly forest.

Amy's hands clenched the back of Devon's head. His tongue found her inner lips. She moaned, his tongue flirting and skirting around her sweet spot until it moistened. Amy could not stand it anymore. Devon emerged from her hips and they stared eye to eye at one another. She had to have him, all of him right now. Her legs crossed she pulled him closer to her until they merged into one.

Devon let himself go; he could not restrain the animalistic side of him any longer. Devon's fingernails lengthened his eyes glowing brightly. Devon scratched at Amy's shoulders blood intermingled with her sweat and he breathed in the coppery, salty aroma. Devon and Amy's bodies merged, their eyes met and their gaze remained locked until an explosion of ecstasy and release made them both yell out.

His energies spent, Devon collapsed and rested upon his stomach on the bed. Eventually Devon curled up in the fetal position and drifted off to sleep, still lying next to Amy on the soft blanket, instead of sticks and leaves, as she hummed softly in her sleep.

32

God's light monastery

James slid his temporary I.D. card in the card-monitor which lit up one unmarked button of several. The elevator groaned then finally stopped and the doors opened at the floor that secured a special type of prisoner. All of the other rooms stood empty. A specially designed floor plan that held only one prisoner, no additional prisoners but her, Soseti, the granddaughter of the First born lycanthrope, Aisos, where the infected blood line had all started.

James unlocked the storage room doors, a cache of silver weaponry wall to wall, bladed weapons, daggers of all types, katanas and spears. On the floor were boxes of ammunition stacked up against the wall. He looked at the L-shaped table filled with shotguns, handguns, a mix of light and heavy revolvers, to 9 and 10 mm Glock automatics and AK-47 machine guns. With a shaky hand he filled out in triplicate mounds of paperwork on a clipboard chained to the wall using his secondary hand, since his AVM had claimed his once dominant left hand. He finally found the IV supplies in a drawer. He searched to find two saline bags and one silver nitrate solution bag before he quietly closed the door as he left the room.

James limped through the hallway with his cane bracing his unsteady weak left side as he reluctantly entered the doorway where So-seti was kept. She was back in the corner on the stretcher hooked up to several IVs and medical machines. Every time he saw her he cringed inside. So-seti smelt like death, James put on the surgical mask to lessen the smell, still his nose burned from odor of decay.

He saw her frail, thin, paper-like skin. She seemed to get thinner and thinner every time he blinked. But this time, James thought, she was almost skeletal in appearance. So-seti's eyes were sunk in and rimmed in dark circles; her cheeks were tight and drawn in, the skin almost transparent. Her neck was so thin he could see the vertebrate as she lifted her head and tried to speak.

"Pleasssse..." spittle flew in the air as she hissed. She tried to move her arms but they were securely shackled to the stretcher bars which were reinforced.

"I... die... soon... pleasssse." Again she spit.

So-seti spent millennia living as a wolf more than a woman. She transformed to human to go in the village to keep up with the times so she could speak broken, sometimes unrecognizable Latin, Samarian, and Mongolian and mangled old English.

"No… give me wet moon no more… I die soon..." the shackles tightened up as she pointed at the silver nitrate in James's hand. Her nails were long and brittle he could see blue veins jutting out in her wrists.

So-seti had been difficult to control for the Lucem Dei until 1835 and the discovery of silver nitrate solution directly in her veins. James reluctantly observed her craggy body. Her breasts were wrinkly old deflated sacks, he could count the ribs in her chest and the muscles in her legs were atrophied. Her whole furrowed body starting to get a sickly gray, he didn't know why but James felt sorry for her. He knew the supply of silver nitrate solution, he could tell by the flashing light, had run out and soon she would have enough strength to transform and no one in the compound wanted that. So-seti was allowed to change every six months to keep her alive but just barely.

James beheld her face and heard the chirping heart rate and blood pressure monitors, So-seti had been right, she was dying. Against his better judgment he set down the silver solution and picked up the tungsten carbide hip restraint. As soon as the custom restraint was secured So-seti knew what he was doing.

"Thank..." her voice was appreciative and softer now, "You."

He stepped back carefully never letting his eyes off her as he unlocked the tranquilizer rifle on the wall by the doorway. He was not done loading the gun and cocking it back yet when the howling began.

Mesmerized by the quickness of it all he stood slack jawed and still, her bare skin transforming to fur in seconds, human visage to Wolf muzzle in the blink of an eye. He was afraid but as the Wolf thing stared into his scared and curious eyes, fear subsided. He saw in her eyes a sincere appreciation for what he had done. The calendar upon the wall told her she had two more months before the Gods Light would allow her to fully transform.

The door flew open abruptly hitting the wall with a bang. A troop of inquisitors with white lab coats stormed in, one took aim at the lycanthrope and fired. A direct hit with a mixture of silver nitrate and tranquilizer and So-seti morphed back to an all human form.

James couldn't believe his eyes. The would-be corpse of the wrinkled woman was now plump and vibrant again. No one knew her age when she was captured but her sparse gray hair was fuller and lighter than before. The color returned to her cheeks and even her breasts were firm again. The wrinkles of So-seti's face and neck filled and became less prominent even her eyes were younger. James tried to gauge her "age", maybe late-fifties, he thought. But it was amazing because before the transformation she had looked ninety to a hundred and extremely malnourished. Her ribs were less prominent but she still looked neglected for food and James guessed if he were to take the chains off that she would gnaw his entire arm off in hunger. His train of thought was interrupted by the man who fired the tranquilizer gun, he knew him as Carson.

"What the fuck do you think you're doing?" Carson yelled. The rage in his eyes obvious, "She transforms on a strict schedule you moron, you could've been hurt or worse she could have escaped!"

The group checked to see if everything was all right and secure then they one by one left leaving just a doctor, Carson, and James in the room with So-seti who was now peacefully sleeping a drug-induced sleep. The remaining doctor checked the monitors for her vitals then also left the room with a reproachful glance.

"You know I have to report this to Byron, don't you?" Carson angrily scorned James.

"Uh...uh...yes," James muttered under his breath.

He checked the chains on the floor up to the bed where they wrapped around and secured by locks. Assured that they were secure he clapped his hands together. James absolutely hated Carson and his shiny bald head, squinty eyes, overly pump features, smug looks, it was hard to believe that Byron Atkins and Carson were not related. James could only tell Carson apart by his smaller stature, goatee and his white lab coat, which he always wore. But he tried to hide his frustration because even Carson was his superior.

Carson would not turn his back to So-seti; he cringed in undisguised disgust while barking orders. "Put a leash on that decrepit woman and report back to the office, got it?"

He motioned behind James where three silver chains and choker collars hung on the wall.

"Oooo...kay," James said reluctantly. Upon hearing this Carson made his way out the door leaving James alone with So-seti. As the door shut So-seti opened her eyes.

"Too much stinging sleep thing, I wake easy." Her broken English was hard to understand but he reasoned the years of being tranquilized repeatedly had made her immune to the sedative. She strained her neck trying to get closer to James.

"You sniff!" She was leaning uncomfortably close to him.

"What?" James shook his head slightly, he didn't understand.

"Smell... smells you... Pleasssse!" It was the first time please was not followed by spittle.

James hesitated but confident she wasn't going anywhere he slowly made his way to her but not close enough to risk her biting him. So-seti breathed in all of his scent once, twice, three times until she was confident she had her diagnosis.

"Wolf strong you. No need my bite you have you blood...Wolf blood in you, strong." She looked into his eyes; she said it again and again until she saw some form of recognition in his eyes from her garble.

James couldn't help but smell her scent too. It was different than before and the smell of decay was replaced with a wild forestry muck and wet dog aroma, though she hadn't been outdoors in a millennium, it was almost intoxicating.

"What do, uh, you mean the Wolf is strong in, um, *ME*?" He couldn't help himself, captivated, he found himself soaking up her strange aroma.

"You like me... understand? Wolf strong in you… fix arm, leg, spirit!" She touched a finger to her forehead to indicate the brain.

The result of her brief transformation, confidence, and better speech now, James could understand her better but it was still broken and garbled English.

A static filled message came on over the intercom, "James Riley you have been ordered to report to the office immediately."

The scolding voice on the intercom distracted him just enough that he didn't notice he had stepped closer to her bed until it was too late; her claws gripped his forearm tightly.

Well, he thought, this is it, death would come at any second and he closed his eyes for the inevitable, but it didn't come. Instead she took his arm so that he looked at her and pointed to his forehead.

"Wolf Spirit fighting to get out…in you, It wagered a war in your head, which is why you are what you are." She let go of his forearm and gestured to the left side of his body pointing to his weak left side.

Again, she gestured to his forehead and touched him, "resistance inside you win, why head burst."

"I, I, uh, um, have to go." James found himself telling her in a genuinely apologetic way. He walked backwards to the door his head was spinning.

"Moon spirit full in three nights, I feel it and you could too, look at it, see your heart." So-seti said meekly.

When she had finished James slowly made his way through the door. He closed the door and resting his forehead against the wall he stood motionless for several minutes thinking. Was she right? He found himself obsessing over the lycanthrope's words as he slowly hobbled along the long hallway over to the office. As a teenager he had had horrible headaches once a month or so, headaches so bad it felt like his head was going to explode and he wished for sweet release of death. When he was twenty he almost got his wish as the veins in his brain literally burst. Then he explored the possibility that the headaches every month coincided with a full moon, and he chuckled aloud. No, that's not right, he argued with himself. The laughter stopped abruptly.

The aneurysm and subsequent semi-paralytic state of his left body made him turn to the church for answers. He found himself, however, in the fringe of the occult. He had always been happy. No, not happy, content till the words of an immortal lycanthrope had him questioning everything.

James pressed the button for the elevator. Still lost in thought he automatically headed toward the direction of Carson's office. He was about to knock on the door when his fist froze. He needed to get out of the dank musty basement of the cathedral and get fresh air. He found himself turned around in the opposite direction heading to the steps that would lead him out of the basement. It was difficult for him to navigate steep stairs and he caught himself unbalanced once or twice and had to steady himself against the wall before righting himself again.

He limped himself upstairs, up the hallway, and pressed the button to the secret door, sliding the marble slab altar from the church upstairs free. A dozen or so feet to go past the oak pews until the double doors of the church swung open and he finally found himself out in the cloudless night sky. James stood still for what felt like an eternity on the steps out in the fresh night air. He breathed a sigh of relief then limped down the cobblestone path to the church gardens. James found himself looking up at a beautiful big silver glowing moon, three quarters full. It was majestic, the hairs on the back of his neck began to rise up and he felt goose bumps ripple up and down his body. Was she right? Was he a creature of the night, someone to fear, up until now someone to watch on the silver screen? Or was this just an elaborate ploy to gain his trust and her freedom? He limped over to the reflecting pond and took a good hard look at his image.

A light breeze blew the branches on the trees and music played softly on the wind chimes. A wave rippled through the cool, blue, man-made waters. James beheld his wavy visage and inwardly took a good hard look at his reflection.

James was fifty-eight years old, the gray hairs on his temples were peeking through and fine lines deepened in his face. He was a handsome man even when he had his aneurysm the telltale droop in the left side of his face was hardly noticeable. He lifted his right arm to his face and stroked his chin. The mirrored reflection had him stroking his chin with the left arm. He couldn't help fantasizing now about his hand and leg. There was hesitation just for a moment. The group Lucem Dei had browbeat into his head lycanthropes are man's scourge on the earth and an abomination. But he let go of all his fears of being ostracized as he could see himself suddenly running on all fours with the soft grass under his paws.

"Look into your heart." James heard So-seti's weak scratchy voice in his mind.

Matt said he had watched several God's Light scientists who had done more suspected lycanthrope autopsies then he cared to count. What if the headaches were the struggles of keeping a pineal gland from calcifying? Besides the genetic physical markings of all werewolves in suspected adults one of the telltale sign is a soft pineal gland, and in the old lycanthrope's brains' they developed many tumorous veins to feed and protect the soft pineal and the pituitary gland. He couldn't believe that he even entertained such blasphemy, but now he was obsessing over it. He found himself walking up to the steps of his house before he realized it.

He slipped his shoes off at the foot of his bed and covered himself up with a comforter, too tired to even take his clothing off. Thanks to the snitch Carson, he would have hell to pay tomorrow explaining to Byron his actions with So-seti. But for now he stuck his headphones in his ears, turned the volume up on his smuggled contraband music player, the thanks due to Matt who had a knack for smuggling anything in and for the first time drifted into a peaceful dream filled sleep.

In his dreams he wandered the woods…stark-naked, exposed to the elements. Walking in the forests barefoot and without his cane, in fact, James could use all his limbs fully when he walked and he danced in excitement. He wandered the massively wooded canopy until he could not continue any further. He beheld the magnificent forest, an amalgamation of all woodland areas all across the world. The Black Forest, Targhee Forest through Yellowstone, Majestic oaks to ash, and willow trees that looked as if they are weeping green tears towards the soil and Spruce trees as far as the eye could see. He breathed in the pleasant aromas of wild flowers and grass. He lifted his left hand in the air and waved it around smiling.

James pulled himself up on the limb of a tree and began to exercise for the first time using both hands for his pull-ups. One, two, up, down, then up again and again, thirty, thirty-one… ninety, and one-hundred, finishing now without breaking a sweat James jumped down to the dirt and looked around steadying himself without his cane. He could not shake the excited feeling and he couldn't shake the feeling of eyes watching him. Cunning, clever eyes watching him concealed and camouflaged in the shadows. A glowing set of eyes fixed upon his back, James spun around just in time to see an enormous lupine head bursting through the thick brush from which it had been hidden.

Intelligent Auburn eyes locked onto James' eyes. He mused at the fact that the brown gray wolf's eyes looked exactly like his own. The wolf's head twisted in curiosity as it slowly crept forward toward James.

"The Wolf strong inside you," So-seti's voice in his head was getting louder, "the Wolf struggling to break out!"

The wolf pounced unexpectedly. Dense ivy with its vines bridged from tree to tree, breaking on the wolf's burly chest. Leaving James no chance to defend himself, his limp arms laid by his side no time to react as the wolf's limbs clutched his body in a snug embrace. In his wakening moments he would've been unbalanced, the left side of his body useless, but in his dreams all of his limbs functioned, his body unwavering and stable with both of his feet firmly planted in the dirt.

James wrestled the Wolf who stood on two legs with its paws around James' neck. He felt the wolf's hot stale breath; the wolf's fur looked exactly the same as James' hair and he even felt the wolf's heart beating fast keeping time with his own heart. He knew his heart and the wolf's were one and the same!

While the wolf and James locked eyes everything froze in time and space. The wolf's body tensed for the impending attack. James did not close his eyes even though the wolf clamped down on his neck, its white curved fangs going through tender flesh with ease. However, no blood spewed out and he felt no pain at all.

Terrible pressure ensued. Like a chainsaw the wolf's fangs ground through James' skin with cold efficiency until the wolf buried its muzzle into his' chest cavity. He strained his neck to see the wolf buried into his chest. Paws and jaws pulverizing his skin until he could only see the wolf's shoulders.

The wolf's back limbs reared up and its huge paws pressed against James' hips. Tail wagging as its hindquarters waved from side to side. The wolf's shoulders finally slipped through James' gaping and exposed breast wound. The wolf then proceeded to occupy James' form. First the wolf's torso, then only a wagging tail as the hindquarters receded into James' body and disappeared. He pressed his palms against his chest; no gaping wound could be seen or felt. The Wolf was gone from the dream world, but it was inside him… In fact, the wolf had always been subconsciously by his side, but was now inside of him. The Wolf and James were one.

James could hear So-seti's voice in his head again, "…Wolf is inside you."

33

God's light ministry

James awoke and stood up, sweating, his clothing drenched from his shirt to socks. Dread came over him twisting his stomach into knots but it was not his dream that sickened him; it was the upcoming meeting with the boss. This thought, and the surreal dream made him move slower than any other usual morning, slower than molasses. In his dream his limbs had functioned fully, that was not the case when he awoke, though, off balance he fell toward the ground before stabilizing his self on the door handle and procuring his cane. He couldn't help but relive his dream as he tried to close the door with one hand while steadying him. The sun rose in the mountains painting the sky a brilliant mix of purple rubicund, auburn, and ginger.

He made his way to the church preparing to face the music. The attendant nervously look away riddled with guilt as James pressed the button for the trap door sliding the altar to the side and entered into the cavernous level below where Byron impatiently waited for him.

"Don't worry, James, I've cooled off Carson. I can forgive you for the blunder; I wanted you to check on So-seti while I was away!"

Byron Atkins shrugged off James's stuttering apology and laughed.

"Curiosity, I get that …" Byron Atkins paused.

"I hear you were almost fooled by the bitch, So-seti..." He slapped a fatty palm to James' back leaving James unstable, his body off balance until his cane hit the floor helping to stabilize his frail frame, "You have a big sympathetic heart but don't be fooled by her helpless nature."

Byron motioned toward the offices coaxing James toward his heavy oak door. James stopped just feet from Byron's desk to let his aching body rest a bit. Byron continued on to his extravagant and expensive, ornately adorned bureau.

"James," Byron patted his sweaty forehead with his white handkerchief from his suit coat pocket, "last night there was a situation of sorts; So-seti had a fit when she found out that you were going to be replaced..."

James stood in silence observing massive amount of religious icons. Dr. Byron Atkins thought being surrounded by religious codes in his office sanctuary would protect him from the monstrosities and evil spirits he had been exposed to on the floors below him on an everyday basis. The Muslim prayer mats called sajjāda hanging on either side of his walls, one in maroon and silver mosque and the other one in black, gold and blue in kaba design. In stark contrast to the Muslim mats also on the sides of the walls there hung Jewish adornments and the Star of David. To Byron's back hung an oil canvas of Lilith from an unknown artist in an unknown period of time and a canvas of Cain cast out into the wilderness. For Christianity an assortment of crosses were tastefully displayed throughout the room. But the Christian crosses were a source of anxiety and sadness for James. For him the cross represented misery, torture, and sorrow instead of resurrection, salvation, redemption, and gratification for all of the Christian church.

"So-seti turned her stretcher onto the floor at feeding time," Dr. Atkins said in a monotone voice.

Atkins cleared his throat and stood to get James' attention. "Would you be willing to go and check in with So-seti full time? I will bump up your security level permanently."

James stood frozen poker-faced but the excitement began building hearing her name. The Dr. had his attention now. Dr. Atkins came between James and the canvas of Cain in which he gazed. But James still could not look Byron in the eyes.

"She calls out for you..." Byron said, waiting until he got James to look him in the eyes, "and you alone, would you be interested in it? The unfettered attention garnered will give us enormous amount of information."

James smiled inwardly; she called out to me by name he thought, responding as he said, "Yes, uh, uh I would, thank you."

"Good," Byron said, shaking his head and opening a globe at the equator revealing several crystal glasses and a lead crystal decanter filled with golden bronzed colored brandy.

Byron took out two glasses and the brandy filling both of the glasses halfway then offering the spirits to James who politely accepted. Only sipping Byron's favorite full-bodied drink for fear of his blood sugar spiking, Byron told a tale of warning.

"Let me tell you a story as a warning before I took charge of the abomination...before I was even employed by the God's Light a continent away, So-seti befriended an employee by the name of Olson," Byron offered James another drink that he accepted and quickly gulped down. Then he gestured for James to sit before continuing.

"He started to trust So-seti and eventually So-seti persuaded Olson to loosen her shackles so she could get more comfortable, that is when the horror ensued." Byron sat on the edge of the desk next to James.

On the edge of his seat James asked, "What, um, happened then, sir?"

"She was able to transform and slip her feet out of her chains, her abdomen extended and twisted around, with her freed legs she was able to strike out at Olson, severely injuring his neck and knocking him out for a moment." Byron stopped to down the last drops of brandy from his glass.

"See, this was before we started to dose So-seti on a week to week basis just to be on the safe side," Byron continued, rummaging through his desk drawers before emerging with a picture. He handed off the picture to James and refilled his drink by the open global drink station.

He saw in the photograph a half-decapitated Olson sprawled out dead in a room not unlike the room that they were in as Byron explained more, "the surprise attack left Olson dizzy and out of breath on the floor, leaving him exposed to yet another attack."

Byron pricked his finger, his blood sugar still in range, comforting him; he smiled as he made himself another drink. He observed James as he took in the picture, reassured James had taken the whole situation in, he continued.

"The bitch instinctively went for Olson's jugular. He didn't have a chance..." Byron stopped sipping his second glass of brandy. James resumed nursing his own drink. "He bled out in seconds and So-seti escaped her confines."

Byron snapped his fingers in a motion that told James to give the photograph back, "All said and done, before she got captured, the death toll of our employees were five dead and two injured... Needless to say this brought about an increase in security and the severing of So-seti's legs permanently by implanting silver screws into the humorous bones so if she ever escaped again, she couldn't go far."

"You see?" Byron raised a bushy eyebrow and James urged him to continue,

"You are a brilliant administrator even with your disability and I'm sure you will manage the extra responsibility of babysitting the bitch and reporting back to me."

James felt like he had finally been validated. He had been employed by God's Light before Byron had been hired. The management change left James feeling insecure, like he had something to prove to his new boss, as though having to prove that half his body being useless did not affect his mind. He dove into his work, researching incidents and sightings, investigating whether or not the sighting had been legitimate or a fake. Delving into reports of the werewolf of Valadez where the werewolf ate road kill on the side of the street or the hoax of the bat kid of England. Until he had the new boss's attention organizing notes then producing brilliant and inspiring report after report so his indiscretions were forgiven.

"I showed you the gruesome photograph to remind of the horrors that she is capable of. Ever be complacent, never be fooled! Don't let her charm you! She is a test subject and nothing more, a lab rat to prick with a needle, study and dispose of when you are done." Byron sat silent for a second waiting for James to respond.

"I'll do it!" James stifled a smile; he did not want him to see the unbridled enthusiasm in his demeanor. He swigged back the rest of his drink and set down the empty glass on Byron's desk.

"Good, you're my best researcher as long as you do what you're told; you're going to have a bright future!" Dr. Atkins slapped James hard on his back, an annoying habit that James despised.

Byron promptly took a coaster from a stack by his desk and put the empty glass on the coaster then checked for any damage done by moisture to the bare wood. He opened the middle desk drawer by his portly legs and rummaged through the top drawer emerging with another ID card, higher up in security; "LEVEL IV special access".

"Thank you again, Dr. Atkins," eyeing the card.

Atkins swiped the card through the reader hooked up to his computer then handed the card to James. James tried to clasp this new ID badge onto his white lab coat with his secondary hand until finally feeling sorry for him Byron helped James clip it onto his breast pocket with a suppressed sigh of irritation.

Now a permanent level IV, he definitely had to gloat to Matt when he met up with Matt for their chess match. He stood staring at the buttons I through VII when a thought came to him. At security III they had James' nose buried in reports and investigations. Matt's level IV had him studying relics, dissecting organs and corpses. Down at Level V there were empty cells dedicated to interrogating live lycanthropes. Then he turned his attention toward the lit unmarked button he turned to see several unlit buttons he wondered if the special levels were dedicated to such clandestine activities and comatose experimental abominations. He wondered how far down the dungeon goes. Thinking about the cruel experiments perpetrated on their own God's Light employees made him livid, white knuckling his good hand on his cane as he hobbled to the elevator.

He roamed the glossy marble halls thinking about this for a moment. Just down the hall he stopped and stared at a large statue of the arch angel, Michael, its cold white marble cracking from age, wings spread out in all its glory, stepping on Lucifer's head. However he was not annoyed with the volunteers. A part of him wanted so desperately the childhood fairytale recipes to work to be validated but trial after trial were all futile.

He stood just a few feet from So-seti's prison putting his palm to the cold brick by the locked door. Just inside the door laid his validation, his proof in the flesh. Writing report after report and studying the arcane paled in comparison to the day when the helicopter blades spun and So-seti came to stay, not just of a paper and then not just of myths.

He stalled at So-seti's doorway to get his breath before sliding his ID badge at the door lock watching it turn from red to green and unlatch with a click.

"Jameeeees!" So-seti hissed, wrenching her neck to see him.

Her eyes revivified and brightened from the black lifeless orbs they had been before. He saw her trachea undulate over her frail tautened, thin skin as she spoke, "you follow your heart… come back for me?"

"Yes," James nodding in response.

He tried to imagine So-seti as a young wild animal, a feral wolf but then he saw her aching eyes. So-seti's eyes still had a milky haze about them; her eyes had been conditioned by torture and hopelessness. But some hopeful light filtered back to the eye, the light of kinship when she saw James, she had been alone for so long.

"Gooooooood..." So-seti cooed.

Instead of disgust when he looks upon her decrepit form he feels grief, tears spring forth from his eyes. So-seti looked like an animated puppet shivering with no blanket, chained up by her neck and waist, exposed to the cold, sterile room. Her blackened eye sockets had sunken in even further from yesterday. Her cheeks were almost like wet tissue paper and transparent in appearance. Her diaphragm mechanically raised and lowered with every difficult breath. Her legs like stumps with amputated wounds long ago healed, swaying back and forth. So-seti's phantom feet resting on the stretcher.

"I have the Wolf inside of me?" James couldn't stand to look at her as he gazed at the EKG machine.

James tore off the lined paper with a diagram that looked like several valleys and crests that monitored So-seti's weak heart rate.

"Yesssss, me can smell the wolf musk, powerfully strong in you..." So-seti pointed a boney finger at James' heart and he did not recoil from her hand.

"Wolf shade wants to come out!" So-seti reached out and patted James' head, "Me teach you how..."

James felt conflicted, guilty but exhilarated. How could this supposed lycanthrope physically transform? Even her long lean nose had sunken in decay, the bridge of her nose all but gone. She looked like a sickly gray-blue zombie, the crawling dead! He began to doubt everything, but he obsessed about his true potential. He could imagine once again using the left side extremities of his own body.

In fact he stopped fiddling with So-seti's processed food supplement, glorified wet dog food he thought.

James poured a milk formula high in protein and fat into a baby bottle complete with small nipple, "Tell me your secrets... Please."

So-seti greedily sucked down the bitter white fluid, formula spilling from her mouth onto the stretcher as she said, "Me tell you my secrets, you do me a favor..."

James hobbled over to the closet and opened it. He emerged with a musky pillow and blanket filled with holes eaten by moths. He slid a pillow under her head and covered her up with the thin blanket which felt more like writing paper that just outlined So-seti's form.

"Do we have a deal?" So-seti asked, the blanket only warming her a little bit but she did not shiver anymore.

"Yes, anything..."

So-seti motioned for him to come closer. Though uneasy, James drew closer while So-seti strained to find his ear. So-seti whispered with a hiss all the precious herbs and supplies for the ritual of the awakening.

34

Before James could meet up with Matt he had an unscheduled stop to make. He had to purchase items! He knew some of the ritual myths he read them as a young man and they were seared into memory! Maybe subconsciously he had been preparing for this, James thought. He headed to the marketplace for supplies. James entered the herbal/library marketplace on the outskirts of the walled Lucem Dei estate. Thrust back in time, back to the Middle Ages even down to the period piece cowbell that alerted the store owners of his presence. The inside of the marketplace was drastically different from the prefab modern structure outside. The hard wood floor, probably stripped from a 17th century church slated to be torn down, creaked. Dust flew through the air in a torrent of particles that made his throat burn as he inhaled it.

Surrounding him on either side spanning from floor to ceiling were bookshelves. The Lucem Dei library boasted the largest collection of occult, metaphysical, and theology based books in the United States. The first bookshelves contained hardbound ancient manuscripts. Some old manuscripts looked new from the care and gentle hands of some previous owner but some manuscripts were falling apart, duct tape running the edge of the spines. The second bookshelf held newer books, but still old from book standards, 1900s to present day manuscripts with the shiny lamination and crisp pages.

He searched the bookshelves obsessively until he found what he was looking for. Between the study of psychic phenomenon, vampyres and ghosts was a study of shape shifters. He found a new book called *Understanding Lycanthropy and Its Disease* by anonymous, two books from his youth that he had read called *Of Wolf and Man,* and *The Encyclopedia of Werewolves.* He picked them up dusted then them off when the shopkeeper finally arrived.

James was taken aback when he turned around and saw the black robes and habit. She was an old nun with thick rimmed, wire framed glasses with a beaded chain across her neck so she wouldn't lose them.

She had pleasant hazel eyes and red rosy cheeks and an unassuming smile. James noticed her lip stick stained dentures when she talked.

She clasped her hands when she spoke, "I'm sorry to keep you waiting," she said, "Can I help you my dear child?"

"Thank you sister," He whispered as he set the books down on a table. The nun reminded him of the library in Holy Family Elementary School and the evil nuns who smacked his hands with the ruler whenever he was talking in an octave too loud for the nuns to stomach. "I am a research assistant, assisting Dr. Byron Atkins, I would like to check these books out and then get help selecting and identifying herbs."

"Very good my dear, I will just need you to sign the books out over here and then I'll help you with the rest."

James struggled to limp over to the counter. His heart skipped a beat as he remembered the sign-in process. The walls of the Lucem Dei functioned as a self-sustaining village apart from the world. If you are in the walls of the Lucem Dei you didn't need any money but you had to sign everything. All you required was covered by private benefactors (some with military ties and deep pockets) going as far back as the late 17th century. It was a shadowy program backed by the Vatican, though if brought public the Vatican would disavow any knowledge of its existence.

He sloppily signed a signature, signing Sebastian Bach one of his idols a great composer that came to mind in a pinch. Too worried he was going to get caught he scratched anything that came to mind, however, she did not give him another look, too complacent from the relative safety of the secure walls, as she closed the sign in book and put it back under the counter. James could breathe again as he looked into her trusting, unassuming eyes.

If the Lucem Dei were governed by the states, the DEA would be knocking down the door for the illicit items under the counter, but the Lucem Dei was a safe haven, not governed by the states and he was safe and secure behind the walls of the Lucem Dei. People would get their milk and bread together with their opium and a host of illegal drugs with a smile and "God bless you" from a saintly nun, all necessary legal sacraments under the rites of God's Light.

The secure walls around him did not give him any solace, however, as his voice cracked worried about being arrested when he suggested under his breath, "I need, uh, um, two dozen copper nails, ergot fungus, wormwood, fennel, anise and um, um, a pint of grain alcohol and perhaps some other things."

"And oh yes, I need uh, lycanthropous flowers..." James said following the nun.

The small fragile nun had no trouble retrieving the flowers imported and cultivated by the church. She turned and proceeded to select the things on James' list. The wormwood and fennel she collected was beside the carrots and potatoes which made James immediately laugh to his self. The ergot fungus was in a glass container by the parsley and oregano. The opium was locked in a safe under the counter amongst the many illicit materials James had selected. The nun, as if realizing James's ultimate plans, frowned making James' heart sink. Dammit, he was too close to realizing his ultimate destiny to have it all yanked away at the last second. He felt sweat beading under his shirt.

"Excuse me for saying this, far be it from me to understand the projects here, but you already tried this experiment eleven times and every time the experiment failed. Tell me in advance next time because I'm running out of wormwood and I have to make a new batch of ergot fungus from Rye seeds before you experiment anymore." James looked into her eyes. Her eyes were full of compassion and concern. She thinks I'm one of the doctors, he thought.

"Seems to me the Holy Ghost and our Heavenly God doesn't want such blasphemy under His roof." She knew she had crossed the line somewhere in the sand and she was worried about retribution. And if it had been anybody else she should have been disciplined but it was James so there would be no punishment today.

"Sister, forgive me, but *all* failed?" the fear in her eyes made him bolder to question such a thing.

"Well yes my dear." Not questioning that a doctor should have known this already.

"I thought the ritual was an utter failure. The basement is full of volunteers that got bitten. Those comatose demonic things," She was lost in thought for a moment and wrung her hands nervously muttering under her breath "but I see you are trying the procedure one last time."

"What?" He had completely forgotten his fear of getting caught, now too wrapped up in Lucem Dei and its clandestine operations.

"Why, the volunteers got bitten or volunteered for the ritual to get infected so they could study the beginnings of the disease, of course."

He didn't say another word, gathering up his supplies including a copper pot and a dozen copper nails and hurriedly left the store as quickly as he could, hobbling on his cane like a man on a mission.

James' head was reeling with the discovery of the clandestine experiments perpetuated by the Lucem Dei. Somewhere in the church turned dungeon of the Lucem Dei there were lycanthropes being held captive other than So-seti. Where were they? How many were there? He shook off his uneasy thoughts and finished up procuring his items. Then, he made his way toward Matt to finish their nightly chess game in the garden by the church.

"Hey James," Matt cheered, "I almost thought you ditched me!"

"Um, um, um now why would I do such a thing?" James set down and pushed the procurements under the bench.

"So I am dying to know, in your conversations with So-seti did you learn anything pertinent to our bets?" Matt questioned while he sat up the last figures of the chessboard, "for instance, the myth of an Alpha in wolves set to a family hierarchy system."

Once Matt set up the board and the white and black figures he looked at James, "Okay, I'll make the first move, Pawn to B-4. So did I win the bet? Is the alpha-wolf just hokum, a myth?"

"Um, uh, Pawn to B-6," James countered, "I don't know um, um I don't know about a natural born family wolves, but did you observe a feral Mongol rogue pack? They could be made up from a mixture uh, of various breeds of dogs, For example..."

Matt nodded and picked up the white figure, "Pawn to G-4... yeah, go on."

James countered, "Pawn to D-7, No family um, at all, just a mismatch of different breeds of a variety of different sizes from a small Chihuahua to a large Greyhound. Large to tiny dogs follow a medium-sized mutt, um, um, secreting hormones because he's a strong, confident leader. But then the mutt gets injured and lame and a stranger amongst the pack takes control."

"Bishop to A-3," Matt countered, smiling because of his friend's more fluid conversation.

James continued, "So-seti told me lycanthropes are partially human and as such they crave structure, like a military structure. The alpha is like the Grandfather and the pack his children. She used to have strong pheromones so the weak willed would do her bidding but she became weak and the secretions ebbed, Pawn to A-5."

Matt quickly made an L on the board, "knight B to C-3, so what you are telling me is you won our bet."

James smiled, "I don't know about him and natural wolves but for all intents and purposes lycanthropes have pheromones and the leader of the pack is considered alpha wolf, Pawn E-5."

"Knight F-3," Matt chuckled, "well, I don't have my wallet with me. How about some time I take you to dinner, get you a couple of drinks, and we call it even?"

James scoffed and shook his head, "okay."

James slid the Bishop across the board. They played chess throughout the night. They laughed and joked but he couldn't help but think of poor So-seti down in the dungeon. James won four games before Matt finally won one.

After losing a record amount of matches Matt got up and stretched his legs, "well it's been fun losing to you, but I have to be turning in for the night James."

"Um, um, um, okay, then," James smiled and awkwardly stood up to shake Matt hand, "good night to you."

James made sure Matt had disappeared into the night before bringing out the illicit supplies for the upcoming full Moon.

35

He came in to So-seti's room and remembered the kindly old nun who told him about the failed experiments. He couldn't hide the signs of shock when he looked up at So-seti's craggy visage, the creases that had deepened since even yesterday.

So-seti spilled out her secrets night after night in preparation for the next full moon. Lucius whispered to her a hidden pathway that led out of the God's Light's walls. She had not been out in the fresh air since she had been delivered to the God's Light compound; however, she repeated whispered directions from an old friend. James could not wait to get out of the basement of the church. Both James and So-seti were silent, anxiously anticipating the sunset and what was to come of the shared knowledge when the full Moon started to rise. James checked the silver nitrate solution, two pints. He replaced the empty saline bag, and then he scrolled a report on the clipboard chained to the end of So-seti's stretcher.

"Thank you," James spoke softly never taking his eyes off her while he withdrew from the room until he locked So-seti in for the night.

James fought back the instinct to stay with So-seti, to comfort her, conflicted between staying with her and testing out the ritual in the fresh air. But in the basement the absence of windows made him grow restless and he struggled into the elevator. A short trip, then a "bing" and the elevator doors opened.

He still had to finish up a report about an upper New York state area "Sasquatch" sighting. In his investigations the setting of a "Sasquatch" showed most sightings were just elusive werewolf sighting. A quick proofread to his finished report then he hit enter and was done.

James flew out the doors as quickly as his injured extremities would let him and he wasted no time finding the fissure in the wall. He finally found what he was looking for by an overgrown weed-filled area behind the General Store. Bamboo trees not native to California, but flown in and planted to increase the aesthetics, hid the great wide gap in the fortification where the concrete fell. Dirt and sediment poured in making a gentle sloping ramp up the ten foot man-made hole.

James made his way up and out to the freedom outside the compound. He found a massive ledge with a dozen or so mature blue oak and ash trees overlooking San Francisco. The altitude and the absence of the oppressive white lights of urban technology made the first signs of the first night of the full moon an impressive sight as he stared up at the brilliant silver moon seeming to burst out of the ground, the moon's lights and shadows of the craters, hills and valleys begging to be touched.

Yesterday in the cover of night James picked a lone, healthy ash tree and then using a silver butter knife scored a circle all around the lonely tree spacious enough that he could dance around it as per So-seti's instructions. With a shaking hand he plunged in his pants pocket, emerging with three copper 6-inch nails in his palm.

He had read several folklores about becoming a werewolf, but they were incomplete legends something for his curious mind to pass the time away. So-seti's complete secrets solidified his resolve to see this experiment through, failure or success. He drew the copper bucket close to the ash tree and carefully stabbed the copper nail through the bark with his only useful hand. He repeated the process until out of nails, nine in all. Then he picked up a rock and pounded the nails a little further until sap came pouring out.

Now he found his ash tree and checked on the bucket, full of sap and illuminated by the light of the full moon. He set the lycanthropous flowers so they could bask in the full Moon's light while he prepared. James crushed the mixture and drank it. Then he proudly chanted the secret hymn aloud. He saw the glowing full Moon while smearing the secret illicit oily substance all over his unclothed body. Dancing around the tree with the help of his cane, stumbling but never falling a dozen or so times, he made smaller circles while orbiting the tree so he could gaze upon the moon without any disruption.

He felt dizzy and unstable, his whole world spinning, he felt a pop deep in his brain just like the feeling he had before when he had had his aneurysm. His anxiety overwhelmed him and his heart fluttered. The hairs on the back of his neck and arms stood up at attention… his heart quickened, his skin thickening and fingernails bleeding as his fingers lengthened.

James' spine began to crack and shatter into pieces as muscle and sinew contorting. Stem cells, satellite cells armed now with blueprints, started to convert James' entire body. He opened his fanged mouth to howl out, a glorious commingling of wolf and human hybrid ready and fit for survival, an apex predator.

The transformation complete James felt electricity, his whole body the source of pins and needles, bizarrely he felt numb at the same time, an orgasmic release and an overwhelming bliss as synapses fired all at once. James knew no fear, no rational thought no consciousness, just the pure instinct that begat unadulterated power. Able to use all four appendages for the first time in a long time he stretched his limbs and scratched into the Earth with all four paws consecutively because he could.

A kaleidoscope of sight, hearing and smell merged into one great sense. James saw in a crude form of heat and night vision and the crisp magnification more than made up for red and green blindness. A lucid vision, like James' mind floated over his wolf form while the wolf peered out at the mountaintop with his brand-new animalistic eyes. He saw the rural road far off in the distance too far for human eyes. Head lights from a stranded car got the brand-new wolf's attention.

Hunger suddenly beset his belly; consuming his every primeval thought process. A low guttural growl could be heard coming somewhere in the wolf's throat. He soon locked onto the stalled car just like an infirm and incapacitated animal cut out from the herd. He could see a motorist furiously changing a flat tire. Sniffing the air all around him, he reflexively cringed. The stale stench of an overcrowded decadent human population nauseated the beast, the pheromones of fear, helplessness and despair. Carbon monoxide exhaust and the faint smell of cheap cologne wandered up the elevation watering his eyes.

Somewhere in his hazy and rudimentary consciousness he remembered a voice whispering that if it could be helped, stay away from the humans until you're more knowledgeable and skilled in the ways of the wolf. Concealed by the darkness in the rocks of the crag the moon's light captured the mountain lion's eyes betraying its position.

Instead of bouncing down from the mountain to attack the stranded motorist he turned to attack the mountain lion. A hiss of warning then a shriek of pain as the wolf swiped the lion in the thigh. A fury of fangs and claws ensued. The lion's front claws lengthened exposing nails, rearing up on hind legs the injured limb hung limp while the lion's good paw swiped at the aggressive Wolf. The claws did not penetrate the wolf's thick fur and tough skin. Now the wolf had two limbs to clutch onto the lion and it was not long before the brawl was over. The wolf's teeth eagerly bit down into the lion's exposed neck, golden fur turning a dark sticky maroon as the rest of the lion's limbs went limp.

He let loose a cry of joy, a howl that could be heard for miles over the mountain tops, he recollected through the fog of consciousness the orders given to him by So-seti. With a full belly the wolf sat on his haunches, content, the wolf's muzzle dripping with lion's blood. He let loose the aria of loss, a tale that can be heard by Aticus, the original target, far off in Louisiana.

36

Outskirts of Pointe Coupee Parish

The black, one-eyed Wolf appeared from behind the Cyprus. Muzzle a rust colored, crusted, congealing mess from his fresh kill. It was not human but it satisfied his love for the hunt. He licked a huge rock. Saliva made the rock melt away, salty molecules falling, hissing and bubbling as they hit the ground. A trick he learned from his sorceress mother the solid mass gave way to Aticus' clothing including his wraparound sunglasses, homemade patch and precious black military style boots. Aticus was dressed before he darted toward the owner, Michael's, shack. The agonizing sounds coming from the shack had him kicking himself; he couldn't believe he let Michael talk him into trying to change Ken, his best friend and roommate. Something about Ken just smelled weak.

Aticus skewered a piece of meat on a spit then tossed it onto a makeshift barbecue pit. The gem reflected through Aticus' wraparound sunglasses as the sun peeked out from behind the clouds. With one quick motion he leapt on top of the tin roof of the shack, the thin tin resonated like thunder as his feet hit. The shack groaned surrendering to his weight as he walked to the edge giving him full view of his surroundings. First they infected the outskirts of Royal Bay then they circled the town of New Roads, then Batchelor, before Aticus set his sights to yet another town. Aticus grimaced in disgust, fangs bared; several improvised dens made a circle on the outskirts of Royal Bay. They were strategically perfect but he found five decapitated homeowners and burned out homes. He knew this bedlam had to be Devon's work but he was staying at Point Breeze Motel the self-imposed save zone. But he considered himself a man of his word so no harm would come to the patrons staying at the Point Breeze but was he to step out of the Motel area and all bets were off.

Michael's shack, an isolated pastoral, stood out amongst Pointe Coupee, West Feliciana, and Concordia Parishes and at the Mississippi state border. Aticus' inner circle consisting of Lance, Montezu, Tomas, Tonya and Aticus' had grown. Oung from China arrived by freighter to the New World. He had blue black luscious hair tied up, braided and ever-growing because of commands of his Tao religion. Then came O-Kami from Japan tattooed from neck to torso with inks infused with liquid silver.

His stature like a general, shoulders high, arched back, legs straight, and his arms crossed as he gazed out at the Parish borders. Except for the shack, which he was standing on top of, there were no houses for miles. A sly smile exposed his long canines an ideal place for the pack's next makeshift den. Michael, the occupant of the shack, had been responding well to the parasite. Now he was excited, he had the plantation in his sights. Lance was off observing the group, including Devon at the Point Breeze Motel. The group would travel back and forth to Raccourci Island with Sarah who was sprucing up her inherited acquisition. When anyone ventured out too far, with Aticus' orders Lance would be in position and ready for action.

The snow white fur shone in the sunlight as a huge white-furred wolf, Montezu, appeared out from the woods, the Cyprus' giving way to his large snout. Ears twitched involuntarily as they zeroed in on the faint sounds of movement. He had six alternating large and small studs that came to a point screwed onto his skull and his dark gray eyes radiating translucent flecks of red, animal eyes. He morphed from wolf to man without stopping. He got a robe and pants from a clothesline near the shack and with one fluid motion he was dressed. His hands gripped the top of the shack and he jumped onto the roof feet first like a gymnast.

"There are five hunters a mile and a half towards the Cyprus, close to the swamp." Montezu reported patting his old friend on the back. "An arsenal of weaponry in their truck, at hand there are three with shotgun, two with rifle, looks like they're hunting... for us."

"Keep an eye on them," Ordered Aticus, "they get any closer. We may have to kill them."

Aticus tried to refrain from chuckling but failed. Montezu's accent was a really strange and amusing mixture of Mesoamerican and French-Canadian. Born 300 BC in Mesoamerica, now Honduras, he had been one of the Nahual tribe. When the wolves retreated further north the tribe migrated too. In time the wolves and the Nahual tribe were hunted to near extinction and truth gave way to folklore.

Sadly the Nahual, once great werewolves, became just another shape shifter legend. And wolves gave way to indigenous animals over shadowing the once great Nahual tribe. Temple carvings that depicted wolves got interpreted as dogs, and carvings that depicted the Wolf man beast got interpreted as donkeys.

When Stefan was killed Montezu headed to the extreme north, tired of the heat and to clear his head. He and his indigenous wolves made their way to Canada. He started a new pack that soon worshiped him like a God, however boredom made him insane. Aticus' howls had made him drop what he was doing and Kill all of his followers and look for Aticus who returned to the new Americas. Being a blood-soaked warmonger He was distraught when Aticus told him that several big wars had come and passed. Two wars specifically, World War I and World War II, which had almost all the countries involved. Montezu kicked himself for missing both.

"Tomas and Lance should be back from patrol soon." He looked at Montezu who was staring at the ground. His body had gone rigid mentally trying to lighten his weight for fear of the roof collapsing under his feet.

"Good," Aticus stomped hard at the roof with his boots making Montezu flinch," Don't worry my friend, it'll hold." He chuckled; amused by the fact this ferocious man had a horrible fear of heights.

He looked up at the full moon still present with the rising sun, just about 5 AM. With his preternatural ears he could hear commotion coming from the tin shack and it pleased him immensely. Up on his feet now the occupant stumbled around the trailer. He didn't even need to turn around he could faintly smell his fellow pack members returning, Tomas retiring from the patrol out from the woods and Lance back from monitoring the hotel where Devon and the others were staying. Aticus jumped from the top of the shack down to the ground as the shack rocked catching him off balance Montezu's eyes widened.

"There is only one main road out of town to the interstate, a back road but it leads to a small creek with a bridge easily gotten rid of." Tomas Reported matter-of-factly morphing from a wolf to man and getting dressed from a clothesline tied up from tree to tree.

Tomas' proud cheekbones and red brown dreadlocks which were more like fur than hair, now hidden when he flipped up the hood on his robe but his cheek and nose visible in the sun light. Navajo born, the last of his line of the legendary skin walkers with natural blue black hair gave way to reddish-brown fur. His canines gaining four sets of teeth several decades ago made his jaw more pronounced. Lance's wolf morphed into a human and put his pants on still shirtless. He liked the way the sun felt on his back and the wind felt through his red chest hairs.

"We found five phone towers and two auxiliary electrical stations leading down to one main station." Lance ran his fingers through his bright red hair. "Say the word Aticus and I can have it destroyed in a matter of moments."

Lance absolutely loved being a werewolf; still young enough that his enhanced senses, preternatural strength, agility and healing ability exhilarated him. Before the change he had been dangerously obese, feverish with smallpox and at death's door, Aticus gave him his salvation. Now he was healthy, lean, and muscular could run a marathon without getting winded. He felt Aticus was a father figure to him and he would stop at nothing to please him.

"I could call the wolves." Montezu suggested.

"No, not yet, patience my friend," Aticus ordered.

He knew Montezu could control and command real wolves, a consequence of his blood line but he felt the time had not come yet. All in good time, as the pounding in his head increased, only minor setbacks Aticus thought, all on track with his master plan.

Tomas and Lance leapt onto the porch spurning Montezu to do the same his confidence increasing when his feet touched the earth. Followed by Aticus, The one eyed leader nodded an order but he was lost in thought, he motioned at the door. The shack door slid open, surprising the wolf-man, Michael Miller, who resided inside. The wolf man's ears twitching he stopped his destructive tantrum as he spun around in the direction of the four intruders. He growled a warning, fangs snapping like chattering toy teeth at four interlopers invading his home.

The monster towered in the hallway he looked like a giant in the shack, arms outstretched with talons scraping each side of the trailer walls making a shrill sound that had Tomas shuttering. Thin and tall, it was the first time the Metamorphoses come upon him but he already had reversed knees, tail, and the short but prominent muzzle.

Aticus crouched down and slowly crept between the sliding door and the hallway. Michael's growl began to get louder, his ears laid back warning Aticus of an immediate strike. He had a tear in his eye like a proud father looking at his baby for the first time. Michael the wolf man had responded to the parasites more quickly than Aticus had ever hoped. Surprised to see the tail and the reverse knee form for Michael so quickly because in his vast experience it usually took two or three Moon cycles before the infected started to see significant lupine-like changes.

Aticus' forearm hairs thickened and his talons burst out of his skin as he shoved Tomas and Lance back targeting his frenzied progeny. He flew forward squeezing Michael's thick hairy neck; the foreword propulsion knocked Michael to the floor. Michael's neck veins bulging as all Aticus' weight pressed down on his chest. His claws tightened like a vice, squeezing the life away from his body.

"Boy! I own you... It would be in your best interest to settle down like a good pup!" His voice was stern but no hint of anger. In fact he was exhilarated to see what rage Michael had in him. "Settle down boy and I'll release your neck."

Michael struggled a moment or two more but then his body went limp and he urinated on himself, a sure sign that Aticus knew he would be complacent. Aticus spoke softly, "That's it, good boy, that's it."

Slowly, he stood up relieving the pressure on Michael's chest allowing him to breathe again. All said and done, Montezu slapped Aticus on the back of the head playfully shoving him against the wall.

"You prick," Aticus said smiling playfully as he retaliated forth with.

Lance made himself home slowly strolling past the small dining room towards the kitchen. He really loved this place and he could see why Aticus had picked it, "In the boonies," He said to himself. After the scuffle Lance made his way to the kitchen counter where the alcohol was kept. Bottles and bottles of alcohol, so much alcohol it was hard to pick just one spirit. Lance picked out his favorite poison then he drank a few swigs from the bottle before pouring himself out an ounce and a half in a shot glass. The quiet surroundings reminded him of his favorite horror movie.

Exclaiming, "No one can hear you scream!" He howled at the top of his lungs then swigged another shot.

Montezu was irritated at the corny "Aliens" reference. It irritated him, Lance's obsession with 20th century movies and television. Most days, Montezu mused, Lance was just a human playing a wolf.

"Lance I need you to take Michael for a walk," it amused him every time he referenced the new changelings like a puppy, "Before he gets antsy again, I'm beginning to get a headache and I need to talk to Tomas privately."

Lance fixed himself another double shot, downed it, and then grudgingly did what he was told, "okay."

"I'll go with you," Montezu had just gotten comfortable on the couch but he saw the disappointment in Lance's face so he got up on his feet, offering his company.

Aticus heard the door slide shut as he attempted to straighten up Michael's mess. He turned over chairs until they rested on their legs. Then he quietly and carefully placed decorative statues upon the entertainment center then headed toward the hallway to the three back rooms of the shack.

He closed his eye as he entered a side room, one of three the fragrant scent of the lilies and fresh pine needles over taking him. Only clairvoyants or those "blessed" with the third sight could see her, Tonya, she wasn't physically in the room but he knew she was there. With his Wolf eyes he could even see her ghostly silhouette sitting cross-legged on the floor.

"*Tonya*." Aticus shouted out in his mind.

His thoughts were answered almost instantaneously as Tonya materialized. Her ethereal figure turning to flesh and blood her smooth caramel skin and naked appearance made Aticus blush as his loins ached from wanton. Her luxurious Raven black hair came down strategically to cover her naked breasts. Her blue wolf eyes gave the appearance of a normal human and they shot daggers towards Aticus' direction.

"*Yá'át'ééh shitsóí, Aticus*." Tonya greeted him.

A Navajo greeting that she knew Aticus couldn't understand. She said hello in her native tongue. But it wasn't just "*hello*" it translated to, "*hello, my young child*," a rib at him as the alpha male. But she said this with a smile and a low smoky voice that Aticus loved so well she hoped he would be oblivious to the veiled insult.

Playing a dangerous game she gathered a white silk robe from the closet but slow to cover her body up knowing Aticus would stare at her longingly. Angry with him for the death of Stefan and furious for the fire that almost cost her life she found herself conflicted. Strong pheromones swirling through the air made her strangely attracted and obligated to him, but she found herself repulsed by him at the same time.

Aticus looked her up and down his manhood stirring but he stopped at her scarred calves and thighs a constant reminder that if she wasn't a shaman and could become ethereal almost in the blink of an eye his impulsive rage would have cost her life. Tonya wasn't going to forget about it any time soon either prancing around him day after day naked for the entire world to see but denying him even a touch.

"Is there any progress with Oung?" He asked. Tonya was terribly close to Aticus now, a deliberate calculation to get under his skin, he thought.

"Oung says, 'Ni hao'." Tonya jokingly smiled as she tried to pronounce the Mandarin language Oung had taught her.

He stifled a laugh as she said this, butchering the pronunciation of the Chinese hello. He didn't know Navajo but he did know Mongolian, as evidenced by his Mongol like features. He could translate many more Chinese dialects even some dead forgotten ones.

Aticus had started to feel small around her, insignificant. But her shaman ability to enter dreams and teleport had become priceless. An intricate part of his plan she could eaves drop on both Oung and O-Kami. Oung able to transport his wolf-self halfway across the world and O-Kami could transport and control a pack of spirit Wolves in his trance like state to crush those who opposed him. No matter how he felt about her she could be aware of them anywhere they were.

"Is Oung out of his trance yet?" As he said this he consciously bit his tongue the desire almost too much to bear but the headaches he suffered had come back with a vengeance. Aticus' body severely shook as if he had mild seizures withdrawing off a dangerous drug.

She spoke in her smoky, broken English voice, "No, not yet, but he has picked up the scent of another werewolf."

"Oung has tracked a lone straggler into the icy forests of Siberia."

Tonya almost touched Aticus' chest the anticipation killing him, too much for him to bear as he flexed his chest. Tonya saw what he was waiting for and drew her hand away teasing him. Tonya's loyalty never in question and it pleased him but since the fire and subsequent death of Stefan she punished him in other ways. When in heat she would run off and mate with real wolves instead of Aticus. The evidence of her infidelity could be seen chained up by the shack, three Wolf pups sleeping peacefully under the porch hidden from the sunlight.

"O-Kami?" His voice broke.

"He is with Oung tracking the Wolf, patience, my sweet Aticus, I've been all around the world already today; my psyche is tired and needs rest before I can teleport again."

Satisfied with her answer he calculated his next move when Tonya spoke again." I'm going to check on MY children and then I'm going to go on a run to clear my head."

The emphasis on 'my' angered him provoking a response, "You're a true bitch."

"True, I'm a bitch," she uncovered her silk robe to reveal her forbidden Garden of desire and her horribly scarred legs.

"But you're a murder." She said this also with a smile, the death of Drake, her son, was still fresh in her mind. At night he could hear her howling a funeral dirge and some nights searching for him in her dreams.

"You know if you make love to me the scars will eventually go away." He said this matter-of-factly, taking full advantage of his special ability.

Only it wasn't exactly Tonya's emotional and physical scars he worried about, he longed for Tonya's ability to enter dreams and teleport. After Aticus was wounded and suckling at Tonya's teat and in between the terrible fire she gained her abilities by having sex with an unknown werewolf. Aticus so badly wanted this power.

"Sure and then you would have the power of the Shaman and have no use for me. No thanks, I'd rather die than have sex with you." And with that she turned and walked out of the room, Aticus closely shadowing her.

Aticus retired into the bigger master bedroom in back with Tomas shadowing with a drink in hand ready to offer it to his leader then he retreated to the rocking chair where he sat quietly. Aticus walked over to the quivering lump in the living room. The quivering form, the paramedic, Cody...

Cody had awoke from his cold, dead slumber, finding himself in a body bag in the morgue the following night when the full Moon though recessing had made its way across the sky again. Dr. Jacobs had just finished pulling out the three slugs from Cody's body and he reached for the rib-cracker, preparing to open his chest but before he had the chance to begin the autopsy, Cody's heart began to beat again, pumping the parasite all through his veins.

The abomination's body shook transmuting right before Dr. Jacobs eyes. Dr. Jacobs froze with a scalpel in one hand and the rib-cracker in the other. Cody started to look like a combination of the paramedic's youthful face and a furless short muzzled, dog-like creature. The forehead gushed with fresh blood from his bullet wound and his cheeks and chin were boiling from the extreme heat of the transformation.

Cody's biceps were engorged, floppy hands struggling to drag his useless limbs off the resting place on the stretcher. The body fell clumsily; his paralyzed feet plunged down onto the cold hospital floor. Dr. Jacobs' terrified eyes could not drag himself away from the animated monstrosity headed straight toward him. The gore pooling up from Cody's fresh bullet wounds in his abdomen. Blood staining the concrete floor as it spread, congealing blood making a trail straight for Dr. Jacobs. Cody's mutating body slithered like a snake heading straight for him. He watched in horror as Cody's spine contorted, arching almost out of his skin then whipping back again. His coccyx lengthened the skin stretching until a small hairless tail emerged out of the reanimated man's nude buttocks. His hands like silly putty stretching, the fingernails lengthening, reached out for Dr. Jacobs. His wild eyes filled with pain, shock and confusion. Skin stretching to accommodate his ears as they began moving, growing, spreading out and reshaping like triangles, then falling in on themselves.

"That's impossible!" Dr. Jacobs found himself shouting. "You were dead! Weren't you?"

Dr. Jacobs hesitated, He did not run, He did not scream as the monstrosity named Cody enveloped him. He managed to drag his paralyzed legs along the way assaulting Dr. Jacobs without any hesitation. Cody's fingernail beds bled as the nails darkened and lengthened. Dr. Jacobs gathered his wits about him just as Cody's bloody fingers tore his white lab coat and cleaved through a button up shirt, tearing the exposed flesh.

Dr. Jacobs could not get out of Cody's deadly embrace. They were locked together in a macabre dance, each one whirling about, Cody's useless legs just along for the ride until they both twirled around knocking down a tray of sterilized equipment contaminating the contents. When the stainless steel equipment hit the hard concrete floor the resulting bang resonated throughout the room. Steel instruments clanging against steel which tore through and violated Cody's sensitive ears. Cody instinctively let go of Dr. Jacobs and put his hands up to his head protecting his ears. Without the support of his hands resting upon Dr. Jacobs's shoulders Cody's body flopped to the floor.

Dr. Jacobs realized with Cody's claw-like hands protecting his ears and balled up in the fetal position on the floor a perfect opportunity of escape and he instinctively made a break for the doors. Dr. Jacobs didn't stop running through the corridor and down the employee only steps until he made it to the cafeteria. Stopping only to catch his breath he realized the scratches he received had broken skin and now he bled through his torn shirt.

Dr. Jacobs wildly looked around behind him again, nobody coming for him. Assured that he had not been followed by this nightmarish monster he sat down on the nearest chair. In shock now and going down the long deep road to madness he hysterically laughed. Chuckling, surely without a body to deal with the center of disease control would be wrapping up their case, he thought.

When a sufficient amount of time had passed Dr. Jacobs got up on wobbly legs and proceeded to exit the cafeteria only stopping when the cashier looked at him wild eyed with bewilderment and noticed his disheveled appearance and noticed the blood on his chest.

"My floor drain, it backed up! It is a bloody mess literally!" Dr. Jacobs tried to hide the bloody scratch marks by putting his palm on his heart as if he took an oath, pledging his allegiance to the United States of America.

The cashier opened her mouth preparing to speak but Dr. Jacobs cut her off, "I think I have it all cleaned up, but now I'm exhausted!" He grabbed a dozen or so napkins from the dispenser then looked her in the eye, "I really need coffee!"

Dr. Jacobs dabbed at the clotting blood with a napkin. He sipped on his coffee. He found himself on autopilot, trying to make his way back to his morgue counting tiles along his way. No trail of blood coming from the exit doors to the hospital.

Dr. Jacobs timidly pushed at the double doors, wholly expecting an imminent attack by the horror inside. He blinked his eyes rapidly, holding the hot coffee cup at the ready, preparing to throw the scolding hot liquid if accosted. He opened his eyes wide to see that blood had pooled on the concrete floor but nobody stirred within, just the two corpses lining the walls waiting to get examined. No monster moving within the room at all.

The advantage of being human was having an ability to rationalize the strange, the unusual, and impossible. As soon as Dr. Jacobs got away the pathways in his brain rerouted with every step he took until delusions filled his mind rationalizing the insane reality he ran away from. A saving grace throughout history when a human being rarely happened upon a lycanthrope fog cloaked his mind until he rationalized the surreal moment. The feeble nascent mind cannot fathom the preternatural event causing insanity. Resulting in a feverish denial, the mind rejects the bizarre and strange probability that they just saw.

Maybe Cody wasn't dead at all! Maybe Cody made up the elaborate ruse to escape the police! Maybe some chemical had spilled in his morgue explaining the hallucinations. He checked several bottles of fluids spanning wall-to-wall on the shelves. Yeah, that had to be it he convinced himself. Unbeknownst to Dr. Jacobs, Cody had mauled another person just outside of the hospital.

Cody escaped from the hospital morgue; he found his way back to the relative safety of Aticus' improvised den, his useless half-formed hairy legs trailing behind him. When the full Moon finally regressed for another month the animated body grew still once more, his heart stopped pumping, the grievous injuries just too much for Cody's body to bear. Yet Cody had come to Aticus so he tried to protect Cody's lifeless body until the next full moon. He somehow hoped Cody would come out of his stupor. With the full Moon the heart would beat once more. A comingling of lupine form would repair the damage that had been done to his severely wounded body. But the brain and spinal cord had atrophied beyond repair even the parasites could not save him. Aticus could tell by Cody's decaying smell and his hazy eyes, His body was rotting away, he would not survive.

Aticus shook his head in sorrow and disgust as he remembered the day and he had come home to him. He stared at Cody's broken form writhing around in agony the parasites trying to heal broken neurons.

"Oh my boy, I will miss you," Hesitating he cocked back both barrels fired both slugs that found its target, entering Cody's forehead.

The antique gun still smoking as he flipped a switch that revealed a silver bayonet and with one well-aimed strike the pineal and pituitary gland burst like a grape under a boot. He went on to sever Cody's spinal column between the third and fourth vertebrate.

Aticus tussled Cody's hair a moment before sitting down right next to Michael's friend, comatose on the couch, "He has no hope for survival."

He found the remote to the radio and turned it on to a metal station oblivious to the comatose body sitting right next to him. The rhythmic electric guitars and the tribal like drums always soothed him and somewhere deep inside exciting him.

Aticus' eye squinted, rolling compulsorily, his fingers rubbed at his stiff neck as he remembered the night he futilely tried to facilitate Ken's transformation. He had been growing weary, impatient and running out of things to try. He clicked the double firing pins into position and rested the antique shotgun barrels against his chin a habit he had every time he grew frustrated.

Michael Miller's "walk" now finished, the moon receding, making way for the sun he had become human again. Aticus heard the sliding door. Michael's legs weak like wet noodles slowly stumbled into the cramped living quarters.

"I really wish you wouldn't do that!" Lance said hoarsely entering the trailer after Michael, motioning at Aticus with the loaded gun resting under his chin.

"Oh you're no fun," Aticus scoffed, his thin, pale lips cracked a smile and put the gun down.

Aticus looked upon Michael with a proud eye, responding well to the parasite, Michael surpassed his expectations. His sickly thin drug-induced body now filled out getting meat on his frame. His long face and dark sunken eyes now Rosy and full, his eyes brightened a bit. Shirtless, wearing only shredded jeans and barefoot his stomach now rounded and slightly plump. Michael crouched down next to his comatose friend gingerly touched his cheek. Aticus couldn't help but remember the events leading up to Ken's body thrashing about going into a seizure.

"I think he had a stroke." Michael said looking at his friend's eyes. Evidenced by the right eye blown out and blood-filled, right cheek sagged and sunk in. His right shoulder prostrate and lifeless as well.

"Dammit!" Aticus had tried every ritual and potion he could think of, whatever it would take to get the parasite to finally respond to his body, but it had been all for naut.

Michael said meekly pointing at the crumpled up pale thing, "He's not showing any signs of change."

Ken, Michael's friend and roommate a boy in his late teens lay in his own vomit on the floor. Shaking slightly, he laid out in the fetal position. Aticus' sharp claws man-handled the boy's head roughly, a vice like grip on his chin; crimson drops trickled down Aticus' palms coming from the pale man's pierced cheeks. Coming up so close to him their noses touched. Sniffing him, licking him, and then looking into his eyes. His face went red with frustration.

"You may be right," Aticus' claws let go of his head leaving him unbalanced his chin dropping down and hitting the armrest with a snap, the bones breaking.

He impatiently unfolded an old fur covered rug, It was a gray and black skin Wolf pelt. He threw the pelt across the meek man's shoulders. He slathered a sticky black solution all over the man's face and hair then carefully put the wolf head rolled on top of his head. Finally it seemed to work, a guttural growl starting in Ken's throat spewed forth louder and louder before his body suddenly stiffened and arched. His eyes rolled back foam billowing forth from his pale lips like a volcano erupting... Now Aticus shook off his thoughts and Ken's pale lifeless form made him sick to his stomach and he felt his migraine coming back.

Aticus turned his back to the man and picked up his gun, "I can't watch this, discard him deep in the forest," Aticus closed his eyes, frustration setting in, his headache worsening, rubbing his temples. This is hopeless, he thought growling with frustration.

Tonya entered as a side door flew open, the trailer rocking and the pitcher frames rattling on the walls, "what are you doing?"

"What?" Aticus opened his eye to see Tonya on top of him.

"He could yet survive, you ass!" She was instinctively beating on Aticus' bare chest.

Quick hands stilled her torrent of blows. He increased the pressure on her wrists until she settled down. "What are you talking about?"

Tonya rubbed her aching wrists, it was foolish for her to challenge her alpha let alone beating him she thought, but she could only take so much before she snapped.

"He could yet survive. He could have changed. It could take six months for a normal human to Metamorphosis!" Tonya spit.

"Sadly, no he is not, if he does transform he'll head home," Aticus said matter-of-factly. He turned his back on her, a challenge and a test.

"But I know medicines..." She was silent now, so her words could sink in. Aticus turned his back to her, she instinctively flinched, then resisted the chance to ambush him. She passed the test.

"You have silver sickness. The headaches, they're slowly..." Aticus interrupted Tonya.

"You are sliding down a slippery slope, careful, my love." Aticus touched her shoulder and she impulsively backed away from him.

"All those lost souls don't stand a chance with your impatient nature, Aticus." She emphasized his name deliberately to see him cringe, and he was getting infuriated with the conversation.

"Don't question me; I know what I'm doing!" Aticus snapped.

"My Liege," Tonya converted to another strategy. "You are powerful, and ancient. With all due respect, I just meant that you were born a Wolf with a Wolf mother that left you orphaned at a young age. You haven't experienced a pack mentality or the secrets that come with a tribe."

She had seen him destroy three young hopeful, but nonresponsive changelings just a day ago and she grew weary of it. Tonya gingerly rested her delicate hand against Aticus' antique gun, making him lower it.

"Enlighten me," Aticus said sarcastically as he made himself comfortable on the sofa and motioned for Tonya to sit on his lap. She declined, remaining standing.

"There are ice baths to relieve the fever. In my tribe the initiate would dream walk bare in the winter to cure the fever. There are herbs that inhibit the healing process from attacking the invaders until they are fully changed. There are chants and rituals to make the élan vital to multiply at an accelerated pace increasing the initiates' chances of success if left to fend for themselves." Tonya was startled when Ice suddenly stood up.

She cautiously continued, "Numerous persons have already survived the initial infection and are thriving. I can see them in my dreams... patience is a virtue, my friend."

Of course for those that followed Aticus' arias and joined the pack he could wholeheartedly help the infected through the fever process. His migraines, occasional bouts of confusion, and lastly the rage from the silver sickness making him a cruel and sadistic pack master. He would obsessively check for genetic markers, for preternatural healing by cruelly slicing the arms or the chests with steak knives or razors to see how quickly, if at all, the infected were able to heal. There would be no room for weakness in his den.

He could sense the others lost in the world on the verge of the change and those comatose dying and decaying. Those animated on the full Moon had just the primitive brain stem and are easily pliable. Dozens upon dozens have been infected, well past the numbers that he projected, and it pleased him immensely. Changelings were alone for the changing; but Aticus reasoned he abandoned the infected to save their lives. He can see himself shooting them in the head if the whining and howling begun and he had a massive migraine.

Killing Cody was a blessing in compassion. A normal bullet had severed Cody's spinal column; he could not walk or feel and would decay until his brain would not function any more. Aticus assumed his injuries would be permanent, injured so soon after infection, so killing Cody put him out of his misery.

As for the murder of Alex, Tracy had recently given birth and was too busy running around her baby to worry about her lost love. Two other women were in the back room their minds in a haze. Aticus had plans for them to breed with the other pack members to strengthen his pack. Yes, there were several murders to worry about and he just had to put a bullet in Cody but as far as he's concerned weeding out the weak and infirm strengthened his pack.

He proceeded to open the curtains to what used to be Michael's clandestine room. An unfurnished room with no TV, stereo, a desk with no drawers, even chairs or a bed… just a foldout table. A beaker filled with an unknown fluid and fan hooked to a hose that attached to the window of the shack sat on a hot plate plugged into the wall.

No coincidence that Aticus and his pack stumbled onto Michael's shack. Aticus could smell the stink of his synthetic methamphetamine coursing through his veins from miles away. Now he had a working lab. Chemicals such as Alcohol, Toluene, Iodine, Salt, Lithium Batteries, anhydrous ammonia in a propane barrel, Lye, red phosphorous and Muriatic Acid could be seen in the corner of the room. Coffee Filters stacked up out-of-the-way and Pyrex Cookware on the floor, enough ingredients and glassware for two clandestine methamphetamine recipes. Aticus turned his attention to the finished product which rested on the table.

Aticus pulled out a decorative double bladed letter opener from his pants pocket then watched his human arm transmute to a lupine limb and huge paw with thick black fur. His skin still bubbling in transition between human to wolf he proceeded to slash his forearm and blood began to spill out filling the beaker until the clear liquid turned to pink plasma.

The surreptitious recipe's operations had changed throughout the years but one thing was the same, wolf's blood. In the old days they used human sacrifice to elicit the fear, adrenaline and what is known as the "impending death" hormone but nowadays, modern science began to synthetically replicate what was precious about the blood sacrifice. Smoke billowed out of the shack from the makeshift science lab. He had a determined look on his face. Blood dripped down from fresh rags on his forearms as he measured beakers, checked temperatures, stirred mixtures. Aticus frantically makes the reddish rock until powder, sweating from the effort.

Aticus wrung his hands, up pacing the floor nervously while Montezu finished filling the last of the baggies with the remarkably special pink powder smiling all the way. He scooped up the pink finished product with a measuring device and poured it into a small plastic bag. Montezu counted the baggies then put them in a black briefcase for his leader. Aticus set the black briefcase with the other briefcases in the closet. Growing furious remembering how Tomas dared compare him to a drug dealer. Soft growls getting louder until suddenly Oung opened the bedroom door startling him out of his train of thought.

"The deed is done..." Oung referred to the tracking, stalking, and killing of a lycanthrope that resisted Aticus' alpha leader status.

Aticus asked, "You have anything for me?"

Oung felt sorry for him, and he immediately spewed forth the gore and the whole bloody brainstem complete with glands and the still beating heart of Aticus' resistor onto the floor.

With a gleam in his green eye Aticus threw himself upon the floor lapping up the plasma soaking into the shag carpet. He greedily consumed the whole heart then consumed glands on the floor like a junkie craving for his next fix. Oung felt sorry for Aticus as the forbidden juices spilled from his mouth down to his neck. He watched Aticus' eye as it dilated, the brilliant green iris just a thin band and the expanding pupil becoming a black hole. Oung watched helplessly, Aticus oblivious to those around him, lost in reverie.

Oung was familiar with the ritual of a lycanthrope consuming one of their own but only when one died or there was a challenge in the pack. Rare and highly ceremonious, all the pack gathered around to eat. Anyone caught ingesting the flesh without such ceremony was still taboo and copious amounts led to ill health. But Aticus greedily absorbing the dead meat, the rush, the high, the pleasure that it contained within, a pain reliever he became numb and nothing more than that, he had become an addict.

Aticus had heard an unfamiliar howl last night but its contents were all too familiar and it tugged on his heartstrings. An aria he heard from his younger days, happy pleasant memories where his brother and beloved sister still lived, a song that had been handed down to his mother by his grandmother. A sure sign his grandmother survived still.

"I need a favor from you my friend."

"Anything for my brother," The one thing he hated as a lycanthrope, it was getting harder and harder to feel the effects of the alcohol as he threw away his shot glass and drank straight out of the half-gallon vodka bottle.

"I need you to go to California, specifically, Los Angles." Aticus waited for Tomas' response.

Tomas was taken aback with Aticus' request. Taking a plane was out of the question, somehow the altitude made a lycanthrope involuntarily change; But Aticus was his best friend, his blood brother. The decision was made before he even thought about it.

"I'll do it. Just tell me what for." He toasted Aticus' half gallon with his shot glass in a sign of solidarity.

"And I need you to persuade Tonya to go to California, it will be easy enough for her," he swallowed before continuing like the words were rancor to his mouth, "with her gifts."

Tomas nodded in agreement, waiting until Aticus finished.

"I want you to pick up my Grandmother," Aticus said under his breath, "Lunacy will reign soon."

37

God's Light monastery, California

The sun high up in the sky; warming James' semi-lupine form, warming his fur before the full moon could not be seen, setting in motion the conversion to a human being again. He slumbers exposed on the hard, warm Earth for two or three hours before finally awakening.

For years after his aneurysm just getting out of bed in the morning had been a chore but not this morning he sat up with relative ease. He felt a strange tingling in his left shoulder and it began to pulsate through his arm to his hand. James rubbed his eyes then his left hand, still groggy, perking up with his left fingers moving independently and intricately… pointer, ring, middle and the pinky finger for the first time since his stroke. His heart quickened, it is not possible he thought. For the first time since the stroke he braced himself with both arms and though unsteady at first he got up without any assistance. Although his useless left limbs had atrophied throughout the years and were weak, they were able to support his weight. He had to think about every movement of his left leg and arm, since the years of inactivity had his limbs complacent, but they functioned normally once again.

His stubbly cheek and chin felt sticky, his belly felt full and the palms of his hands were stained with blood. The night's events were hazy at best and some memories he could not recall at all but exhilaration pulsed throughout his body bringing him a well-deserved harmony for the first time he could remember. He saw a half-eaten mountain lion a few meters away from him sparking last night's events.

James thought of the mountain lion and the powerful beardless wolf-man amalgamation. No thoughts, just instinct, a pure primal urge driving him on. He had so easily overpowered the meeker lion and he consumed him. Only hunger and rest concerned him, a freedom he longed to feel again. He scooped up the lion onto his shoulders then headed back home via the hidden sloping dirt route, a disruption in the massively tall wall to the God's light compound. He had grown quite comfortable in his birthday suit, it seemed so natural, so primal, so liberating. However, the closeness of the God's Light compound made him keenly aware of his nakedness.

James rested his stiff leg. Traversing the slope proved difficult without his cane, but he happily passed through it back to the gardens. The town clock gonged five times, 5 AM. He stuck to the shadows of houses as he could not very well explain away his nakedness and the carcass that he held in hand. The ease of which he could sense human or animal presence flabbergasted him. He could hear private conversations coming from a dwelling, a conversation not meant for the public but easily deciphered through his modified sensitive ears. Breathing in an assortment of odors and aromas he could distinguish three distinct human beings and one dog. James closed his eyes and concentrated; one man in his 20's exuded health, vigor, and fitness but the other one had the peculiar pungent scent of illness though still in his teens, a dangerous heart murmur revealing itself with a faint odor of decay in the sweat. He now whiffed a unique mixture of blood of the third stranger. Still a boy, puberty had not come upon him yet. He could even smell the fleas that infested the hairy dog. He could smell the skin flakes, dried blood, and feces of the fleas. His confidence rising, James triangulated the smell by wind patterns and heard the faint conversations and was able to determine that they were three blocks down and one block to the right of him.

James' naked form simply snuck past the group and the dog. The dog scented James' ominous presence and instead of barking it backed up in between the younger boy's legs started trembling. He hoisted up the carcass with his left hand, smiling, as he fumbled for the keys with his other hand. Eventually finding the keys he unlocked the door and headed into his house.

James already missed the raw power that came from his transformation. Even though after his transformation he had blacked out a lot of physical memories he was able to remember the potent feelings it had brought forth. With every swipe of the knife to dismember his prized corpse to manageable parts James felt the remarkable power of last night surging forth from his body.

He got dressed in a simple gray sweatshirt and sweatpants combination then wrapped the parts in paper, opened his igloo container and put the wrapped parts inside. If the security were to stop him he hoped his lunchbox would not raise any eyebrows. Satisfied the lunchbox would pass by the security staff, if they didn't rummage too far back, he placed the container into his backpack so he could use his cane. Although with practice he was able to maneuver the left arm again he wanted to hide his functional arm from the staff. James quenched his thirst for water for the third time and then out the door he went.

The Lucem Dei's estate felt smaller somehow. When he enthusiastically joined Lucem Dei the acres and acres of its walled property felt huge to him. The walls that used to protect him were now smothering him and closing him in. Anxiety started to take a toll on him until he came to the church.

"Get it together man!" He said out loud pressing the button to move the altar and unearthing the trapdoors that led to the inner bowels of The Lucem Dei. With only a brief glance from the security staff at him he sauntered inside. James pressed the button on the elevator that led to So-seti's prison.

So-seti could smell James and the fresh meat walking down the hallway before he entered the room. Her eyes fixated on his backpack where she knew the fresh bloody game had to be, her mouth was watering in expectation, but in utter confusion. She had been sustained on a diet of basic kibble, a mixture that was just shy of glorified dog food, for decades, to keep her weak and she was not expecting anything more.

James avoided eye contact with So-seti as he went about the makeshift prison cell turning dials, checking numbers, and replacing empty IVs. It was hard enough enduring new smells and the dizzying array of beeps and hums of the makeshift dungeon let alone looking upon the weakened and legless atrophied form of So-seti, who he now regarded as a majestic and beautiful creature. Too much for him to handle, his heightened senses on overload. His shaking hands turned the IV knob until the silver nitrate trickled no more. He pressed a series of buttons on the numerical keyboard. James entered a code that he had only just managed to memorize last night while distracting Dr. Atkins to override and stop the flow the silver nitrate. He could hear the buzzing of the overhead florescent lights and he could smell her salty tears, the tears of excitement and gratitude.

So-seti was truly weeping now as the incoherent fogginess of her drug induced haze lifted. The silver nitrate poison dissipating in her veins. James checked the IV lines that ran up to the wall and over to a corner away from So-seti's shackled bed. The IVs were deliberately bolted to the corner so no staff members would be forced to turn their backs to her and risk their life if So-seti should somehow slip her bonds and attack. Her nose crinkled as she sniffed the air, breathing in all of James's scent. He smelled different, she thought; the Wolf was now inside him and it thrilled her brittle bones. His stature and stance was different and his cane once vital for balance as he walked was now just a glorified ornament as the cane hovered above the floor. So-seti noticed his left arm still hung limp at his side but the shoulder was different, higher than before. The shoulder muscle that had been smaller the cartilage and muscle that had slipped from the bone was fuller and more pronounced now, anatomically symmetrical.

"Move sssshoulder." She was choking back tears when she said this. "Me knew you were sssstrong!" She knew in her heart James was now a changeling.

James froze, startled, interrupted from his busy work of straightening and filing papers but he rotated his shoulder fully then walked towards So-seti. Without a word, he raised his arm and wriggled his left fingers and with a smile, he began to get the meat out of the lunchbox and carefully unwrap it.

"I knew you had to be famished." He said as he watched her devour the meat almost before James had finished opening it.

"Thank you," she said as the blood trickled down her chin.

She noticed that she had just the minimal amount of shackles and more importantly she wasn't wearing a choker, a safety precaution during feeding time that she had always dreaded.

"Come here, my prodigy. Come here, that I can smell you," So-seti whispered, choking back her tears.

Pieces of meat spilled out as she said this. She saw a difference in his physique; He was somehow thicker than before. The subluxation in his shoulder apparent, the muscle had slipped one-inch from the bone, and the hypo flexion of his arm was obvious but the shoulder muscle was now engorged. Yes! He was now a changeling she was sure of it!

He stopped just short of her face and lingered. She tried to touch James's cheeks but the chains tightened. So-seti breathed in his scent deeply, and then held her breath to take it all in. She had begun to feel tingly and euphoric… a sign that the silver nitrate had left her system.

In fact, she could transform and escape now but with the silver rods through her thighs she could not regenerate her legs. Making her effectively legless, underground at least three or four floors down, without legs it would be far too ineffective to attempt escape so she lay motionless for a while, then she spoke to her Savior.

"Me know the Wolf is inside you now! Tell me, exhilarating, isn't it? Can, use your arm and leg?" She stared into his eyes but then her attention turned back to the rest of her dinner.

"Yes," he was staring off in the distance, pleasant feelings running through his mind. "I brought you my first kill. It is a mountain lion."

"Yes me know," she looked upon him lovingly, "It is a strong adult lion too, me impressed."

He opened the last of the meat and fed it to her like an ailing grandmother that he loved unconditionally.

"Your prize lion that you have so generously gave to me, a strong lion, Yesssss?" She hissed as she said this, her undying gratitude evident; James could see it in her eyes.

His eyes lit up, remembering the claws of the lion tucked away in his backpack. He pulled out three magnificent curled nails to show her.

"Your puissance very impressive. You survive your first change and the Wolf inside you is powerful." She said as she tore a piece of meat with her teeth dangerously close to James's fingers.

"I have some questions." James said. He watched So-seti as she devoured the last of the meat.

"But first I have to say that I am truly and horribly sorry for the things they were doing to you." Now, his eyes welled up and he began to cry.

Taken aback from his tone and honesty she felt the tears welling up again. "Me will teach you if you permit me, since my captivity leaves me idle and it would be great company, for so long all me had was just my own voice to keep me from going insane."

A modest man, he did not mean to, but he glanced at her breasts. He felt a growing heat in his cheeks and a stirring in his loins. Yesterday the site of her body repulsed him, now after his change she appeared strangely more attractive to him. So-seti noticed this and smiled.

She closed her eyes and her mouth opened revealing fangs as her back arched. James could see fine black fur cropping up over the length of her body. Three pair of tiny teats sprung up on her chest and abdomen. Her claws scratching the stainless steel gurney making a screeching sound that made him shudder reminding him of nails on a chalkboard. As quickly as the transformation started the fine fur receded back into her now taunt smooth body. Fangs gave way to teeth as she licked her lips slowly with her tongue; her lips were supple again and had the pinkish hue where once a cracked sick gray had been. She deliberately tried to reach out and touch James's face but the restraints stopped her just short of that. James got the clue and immediately made slack on the chains so she could touch his cheek.

"Am I going to be immortal too, just like you?" His hands reached up and touched hers.

It had been fifteen years since any significant gains to his weak side and he had resigned himself to living the life of a cripple with the hardships and scrutiny that comes with the stigma. But now, in this very morning he noticed real changes. He had the stamina, senses and the strength of an Olympic athlete on anabolic steroids, even his atrophied muscles started to fill out thrilling him immensely. He closed his eyes, swallowed and then held his breath before asking her a dreaded question.

"Will I be whole again?"

"No, not yet, my sweet, sweet child." Her voice was smooth and sexy as she wiped a tear from his eye she said, "The Wolf shade is still changing you."

So-seti craned her neck still worried that at any moment the alarm would sound alerting the staff who would rush in to secure her. She shuddered just imagining the silver nitrate solution burning through her veins as the staff pushed the plunger down. James held her wrinkled hand assuring her everything would be all right. She could see the confusion in his face so she elaborated more about the subject as best she could.

"Young lycanthropes just starting out, their wolf shades are still invading their bodies. Are separate in their bodies and minds, they're effectively two beings until they merge. My Wolf and I were one and the same, we merged together long ago, do you understand?"

"No." He said simply, wiping his tears away.

A noise coming from the hallway startled him and quieted for a second. He exhaled, breathing easily again; just lowly staff members chatting and walking through the hallway. His heightened sense of hearing alerted him. He put his finger to her lips to ensure her silence. As a new changeling, frustration set in, trying to home in on the suspicious noise until he zeroed in on the source. But it wasn't this hallway where the sounds were coming from; the sounds were coming from three floors below. The noise he heard quite clearly astounded him because in the basement the walls, ceilings and floors all were soundproof. A couple of seconds more, just to be sure he wasn't wrong that at any moment the staff wouldn't burst in interrupting them, then he gave So-seti the signal to continue.

"Now the Wolf spirit inside of you has awakened and coursing through you, but you are not one and the same yet. Understand?" So-seti choked back a sob.

So-seti closed her eyes as James gingerly caressed her cheek. James didn't say anything but his facial expressions told So-seti that he still didn't comprehend what she was talking about.

"Some lycanthropes Wolf shade slumbers deep inside," So-seti's bony pointer finger touched her wrinkled forehead. James was still brushing her cheek with the back of his hand delicately. It had been an unfathomable amount of time since any affectionate touch and she didn't want it to end so she rattled on, "They live their whole lives and die still separate from their wolves."

"First, let me tell you the abbreviated version of the incipient lycanthrope, the werewolf who started it all." James was surprised at the ease of which she spoke; she was articulate and almost poetic with the silver nitrate gone from her system, neurons making new pathways in her brain.

She had been in captivity under the ward of the Inquisition since 1800 A.D. until she moved here to the Sacred Lady of the Light on Diablo's Mountain range and its sprawling acres of land. When she talked the perfect Queen's English spilled out now, she had fooled everybody. James couldn't help but laugh. Of course, they thought she was a wild beast so she gave them a wild beast. All the while listening to the conversations and probably strategizing a way to escape. He wondered how many conversations through the millennia she had overheard. He wanted to ask which people had their dirty little secrets and hidden affairs, but it would have to wait as she continued.

"I am the great granddaughter of the first true lycanthrope; my kindred are those who are a distant relation to the first werewolves. My great grandmother threw herself into the depths of the ocean. My great-grandmother, Aisos, tired of this world and faced with the fact of immortality she threw herself into the briny deep. Her body sank like a stone before she ultimately died and began to decay. She had six surviving children that set out on this world and sired more children.

The ocean began to evaporate water molecules began to condense into rain clouds, the invisible parasites lighter than water vapor began to condense too. The tiny animalcules rode the Jetstream until they condensing enough to form rain clouds and parasitic rain fell down. The animalcule invading unsuspecting villagers made humans carriers, effectively the parasite spread all around the land. But the carriers of the parasite were diluted through the years even the Wolf Cults thinned out through the millennium. The first wolf Cults spread out across Asia, two in Europe, North America, South America and Africa. Aisos' lineage began to dilute as the human population exploded then infighting threatened to exterminate the cults, the only saving grace was that every single human in the world now had the animalcule inside them lying dormant. However, you'd have to know the secrets of the beginnings to unlock the metamorphosis… And the six packs guarded the secrets fiercely…or you must get bitten," She pointed to her forehead right between the eyes. He was staring at her eyes, her delicate caring eyes.

"You could seek the infected out if you were so inclined. They would be colorblind but they could see a small bird 100 miles away. Some have pointed ears, could hear a whisper in a crowded room, the same length of digits on his or her fingers, those that late at night long for the outdoors, for the hunt, the outcast, the distant genetic relatives. Lucky ones are the kindred possessed of Wolf's blood inside them."

"Every once in a while a brave soul might muster up the courage to research the forbidden art but without the help of the packs to unlock its secrets they shall not be successful…" So-seti beheld James' hungry eyes, eyes thirsty for knowledge, "You possessed the wolf shade and you're lucky enough to find me to unlock the secrets within you."

He could envision the bitten ones, their pain much more unbearable as the Wolf blood slowly creeps in and violently mutates through their veins.

"People that generally don't survive to realize their first transformation, the lucky few feel like they've been cursed."

He could just imagine that unless the biter comes to the aid of the stricken they don't survive.

"A fatal self-inflicted gunshot wound to the head or angry mob's torches does the werewolf in before the year is done. If they survive without a guide they live their lives to the moon's phases, growing older without a mentor,"

"Tell me more..."

James eyes were ablaze with expectation; So-seti lay quietly for a moment letting him contemplate the remarkable circumstances. James pushed his sweat shirt sleeves up, first the left then right before realizing his left arm pushed the other sleeve up by habit for the first time. So-seti saw the fine hairs rising, all of them spurting up and down his arms and she could hear the intensifying rumble coming from his stomach.

James remembered the broken and staggered secrets So-seti whispered to him and now he understood, "The Wolves shade rains fell down. The animalcules soak into the roots of the ash trees. They slumbered in the ash tree sap..."

"You follow, yes?" He nodded acknowledgment so she continued. "The animalcule rests in the pineal gland. As a child grows into a young man the pineal gland calcifies trapping the Wolf shade, the ability to transform an almost impossibility."

So-seti caressed his face with her hands, "I've eave dropped on many a scientist's conversations through the centuries coming up with this breakthrough. If a lycanthrope bites you the animalcule invades the bloodstream and the enzymes that were created soften the pineal gland. They awaken animalcules from slumber and fusion with the invaders... Or so I am told, ha, ha. I tell you my sweet it is a surreal experience to listen on to other people trying to explain what I am gifted with."

"So you understand," So-seti continued. "Every man, woman, and child had the animalcule dormant inside them at some time before the time when human population exploded. I could smell you, one of six pack's descendants. I could be definitely sure about that."

James finally broke their mutual stare. He looked to the door to ensure it remained closed, the hunger pains getting the best of him. "Okay I understand so far, So-seti."

"A person could find a copy of the rituals penned down by the six packs or a person could be bitten and if they are lucky enough to survive they become a lycanthrope. That is the reason the God's Light has a vested interest in me but I could smell with my preternatural senses that all of the test subjects failed horribly!" So-seti paused so the message would sink into James' mind.

James' mind reeled thinking about becoming a Wolf-thing last night but he had turned back into a puny human once again making his heart sink. He couldn't help but imagine the God's Light test subjects, alone, without anyone to instruct them they were stuck in limbo in most likely a vegetative state, the two halves, Wolf and human warring with each other. He thought about the people in the basement who would not survive the first night their heart exploding or like James there is bleeding in their brain. He could just imagine row after row of patients down below the God's Light compound in a vegetative state or in a coma just like James once found himself in years ago.

A light bulb went off in his head, it sunk in, God's Light needed So-seti for their failed experiments and they desperately needed her secrets. The guinea pigs of the Gods Light could learn from her easier rituals and be in less pain when they finally transform. Maybe even come out of their comas! She could pick and choose the staff members according to their smell. With the right mentor the person can be instructed to merge with their Wolf self instead of resisting the wolf animalcules. They could be taught to transform at will, at ease and becoming immortal of sorts, because the human side dies as the Wolf side is born again and vice versa, every time the lycanthrope morphs.

"Hungry, yes?" one look into his eyes and she could tell James' pain, excruciating unbearable hunger that made her heart hurt.

So-seti drew closer her mouth opened. Mesmerized by her eyes James didn't realize what was happening until their lips touched and she regurgitated into his mouth. James first instincts were to gag, to quell the peculiar feel of the warmth cud as it surged down his throat. Sticky, thick, the consistency of oat meal and sour to the taste but the cud had been condensed and concentrated… full of abundant vitamins and minerals it pacified James. Their lips locking in place suctioning together like interlock in a submarine so So-seti finished feeding him. The hunger that racked him so severely had been quenched.

James swallowed, "Thank you."

"You find for me the others! Now you can learn all you can about this accursed place, yes?" So-seti spoke as thick splotches of oatmeal-like dribble flowed down her bony neck.

"I will," James said staring at her hopeful radiant green eyes, his hunger pacified.

"Thank you..." She said softly, almost at a whisper.

"You're welcome." James whispered.

No more silver nitrate running through her veins her pheromones began permeating through the air. James could not help it, unable to break away from her stare. Such a strange but mesmerizing creature, he thought, she looked famished herself James thought. He could count her ribs and look upon her beating heart through a brittle sternum and paper-thin skin.

Her dry lips cracked, splitting apart, bleeding her loose jowls flopped as she spoke, "see what they're doing to our kind... so you will be ready!"

He twisted his head in confusion, "Be ready?"

"Did you sing my aria for me?" So-Seti questioned.

"Yes, I think I did," James searched his memory, recalling the song coming to him like a dream. A fleeting memory, with his belly full and atop his prize, the dead lion, James' wolf threw his lupine head back and howled out, "yes I definitely did!"

"Then my progeny will come!" So-seti flashed a wrinkled smile exposing canines.

Without any hesitation he walked over to the phone on the wall and pressed for the operator. He had a brief conversation with the receptionist to patch him into Dr. Atkins cell phone. James said in an authoritative, but deliberately stuttering voice, "Yes, Dr. Atkins, uh, um, this is James in the lower level."

"James, what can I do for you?" The voice on the other side of the phone said.

"I'm well aware, uh, of all of all the theoretical lycanthropy myths but now, um, face to face with a real lycanthrope for the first time in my life...I would like, uh, to study lycanthropy closer with a scientist so I can better understand, um, So-seti." James lied easily.

Dr. Atkins thought about this for several seconds. James had been a loyal employee and his disability made him no threat. Ironically the only thing that stopped Dr. Atkins from promoting James had been his disability. "It wouldn't hurt. Tell you what James; I will call over to my scientist, Carson Milton, on the third floor in the East Wing to alert him you are coming, okay?"

James grimaced when he earned the name Carson but then glanced over to So-seti and flashed a symmetrical smile, "Thank you Dr. Atkins, I do, um, appreciate it."

James presses the elevator button for the third basement floor East wing, conscientious to fake a limp and use his now ornamental cane as he walked into the elevator. He wasn't sure he could stomach the experimentation of his new blood brothers; nevertheless So-seti wanted to know their whereabouts and wanted him to learn in a way that he understood, scientifically, all that he could about his new found abilities.

The elevator doors opened. James looked around the room as if for the first time. He touched the cold smooth stainless steel walls feeling the minute textures not apparent to human beings. Smelling the sterile but stagnant air had reminded him of a Lysol and alcohol mix. The flashing lights that spanned the length of the hallway always seemed too dim to him now too intense he had to shield his eyes. The glare so intense he had to squint. The bare steel walls with no pictures that can be seen anywhere magnify the reflective radiance. He smiled thinking back to the fact that only yesterday he had clomped clumsily as he walked, a consequence of his left side weakness, now he swaggered through the hallway without a sound. He stopped at the edge of the glass doors where a staff member labored away with his back to James. He did not notice the intricate arcane sigils carved into granite covering the walls edge to edge. James could smell the faint oil-based paint and strong silver smell that assaulted his nostrils coming from the decorative sword held in the arch Angel Michael's hand; it had been painted the exact same color as the marble statue a long, long time ago. He slid open the glass doors startling the oblivious scientist who was working in the room.

"Ah, it's you, I got a call from Dr. Atkins and he told me to expect you." The scientist Carson motioned to the ceiling, "I guess it's nice to have somebody to talk to. I've been so lonely I catch myself talking to nobody in the room and you know what they say about the person that talks to himself..." He trailed off awkwardly.

"I heard you're only crazy if you answer yourself," James said unaware the stuttering had gone away, as they shook hands. "Let's start at the beginning I feel like we got off on a wrong start, I am James and you are?"

"Okay I will play, its Carson, nice to meet you James and sometimes yes, I do answer myself!" Carson pushed the wire rim glasses further up the bridge of his nose and flashed a smile, "in fact I'm in the midst of an argument with myself right now!"

Carson the baldheaded scientist said, sneering, "So the boss tells me that you need some experience in the autopsy experiments, that it?"

"Yup," James said simply, hiding his rising disgust with the mere thought of a real-life autopsy.

"I am in charge of the brains, glands and organs, specifically pineal and pituitary. I study the parasite's behavior," Carson laughed.

James body shivered from every one of the countless jars that held cross-section brains in formaldehyde, the mounting smell too much for him to bear. Dizziness over taking him, he grabbed the autopsy table to steady himself dropping his cane in the process. To make matters worse, the dreadful hunger twisting in his stomach once again making him dizzy and hard to think.

"Yeah, we found the parasite by accident; first accidently found by electron microscope. We and the general population including all the doctors are not generally taught to look for a parasite. Even the general tests don't register either unless the parasites are sloughing off. With its miniscule size it's a wonder they caught it at all. We are studying the dwindling specimens to see how it functions, and if there is a cure to be found," The scientist said, "We have made great strides in the study of lycanthropy. The parasite is an Arthropod with a dozen or so legs… we haven't counted them yet, the amoebas rest in the pineal gland."

"The parasite larvae are dormant sleeping in the pineal gland until the full moon. When the Moon is bright and full in the sky, amoebae apparently awaken from cryptobiosis and flood the blood stream maturing to adult parasites. For all our investigations the parasites are like the microscopic tardigrade or waterbear, found everywhere and able to survive even the harshest habitations throughout the world." Carson shook his head in astonishment, "You know one out of three people have a parasite inside them. You'd be surprised to find so many unsuspecting stowaways in the human body, bacteria that live in the digestive tract, it is said almost all of the human population has the Schistosoma mansoni, a parasite that lives in the bloodstream. They do not know it's in their body until they get dementia and a whole host of other diseases that comes with that particular infection."

"That's truly disgusting to think about," not quite so fascinated James made a nauseated face.

"Through our studies we think that if the horrid beast bites you, the enzyme that the parasite puts out reanimates the dormant parasites in the bloodstream." Carson explained; giving him more of a scientific answer than So-seti had already given to him.

"This parasite is extremely unusual. The parasite is asexual, it reproduces more amoebas in its segmented many legged body. We have been unsuccessful in definitively sizing the parasite thus far; it can only be seen by electron microscope analyzing it through supercomputer. The parasite rolls up into a ball when it's dried out and hibernating. In ball form and dehydrated we're unsure if it is an amoeba or a full blown adult and we waste all the samples analyzing it," Dr. Carson said as he continued.

"I think that's why we have some problems infecting the volunteers so we could come up with a cure. We don't know if it is amoeba or an adult, if it's rolled up in a ball and dehydrated, if it is best night or day by the moon's various phases. We're not even sure if it worked on the subjects in a coma." Carson is silent for a moment then looked over to James and continued.

"Hey check it out, James." The scientist patted him on his left shoulder as he filled beakers and carefully began pinching liquids from a dropper, his eyes filled with excitement. "The parasite is almost magnetic; it binds and concentrates iron, watch this!"

Forgetting his cane that fell on the floor and his fake limp James walked toward Carson putting his once lame hand on his shoulder as he watched, curiosity getting the better of him.

"Think of this as a normal human body with normal water weight." He then proceeded to pinch the dropper until the red liquid ran out of it. "Then this is an approximate of human blood supply."

James watched in fascination since, he had gone through the metamorphosis himself. The scientist removed a giant magnet plugged it in and then placed it three-feet from the beaker. The beaker slid over to the magnet, instantly attracted by it. James knew what the magnet represented before the scientist said anything.

"The magnet represents obviously, the moon." The scientist unplugged the magnet for just a second and proceeded to get a faux skin and wrap it around the beaker then plug the magnet back in again. This time a dramatic difference in the behavior, the beaker didn't move toward the magnet but the blood pressed against the glass moving in circles frantically darting to and fro.

"Exciting right?" The scientist gestured to James to wait a moment while he powered up the machines then motioned for James to approach. James stared at an image marked as "unknown lycanthrope #1". A parasite still in stasis attached and threaded all throughout 46 chromosomes of his DNA.

"We were lucky to test this captive before the full Moon had arisen. He flew into the rage and eventually we had to shoot and kill him because he was trying to attack the staff." The scientist said, "By the time it was over two of our staff lay eviscerated. Their livers were swallowed whole."

"I believe the parasite feeds on salt and iron, that's why I think that iron has such strong play in the process of transformation." Carson ignored James, now preparing one more example.

"I think we have had a breakthrough in regards to transformation." The scientist said with a smile, he was anxious to show James what he had found out. "Parasite larvae in the pineal gland are responsible for waking adult parasites attached to the ladder of DNA from stasis."

"I'll just be a moment." Carson said excitedly.

With a few strokes on the keyboards the big screen came to life. He proceeded to pull out from the freezer what look like a bundle of glands and connective tissue. He hooked it in place with wire and string until it looked like a grotesque 3-D instruction manual, a human monstrosity complete with wrinkled hydrated eyes and plasticized heart. Then he carefully removed two human arms one left one right cut off at the elbows but intact with the arteries and veins.

Carson maneuvered the 100 Neodymium 3/4 inch Magnets closer to the glandular veins with eyes and heart then he found a floor lamp and screwed in a high-powered ultraviolet light.

He unfolded his pocket knife and proceeded cutting his submarine sandwich in half offering half to James. Although disgusted at the site of the sandwich and smell of ammonia mixed with decay he took the sandwich anyway and proceeded to wholeheartedly devour it with one gulp. Carson turned the monitor so James could see it. There for James' eyes was a plasticized human glandular system complete with eyes and a heart!

"The magnet represents the gravitational pull of the moon and the UV light represents the light of the full Moon, watch this." Carson explained.

"Meathead," that is what our Carson lovingly referred to the bundles of veins and plasticized arms, "magnets represent the moon. When it's not plugged in it represents daytime, when the Moon is extremely far away. Look closer at Meathead's arms, they are not changing."

He turned on the electromagnet and moved the group of magnets even closer, "this represents the movement of the moon in the sky. Now it's directly above Meathead representing nighttime. Look closer and you see the veins and arteries pulsating like a fire hose being turned on."

"I learned with the help of Meathead and others that the human parts of the victims start to feel tired and lethargic when the sun sets because of the release of hormones and serotonin in the uncalcified pineal gland and pituitary gland, putting them in an easily pliable trance-like state. A lycanthrope's eyes have a range far greater than humans so when the full moon is in the sky it filters the light through the eyes and into the uncalcified pineal gland effectively setting the hormones in motion to awaken and release the parasite!" Carson rubbed his bald head and continued with his practiced and well-honed speech.

"Watch, James," Carson flipped the UV light switch to on.

An instant sheen could be seen on Meathead's veins and arteries as the parasites awakened and a visible spike could be seen on the computer screen. James' eyes widened in disbelief as Meathead's pineal gland released a flood of invisible amoebas. Raisin like eyes rehydrated looking more like large grapes. Meathead's decaying heart beat again. The dead human arms begin transforming to true wolf paws. James could not help himself he had to pat Meathead's soft fur. Looking over at the jumble of eyes and arteries a horrible thought went through his mind, he could also wind up as just a bundle of parts to experiment with and that horrified him.

"Even in death the live animalcule somehow recognizes the full Moon light frequency." Carson continued, "But of course we have to immerse "Meathead" in a vitamin soaked solution when we're done experimenting or the adult parasites attached to "Meathead" will dry up and eventually die."

James tried to shake off his horrible thoughts. He hobbled toward the waist high gray filing cabinet that he saw. Opening filing cabinets pulling out several folders and paging through reports that had caught his attention then scanning through a computer screen adjacent bolted onto the desktop. He read that the parasite's many, many legs mimic molecules that could replicate lupine genes and chromosomes so they can bond with the host DNA.

"So-seti's experiment led to a breakthrough as well. We amputated her extremities. Again and again, when the full Moon raises her stumps grow back," The scientist mused. "The lycanthrope's spine shatters and stem cells emerge constructing new lupine DNA resulting in an almost lightning quick healing factor."

"Meathead's heart, arteries and veins used to have a spine and skull but on the first full moon after he had been dissected before we could experiment with him the spine shattered." Carson mused.

The scientist Carson haphazardly threw Meathead back in a solution then into the freezer and wheeled out a cart which had a flat screen TV, DVD combination to the middle of the room.

"Check this out," his body shook with excitement he could not contain himself. "The one and only experiment that involved So-seti was recorded for prosperity. The Computer analyzes all the information and animated the information for us.

"Look, her spinal cord cracks and stem cells are able to make the Dire Wolf's blueprint, until we amputated her legs once more. So-seti's missing legs as she morphs into new wolf's limbs. Eventually we amputated her legs and stuck silver rods in So-seti's stumps to inhibit the regeneration. Of course that was long ago all before we gained custody of the beast." Carson said proudly.

Carson put in a DVD showing a young, vibrant and wild captive So-seti. He could not suppress his feelings any longer as the tears sprang up from his eyes. James whipped his head around trying to conceal his moist puffy cheeks.

James watched the animation on the computer that showed alien DNA, presumably from a younger So-seti, chromosomes. The DNA ladders begin to polarize the individual sets tear apart. The parasite legs mimicking chromosomes attached to the ladders that were torn apart and fused together.

"The parasites in her DNA would reverse the chromosomes until she had the normal amount of chromosomes that made her a woman. No traces of Wolf remained. However, she could transform any body part to Wolf or human at will without the moon's influence. I was intrigued by something So-seti said, 'My wolf and I are the same.' "Carson spoke in monotone, mesmerized by So-seti's torture.

James could not tear his eyes away from the screen. He tried to make sense of the onslaught of data. Carson continued, "The Rome chapter of Lucem Dei would starve her and drug her so she had trouble transforming. Eventually, we learned So-seti's DNA had one-hundred and twenty four chromosomes in a unique structure. I can only describe her unique double helix with missing ladders or half sets of runs outside the sugar phosphate backbone as two entwined roses the runs outside the latter like thorns. But eventually the unique double helix died from starvation and the lack of regeneration. Her elongated chromosomes died, no longer able to transform at will. However, the parasite larva always exists in her pineal gland and when the Moon is full would flood her bloodstream with adult parasites that mimic wolf DNA and they fused to her human DNA if we didn't flood her bloodstream with the silver nitrate solution."

"So far our working hypothesis is the parasite feeds on sodium, iron, and creatine and replicates. When the Moon wanes those parasites attached to the DNA go into stasis again and the larvae heads up to the pineal gland curled up in a ball and goes into cryptobiosis. It gorges itself with protein, iron, sodium and high levels of creatine, also found in striated muscle. The parasite tries to invade all the human organs until the parasite and the human are one and the same. Imagine the human DNA as a zipper. Now imagine the parasite an inside out zipper with wolf's blood DNA in its tabs. The wolf's blood DNA zips up with the loose chromosome bonds."

"That's why we found that silver, anything electrical really, being a natural powerful conductor of electricity, disrupts the parasites insertion process, since the human is basically a bio-electrical being. I was there when this particular captured werewolf metamorphosed before we shot him to death, the whole experience looked painful." The scientist spouted off an almost exact definition in the book, titled *Understanding Lycanthropy and Its Disease* the God's Light manual, while still watching the screen with interest.

Screams and wails on the T.V. coming from a tortured and miserable So-seti had him at his breaking point. James tried to calm down; breathed deeply, closed his eyes, but he could still hear her screaming.

"The group had been lucky enough to draw blood from a changing lycanthrope and So-seti without getting mauled. When the moon is full the lycanthrope's pineal gland floods the blood stream with magnetically charged iron parasites that release a torrent of hormones all at once that resemble metylenedioxyamphtetamine, Methylenedioxymethamphetamine, Psilocybin, Phencyclidine, Mescaline, and lastly Lysergic acid diethylamide. The cocktail of chemicals is the Parasite's waste product. It awakes because of the cocktail and latches onto and invades their DNA." The scientist told James as he carefully read the drug test results, flipping through papers.

James's eyes widened in surprise at the report, exclaiming, "Ecstasy chemical types, peyote and PCP, are the active ingredients for mushrooms, and acid!"

"Not exactly but they're so similar the drug tests make a positive. No wonder some volunteers have their hearts explode." The scientist who looked hilariously like Byron scoffed to himself.

"The cocktails of drugs, amounts of which we still have yet to determine, flow through the bloodstream. The larvae come out of stasis and pineal producing Dimethyltryptamine or DMT..." The scientist hesitated as he calculated some imaginary equation, "the death drug. That's when all hell breaks loose!"

"Imagine them as the walking rocks of the Racetrack Playa in Death Valley and ice is like the drug cocktail. The rocks are stationary, hibernating until night temperature drops making ice where there used to be hot sand. The unmovable rocks could move around now sliding back and forth with ease. The amoebas escape the pineal gland, some forming adult parasites. We understand the process in theory, the amoebas infect people and the adults invade their systems. But we have yet to successfully carry it out, all the experiments thus far are an utter failure."

"So, what of So-seti?" James asked.

"That's the amazing thing," the scientist talked fast in his excitement. "So-seti could control her body of sorts. First, she could release Metylenedioxyamphtetamine, when the levels raise enough they triggered a release of Methylenedioxymethamphetamine." Carson calmed down now, "the body then releases Psilocybin which then releases the parasite which produces a type of natural Mescaline, Phencyclidine, and finally Lysergic Acid Diethylamide in a controlled dose. Her special set of double helix, the astronomical amount of magnetized iron and her cocktail of drug-like hormones allowed So-seti to change at will. To polarize her chromosomes and fuse other connected chromosomes back together again, on and off like a light switch, made her a dangerous woman. The x-rays show her pineal gland is as hard and concentrated as iron. I think if she would have received a gunshot wound right between the eyes with a normal bullet it would bounce off."

"This is amazing," said James.

Excitement ran through James as his heart raced to the point of arrest. You shrewd, cunning girl! He proudly thought, So-seti may be incarcerated, but she had listened and learnt all that she could about her gift that she didn't already know before!

James said staring off in the distance as he muttered under his breath again, "So-seti is an amazing person!"

Carson stopped what he was doing and gasped, "She's a beast! She is an abomination! An affront to God! She's not even human! Her DNA and the parasite infestation prove it!"

James watched in horror as the realization hit him like a ton of bricks. He finally understood almost everything. So-seti had had one hundred and twenty four chromosomes *before* confinement instead of forty six, for a normal human, or seventy eight for a Wolf. So-seti and the wolf had merged until inactivity destroyed the unique cells in her body. He understood how stem cells behaved after they broke out of her spine. The only thing that kept her alive were the parasites inside her now, the apparition of Aisos' dire wolf bent on survival, He almost understood everything but it he had gotten harder and harder to think rationally as his stomach reeled in pain and hunger.

What is going to happen to me, James thought, I am a beast. I AM a beast now! James growled under his breath, "She's no guinea pig!"

"What did you say? I'm sorry, uh; I didn't mean to strike a nerve. Tell you what, I'm going on break…you need me to bring you something the back when I return?"

"Yeah, could you bring me back another foot long sub?" James' lighthearted mannerisms and demeanor put Carson back at ease, all though his teeth clenched and his stomach growled with hunger.

"All right," Carson laughed.

He tapped several papers together so they would be even. He looked around the room to ensure he did not forget anything, took off his white lab coat, neatly folded it over his chair then headed out the door with a backwards wave.

Finally alone with his thoughts he stared at the freezers on the wall, one freezer particularly, the one that housed Meathead's "body". Then James glanced at the clock on the wall, 2:00 pm. Meathead's misery ends today! He rationalized in his head. Meathead only had glands and a brainstem but no brain. He isn't alive doesn't feel pain anymore. Only the parasites cohabiting and reanimating the mass of veins that led to just his arms. He could not feel pain anymore, could he? He jerked the freezer door open; a blast of cold air assaulted his face fogging up his glasses.

When James' glasses cleared up he carefully scooped up the remains called Meathead. He cautiously crossed just feet from the freezer door before setting Meathead down on a floor basin. He needed fire to burn Meathead so he could finally be free. James soaked meathead in an ethanol alcohol solution. White phosphorus, he thought, then immediately began working on freeing the White phosphorus from a glass container. A bright idea hit him through his fog covered mind… find the keys.

James obtained the keys in a desk by the corner then turned his attention to the glass container by the table on the adjacent wall. Embarrassment washed over his face as he easily unlocked it. He obtained a small amount of powdered white phosphorus in a glass. He hesitated for only a second to be sure that he wouldn't be caught in the blast then threw the glass into the basin.

He stumbled back from the swift heat and flame the sudden flash hurting James' eyes. No turning back now as he watched Meathead burn. No chance to explain this away!

"Rest in peace!" A sudden horrid stench stabbed his stomach and brought him to his knees.

James frantically searched around the sterile room. A twelve foot by six inch shelf sat almost eye level on the wall and held all the ingredients. Bottles and beakers some sealed up with corks all labeled and numbered. Powdered creatine tempted his eyes. He could see a brown large pill bottle labeled "IRON 100 I.U.". A gallon jug labeled "PROTEIN" dominated the shelf-space.

A protein, iron and creatine combination smoothie he thought as he found himself going through bottles and jars to find a glass. James turned on the faucet turning on the water. He poured in the combination then stirred. A mound of white crystals whirled upwards like a mini tornado as it diluted to a clear liquid.

Swallowing up the homemade mixture with one gulp James' thirst was satisfied and his hunger completely pacified again. Hastily he grabbed all the useful transportable small bottles and powders that he could and put them into his pockets. Almost out the door when he remembered one other thing he needed, the UV lamp, oh and his cane!

Only authorized to go down to the fourth floor James knew he couldn't go down to the fifth special floors by elevator. The emergency stairwell is guarded by only a security-key, however. With his disability Dr. Atkins trusted him. The Dr. knew he would not able to navigate the stairs. But James had two functional legs now, and the equilibrium of a trapeze artist. He quickly searched for and found the keys to the stairwell behind the door on the wall hanging on a hook.

He stopped in the stairwell to get his bearings; once underground, God's Light compound is a cavernous place comprised of a vast lobby, the elevator, stairwell, North, South, East and West wings, a carbon copy of her sister compound in Rome, Beijing, and several others dotting the landscapes. Until yesterday he had spent most of his days on the third floor, right wing, or limping off to the library. I don't even know where my brethren are held, he thought and then he chuckled to himself, follow your nose, it always knows!

James anxiously clutched the keys that would unlock the stairwell. A moment of unease as he gathered his confidence then quietly slipped out the door. He crept slowly and quietly down the hallway until he came upon the emergency stairwell.

James flung the Oak doors open his eyes widening with shock staring at rows and rows of stretchers, every one filled with comatose patients, six unlucky volunteers laying side-by-side. He hesitantly hobbled over to one particularly miserable young man. Touching the test subject's face, he felt so cold forcing the subject's eyelids open, so vacant, so hollow inside.

With So-seti's knowledge shared with him he could save them! He began to measure various powdered substances diluting the mixture then injecting the mixture directly into the comatose patient's veins. He flipped off the light switch and plugged in the UV lamp when he heard something coming from down the hall.

"*James, James, James,*" a voice in his head beckons, "*James, James, James.*"

Navigating the hallway towards the source James could smell the decay in the basement, drawing him ever closer to another room. It had an electronic security code but he checked the doorknob anyway, locked. James turned around about to walk away when he heard a beep and then a click. He checked the door once again, this time it opened with ease!

"*James.*" Now in the room the voice in his head spoke louder.

No furnishings in the strange room except for the twenty or so cages on the floor by the wall. No beds, drawers, or tables… not even a picture hung on the wall, just rows and rows of cages filled with… rats.

"Is anyone there?" James called out in a calm whisper. He noticed the rats all in their cages all with their red eyes trained on him. Each one moved their head's in unison to James' movements.

"*It is Lucius, Vampyre and ally.*" the disembodied voice said again, this time it had come from various imprisoned rats.

"I am James, excuse me a moment but with all my investigating I thought the Vampire and the Werewolf were mortal enemies?" Lucius laughed in James' head loudly.

"*No, no, we are brothers and we are the children of the night, we learned to get along centuries ago. Lycanthropes have toxins in their special blood that if a vampyre drinks, they would be horribly sickened. Their blood tastes unpleasant; unpalatable. We have learned long ago we have mutual prey, a mutual enemy, humankind.*" Lucius said in his mind.

James examined the cages. There were twelve cages, six rats in each cage all draped with a light silver screen. Each rat in the cages stopped its incessant circling and peered at him through red beady eyes. He deliberately moved side to side, the rats moving their heads accordingly watching his every move.

"*Let me out, let ALL of me out.*" Lucius said in James's mind referring to the caged rats, "*I fulfilled my obligation to So-seti. I gave you to her, now let me out, I beg of you.*"

Against his better judgment and slightly confused he started to unlock the cages and take off the silver screens that prevented the rats from escaping. He managed to systematically unlock all twelve cages. He rolled back the light silver screens and picked up and gingerly sat down the rats two and three at a time. Instead of running away to safety these rats pushed onto one another growing like a living pyramid as they ran into one another. The rats continued climbing up on each other.

"What the?" James questioned under his breath.

The rats seemed to get denser until all individual features were lost in the pile. The bottom circle of rats began to melt onto the floor. He took hurried steps backwards and ran toward the stairway. He felt it had been right, but he needed to flee this room for his own sanity's sake now. He needed to seek out the one person who could calm him and then tell her what he found out.

Without a second thought he navigated the steps up and ran down the hallway. So-seti widened her eyes in surprise when James busted through the door. His hands rested on his knees trying to catch his breath.

"Vampyre… He is Awake…" Breathing in.

"I found… six test subjects," Breathing out.

"Listen," she said softly, "the moon will be up, before the sun sets, I feel it. And you're not in control of your Wolf yet. You need an excuse to get out of here and get to somewhere safe for the transformation. Can you feel it coming on, the change?"

Now that she said this he could feel it coming on the sweet seduction of the change, he shook his head yes.

"The last favor, my sweet," So-seti whispered, "unchain me."

She had a delighted look on her face as she consciously put a hand on James' left arm. She could almost feel the electric tingling and she heard a low growl churning in the pit of his stomach and his increased heart rate. She could feel a marked increase in in his temperature, although the temperature in the room was a constant 69°. Although his body felt hot a sudden chill came over him as he could see why new lycanthropes die before the first year is up. If it wasn't for So-seti he probably would have had the change before he was ever out of the estate. He would be amongst the Inquisition and their many forms of torture. If he was lucky he would die, if he was not, he would live. He would be one of their living science experiments… just like So-seti. Without her he would probably not survive what is happening to him or the transformation to come.

He had enhanced senses and the beginnings of enhanced strength and balance but he was still a broken man. His side was still weak and try as he might he still couldn't use his left hand for any intricate movement and his foot still all but useless. The Inquisition would make minced meat of him immediately.

So-seti hissed, "don't worry, I'll take care of you and teach you the ways my child. But now you have to get out of here*!*"

James quietly obeyed, unchaining her, and then with just a second glance he punched in the numbers to her prison cell door. He hurriedly walked through the hallway with his now decorative cane in hand. He saw Lucius out of the corner of his eye, a green hospital robe covering his nude form, his one good arm rubbing against his stub.

He stopped, mesmerized and hypnotized by Lucius, his unearthly eyes. Only the bang and shatter of the emergency stairwell doors forcefully opening shook him back to reality. Six patients rushed into the hallway like a tidal wave rushing down the beach. The double doors slid swaying back and forth broken from the force; James looked around at the subjects' eyes, still so vacant, so hollow inside.

The test subjects turned their heads in unison. Their spines arched back, fine hairs protruding through their nude and emaciated chests. One subject observed James suspiciously through animalistic eyes. He crouched in the corner; his back to the wall, giving commands to the less evolved freed test subjects with grunts and growls. James could tell this subject called all the shots. The test subject that led them stood on two feet. Not yet in his true lupine form, it lacked some key components... having only a tail, reverse knee and long muzzle, looking like a thin and wiry gorilla instead. The hairy monstrosity growled at him but did not make any move to attack. The monster stuck his wet muzzle against James' chest sniffing the length of is body, still untrusting but the monster backed off. James let out the breath he did not realize he had been holding.

Lucius materialized into So-seti's wall and floated through the pack unmolested to her stretcher. He scooped up So-seti's broken body in his arms. Without hands the door in her prison slowly opened as Lucius left the room while James helplessly watched stunned.

"See, *I am a man of my word my dear So-seti*," Lucius whispered in her mind, no emotion whatsoever as he carefully cradled her in his arms.

So-seti yelled out her commands, her voice growing ever stronger howling... "Tempus! Filioli filiorum et filiarum lycanthrope surge! Align evertant sacer Dei Luce members. Free sanguine tuo, Mater et adolebit Seti-huius agri in terra, howwwwwwwwwwwwwwwl!"

So-seti's broken Latin lupine speech still said it all to the great prisoners of the God's Light compound. James just roughly translated this, "It is time! Sons and daughters of lycanthrope rise up! Transform and overthrow the accursed God's Light members. Free your blood mother and burn this estate to the ground. Howwwwwwwwwwwwwwwl!"

He saw Lucius with his pallor complexion and perfectly sculpted cheeks, his brooding catlike crimson eyes blazing under the fluorescent lights. Staring into the vampyre's eyes time seemed to slow down and stop, something inside James stirred, he felt peculiar.

"Go!" Lucius commanded, violently making a motion with his pointer finger.

The terrible hunger kicked in again, his hands clenching his stomach as if the pressure would help with pain. Something about Lucius made him feel peculiar. His whole body was in a state of flux between human and lupine when he stared at Lucius' haunting eyes and he had to get out. He had to get out and get some fresh air a chance to cool off. The surrounding hallways were unfamiliar to James and he blacked out several times before locking in on the sweet perfume of night air too tempting a mistress the smell of freedom. Eventually James flew out the church doors stumbling down the steps. He staggered into the garden and stepped on the cobblestones before he started to feel normal again.

He saw the penlight eyes just behind the bushes by a great stone wall that protected the village. Only the eyes were visible obscured by the bush but he knew it was a Wolf and he felt its draw. A black muzzle broke through the bushes. A blue raven-black furred hybrid-wolf revealed itself instantly transmuting to a scarred attractive woman.

The transformation seamless, with her smooth skin she looked like a granite statue, Venus come to life, James thought, if he touched her skin it would be so smooth, so tender. She reveled in her nakedness and got precariously close to James. He breathed in her intoxicating aroma and he felt her alluring heat.

"Was it you who sang that song?" Tonya softly inquired.

"Yes, yes. So-seti asked me to." James said timidly.

He closed his eyes, her physical presence too much for him to bear. Realizing with great clarity Tonya represented all that lycanthropy embodied without shackles and chains. Instead of So-seti's wrinkled physique and decaying body he envisioned Tonya's supple body. So-seti should be free, to heal, to regenerate and Tonya had become a living embodiment of that. He could just imagine Tonya as So-seti.

"Oung!" Tonya called the Wolf by name.

A speckled black colored Wolf with light green eyes that looked like a large foo dog with fur that almost touched the ground ambled out from the shadows.

"O-Kami!" Tonya called another one by name.

Several spirit-wolves materialized, they glowed like a bright full Moon above them. The wolves moved silently traveling right through the locked doors of the church.

The courtyard brightened as the full Moon traveled up beyond the suppression of the numerous trees. James had a strange compulsion to look up into the dazzling moon light. His body, the very nerves, muscles and bones exploded with electricity. His blood boiling as he arched his body beyond familiarity. He saw through a thick veil of fog, like a lucid dream now as flashes began to be seen through the church windows.

His human skull had burst into a million pieces then reformed itself into a mixture of lupine and man. The human bones of his feet had liquefied and began lengthening before congealing again. Tarsal and metatarsal bones stretched to ridiculous extremes; he planted his preposterously long broad feet upon the ground. Long footprints giving rise to the Bigfoot myth. James paced around the garden, his large head a monstrous creation. Lengthy pointed ears extended, a smashed snout on top of a medium muzzle, accommodating full large curved fangs. An outsized red tongue jutted out and slithered around his mouth. His thick broad neck craned to see the employees that escaped the fire were running around in circles until wolves materialized out of thin air and gobbled them up. James crouched on his knuckles. He had the skin of a Wolf and the skeletal structure of a man except for the skull and the feet.

The shadows from the courtyard danced as the light from the church fire intensified. The mounting heat too great to sustain a cohesive bond the stained-glass windows in either side of the stone church burst into dozens of deadly shards with a bang and rattle.

Carson the scientist stumbled through the heavy oak doors hands covering his mouth as he coughed up soot and debris. He ran down the steps away from the church before collapsing onto cold cobblestone ground. Carson struggled to get onto his knees and eventually he got up and dusted himself off. He smiled, burst into a chuckle, then a full-fledged laugh, he had actually made it and he survived. Carson looked up in the night sky a cold chill ran through his bones and he shuddered.

Carson's eyes tried to adjust to the extreme glare of the inferno then the immediate and overwhelming darkness outside. The full Moon though prevalent was hidden by the trees. He heard something moving in the midst of the sunflower garden the long thick stalks and massive white flowered heads masked the wolf's presence.

A growl coming somewhere from the garden got Carson's attention. He instinctively patted his chest to see if he still had his concealed weapon, a Glock 10, against the pit of his arm; though he knew for a fact he had checked it in and locked it up at the end of the day.

James' wolf abomination burst out of the sunflowers growling. Surprised, Carson fell on his ass. He scrambled to get away on his back on the cobblestone. His neck through his shoulders tightened as his white lab coat stuck on branches of bushes lining the walkway.

Carson struggled to tear his lab coat apart to free himself as James the werewolf pounced upon him their eyes locking onto each other. Werewolf saw Carson's eyes panicky and full of disbelief. He had worked on, experimented, and even killed lycanthropes before in a clinical setting but seeing the powerful werewolf without shackles and bonds horrified him. What shocked him more than anything; however, he saw the eyes of his colleague James in this monstrous form!

As he remembered all of his brethren and So-seti's wrinkled defeated form James saw red. He snarled at the scientist. However, the whirl of a helicopter grew closer and sound made the werewolf yelp in pain.

James' paws rubbed his lupine ears from side to side on the ground, the pain too great for him to bear. Carson began to tear away his lab coat and twisted around until he managed to get up on his knees.

A helicopter with a chain attached to a yellow metal container swinging like a pendulum slowly maneuvered over to the burning church then opened a hatch spilling its payload. A cascade of warm lake water soaked James' fur. The force of the falling water knocked Carson on his ass yet again.

James lunged at Carson's prone body still stunned from the force of the water that fell from the sky. Sharp fangs snapped onto his thigh and twisted flinging him around and onto his belly.

"James?" Carson questioned, looking into the abomination's eyes, he had seen just those eyes staring back at him just moments ago in the lab.

James growled and said, "I won't be tested like a guinea pig!"

Carson took advantage of the man-made rain and ran getting a head start toward the smoldering church. An animal instinct older than the first signs of civilization kicked in and the abomination gave chase instantly pouncing upon Carson like a lonely wounded gazelle.

"No! Please!" Carson pleaded.

Before James tore Carson's trachea silencing him forever. The light from his eyes dimmed and the iris dilated, then fixed, but James did not stop mauling him.

The double doors swung open again to reveal Matt caked from head to toe with soot; he covered his mouth with a fist hacking his lungs out. His lab coat practically split in half in back one sleeve gone altogether.

"James!?" Matt sputtered.

Deeply burrowed in Carson's neck Matt could only see his friend's eyes watching his every move. His twitching ears set back and Matt knew if he moved even slightly the predator would pounce. His furry forearms coiled so that a minor jerk would initiate a predator and prey dance, a dance old as time.

Matt did not move a muscle, Matt questioned, "James?" He called, wiping at his soot covered face.

Daring to peer close enough that Matt could get a better view but far enough away there would be no danger of James shredding Matt's face off he stared into the monster's eyes while James' powerful jaws tore into Carson's trachea.

"Yes, am friend!" James bellowed a garbled growl.

A moment of awkward silence ensued as James and Matt stared at one another …

…

…

"Change me, change me please!" Matt pleaded.

James the lycanthrope broke the staring contest first, something within him, broke through the fog of his mind, Matt had been a loyal friend. He knew in his heart he couldn't harm Matt at all. Oung and O-Kami with his spirit Wolves emerged through the double doors of the church followed by Tonya as the structural supports gave way. As smoke bellowed out from the gutted and burned-out church the pale white faced and glowing eyes and pallor nude and blood smeared bodies emerged from the wreckage along with Lucius carrying So-seti, no surviving staff members could be seen among them.

The lunatic patient who had been crouched down giving orders to the other changelings before they escaped the God's Light compound noticed Matt. Preoccupied Matt did not see the lunatic about to attack him but James did.

"He's mine!" James spat drool dripping from his fangs.

Snarling James pounced as the lunatic leapt for Matt's jugular vein. Matt only had time to put his arms up and crouch down in defense. Matt could feel the heat and smell the musk of the lunatic before James jumped after him and threw him down onto the soaked Earth, a close call.

"He's mine!" James reiterated.

The lunatic whimpered, retreating from the powerful and well developed monster towering before him. James' torso twisted around to see Matt's and jumped towards him.

Matt pleaded, his hands in a prayer position, his eyes wide, begging, "Make me a werewolf, please!"

James dropped onto all fours, looking like a true Wolf now with long furry withers and powerful shoulder blades except for the missing tail. He sniffed Matt's crotch, nestling his wet nose and whiskers against and tickling his groin. Huge shoulders broad limbs and paws crowding Matt's legs he truly felt fear for the first time.

Satisfied with Matt's aroma he pressed his paw firmly on the wet grass until he made an impression. Saliva from his long muzzle dripped down and mixed with the moisture of the indentation forming a pool. James looked down at the Paw impression and water saliva mixture then looked at his friend.

Without any more instruction Matt knew what he had to do. He scooped up the muddy mixture and drank it as the church smoldered.

38

The Ruins of the God's Light Monastery, California

The pair huddled up next to each other, James and So-seti, human again, laying on the grass the smoldering smoking remnants of the God's Light ministry hovering in the blue sky.

Matt sat on the cold soil with knees pulled up to his chin. The change had happened to him and swiftly and just as swiftly had stopped abruptly. Matt had converted back to human again. His head a pin cushion, sudden stabbing barbs through his forehead. Squinting from the intensely bright noonday sun he threw his arms together in a gigantic self-induced bear hug. He could not remember anything he did last night but he felt every powerful sensation… the unadulterated power, he was already missing the experience. Like a prolonged orgasm he had not experienced anything like it before. His headaches felt like he would die, and it would give him sweet release but he would not change the experience for anything at all, and he thanked God that he was given a second chance instead of his good friend simply mauling him to death.

The lunatic test subjects had gone running in a straight line for Louisiana. Lucius, his pact fulfilled, had floated off in a different direction. James and So-seti veered towards the God's Light village. So-seti thought clearly enough to get the two spare crutches, a backpack full of clandestine supplies. Thanks to So-seti's secrets James had not transformed back again, still in his hybrid-Wolf form a perfect workhorse to carry all the supplies. His claws and arms full to the brim he carefully traversed the break in the wall and successfully escaped the God's Light compound.

Though human again with shredded clothing Matt waited outside the wall for James and So-seti to arrive. Matt felt loyal to them like a cohesive pack. However, Matt had become extremely tall but puny in comparison to last night and frankly felt intimidated and terrified looking at James and So-seti. He tried to stay in the shadows by the oak trees quietly observing them and trying to make himself small enough that he would not be noticed.

Last night her heat with all the pumping adrenaline, excitement pheromones interlacing with their wild powerful musk twirled all around and infused the strange couple. James and So-seti copulated, a co-mingling of a legless wrinkled hybrid-Wolf and wolf man. An awkward beginning to their fornication So-seti had no calves, amputated below the knee. She had a lower focal point for James' bipedal wolf-man's manhood to concentrate on. He got down on his knees as she backed up to his groin. His engorged member entered her, determination and lust getting the job done.

Eventually with his load spent they collapsed on the ground, James hugging her, his arms squishing her sides his claws gingerly pressing her teats. So-seti panted with exhaustion her tongue licking his muzzle, her tail wagging in satisfaction as they lay lazily on the soft grass. The wolfman and the disabled Wolf stared at the Moon content and free until they drifted to sleep snuggling, So-seti finally enjoyed a peaceful slumber without silver nitrate in her veins for the first time in centuries.

Matt made the most of his powerful form while James and So-seti were indisposed for a moment, killing every wild animal, big and small he came across. Running about on all fours, though he could still walk upright, stalking rabbits and field mice to his heart's content. He felt uncanny power, every sense and sensation new like a baby, so surreal.

They stayed on Diablo Mountain by the new ruins of the God's Light church until the sun came up the next day. By the time James had stirred the sunlight warmed the whole of his bare skin. As he wiped off the caked up sleep from his eyes he couldn't help but notice So-seti. Her skin had a glow that he had never seen before. The deep wrinkles were gone and just faint lines remained. Her face somehow more pliable and flawless her neck filled out. He could no longer see every movement of her spine and arteries. Her thin brittle hair somehow fuller and black as oil. He had seen a sneak preview before when he interrupted the flow of silver nitrate to her IV and she transformed temporarily. She looked different. Though he was generally really bad at gauging ages she appeared to be in her 40s maybe even late 30s, a skin-brittle and skinny 90-year-old who had reverted to her youth.

He listened to her strong powerful heart beating slowly and consistently. He couldn't help but stare lower at her bare taunt navel, his eyes lowered to her firm smooth thighs. His eyes reverted toward the silver posts impaled through her bones, two in each stub and his heart sank. Even with the silver nitrate gone from her veins she remained hobbled.

Matt had summoned his courage to walk up to James and talk to him while So-seti still slumbered, "Thank you… for this gift you have given me."

James did not flinch; too busy examining the studs that went through the bone, pointing to her stumps Matt remarked, "You know…"

"The spikes have been permanently fused to the bones…It's ironically called Wolf's law, when the bone breaks then heals it becomes harder than before." Matt pointed at her stubs and the shiny silver posts traveling through her skin and bone, "it's called bone modeling. They found out awfully early on when lycanthropes start their transformation the bones break, they shatter into a million pieces. When the lycanthropes turn the bones harden again and condense thicker and stronger than before. This process starts over again every time they transmute. So with every transformation the bones break and reset until they are like steel, tungsten carbide, or something much harder even than diamond. The down side is when you impale silver rods in the bones the rods adhere to and fuse together. Doubly, the conductive silver interferes with the parasites and they're disrupted so that the legs or arms don't grow back."

James could not hide the fact that her missing legs and the horror that she endured made him sob like a baby. The weeping woke So-seti. Her hands impulsively stroked James' cheek to comfort him. Now that she was awake Matt tried to make his body smaller, less noticeable because in his mind until last night for all intents and purposes, he had carried out orders as a God's Light employee and he worried So-seti would take out her anger and frustration on him.

"Oh my child it's going to be all right." She consoled James, but she stared daggers at Matt. James could feel icy tension in the air the oxygen leaving the trio like a vacuum in space, "you've already freed me from the burning poison in my veins and for that I am extremely loyal to you."

Matt knew that she could instantly maul him, he would exsanguinate from a severe wound from her sharp claws. His fragile neck flayed open by a surgical strike to several arteries. He would die before his feet left the ground but she resisted her instinct for a friend of James she would spare his life. James realized she had an extreme loyalty toward him; she viewed him as a mate. James viewed Matt as a friend. But he purposely moved between them, just in case, a reluctant referee.

It still amazed him as he breathed a faint smoky air and listened to the faint noises of traffic and commotion at the bottom of the mountain. Every sound and odor exceptionally magnified. If he wanted to he could hone in on one particular car horn, engine and conversation and follow it indefinitely. He could single out the faint nuance of smells such as smoke, a flowery fragrance, and flesh, and easily follow it. The train of thought shattered when So-seti's familiar sensual and stimulating musk seared through his nostrils. Her nakedness had him nervous.

So-seti whispered in his ear, "I can smell the road, we are getting close."

Her nonchalant attitude for nakedness and closeness had him anxious. He tried to train himself to look upwards at her eyes, a bright brilliant green, but he found himself staring at her breasts instead. He cannot help it, after he unplugged the silver nitrate drip her drooping sagging breasts, the breasts of an 80 or 90-year-old now lifted a little defying gravity and had become firmer, now the breasts of a 40 or 30-year-old. James felt a stirring in his loins until he looked down at her amputated legs and tears sprung up in his eyes once again.

"I smell a stranded car..." without the silver nitrate running through her veins for quite a while now she had become calculating, shrewder, "from the sweat it is a man... weak, scared and anxious, and more importantly, he is alone."

He reluctantly turned away from her naked form and looked down from the mountain. His eyes squinted trying to see the highway below. Even with James' enhanced eyesight with massive sturdy branches that obstructing his site he could only get a fleeting glimpse of the cars and trucks like tiny ants speeding by this way and that.

"On the highway there is a yellow car, the occupant sitting in the driver's seat, you can smell the smoke from the stale cigarettes. Do you see it?" So-seti questioned James.

He focused his eyes straining to see the car amidst the thick branches, "No, sorry, I can't."

"Do not think, just smell the burning oil and coolant, hear the radio in the distance then let your eyes naturally find the stalled car." So-seti instructed, limping with her crutches over to the cliff edge to teach James some of the secrets of the changeling.

"I can't see..." James frustratingly snapped, then froze and yelled excitedly, "Wait, I think I see the car and I hear a flint striking and I smell smoke!"

He began zeroing in on the yellow car like he was turning the knobs on a telescope, a Volkswagen beetle with its hood up. He could even see the heat plume, wave after wave distorting the air around the ruined engine.

A tow truck with his flashing lights emerged through the trees and stopped to help the stranded motorist. The backup lights lit up and the tow truck maneuvered in such a manner that the driver could lower the boom.

"There are two now and a functioning truck. This is a test for you, James," she pointed to the tow truck and Volkswagen beetle, "Howl out, grind your teeth, dance around with wild abandon, do not think what you're going to do, let your body do all the work for you. Purposely travel back into your subconscious, let your mind go and The *Wolf Blood* will awaken inside of you."

So-seti coaxed James down onto his knees so they would remain hidden, "do not think, just feel. Can you hear your heart beating?"

A bend in the road concealed So-seti and James discussing the procurement of the tow truck, "change, my love, without the moon's influence changing you!"

"I don't understand!" James said in frustration.

"Go into a trance, a daze, and a dream-like state… it is easier that way. Visualize the Wolf inside you." So-seti instructed, "Try to flex and strain every muscle in your body as if being drawn and quartered by four horses running in different directions. The end result, envisioning the inner wolf flooding your being…"

James' heart raced, his hair stood on end, his blood started to boil as he watched the VW bug owner's backside but he beat his fists on the ground frustration ensuing, "I can't change!"

So-seti fumbled for something in the backpack until she found what she had been looking for, "here, take this, is going to be easier for you to change if you're out of your body… Here!"

So-seti force-fed a black powdery substance into James' mouth, was it Ergot, Peyote, Opium? He could not see what she gave him but in a moment a mild hallucination ensued. He began to feel dizzy and disoriented. His heart began to beat harder as he found himself emerging from his hiding place between the rocks. James looked at the tow truck driver securing the bug. The owner of the disabled car obliviously yelled into his cell to some anonymous person on the other end while sucking on a cigarette.

Suddenly she dove off the cliff with her crutches in hand. Like an Olympic gymnast she weaved and twirled down the cliff. She used her crutches as a brace to stick between branches her stumps swaying in the air. The branches groaned with the added weight before she leaped off again. The branches split in two, leaves freed from twigs floating down towards the traveling cars on the highway.

James inched closer to the edge psyching his body up enough to jump off. Even with So-seti's missing limbs she jumped from tree to tree like a flying Fox. She gradually drifted down towards the mountain's edge rolling over any gradual decline until she blindly leapt off the cliff again.

He looked over at Matt who stood hidden behind a tree. His eyes black as coals, sunken and bruised things, no lights of consciousness could be seen. Nevertheless Matt's manners told of an undying loyalty for his Savior.

He beat himself in the chest several times to psych himself up, jumping up-and-down for the first time since before his accident. He had to catch up with So-seti several yards down the mountain now. His teeth clenched as he found himself growling involuntarily. Hairs all over his body began erecting and fever progressed. He gathered his nerves and took a good long breath as he jumped.

James didn't remember anything until his feet landed upon the ground safely. Sizing the mountain up, he apparently scaled down a 300 foot cliff, astonishingly landing on his feet without breaking his neck. He quickly scanned for So-seti then searched for Matt who still looked at him up on the ledge of the mountain.

The site of the nude man just materializing from thin air left the tow truck driver slack-jawed and silent for a moment before he yelled, "what the hell!?"

He let his body go as the woman's voice instructed him. He did not know if it was a mixture of drugs, unleashing his unconsciousness, or the combination of heart racing adrenaline but his human arm had changed into a fusion of something monstrous and half-lupine. Fur sprang from his forearm. His nails had grown talon-like claws.

James did not think, only reacting, on autopilot. He hyperextended his left hand, the hand had just nights before hung useless by his body. Before he knew it he could see his arm as it lashed out in an arc. James saw all of the attack as if detached.

A consequence of the magnetic Moon nowhere in sight his arm felt heavy like bricks, he felt as if his whole body was moving slower than molasses and a million needles stabbing his body all at one time. Yet his arm instinctively slashed for the second time at the wounded and frightened VW bug owner which severed the man's shoulder to the bone, reminding him of the killing of the mountain lion.

Even if he felt like he moved in slow motion the human victim's reaction time was no match for his uncanny lycanthrope speed. A thick spurt of warm crimson blood shot out from the stranded motorist's partially severed shoulder his cell phone twirling towards the ground before he finished dialing 911 for emergency assistance. The spray felt tingly and delicious on his tongue. A strange warm fantastically copper metallic taste that satisfied a hunger he did not even know he had.

The delicious spray had set off a domino effect; James flew towards the injured man's body in a frenzy knocking his body off balance. His lips stretching as his mouth swelled then popped. The jaw dislocated to accommodate more teeth. Thick teeth turned into large protruding fangs which sunk into the stranded and now wounded man's exposed neck, easily sinking into tender human skin. James' pupils dilated as he gulped down torn muscles and flesh.

The bright sun physically hurt James's dilated eyes temporarily freezing the new changeling's horrid onslaught long enough so the wounded man could make his escape. As the driver's door opened the high frequency screech like nails to a chalkboard made his ears bleed wailing out in pain.

From the combination of a blaring radio station, blind spot in the window and paperwork the tow truck driver had been unaware of the commotion, the lethal conflict that transpired until he heard a thump and the truck rattled. A burly man with three years growth of hair on his face opened the glove box to reveal a small 9 mm. He had oily, dirty overalls he threw his clipboard onto the bench seat, and cocked his gun and stepped outside on the shoulder of the road.

A white halo of dazzling light an unpleasant bleached brightness all around had James dizzy, unsteady on his limbs. It made him blind and the temporarily high frequency made his ears ring but he could still smell. He could smell the fresh blood coming from his victim and the burnt antifreeze coming from the disabled bug to the back of him. He could smell the hydraulic oil and lube coming from the tow truck to the right. Suddenly he smelled the overabundance of body spray several yards away and the unmistakable aroma of gunpowder directly in front of him.

A loud bang and James reacted instantly dodging the projectile. Another bang another dodge and the aroma guided him like a roadmap and James had the tow truck driver in his clutches. Another quick bang, this one muffled as James slammed into the burly man. The jolt forced the gun from his hand and it fell on the ground harmlessly. The burly man's eyes widened in shock, disbelief and fear as he a saw James' monstrous eyes. No empathy could be seen in his eyes no compassion no human thought remained. Just lupine thought and animal bloodlust he knew the last shot hit him, but no pain had registered in his eyes.

A thought ran through the tow truck driver's mind as the monster crushed his' head again and again against the truck window frame… if eyes were a window of the soul, then what about this monster's eyes? He saw bright golden eyes, the eyes of a wild animal, frantic, frightened, desperate, no forgiveness in the eyes only an insatiable hunger to live. After the 13th time of his head smashing in on the door frame, his skull cracked. He looked into the lunatic's eyes for the last time as he slipped into unconsciousness. The tow truck driver's blue eyes seemed red now, a vivid crimson as blood stained and filled in the once white part of his eyes. A laceration on his scalp bled down his forehead like a viscous waterfall. He slumped over but stayed on his feet, his arm wedged through the seatbelt he exhaled a last breath standing upright.

James' heart rate slowed affecting his feral state. He turned around then promptly collapsed onto his knees. From a large bolder he saw So-seti sneaking out from hiding to inspect the bug owner's dead body.

Hunger and curiosity forced Matt to gain enough confidence to come down the mountain as well. He snuck cautiously and slowly over, drooling hungrily over to the body.

So-seti tore off the lips of the dead man and greedily devoured it. Her eyes still slits of discontent but So-seti knew James trusted him, so she learned to get along. After she finished, she grew claws and tore the rest of the face off and offered the bloody meat to Matt which he gratefully but a little timidly accepted.

James smiled; he thought the kids were playing nice. The pain hit him suddenly and without mercy. He felt a stabbing sensation in his lung every time he took a breath where he had been it by the bullet. So-seti and Matt turned around in time enough to see James collapse.

He awoke feeling disoriented with a severe headache. The sun had set and he could see again. He remembered being shot suddenly and he pressed his palms to his chest feeling only a scar.

"I tried to clean you up a little, Matt tended to your wound, and he got the bullet out so you can begin to heal normally. With a foreign body I was afraid you couldn't heal at all, my young changeling, your blood being so young," So-seti comforted and soothed him while stroking his cheek and hair, "when the Moon is full again, you should be healed when you change…or sooner than that if you learn to metamorphose early."

He looked up at the night sky through the window of the tow truck. In the driver's window bits of brain and crusted blood blurred the light pouring in from the street lamps passing by. He wasn't exhausted but his body hurt everywhere. For one dreamy encounter in the ambient light of the truck So-seti seemed flawless, her body felt firm and tight. So-seti's lips were fuller and her green eyes brighter still like sparkling emeralds but then he looked down at her amputated legs. She probably gorged herself on human flesh and metamorphosed, James reasoned.

Matt was a different story altogether. He looked pale his eyes sunken in there would be no metamorphosis, he was a drone, a ghoul, no intricate thought it all. He did what he was told but there would be no transformation before the next full moon. However, he had been a loyal friend and ally, he'd follow him anywhere. He slipped into unconsciousness again.

"Don't worry my dear, I'll teach you; the wolf's blood inside you is strong. Remember to go into a trance your heart rate and breathing is paramount. I'll be there guiding you all the way, I promise." So-seti whispered.

With So-seti's instinctual directions Matt turned down the interstate as James lay on So-seti's lap somewhere between consciousness and a dream on the way to Raccourci Island, LA, headed towards Sarah's inherited plantation.

39

The specifics were fuzzy to say the least and throughout his body and mind a powerful ache threatened to split his brain open. He felt like his body had been poured into concrete and set. Weakened and sickly, he felt as if he had one foot in the grave.

Atkins stared at his hand or the lack thereof, a mangled, broken, flattened hand… a useless stump of a hand, his body shaking. He adjusted his eyes to look around at the confined space he found himself in reminding him he had been hiding in a closet at The God's Light compound.

He couldn't help but flash back to the conflict between him and Lucius. He could not remember any detailed event but Lucius' inhuman malevolent, shining cat-like eyes were seared in his mind. Atkins stared at the cat eyes; his body had materialized no more a dark specter. Could his mind play a trick on him; Lucius could not be out could he? Byron Atkins steadied himself to some form of a dream or a nightmare trying to recall the horrid offense. Dizzy, sickening, weakened and paler with each heartbeat that Byron's body made.

Byron looked around with real effort, as he did so smoke billowed forth from the ceiling. The sirens blaring in his ear, oscillating red lights, alternating beams making shadows dance on the wall affecting his equilibrium.

"Ah, hello Mr. Atkins," Lucius' voice box shivered not yet used to physically talking. With his cold, complete hand he touched Byron's cheek; Byron couldn't help but notice the other arm with interest, a missing hand as Lucius continued, "my darling So-seti has slipped her chains, as have I."

He had many questions but in the end he asked only one, "who let you out, Lucius?"

Instead of talking clumsily out loud, Lucius used his specter-self and violated Byron's mind, *"Wouldn't you like to have the answer to that, Byron!"*

Atkins' pulse began to get weaker as Lucius' pulse began to get stronger. Byron heard a beating pulse but pulsing wasn't coming from Lucius' heart which had stopped dead eons ago. His heart beat no longer, the sound Atkins heard was pure vibrating energy running through Lucius' veins, currently being siphoned off from Atkins' own body. Lucius did not need to feed in any traditional sense; a long time ago he became able to feed on the lifeblood energy without even biting his prey.

Lucius's body was whole again all but his missing forearm, able to unify with the majority of his rats. He had consumed unsuspecting staff members just a floor below until he went from a skeletal, mummified figure to near perfection.

Lucius nodded his head, forcing Atkins off his feet, flinging him into the wall, "Where are the other rats?"

Atkins winced; an invisible force left him breathless from the wind being squeezed out of him. He could not say a word, for a lack of oxygen if nothing else. He clutched his neck, his face going through the colors of a twisted rainbow. First pink, then a deep red, followed by a pale purple hue graduating into a deep purple, finally a black face, his veins bursting in his eyes. Then the force squeezing his neck inexplicably relaxed.

"No matter... in time without nourishment my rats will eventually die and decay, then I'll have forearm and hand back again... Dust to dust, as they say." Lucius whispered then stomped down on Dr. Atkins' left hand.

"Ahhhhhh!" Atkins tried his best to be silent, to grin and bear it. But then came more than he could stand as he yelled out like a baby.

Lucius began to smile, his glossy canines glinting under the fire, "Now you have a useless arm just like me! I would kill you, but I need you to spread a message for me to The God's Light all over the world."

Lucius continued, "Lucius, Cain's apprentice, is loose and has set free So-seti. The lycanthropes are ready to wage war on humanity. Run and hide if you want to live but tremble with fear! The horrors that were waged on the children of the night come to haunt you!"

Atkins shivered as he remembered that, and the night's events. With trembling hands he searched for his cell phone with his good hand.

He calmly looked around calculating his situation, and while waiting for the phone to pick up, nervously smiled, lucky to be alive, support beams rested just inches from where he stood. A dozen or so holes intermittently graced the scorched floor and ceiling. The walls that made barriers to the rooms were no more, just an occasional doorframe remained. The five million dollar custom bunker complete with an imported brick church had been destroyed in only hours. Now it was just a huge grave with charred debris.

In fact; the heat of the Inferno coupled with massive smoke inhalation he should have died hiding in the closet were it not for the fact that Lucius obviously put a spell on him. He would survive so he could deliver Lucius' message. Then he thought of all the innocent employees, he saw flashes of Kathy the receptionist, clotting crimson gore all over her body, reflected in her pale flesh. Somehow he knew nobody but he remained alive here.

First he called God's Light with exact coordinates so he could be picked up. He stood still as a deer in headlights estimating he was forty feet underground with another sixty feet or three floors above. He dared not move an inch or he could fall further into the flimsy structure should there be a critical failure.

"Yes, Dr. Atkins? What can we do for you?" The voice on the other line, a man called Hunter asked.

"Hunter, the ancient bitch So-seti has escaped! Seek and destroy her and any lycanthrope you find and immediately report back to me, is this clear to you?" squinting, Dr. Atkins did a salute to shield his eyes from the sunlight seeping in from the holes around him.

"I have just found an ancient lycanthrope with a red tattooed face. He has been stalking around the Point Breeze Motel, he could replace what we lost sir; do I capture him or destroy him?" A disembodied voice asked the leader of the Western God's Light chapter.

"Destroy him…destroy all of them, and report back to me!"

"Yes sir, I'll call you with my progress …over and out," The disembodied voice hung up the phone.

A whirl of the helicopter could be heard from the distance, raising Dr. Atkins' hopes. A lever dispatched the ladder that came down swaying in the wind. He watched the ladder as it easily threaded through the gaping holes in the floor.

He slid his cell phone back into his pocket, stabilizing his feet on the bottom runner of the ladder whilst crossing his forearm on the chest-high runner with his useless hand. A sudden jolt and Atkins grasped his other hand firmly on the rope and closed his eyes as the ladder lifted up from the ground.

He opened his eyes long enough to see an aerial view of the ruined compound, the first time in his life he felt any humbleness and helplessness. He saw more corpses, dead receptionists and scientists could be seen on every floor, on every level.

"God help us, God help us all!" Atkins said under his breath closing his eyes again feeling the sun beat down on his bald head as the wind swirled around him.

His body slackened under the warm, healing rays of the sun that assuring him that he would not be attacked. He clutched the ladder for dear life until he felt the ground again. People on the sidewalk were pointing and gossiping. Word spread about the deaths and the church Inferno before the sun came up, but luckily there were no pedestrian casualties. He breathed a sigh of relief, the market and houses were all untouched just the compound which had been utterly destroyed. The ladder wound up and the roar of the helicopter faded away. A crowd of people had gathered around to watch the aftermath, making Dr. Atkins spontaneously smile. The monstrous captives were all preoccupied with escaping; no harm had come to the residents at all. Dr. Atkins sat on the cramped ground and crossed his legs. He cradled his wounded hand and had to take a moment to think, to strategize his next move before he passed out and went into a coma from exhaustion coupled with his diabetes.

40

Batchelor, LA

Sitting at the kitchen table Detective Jenkins stared at the house phone in his hand as it rang incessantly before he made the decision to press the button to mute the ringer. He knew he had a moment of silence before his cell phone started to ring again. His cell phone rang out, "sing a song about the Southland" sounded as Lynyrd Skynyrd wailed. He shook and lowered his head as he bit the bullet and answered the neglected call.

A small staff of police officers a smaller staff of detectives, made smaller still by Detective Jenkins' absence at the Batchelor, LA. Police Department had the staff Sergeant's patience wearing thin. Though sympathetic, he called wondering when Jenkins would be available to work again.

"Detective Jenkins," he answered the one-sided conversation in a monotone voice, "yes Sir, yes Sir, next week Sir, Will do, Sir, Goodbye." Detective Jenkins grimaced as he ended the call.

The brass had been on eggshells since the officer involved shooting a few months ago that killed the paramedic, Cody, and the immediate disappearance of the body threw them for Loop. The CDC and the Point Breeze Parish Sheriff's Department had their hands full since his disappearance. A whirlwind of confusion had set in as they investigated. Those at the top of the chain of command rationalized that it was no dead body at all, only a coroner's mistake, the police called off the search and doctors double and triple the checked many of the test the results which held no trace of a contagion so the CDC headed home, rationalizing the few months were just localized mass hysteria. Detective Jenkins would not be so easily convinced, however. His body shaking, it had been the second time he fired his weapon and it mirrored the first, welling up painful memories. The sins of the past had arisen evoking the ghost of his long dead son, Phillip Jenkins.

Since the second shooting Detective Jenkins went into hiding, a self-induced isolation, burning off sick days in a drunken stupor. A righteous shot, he heard somewhere in his mind. They called it a righteous shot a second time! And the first shooting he could blow clean on the breathalyzer but if they would have blood tested him, they would have found a cocktail of valium, tranquilizer and Ambien… legally intoxicated, unable to legally drive let alone handle a gun. A decorated detective, the pride of the force his word gospel, they had declared it a "righteous shot" as his son lay dying; bleeding on the kitchen floor the damage had been done. Except for the drug-induced haze it happened exactly how he said. But even without his son's hood he would not know him from Adam anyway. Labeled a pariah he quit the Louisiana State Police Department and moved to Batchelor, LA. Where he promptly got a divorce; the loss of their son more than his wife could bear. He procured another job at the smaller hometown Police Department where he could get a fresh start, unknown to the other officers but his son haunted him wherever he went.

He knocked back another shot of brownish liquor then refilled it from an almost empty gallon jug of the stuff. His kitchen tabletop looked like the display unit in the liquor store. Aftermath of bottle after bottle of alcohol of varying sizes, Half-pint, pint to fifths, row after row of hotel sample-size spirits even one gallon jug that Detective Jenkins had poured his shots from.

He had been in the process of getting better. Regular jogs every day at dawn had his head clear for the first time in years. He had even quit smoking cigarettes! Then a second shooting, a second shooting that reminded him of the first shooting and the day his son died by his hand. He was supposed to be away! He was supposed to be away at school learning, laughing and living, just living. It was no excuse, Jenkins thought, but his son had been higher than a kite and had a blood alcohol content of .16. No excuse! No excuse! He beat himself up inside.

He heard the electronic noise and the crooning of a rock band in the radio, "hate me today, hate me tomorrow…" sung on the radio somewhere in the house.

He remembered all of the terrible fighting that ensued, culminating in the couple's bitter divorce. He remembered Mary and her accusing eyes. Everybody in his old accursed town accused him whether openly or with their eyes.

That is why he moved to Batchelor, Detective Jenkins thought, am I a magnet to these things? He wasn't on anything this time and it had happened again! He did everything right and by the book! But he had been unarmed! No, he wasn't! Detective Jenkins argued to himself, he had huge claws, like a bear's claws.

Detective Jenkins downed another shot; consumption of the draught becoming double digits at this point. Months had gone by but the guilt had him to the breaking point. All of his colleagues were there canvassing the scene and they came up with no other weapon but the knife anywhere. He remembered his own knife. It wasn't meant to be a drop knife at all. He had it with him strapped to his thigh along for the jog as defense against a rogue boar or crocodile. He remembered tossing the knife on the ground by the unfortunate suspect.

Why did he plant the knife on the body anyway? He identified himself as a police officer, but the perp. didn't stop when ordered and in fact he lunged forward! Detective Jenkins thought he was definitely armed, and very dangerous… he saw the claws! No that was the right thing to do he thought. If the fatal shot had driven him to the breaking point then the missing body that he had just shot drove him to a slow and steady spiraling descent into madness.

"You know I hate to tell you this but you are already crazy, ever since I died," A disembodied voice knew his thought process.

The investigation concerning Cody's body had been lukewarm optimism at best. The shooting broadcasted unwanted attention on the department. Without a body to cast light and criticism upon the top brass hoped the people would eventually forget the embarrassment that detective Jenkins had caused them. Especially since the man who caused the shooting had killed a boy before, still fresh in the public's mind.

Though the search had been called off months ago he obsessed every day and every night over the whereabouts of the paramedic. He hoped the location would be revealed tomorrow when he picked up Dexter, a German shepherd with the Louisiana State police canine unit. Today, however, as he downed another shot, if he stood up to do anything at all he would likely just pass out.

"You're so pitiful! No wonder my mother left your sorry ass!" the voice scolded Detective Jenkins, "But I guess I don't blame you."

Hearing the voice of his son, Jenkins flinched and closed his eyes. He felt dizzy now and the mocking from his son did not help. Closing his eyes would not help the barrage of insults to come.

"Geez, why don't you kill yourself already?" Suddenly, empty alcohol bottles shattered and full bottles fell and rolled onto the floor. The ghost of his son materialized and floated forward to the kitchen table.

"Well you've outdone yourself this time, Daddy!" the ghost of his son said slamming his fist on the kitchen table, knocking over more bottles to get detective Jenkins' attention. But he stood the bottles up again without flinching.

"I can't believe that you actually killed again, Daddy!" His dead son's ghost smiled a translucent smile, "But I hear he just got up and walked out of the hospital, imagine that!"

Tired of whispering accusations and insults it would all come to a head tomorrow, he thought, confident he would find Cody's body or at least a suspect. Detective Jenkins had had enough, promptly standing and stumbling for a minute while he got his bearings. His blood pressure plummeted. The double vision came upon him suddenly; his eyesight darkening as he fell toward the ground. He managed to miss hitting his head on the refrigerator by mere inches. For several seconds he didn't move at all then his head stilled and snoring ensued.

"Dad, you're truly pitiful." His son, Phillip said softly as he evaporated.

Lynyrd Skynyrd incessantly sung until he stirred. Awake, his head pounding, lying there on the floor where he had so gracefully passed out the night before. His shirt was wet with drool, his hair a rats nest and greasy.

"Yes?" detective Jenkins said as he frantically searched for his cigarettes and lighter.

The other side of the cell answers and introductions were made. A short conversation ensued.

"Good. I will be there shortly, I owe you one."

"Coffee," He said to himself aloud, "I need coffee."

He did not wait for the coffee to finish brewing and fill the decanter, instead he precariously perched his coffee cup directly under the flowing scolding black coffee. Two imitation sugars and a dash of cream and he carefully sipped his precious caffeine beverage.

"Not gonna drink today, right?" The apparition of his son questioned accusingly.

"No, I'm not going to be a lush today. I have things to do." Detective Jenkins said nonchalantly.

For the first time since the shooting detective Jenkins headed into the bathroom determined to shave the stubble from his face. Slathering shaving gel liberally onto his face he looked into the mirror took out a straight blade razor and carefully started to shave his cheeks.

"What are we doing today, Pops?" He could see his son materialized in the mirror.

He glanced up at his dead son for a moment then concentrated fully on his own reflection. A true bum he scoffed looking at his graying curly hairs on his chest and white wife beater, which had become crusty and stained. His empty hand rubbed a half-shaved chin. Detective Jenkins stared at his own reflection instead of his dead son, the lines on his forehead a little deeper his close cropped graying hair receding further since the first unfortunate shooting.

"I'm going to find the body today, how about you, son?" Detective Jenkins said mordantly as if talking to his dead son the most natural thing in the world. But his son had vanished for a while.

He plunged the razor full of hair and used cream into the milky water shaking it around until shiny and clean. He hesitated a moment to get in position before getting started again. The razor made a clean wide trail and where once grey stubble used to be became smooth skin.

He looked into the mirror. His face made him look young again, more youthful. He let out a deep breath, grateful his son had left for a while. He'd be back, but for now, Jenkins could get some peace and quiet.

With the sudden disappearance of his son he entertained the same notion he had a thousand times before. He pressed the straight razor against his neck. A little more pressure to nick the carotid and it was the all over the pain would go away.

"Give it up, Dad, you and I both know you're not going through with it today, now hurry up or you're gonna miss your meeting up with Carl Goodman and his dogs." His son warned.

The disembodied voice came from somewhere in the house. Detective Jenkins could not see his dead son in the mirror in the bathroom anymore but he learned from experience to expect him in the bedroom.

When his better half left him she got all their furniture and appliances in the final divorce decree. He had to scrounge around in the storage unit to find his old furniture he had kept from his youth. He arranged his bedroom to be a montage to everything great or horrible in the 60, 70 & 80s. His water bed with giant mirrored backboard to his velvet oil paintings and blacklight posters littered the four walls in various shapes and sizes. He went with this theme going hog-wild throughout the room, even plugging in a lava lamp and a blacklight for the posters. His bedroom turned out to be the only fully furnished room in the house.

He splashed down on his waterbed and picked up a simple dumbbell trying to ignore his apparition in the corner of the room. He did a series of bicep curls with his right hand then the left without counting. Sufficiently pumped, his biceps burning, he dropped the dumbbell on the floor. Detective Jenkins checked his alarm clock by his bed.

A huff of disapproval rolled out his mouth, almost afternoon and he still felt like shit! The apparition sat down upon the edge of the water bed. Gentle waves rolled and crashed on the edges of the bed. Sliding his feet into his steel toe boots mindlessly tying them in functional knots Detective Jenkins got up and opened a closet. One of two, his and hers, one that was empty filled with cobwebs from ceiling to floor and the occasional moth that wandered in by accident the other one filled to the brim with uniforms and jeans. He chose a clean shirt to replace the filthy one he currently wore putting it on then he looked at his hair in the mirror. He deliberately tried to ignore Phillip who lay down on the bed.

"It is a little petty that you ignore me now." Phillip sulked.

Something in Phillip's tone struck a nerve and he would be silent no longer. Twirling around throwing his filthy shirt at the bed as the flood gates opened and a torrent of irate words like daggers followed.

"I'm not ignoring you!" Detective Jenkins argued, "I've learned to live with it, believe me!"

Rubbing the deodorant on his underarms then liberally spraying on Cologne to mask the night's events he continued his barrage of ridicules then was silent once more. Looking at his reflection in the mirror then at his son, sometimes he thought there had been no chance for closure, no time for grieving, the apparition of his son was so real, so material. No wonder he hallucinates when he makes the same mistake all over again!

"Did you ever think that I am your Guardian angel?" Phillip smiled.

He lit another cigarette and poured himself more coffee, which he quickly downed to a drop. He checked for the keys in his pocket then he said, "no, no, I didn't… more like you're a demon in disguise, come to haunt me."

On autopilot now he trudged out the house door and starting his engine before he knew it. With engine running he waited in the driveway until Phillip caught up with him. He tried to tune him out driving down the road, his dead kid sitting next to him chatting incessantly. Trying now to ignore the yellow house the crime scene coming up the road Detective Jenkins engaged in small talk with his imaginary son until the house could only be seen by squinting into the rearview mirror.

Detective Jenkins could see Carl Goodman wave as he appeared over the hill his slack leather leash in hand. Dexter, his well-trained and well-behaved German shepherd, sat patiently on the grass. Dexter excelled in finding missing persons and cadavers. Taught by the Louisiana State Police Department K-9 unit but since then retired by them for his age Dexter had become the perfect dog for the mission.

Gravel had kicked up from the tires gathering dust up into the air. Several canines caged in the kennels out back bellowed their warning howls, their low-tech intruder alert. Rocks kicking up and hitting the side of the truck sounded the sound of popcorn pops or rice crispies getting chatty with milk echoed throughout the lonely swamp land. The truck came to a rest in the parking lot by a faded sign that said "Canine Inn, Training and Obedience."

Both of the doors closed in Detective Jenkins' truck as he headed toward the dog trainer Carl Goodman, but Carl saw only one door open. Dexter observed their chat back and forth patiently although a new face excited him. Carl pushed his wire-rim glasses back on his bulbous nose and rubbed his obviously receding thin and wiry blonde hair.

"Jonathan, how are you?" Carl Goodman greeted him with his free hand.

"I'm good. How are you?" Detective Jenkins returned his pleasantries shaking Carl's hand.

"He's lying!" the translucent Phillip argued to deaf ears.

Phillip silently bent down to rub Dexter's underbelly, unseen by Carl, but Dexter's tail wagged, barking excitedly at an unknown presence.

"Thank you, for Dexter's help in the search." Detective Jenkins bent down and began rubbing Dexter too.

"Don't mention it my friend," Carl consoled Jenkins, "I owe you one, besides Dexter here needs to get out and stretch his legs a little since his retirement."

It was true that Detective Jenkins did so many favors for Carl Goodman he had stopped counting a long time ago. Between fixing tickets and dismissing D.U.I.s. however, he had a funny feeling about the borrowing of Dexter since his dream last night, where an unknown emaciated dog was killed and then his limbs amputated by monsters. Despite his reservations Detective Jenkins needed Dexter for his tracking ability.

Carl handed off the reins to Jenkins for Dexter who obliviously consented to the change in leadership. With his tongue out and wagging his tail Dexter followed Jenkins to the truck.

"Take care of him." Carl smiled.

Bending a knee so he could pat Dexter on the back one last time before Jenkins opened the truck door. Dexter immediately hopped into his front seat with the ghost of his son. Anxiety grew as he put the truck into reverse and rolled out of the lot. Dexter leapt down into the floorboard finding and eating the dry food and water that Jenkins had already obtained for him.

He did a U-turn remembering his daily jog and searching for the unincorporated road. Jenkins stepped on the break when he turned into the neighborhood where it had all happened. Just shy of the Batchelor, LA City limits he slowed down as he came upon the yellow house where crime scene tape wrapped around the entire yard. Going up the driveway he stepped on the break, put it in park as he stared at the yellow house with the boarded up windows.

With his hands firmly on the leash Jenkins stepped down from the truck coaxing Dexter to follow. The grass had grown up high enough to conceal Cody's blood. Dexter hesitated on the sidewalk trying to get his bearings.

"Come on boy!" Jenkins commanded, smacking his hands on his thighs.

Jenkins fished out a copy of the house key then unlocked the door. The front door gave way easily and Dexter's front paws echoed across the hard wood floor. An eerie silence enveloped him as the stench assaulted his nose almost knocking him to his knees.

Jenkins' eyes had to adjust to the dim light a moment until he could see the hectic mess before him. The entertainment system was knocked over on its side, the flat screen TV crushed. The glass coffee table lay shattered in a million pieces.

Dexter barked three times then enthusiastically sprinted toward the source of the smell. Jenkins almost let the leash slip as Dexter headed off in the direction of the kitchen but he battled for control of the end of the loop of the leash again.

Dexter lapped up the rotten spoiling meat on the floor by the broken refrigerator where maggots made their home. The door to the refrigerator had busted at the hinges and the light could be seen in the seams. Open, broken cabinets and broken dishes were on the floor.

It was clear to Jenkins when he walked about looking room by room some kind of conflict had ensued throughout the entire house. He found himself in the bathroom where a broken mirror's shards of glass were strewn about the floor. The medicine cabinet mirror completely destroyed, leaving Jenkins to believe it wasn't so much an external conflict with an unknown intruder, but an internal conflict in Cody's mind.

No sense stalling any longer, he thought. Jenkins and Dexter made a beeline for the bedroom. Cody's door was in splinters with only the doorframe remaining. Jenkins tried to control the leash while Dexter ran around in circles the aromas making the dog crazed. The stench overwhelming him, he instinctively pinched his nose against the powerful smell of ammonia.

Cody's dirty clothing was strewn all across the piss covered floor. A grouping of five deep scratches crisscrossed the length of the walls, a dozen or so in number littering the paneling. Jenkins looked at the boarded up window that Cody shattered while escaping.

Jenkins gathered some of Cody's clothing putting them in a gym bag as a thought ran through his mind, if there is not a new horrible disease in Batchelor's midst then it's not unreasonable to think there is a new designer drug sprouting up in the shadows and that frightened him.

"Let's go boy!" Jenkins said, slapping his palm on his thigh.

A strange fleeting aroma like a wet wild dog caught Jenkins' attention for a second then vanished. Dexter smelled the strange scent too, stalling until Jenkins yanked on the leash to coax him to move. He packed up Dexter and double checked the straps on the ATV before heading out to his next destination, the Pointe Coupee hospital where Cody's body first went missing.

Before opening the door to let out Dexter in the hospital parking lot Jenkins opened the tailgate and placed the ramps on the gravel parking lot and slowly rolled out the ATV. Pointe Coupee hospital was where Cody disappeared and where Dexter would get Cody's scent.

Jenkins sat upon the red 2000 Honda TRX300 ATV. It had a 281cc motor and dirt encrusted fenders. A dinosaur of sorts but it had a well maintained engine with sleek new tires with thick treads it would get the job done and it had a rack in back to let the dog rest while the detective crossed the topography.

Gathering Cody's used clothing he opened the door to let out the anxiously awaiting Dexter, "Let's go boy, breath in Cody's scent and lead the way."

Wagging his tail in anticipation and excitement Dexter stuck his muzzle into Cody's shirt drawing in a strong scent of his essence. Instantly Dexter had his direction. Jenkins twisted the throttle slowly, just enough to follow Dexter on his leash. His nose to the pavement Dexter paced in the median like a madman on a mission.

Dexter led the detective to a wooded area leading him to a shortcut to a rural side gravel road back to Batchelor. The dog circled around to Jenkins' old jogging route and back to where Jenkins had shot Cody. He remembered the cold body on the over grown grass. Losing his mind as Cody spouted fangs and claws. He remembered his knife as he kicked it underneath Cody's body.

The ATV rolled along by Dexter who slowly trudged out into unincorporated borders. He remembered Capt. Rogers and his involvement in the shooting of his son and the crazed paramedic, his compassion and understanding. He knew he could call on Capt. Rogers if things got hairy.

Dexter sat on his haunches; Dexter stoically still until the winds had changed and he caught another strong new scent exploding into motion and b-lining away from the neighborhoods. Jenkins nimble hands throttled the engine moving quickly enough to keep up with Dexter.

The worn shocks coupled by the speed of the ATV, rocks and branches caused the ATV's body to jar back and forth as Jenkins observed Dexter's muzzle on the ground. The GPS hooked up on Jenkins handlebars went blank, uncharted territory until Dexter locked onto a familiar scent.

In the distance Jenkins saw a dilapidated shack. He sensed a strange and sinister presence all over the area. Where the thick trees stopped sat a neglected privacy fence spanning the length of the property, abruptly turning ninety degrees where a full deck ran flush. Where the steps to the deck ended a privacy fence stood open. From a decrepit shed in the corner of the yard a bonfire peeked out. The dancing flames casting shadows on the termite infested rotten boards. Jenkins pressed the break stopping the ATV. The choker tightening as Dexter stubbornly pulled against the leash following Cody's scent.

"Whoa boy, heel." The detective demanded. Reluctantly Dexter obeyed with a whimper. Jenkins got off the ATV but left it running.

With Dexter leading him on an unfamiliar route and the GPS not computing Jenkins wasn't sure if the area around the shack fell under the jurisdiction of Batchelor or not. Besides, Jenkins thought, technically he had been off the job he had to call someone. He had no time to think about his options when the screen door opened unexpectedly.

In the front of the shack a screen door swung out, worn rusty springs did little to inhibit the open screen door from roughly closing with a bang. This startled Dexter who immediately stood still, ears at alert, his tail erect. Dexter's cautious nervous eyes were trained on Aticus who stepped out onto the porch.

A stitched do-rag, a custom Bandana of sorts, could be seen over his extra dark sunglasses that hid the emerald gem inserted in his missing eye. He had one long pointed ear the other one covered and concealed by the do-rag. He saw his sharp cheekbones and long nose, long thin lips. He incessantly licked his lips almost panting in a way. Only six foot four, but he had a presence that made him seem nine feet tall. The detective couldn't help but shield his eyes from his shirtless and extremely pale but well defined torso. He smelt a musk that reminded him of something wild, something feral. He couldn't shake the sinking feeling he had come face to face with a primeval malicious entity.

"Can I help you?" Aticus said with an accent thick and strange. He had a sinister toothy smile as he bit into a bright shiny apple.

Jenkins noticed Aticus' long black fingernails and a cold chill ran down his spine. He could smell something strange but familiar from the bonfire, like a smell of burnt barbecue. He peered into the fire. Was that an arm? No, he thought he must be crazy. But something is strange here!

"Sorry, let me introduce myself. I am Detective Jenkins and I am investigating the disappearance of an ambulance worker." Jenkins offered. His eyes trained on him, his brain trying to process the strange entity.

"Oh, I see." Aticus turned his attention to Dexter while slowly ambling off the porch near the privacy fence gate. When he stepped off the porch the dog yelped, skittish of his presence, and suddenly intimidated.

Aticus slowly bent down but his one eye never left Detective Jenkins' eyes. He reached out a hand to pet Dexter but the dog recoiled to the safety between Jenkins' legs.

Detective Jenkins pulled out a photo from his pocket that he had gotten out of Cody's house and showed it to Aticus. He moved in to have a closer look prompting Dexter to piss all over himself, and rollover onto his back in an act of submissiveness in Aticus' presence. The canine's fear did not thwart his efforts to pet the shivering dog until Detective Jenkins shook his head in disapproval.

He warned Aticus too late, he dug his filthy nails into Dexter's soft fur immediately making Dexter frigidly still and whimpering like a puppy. Jenkins felt the dog severely shaking like he was an extreme epileptic.

"I don't think it's a good idea to touch him!" Detective Jenkins warned.

"Cute dog you have there." Aticus said, stifling a growl as he stood up. He turned his attention to the photo and tapped the photograph. "I do not believe I've met him."

"Would you mind terribly if my dog and I search your property?" Detective Jenkins asked as he tried to coax Dexter into standing.

Aticus slyly strolled over to the gate and kicked the privacy gate closed concealing the bonfire with the supposing amputated arm with in.

"Yes I do." Aticus told Jenkins patting him on the shoulder firmly.

Taken aback from Aticus' response Jenkins stepped back and instinctively put his professional game face on. "You know if my dog sniffed out anything suspicious I have the right to enter into your dwelling."

Aticus could not suppress the growl in his chest, "I do not think your precious dog is going to find anything anyway."

Aticus looked down at the frightened dog still shaking uncontrollably. Dexter had crawled back in the safety and security of Jenkins' legs. Suddenly Dexter jumped and darted toward the ATV. The leash in his hand tightened to the breaking point. His hand bleeding as the leash forced it up the length of his wrist, Dexter lie down on the rack and submissively put his head in his paws, his eyes lowering.

Aticus pulled out a combination lock from the tan leather pants pocket and proceeded to latch the gate. Aticus whipped his head around and took off his dark glasses to see his animalistic eye. He flipped up his do-rag made of human skin to reveal a gleaming green gem stuck in his eye socket.

Not prepared for this moment, Detective Jenkins stepped back, taken aback a bit. The investigation surprised him to find a menacing fiend, a malevolent presence, which made him regress to the point of a child leaving detective Jenkins helpless.

He knew he should retreat from this place and call Captain Rogers, a state police officer. Being a Batchelor city police officer he had no authority whereas state police officers had the authority to enter into the shack where the boundaries had changed.

He looked at the frightened dog, Dexter, who buried his muzzle in his limbs his tactics changing, "I'm sorry to have bothered you, your name is again?"

"My name is Aticus," he tapped at his shiny jewel in his eye socket smiling at Detective Jenkins, his canines prevalent, "my friends call me Ice, but you can call me Aticus…"

Aticus stood on the porch his hand clutching the top of the locked gate. For several seconds A Mexican standoff occurred, each one eyeing the other. Before Detective Jenkins flinched first and turned his head.

"You know you should be careful, you might not like what you dig up." Aticus said under his breath as he headed into the shack, the screen door closing behind him with a loud clack.

His head reeling he had a strange gut instinct that told him to beware. Without backup he was weary and Detective Jenkins slid his legs over and plopped down on the seat of the ATV. He kicked the gearshift into neutral then slowly rolled from the rock driveway to the gravel road.

From the ATV rack Jenkins pulled out the binoculars then he moved to the safety of concealing weeping Juniper trees. The privacy fence now closed he couldn't see the bonfire but he could see the heavy smoke coming from it. With the binoculars in one hand he fished out his cell phone with the other and proceeded to call his friend Capt. Rogers.

Capt. Rogers picked up the cell and was now on his way to meet Detective Jenkins. He continued to peer into his binoculars to spy on the house though the privacy fence obscured the right side of the house and the yard. Dexter was content for now to cower on the grass at his feet.

He heard footfalls on the road distracting his surveillance. Capt. Rogers had parked a mile back so as that anyone in the house would not be tipped off by his presence. Jenkins looked Rogers up and down;

he was definitely off duty due to the fact of his civilian clothing. They were roughly the same age; however Capt. Rogers and Detective Jenkins had aged drastically different. Both Captains of their respective football teams in high school they were brawny and solid. In fact, in high school they faced off against each other occasionally. However, that's where the similarities ended.

After high school Capt. Rogers went to college on a full athletic scholarship, Detective Jenkins went into the police Academy and found the love of his life. He found a job in the Baton Rouge Police Department but downsizing led to a layoff and a move to Lafayette where he eventually landed another law enforcement job. Now burnt out and just going through the motions soon this job too stalled out until tragedy happened and he killed his son. This brought about the reunion of Jenkins and Rogers for the first time since high school.

He could no longer show his face in Lafayette and the stress of the loss of their son had led to a divorce. This correlated in a three year long alcohol binge until he eventually landed in the Batchelor Police Department. The loss, stress, and the boozing had prematurely aged him. Though he had line-backer shoulders they were slumped and defeated. The defined lines and bags under his dead eyes droopy and bulldog like jowls. His receding and disheveled salt-and-pepper hair seemed thinner day by day.

A lesson in opposites with Rogers though; he had only climbed to Captain in the Police Department but no further. After Captain, his wife wanted him to climb the ranks of the Police Department. She could see him becoming Major, Commander, Deputy Commissioner, even Superintendent. She even tried to get him into politics, entertaining the idea of becoming mayor or even a Senator of Louisiana someday until she contracted cancer. As he tended to his wife's needs he had no ambition in climbing the ladder any higher. Brought up to be a simple man with simple ideals he had no stomach for the hoops that he was required to jump through and eventually he squashed the dream or as he defined it, the nightmare, as he took care of his wife's health needs. When the stress seemed too great he had an affair which did not detour his wife. A perpetual child, Peter Pan syndrome, he seemed ageless as worries slid off his back not a care in the world.

With all his stresses he still stood up straight in stature his tall powerful linebacker shoulders, wide and proud. The worry and frown lines in Detective Jenkins were not evident in Capt. Rogers' shining complexion with his wide large shining eyes full of life. He always smiled with a mouth full of bright white teeth that accentuated the dimples in his cheeks and indentation in his chin.

"So fill me in, what's the 411?" Capt. Rogers whispered, extending a hand to Dexter.

From the very start of the incident of Cody's shooting Detective Jenkins and Capt. Rogers shared information with one another. Detective Jenkins bent down to unfasten Dexter still startled and shivering from the meeting with the eccentric stranger.

"Before the Doc went off grid for going on months now, he had reported Cody coming to life and attacking him with claws and nails. He had planned to use his unused vacation days to find Cody before he too then went missing." Jenkins watched the shack like a hawk while he waited for Rogers thoughts.

"He thought his sickness had him hallucinating." Capt. Rogers reported this, his manner stern and cohesive, very matter of fact.

Capt. Rogers smiled when he looked into Detective Jenkins clean-shaven face. Beaming with pride, delighted with his friend for professionalism; he could not think of the last time he had been shaved and clean since the shooting accident.

"Okay right, run it through to me again with fresh eyes, so to speak. You got up for a run morning of the shooting. What did you see?" questioned Capt. Rogers, as he tapped Detective Jenkins on the shoulder and gestured to obtain the binoculars.

One look into Capt. Rogers eyes and he could not shake the sinking feeling of cruel and humiliating judgment. Now with his second shooting…

Capt. Rogers did not feel the same way, though. When it comes to the men and women of the Police Department everyone bled blue. He took Detective Jenkins at his word. He trusted him and backed him up. He considered him a friend and colleague just needing the new specifics that Jenkins could provide.

"In the morning I went for my daily jog, fifteen miles or so to sweat out last night's alcohol." Detective Jenkins said, handing Rogers the binoculars, "I'm unsure of what I saw until Dr. Jacobs verified that Cody had a fangs and claws as well."

You run 15 miles a day?" the odd conversation interrupted as Rogers' eyes widened in amazement, more a statement than a question Rogers exclaimed, "Look, there's smoke!"

Alerted to the rising smoke coming from a window in the shack Detective Jenkins exclaimed, "shit, Call 911 I think the shack is on fire!"

Jenkins ran toward the front of the shack without thinking; unincorporated it will take a while for the fire department to respond. Capt. Rogers called for assistance while running towards the deck side of the house by the locked privacy fence. Rogers beat his fist against the privacy fence, the fence blocking his access to the backyard.

"Hey, police!" Jenkins banged on front screen door, then frantically looking back at Capt. Rogers who was still barred at the gate.

Rogers cradled his cell handset sandwiched between his thick neck and shoulder still calling to 911 while he folded up his long-sleeved shirt, revealing his faded tattoo on his forearm; it looked like a homemade jailhouse tattoo, a phoenix rising from the flames. In the back yard in the distance somewhere by the shed Capt. Rogers heard a two-stroke engine firing up.

"Hey, something's happening!" Capt. Rogers firmly jerked on the combination lock but it would not give.

The shed's borders exploded, the roof collapsed onto the oil soaked floor. The tin sides burst sounding like thunder as they fell on the ground. A camouflage green ATV emerged with several passengers who held on for dear life.

Capt. Rogers used his gun as a lever to bust the latch secured with two inch nails in the privacy gate. He eventually managed to twist the lock to the breaking point. Rusty nails and rotten boards splintered at his feet. He shoved open the privacy fences with wild abandon just in time to see the ass end of the ATV disappearing into the forest thickets.

"Several people are escaping on an off-road!" Capt. Rogers adjusted his binoculars craning his neck on the phone with emergency services the ATV now long gone from his sight, "I could see what make and model the off roader is. Before it disappeared I could see four or more people!"

Detective Jenkins threw open the screen door had no luck and jiggled the locked knob of the front glass door. He balled a fist preparing to shatter the glass when a figure emerged from the smoke. The stranger put his cheek to the glass. He had tanned skin and high cheekbones. A Native American appearance with long brown dreadlocks he slyly smiled a mischievous toothy smile before he smacked his palms against the glass. His fingernails grew into thick black sharp talons then he proceeded to scratch down the glass permanently scoring it.

"I knew it… Claws, the fucker has claws, I knew it!!!" Detective Jenkins gasped wide eyed in a combination of surprise and validation.

The leaves stirred in the shadowy edge of the fenced in backyard revealing a naked man. He had strangely pale Latino features with long white hair and glowing red eyes. The albino Latino started towards Rogers' direction on a single-minded mission to destroy. Capt. Rogers withdrew back to the safety of the privacy fence's borders.

Detective Jenkins attempted to block the door while fumbling for his civilian gun, a snub-nosed 38 caliber revolver at his ankle. The Native American with brown dreadlocks repeatedly kicked the front glass door trying to smash the glass out until the frame groaned and the entire door gave way. The falling glass door left Jenkins off kilter, off balance and he fell off the porch onto his back. Jenkins' arms shook like a nervous Chihuahua as they try to prevent the heavy glass frame from crushing his chest.

The albino made his way to the privacy fence. Rogers eyes blinked rapidly his mind could not conceive the strange happenings. The white haired ashen bodied figure dropped to all fours, fur sprout all along his spine. Capt. Rogers could see the muscles on his back and shoulders until thick fur spread all along his body concealing pale flesh. The albino altered into a canine monstrosity, tailless with his face changing into a long muzzle complete with long, curved drooling fangs. The white beast's body built for battle and conflict. All four feet on the ground, its upper limbs still had long fingers with talons instead of paws. The albino monster was a massive wolf thing now but it was engineered so that it could still brawl and stand up right like a man!

Rogers groped for the fence to close the gate, temporarily confining the creature. He put all of his weight into the gate dropping his cell by the fence.

"Jonathan!" Captain Thompson Rogers shouted as the gates swayed back and forth violently the albino Wolf-thing trying to get through the closed fence.

Meanwhile, from the front of the shack black acrid smoke billowed out from the open front door. Jenkins lay on the ground his eyes locked onto the Native American aggressor while he desperately searched for his spare gun. He broke the stare just long enough to find and pull out his revolver, then turned to look into the aggressor's eyes again to find they were not human eyes anymore. He stared into the vicious eyes of a Brown hued huge Wolf and its yellow eyes hungrily staring back at him.

A Native American Wolf, called Tomas, tried to render Jenkins' bare throat snapping and biting but the clear barrier hindered the wolf-thing. The prone detective could see spittle that dripped down, pooling around the glass. Scared shitless he couldn't help but void his bladder as he evaded snapping fangs and claws while he tried to aim at a solid mass.

"What the hell is going on?" Rogers exclaimed, known for being cool and calm under pressure, his body shook with fear. He took a deep breath, rolled his shoulders, planted his feet upon the Earth, cocked the hammer of the gun back as he prepared to squash his fear and prepare to fire at the closed gate.

Detective Jenkins strained to understand the bizarre sight of the monster Wolf. He tried to yell out to Rogers, but all he sputtered was, "Claws! I knew he had claws!"

In the front lawn Jenkins pushed the revolver up to the glass closed his eyes and fired. Shards of broken glass rained down on his face. He breathed in with no constriction so he opened his eyes to see the wolf-thing standing up right. He stared at the crimson wound on its thick brown fur giving him confidence to shoot again. Two, three, four then a thump as the beast went down.

Capt. Rogers fired. A small perfect hole permeated the wood. He fired again twice. Sunlight peeked through the second and third hole from the faded and neglected wood. He heard a yelp, then a thud; instinctively prompting him to lower the gun.

Detective Jenkins slowly staggered up to Capt. Rogers as he opened the bullet ridden gate. In the lull of excitement they had a chance to gather their wits about them. Rogers planted both feet firmly on the ground while reloading a full magazine clip. Despite his better judgment, he warily looked over at his friend Detective Jenkins and the shack on fire burning bright.

The broken glass door now just a broken frame rested on the concrete. The oxygen that rushed in fed the dwindling fire re-sparking the dying flames by the living-room. On Jenkins' back side oppressive heat, on the other a severely bleeding wolf-thing lying in the grass as a circle of crimson gore continued spreading rapidly.

Detective Jenkins had a chance to look at the beast more closely. He had a brown furry long torso with the head of a huge Wolf all of the extremities were covered in thick brown fur. Its shoulders, arms, hands and legs looked humanoid except for the feet. The wide feet they were extremely long the heel of the foot could double as a reverse knee. He cautiously moved closer to the wounded beast his feet did not leave the ground scraping the concrete.

The privacy fence squeaked open and Capt. Rogers rested his pointer finger firmly on the trigger ready to fire. Detective Jenkins bent down the brown beast stirred startling him. Capt. Rogers locked onto the white beast. Patches of blood could be seen on its fur confirming the fact that he hit it though the gate had been closed.

In the distance a blue-winged Teal perched in the Cyprus trees where below squirrels ran under the moss. An alligator sat sunning itself on the river's edge while watching the mallards swim. The pair of Wolf-things perked up, their ears oscillating, homing in on the faint reverberations. There came a howl, a command, an order to come back to the pack. Both the brown and the white monstrosities turned to face Detective Jenkins and Capt. Rogers respectively.

Detective Jenkins trained the handgun at the brown beast but froze, mesmerized by what he saw. The fur receded from its body, cracking and popping as its muzzle reverted to a human face. A humanoid visage with long Brown dreadlocks, glared at detective Jenkins. The massive wounds of the Wolf changed into a human chest and abdomen pushing out the foreign projectiles. The bullets fell down onto the grass and the skin seemed to heal itself until only a red blood stain remained.

So, too with the white wolf as it reverted into its human form the bullets fell to the ground leaving the pair of policeman speechless. Though in denial, dazed, and in disbelief both men were prepared to fire again if attacked. However, with a growl they turned around and on all four limbs they ran off into the safety of the woods, the brown haired man had turned left behind the shack and into the woods also leaving the Officers to deal with the fire. No hesitation, no thought at all, both men entered into the shack, with Detective Jenkins going in first.

"Thompson, find the fire extinguisher if they have one!" Jenkins yelled as he tried to find something to quench the flames.

Thompson Rogers ran around room to room trying to find the extinguisher. He finally found the extinguisher on the floor gathering dust by the living room closet. Scooping up the canister he squeezed the handle fighting several deliberate fires. Finally, they heard the line of sirens getting closer.

Rogers looked at Jenkins' smeared soot covered face with an ear to ear smile. The soot concealed the numerous lines on his face remembering how long it had been since he had smiled. He felt good for his friend, irrefutable evidence had been seen by both and the experience somehow softened Jenkins eyes a little bit.

"I can't believe…" Rogers shook his head.

"I know, right!" Jenkins interrupted Rogers and looked at him.

Jenkins too covered in soot from head to toe a funny but satisfying feeling came over him. They were equals. Even if the experience turned out impossible to prove Jenkins knew in his mind that Rogers now lived through the strange experience too.

The whining of sirens and the hectic commotion by the front door told Jenkins and Rogers, the fire department had arrived. Several firemen rushed them outside to safety. They were forced to twiddle their thumbs until the fire chief gave the all clear.

The report from the fire Chief had been a sobering experience. Apparently the people in the shack had been cooking some type of synthetic drug just mere hours ago. He moved toward the lumpy blood soaked couch and bent down to move the bloody comforter. Jenkins smiled even wider. He had a lot of questions, but at least he had found Cody's body.

"Well, I'll be!" Rogers said.

Stepping over the debris in the hallway the closet to the back bedroom the stronger the ammonia smells were. He wisely put on his officer issued latex gloves and went around tracing the secret sigils but careful so as not to touch the walls and contaminate the crime scene.

"Damn it, Amy is right! We were this close to finding answers!" Rogers remarked to himself.

"Capt. Rogers, Capt. Rogers," a uniformed officer tried to get Capt. Rogers attention while the Capt. stared at the weird markings on the wall, "we're missing the owner of the house, Michael Miller, the brother of the distinguished Col. Miller who went off the grid a long time ago."

Jenkins and Rogers huddled together exchanging secret glances as they exchanged shortwave walkie-talkies.

"Way to go, Dad, you made a friend." A clean perfect translucent face untouched by the soot and smoke whispered into a grieving father, detective Jonathan Jenkins' ear.

The apparition gestured to the dual walkie-talkies Rogers and Jenkins clenched in their hands.

41

Raccourci Island, LA

Schools were in full swing but the friends made a decision, albeit Tommy begrudgingly, to take a respite for a while to finally fix up the plantation. Sarah sat down lifted her legs and crossed them on a dusty chaise lounge. She envisioned her great-grandmother sitting on this very chair. She had no electricity, only the light filtering through the dusty panes of glass. She strained her eyes enough to see the words on the page pacifying her curiosity from the worn-out pages of her found diary.

Sarah flips the well-worn pages, page after page in sequence. She looks outside for a moment to see what some of the others are doing before looking down at the diary again. She blew off the fact that she found the diary from a magic rock after it disintegrated. She reasoned the magic rock wasn't magic at all; dust and the elements from many years of neglect concealed the diary but Sarah somehow disturbed the settlement revealing the diary. But she couldn't shake the fact that the diary had been hidden in Alicia's room lying hidden even after her family had fled. She scanned the yellow sheets before periodically looking out at the world again.

Sarah closed the pages of her ancestors' journal letting out a yawn and stretching her numb, tingling legs then stood up. Her eyes hurt from reading in the dim light and her legs were still wobbly from immobility as she listened for movement upstairs. She couldn't take the chance on waking her other friends. The girls, Roxy and Tequila, dead set to go to the legendary French Quarter took the opportunity to go to New Orleans and see the sights last night. Staying out all night they staggered into the room at the hotel at three o'clock they then reluctantly drove over to Sarah's new house but now they were sleeping off their fun in Alicia's room.

The others were out in the yard; Desiree, Tina, A.J., Garrett, Jac and Tommy who reluctantly worked on his knees trying to landscape the huge, neglected garden by the right side of the manor. She could go back to her book in a moment, she thought, for now her throat felt dry and parched and she needed to get a drink from the shared cooler. As she stood with her soda she looked out on the yard where Jac and Tina were shamelessly flirting with each other while they worked.

"Tsk, tsk..." Sarah shook her head, finished her soda and smiled before plopping down on the chaise lounge again to read her precious diary.

Jac whipped his head around fist full of weeds in his hands and sheepishly smiley at Tina, "what do you think? Is it time for a break?"

Tina wiped the sweat from her forehead and as she did thick dirt smudged her cheeks making Jac laugh hysterically.

"Um, you have something," Jac gestured at Tina's cheeks "on your face..."

Tina's mud smeared cheeks brightened to a reddish hue of embarrassment; Tina stood up and dusted off her faded jeans with a rip strategically placed to show the knee.

A peaceful cone of silence in the living room broke as the dusty screen door slammed closed sending particles swirling about this way and that startling Sarah. She slammed the diary shut and clutched the diary with a death grip as she pressed it to her person like a little boy getting caught with his father's stack of porno magazines.

"Tina, you scared the hell out of me!" Sarah managed a smile, "what do you need?"

"I just wanted you to know that Jac and I are gonna run off towards the stables." She smiled a mischievous smile that told Sarah she shouldn't go anywhere near the area, "I'm just warning you."

"Oh. Okay," Sarah couldn't help but laugh, smiling, "well I need to stretch out my legs a little and read more in the sunlight. I assure you I will not disturb you two."

Sarah saw Jac and Tina walk over and open the van door. With a small can-am side-by-side 4x4 secured inside they had had to take out several seats in the van, which made for a cramped ride. He grabbed the handle bars and pulled out the newly rented four- wheeler as he pointed at the stables and the abandon tow truck with a bug in the field far off in the distance.

"I don't remember there being a tow truck on Sarah's property." Jac mused to himself before getting sidetracked by Tina as she jumped up and hugged him.

She watched the pair tear off in the direction of the stables. Needing direct sunlight for her eyes and to stretch her legs Sarah set off after the couple until she got within twenty five feet of the stables entrance careful not to wander too close so as to interrupt the love birds. With the stables blocking her view she could not see the tow truck gathering weeds. Satisfied she had enough light to read by she took a gulp from another soda pop and plopped her butt against a willow tree turning her attention back to the book,

"I vanished into the sugarcane fields today; it is a wonderful day and if I am seen I'll be forced to go inside. Sucking on a cane I entered into the forest. I could smell the sweet and succulent honeysuckle near me and I could hear the river's fast-moving waters in the background. I thought I saw movement in the corner of my eye. I twirled around and what I saw took my breath away. Feet away a stunning black Wolf with emerald eyes stared at me. My heart quickened, I could see the ivory of its fangs, but it didn't attack me it just gazed into my eyes. I reached out and carefully placed a palm on the Wolf's head. Slowly I rubbed his muzzle counter clockwise then his soft fur on the top of his head and scratched his ears, his tail wagging with excitement. But then growing skittish, it burst off into the brush and was gone from site."

This passage took her breath away. She pulled out a cigarette from her pack and striking the lighter put flame to it. She pulled in a few more drags then went back to read a little more, captivated and mesmerized now.

"I tried to make an excuse every day to go outside into the woods again to the same exact spot that I saw the majestic wonder. My patience working for me when I saw it again… a huge, beautiful male and he did not seem to see me. Oblivious to the world he rolled on the tall grass like he had no care in the world, wagging his tail about. Suddenly his ears twitched and turned to an inaudible sound. He wrinkled his muzzle sniffing the air all around him. He set up on his haunches turning around to see me. The majestic wolf bowed his head, his forelimbs bent down like compressed strings about to explode. My blood ran cold and I close my eyes as the inevitable attack drew near."

Sarah paused for a moment to get a drink of her pop, unaware of the imminent danger inside the mystically concealed barn. The van's stereo blared heavy metal music which melded into the back ground noises of the forest. Sarah licked her tongue on her pointer finger, flipped a page, unconsciously tapped her foot and ignorantly read on.

"I kept my eyes closed as a rush of air threatened to knock me over and briefly I felt the wolf's soft fur. I heard snarling, growling, hissing and splashing... signs of conflict coming from behind me; still I did not turned around. I turned my head slightly just glancing from the split of my eyelids, a chaotic blur of intermittent green and black splashing about before submerging to the murky depths. The Brown waters giving way to a Crimson tide. I couldn't help but peek and what happened next took my breath away... The tail of the alligator whipped about as the alligator went into a death spiral. Then I blinked two, three times not believing what I saw. A human arm burst out of the water in an arc making a fist and struck the alligator on the top of his head! Eventually the disruption over the rough waters smoothed out. All was calm but the wolf that wrestled the alligator did not surface. Nervous, I bit my nails until they were all but bleeding..."

Sarah paused for a moment before reading the passage from Alicia again, ***"The Wolf soon emerged from the water with the dead alligator in his jaws. He looked at me then dropped the limp alligator in the mud. Before I knew it I dropped down on one knee. I opened my palm and timidly reached out for the drenched wolf."***

No sooner than Jac had open the wooden gates Tina embraced him enthusiastically, her anxious lips trying to find his lips, the weeks' worth of stubble tickling her cheeks. Jac grasped onto Tina's backside and twirled her around until her body rested against the termite ridden boards. She crossed and locked her legs against Jac's back, putting all her weight against him suspended off the dirt floor pelvis to pelvis.

"I love you," Tina let slip out in the heat of the moment. No sooner than she said those words she hesitated looking for a sign in Jac's eyes that validated her.

The validation came when Jac looked devotedly, compassionately and fervently into her loving eyes and countered, "I love you too, of course."

In the throngs of a passionate kiss they didn't notice the others so tantalizingly, dangerously close but hidden from sight, watching their every move in the stables. The music had slowed down, a song appropriately called "I'll Stand by You" by The Pretenders. They could hear it from inside the barn so they swayed together a happenstance of sorts keeping time to the music.

Jac twirled a half circle when a human figure caught Jac's and Tina's eyes making them involuntarily gasp. The figure melded into the darkness of the corner glowing eyes burning in the darkness like a predator's eyes caught in headlights. Tina could tell they were human, but she could not make out anything more than that.

Instantly Tina's hands clutched Jac's shoulders, "Jac, look!"

She frantically shook Jac's shoulder to get his attention pointing into the darkness. Jac adjusted his eyes to find two nude and pale men in the middle the stable.

"What are they doing here?" Tina shrieked, as she pointed to the figures in the stall.

"Why are they in there?" He echoed Tina's cries, "Get out of here, Tina." Jac yelled, shaking Tina within an inch of her life.

Sarah's bare legs curled up in a ball, chin to her knees, resting her back against the side of the tree. In her younger years she always felt safe curled up as she read her latest Harlequin novel while her latest foster family beat the hell out of each other. Now she was lost in the pages of a real-life romance unaware of the conflict starting just a few yards away.

"Several minutes went by as the Wolf stood still a caw from a crane in the distance startled the black Wolf, he jumped off into the sheltering of the forest. Still reeling in the moment I suddenly heard a rumbling in the dense Cyprus. I imagined the black wolf had returned. The wolf could not pass such an easy meal rending my tender flesh to pieces so easily like an alligator. I closed my eyes braced myself and began to pray. However, it was not fangs or the claws of an animal; I felt delicate warm human hands upon me... wearing only a loincloth to conceal his nakedness, His kind green eyes glinting from the sun's bright warming light. He had a bizarre wildness about him that allured me so. With his blatant nakedness on display I should have been afraid and horrified; forgive me my blasphemy dear lord, but... in the seclusion of the forest his body looked like a God had come to life. I could not help but to admire his solid statuesque form. No fat could be seen anywhere, flawless from head to toe save for the faint pink scars crisscrossing his figure; but they were barely noticeable on his otherwise perfect physique. The

stranger made me melt, made me weak in the knees. Encroaching uncomfortably close to my body but I didn't move. The angels sang when he spoke…

"Excuse me, but I must know, are you okay?"

His voice so soft, smooth and comforting with an accent that I could not place and his dark green eyes… something about his green eyes which were so comfortably familiar.

"I was wandering through the woods and I saw you oblivious to the crocodile about to strike."

I could only shake my head to say yes, everything was fine… If it wasn't for the black wolf saving me…

I would surely be dead. It seemed like forever staring at his eyes. Exhilaration went through me something electric when I touched him.

"Like I said, I saw the struggle, I'm glad you're all right…

My name is Aticus… forgive me for saying this, but you are beautiful."

Alicia's voice echoed softly in Sarah's mind***," suddenly this Aticus had become a drug and I had become addicted. I had to be careful sneaking out at night lest I incur Poppa's wrath, but I had to see Aticus."***

Sarah paused; she thought she heard a muffled sound from far away. She grew still a moment, but she heard nothing only the music coming from the van. She hummed along with the vocals of a song by Jonathan Davis and a band called "Korn".

Jac and Tina broke their embrace staring at two figures one with amputated legs standing with the help of crutches by the stall, still no aggressive movements at all. But another figure emerged from the darkness and quickly blocked their exit. Assured they had no escape a tan figure with long-haired dreadlocks progressed toward the terrified couple making them back up.

Jac and Tina, both finally inquired after they had the courage to spit the words out, "Who, who are you?"

Tomas seized Tina's face, "lovers I bet and Aticus has a soft spot for love… a diehard romantic, too. That's too bad; you're going to die!"

The figure came uncomfortably close to Jac's face. He saw Tomas' lupine eyes, his twisted lips in an evil smile; his lips looked a bright red like he had sucked on a red Popsicle. His sharp Navajo cheekbones rose equally he could see his sharp canines that protruded out from behind his lips.

"I'm Tomas," Tomas Growled at Jac spittle flung at his face.

Tina clung close to Jac her arms shaking in fear Tomas' hands still clutching her cheeks, "what's going on, Jac?"

"I don't know!" a frightened Jac answered.

Montezu had heard a commotion and ran out of the barn into the stable interrupting Jac and Tina, his bleached almost opaque hair in his face as he barked, "Let's just kill them immediately so they don't escape; besides in the barn the greedy children are starving!"

Jac summoned his courage and attempted to swing out at Tomas with a closed fist. Like lightning without ever blinking Tomas lashed out and blocked his puny punch, slamming Jac's windpipe, knocking him flat on his back. The soft hay buffered the sound of him landing.

Tina's whole face shook and squirmed until she broke Tomas' grip. She turned to run but Montezu silenced her coming scream with his huge palm then shoved her with his shoulder. His uncanny power surprised her; her feet lifted off the ground and into a wall shattering her lower spine effectively paralyzing her and stealing her breath away.

From the upstairs girders in the darkness there appeared a huge coal black canine. His large pointed ears twitched, one ear misshapen, one green eye trained on Tina who remained standing but restrained. The huge misshapen Wolf jumped down from the rafters a folded up robe snugly in its muzzle. With one fluid motion he altered and dressed before he headed to the human laying on the hay.

"*I must be dreaming*," Tina said in her hazy mind, she couldn't believe her eyes watching the strange events, her mouth still restrained by Montezu's huge hand.

Tina observed the one eyed stranger's commanding gestures and she assumed she had come face-to-face with the leader of the gang.

"What are you doing, this is Sarah's property!" Tina's shrieked.

Aticus answered her question, "Oh, my dear, it isn't Sarah's property. I was here long before you, and I will still be here long after you're gone."

Jac started to stir, which started a horrid chain of events that sunk Tina into madness. Jac lifted his knees and put his arms on his forehead to shake off his dizziness. A rush of air made Tina instinctively turn her eyes to see the commotion. She squinted and strained her eyes, but she could only see a furry blur.

Tomas who used to be a man now a brown wolf with dreadlocks, the wolf's forelimbs trapped Jac's arms, its furry brown chest pressed down on Jac's sternum squeezing the life out of him.

The wolf's muzzle bore down on Jac's exposed neck. He tried to scream but the wolf twisted his head back and forth until Jac's windpipe tore free. Every time he tried to speak pink bubbles swelled out and popped, sticky liquid traveling toward his neck and dripping down into the hay.

Tina's eyes widened in fright, tears welled up in her eyes at the loss of her love, Jac. Montezu released his huge hand against Tina's mouth and put a finger to his lips, "Sssssssssshhhhhhhhhhhhhhh!"

Tina obeyed; she didn't make a sound, wasn't sure she would have been able to anyways as Montezu transformed into a Wolf with beautiful white fur as well and fell upon Jac's leg. She heard the sound of fabric tearing as fangs tore through skin. The Brown Wolf shredded Jac's neck while the white Wolf feasted upon his leg until the only movement Jac made, a sick twitch while the wolves dug into the fresh meat.

"I'm sorry, about all this…" Aticus said, fangs emerging from his mouth, "but I can't let you leave!"

He fell upon Tina before she could react. His unusually large arms and hands smashed the stable walls and trapped her trembling body. She instinctively tried to curl up in a fetal position and close her eyes. A sudden pressure in her neck then numbness, in fact no pain anywhere in her body at all. She couldn't breathe as warm thick fluid ran down the back of her throat, darkness over-taking her.

The brown Wolf had finished sucking the marrow out of Jac's spine and now the bloody Wolf sauntered over to the white Wolf. The pair latched onto Jac's lacerated leg and shook it in opposite directions until the knee fell off at the joint.

"Come!" Aticus gathered the corpses, "Let's go to the barn. The kiddies need to eat."

The barn doors opened to reveal Aticus, So-seti, Tomas, Montezu and lastly, James consciously trying to give a wide berth to Aticus. Inexplicably irritable when they interacted. Even mated with his matriarch James glanced at Aticus' eye full of an untrustworthiness hate and murder. James made his way towards his friend Matt as if there would be safety in numbers. Matt timidly climbed down off the girders by the ladder. While Aticus headed off in the corner shrouded in shadows and converted to a human again. He threw Tina and James' fresh corpses to the undulating mass with their glowing eager eyes. A tidal wave of greedy arms grabbed the corpse and pulled it into the shadows.

Two figures sat motionless by the wall. Oung with his ability to materialize his Wolf-thing anywhere around the world when he was in a trance and O-Kami who could materialize a ghost wolf pack anywhere around the world was in a trance as well proved invaluable to Aticus. They sat still, unmovable like a tree rooted to the Earth.

Oung opened his eyes and immediately threw up the heart and glands of another dissident while O-Kami's eyes remained closed in meditation looking for even more rebels. Aticus was upon it instantly, devouring the heart and gland whole. His eye dilated and his headaches subsided as his body mended on the nourishing juices, the pack turning a blind eye to the taboo of assimilation. Aticus wiped the blood from his lips with his forearm.

"The perigee moon, the Super-Moon, will once again soon be upon us, at its brightest and closest to the Earth. I know a ritual that will summon the great shaman, Aisos- the first of our kind. She has the power to heal my wounds," So-seti informed Aticus looking at her pale and shaken, her grandson's one green eye gleaming, looking desperately upon her, "and your wounds as well."

"It's just a myth that people are personally affected by the full Moon so it stands to reason the super Moon is just a celestial event!" Matt said meekly, reasoning scientifically from out of the darkness.

"How can you actually believe that, Matt, working where you work? The powers that be made it a myth so that people do not have an excuse when they do something bad! But when there is an approaching full Moon it has an effect on water. The tides rise, even the earth quakes, as opposing magnetic poles increased. People are made up of about 65-70% water, ironically the Earth is too. So it's only natural that each of our own tides rise, we're more prone to feel angry, pressured, irritated, frustrated over the little things at this time. If it feels overwhelming, breathe and breathe again after the full moon the pressure will stabilize and you will go back to feeling like yourself. So whatever ritual So-seti knows the super Moon could be a substantial help in raising Aisos."

"Good, good." Aticus smirked, picking up a stack of papers that he had ordered one of the mindless automatons to replicate, "Tomas pass out those flyers for the Wolf's Den at the motel, quickly!"

Tomas skinned Tina's scalp and carefully placed it on his own.

Sarah stopped reading and listened for a moment, did she hear a noise coming from the stables? Maybe Jac and Tina need help, she reasoned. She got up off the ground dusting herself off she peered at the stables. The gates suddenly burst open and the can-am roared out with two occupants.

Sarah could see the long blonde curly locks coming from the back, Tina's hair.

"Jac, Tina! Guys, wait!" Sarah yelled, but they were gone, obscured by weeds and branches.

42

Wolf's Den Tavern

Amy had finally left the cabin to do yet even more research like she did every day leaving Devon alone to his own devices. He was free to spy upon the group, specifically Sarah. He watched Sarah and Desiree, Roxy, A.J., Garrett, Tommy and Tequila go into the Wolf's Den bar after some argument that he reasoned had to do with the disappearance of friends Jac and Tina. They were still missing going on weeks without a peep from them.

The last of the group had gone through the swinging doors. The white Wolf concealed in the bushes felt safe. Devon looked around one more time then came out from the weeds and thickets, standing upright and stretching his stiff muscles before getting dressed from a satchel loosely hung around his neck. The air all around him smelled of lupine stench. Apparently it's been lycanthropic for some time now. This was Viddarr's lair and if Viddarr had aligned himself with Aticus his body would surely be pulled apart when he stepped into the Wolf's Den.

Devon started off to find Viddarr. His human nature had long since passed. Devon's stomach began to churn remembering their last fleeting encounter. His biker jacket had a peculiar but familiar scent. Then he started to uncontrollably gag when he first realized what material it had been stitched from.

Viddarr tugged on his leather jacket remarking, "Human skin, it is made with human skin. I have a really excellent tailor with questionable morals," he told him, answering the question before Devon had asked.

"Bring him the materials and an obscene amount of money, and you'll get a magnificent wardrobe no questions asked."

"I'm a wolf... in human clothing." Viddarr made a toothy grin while gesturing at his human leather coat. He shivered thinking about the surreal experience, and then before he realized it Devon was staring at the swinging doors of the bar. Opening the doors he slowly eased in, trying to blend into the crowd.

His preternatural senses found Sarah who sat at a stool with A.J. As she sucked her fruity drink that she had ordered only moments ago. Devon politely put his hand up in protest at the cocktail waitress when she suggested a drink. Although he did not order the waitress did not leave. She stared at him in awe.

Devon's outfit would have had no extravagances. Generic cheap mass-produced clothing, no head would turn looking at his long-sleeved shirt and pants with sneakers. His tattooed face would scare off males but not females and cocktail waitress. The musk all around her and the preternatural aroma permeating her senses combined with his strangely animalistic eyes had her in heat, a bizarre affect that came along with all lycanthropes. He gave her a quick kiss on her forearm to pacify before he shooed her away. She only blinking back with disappointment once then she headed off.

"I just worry about Tina and Jac is all. They took off and now are completely gone the four-wheeler included." Sarah sucked down more of her bright green drink while A.J. put his hands on her forearms to comfort her.

"You went to the police. Besides we're in a tempting town, Sarah, I expect they'll turn up sooner or later. I'm sure they just wanted to be alone and not stuck in a group, if you get my meaning." A.J. said his voice soothing enough to reassure her.

"I think you're right A.J., I shouldn't be worried, but I'm going to call it a night anyway, if it is all right with you. I'm going to take a cab to the motel and read a while before I fall asleep."

Sarah's thumbs were busy dialing the number for the local cab company so A.J. gave her a quick peck on the cheek, "well, I'd be lying if I didn't say that I'm a little disappointed you're not going to finish out the festivities, but get some rest, okay?"

She nodded then finished her drink, smiled and stood up from her stool.

Like a gentleman A.J. went outside to wait for the cab to come pick her up so she wouldn't be lonely. He smiled and waved as the door closed to Sarah's cab. She couldn't see the bright animalistic eyes, staring daggers at her in the darkness. The bright red taillights mimicked the two wolves' eyes. The cab's two red eyes faded into the night while two bright pair of eyes crept ever closer out of the woods towards the parking lot and A.J. But he eluded the advancing wolves by going back to the safety of the building.

Devon let out a deep breath as he saw Sarah leaving out the far window. She didn't notice him sitting at the bar. Confident that Aticus would honor his promise and leave Sarah alone when she arrived at the motel room. He scanned the floor for the remainder of her friends: Desiree, Roxy, Garrett, Tommy and Tequila gyrating out on the dance floor. He mapped their individual scents so he could keep track of them while he searched for the proprietor, Viddarr.

The music tore through his head like a blade, some type of new wave electronica, it was all he could do to concentrate and scan the area against all the turning, whirling, dancing mortals to find Viddarr. His heart quickened, the target of his search was already peering at him through the wave of people between them. A cold shiver ran through him and a nervous anticipation stood the hairs up on the nape of his neck. He couldn't kill him in public, could he? Devon hoped so as he remembered the moment that they met.

43

The baying of wolves called for help to any lycanthrope within earshot. Curiosity got the best of him and he was drawn to the graveyard. Glowing eyes appeared and vanished by the gravestones. The smell of rotting flesh over powered his preternatural senses. Then the glimmer of glowing eyes and a glimpse of silver fur caught Devon's attention as something dashed for cover under an ash tree. He sniffed the air trying to pick up anything beyond the smell of an unburied corpse but despite some shape that followed him he could not pick up anything human or animal.

Hair stood up on the back of his neck as he twirled around just quick enough to see a huge silver furred figure run a half mile down the hill to the mausoleum then melt and disappear into the door of the dilapidated crypt. Nervous apprehension triggered an involuntary transformation, slowly the fur rippled up and over his flesh. The searing heat of his blood made him double over as he swiftly contorted and fell upon four paws.

A warning howl emanated from everywhere. One by one, from behind each gravestone they stepped into view. Thirty or forty transparent wolves with eyes like red lava crept closer to him. Devon, now a wolf, spun around with his tail tucked between his legs as he rolled over in submission.

No warning, no scent, the wolves materialized just inches away from him and he surrendered... his body tensed as they slowly and strategically circled and enclosed around him. They yelped and howled back and forth amongst each other in a system of speech he couldn't comprehend. Then ten of them broke off from the pack, he could see the ash trees and tombstones, transparent ghost wolves, smaller in stature as they ran down toward the mausoleum, presumably to lead the way for him. The bigger wolves turned back around and stayed behind and stood guard on the interloper.

Devon's tail stiffened as he yelped out a signal as if to communicate, "I am a friend." Why were the ghost wolves here? Why so many? And where was the over overwhelming stench coming from? The wards at his front slowly approached then took position alongside their other ghostly pack mates. They turned and slowly took position alongside one another in a straight line simultaneously. Slowly, like a funeral procession, they marched one by one together down the hill. The two wolves making up the rear stopped and glanced back as if to urge him to follow them.

They were all, one by one, walking through the wall and into the old crypt. Devon stopped before the entrance and swiftly morphed back to a man. If he were to go inside he was going to need his hands to open the door. He couldn't quite go through the wall like the ghost wolves had.

At the crypt doors the unmistakable and overpowering stench of death caused convulsions in his stomach. The smell originated just beyond the metal doors of the crypt. The brass doors, of course, were locked but the bolts gave way to his superior strength. With a groan then a snap the doors swung open, creaking on unused hinges.

He wasn't prepared for the sight before him; he stood horrified yet unable to pull his eyes away. Six feet away from him he spotted a decayed corpse as bile pooled up from his stomach to his esophagus he tried his best to choke down the vomit. Ten transparent wolves stood still as statues packed one on top of the other in the painfully small crypt. Devon figured the huge transparent silver wolf with red eyes, withers, and royal mane protected the once extremely powerful decaying lycanthrope. A brilliant flash made his hands instinctively cover his watering eyes. He squinted at the dazzling light beams as the smaller ghost wolves vanished. Once the smaller wolves were gone the huge dazzling silver wolf stood up and circled around then jumped at the decaying corpse. Now that the ghost wolves had disappeared the smell of decay grew into something stronger, a strange aroma, unlike normal decay. Devon peering as closely as his nerves allowed him found the body's thick decay only superficial, the organs within, except the heart, fossilized. Every so often he heard the heart. Though impaled the heart quivered and seemed to make a faint beat every so often.

The corpse was skewered by a spear from buttocks to collarbone. The corpse's arm and leg stumps swayed though no wind could be felt, like a morbid marionette. His body suspended by the makeshift spear supported by the crypt wall and the marble floor. A large granite statue with a sword held in the hands of the statue of The Arc Angel, Michael, had fallen impaling him through the heart.

Devon studied the rotten corpse for several minutes in stunned horror, who did this to him? The form, once a man, too much for him to bear, his skin had drawn back tight to the bones and rats made a meal of his face, his eyes were missing, spider webs replacing them in the sockets. His arms and legs had been amputated. Sawed off the bone missing and his legs were charred, the flesh on them almost black and flaking off.

His arms and legs were missing from just below the elbows and the knees. The skin jagged edges and stumps of bone were exposed at the ends. The corpse's head tilted up so that his missing eyes sockets looked permanently up at the ceiling. Its face twisted in a mask of rage and pain made all the more pronounced by its state of strange decay. He could see sparse hairs that had not fallen off yet, long wavy brown hairs on its head. Its mouth was open as if it were still screaming, now some silent scream only heard by the dead.

A powerful old lycanthrope, which is why the wolves led him to the corpse, Devon realized. Somewhere deep in his soul a primal instinct told him this man was an acquaintance, say a fellow lycanthrope, bound by blood, the poor tortured brother.

He had to remove him from his place of demise and place him on a pyre and burn him until ash, as decreed in werewolf custom. His heart ached for an obviously majestic pack mate. Slowly and with great care he pushed back the statue until up-right, freeing the corpse from its place of impalement, the body stiff and frozen in its position. He then gently removed the pole from the ground and the body fell to the dirt. He used the pole at either end of his body to carry him out the crypt doors to the forest nearby.

At the top of the hill he saw the ghost wolves again watching with silent approval. The largest of them threw back its head and let out a solemn dirge of mourning, the others leant their heads and voices to the sky in a beautiful melody of song that stirred his heart. The wolves' howls were telling the passionate tale of a great werewolf's life.

He walked for hours into the darkening forest with the canopy of trees so thick no light could pierce the veil and the earth beneath him turned to dirt. No grass could grow beneath the thick cluster of trees. His arms ached from the weight of the corpse but he pressed on until he came to a place with a clearing wide enough between the trees to dig an improvised funeral pyre/grave. He slowly laid the man down on the soft earth and turned to the task at hand. His fingers becoming claws, he instantly began to dig. He had dug a two foot deep hole into the ground when he stopped to catch his breath.

A rustling in the trees turned his body around reflexively to investigate. He knew he was the only person in the murky darkness. His eyes widened, slowly beginning to glow as they refracted the dim lights around him, as he become more lupine in appearance, his ears perking up, scanning the area.

He crouched low and slowly glanced from side to side scanning the area like a spotlight. There was a rustling in the leaves again, and deep gasping breaths coming from close behind him near the corpse. He could hear the faint rhythmic beat, a drum beat? He spun around quickly, nearly slipping in the loose dirt beneath his feet, trying to focus in on the rustling, beating, and breathing.

A chill ran through his spine as he registered in his mind what his eyes briefly caught. The stubs that used to be arms moved ever so slightly stirring beneath the corpse. Then suddenly a harsh raspy gasp for air again, the corpse was trying to breathe with its deteriorated lungs…

Devon felt weak on the verge of collapse, surely his senses deceived him, even as long lived as he was he couldn't fathom what was unfolding before his eyes. He had seen Blood brothers that should have died from injuries that would've killed an ordinary human or even recently dead Brothers springing back to life to heal their grievous injuries if the full Moon had not yet thoroughly cycled through. Never from such extreme state of disrepair that this poor soul was in! Maggots squirmed from the corpse's skull-like face, falling down to the ground as the corpse gasped for breath yet again.

The corpse seemed to come alive, its chest rattling up and down in such small minute motions that it was almost unnoticeable. Its legs twitched then a twitched again, then a violent jerk that lifted what remained of his legs up off the ground and down again. Its head snapped back with a pop the mouth widened and it took in its deepest breath yet, a breath that sounded more like a snarling growl.

Devon could've run at that moment but he was captivated. Thoughts were racing a mile a minute through his head; the repercussions of the corpse's sudden motions were staggering. He found himself re-thinking even life and death itself as a werewolf. Devon was startled when without warning the thing convulsed, wildly jerking side to side then turning around on its back. Now it could see the treetops if not for its missing eyes.

Writhing about on the ground a sickening chorus of pops and snaps came out from its decayed stricken shell. Foam bubbling up from its open mouth as a blackish mixture of bodily fluids began oozing from open wounds. Devon could see the corpse's heart beating through a gaping hole from the granite sword that used to be in its body.

Wriggling new hair grew like snakes from its scalp. His arm stubs dug firmly into the ground as if it wanted to try and sit up. The living dead corpse's head turning in a jerking mechanical twist. Pus like mixtures of fluid spilled down, the movement of its neck disturbing the brass spear impaling its torso.

A network of atrophied veins, arteries, and nerves inflated and crisscrossed in its eye sockets. Wires that slithered wildly around until they immerged themselves in a stagnate pool of fluid in the sinus cavities. Sparks made the pooled blood bubble up. Globules in its hollows expanded, congealed and solidified until translucent orbs resembling primitive eyeballs appeared. The living dead's now opaque eyes blazed with crimson brilliance then fixed on Devon.

"He's staring at me," Devon thought shuddering. "I know it's crazy but he is staring right through me."

It tried to usher forth words from a mouth that had but just a stub of a dried and atrophied tongue. The rats had eaten part of his voice box. The sound that it issued forth almost incomprehensible but Devon perceived and interpreted what he thought the living corpse had tried to say.

"PAIN!" Drool poured down its chin.

Devon left the corpse-thing that was wriggling about on the ground and ran. What was he to do? Surely this thing was beyond repair wasn't it? Put it out of its misery? But how? Or try to help it? What could he do? The only logical thing came to him suddenly; he made a mad dash for the graveyard. He glanced around hurriedly from gravestone to gravestone until he found a flower pot big enough to suit his needs.

He easily broke the flower pot from its base at the slab of the gravestone careful not to damage the integrity of the interior so as to not hold water. Devon then ran to the only running fountain in the graveyard. He dunked the bowl the best he could into the shallow fountain. It was still questionable as to whether or not this would do any good but with water in hand he rushed back to the living corpse.

He stopped short of the man-thing to take in all that he saw. The color had returned to the bulk of his body, the color of a normal human's hue. Although he was still pale as a ghost it wasn't a sickly black and gray color anymore. Its skin and the sunken black of its eyes sockets and cheekbones were nowhere near as pronounced. Newly formed eyes were bloodshot with a golden brown color in them. The convulsions had ceased but he still lay on his back.

The rigor mortis working itself out, the blue black bruises faded away to a pinkish hue, the little bit of blood that the lycanthrope had left circulating itself around. The corpse thing's breath was shallow and labored. Breathing seemed better now, not the liquidity, gurgled, wheezing Devon heard before. Since the unholy resurrection unfolded, Devon was so enamored by the process of it all, he realized he hadn't heard a scurry or peep from any animal or birds which were surely frozen by the preternatural spectacle, the only sound coming from a light breeze blowing through the trees making a spectral like moan. He could see the thing's heart slowly beating in the massive hole in his chest.

Devon looked on in amazement as the skin and muscle stretched in an attempt to close up this gaping wound, skin and muscle struggling to adhere to torn ligaments and veins that reminded Devon of the ocean tide ebbing and flowing. Wave after wave of skin covered up the gaping hole then receded. The breastbone reminded him of a stalactite growing in almost a blinding fast forward motion until Devon could not see the heart anymore just new white bone. That's when Devon realized what he had done. He had taken out the granite sword that had impaled him through his heart.

Somewhere in the distance Devon heard one brave bird still rummaging for grubs. All five senses merged together as one coherent radar-like sense. Nerves, muscles and tendons fired in unison zeroing in on the hungry red Cardinal. He moved in a blur of well-honed hunter instinct he leaped several yards from the undead thing to the feeding Cardinal. The makeshift clay bowl of water still in his hand, he snatched the young bird up before it knew what was happening. With a twist and a snap of his now fanged teeth he beheaded the bird before a chirp came out of its beak. He squeezed the animal like a wet towel; warm salty droplets of blood filled the clay bowl. He needed something more than water, Devon thought, but the thing was not strong enough to devour flesh yet.

He came back to the undead-thing with bloody water in hand. He discarded the now lifeless Cardinal on the ground. The man-thing's wounds and mangled body seemed too weak, too sluggish, but the rotted flesh seemed to be shedding like a snake's skin, flaking off all over. The wounds were all wet with a fresh blood supply pumping to them but they began to clot quickly staunching the excessive bleeding.

Devon was spellbound because in all his long-lived years he'd seen a lot of strange things but this took the cake. Devon gently lifted the man thing's head, he found no resistance. Devon offered the blood mixture up to the corpse thing's parched lips which it accepted, greedily gulping down the liquid as the excess ran out the corners of its mouth.

It's glossy and empty, opaque dead eyes immediately seemed to liven up, a spark of life inside them; they dilated and began to glow. The man-thing finished off the blood water mixture in the pot, lapping at the last drops with its tongue and then muttered in an almost incoherent growl.

"MORE!"

Devon obliged, sprinting up the hill again to obtain more water from the fountain and hunting small game until he came back with more.

The man thing was up on his knees the best he could with the spear like object that still skewered him. The object dug a line in the dirt wobbling back and forth his stumps for legs no help keeping his balance. Again Devon offered him the mixture of blood and water and Devon helped him consume it all.

Suddenly the man-thing groans, a noise that sends shivers through Devon's spine. Pain seemed to double it over and even Devon's aid wasn't enough to keep the man thing up right as it fell down on his side. The zombie thing's head lurched back, it jerked its jaws back and forth as a mouth full of lupine teeth emerged and let loose a howl that startled birds from miles away leaving their nests as they flew away for safety.

The stubs from the thing's arms grew bone at an accelerated rate, the ulna and radius looking like sharp twin daggers lengthening and broadening. Milky white cartilage bubbled up to support the new carpals from the milky solution like tiny islands cropping up in a tumultuous sea of superglue until growing to form the bones of his wrist. Ligaments began to form, then meta-carpals more ligaments then phalanges forming, the thing now as rudimentary as skeletal hands.

Devon stood absolutely still, wide-eyed at the unbelievable process taking place. A red rough sheath began to envelop the new skeletal hand then snakelike nerves ran through them like a downed live wire. Then the red sheath like substance began to inflate like a balloon as slowly twitching muscle began to form and snake across the forearms. Cord-like soft tissue, tendons, began to attach to the skeletal hands.

The animated corpse moved its forearms and flexed its skinless hands like a new born baby in awe, just figuring out what he could do with them. Then it groaned and patted his newly formed hands on his head then he clenched the spear that had him impaled. Muscles quivering from the strain and oblivious to pain the spear began to lift up from his head putrid gray brain matter oozing down. It moved the spear out from his head until outstretched arms allowed no more movement. It re-positioned its hands when it was unable to move it more and tried a second time until the spear lifted up from its body. The thing threw the spear down with a thump as it landed on the ground. Woozy with the effort he fell on his back his stump legs seemed to be re-constructing too now at such a dizzying rate Devon's eyes couldn't keep up. Connective tissue circling and forming around the new bones like snakes winding around the limbs of a tree, then muscle tissue, nerves and skin continued to grow in consecutive order trying to keep up with the new skeletal frame. In a matter of minutes the corpse thing was almost complete down to the thing's fingertips and long ivory claws.

The thing lifted its stiff neck. Turning around, the thing's eyes once as wrinkled as raisins were now plump as grapes, and took on an animal-like quality. They gazed upon Devon who cowered uncontrollably at its visage. The man thing's skin was thin and taunt as if touched it would crumble to pieces. The man thing's mouth opened but now Devon knew what to do. He was back in moments with fresh water and blood mixture again this time new hands gripped the bowl and immediately drank from it unassisted.

The ears began to grow where there were once stubs before and slowly twitched and lengthened. The veins in its forehead began to throb once dry cracked taunt skin became fatter, fleshier; the skin's sickly gray color developed a healthier glow. The scent, once of decay, now a different smell altogether that of a wild wet dog. This smell grew as thicker, darker, brown-black hair began to grow from his scalp. Devon could place his face now. It was an East Slavic born, turned Viking chief: Viddarr. He recalled the fight where Viddarr had mercifully spared Devon's life so many moons ago because even as they fought for different clans they were blood brothers… both lycanthropes.

"Thank you," he said hoarsely first in his native tongue then English, his mouth still dry from dehydration, the little water that he had drunk hydrating his entire body. "I owe you my life."

Slowly and apparently painfully the bones of his face contorted while cheeks rose in an unnatural manner the nose and jaw jutting forth into a hairless small muzzle. His face was turning into a twisted version of man and wolf. Fangs protruded from Viddarr's mouth as he hungrily devoured bones in all the corpses of the nearby drained birds, squirrels and rats that Devon had discarded onto the ground.

The process seemed to slowly drift down from his face like a wave through his body, his neck thickening, shoulders widening, and coarse fur rippling over leathery flesh. His chest heaving and expanding, all the while the wound in his sternum, the new chest plate that held his beating heart, bubbled with fluids that contorted, conformed and closed, in response to Viddarr's new shape. Viddarr's Wolf thing seemed completely healed as the wolf that used to be Viddarr shook off the pain and threw its head back in a cry of victory.

Viddarr's wolf a beautiful dark brown color with a crest that appeared mane-like, his wide reddish brown eyes were fierce and his long lupine ears set far back. He had a short muzzle and a short tail but every bulging muscle built for speed and power. Devon was impressed by this being, more so impressed when the Wolf cocked his neck back and dug its muzzle into the backside of Devon's palm, a sign of respect. Devon stroked the wolf's soft fur for a moment until the Wolf collapsed with exhaustion.

44

Viddarr greeted him at the first floor main bar just near the dance floor. Devon laughed as he realized Viddarr was probably aware of him from the moment he had walked in the door of The Wolf's Den Tavern. He was startled by how Viddarr looked, it had been years since they had last seen each other and there was a remarkable difference in his appearance.

Viddarr's complexity once enthralled him; Viddarr's spirit sought for lycanthrope's through his mind even when his mutilated body was technically dead. Devon was the first one who heard his call. Devon had tracked down Viddarr in hopes that he would help him with Aticus and his growing problem. With every full Moon Aticus' infernal pack rose in numbers. He had high hopes Viddarr was just the edge he needed to defeat the pack, but when he first entered the club his heart sank. Ice and the pack's scent were radiating all through the place, he had marked the territory as his. Viddarr looked shocked for an instant then returned to his prior composure.

He gauged him to be about 6'6" tall, a full three inches taller than when he first met him. His dark brown hair was longer now, draping over his shoulders, the sides shaved and he saw a tribal tattoo on each side of his head. Six studs were screwed onto each side of the shaved hairline. His bangs as long as the rest of his hair was pulled back and separated in a braid. His ears were pointed and high up on his head. And his eyes seemed to glow golden with the black lights, but they were a deep dark brown with a circle of black on the irises that made his eyes seem even darker.

Viddarr motioned with his hand for Devon to approach. His fingers were all an even length and the nails were long, pointed like daggers and black. His eyebrows hadn't changed, only wilder but still had an almost triangle look to them giving his eyes a menacing and a matter of fact expression to his face.

Viddarr took a gulp of some vile concoction from a flask he carried in the black worn leather jacket he had on. He wore it loosely off his large chest and broad shoulders. Another tribal tattoo, black and silver nitrate ink mixture for permanence, was visible going down the length of his sculpted washboard abdomen.

"Good to see you, again." Devon slid onto a bar stool beside the powerful animalistic figure, so out of place he seemed even amidst the mortal misfits that surrounded him. Viddarr extended the flask to Devon without a word his eyes still scanning the number of women that caught his attention.

"Well what is it?" Devon cautiously smelled the flask, a bitter medicinal smell and sharp alcohol vapor.

Viddarr smiled but didn't say anything, just gestured again for Devon to drink from his flask.

He took the flask. One edge of his mouth curled up as he slowly glanced at Viddarr then gripped the railing in front of him with both hands. His hands too seemed an inch or two longer; Devon studied him intently, amazed and intrigued by his friend then turned the flask up to his mouth for a small drink.

The concoction almost made him gag as it went down, followed by a warm burning sensation going through his throat and settling in his gut, suddenly the mix coursed through every pore of his body, his head swam as if he were suddenly drunk. He could taste the powerful mixture of unknown stimulants, painkillers, herbs, and grain alcohol mixed together. His eyes dilated like headlights in the darkness they began to involuntarily glow. Enhancing his heat vision and improving smell even better than his preternatural senses. He could instantly detect each and every individual patron that moved, before he had consumed Viddarr's mixture. The dance floor came alive with undulating vibrations moving with the beat of the music. The hair on the back of his neck began to tingle and grow. He knew he was going to involuntarily change form. It took all this might to stop this, his mind racing and in ecstasy. He could close his eyes and still "see" with his now heightened senses. His muscles and tendons tightened until they were about to burst. He began to hear howling, surprising him because the howling he heard was coming from within his throat. The room seemed to shift with colors, emanating from the crowd. Devon was beside himself. He felt himself getting even stronger and more aware of every inch of himself. He could feel every pore and every hair follicle, a sensation he only recognized during the change when his body was alive with the metamorphosis. Time stood still as he tried to control the awakened beast until Viddarr placed his hands on Devon's shoulder bringing him back down to earth.

He smelt the strong musk of Stefan's killer, Aticus, about the tavern. A faint odor hung in the air all around The Wolf's Den. Special shots passed around the dance floor. The formula little different than he remembered minus the parasite amoebas, but he knew what it was, a potion long forgotten except by a select few. His stomach tightened in a knot, from the smell he knew Viddarr swore his allegiance to the new-fangled pack Aticus was trying to create. There would be no information forthcoming about Aticus.

"So you're in league with Aticus?!" Devon tried to ask, but Viddarr motioned him to be silent and waved out to the crowd.

"I'll tell you later. Just enjoy!" Viddarr laughed a deep throated laugh; it sounded more like an order then a request as he tossed his jacket onto the back of the chair and took a deep breath extending his large chest.

His chest had a light patch of reddish brown hair that led down to the tribal tattoo on his abdomen, his arms had short light hair covering them as well but not as noticeable from the tattoos and brands put on them. Viddarr offered Devon another drink of the mixture then rested his arms on the rail.

Devon politely accepted another drink and looked around at the crowded tavern while Viddarr tended to the affairs of the bar. Devon turned back to the crowd, indeed his already heightened senses seemed to expand until coming together sight, sound, and smells mingled and registered as one automatically. Even the air around him felt alive with vibrations and he could feel the movement of the crowd at a distance. It seemed he could see in all directions at once and he couldn't help from having an orgasm, this he thought as the mixture that Viddarr made, the lycanthrope's drug of choice fuel for the parasites, ran through his veins as his eyes rolled back into his head.

"You are so drastically different from our last encounter..." Devon finally managed, "so tell me why it is you are siding with that crazy monster and murderer?"

"I assume you are referring to Aticus?" Viddarr grumbled.

Devon nodded yes.

"Simple, his plan is so grand... Aticus' efforts are so passionate and clear..." Viddarr paused for a drink from his flask, "The human civilization disgusts me. It's time for a change."

"See, I'm Vargr," Viddarr paused for a second as he waited for the meaning of this one word to sink in to Devon's mind. "I am the last of the Úlfhéðnar, the last of the Wolf clan."

Viddarr turned his back to Devon interested in two women coming towards him dancing seductively.

"But, Viddarr, then by nature you are an outdweller. I can't believe you resigned yourself to join a pack!" Devon argued.

Devon knew he was treading on unsteady ground. Viddarr was known for going berserk without any provocation, but he couldn't help himself.

"No matter who you're around you're outside of them, remember that you are Vargr!" Devon said.

However, Devon's pleas fell on deaf ears when Viddarr caught the faint scent of honeysuckle, sunflowers and blueberries combined with a woman's natural scent. He turned to see Desiree, Roxy, and Tequila dancing with each other while A.J. and Garrett were upstairs at the auxiliary bar watching the women.

Tommy sat on the stool of the second floor table in the corner sulking, already half drunk. Sarah giving him the cold shoulder every time he walked into the room combined with Sarah's refusal to sell the Raccourci Island property had him at his breaking point.

45

Sarah lay in the bed in the midst of insomnia rolling restlessly, worrying about Tina and Jac's whereabouts, cradling her book. By now Sarah started to naïvely believe that Tina and Jac had just left Louisiana to started college for another year. Alone in the hotel room she read her found diary while everybody else went out to blow off steam.

Meanwhile at the bar Desiree closed her eyes, threw her hands in the air seductively smiling as she gyrated to the slow rhythmic bass beat. Her eyes wandered over Viddarr and his eyes locked onto hers. When she opened her eyes, she couldn't help but be drawn by Viddarr's animal magnetism.

"Who is that?" Desiree inquired, gesturing to Viddarr at the bar.

Desiree broke from Tequila and she did not even wait for Roxy to respond back before twirling off the dance floor and dangerously closer to Viddarr who saw her in the corner of his eye.

"Hey, wait for me, bitch." Roxy smiled as she ran to keep up with Desiree.

Viddarr ignored Devon's pleas as he watched Desiree and Roxy slide up to the bar. Whole conversations lost to Viddarr as he paid no attention to Devon anymore. One woman, Desiree, impulsively clawed at his pants and the other woman, Roxy, stroked his bare chest.

"Hi, I'm Roxy," she batted her seductive eyes, and then she pointed with open palms to the suddenly shy woman. Her whole body paralyzed she couldn't even tell Viddarr her name, "and this is Desiree."

Roxy motioned towards her scantily clad friend, still tongue-tied and shy; she looked mesmerized by Viddarr's presence.

"It's like Desire with an extra E." she said smiling shyly when she summoned up the courage to talk to Viddarr.

Viddarr guessed she used the line a lot, but she was more desirable than Roxy. They were barely 19 or 20 not yet old enough to drink legally which he could tell by the pink band on their wrists but old enough to enter The Wolf's Den, which had an 18 and older policy.

He held both women's hands and soaked up their appearance. Roxy had blue eyes and long recently bleached blond hair with pink stripes and bangs. She smelled of cigarettes and had an artificial tan that Viddarr with his preternatural senses could smell the decay and looked at the lines that had already begun aging her before her time. She covered the minute lines on her lips and eyes with sparkly pink makeup.

His eyes gravitated towards Roxy's lip liner and the shine of her plump full lips. The tightness of her rhinestone black shirt made her small but perky breasts more prominent. Viddarr cringed when he read her shirt, "vampires suck, but I like it!" She had delicate curves that her zebra stripe spandex pants accentuated.

He slowly raised her arm up and gingerly kissed her hand and took in her fragrance, then turned his attention on Desiree. Her appearance was obviously more appealing to him. Shorter, she stood about five foot; her obviously dyed black hair was put up in braids. Her pale complexion made more striking with powder white foundation. Her blue eyes made even deeper due to the purple-black eyeshade and three piercings. Her thin pierced lips colored black still had her trademarked shy smile. On her neck was a necklace, she wore a jewel encrusted pentagram. Her black tank top was a belly-showing baby Tee. Viddarr stared at the push-up bra but his eyes darted down to her exposed pierced belly button and her low slung green and black plaid skirt. The skirt was the colors of her Catholic high school of Pointe Coupee, her old stomping ground where she went before going away to college. That was why when Sarah suggested a trip to New Orleans she had been gung-ho for a road trip and it certainly showed in her exuberant face. A colorful tattoo peeked out from the top of her skirt on her hips. Fishnet ripped stockings and black platform military boots. Viddarr took in her fragrance too and it was all that he could do to contain himself her nearness all but driving him insane. He put his hands on her exposed hips, and then he turned his head and kissed her, a lingering kiss on the side of her neck.

"I am the proprietor of The Wolf's Den; my name is Viddarr, pleased to meet you, Desiree. Care for a drink?" Viddarr said with a proud huff.

"Thank you, I'd love a drink." Desiree softly whispered her voice smoky, oozing sexuality, her brain a swim with pheromones.

Roxy looked down and playfully pushed Desiree, "hey look at his feet! They're enormous... You know what that means!"

Desiree's cheeks turned a bright red in embarrassment, "Roxy shut up!"

Roxy didn't disguise the fact that she was boiling up with jealousy. Her eyes staring angry daggers at Desiree but she didn't care, something about Viddarr was mysterious and untamed. She had goose bumps and a warm longing in her nether region.

"I hope your drink isn't laced with roofies." Roxy said obnoxiously under her breath.

"I'll just be a minute." Viddarr said ignoring Roxy's spitefully riposte.

Devon patiently waited on the bar stool as Viddarr reached down under the bar to get a homemade liquor bottle and a custom glass. It was a fifth with a homemade label that said "190 proof" and on the glass a deep impression of a wolf's paw made with clay. Viddarr popped the cork on the bottle, poured the liquor and added a pink powdery substance, Desiree assuming it was some type of granulated sugar, and then he stirred the mixture until diluted. The black lights made it flow a mystical purple as Viddarr offered the shot to Desiree. She grabbed the drink with both hands then gulped down the entire concoction.

"Wow!" Desiree spontaneously shouted in surprise as the shot emptied down her esophagus settling in her stomach.

Desiree staggered and put her arm on her jealous friend to balance herself. She thought she could feel the hair on her scalp growing. She squinted at the suddenly bright room; she thought the house lights had been turned on until she realized the house lights were and still off but she could see in the dark. She could see the world for the first time in the way it should be… alive with color and light. She could hear the crowds of people far away like they were whispering in her ears and she felt exhilarated.

Devon sat quietly on his barstool watching Desiree. Her eyes were dilated and they had a preternatural glow to them. His stomach twisted in knots as he saw half a dozen pair penlight eyes in a sea of people. He realized Viddarr had been recruiting reluctant and unwitting individuals he deemed worthy, new werewolves for Aticus' army. He had hoped that Viddarr would see his side of things and the balance of power would change but he looked in Desiree's glowing eyes and for the first time he felt completely hopeless. New questions arose, how long had this been going on just 100 miles from Royal Bay, how big had this gotten?

"What was that? Some form of absinthe?" Roxy didn't wait for an answer to interrupt again, "Can I have a drink?"

"Yeah, sure," instead of handing Roxy Viddarr's special drink he grumbled as he reached out begrudgingly over the bar grabbed a bottle of top-of-the-line vodka and two shot glasses with his immense hands and said, "Here, it's on me… Now if you'll excuse me I have some business to discuss with my friend but don't go anywhere when I am through discussing business I still would like to talk to you ladies."

Roxy begrudgingly said yes but Desiree said nothing, too busy staring at her hands with amazement she just nodded. Roxy had to coax her back onto the dance floor. Finally Viddarr returned half his attention to Devon to resume their conversation. Now and again his eyes glanced back at Desiree her eyes aglow and still staring at him in awe from across the room.

"I think I love that girl; I think I finally found my lost soulmate." Viddarr said matter-of-factly, taking in all of her essence, "you can have the blonde one. Although be sure to use a condom, from the smell of her I don't think her body could survive the change, besides that, she annoys me."

Devon laughed nervously, "I appreciate the offer, but no thanks."

"There is a sense all throughout the area of Aticus' presence, have you met with him?" Devon paused for he already knew the answer.

"Yes. You know I don't agree with everything that Aticus is doing. I think he is ailing and that makes for immense and impulsive mistakes. I think that all of Aticus' pack is like fruit flies; frankly all of the infernal pack means little to me. If they anger me I will smash them with my boot like bugs, but..." he paused as if searching for the perfect words, "together we are the Dogs of God! I want vengeance upon humanity and civilization itself. You of all people should realize that"

"I understand." It would be no use in arguing with him. He was known for his stubborn headed and hot blooded nature and he didn't want to be on his bad side.

Devon put a hand on the strong unyielding shoulder of his old friend. He got the fact it gave Viddarr a chance for revenge for what the humans had done to him. He knew Viddarr felt the power of the sense of being part of a grand divine plan. But it did not change the fact that Viddarr would not be on his side.

The barstool scraped the floor as Devon prepared to leave; he didn't notice several wolves disguised in human clothing strategically staring at Sarah's group. Dammit, he thought, I didn't even fight for Viddarr's allegiance. If he left now and didn't say anything he was going to regret it.

"Fuck... Viddarr, Aticus is crazy. I can smell the silver sickness and forbidden spoils' exuding inside him and any allegiance to him is foolish!" He didn't know he was shouting until Viddarr's eyes glowed red with anger.

He instinctively stood and launched the barstool so hard it hit the wall and splintered. He was face to face with Devon before he could respond, drool spilled out of his mouth as fangs grew in. His body still, rigid, as he searched for the will and self-control to stop the anger and rage that threatened to transform his powerful body to a sleek engineered killing machine intent on tearing Devon's body apart.

"I have no sympathy for humans! Humans slayed my fiancé long ago and I have been hunting for my soul mate's reincarnation ever since! Pathetic humans mercilessly hunted me down! They cut off my arms and legs setting fire to my body sealing me up to die! It was a blessing that

I was sealed in. The lack of oxygen starved the fire out. Hell you were there they fucking skewered me through my ass! Yeah, sometimes Aticus is impulsive and a moron but he is also a means to an end! The only reason I didn't tear you apart when you first entered my club, old friend was because I owed you my life for saving me. You deserve safe passage." Viddarr had calmed down now, partly because of their long standing friendship, and partly because he knew Desiree remained watching. "I'm sorry about your sire, Stefan, I truly am. And if you get the opportunity to kill Ice I won't retaliate but until then Aticus' plans continue."

"Thank you, for a safe passage, an oath, then," Devon put his hands on his shoulders again.

Devon finished his drink. He slammed the shot down on the table and got up to leave with his head slung low, defeated and turned to face the exit.

Viddarr stopped him and twirled him around, "you sure you don't want Roxy?"

"No thanks, my friend, maybe next time." He said anxiously laughing.

Devon knew he had to make a new battle plan for dealing with Aticus but first he had to get out of The Wolf's Den before he imprinted his scent in the air where Aticus' fledgling pack could find him anywhere in the area.

The double doors of The Wolf's Den slammed shut behind Devon as a sense of foreboding grew. Viddarr watched the wooden bar door close behind Devon leaving him alone to observe both gorgeous women from Sarah's group. He began to pour another special drink for Desiree and then proceeded to fill a shot glass full of vodka for Desiree's shadow, Roxy. Viddarr motioned for the girls to come back.

Desiree never took her eyes off of Viddarr even when Devon and Viddarr met or even when Roxy dragged her away. Now magnetic attraction had thrown Viddarr and Desiree both together again. In the pulsing strobe lights in a dark corner Michael Miller and Tracy Seller looked over at Lance and Tomas for their orders now that the threat, Devon, had gone.

She drank from the Wolf's Paw before Viddarr offered it, her alluring voice made the longing stir up again, "I missed you."

Viddarr laughed.

"Was that your business partner?" Roxy asked between shots.

Viddarr politely shook his head no.

"Viddarr, isn't it?"

"Yes its Viddarr or Viðarr, among other names." He said, while trying not to respond to Desiree's flirty dancing, so torturous, trying to talk to Roxy while Desiree writhed and slithered for Viddarr's benefit dangerously close to him.

"Oooh, you're so mysterious." Roxy said sarcastically, clearly irritated by his lack of interest in her.

Viddarr deliberately tried to ignore her as she paced the floor about ready to go after the last ditch effort to gain his attention, "what's that tribal tat all over your body stand for?"

Roxy overtly attempted to touch him on his exposed hard, marble-like branded and tattooed stomach.

"It signifies my involvement with the Úlfhéðnar. You heard of the Norse berserkers, haven't you? Well we're an exaggerated line of werewolves. Warriors, a part of the Norse," although Roxy asked the question Viddarr answered Desiree directly, keeping eye contact with her at all times, "A little more North and East originally."

Viddarr made no attempt to hide his lupine nature to Desiree. The fog of denial even now with the digital age, the truth that lycanthrope's are real and among them often fell to the wayside. Now just myth, legend, and movie fodder, besides, he felt confident in the relative safety and protection in HIS Den!

Roxy staggered and slurred when she spoke, "Oh you're into werewolves. I'm a vampire person myself."

"So you know dead things well, huh?" Viddarr growled.

Offering up Desiree's obscure knowledge of the occult and trying to get Roxy out of trouble for her smart mouth she said, "Do you know that there is a legend that if a werewolf dies he comes back as a vampire?"

Viddarr's eyes widened in surprise and respect, Viddarr acknowledged Desiree with a shaking of the head, "yes, yes I did my dear… I have seen many mystical things. Ghosts, poltergeists, vampires and (He said this loud, slowly and distinctly so Desiree could distinguish the reference) vampyres. I profess that I still do not understand them all… But sure, I tell you they exist."

He didn't have the time or the energy to explain the complex nature of it all; his hands rubbed Desiree's outer thighs as she pressed her back to him. He breathed in her intoxicating scent of honeysuckle, sunflowers, blueberries and a natural womanly scent.

She spun around to face Viddarr. The closeness momentarily surprised her she felt a jolt of electricity at his sheer closeness, captivating her. She snapped back into reality and spoke. "Ya, I read that passage somewhere in one of my occult books. The myths sprang up somewhere in Eastern Europe I think."

Sure he could smell her, Desiree had definitely been reincarnated, his lost love come back to earth he trusted her with a secret, whispering in Desiree's ear, the mere mention of werewolf captivating her, "I am a lycanthrope I am glad I didn't die coming back a bloodsucker."

"What …?"

Viddarr laughed the conversation off, he flipped her dyed hair back, exposing her slender neck and whispered, "It's all a technical process of evolving, exsanguination, heart stoppage and sometimes burying the body in the nutrient rich Earth…It is all a confusing and technical mess... Maybe I will explain it to you sometime. Let's just say I'm grateful I still breathe life!"

She was enthralled by him, partly from the drug laced drink and the rest instinctual.

"I would love to be a werewolf, the raw power and freedom of it all," their closeness hard to bear but she had no intention in backing away from him.

"When I was a kid I used to imagine running around in the woods on all fours and..." she was interrupted before she could finish.

"Desiree, you couldn't stand to be a werewolf, they're too hairy! You couldn't stand it; you are always waxing your legs. Hell, you even wax down there!" Roxy tried to lift Desiree's skirt up to show the crowd for all too see and embarrass her, but Desiree slapped her hand and backed up, blushing.

"It's all such bullshit," Roxy was now beyond trashed and belligerent. "The silver bullet and immortal werewolf only came about because of Hollywood films."

"Oh no, dear lady, you're bullshit; Jean Chastel blessed three silver projectiles for the beast. By blessing the bullets it only took one lucky silver shot to take down a lycanthrope they nicknamed the Beast of Ge'vaudan," He laughed to himself, "but I knew him as Pierre."

"He took three silver bullets with him, but in blessing them it only took one slug to hit him in the head, thereby killing the legend of the Beast. I would have torn Jean Chastel apart, but I didn't too much like

Pierre, he was an asshole." Viddarr wrapped his hands around Desiree and whispered, "I say good riddance to old trash."

In the midst of their current conversation Roxy had found someone else as drunk as she was to tongue wrestle with. Now Viddarr could devote all his attention to Desiree.

"As for living forever… it's a host of information out there, you just have to look between the lines. Cursed to walk forever, blah, blah, blah first off, if living forever is a curse than I'm cursed and I love it. Young changelings die in some way in a year or two before the wolf's blood makes them resistant to all but silver. Luckily it is in the wolf's nature to survive." Viddarr went to get a knife to cut lemons and limes.

"Watch this." Viddarr said.

Viddarr looked around to see a distracted Roxy dry humping a patron that got more attractive with every shot that she drank. The tempo increased and people were crowded on the dance floor unaware of Viddarr and Desiree. He turned around and proceeded to cut his forearm. The knife scored along in a line continuing through until he stopped at the wrist. He nicked the artery; blood spurted out before Desiree. He growled, fangs bared, blood was already pooling on the bar spilling down over the railing. Desiree was horrified but she couldn't look away.

His hand stretched, widening until it looked like a huge twisted paw. Talons appeared as fur rippled up his bloody arm. The gaping wound began to heal itself like a zipper leaving just a matted mess of fur on his healed arm. Then suddenly the fur receded leaving a barely noticeable red scar the length of his arm. Desiree watched this, mesmerized.

She believed anything that Viddarr told her. "Some old ones have died from severe, mortal wounds, other than silver wounds. I cringe when I see a silver bullet headed for my forehead or an inferno…. But being Úlfhéðnar, fire won't destroy me or though I fear it still, even a silver bullet to the brain; I have been around a long time."

"Make me a werewolf." She spoke softly, her eyes wide and hopeful like bright stars in the sky, "please."

Her arms wrapped around Viddarr's massive neck. They were face to face now and she was touching his entire body.

"I have already made you lycanthrope. Follow me and I'll guide you through the trials and tribulations," Viddarr quietly said, He couldn't stand it anymore he pulled her closer. Viddarr's lips smashed into hers as her lips yielded and parted reciprocating his fervent kisses.

A long lingering passionate kiss made Desiree warm with excitement. She explored Viddarr's mouth. He felt the stainless steel post as he further explored her tongue his member ached for her. Her fingers slid down to his buttocks as she pulled his waist in to her until she felt his hard manhood through her skirt. With one hand he scooped her up to his waist then with the other hand brought her legs up to his pelvis. Her inner thighs wrapped around his hips, her ankles interlocked.

Their lingering kiss stopped and Desiree softly kissed his exposed collarbone. Viddarr gripped her hair and pulled her head back, his tongue circling the nape of her neck. His hot breath giving her chills as he effortlessly walked with her to his office.

Viddarr checked the door, locked. He jiggled the doorknob for good measure. With one good forceful shove the door broke open wide. Splintered fragments of the doorframe rained down on the expensive carpeted floor. He and Desiree were in now; he didn't look back as he slammed what was left of the door shut with a moan that echoed around the hot lovers. He didn't waste any time, as soon as he entered his office he pressed Desiree against the wall. His eager hands tugged at her stockings, as Desiree nibbled his warm salty chest. He gripped the waist band of her stockings and panties. With one strong jerk the fishnets and underwear tore to pieces settling on top of his boots. The stockings hung down like a spider web from the floor up to her platform stilettos.

"Oh God," She said breathless.

Now Desiree's smooth, wet, pink flower of desire only inches from his jeans. Frantic hands fumbled to unstrap his belt buckle. With one hand still secure on her firm buttocks, Viddarr helped her with the other hand to undo his belt and unzip his pants.

His large engorged member now exposed to her. Desiree's hands slowly stroked his manhood as she pulled his hips closer to hers. She wanted all of him, every inch of him so Desiree impatiently pulled him into her.

She gasped as Viddarr entered her. His thrusting cock was almost too much for her to bear, enveloping every inch as she rested her shoulders against the wall and straddled his hips. She closed her eyes arched her neck and sang out songs of longing ecstasy. Their mouths met and lingered again oblivious to office walls and windows that rattled as pitchers fell to the floor and shattered.

Supported by the wall Viddarr started rhythmically grinding. He stopped supporting Desiree's body they were two persons in one. His hands rubbed up and down the length of her glistening taut thighs then made their way to her shirt, lifting it to expose her bra. One hand made short work of the white push-up exposing tender perky breasts. Small, pink Areolas and nipples excited him further. He hungrily devoured one nipple before he consumed another.

Desiree could hardly believe she was doing this; at 17 years old when she had sex for the first time her boyfriend promptly dumped her after the two minute coupling. He ran off as soon as the deed was done. She had sworn off sex ever since as a nasty and painful experience. But she could hardly contain herself around Viddarr. She couldn't help herself with his strong animal like magnetism. She breathed in his intoxicating scent. She could not shake the fact she knew him in a dream, another life. She knew that she would do anything Viddarr would want her to do. Wave after wave crashed over her as she moaned through an orgasm, her toes curling with enjoyment.

Viddarr couldn't help but bite her on the top of her breasts, Desiree squealed with excitement. A sharp quick bite but she knew it drew blood as a warm sticky liquid trickled over her breast, "aahh!"

"Am I out of line?" Viddarr grunted an impassioned question. She could tell by his voice that it was an apology as well as a question. But the knife and spontaneously healing forearm intrigued her. She somehow knew she had trusted him with her very life. She shook her head no and gave him a come hither smile hard to resist,

"No... You can do it again if you want," The conversation didn't break their rhythm as he thrust into her, as if trying to consume all of her body.

Large beads of sweat now formed on her forehead she glanced at her lover, not even breaking a sweat. He now bit her other breast, harder still but careful not to use his fangs or he would cut too deeply into her flesh. She was dizzy now but she didn't want it to stop. He now lunged into her with reckless abandon once, twice, three times as his white hot fluid spilled into Desiree.

Panting, his seed spent, Viddarr rested his head upon Desiree's shoulder. Breathing in her scent of sex and wild flowers perfumed with salty perspiration. Still inside her; reluctant to pull out and destroy the oneness that they had become, but he withdrew and Desiree's trembling feet hit the floor.

Viddarr couldn't help but stare at Desiree and breathe her familiar scent. She bore a striking resemblance to Amelia, who had been lost to him when she was so brutally murdered. He slowly slipped into madness with his loss. He sought for a soulmate for years until finding her as a young Veronica, his mate back in the 1600s. But her life was tragically cut short as well. Viddarr searched the world for whatever form she took, for his soulmate, frantically smelling her fragrance lest he forget her. Now the search was over, he finally found what he had been searching for; strangely she too felt the same way as Viddarr,

"I love you," Viddarr and Desiree said simultaneously.

He licked Desiree's wounds on her trembling left bosom until only a faint scar remained. He then proceeded to the right breast. Slowly and methodically he softly licked the other tender bloody bosom until it too began to heal. His tongue proceeded south to her belly and shiny jeweled piercing. She closed her eyes and pulled her skirt up again revealing her mound as his tongue opened the folds of her flower his eager tongue tasting all of her.

Viddarr was getting an erection again as his tongue slowly circled her folds, Desiree's back arched, moaning, drunk with bliss. Her hands combed through his hair as she pushed his head further between her thighs. Explosions of euphoria come over her. Viddarr lifted his head from beneath her skirt and pulled her body onto her knees, to the floor, her elbows folded on the carpet.

Her heat filled him with lust as his organ entered her again but this time he entered her from behind, a much more familiar position to him, used in the many meaningless, but lustful trysts with wolves and humans alike. However, something was different from all the encounters he had in the past, Desiree's aura and familiar perfume was special and he knew in his heart the words he spoke were true. He thrust his organ into her until she began to experience wave after wave of delight, Nirvana. Viddarr's hands gripped her hips as the lovers finished simultaneously. His hand transforming to a wolf claw and it tore the carpet on the floor to his office as he howled with excitement. Cheering erupted from the crowd who had mistaken the howling as some type of floorshow for the establishment so aptly named. Her mind willing to continue but her body physically exhausted she collapsed on the floor.

There was a knock on what used to be a door now caddy cornered and off its hinges destroyed only moments ago. Viddarr and Desiree pulled away from each other; Desiree desperately tried to fix her disheveled appearance as Viddarr opened the door that expanded like an accordion.

It was Roxy, she had wandered around trying to find Desiree; she had finally sobered up since the bartenders cut off the free alcohol.

"There you are! Desiree, I was wondering where..." Her train of thought had gotten derailed she had a horrified look on her face pointing to Desiree's obviously bloody tank-top, "what happened?"

"What!?" Desiree felt her breasts, tender but healed. She totally forgot that they once were bitten. She looked at her bloody shirt then back to Desiree, "no, I'm fine we were just... Um...talking."

Roxy looked Desiree up and down. Her hair was tangled and several rubber bands had broken. Her makeup was smeared from sweat and her black glossy lipstick was now nonexistent leaving her pink lips bare and her legs were shaking from the effort she exuded from making love to Viddarr. Roxy turned her attention to Viddarr who was buckling his belt.

"Oh, I get it..." but turning a judging eye onto her bloody T-shirt, "sort of. I hooked up too. His name is Michael Miller and he invited me to a party on Halloween night. I think it's called the Blood Moon Festival or something like that."

Viddarr was already walking to his desk to retrieve a handful of flyers, "Ah yes, it's sponsored by The Wolf's Den. All of the free food you can eat and unlimited alcohol. We still have room for more musicians and the location is yet to be determined though."

Without a second thought Desiree offered, "I have the perfect place for the party. My friend Sarah just inherited this property that would be perfect, so large you could lose yourself in it."

"I will ask her if it's all right, but I know she'll say yes." Desiree's caring eyes turned to Viddarr.

"That would be wonderful! Of course she'll be heavily compensated for it." His eyes bore into hers and he bit his bottom lip as he smiled.

46

Sitting in the corner, Tommy brooded over Sarah, sucking back the third beer of the night until only foam remained; he tried Sarah's cell phone with no answer once again. AJ and Garrett gripped the upstairs railing watching Tequila drunkenly dance on the downstairs dance floor slipping only two or three times before getting into the rhythm of the dance.

"Dammit!" Tommy beat his fist on the table knocking down empty bottles in the process.

"What's the matter, buddy?" AJ questioned turning around from Tequila's comical drunken dancing to see what was bothering his friend.

AJ motioned for the cocktail waitress to get him yet another shot from the upstairs corner bar. She retrieved it and brought it to him with a smile. AJ looked over at the pitiful puffy-eyed Tommy. He rubbed his dirty blonde curly hair. Tommy had let his hair grow out the last time Sarah had broken up with him when he usually kept his hair cut short and business-like. Now, his hair had grown out to his shoulders. However, the dirty blonde curls and glasses did not achieve the look Tommy desired. He looked like a dirty hippie. AJ felt sorry for him. With his unkempt appearance, unshaved face, his long blonde hair and black glasses, he reminded him of shaggy off the Scooby-doo reruns he loved so much. He just needed to get a green shirt. AJ was left with the thought of this taking another drink of whiskey.

Tommy put his hands up in disgust, "oh, nothing!"

Tommy squeezed his cell phone with enough force that he heard a crack and the screen went white imagining squeezing Sarah's neck, "she's not answering her cell or the motel room phone either!"

"Listen, man," AJ slid his arm around Tommy to console him but cringed as Tommy instantly froze up, uncomfortable with his closeness, "don't worry about it, man. We are in Louisiana, half a click from New Orleans; you should make the most of it."

Tommy's relationship with AJ had been strained at best. Tommy and AJ's relationship with Sarah overlapped when Tommy and Sarah had broken up for a time, and if AJ would not have been cheating on Sarah she wouldn't have left him and gotten back together with Tommy. But AJ's crooked smile and carefree attitude made it difficult for Tommy to stay distraught, and to whine and mope into his beer.

"I can see the enthusiasm and excitement in her eyes every time she is working on fixing up that fucking pigpen. I tried to convince her to sell that godforsaken place; it is in her best interest, really, with the debt that she has accumulated and all. But the immense acreage and a house of her very own coupled with the diary have her dreaming of a yesteryear and a simpler time. She's a damn irresponsible daydreamer."

"Hey I think I'm going to go down there and show these girls how to dance!" Garrett muttered pushing away from the rail. He had heard enough of Tommy's whining and he quickly downed the last of his imported beer whole. He wiped up the spillage with his forearm, staining his expensive black felt button-up shirt sleeve.

AJ turned from Tommy to Garrett, enthusiastically responding, "Go for it, man!"

He would like nothing more than to go with Garrett to pick up women. In his experience playing in his rock band, affectionately titled "Leviathan", the drunker women became, the better chance of success using corny pick-up lines and flattery. With a wingman his chances of picking up a woman grew astronomically but he stayed with his downtrodden friend. He felt partially responsible for Sarah's decision to nix the money that could be made from the sale of the fixer-upper plantation property, her decision to stay partly due to their conversation in the woods, back at the motel.

"Tommy and I are gonna talk for a while." AJ said, patting him on the back and waving for Garrett to go ahead.

"Have it your way!" Garrett scoffed as he headed downstairs, the music going up in Tempo.

Tequila had gotten off the dance floor and had attracted the attention of Tomas. He managed to brush her shoulder only briefly. She thought electricity flowed through her body as goose bumps awakened on her neck from the short encounter. The musk that Tomas exuded intoxicated her even further than the cheap drinks that she had consumed throughout the evening as he sidled up next to her.

"My, my, but you are a gorgeous one," Tomas flirted with an unrecognized accent, mysterious and alluring to her, "what brings you to these parts?"

A simple icebreaker that she had heard before, but somehow with Tomas' accent she found it quite charming. Tequila glanced at AJ and Tommy briefly then back to Tomas. His clothing and demeanor made him look out of place with the normal patrons in the bar. His features intrigued her. His features made him ageless and Tequila had trouble judging just how old he appeared.

Mesmerized by Tomas' cunning, radiantly animalistic eyes Tequila only glanced for a moment at his dreadlocks. She saw shiny silver studs hidden under his full-bodied Brown dreadlocks flowing down his back before she inevitably stared into his eyes again, his remarkable eyes that seemed to change color depending on the light.

"Well, I am originally from New York City. I am going to college. My friends and I are just down here for my friend, Sarah. She just inherited some property here in Louisiana," Tequila put her head down and shyly smiled, "my name is Tequila, by the way.... what's your name?"

Her cell phone rang in her pocket interrupting their conversation and startling her. She signaled at Tomas to excuse her and answered, "Yes?"

On the other end AJ answered, "Hey, Tequila! I think Tommy is plenty drunk enough. I'm going to call it a night. I'm going to get him a cab and get him back to the motel safely. I am taking the key to the van with me. In case you get the bright idea to drink and drive. I'll be back for the van tomorrow. I'll pay for all of you to get cabs for the night. I just wanted to let you know, sweetie."

"It's awful sweet of you AJ. Thank you," Tequila said still staring at Tomas' eyes. "Hopefully, I won't need a cab at all though!"

Tequila and AJ said their pleasantries to one another and hung up, "now, where were we?" She leaned in and bit her lip. Tomas pulled her onto the dance floor.

Tequila stared at Tomas, his hemp poncho and his homemade drawstring baggy pants. He looked as if the clothing had him uneasy, edgy and uncomfortable. He looked as if he would be quite comfortable unclothed and unrestricted by the materials that restricted him. The other patrons had noticed this too, but instead of making him the outcast they were intrigued and drawn to him like a wild animal let loose in a school, the children wanting to know him, touch him, excitedly circling around him.

All eyes were on Tequila too, thrilling, exciting her. By reflection the other patrons were quite jealous of her.

Lost in Tomas' eyes she almost didn't hear his question, "would you like to run away with me? We could get out of here."

The words come out of Tequila's mouth before she could think about it, "yes, yes I would run off with you, just say the word."

Tomas reached out his long black nailed hand as Tequila reached out her hand to meet his, while wildly jealous eyes watched on.

Garrett watched through the crowd of people as Tequila and Tomas went off and left through the double doors out of The Wolf's Den Tavern.

"Hey, handsome!" Tracy smiled as she took Garrett's hand.

Time seemed to stop when he noticed her. Tracy Miller, now a widow, had conceived her baby earlier than the nine months gestation period due to her recent affliction. The lupine, just like the lycanthrope had a two month gestation period so she had given birth to a healthy, albeit small baby, human-lycanthrope.

The new born baby had been ripped from Tracy's hands by Lance at an early age while the pineal gland was young and pliable. So the baby could learn the secret of the lycanthrope, to learn the wolf's ways.

Tracy had just given birth to a son when the next full moon arose she had transformed into a complete lupine for the first time. When the full moon set she involuntarily transformed into a human woman. Yet unable to voluntarily transform until the next full moon but somehow change body and mind. Her excess skin that she had gained from the birth of her son easily shrunk back. No stretch marks could be seen in her taut skin, muscles firmer now. Her human skin had no imperfections, like Aphrodite De Milos; as if she was made from marble statue.

She made full use of her attractive body. Among the many articles of clothing in one of the houses that had been converted to an auxiliary den she had gotten a tight mini-skirt and a tank top two sizes too small now she wore it to her advantage. Garrett could not help but be entranced by Tracy's seductive eyes. Then like gravity his eyes wandered down to her bare stomach. She had the classic hour glass shaped curve to her that appealed to so many men. His eyes lingered on her legs, muscled tight thighs and calves, runner's legs fit to run a marathon.

Tracy slowly and deliberately sauntered closer to Garrett. Her breath warm and minty, "it's awfully crowded in here, or is it just my imagination?"

Garrett glanced about the dance floor, pulsating lights alternating in color made his eyes hurt. The people moved like waves in the sea, ebbing and flowing to the DJ's beat. He breathed in her sweet aroma, intoxicating and mesmerizing aroma until he began to feel an ache and a stirring in his pants.

"Yes, yes, it is kind of crowded. Let's get out of here. I gotta a make a call first, though, um, real quick..." Garrett stuttered not used to aggressive women making the first move.

Garrett's fingers could not dial the numbers in his cell phone fast enough. He put the phone to his ear, the hesitation threatening to kill him, until Roxy answered.

"Speak to me!" the disembodied voice of Roxy answered at the other end.

"Hey Roxy, I just wanted you guys to know I'm taking off. Don't worry about the van, okay? AJ is willing to comp for your cab fare. Have a nice time and stay safe, okay?" Garrett yelled out, competing with the music. His eyes locked onto Tracy's mysterious and hungry eyes.

"Will do, I will tell Desiree!" somewhere across the crowded room Roxy quickly hung up with him.

"Well handsome, are we good to go?" Tracy whispered seductively, her warm breath blowing on the nape of is neck.

"We are set, lead the way." Garrett said smiling like it was his birthday.

"Follow me," Tracy said with a mischievous smile, "I'll give you a night that you won't forget."

Like a racehorse with blinders on Garrett could only see Tracy as she guided him toward the door. Garrett shivered as a strong wind whipped through him and a cold chill ran through his spine as they stepped out into the parking lot. The wind changing direction gave Garrett a chance to breathe in her alluring, mysterious aroma, calming the chills.

Tracy squeezed his hand, "come on baby, my car is a little bit further."

Looking around the almost barren parking lot Garrett glanced at his watch, 1:30 a.m. It would soon be last call in the bar anyway. Garrett questioned, "Which car is yours?"

"There it is!" Tracy whispered, then stopped and pointed in the direction of a little silver two-door sports car.

Garrett and Tracy broke hands. She headed toward the silver car's trunk he headed toward the passenger door.

It took a moment for Garrett to adjust his eyes to the deep shadows between the parked cars. He squinted. Though he could make out no details two shadowy forms could be seen one still and the other swayed back and forth in front of him. He thought he heard a faint slurping noise alternating with a low growl.

Garrett did not notice Tracy moving closer to him when he knelt down to get a closer look. Was that a body on the ground!? His heart quickened, was that Tequila lying motionless? His mind going a mile a minute he gasped, definitely Tequila, Garrett thought he could tell by the blood stained shirt that she wore, he could see the gaudy shiny rhinestones that had decorated her shirt.

"Tequila??!!?" the question left his mouth but he feared there would be no answer. Now that his eyes had adjusted to the darkness he saw a massive amount of pooling blood and Tequila's hazy dead eyes staring up at him. He fell back a step, out of breath.

Garrett felt Tracy's delicate hands press down upon his collarbones. He froze as in the corner of his eye he thought he saw a movement, fleeting though it had been, at the edge of the silver car's rear fender.

The smell of a feral lupine, like a wet dog jumped down near the shadow and Tequila's dead body. He tried to recoil but Tracy tightened her grip. Garrett had no time to think as a monstrous brown head with starving yellow, glowing eyes looked hungrily down at him. He tried to move again and to no avail Tracy's long fingernails sunk into his shoulders.

"What the…?" Garrett struggled to be free, but with every movement she tightened her grip.

The monster animal stood up on hind legs. His mind harkening back to his youth, creatures of the dark and things that go bump in the night, he stared eye to eye with a werewolf whose hot putrid breath assaulted his senses. The claws of the werewolf struck his cheek. It's impossible, he thought, and the new Moon not in sight, weeks until the full Moon rose again he was seeing things, wasn't he?

Tracy wanted more than anything to change form to please the orders of her master, Aticus, but although her blood was boiling and her hair stood on end with no full moon in sight the change would not come to her. However, she still had an uncanny strength that she used to restrain Garrett. He strained against her. He had probably eighty or more pounds on her but Tracy had a preternatural strength that held him prostrate.

He looked from the monster's menacing eyes down to Tequila's lifeless body then back to the monster again in time for the monster's claws to grip Garrett's neck and force his neck around until it snapped, cutting off the path from his brain to his spine. The weight of his body crumbled to the ground.

A roar from the woods grew louder until the commandeered Can-am side-by-side ATV burst out from the trees, driven by Aticus himself, "get on!"

Without a second thought Tracy quickly obeyed, she slid onto the ATV as Aticus got off it and with one hand picked up the two corpses from off the ground and dumped them into the oversized basket on the back of the ATV blood spilled out the basket dripping onto the gravel.

Aticus throttled the engine as the brown wolf with dreadlocks whipped its muzzle back and howled, blending in with the music coming from The Wolf's Den Tavern in the background.

The ATV navigated deftly through the high grass down a shortcut with the huge brown Wolf on the ATV's heels until they arrived near Raccourci Island and the barn. Two sets of glowing eyes, Lance and Montezmu, stood watch as Aticus turned off the engine.

Montezmu's wolf's muzzle manipulated the barn door with his nose and pushed it open. Aticus and Tracy both picked up the corpses out of the basket and threw down the bodies with a thud once they entered the barn.

Smelling the air around him, he determined Oung and O-kami still searched for any reluctant member, meditating in their minds. Soseti and James were out walking the fields, her teaching the secrets of transforming at will which involves a powerful and discipline- dedicated mind, which James had in spades. Relief washed over Aticus, grateful for James' absence. He crinkled his nose in disgust every time James had walked by him. James' odor smelled odd. However, the alluring aroma coming from the corpses brought out the hungry glowing eyes of the filthy and nude infected human group.

"Come and get it, my pets!" Aticus yelled. He kicked one corpse towards the hay with a thump. It wobbled toward the group.

Tracy knelt down before the others and with human hands started to devour the human flesh and then one by one they got down on their knees and started to devour the corpse too.

"Good, eat up!" Aticus watched with keen interest hoping the blood and protein may satisfy the group's hunger, awakening the group's transformation, "In a couple of months the perigee full Moon will be near and then I will harken back to the Earth our lycanthrope mother, Aisos, and she will heal my wounds and comfort me!"

47

Sarah sat at the window, watching the upcoming dawn and drinking her coffee or a simulation of it. Coffee, by definition alone, she held in her hands the equivalent of last night's mud. She had not yet gotten dressed this morning, her unkempt raven black hair undone from the day before. Eyeliner and thick mascara smeared by intermittent crying coupled with the large bags under her eyes made her look like a Goth rocker or an "Emo" Queen.

Sipping her mud and clutching her cell phone she waited for the State police department to call her back. She had been on and off the phone with detective after detective since she had gotten up, now a daily ritual that she had grown accustomed to since Tequila and Garrett's disappearance. Her friends were dropping like flies. Roxy and Desiree made it home late that fateful night but now Tequila and Garrett were missing. Tina and Jac were still missing but her heart sank when the local police office told her that her friends were considered adults and from "out of town", a matter for their local Police Department, or at least the State Police. She finally found an officer that would hear her problem. She waited for their call back now, trying to hold back the bile in the back of her throat.

A tear formed in Sarah's eye. She started to cry and once she started she couldn't stop. It was all a huge mistake coming down to New Orleans. Nostalgia, a trip back in time, her found diary and a place to call her very own. She took full advantage of the lawyer's fine print condition that she would get paid a bonus fifty grand if she had decided to stay and fix up the estate. She felt giddy to pay off her mounting debts, but now it felt like it was all such a horrible mistake.

She tiptoed through the kitchen to brew another pot of coffee, careful not to wake AJ. To stave off Tommy's drunken advances every night AJ had moved into her room but in different beds. The TV off and the radio at a comfortable level Sarah sat pondering her next move when her cell phone rang.

"Hello?" Sarah answered, cautiously optimistic.

"Miss Sarah Poirier? This is Captain Rogers returning your call, what seems to be the problem?" The Captain asked in a monotone voice as if the call disinterested him and that enraged Sarah to her core.

"Yes! My friends are missing and I wanted to know what you are going to do about it!" Sarah said in an octave just under shouting.

"Oh, I apologize Miss Poirier," his voice sympathetic, "your friends are missing, tell me their names and I'll see what I can do."

"Two of my friends, Tina and Jac, were the first to go missing," she downed the rest of her mud, flinching just a bit as it made its way down her throat.

Sarah said their last names, where they went to school, and where they lived, before continuing, "Now my other friends, Tequila and Garrett, are gone too!"

A stirring in the other room, she heard AJ as he struggled to get out of bed. A clunk first, one foot then two hit the floor; he had fallen asleep with his boots on.

"Hey, we have coffee?" AJ yelled from down the hallway.

She covered the receiver with her hand and responded, "yes and no, fresh coffee is still brewing last night's coffee tastes like dirt. But I'm sure there's some left."

Sarah heard a grateful mutter of relief then a scuttle as he stumbled into the kitchenette, "what are we going to do about the Van? It's been parked at the bar for going on weeks now. Apparently Garrett had the keys!"

Sarah shrugged for now they were getting by using cabs, "I don't know. The van is rental; it has been such a headache to try and get it rekeyed without the proper paperwork..."

Sarah paused to give all the information to Captain Rogers that she knew of. Her confidence growing as she heard Rogers furiously typing. To get to the bottom of the case Rogers made plans to meet up later.

"So you'll be there two PM right?" She confirmed with Captain Rogers, her eyes traveling off in AJ's shirtless direction.

"Thank you so much, AJ and I will meet you at the van's site at two, then." Sarah said, smiling as she pressed end.

She stood up to stretch her numb legs, pins and needles instantly stabbing her over and over again.

AJ patted his shiny dark brown hair full of gel, downing what was left of the muddy coffee mixture in the glass carafe, "Hey, have you seen Tommy?"

"No..." AJ said, coffee trickling down his chin and neck, "I need a shower!"

He rubbed his wet curly chest hairs, soggy from the spilled coffee, "when we got back, I turned my back on him for two seconds to make some coffee and when I turned around he was gone. I didn't worry about it, though, he didn't have any money to speak of and no car so he wasn't going far, then I guess I passed out... With everybody vanishing though I guess I should have checked up on him!"

"Hmmmmm..." Sarah's said scratching her head, lost in thought, she was pleased with Tommy's absence but she worried for his safety since two more of her friends had gone missing, "AJ, can you call a cab that could take me by my house then go wait by the van for the police today?"

"Sure I can, honey, I just gotta hop in the shower first," AJ turned around, looked at Sarah with a naughty smile on his face, "ya know, you can shower with me to save some time, right?"

He laughed as he saw Sarah's disapproving face.

"Oh, Hell no!" She uttered caught off guard from his comment, "I mean thanks for the offer, but I'll have to decline, thank you."

Sarah's cheeks were starting to redden as she remembered all the tawdry details of their once torrid love affair and embarrassment began to creep in.

"Okay, you don't know what you're missing," AJ give Sarah a mischievous wink, "when I am out of the shower I will call a cab for you."

Leaving the door open Sarah could not resist but peek as she watched AJ enter the bedroom and undress. She frowned when he shut the bathroom door behind him and turned the shower on, the exploitation over.

"What is wrong with you?" Sarah mumbled to herself a guilty smile on her face. She knew in the back of her mind sleeping with him again would be a disastrous thing to do. She had to get out of the room before she regretted her actions.

Sarah bit her knuckles to resist the urge to follow him. Instead she headed toward the front door. Without a second thought she was out on the deck of the cabin. The flowers of late August bloomed in flower boxes waist high along the wall of the cabin. She rested her arms on the wooden rails closing her eyes to warm her cheeks in the sunlight. Eventually she opened her eyes, the long stilted deck creaking as she stepped off the deck and onto the steps.

She casually strolled down the wooden stairway sliding her hands down the wooden banister. She stopped for a moment at the sidewalk to look at the other cabins nearby. She saw a row of three-foot tall Sunflowers warming in the morning sun. In another month or two the sunflowers would grow fifteen feet or more to block the windows on the other cabins. She turned her gaze on the Lake called False River, aptly named for its horseshoe appearance as it traveled down Louisiana, and then abruptly curved and stopped.

Maybe working on the estate would help keep her mind off of her missing friends. She had replaced the scorched floorboards, cleaned the windows, and mudded the holes on the burned walls. Old rags, a lot of bleach and old-fashioned elbow grease and the living room felt warm and pleasant once again. Maybe it was a waste of time to worry at all, AJ said Louisiana was a notorious party state. Perhaps the hard labor and her slave driving ways drove her friends into hiding.

"What time is it?" AJ asked as he dried his clean wet hair with a complementary towel, "if we have time I need to eat something."

"It's still only ten or so, we have plenty of time before we have to meet the police officer, what are you hungry for?" Sarah's face turned flush before the words left her mouth.

She turned to look at AJ, but the play on words was not lost to him. Sarah braced herself for the onslaught of filthy comments to come with AJ's mischievous smile as he opened his mouth.

"I don't know, maybe I'm hungry for…" AJ was interrupted by the yellow cab, throwing up dust continuing until it stopped at its destination, The Point Breeze Motel.

Meanwhile Montezmu peered over the waters of the hotel watching every move that AJ and Sarah made, with his arm around Tommy. His bare chest shone white as a ghost, and his yellow eyes reflecting red from the sunlight. He wore white robes that wouldn't interfere with the transformation to wolf, hybrid wolf-thing, or to a human. Montezmu's ghost white appearance from the top of his long white hair to his pale chest and white robes made him look like a Renaissance statue of a God come to life.

Tommy's button up shirt had been shredded and hung caked with mud and dirt. His cuffs from his dirty shirt were torn as well. His blue jeans had been torn in two spots at the knees and ankles. He had lost his shoes the night before and his feet both were bloodied and caked with mud. Tommy had been given a chance to drink a special solution that invigorated him. Last night he ran around in the forest in a state of lunacy. With the Crescent Moon there would be no transformation, however, the wolf's blood entered Tommy's blood system invigorating him, empowering him and altering his mindset.

"I feel strange, I feel strong…" His fists began to clench, "Are you sure I will be able to get the attention of Sarah?" Tommy asked.

Tommy already could see much further than before and he used it to stare over the lake at Sarah. Oh how he longed for her, he would do anything for her, Tommy silently vowed.

"Stick with us and you will be powerful, you do what we say, you'll get what you pine for!" Montezmu spit when he talked, and it was hard for him speaking English, he sniffed deeply before he continued, "follow us, we will teach you the ways and you'll get what is coming to you."

48

She turned the volume up on her iPod so that the beat of the music might bolster any hidden energy and she could finish buffing the hard wood floor in the living room. The mesmerizing melodies of the bass guitar coupled with the thump, thump of the bass drum and haunting melancholy chants of a dozen monks quickened her pulse. The twang of steel strings on the electric guitar assaulted her ears but stimulated her at the same time. The quickening blare of the rhythm guitar until the lead vocal growled his dark poetry. The blaring music in her ears worked its magic, she picked up the pace. Before long Sarah had all but finished the first floor. Only the hallway remained.

Sarah stood halfway up on her knees, dropped the rag on the floor and wiped off the dust from her hands. The intoxicating music had her body swaying intuitively to the dark rock beat as she regarded her ancestor's portrait, free from dust and shining. The artist had captured all the beautiful exotic traits of her façade. Her hair was golden and lush; she had nonsensically high, proud cheekbones that gave her an air of nobility, dazzling dark blue eyes that could see into your soul. The artist had rendered an air of innocence all about her as well.

The discoloration on a large portion of the wall told her, her family had taken a large picture, presumably of the entire family unit. She saw the similar discoloration on the walls in front of her. That led her to deduce that the family had taken individual family members down off the wall, taking the pictures with them when they fled, only leaving the beautifully rendered portrait of Alicia behind.

Why was the portrait of Alicia the only picture that remained on the wall? It puzzled her. Two semesters of psychology had her entertaining the thought that the head of the household had subconsciously forgotten Alicia's portrait in a passive aggressive attempt to discipline the child.

She could just envision some sort of catastrophe that was brought on by Alicia's actions. The psychological mystery that left her desperately wanting to read a little bit more of her diary. She had had enough of the stuffy dusty living room for a while. She got up and retrieved the diary on the floor by the screen door.

She managed a weary smile, "Well, I think I deserve a break."

Sarah wiped the sweat from her forehead, then clutching her diary she opened the screen door and stepped out onto the deck. She had moved an antique rocking chair out on the deck so she could get some sunlight and fresh air during her breaks from working in the old house. She loved the smell of fresh paint drying on the walls, of the house's oil-based sealant on the deck, and the smell of freshly cut grass soothed her immensely. For just a little effort and for such a low cost she had managed to revive a decaying estate and though still uninhabited the house felt like a home again.

"Every chance I can, I sneak away from my family ..." Sarah read out loud, ***"I travel to the forest, so I would not be seen with him, my love, Aticus."***

She took a long, deep, breath in then stopped rocking back and forth in her chair. She knew her friends were missing…but here, on her inherited land, the reconstruction and remodel keeping her mind preoccupied it had a calming effect. The scenery so quiet, so serene, she had not a care the world.

"Aticus… Aticus. He has such an exotic and unusual name. He tells me he was not born of this land, he tells me secrets that I think he has never told a soul but I think he is still hiding something from me. I do not care what he is hiding; I think he is my soulmate." Sarah whispered with a sigh.

The leaves of trees swayed back and forth, she imagined she was back in a simpler time. She imagined herself as Alicia. She couldn't help herself, as she began to read more.

"It was a beautiful night and I could see the stars, the moon in the sky was at its crescent. I was alone in the forest, at night, but with Aticus I felt safe, secure. A clear cloudless night I saw brilliant stars falling from the sky. Dozens upon dozens of shooting stars fall… I couldn't help myself so tantalizingly close to me I kissed him." She paused, crossed her legs, and licked her lips. Then she continued to read on, silently this time, ***"Our lips lingered; the electricity was almost***

too much for me to endure. Goosebumps surged throughout my body. I knew this night would be the night that I surrendered to him, my lover."

"My soulmate takes me by the hand, to lead me further into the forest. I should be scared the further away I get from the well-lit star filled sky. We moved closer to the growing darkness but excitement kept me trudging through the blinding obscurity until I adjust to the miniscule light."

"Aticus turned around and held out his hand to me. For the first time I could see clearly. His dazzling emerald eyes glowing brightly like flashlights. Those unusual green eyes sparked a flash of memory of a black Wolf in a life-and-death struggle with an alligator. Then I saw something amazing, confusing moments where a human arm splashed out of the water and eventually saved my life. His eyes were same as the wolf, animalistic eyes filled with ferocity before he blinked. Then when he looked into my eyes his vicious eyes melted away." She carefully slipped a bookmark into the pages of her book, time for an intermission.

Sarah kicked her flip-flops off and hopped off the porch, careful to secure her diary in the process. She could feel the soft grass between her toes. She walked. About a hundred yards from her house there sat the woods. A small, ambiguous dirt road led to the Wisteria trees their vines finally blooming to a royal purple leading to the concealed barn also owned by Sarah. The invisible barn with rows and rows of vines that resembled swirling white and purple cotton candy falling down would be ignored making a great den for Aticus' brood. She moved gingerly while searching for landmarks Alicia had written about. Clearing the sticks and debris so she could comfortably sit, Sarah picked a Cyprus tree and rested her back upon it. Now In the middle of the peninsula, in the heart of the forest she felt peaceful and quiet, a good place as any to continue.

"Instead of this sullen, temperamental creature that I had come accustomed to, he turned into a caring, loving, deeply compassionate lover. In fact, whenever his eyes fell upon me, his deep dark green eyes, I could not look away." She paused for a second as the robins chirped and sang somewhere in the distance.

She flipped the pages until she came to another passage that interested her, continuing, ***"When I looked into his eyes soaking in his fragrance something wild, exotic and exciting. I felt like we were the only people on earth we were alone figuratively and literally in***

the woods. In the woods even Poppa couldn't find us, stop us; stop the love that we had for one another. Tonight I determined to seal our love, desire intermingling to become one."

"Though the darkness was enclosing us, he somehow scratched our names into the bark of a gigantic Weeping Willow tree. Alone, standing tall in the midst of several Cyprus wisteria vines his glowing green eyes were all I saw as I explored his body. I ran my hands through his thick, black hair and in the safety of the canopy of the huge weeping willow tree we made love, for the first time in my young life I gave myself to a man body and soul." Sarah closed Alicia's diary, careful not to lose her place.

She had found the tree, a huge weeping willow tree which had their first names scratched deeply into the bark; Aticus + Alicia. It had come to life from the pages of this diary. Its branches had grown until they touched the ground and swayed back and forth blowing slightly in the wind.

Aticus and Alicia were real, not just a fantasy written from a young girl's imagination, scratches on the bark made the story more carnal. She skipped a few pages, a few weeks going by in a flash then read aloud this time, "***In one of our many trysts by the Weeping Willow Aticus stopped, twirled me around and took my hands. What happened next tested my sanity."***

"Aticus told me a secret in confidence; he said he had come to the Americas for vengeance, that we were the descendants of a family who had done unspeakable torments to his family. They had hunted his family just shy of annihilation. Our family slaughtered all of his bloodline so he was hell-bent to exterminate all of ours. My love Aticus, coolly confessed without any emotion whatsoever; I will never forget those words… I stalked you, waiting to end your life… but thank the alligator for moving, for setting off my instincts to give chase… Then when I got out of the water and looked into your beautiful face…"

"I couldn't comprehend what Aticus confessed! Did he confess to being the black wolf? Had he confessed to plotting to annihilate my whole family like my family had murdered his relatives? I should have been sick, thrust in a dreamlike fairytale, horrified and scared for my life…"

"… Silence, my heart melted at the same time I fell forever in love with him he said, 'your innocent eyes, I fell hopelessly in love with you and I swore then and there that I would protect you'…"

A crow cawed its warning at the same time her cell phone wailed, startling Sarah.

"Hello?" Sarah half expected to hear the county sheriff's office calling her back or her long-lost friends finally checking in, but she heard AJ's voice on the line instead.

"Hey, Captain Rogers took our report. I'm in the taxi and I am picking you up. I need to talk to you. Stay put, okay?" AJ said.

Impulsively smiling Sarah responded, "Okay, bye, fill me in when you get here."

As she pressed the end button on her reflective phone she caught the reflection of the sun's light. She beheld her reflection, straight raven black hair and her dazzling deep green eyes; she imagined Alicia and Aticus' love affair, Alicia's descendant?

Aticus had transformed into a mammoth of a Wolf. A huge and vicious, sleek-lined canis dirus a "fearsome dog" mimic, true form in almost every way save for the shorter than normal muzzle and bushy tail. Aticus' ankles/feet converted into reverse knees. Shorter than normal, even though the actual foot had lengthened and his toes now rested on the ground, converted into paws the balls of his feet changed to thick pads. But in the distance Aticus' huge Wolf looked normal, normal save for its missing eye and ear.

The Wolf stalked Sarah's every move. It peered at her through the concealment of the dense trees, mesmerized and captivated by her hauntingly familiar looks. He stood up on his hind legs, converting back to human. He clutched an Onyx pendant in his sharp pearl white teeth.

Aticus excitedly stepped forward, and then froze, anxiety getting the better of him. He touched his missing and scarred eye socket and then his horribly scarred and mutilated half lupine, half human, ear. Aticus' strong heart raced with panic, fear and anxiety. What if Sarah was horrified with his appearance? What if she ran in fear from his grotesque mutations? His blood boiled with reservations and misgivings. He couldn't help it, he was shaking uncontrollably. His eye dilated with adrenaline, with rage, his black hairs stood on end again. His nervousness hit him like a tidal wave and he couldn't stave off the involuntary conversion to a bipedal wolfman, a release for his anxiety. He retreated back into the shadows of the trees so he would not be seen by Sarah, so he could calm down enough to convert back to a human again.

She put her cell phone in her jeans pocket then rested against the scored tree for just a second, head swimming with outlandish thoughts she clutched her family pendant then turned around and ambled toward the treeless meadow and her estate.

She stopped in between the woods and the clearing, eyeing her house in the distance. The cab sped by, disturbing dust on the ground, like a vacuum small granules flying up, getting stuck in the undercarriage.

She clutched her necklace as she met AJ and the cab halfway from the driveway to the house. AJ pressed the passenger side button rolling down the window and rested his left elbow on the passenger side door panel. He paused for a moment, smiling nervously, and then spoke.

"Well, I met Captain Rogers at the van. I must have been really sauced last night because I couldn't find the tavern to save my life. I think this Captain Rogers guy is taking the disappearances seriously. He left a cell phone number to reach him." AJ smiled ear to ear, "can I offer you a ride?"

AJ, being the unceasing gentleman, opened the back passenger door for Sarah. With an outstretched hand AJ coaxed Sarah to get in the cab. She held his hand and jumped in the back passenger seat.

"Why, yes, thank you, I'm starving!" She exclaimed to herself as she shut the cab door.

"Good." AJ instructed the cabbie where to go and the driver turned around onto the road and they were off in a cloud of dust.

Aticus beheld his reflection on the back of the pendant, his skin quivering like the sea's tides. The bones popping and cracking back into place until it resembled a human chin. He clutched Viddarr's amulet in his long black talon hands, he stole the runic talisman to make her remember as if she were Alicia in her past life ... Then when the perigee Moon is full So-seti would also invoke the mother of lycanthrope, the necromancer, Aisos, to heal his ear and eye so he might have the self-confidence to finally meet the incarnation of Alicia, the woman responsible for his haunted dreams.

49

Captain Rogers sat at his desk staring at his hand that held the sealed baggy. A clear plastic bag that said "EVIDENCE" in big black block letters held a commandeered motorcycle license plate. Blue uniforms with shiny badges entered and exited the area without disrupting him in his office. He alternately inhaled the fragrant coffee and carefully sipped the hot black brew. He released the license plate and began reading the reports with interest. The CSI technician checked the tire mold and based on the width, the size, and dimension of the tires he had determined that it could be the exact make and model ATV that escaped from the inferno at Michael Miller's shack. The plate's numbers registered a 4 x 4, side-by-side owned by A-1 Rituals and was rented by the woman that filled out the first missing person's report, Sarah.

He drank from the small, white Styrofoam cup then scratched his head while staring at the license plate yet again. He had found the license plate beneath the undercarriage of the Van, the white Van driven by Sarah and her group. Months ago she had reported two friends missing and now two others had went missing from the group as well. The results of the license plate registration deliberately threw Sarah into the midst of the confusion, from innocent victim to perpetrator, but to what ends? His mind raced a mile a minute, Captain Rogers's bloodshot eyes watered. He hastily picked up the black outdated and corded phone and began to dial a familiar number.

"Hello, is this Detective Jenkins? This is Captain Rogers, do you remember me?" Rogers questioned while putting his feet up on the desk.

"Yes, yes I remember you, what's up?" Detective Jenkins slurred his question. Tired of Phillip's constant ridicule the detective had already drank a significant amount of alcohol for breakfast.

Rogers looked up at the clock inside his office, 9:30 a.m... Jenkins was pretty sauced already, he thought to himself, "I got to check out a lead, you wanna team up with me on this?"

Rogers' phone on the other end went silent for several moments, Captain Rogers' mouth hung open about to respond when Detective Jenkins slurred, "Yeah, sure, I'm sure, and we'll get Dexter again. If it is the same culprits, Dexter has had experience with them before."

"Good." Rogers said with an authoritative voice, clearing his throat.

"We have got to find and talk to Dr. Jacobs, first and foremost." Jenkins said and Captain Rogers was amazed by Jenkins' logical and coherent idea despite his blatant drunkenness, "He was on scene when I had to fire on the lunatic. Since his alleged attack and the missing corpse incident he's left work. Dr. Jacobs had been researching some off the wall monster myths before he fell off the face of the Earth."

Captain Rogers and Detective Jenkins both stayed on the phone for several moments silently contemplating their next move. On Jenkins' end, Rogers heard loud classical music blaring at an uncomfortable level. On Rogers' end he could hear typing, muffled conversations, and the dispatcher wading through her calls, a relatively quiet day fielding sparse calls for the EMT; a heart attack, a missing kid, a four car fender bender.

"When you sober up we can plan our strategy. ..." Captain Rogers paused for a moment, shaking his head, "I know in my rational mind I should report this to the proper authorities, but nobody would believe me, not after what we experienced..."

"I'm just glad I have company now," Jenkins sounded more coherent and upbeat, no longer in a deep depression, suddenly a man on a mission. Before he got off the phone with Rogers he had just one more question, "I always wondered, your first name is Thompson, it just sounds like a last name, there has got to be a story behind it, just curious about that."

"Nothing major," Rogers laughed, "my mother still wanted me to be named after my maternal grandfather. His name was Jules. My dad thought it was a girl's name, so they named me after his surname, "Thompson". Simple as that...." The two men laughed together as they mutually hung up their phones feeling a little more hopeful.

50

Detective Jonathan Jenkins put down the bottle of alcohol as soon as he hung up with Thompson Rogers and put some coffee on to brew, time to sober up he thought. First things first, find Dr. Jacobs. Maybe he could shed some light on the strange events periodically plaguing the small parish.

A master at multitasking, Detective Jonathan Jenkins set out zealously on the phone to procure Dexter's services again as he feverishly typed on the computer to find Dr. Jacobs. With the use of Dr. Jacobs' cell phone he would track him down using GPS. He had been lying in a flea bag motel in the outskirts of Royal Bay. He stopped and took a quick whiff of his clothing; the alcohol had exuded from his body, soaking his clothing but he declined another drink. He decided he would take a hiatus from getting drunk, he wanted to keep it professional and he had an obligation to keep his partner safe. This time he felt a growing justification because he saw and believed the bizarre events and would be backed up and then everybody else would believe him.

He felt the gray stubble growing on his chin. No need to shave this time, he thought, satisfied the stubble had not grown out long enough to make him look like a homeless man. He picked out a black T-shirt among so many black shirts from the laundry room; he took off his old musty shirt and put on a clean shirt then went over to the bathroom medicine cabinet. Next a vigorous almost obscene spritzing of his body spray to mask the alcohol smells that he had sweated out. He had picked up another personal firearm since the police confiscated his snub-nosed 38 caliber revolver after the shooting at Michael Miller's shack. Though technically he was still on hiatus from the Batchelor Police Department he grabbed his badge. He blew on the disposable plastic straw hooked up onto a breathalyzer. Unconsciously tapping his foot as he waited the results, it finally beeped, "good" he thought aloud, it was at the legal limit and going down.

He finally made his way out the door and was checking the ATV now. A squad car would be impossible in this instance. Dexter may pick up a scent that takes them into terrain made impossible to navigate in any other vehicle except a 4 x 4 again. Newly washed, shiny and clean, with a 281cc motor and was secured in the bed of the truck. Jenkins jumped in, inserted and turned the key in the truck, plugged in Dr. Jacobs' address into the GPS then he rolled out of the driveway, finally on his way.

"You know, it doesn't vindicate you at all..." the ghost said to him, sitting in the passenger side of the truck, eyes forward, watching the road ahead, "just because you didn't hallucinate the fangs and claws coming toward you this time, you did shoot me, your only son, and I don't have fangs and claws."

Jenkins searched for his cigarettes and lighter, trying to ignore his son. Finding a box of Generic full flavor 100's he quickly put a cigarette in his mouth, putting flame on the tobacco until the end of the cigarette began to smoke. He angrily breathed in the thick smoke then calmly exhaled the cancerous plume.

The scathing comment had been made by his own imaginative ghost, but it hurt him deeply anyway. He sucked on his cigarette, drag after drag, trying to ignore the ghost of his son, he didn't turn his head and acknowledge him whatsoever but he knew his son sat beside him. All around him he felt his son's presence.

He had mixed feelings about teaming up with Capt. Thompson Rogers; he had an uneasy feeling about his growing relationship with him. He worried his relationship would only bring Rogers down, ostracizing him. He worried about all of the bridges that were burned, all over the state, black flagged in all of Louisiana. He worried his association would forever ruin Rogers' career.

"Boy, you're pretty hard on yourself, Dad." The ghost said, as if he could read Jenkins mind. Thc ghost placed a hand on his shoulder and detective Jenkins felt a cold chill run through him.

Jenkins ignored his dead son as he finally arrived at the motel. The place looked as if it was abandoned. The grass had grown out of control. The weeds had grown wildly and were overtaking the once manicured gravel parking lot. The sidelights and the vacancy sign had blown out. Even the letters making up the sign for the motel had been stolen long ago. He saw a drastic difference to the property lines scattered throughout the area. A gun shop, a payday loan hut, and a pawn shop all had a straight manicured line all the way to the yard, in contrast to the unknown motel's unkempt lawn.

Detective Jenkins opened the truck door and stepped out onto the overgrown lawn taking his time to look around at his environment. He didn't see it, but he felt sure that the ghost of his son got out too.

He had seen Dr. Jacobs' car before, a cream M6 BMW with beige, leather interior. He knew from just his brief interactions that this car was the doctor's pride and joy. He washed it once a day at least, probably twice if it sat in the parking lot under a tree. His finger trailed down the rear bumper quarter panel to the hood of the car. He looked down at the grime coating his finger he could tell by the grime and dust that Dr. Jacobs' hadn't driven it in a long while.

The proprietor had informed him of Dr. Jacobs' room number. He looked into the windows. Dust and cobwebs graced the panes of glass. Dr. Jacobs had wrapped the inner panel of the windows in aluminum foil, in what he supposed was an attempt to block out the sunlight.

"Something is really wrong here, I can feel it!" warned the ghost.

Again Detective Jenkins ignored him. Although he didn't turn around he knew the ghost still wore the same clothing, dark sweatpants a hooded sweatshirt. It was what he wore for his homecoming where his father, Detective Jenkins, had accidentally shot him. The blood stains were still there, though strangely there were no bullet holes in the fabric. In fact, he learned long ago not to look at him closely because when he did, sudden flashes from the night of the shooting ran through his mind's eye.

Of course he hated to admit it but his dead son's comment rang true. Farmland as far as the eye can see ran adjacent to the main highway and now only a few houses dotted this side of the street for mile or so. The well-maintained, tidy house with the clean lawn stood a half an acre away leaving the motel lonely and foreboding. The once inviting flower garden with its roses, lilies, and daisies now neglected and dead, no pedals remained. He likened it to an old B-horror movie, the old ax murdering, cannibalistic, inbred murderer, or alleged haunted house from myth and legend. The kind you whispered about in your misbegotten youth. Suddenly he busted out with laughter standing at the edge of the lawn imagining that at any moment the door would burst open and out might come a hook-nosed witch waiting to turn him into a frog.

"Regardless, I need to see him, son." Detective Jenkins said opening the screen door.

He froze for a moment his arm rested in mid-air, making a fist, ready to knock on the door, though, gathering his wits about him before he knocked quietly.

Although he himself could hardly hear the knock the door opened almost at once, revealing a disheveled and wild-eyed Dr. Jacobs. He had opened the door so swiftly Detective Jenkins gasped wide-eyed for a second before regaining his composure.

Detective Jenkins could tell Dr. Jacobs had not changed his clothing nor had a shower in days. Dr. Jacobs tried his best to shield his eyes, sunken blood-shot orbs, from the blinding sun.

"Detective Jenkins, um, oh, what can I do for you?" Dr. Jacobs quietly asked, squinting from the light, as if the sun rays actually stabbed his eyes.

Dr. Jacobs's appearance hit him like a ton of bricks. Detective Jenkins had had dealings with Dr. Jacobs from time to time. He thought he knew what Dr. Jacobs looked like but this incarnation of the doctor had him dumbstruck. Instead of Jacobs' familiar brown hair, which had a multitude of thinning gray hairs on the temples, his hair had become fuller, but was now completely silver in color.

Detective Jenkins eyes gravitated towards Dr. Jacobs' belt examining the prongs protruding out of the improvised hole in Dr. Jacobs' belt. The doc had punched several different holes in the black leather belt to accommodate his shrinking size. Three amateurish holes of varying sizes told Detective Jenkins Dr. Jacobs had lost weight at an accelerated rate.

He had lost all natural, healthy color from his skin, his skin now ghost-like in complexion, almost sickly, though no lines of age could be seen anymore. He momentarily wondered if the doctor was not wearing makeup but dismissed the idea. His T-shirt was stretched around his thick neck, trapezius and chest, however, his shirt hung outrageously loose in the mid-drift, but revealed his bare skin, stopping short before his hips.

"Yes, Dr. Jacobs, I just wanted to speak with you for a second. You have been a hard man to track down. May I come in?" He asked politely.

He looked into his eyes. A brilliant dazzling gray with flecks of green, he tried to remember, were Dr. Jacobs' eyes always that color? He had a surprisingly hungry and aggressive glint in his eyes, cunning and self-assured eyes; animal-like eyes.

"Come in, come in." Dr. Jacobs said finally, holding his arm out to hold the screen door open to accommodate the detective.

Detective Jenkins notice Dr. Jacobs' engorged biceps and forearms. He had well-defined muscles that had the veins protruding on his arms, a stark contrast from the flabby, soft upper arms that he seemed to recall. If he didn't know better he would've sworn that he had used a lethal amount of steroids to get inflated so quickly. In fact, despite his sickly appearance, his all-around pasty visage his spine now stood up straight and tall. He had a spring in his step. He blinked rapidly unsure his eyes were playing tricks on him as he examined Dr. Jacobs' ears a little closer. They seemed to come alive with every minute sound nearby as the motel room settled with age. His ears were moving like a radar dish able to focus in on a signal.

As Detective Jenkins stepped past the doctor and into the room, out of the corner of his eye he noticed his dead son standing immobile, motionless. Like an uncanny force, a powerful presence, this had Philip spooked.

"If it's all the same to you, Dad, I'll wait here." The ghost of his son said quietly, his head turned downward toward the ground while kicking rocks at his feet.

Detective Jenkins acknowledged the ghost of his son with a nod. He guessed he would have to go into the house alone. He entered the room and shut the front door behind him. Dr. Jacobs walk into the kitchenette. Jenkins would have lost sight of him were it not for a windowless partition stopping waist high in the bedroom room.

"Forgive me, would you like a drink?" Dr. Jacobs said, and didn't wait for the answer before pouring two glasses of homemade sweet tea, offering one glass to the detective.

"Yes, please..." Detective Jenkins stuttered, taking in the doctor's remarkable transformation head to toe, "I would love a drink."

An uncomfortable silence hung in the air as both men sipped on their tea. In fact, both of the men sat in silence for almost five minutes before the doctor took out a sphygmomanometer, a digital blood pressure cuff, fastened it onto his bicep and pressed the button to inflate it.

The floodgates came open when detective Jenkins asked three simple words "Are you sick?"

Dr. Jacobs stopped what he was doing for a moment, then he answered, "well, I guess, technically I'm not..."

He checked the blood pressure display, 99 systolic over 66 diastolic pressures, his heart rate read at 61 beats per minute. Satisfied with that reading he explained further, "I feel fine. In fact, my body feels extraordinary."

He took a drink of his tea and leaned forward. "I tested myself for various types of flu, typhoid, rabies, lockjaw smallpox, even the human immunodeficiency virus, down to the bubonic plague, and all came up negative ... We have had a visit from the Center of Disease Control, but finding nothing coupled by the fact that eventually I and all the sick patients got better, they too were at a loss..." Dr. Jacobs said quietly, more for himself than for the detective.

Before continuing Dr. Jacobs gulped a massive amount of tea from his glass, then he felt he had to validate some of the worry and doubt plaguing Detective Jenkins...

"Listen I think I saw what you saw in the morgue..." Dr. Jacobs paused turning his gaze away from detective Jenkins and down toward the kitchen table, "fangs and long blackened claws, but coming from this animated abomination that I thought you had already shot and killed!"

He shivered just thinking about the day that the corpse sat up and dragged itself toward him. He would not even believe his own eyes were it not a fact that he had been mauled.

Suddenly an exotic aroma wafted in and faint music could be heard. His eyes instinctively locked in on the scent but Jenkins made his way in the darkness and found a light switch which turned on the lights in the room. A suddenly dazzling incandescence light above the doctor made him squint even with the dark sunglasses to shield his eyes.

Dr. Jacobs had been used to the dark for so long he howled out in pain, "Fuck, turned the lights off, please!"

"Are you all right?" The detective asked with sincerity in his voice.

"I was attacked by that kid, Cody, but as I told you I tested myself and I felt fine or I thought I was fine until the first full Moon," just saying this string of words filled him with embarrassment, an uneasy smile crossed his face imagining he was in a low-budget horror movie.

Phillip the ghost had seemingly mustered the courage to step into the hotel room and was now standing between the bedroom and the kitchenette. When Dr. Jacobs stood up Phillip rushed to his dad's side to protect him.

"Pssst!" Phillip nudged his father to get his attention, making cold chills run down his arm.

Phillip had diverted Jenkins' attention to the doctor's dirty old Dockers slacks, now high waters. He could see the doctor's socks and hairy legs, was the doctor always that tall? He wondered.

Already the detective's mind raced; there were so many pathogens that could catch a ride on dirty nails, including blood. He could not count the times that a suspect was apprehended using the DNA from the victim's fingernails... The doctor spoke further, interrupting his train of thought.

The detective thought that the doctor was reading his mind when he said, "I'm not sure but I think I may have been infected by a blood born pathogen... I know when I looked at that monster's claws they were growing and bleeding." He began to pace as he spoke, making the ghostly form beside Jenkins tense up.

"That's when I started to test my DNA... I figured I would catch this little bug somewhere in the process. But it was an utter failure, it remained hidden. However, now my DNA is somehow changed, every time I tested it, it spits out a tainted, contaminated or inconclusive result." Dr. Jacobs paused a moment eyeing the empty glass that sat before him.

"He only scratched me! But in a few weeks I started to feel strange..." The doctor paused for emphasis, "I went outside to get some fresh air. I felt drawn to look up into the sky, an urge to look at the brilliance of the full Moon that's when something strange took over me..."

Detective Jenkins took a small drink of his tea, careful not to consume it all and gestured for Dr. Jacobs to continue.

"Like I was saying, I went outside and looked into the full Moon for the first time since I was attacked and… I lost time, somehow. I found myself at a strip mall in a parking lot and I was confused about how I got there." Dr. Jacobs confessed.

"My limbs unresponsive I watched helplessly while my body instinctively responded fueled by instinct and senses. I heard the sound of a huge raccoon and I cornered it in the open-air atrium next to the theater… stopping to look at my reflection in the coming attractions poster I become horrified with what I saw!" He clutched the back of his chair.

He described the horrid scene. The doctor described the appearance of a mutated freak, his skin stretched and thickened, his forehead lengthened, his eyes widened. The doctor's nose had simultaneously elongated and flattened, leaving his nostrils broader. He had a massive chin and on his lips an eerie smile. His arms and hands were below his waist. His body had stretched out. The change had been drastic, but he could pass for human, or at least an ugly bipedal humanoid.

The noise of a passing train combined with a boisterous crowd from a movie theater nearby made him come to his senses just in time for the moon to become obscured by the gray clouds. Panic overwhelmed him, a fear of being seen. He whipped his head around wildly examining his surroundings. Where he stood on the sidewalk streetlights graced either side surrounding him in light. Nevertheless, a wastebasket and large bush cast a large shadow on the brick store wall. He stepped back onto the grass where he would be hidden. The skittish humanoid managed to crouch down between the bushes and the wastebasket, but a large group of intoxicated individuals saw a large form in the shadows and headed towards his direction.

"Hey you!" Freddy, the tall, fat tattooed man who was obviously the leader of the group with black, cutoff sleeved shirt and dirty, torn jeans yelled with a thick southern Louisiana accent, "hey you! You sick or somethin'?"

Shadows concealing Dr. Jacobs's horrid form he turned around to face the tall man his heart rate increasing. Against the protesting group the tall man pulled out a large hunting knife.

"Why don't ya giva me all your money!" The fat man spit.

"What's wrong with him?" A young girl whispered to her friend who just shrugged with uncertainty, she couldn't help but stare at his face still obscured by shadow.

The crowds had broken off and went in separate directions, thinned out and dissipated. Nobody noticed the group as they got into their cars and drove away. A thinner, shorter man named Jake with worried brown eyes and a grey goatee came up to the leader and placed his hands on his shoulder.

"I don't know if dats such a good idea. I think something is severely wrong wit him. He looks like an escaped mental patient if you ask me." the man with the worried brown eyes warned.

According to Dr. Jacobs, he heard a strange growl, a deafening warning, but it shocked him because the growling had come out of his own throat. Breathing quickened his heart racing out of control. The synapses in his limbs shut down no longer under voluntary control just instinct. No thought just reaction, Freddy attempted to thrust his blade but the Doc moved with blinding speed, crushing the fat man's hand.

"Ahhhhhhhhh!" the fat man's eyes widened as he sought help from his friends "help me, Jake!"

"I'll save you, Freddy!" A short, thin man exclaimed instead of running away like the rest of his friends, who fled at the first sign of trouble.

The plea too little, too late the Doc still had control of Freddy's shattered forearm and pulled the man closer. His dangerous teeth bit down on the man's fleshy tattooed triceps like a vice. His pleas turned into curdled screams, blood spurting out like fountain.

The lunatic Doctor threw the fat man into the store front. The wind left the fat man as he slammed horizontally into the plate glass window. The glass relented and smashed into a million pieces. Alarms blared as the fat man named Freddy hit the glass strewn floor like so much discarded litter.

Jake, the thin man, whipped out a small caliber handgun from his pants pocket but the doctor pounced on him before he could fire. His body crumbled onto the sidewalk. His chest and arms pinned down by the drooling mutation Jake shut his eyes waiting for the inevitable. But the cornucopia of sound had the doc's ears ringing. He could not stand the noises any longer, putting his elongated arms up to cover his ears. The piercing noise of the alarm and the police sirens growing closer the doctor hit his chest as a warning then jumped off Jake's body and ran towards the shadows on all fours.

Detective Jenkins could just imagine eyewitnesses and investigating police officers on scene. Though some had dealt with him daily he knew from just looking at the Doc in the hotel room they would not identify him. His face so twisted, even his own mother wouldn't recognize him.

"I can hear the howls calling me, instructing me, sometimes even ordering me to do things that only my sensitive ears could hear. Then my heart rate slowed and steadied again and I regained my senses." Dr. Jacobs explained.

Dr. Jacobs turned his back to detective Jenkins, "I forgot all about that strange experience until his bloated corpse came into my morgue. When I saw his face frozen in horror that horrible flashback knocked me on my ass… I remembered killing him then, disemboweling him. I did that monstrous thing …" Dr. Jacobs softly whispered.

Babbling now, Dr. Jacobs continued, "Though I was still human like in appearance, I know because I looked into the reflection on the car, I felt so potent… Like a power lifter on steroids…"

"My curiosity as a scientist got the better of me," Dr. Jacobs motioned at the heart monitor, "I could almost reproduce the nearly orgasmic experience by controlling my breathing and heart rate…but…"

He poured more tea as Dr. Jacobs confessed, "my dad was a man of science and my mother was a woman of faith so I inspired to be both. But I studied medicine first, and then got a job dealing with death all day long. I believe in God, but I also believe in the physical world, where death is a certainty… it left me a little jaded."

"With my own eyes I saw a corpse come alive healing the numerous wounds that killed him in the first place… Only God should have control over such miracles…" Dr. Jacobs' muttered a Bible verse, with gray eyes that seemed to implore his help in some way, "God made man in his image"…

"I think I'm becoming a monster!"

"But you're afraid of the beast inside you. Are you not?" Detective Jenkins questioned.

"Yes… I'm afraid… But not of the beast inside of me, I'm afraid when I let loose the beast I'm going to like it! Eventually it will overtake me I will revel in its immense power. I have been raised as a Christian, I am afraid for my immortal soul!" Dr. Jacobs confessed his face contorted in agony.

Detective Jenkins reached to put his arm around Dr. Jacobs to comfort him, "I don't think you have anything to worry about!"

The detective walked away from Dr. Jacobs and paced into the front room where aluminum foil covered the windows. Dr. Jacobs was a man conflicted, two minds at odds with each other. He could do worse than to recruit Dr. Jacobs he thought. Dr. Jacobs looked human, nothing like the monster that he encountered, he would be fine. He had already learned a great deal on the inflicted by Dr. Jacobs' actions, sensitivity to light could come in useful. Altogether three dangerous encounters had been narrowly averted and it would help to learn all that he could about "the affliction".

Detective Jenkins had already dialed the number for the dog kennel. Despite his better judgment, he found himself offering a partnership, "come with me, we could use all the help we could get."

Dr. Jacobs thought about this for a second and then he nodded, maybe helping him would go a long way for Dr. Jacobs' salvation, remembering the corpse thing from his morgue. Maybe if Detective Jenkins could find others suffering the affliction just like him he could study this disease and find a cure. Doubt plagued him, but he would not give up hope.

"Okay," Dr. Jacobs said reluctantly, "I better bring my sunglasses; the sun hurts my eyes something awful."

51

Dexter panted, excitedly wagging his tail as he looked up at the detective lovingly. Detective Jenkins picked up the dog from the kennel with Dr. Jacobs. They arrived where the Van had originally been in what they thought was an abandoned parking lot, but in reality was home of The Wolf's Den Tavern, protected by an ancient incantation to shelter it from prying eyes. He had called Capt. Rogers and now he waited for his arrival.

"You know, I thank you because you are the third person that knew without a shadow of a doubt that something strange was truly happening..." Doctor Jacobs paused for emphasis before continuing, "You know it wasn't your fault, don't you? I have seen their eyes, full of frenzy. Cody wasn't in his right mind from what you're telling me. I don't know that there was anything you could have done differently, or I, for that matter." He mused.

"Yeah, I've seen Cody with my own eyes and truthfully I wouldn't have believed what is transpiring!" Detective Jenkins scoffed. He scrounged around for his crumpled half pack of cigarettes from his pants pocket beating his crumpled cigarettes on his thigh then offering one to Jacobs.

"No, thank you." Dr. Jacobs politely declined.

Jacobs could only smile as he started to think about his own encounter. He knew he acted out of instinct. He acted in self-defense when he killed Freddy by the theater. It wasn't technically his responsibility but in his heart it was his fault. It worried him when the lunacy overtook him he had begun to love it more and more and that vexed his soul, his very faith in his own humanity.

Dr. Jacobs had helped Detective Jenkins get the ATV down and now he sat patiently waiting for Capt. Rogers' arrival, his dark sunglasses keeping safe his sensitive eyes from the harsh sun light. The minute sounds and faint smells of the forest were exhilarating him. He could zero in on the tiniest mouse hastily making its nest. Astounded he could tell by the sounds and smells how far away the mother sparrow tweeted for her babies to feed, in fact with every inhalation he could tell how many animals belonged to each family. Now, so sharp, so potent the odor, it gave him goose bumps on his arms trailing down to his hands.

He felt as if he would just jump out of his skin. His wrist watch which tracks heart rate beeped incessantly. Dr. Jacobs' curious nature led to relentless experiments with his unholy gift. He knew that if he could go into a trance like state and increase his respiration his heart rate would quicken releasing endorphins, awakening the parasites inside of him. He would successfully transform into a powerful humanoid, a beast like-Neanderthal with no worry, no cares, just running on pure animal instinct. It had become surprisingly easy to transform, more control each time. As more and more parasites flooded his veins he started a low guttural growl, which worried and concerned the man of faith so he took in a deep breath trying to slow down his heart.

"I have seen the colossal power that the inflicted possess and there are at least two of them. Capt. Rogers is on my side, he too has seen what I've seen," Detective Jenkins ambled over to Dr. Jacobs. He couldn't help thinking that not only his medical training but his exposure with this mysterious bug would be an asset whenever they came across the suspects again.

He paced away, a calm silence filled the air Detective Jenkins deep in thought until the ghost of his son spoke, breaking through his concentration, Philip questioned. "What is it you're looking for, Dad?"

Detective Jenkins' body jumped into the air, he had all but forgotten about the ghost in the midst of his musings. Jenkins started to protest, "I'm not looking for anything per say, I'm just… Well, I'm just stalling until Rogers gets here."

Capt. Rogers' paperwork for his quadrant, Pointe Coupee through West Feliciana parish, which consisted of over five hundred square miles had stacked up of late. Since the arson at Michael Millers he had seen two of the alleged cult member's faces or an extreme facsimile thereof and he felt in the pit of his soul he would soon unravel this mystery. The Capt. let out a satisfied groan when he finished up the last of his tedious paperwork pushing off from his desk and stretching his legs before he headed out to meet up with Detective Jenkins as planned.

Concealed by a multitude of Cypress trees, Capt. Rogers couldn't see the Jenkins as his truck sped along Route 1 until he turned the wheel onto a side road toward the parking lot and the concealed Wolf's Den. Capt. Rogers and Jenkins caught sight of each other. Jenkins adjusted his eyes to look at what he imagined to be a little red matchbox truck. Further still and the truck look like a red snap-together model hurtling towards him. He unclipped his walkie-talkie to say he had already arrived as Jacobs quietly stood beside him.

"Well it's about time, Thompson; I thought you weren't going to make it!" As the truck came into view he couldn't help but smile ear-to-ear the pair had become a trio, the three musketeers. Jenkins scoffed or more than likely they would be the hilarious three stooges.

"I had to finish my reports after work, I still haven't had the chance to change out of my uniform yet," Capt. Rogers looked up at the gathering gray cloudy formation, "I hope it doesn't rain on us."

Dexter led Detective Jenkins down into the ditch, his tail wagging. The chain snapped taunt, the eager dog leading him up on the shoulder of the road. Jenkins aggressively tugged the chain until the dog froze. Jenkins waved his hand in the air so Capt. Rogers could easily spot him and put on the brakes.

"Who the hell is that?" Capt. Rogers questioned. He had parked on the shoulder of the road and gotten out of his dusty truck and now he stared daggers at the presumed stranger.

"Don't you recognize him, Thompson?" Jonathan Jenkins remarked pointing at Dr. Jacobs.

Thompson Rogers scrutinized Dr. Jacobs' outlandish appearance, "Who?"

Rogers did not recognize the doctor right away. He had been used to Jacobs' clean and well-fitting outfits but the stranger had on an ill-fitting, dirty uniform. He had gotten taller and leaner. He now wore a grungy lab jacket two sizes too big for him and the length of his pants two sizes too small on him. Rogers had been used to Dr. Jacobs' thinning and receding hairline. This stranger had thick, silver-gray hair, and bushy gray eyebrows that appeared as one eyebrow instead of a pair.

Dr. Jacobs took off his sun glasses. They were no longer the familiar loving and compassionate eyes. They were tired and anxious but the very structure of his eyes had changed; his new eyes had a keen intelligence, somehow mixed with cunning instinct. Even the irises changed to a glowing golden brilliance. No more wrinkles that had come with age his face tightened and smooth. A whole different person altogether, Rogers thought. Dr. Jacobs' new visage, his confident stature with his smashed fighter's nose and high cheekbones he looked almost dangerous.

Dr. Jacobs stepped over the ditch and got alongside the truck asking, "You don't remember me Capt. Rogers?"

Capt. Rogers squinted as if peering closer, "Dr. Jacobs?"

The doctor's voice lower and deeper than normal, "Don't you recognize me, Captain? I'm Doctor Jacobs."

"Hell, um, right… Lord, have you changed!" Capt. Rogers couldn't believe his eyes.

The man's conflicted behavior and his body language aside the white uniform sparked Rogers' recognition. It was Dr. Jacobs' mind but the physique had changed somehow. Capt. Rogers saw Dr. Jacobs' conflicted expression, as if his eyes had been at odds with two persons trying to possess one physical body.

Detective Jenkins smiled as he regarded Capt. Rogers' dark navy Jacket and pants suit so perfectly cleaned and neatly pressed. Jenkins saw his bright white, starched button up shirt, dark blue silk tie, shiny brass cufflinks; he looked so professional, at odds with their bizarre reunion. In the back of his mind he welcomed the mounting support, Rogers and now Jacobs believing bizarre events occurring.

Capt. Rogers shrugged his shoulders in a submissive gesture relating to all the unbelievable things, things that he had seen far. Teaming up with the expertise of the doctor to investigate the mysterious strangers seemed like a good thing. Through Dr. Jacobs he could scientifically report back the findings anonymously to Amy Anderson so she could lead with a breaking report of the phenomenon she had been looking for.

Capt. Rogers had recently obtained several items of value to Tequila and Garrett procured by their friend, AJ, commanding, "here boy, get a good whiff!"

Capt. Rogers whistled for Dexter. Detective Jenkins released the dog from its chain who instantly and enthusiastically responded. Capt. Rogers bent a knee and gave Dexter the clothing, who greedily inhaled their scents. Eventually Dexter had a trajectory and the dog's tail rose up and stiffened.

"Okay, here is the game plan…" Used to giving out orders, Capt. Rogers spat out commands, "Jenkins and Dexter will go on the ATV, Dr. Jacobs and I will follow you on side roads suitable for my truck, communicating on radio."

The trio nodded and Dexter barked as if he understood.

"Forgive me, but Captain Rogers is right… you have drastically changed. Do you still feel the same?" Detective Jenkins tried to play off his concern, worry still evident in his cracking voice as he turned the key to the ATV.

Dr. Jacobs thought about the question a moment and spoke, "no, I feel fine… great, actually. I am still me, strangely, only in a new package that changed for the better; it's actually quite fascinating clinically!"

He managed a smile, "All of my faculties are working fine and I have all of my long-term memories but…" He shrugged and looked down at his distorted body, his lips quivering because he knew his rational thought was starting to conflict with baser animal instinct.

Detective Jenkins looked into his eyes and smiled a toothy smile, as he pats Jacobs' shoulder for comfort. Jacobs' heart rate quickened, the hairs rising on the back of his neck. Somewhere he heard a growl of warning and was momentarily alarmed until he realized it came from his throat. For just one moment he had thought the detective's exposed teeth were a sign that Jenkins was somehow threatening him. And his staring into the doc's eyes had seemed a sign of superiority or dominance. The Detective's social clues of comfort were unconsciously mistaken as signs of aggression, making the doctor severely uncomfortable, invading his personal space, both frightening and enraging him. He realized all this and had to restrain himself from striking out at the detective's neck… 1, 2, 3… the Doctor counted silently; he had to calm down, and inhaled slowly. His heart rate slowing until he came to his senses.

"Are you coming?" Capt. Rogers questioned, already in the truck with the engine running.

"Let's go!" Dr. Jacobs climbed into the truck and sat down then wrung the used clothing in his clenched fists, he breathed in the familiar clothing too.

Detective Jenkins and Capt. Rogers conversed by radio, the truck stayed on the neglected but passable pathways. Dexter ran through the fields using shortcut after shortcut until the dog came upon Gerome's manor.

"Hey Rogers, Dexter has stopped over at Gerome's old plantation…" Detective Jenkins squawked.

The Captain shivered at the myths of his childhood but he remembered the legends. Gerome's place lay abandoned but in the full moon's light a sorrowful howl could be heard coming from inside of the house. The howling had stopped long ago before he was born and he had long since grown up but he knew the myths well.

Detective Jenkins called, "You have to see this, get here right away; copy?"

"Copy, be there right away, over and out." Capt. Rogers turned off the radio and looked over at Dr. Jacobs who stretched his head out the window oblivious to him as he sniffed the air around him.

"It's gonna rain cats and dogs, I can feel it." Dr. Jacobs closed his eyes and looked up to the sky.

Capt. Rogers continued slowly on a poorly maintained dirt road until he came alongside the ATV. He still sat on the seat of the ATV and Dexter stared off in the distance with his tail between his legs, too scared to go any further, involuntarily relieving himself upon the grass.

Detective Jenkins could see strategically placed Weeping Willow trees that had been planted a long, long time ago in the distance concealing the whitewashed walls of Gerome's old place. Capt. Rogers observed the white van in the gravel driveway. The gravel drive spanned the length of several football fields, from the van to the thick wooded area. The driveway abruptly serpentine, conveniently obscuring the barn that held many infected, including the pack's inner circle, between the thick woods and the white house.

"Dexter had a strong scent; he rushed me around through the trees but then it was like the Millers incident. The dog stopped, shaking, and Dexter started circling around me his tail between his legs. He was a professionally trained tracker! Not easily sidetracked or frightened until he got to the Millers shack and Raccourci Island." Jenkins remarked, he had let go of Dexter's leash and he promptly jumped into the truck bed. "I tried to coax him to go further but it was useless!"

The first large thick cylindrical raindrop fell to the ground and Detective Jenkins, Capt. Rogers, Dr. Jacobs and Dexter the dog, looked up into the dark, cloudy sky as a torrent of rain began to fall. While Rogers and Dr. Jacobs were protected by the windshield from a good soaking, it got the clothing of Jenkins uniform and Dexter's fur. Even Jenkins' ghost son looked up into the sky in the bed of the truck, so the raindrops fell down on the bed liner.

"I think it's time to go!" Capt. Rogers barked his arm outstretched across the rolled down driver side window.

"I'll help you load up the ATV. Then you can get in my friend." Rogers signaled Dr. Jacobs to step back.

Dr. Jacobs stared at the wooded area behind the white house. Almost in a trance he spoke softly under his breath, "they are here somewhere in the wooded area, I can smell it…"

Nobody heard Dr. Jacobs' soft-spoken warning. Detective Jenkins and Capt. Rogers had just loaded up the ATV when headlights of the van quickly approached.

"Hey, Captain Rogers! Do you and your buddies want to come out of the rain? I am heading back toward the motel."

Detective Jenkins and Capt. Rogers did not respond, but Sarah would not take no for an answer, "come on, I just got my van back and you can't all fit in the cab of that truck, I'll take you wherever you need to go after we get back to my dry room."

The motley crew offered no further resistance as Rogers shrugged and climbed into the van and before he could shut his door, Dexter jumped out of the bed of the truck and hopped up on the seat with him. Sarah grinned at the dog who looked quite pleased for securing a warm, dry seat.

52

Detective Jenkins and Capt. Rogers had been taking turns drying off their hair with Sarah's towels and shaking out their wet clothing as they quietly listened to Sarah's rant. For almost an hour the rain had not relented. Dr. Jacobs stood on the porch eerily quiet, mute even, staring at Dexter who was curled up in a ball outside by the wall of the hotel room trying to stay out of the rain.

Dexter kept an un-trusting eye on Dr. Jacobs. The dog had nowhere near as violent reaction to Dr. Jacobs as it had to Aticus but the dog still kept a healthy distance from him. Any closer and the Doc would be greeted with exposed fangs.

"So…is there any progress?" Sarah hesitantly asked, sipping hot chocolate out of a mug.

"No, ma'am." Capt. Rogers with his back to Sarah answered before the detective could respond. Sarah had lent her ancestor's diary to the detective. He thumbed through the pages with growing interest.

"This morning I felt nauseous and I haven't yet bled. I have to hide myself from my father… I am not sure, I may or may not be with child, but Aticus seems sure of it."

Detective Jenkins all but ignored Capt. Rogers, who sat down in a rocking chair, engaged in conversation with Sarah. Dr. Jacobs had come in from the rain, but ignored everybody and gazed at the darkness out the window.

"It has only been one and a half months and already my child is lively and moving incessantly, yet I barely show and I hide easily my sin. My extraordinary baby seems to be growing at an alarming rate and I fear Aticus knows it, as well he told me he can smell it in the air around me. I felt pangs out of this Earth, it has been only a few months but I fear I will soon deliver! I need to bathe and get some rest, but those familiar glowing green eyes outside will make it hard to sleep."

"Aticus, he said his name is Aticus… And that's impossible," detective Jenkins sat on another rocking chair and softly whispered, he looked up, interrupting his reading when the door opened.

AJ and Tommy walked in, their fishing poles in hand. They immediately dried up with towels then AJ set the fishing poles in the corner of the room to greet the men while Tommy strolled toward the kitchen with the fish that they caught in hand.

Laughing, AJ asked Sarah under his breath, "What's up with your boyfriend? He's acting weird, even for Tommy's strange ass."

"He's not my boyfriend," Sarah scoffed playfully hitting him in his chest; Sarah turned her head toward Tommy, whose back had been turned from the group, "be quiet, he will hear you."

Sarah instinctively did a double take as Tommy turned the corner. She admitted he had drastically changed and in most respects for the better. He seemed self-confident. Not a scared, shy, bumbling boy she knew him to be.

"This is a might unusual and informal in the extreme, but I am Detective Jenkins and I think you have met Captain Rogers." He introduced himself and extended his hand, which AJ graciously accepted.

"Is there any progress with finding our missing friends?" AJ asked the officer.

Capt. Rogers looked over at Detective Jenkins as he exclaimed, "We are working on it, trust me!"

Tommy caught the gaze of Dr. Jacobs as he walked out of the kitchen after he put their fresh catch in the refrigerator and for a moment their eyes locked. Tommy froze as they stared at one another, each one sizing the other one up for dominance and control. Odd sensations came over the Doc. He felt tested in some manner. He felt he was being threatened, threatened for his territory and threatened on seniority. A tense couple of seconds crept by until Tommy, the weaker one, looked away.

"In the back of my mind I cannot help but imagine those emerald eyes watching from below me assuring that our baby would survive my family. I'm nervous; I worry in the pit of my gut I feel a conflict beginning that would tear me and Aticus apart." Detective Jenkins stopped reading as a nervous unease twisted in his gut.

Tommy had finished putting away the gear and returned to the living room. He tried to ignore Jacobs as he parroted the words that AJ asked the detective, "Any progress finding our friends?"

"Capt. Rogers is working on it." Detective Jenkins stood up from the rocking chair and sized up Sarah's friend Tommy.

"I don't trust anything he's got to say!" Phillip exclaimed in Jenkins head, "I…"

Detective Jenkins interrupted Phillip's ghostly voice, "So you and your friends are staying at this motel instead of your inherited property?"

Jenkins question had been directed at Sarah. She was taken aback a moment, she didn't remember telling the police that she inherited the property, and then sensible reasoning sunk in. They were the police; they made it their business to gather information. Maybe she did tell him about her inheritance. It didn't matter now, they were here and she was grateful.

"I decided it would be better to stay at the motel while we fixed up my place. I worried about the health of my friends between the lead, asbestos, and the possibility of there being black mold on the premises… I would kick myself if something happened to them…" Sarah paused for a second as she thought about her missing friends and the obvious irony of her statement.

Tears ran down her cheeks, threatening her calm composure. She tried to rapidly blink her eyes but they were quickly inflamed and reddening, "we had five rooms in the motel, I wanted to keep them all in case someone came back but… we just have two rooms now."

"So is it you and AJ in one room and Desiree and Tommy in the other room?" Detective Jenkins skeptically inquired.

Sarah quickly countered, "You're right, sort of! AJ sleeps on a cot in the living room by the TV," she involuntarily glanced at Tommy and under her breath she continued, "To protect me at night."

Though Sarah said her comments quietly Tommy heard her scathing remarks and quickly added, "I used to share a cabin with Roxy now I am in Desiree's room … He looked over at Sarah cutting the tension with a hearty laugh, "oh but don't worry, I have no interest in you anymore. For that matter I'm not into Desiree either. In fact with all the time she spends with Vlad, Vad, Viddarr or whatever the name is of the guy who owns that dingy Wolf's Den Tavern. I basically feel like I have the room all to myself."

Sarah crossed her arms as she looked over at Tommy, thinking a moment. He was telling the truth, she could see it in his eyes and his mannerisms. He felt no passionate interest in any one of them anymore. Just a protective sort of kinship that she could see every time he looked at her now that reminded her of an older brother watching out for their younger sibling. The circumstances that surrounded Tommy's abrupt lackluster interest should have felt odd since he had been chasing her around like a little lost puppy ever since college, but she felt tremendous relief that he was not stalking her anymore. She abruptly turned away from Tommy and walked toward the refrigerator, emerging with a peach wine cooler and quickly downing the bottle quenching her thirst.

With the first question out-of-the-way Detective Jenkins dusted off his investigational chops, almost attacking Sarah, "So how long did it take for you to let their cabins go after they didn't come back? You throw away all of your friends things as soon as they went missing? Where are their things? You still work on the property, even after your friends went missing?"

"No, no, no! We took all of their things and put them in the van, careful not to damage them. You can have them if it will help you in your investigation." Sarah peered at detective Jenkins' for the barrage of questioning visibly hurt and betrayed but she quickly shook it off. "My lawyer, Richard LeBeau, told me he would pay any expenses as long as we fix it up and I kept the place, I wanted to hold onto the rooms a little bit longer. Yes, I do still work on the place; physical labor seems to help sidetrack me some so I don't go crazy with worry."

Capt. Rogers scratched his chin deep in thought. Detective Jenkins told him about her diary and the connection to Aticus then and now. Somehow he knew the disappearances, the arsons, the murders were all connected to Sarah, to her diary and to her inherited property, but he feared it would take more proof to substantiate his theory.

"All roads lead to her, you know that, right?" Phillip questioned under his breath as if they could hear him.

Detective Jenkins couldn't deny it, Phillip had been right. Dexter had made a beeline straight for Sarah's property when they were investigating the disappearances. However, Detective Jenkins still didn't know if Sarah was an innocent bystander caught up in this madness or the mastermind behind it all.

As if Philip had read his thoughts, "good luck trying to substantiate this madness, it is like the fairytale, The Boy That Cried Wolf, literally," Phillip laughed nervously, "Adults have a hard time rationalizing the unexplained. They have a habit of denying the supernatural, even if it is thrust in their face!"

"Yeah, you're right, son." Jenkins said to himself.

The phantom conversation had not gone unnoticed with Capt. Rogers, Sarah, and the others, they just silently stared at him.

"Well, I don't know about you guys but the rain has let up and I'm hungry. I'm going to fix a fire in the fire pit. It was nice meeting you guys." AJ said saluting them as he walked out.

As if on cue Detective Jenkins and Captain Rogers looked over at each other and both spoke, "well, we should get going. We left our cards on the table. If you have any more information, do not hesitate to give us a call."

Sarah followed Detective Jenkins, Capt. Rogers, and the Doctor out the door. AJ made quick work of the fire, now a healthy mingling of yellow, orange and red flames dancing around one another, producing heat for the fish. After Tommy gave the fish to AJ he went over to his and Desiree's cabin, closing the door.

After everyone had left Sarah looked up at the Crescent Moon, what a lovely sliver of Moon she thought as she walked over to AJ and the fire.

53

Aticus stood in the doorway of the barn, trees obscuring his view of Sarah's manor. The bright red barn, now dull rust-brown faded from age and neglect. Flimsy boards that were brittle had colonies of termites that had made this their home long ago. The dim light from the windows cast dancing shadows as the flames from the lanterns on the wall moved to and fro. Looking up at the half-moon he couldn't help but smile ear to ear, a toothy smile full of jagged teeth and short fangs, his one good eye glinting green in the moonlight. He inhaled the air around him.

Orphaned and lonely, he found solace with military kinship and learned to think like a General so he thought with military precision and made his battle tactics. Things were going according to his plans. He could smell many more infected in the area. They were strangers to him, except for the distinct aroma surrounding them. He even sensed many more people that were not thinking as radically, Aticus had no hold over them yet, the infection slower to invade their systems. He knew that when the full Moon rose they would go wild and wreak havoc on their towns. Oung and O-kami destroyed any opposition with the strong-willed and resistant to Aticus' demands.

The generator hummed to life again. They were careful to be sure that Sarah, AJ, and Tommy, minus Desiree, were done for the day and safely down the road before they turned the generator back on. James worked with Michael on the next batch of Wolf's Blood crystal. James instructed Michael in a new way of creating the Wolf's blood, full of Lycanthropus Snapdragon flowers and opium that he managed to save before he had exited the compound. Although Matt was silent now and huddled in the corner since he had come to his senses, with his knowledge they had made a mixture of the old world traditional potion with modern pharmaceuticals. Along with So-seti's instructions the larvae combined with the crystals were turning out to be really powerful and extremely infectious.

From the shadows in the corner of the room So-seti quietly and with great care instructed and reassured the growing infected and the children. The children, almost adolescents, were growing rapidly with lupine blood a result of the full moon and pheromones spiking. The resulting lunatic males found the females, breeding in a mass orgy of copulation. Four children sat cross legged, quietly listening to the wisdom and instructions of their elder.

So-seti coddled the adolescents, it fulfilled a desire in her she had noticed since capture, the desire to nurture and protect children. Especially since So-seti's abdomen had grown taut. She could tell that life resided in her compliments of James. She prepared for another quick two months, the conception and labor of a true wolf-thing.

Tonya seductively sauntered over to Aticus, his back turned to her. She resisted the urge to gag and cringe in disgust with the nearness of her murderous leader; however, she would obey her leader. She constantly teased the hell out of him; he could smell her fragrant perfume and the deliberate closeness of her body always killing him as she denied his advances every time. She slowly slid her hand around his thick neck imagining choking the life out of him, but massaging him instead.

Stepping back some Tonya reported, "Oung and O-kami have a line on another dissident in the middle of the black forest. It will be twenty seven that have actively resisted your rule."

"Good, good…" Aticus mused.

Oung emerged from the shadows, his complexion ashen with bloodshot eyes oblivious to everyone. He had just finished regurgitating the glands and heart from another slain resister. He paused, outstretching both arms, his hands against the wall stabilizing him. His long, straight black hair was pasted on his forehead and down against his face as he closed his eyes to get his bearings.

"For you," Oung feebly said in broken English as he flung his arms in the general direction of the thick shadows, "O-kami and his pack of spirit wolves are on the trail of another ancient lycanthrope, I think he is the leader of his den."

"Well done!" Aticus exclaimed pleased, seven separate dens, proud distinct individual dens that were around for millennia that held their separate myths, rituals, beliefs, and rules that govern soon would be united within Aticus' powerful grasp.

Aticus could smell the sweet, sweet flesh that could relieve his hammering headache. He stopped listening after he heard "for you" in Oung's infamous broken English. He could smell the gory entrails on the ground in the corner where O-kami still sat in meditation.

"Good, good," Aticus said under his breath to no one in particular. Like a junkie craving his next fix he fell down on his knees, the junkie digging through the shag carpet, tiny pebbles and lint for an imagined crack rock.

Aticus' heart skipped a beat as he found what he was looking for… two testes, an adrenal gland, thyroid, pituitary gland and he found hiding in the thick shag the Holy Grail of glands, the pineal gland housing the impenetrable parasite larvae. He plucked each and every the gland obscured in the carpet with his fumbling hand then the gulped all six glands down whole. The intricate glob traveling down his gullet and as soon as the glands digested in his stomach his one green eye dilated. Goose pimples traveled up his arms, up and down his spine, and for a moment time stood still. The pressure of small slivers of silver fragments burrowed deep in his brain eased, released him from his pain and agony for just one moment of bliss.

Except for the shaking his body stood rigid for just one moment then he bent down on the carpet again, wildly in search of the heart. The infected and the children shielded their ears as they heard the involuntary growling and disgusting chewing sounds as he swallowed torn pieces of the intricate muscle.

"Excuse me, Aticus," Tomas with Montezmu walked toward the kneeling junkie, Aticus, and waited silent for a moment before they continued in unison, "Aticus… Michael and James are finished with another batch of Crystal."

Aticus wiped his mouth of blood and with one knee twirled around, still kneeling as he acknowledged Michael and James. He had tried to wipe the gore from his chin and cheeks but when he opened his mouth to speak blood and drool pooled from the corners of his lips escaping down his neck and chest.

"Good, Tomas," Aticus looked up; his one good eye looked crazed and luminous, terrifying Tomas and Montezmu who impulsively stumbled backward. Abundant straw piled up like a soft pillow on the dirt floor moving like a tidal wave, a shhhhhhhh sound like a moving snake.

He looked crazy, like a rabid, feral animal, "You and Montezmu take the surplus crystals to Viddarr's establishment. He has connections in Washington and California which could establish our new type of drug in the streets."

Suppressing his fear and mustering up his courage, Tomas held out his hand offering up a baggie full of Crystal. As Aticus quickly snatched the baggie from his hand Tomas could not hide the gathering disgust for his friend's situation. He was addicted to the ecstasy and the escape from the pain that he always felt in his head that came with swallowing whole his fellow lycanthrope.

"I worry about you, Aticus," Tomas said sincerely, Montezmu just silently observed.

In Tomas' culture they only consumed the flesh of their kind if someone died or to decide who was going to lead the pack, the one that loses dies and in a highly ritualized ceremony everybody partakes of his flesh. The segments of flesh divided up by the den, so little there was only a mild buzz felt. In his whole long life this happened only twice.

Consuming all of the lycanthrope's glands and heart by his self was paramount to main-lining a powerful hallucinatory anesthetic. The quick high that he received was accompanied by a drastic low, forcing an unwelcome withdrawal… to chase his high Oung and O-kami killed everyone against him and he hungrily devoured them whole.

"Don't worry, my friend," Aticus patted him on the shoulder while wiping off the rest of the gore, "my grandmother is a shaman and in less than two months she assures me the combination of the perigee full Moon and all hollow's night where the line between the living and dead blur, she will conjure up Aisos, the mother of us all and a more powerful shaman. Aisos should be able to disintegrate the silver screws in her missing legs. Then she can grow her missing limbs back. And she can do something with my missing eye."

"My sweet Aticus," Tonya cringed when she said this, "it is almost midnight."

With a smile Tonya motioned to the rafters, "come with me."

Tonya offered out her hand and Aticus accepted as they climbed together up the ladder to the rafters. They sat cross-legged together, the rafters creaking at the increased weight. He stared at Tonya's beautiful dance, a secret ritual passed down from generation to generation. She could enter someone's dreams. In a trance, properly in tune and along with Tonya's touch, Aticus could enter someone's dreams as well and although hesitant he took her hand to travel into ether.

54

The school bell rang at Pointe Coupee Catholic High School before Kevin had even made it to the doors, stumbling on the bottom step. He made his way to the double glass doors stopping once to take a puff off his prescription inhaler before he made his way inside the hallowed halls.

Kevin had a lanky body and a scraggly appearance. His dirty and unkempt blonde hair stopped just above his uniform collar. He had a green uniform jacket and white button-up shirt that was left un-tucked from his khaki slacks. His worn dress shoes had seen better days. He could not shake the vivid dreams he'd had for three nights now; the mysterious hooded man in the forest with one eye. The dreams were imbedded in his mind. Lucid dreams about the mysterious man in the forest, wolves, a ghostly woman, and running… so much running as he tried keep up with them. He could see himself running on all fours, his hands and feet on the ground, running for miles without tiring, without taking a puff of his inhaler to open up his closing airways. The ghostly woman ran effortlessly keeping pace in the mystic forest of his mind as she laughed. He remembered feeling unstoppable and powerful and he wished the dream would go on forever. It exhilarated him until his alarm clock rang out and he had to get up for another grueling day.

Now he was at school, it was so hectic so noisy. He could barely stand it. He sat down at his desk and tried to ignore it, the teasing and ridicule he received every day. Kevin snuck a peek at his secret crush, Tasha, two rows ahead and to the left of him. He could only see her back but oh what a beautiful back it was, Kevin thought. He had to suffer through three semesters viewing her greatness from afar. He could only see her golden tresses, feathering down, but he could imagine her doe-like blue eyes and warm smile. She didn't know that he existed, but an image of her had been burned into his mind.

"Hey shithead, that's my sister you're staring at!" Brett, the twin sibling of Tasha spat out venomously. "I've had to look at your ugly ass for three years now and I am sick of you!" Brett Traiteur shouted.

Brett had a dimpled chin; high protracted cheekbones on a face that made him look like an over-filled balloon. He had an athlete's physique, a quarterback's frame, a thick neck, a real jock with engorged shoulders like he wore his football shoulder-padding though he wore only a tight T-shirt. He had Tasha's blue eyes, but on his face the blue eyes were cold and brutal, a real goon.

Brett stood up from his desk, one hand held a heavy hardback book, the other a clenched fist. Kevin desperately searched about the room for help, the history teacher Mr. Phelps was nowhere to be seen.

"I meant no disrespect, Brett," Kevin tried to retreat, strategically trying to get between desks and an angry brother, "I didn't intentionally mean to stare at your sister just deep in thought, man..."

"It's time to throw down!" Brett hissed as he faked throwing the heavy history book prompting Kevin to duck down and cover his head.

He spastically stumbled backwards; he craned his neck looking around for any possible reinforcements. However, his hopes quickly sank, no students appeared to be concerned with the squabble or they chose to ignore what was happening close by. Even Brett's sister, Tasha, had her back turned to him, hoping that he would just leave Kevin alone.

"I don't wanna fight you," he meekly pleaded, sliding the desks between him and his aggressor. He stumbled backwards off balance and fell on his ass onto an empty desk seat.

Brett snatched the ends of the desk with his enormous meaty hands. Then he slid the desk forward so he and Kevin were face-to-face. Brett's biceps strained to get the desk halfway up in the air like it was a bicycle popping a wheeling. Kevin suddenly saw the incandescent lights from the ceiling above him before gravity had a hold of him. He felt himself falling backwards, a hard thump smashing his head on the hard ground. The desk now horizontal papers and pages were flapping through the classroom like birds as darkness enveloped him.

When he came to he found himself seated on the desk class in session confused and delirious. Kevin looked for Tasha who stared at him with pity, her blue eyes moist with concern.

"Kevin?" All eyes were on Kevin as Mr. Phelps stopped a well-practiced but monotone and boring speech to form the question.

Mr. Phelps waited for Kevin to respond. Phelps was a tall, dark skin African-American, who was well-traveled and spoke with a French accent. His pristine bright white collared dress shirt and light tan Dockers made an even more noticeable contrast with his dark skin. He had a creased and furrowed face, as his sixty-two years suggested. He had short black, curly hair and extremely big ears. One large gold hoop earring helped to offset his lazy eye, the other golden eye trained on Kevin.

No response...

He formed the question again, this time hushed whispers could be heard in the classroom, but no response came from Kevin.

"Kevin?" Mr. Phelps queried his voice authoritative and stern.

Phelps had grown tired of Kevin's absences. He was out of the classroom more than he was in, and when given his assignment his daydreaming and procrastination had become annoying. He had had enough; he blew up at him the likes of which the world hadn't seen since the Great Explosion of the Krakatau Volcano in Indonesia.

"Kevin Reynoll, I am talking to you! Can you hear me, boy?" Phelps yelled, "I'm tired of you ignoring and disrespecting me in my own classroom!"

"What... Excuse me?" Kevin came to his senses just in time to see Mr. Phelps staring at him, his ranting foreign to him.

Kevin had a splitting headache and a severe concussion from hitting his head, his whole world in a spin. He couldn't comprehend what Mr. Phelps had asked him. He beheld Brett, who tried ignoring Kevin and pretending he wasn't involved in a scuffle.

"I just about had enough of this!" Mr. Phelps bent down and hastily scratched out a reprimand on his notepad, "if you're not going to pay attention in my class go to the principal's office, I will stand for no more distractions."

Mr. Phelps beat his fist against the top of his desk, graded pages flowing up in the air like a butterfly catching the breeze, taking flight. Kevin jumped straight up out of his seat. Phelps gave Kevin the pass forcefully, which he begrudgingly accepted.

Kevin didn't fully understand what had taken place, but with the tone of Mr. Phelps' voice and the familiar yellow slip he complied, "yes, yes, sir..."

A brief discussion in the principal's office validated what he already knew would happen; a five day suspension. Kevin waited outside in the hall until the bell rang, freeing the students. He went to his locker and put away his books. This was his chance, he thought. He snuck out into the courtyard and sidled along the sidewalk.

Playing hooky from Pointe Coupee Central High School, home of the Cougars, John Chism was free to answer his cell phone. He sat astride his bike in the back of the strip mall by the railroad tracks, at the area the kids' affectionately called "the dips" where they could off-road and get wasted. The call prompted him to cross over the railroad tracks and head east on Highway 1, zigging and zagging until he arrived at 504 Fourth Street West, Kevin's Catholic High School.

"Hey buddy! What's up?" John Chism's steel-toed boots came into contact with the gravel, stabilizing the silver BMW, 2013 R1200GS Enduro motorcycle until it came to a full stop then he pulled off his helmet.

"Can you give me a ride home?" Kevin questioned.

Kevin Reynoll and John Chism were childhood friends, they went to the same Catholic grade school together, played together, even stayed the night at one another's place when they were young. But a messy divorce split the pair up. The broken Chism family bowed out of the Catholic experience and registered with Pointe Coupee Central High School, John had started another life, but they couldn't help but keep in touch with each other. Kevin started to pull away from their straining relationship because of John's suspected drug use and his new unsavory friends and they hadn't reunited for three months until Kevin's call.

However, today, Kevin needed a ride and John faithfully delivered, with a grateful attitude he said, "Of course I can!"

Kevin hopped on the BMW and they were off. The Enduro roared through the back streets and off-road until he arrived at Kevin's trailer.

"Well man, I hate to drop you off and run but I think I fucked up something on my bike when I jumped it at the dips and I need to get home and check this mother fucking thing out," John waited until Kevin got off his bike before continuing, "Maybe we can get together sometime soon since you are suspended from school." John said with a grin.

"Yeah," Kevin hesitated, smelling the pungent aroma of marijuana coming from John's jacket, "yeah, yeah, we'll see, thanks again, man."

He opened the door and said his hellos but nobody responded. He could feel the fire burning in his lungs, a horrible feeling he had been growing accustomed to, his lungs closing up on him again. He clutched his hand to his chest. His heart rate was increasing. He searched for his emergency inhaler in his pocket, looking around at the quiet and empty living room.

His grandmother, Betty, the one who had raised him had been hospitalized yet again and he had the house all to himself. A precious secret that he guarded fiercely lest a nosey bystander, children services, or any friends find out he managed a household all alone.

He thought about his emergency inhaler and headed toward his room. Greeted with wall to wall horror posters a normal child would be frightened, even the mirrors were covered with the latest gory flick, but not Kevin. He practically pole vaulted to his bed plopping onto it with his entire body. After taking a puff he wasted the day away watching videos and cable television until he fell asleep.

Pretty soon a cacophony of howling across the dreamscape chilled Kevin to the core, but not in a bad way. Excitement ran through him as he beheld the familiar surreal full Moon of his dreams again. The Moon undulated, following him, alive with colors bolder, brighter, exotic colors throughout the night sky. The big strange Moon followed Kevin through an enchanted forest. Soothing bells could be heard on the calming winds. Dream catchers flowed from side to side on trees like they were forbidden fruit.

"Kevin," the disembodied voice of a woman called out to him, "come… come to me."

He searched around for the disembodied voice so inviting and comforting, "where are you?"

Slow rolling fog in front of him. Suddenly he heard a sound coming from the brush behind him. Soft footfalls made him twirl around to see a woman who was unclothed and terribly scarred. The scars traveled down the right side, right arm on down to the thigh, ending at the knee and her cheek seemed to have mild sunburn. The essence of beauty nonetheless, with her hour glass figure and seductive smile, who could resist Tonya's charms? Her almond eyes were huge and unusual with her Navajo ancestry and her glowing eyes changing color in the moonlight.

"He has a gift for you, sweetheart." Tonya whispered softly in his ear and pointed into the darkness. Kevin peered at the thick fog obscuring his view.

He could hear footfalls coming from directly in front of him, instantly putting him on guard, his body went rigid. The rolling fog dissipating until he could see a dark shadow take shape, human in form.

"Do you wish to be all that you could be?" The stranger's visage obscured by shadows but his one glowing green eye showing through the thick fog.

The stranger thrust his hand into Kevin's hair and finding the large lump in the back of his head. His eyes adjusted to the dim light and he could see the cloaked figure more clearly under his hood. He saw the stranger's one brilliant emerald eye, in it a look of savagery and vicious cunning.

"You are man enough. I have something for you. I can make you powerful; I can make you strong without compare…" The stranger pulled forth from his cloak a Wolf print mug full of glowing liquid.

The woman sauntered up next to Kevin, gingerly placing her hands upon his shoulders, "Aticus could bring you vengeance from your bully called Brett. He could bring vengeance upon everyone that ridicules you."

"What did you say?!" That's impossible, Kevin thought, but then he came to his senses, "of course she knows my thoughts and experiences, I am dreaming."

He could see Aticus' feet through the sparse fog. Aticus' feet were not feet at all but large furry paws. He began to hyperventilate. Just dreaming, he told himself, but his lungs began to close up.

"Inhaler!" He searched for his life saver but had no luck.

"I can make you werewolf…" Offering the large mug to Kevin, "I can make you a werewolf strong and bold… You can get your vengeance upon Brett."

As he stood wheezing and gasping for breath Kevin pled, "Make me a werewolf then, I beg of you."

Aticus produced an unknown, powdery substance and began dropping it into the large cup filled with the flowing liquid. He swirled the mixture around and spit into the cup for good measure. As he offered it, Kevin gratefully accepted it. He greedily gulped it down. Instantly he gagged his throat on fire and his lungs inflamed.

"Now you're a werewolf..." Aticus smiled his mischievous smile as Tonya howled.

Kevin's body began to feel strange as Tonya howled Aticus' orders. He felt his lungs beginning to inflate once again, his muscles began to engorge then he blacked out.

The sun warmed his face when he awoke. He convinced himself it had been just a dream. However, he found himself outside, shirtless with torn jeans and no shoes.

"What sorcery is this?" He had gone to bed in his room dreaming of wolves and a man in the forest who gave him a drink that gave him extreme power, but it was just a dream, wasn't it? Did he sleepwalk all through the night?

Dazed and confused, his hands gripped the grass that was still wet with dew. He had remembered going camping when he was younger, waking up in the morning wheezing and trying to catch his breath, then two or three puffs off his inhaler before he could enjoy the day. But this morning he could breathe naturally in and out, unhindered by his asthma. He found himself breathing strongly and naturally.

Confusion set in, looking around at the strange town he found himself in. He saw a sign that said "Welcome to Plaucheville, Louisiana-Population 248 souls". From his calculations he had to walk almost fifty miles before making it back to his hometown of New Roads. It's a good thing that he was suspended from school and no one would be home. Instead of walking he thought he would try his luck running with his new found lungs and legs. He couldn't place his finger on it but he had changed somehow, for the better. In fact when his suspension had lifted he thought he might even try his luck at track.

55

Maurice Jackson sat at the Gas -N- Go, a week's worth of stubble on his chin, sipping coffee. He remembered a storm not unlike this one that poured down. He remembered huge wet drops sadistically in nature beating down those that were unlucky enough to be outside. Maurice ran for the closest shelter out of the rain, another gas station with tables so he wouldn't get soaked. He shivered as he recalled his strange encounter. From the corner of his eye he saw the blonde girl from the emergency room in the plate glass window obscured by the steady rain. He had an uneasy feeling that he had been followed.

The onslaught of rain concealed her form from the alley where she stood wet and naked. Maurice peered at her from a safe distance across the street. The short blonde girl crinkled her nose and inhaled. She had tracked Maurice's familiar scent for days. Now, she found him in the flesh. She quickly snapped her head toward Maurice, pointing her finger at the obscured window of the quickie Mart where Maurice sat. Even though the window panes were hazy with fog he could see her shining yet hollow, animalistic eyes.

"It's miserable out there isn't it?" The cashier innocently questioned, her elbows resting on the counter, hands tucked under her chin.

"Yes, you don't mind if I stay to weather the storm in here, do you?" Maurice asked finishing his bitter cup of coffee and hoping desperately there was 12 ounces or more in the carafe left.

"Oh, I don't mind, you can keep me company." The cashier laughed, she read his mind walking over to make a fresh pot, the rich and bold aroma filling the store. "The rain is keeping most my regulars away it seems."

Maurice looked over at the window to search for the girl again and was startled. Two more figures had joined the blonde girl. Two pair of penlight eyes stared at Maurice through the foggy window.

"So how is your morning starting off?" The perky cashier's eyes turned to Maurice, trying to start a conversation by the coffee maker but Maurice didn't hear her.

"What...Sorry, what did you say?" Maurice questioned, returning his eyes to the girl, he searched for the other frightening strangers who were now nowhere in sight.

The bells ringing gently as the doors to the store swung opened, letting in harsh stinging rain and saturating the large rugs all over the shiny polished floor. A musky aroma inundated the room. The cashier stopped cleaning the counter and looked up. A strong wet dog odor flooded the store that made the cashier involuntarily blink her eyes and wrinkle her nose.

"Good afternoon," The cashier shivered uncontrollably as she looked over at the odd men coming in out of the rain.

Tomas only nodded respectively in recognition shaking off the mud and water on his boots as he headed toward the unwashed tables and Maurice. He sat down on the bench adjacent to Maurice and folded his hands and smiled at him.

"Good afternoon to you," Montezmu replied in a smooth voice, eyes that seemed to change with his mood shown a faint Yellow reddish hue stared at the cashier wantonly. He proceeded to turn the sign from "open" to "closed" then latched the door, "we'll just be a moment here."

"Suzy, it is Suzy, isn't it?" Montezmu turned to face the frightened cashier gesturing at her disposable ID stuck onto her white colored shirt and flashed a smile, "you are a beautiful woman; do you know that?"

Suzy stood frozen with fear, her face flushed an ash color making her that much whiter in her bleach white uniform shirt.

"Is this…" Suzy hesitated, her heart racing, "a robbery?"

"No, no, my dear," Montezmu said, holding her hand and then softly blowing his long hair back from his eyes.

Maurice sat mesmerized, there before his eyes were the creatures that night after night he dreamed about. He saw several transdermal piercings in their skulls, noticed their strange dress, Montezmu wore a homemade tunic and pants made out of a strange leather. Tomas wore loose fitting pants and a handmade hooded robe.

Montezmu's pheromones and liquid voice were intoxicating and with every breath Suzy felt dizzy, off kilter, a little less on edge each time she breathed in his aroma. Her loins began to feel warm and against her better judgment she was exhilarated, goose pimples running down her arm with his touch.

"I am proud of Alle for finding you!" Tomas motioned over toward the blonde girl across the street, I am proud of her skills; she is becoming a superb tracker."

All of Maurice's dreams come flooding back to him, *I'm coming for you.*

"We have a proposition for you," Tomas said, he had just eaten and his sour breath smelled like decaying game, making Maurice recoil as he patted his shoulder a little bit too hard, making him flinch in pain.

Maurice did not say anything to Tomas but turned to the window to see the girl motionless, her hair soaked by the rain as she stood statue-like, as though she was obeying some silent order to be still. He silently stressed about Suzy, the cashier who had taken Montezmu's hands and was being pulled backwards toward the back room. In a trance-like state Suzy stared into Montezmu's eyes. Maurice could tell from her frightened but somehow exhilarated eyes that in her mind she resisted this bizarre man but her body had other plans altogether.

His powerful preternatural pheromones were intoxicating her, reminding her of a spring time rain or summertime mist and sending her subconscious into wild abandon as she walked backwards on autopilot toward the employee door. Montezmu had a dominant presence and he seemed to tower over the trembling cashier as he pushed open the swinging doors for Suzy.

"I see you were bitten, weren't you?" Tomas grabbed Maurice's scarred forearm, his dark smoldering eyes like an animal's eyes frightened Maurice he felt like a tiny midget staring up at a monstrous giant.

Maurice felt an urge to reply, like he had to oblige him with an answer, "yes."

Tomas examined and scrutinized Maurice's wound, "it is not, healing is it?"

Tomas' inquiry had been more an observation than a question so Maurice remained silent, he just shook his head no and intently listened. In the back of the store he heard the sound of struggle. Sounds that reminded him of dogs, clanging water and drain pipes from the bathroom sounding like a rattling cage in the animal shelter. By the employee back room there came a horrid snarling, growling, yapping and moaning. All of the turmoil sounded like a stray dog scrounging for delicious scraps of meat. All sounds except for the moaning, a decidedly human sound that amplified in pitch and frequency until a crescendo.

"You are lucky you are not to be meat for the Wolves. You are kin to our pack." Tomas flashed a smile.

Again Maurice remained silent.

His teeth reminded him of a nursery rhyme, how does the nursery rhyme go? Maurice thought *my how many teeth you have...* No, no, that's not right! *My, what big teeth you have*, he thought about the stranger's teeth which were peculiar and plentiful, too numerous to be human, Maurice thought. Certainly they were too sharp.

Ignoring the sighs and moans coming from the back room Tomas continued his proposition, "For sparing your life, we need something of you. Come with us and meet our leader… Aticus. He has a job for you."

Suddenly bright white headlights pierced the rain and in the parking lot a SUV was heading to the gas pumps. Nobody noticed the "closed" sign on the door or the two men seated in the store, the substantial deluge obscuring their view inside. Tomas sniffed the subtle changes in the air all around them. He whipped his head around searching for the petite blonde girl getting drenched by the rain. She had moved back into the shadows so she wouldn't be seen by anyone but she still waited as instructed.

"Come now, we must go to Raccourci Island, before we get caught!" Tomas instructed reaching out his hand toward Maurice.

Maurice felt weak with all the staggering new information. He felt shaky and dizzy but he complied taking Tomas' hand.

On his feet before he knew it. He found himself being dragged like a children's cherished blanket or a stuffed bear to the back room. The swinging door slammed into the wall knocking mops and brooms down like dominoes.

Tomas proceeded forward to the restroom doors, alerting Montezmu. He opened the door immediately expelling the aroma of sex, gore and robust wild mongrel. He stumbled out of the bathroom disheveled and clutching his tunic. Maurice's color drained from his face at the sight of this half man, half beast. He had a lupine form, elongated pointed ears, glowing red eyes, enormous ivory fangs with snow white fur from its head on down to the base of its spine. He had snow white fur until an extended muzzle which was soaked in crimson blood.

There standing before him in flesh and blood was the monster of his nightmares, coming face to face with the flesh rending Wolf-thing he had an odd calm come over him, he looked into Montezmu's yellow eyes and he was assured he would not attack. No longer afraid, Maurice came to his senses.

"Get the security tapes!" Maurice yelled, even though he had no naturally occurring fingerprints the security tapes would show everyone's faces.

Bubbling and cracking, Montezmu's lupine face already reverting to human form, he growled, "Do what you have to do, we will wait for you in the shadows of the parking lot. If we get separated the girl will find you and then instruct you on where to go."

Maurice was already heading into the office and just nodded, he understood. He saw one outside monitor, another inside monitor. Pressing eject for both DVDs he heard people trying to open the doors. Probably the two men that wanted to get gas Maurice mused. He had worked enough jobs in the gas station /convenience store industry that he knew a trick or two to unlock the cash register. He pressed a hidden button in the cash register bottom till slid open with a happy "Ding". He seized a miniscule amount of money, at least, he thought, when the police get here they'll think it's a robbery.

He didn't want to stick around and find out. Keeping low and making sure the counters came between Maurice and the windows he slowly crept toward the back room. As soon as the swinging doors swung closed Maurice got up on his feet and was headed toward the exit door when he heard moaning coming from the bathroom.

Even with his dark complexion he could not hide the embarrassment of his reddening cheeks when he saw the unconscious body on the floor in the corner of the room. The cashier had her clothing torn off and was lying spread-eagle on the floor. Maurice saw blood everywhere, on the walls, on the floor, even on the ceiling. Her eyes were closed; blackened masses of bruises could be seen on her neck, breasts, and inner thighs. Peering closer still he could see deep fang marks before his modest sensibility got the best of him and he covered her up with her torn clothing.

Looking at the broken and battered, beaten and bruised prone body of the cashier, Suzy, an unusual aroma began to invade Maurice's senses. It didn't take long for Maurice to formulate his theory. She had been bitten extensively, breaking skin, and was raped mercilessly. However, he could smell the almost mortal wounds which were already beginning to heal. She was becoming one of the things of his nightmares, he just knew it. Then she opened her eyes and it was confirmed... Glowing bright animal eyes looked over at him before she closed her eyes and moaned, slipping into unconsciousness again.

Maurice found himself out the door and running in the parking lot. Alle, the blonde tracker, ran beside him instructing him to their den on Raccourci Island.

Maurice shook the memories off. He found himself exhausted and in Hessmer, Louisiana now sipping lukewarm, bitter coffee to keep his energy up. He clutched for dear life the contraband as he got up from the table, strolling through aisle after aisle. Although he seemed oblivious to the infection he had new gifts anyways and one of them being that he could smell the infected and the healthy alike.

He impatiently waited for the rest of the Mexican Mafia, the Surenos, with their connections to smuggle contraband through to Alexandria, Louisiana, then on Houston, Texas then through California and Mexico. He had done this run a dozen times now but he still felt nervous. A persistent knock on the store window startled him. He unlocked the door to let a brown scraggly haired Sureno with an outrageous mustache in.

An older Mexican with a handlebar mustache asks, "Hey friend, ya got our product?"

"Yes, yes, I do." Maurice handed over a brown paper bag and the Mexican nicknamed "Knife" brought out and carefully opened a vacuum plastic bag full of pink crystals which he greedily inhaled through his nose.

Knife's body began tensing, muscles began to engorge and his eyes began to glow, "good, good... This is some amazing shit!"

56

Deserted Wolf Town

The Hunter slowly drove by on his Can-Am Spyder, 3-wheel motorcycle with oversized leather saddlebags that held the rest of his trapping and assorted supplies. Riding on the bike he could smell the roses and the aroma of lily flowers and also the infected all around him. He had on a German motorcycle half-helmet exposing his long silver hair that hung in a ponytail. He had squinty eyes that seemed somnolent, golden in color but they looked wise, oppressive with a constant look of steely determination. He had a scruffy appearance, with a weathered look to his forehead. He had a bulky leather satchel strapped on his right shoulder. He didn't bother to conceal the fact that he had a sawed off shotgun on the right side, a rifle on the left side, and two handguns in his waistband.

After receiving what amounted to a desperate phone call from his superior, Dr. Byron Atkins, with the green light to search for, find, and destroy any lycanthropes that may have come to Louisiana he tried to smell subtle changes in the air. He had a line on the red marked and white haired stranger staying at the Point Breeze motel. He had staked out the motel for months but as of yet he proved elusive to capture and kill. When the reporter had gone for a day of research several times he had broken into her motel room to capture the white haired stranger, but as always, he disappeared. Downwind from the Hunter he could swear that the stranger had watched his every move. Eventually he had to keep moving. There was the matter of several escaped lunatics and the ringleader to deal with. He carefully navigated the overgrown brush and neglected gravel pathways through a hundred yards of thick trees and neglected farmland leading to the forgotten sugarcane plantation.

The Hunter slowed to navigate the overgrown weeds and the potholes in the road. He put his feet down on the grass to stabilize the bike as he bumped on down the gravel road. He explored the outer perimeter of the island first.

The motorcycle came to a crawl due to the rocks and weeds reclaiming the gravel road but still the bike staggered onward. The bike lurched forward and faltered, he leaned on the handlebars before righting himself again. The ground began slowly absorbing the wheels then his feet, water creeping out like a sponge. Leaving the rifle and shotgun, but patting his waistband to assure that he still had two guns in the holsters, he abandoned the bike before the three wheels could sink up to the spokes and the driveshaft. Carefully trudging through the forest he found the first shack by the swamp near the river. It was an old hunting shack he assumed from the isolated placement and had burnt down to the ground and long since been abandoned. He walked a mile and half away before he found the first of six servant shacks. They were long since abandoned too. He broke out from the thick jumble of trees to see the white manor in the distance.

His legs ached from the efforts of traversing natural obstacles, through the weeds and muck. He scrounged around on his knees carefully moving blades of grass looking at the dirt for clues of the lycanthrope's existence. An unknown werewolf marked this territory acre to acre, north to south, east to west. A unique and very faint smell to a human being, but the Hunter had tracked the supernatural for years. He had become accustomed to the familiar pungent odor and now for him it felt like the primate enclosure at the zoo. He surveyed the clearing.

He could see the renovated manor. By the look of things, he could tell the occupants were there every few days or so fixing the house up but nobody appeared to have been there today.

There were no telltale signs of the werewolves' presence either. No deep scratches strategically placed wall to wall, a secret lycanthrope language of their own, an indication of their den, suggesting only human habitation. He brought out maps of the Raccourci Island area. He had found a burnt hunting cabin, six servant shacks and the manor itself. However, he saw a clearing that was large enough to accommodate a barn, and caught the strong stench which hung heavy in the clearing, but he couldn't find the barn itself. Perhaps the barn had burned down in the war, he thought.

He grimaced; there were signs of a heavy werewolf presence, but no clue to their whereabouts at the present time so he backtracked. He sluggishly trudged over the spongy wet ground until he saw his motorcycle again. Hopping onto the Spyder he slowly backed it up until he hit firm ground.

Observing town after town he had come to the painful conclusion that the infection had spread beyond the several purposely burned down shacks, trailers and houses. He drove down to Belcher, with six-hundred and seventy people the streets were empty outside and not a car in sight. Then on down to Plaucheville with nearly three-hundred residents, the same thing as Belcher, each neighborhood looked empty, abandoned. He pressed the clutch in, down-shifting the motorcycle to ride slower, inspecting the area of Pollock with three-hundred, seventy six residents. On down to Saline, Calvin, and then Ida, Louisiana which all had less than three-hundred residents, and on to the border of Arkansas; all a virtual rural wasteland, everywhere he stopped now were ghost towns.

He crisscrossed the land, gathering more clues to report to his superiors. The engine sputtered and coughed, severe punishment of the drive almost too much for the motorcycle to endure until he came to Hessmer; with a population of eight-hundred, where he gave the bike a rest, parking at the US Post Office. He could smell the newly changing. The weak-willed exhibited some manner of normalcy, never knowing the beast that raged inside them.

Residents in this town went on with their daily lives, going to work, doing yard work, cutting their lawn or just rocking on a porch swing. He felt several eyes staring at him. He glanced around and saw six people in the corner of a gas station/Laundromat. Latino or Hispanic features. They were dressed the same with pants drooped down to their boxer shorts, white wife beater tank tops with brown shoulder holster peeking out from a button-down blue checkered shirts, and had blue bandannas, intently watching Hunter's every move. A gang of some sort, Hunter thought. By the smell of them those men were not aware of the beast that raged inside of them but due to extreme neurological changes they were obligated to fulfill the alpha wolf's beckon and call, kin through the blood he thought. There were too many of them, he thought, he didn't want to wear out his welcome just yet.

He turned onto Highway 1, stopping to check for clues at New Roads through Batchelor, LA. The sun set as he arrived at another small deserted town, Royal Bay. The streets were empty, newspapers piled up in yards. Cars resting in driveways, dust covered, where the occupants left it. A soft breeze blew across Hunter's face as he stopped in front of a house its lights were on in broad daylight. He cautiously walked up the driveway.

A Rottweiler, obviously a guard dog, threw itself against the window from the adjacent house nearby and barked his alarm. Hunter stepped and stumbled as he looked at the crazed dog. Signs of neglect were painfully obvious. He could see the bones protruding out of his side as fleas hopped across his dripping muzzle. Scars on the lips that had bled and scabbed up told him he had been trying to eat his own face. Signs the dog had been trapped in the house for weeks. Barking furiously as the Hunter approached the neighbors' front door.

Shaking off his initial start he withdrew a gun from its holster as he checked the door. It was unlocked. He swung it open, opening wide into a well lived in house. The TV still blared and it felt hot to the touch. Popcorn and beer sat on the coffee table. He scooped up and consumed a handful, the kernels were stale, and then he sipped the warm flat beer. He switched the TV off with the remote, the house warm and toasty but there were no signs of life within.

"Hello?" Hunter called out but silence was the only reply.

He walked over to the next room to discover the source of the heat. One of the burners on the stove top was still on, red hot, like a bright bull's-eye. The pots that sat on the other burner were smoking as the last of the water had evaporated. He shut off the stove, sweat already shimmering on his forehead. He wiped his head with his sleeve and shrugged his shoulders. He assumed the owners of the house had left in a hurry.

Damn, something was really wrong he saw it as soon as he entered the living room. A bird cage hung on the wall near the fireplace. Bars broke and bent out of place. Two large birds lay motionless upon the fresh bloody newspaper in the cage. The colorful exotic birds were decapitated, lying in their own fluids.

A chill ran up his spine, the hair tingling on the back of his neck. He tightened his grip on the revolver as he climbed up, the stairs groaning under his weight. As he turned the corner with his hand still on the stair rail he saw them. An older couple lying on the bed, the bedroom door opened before them. His pulse quickened, unsure what to make of the scene. He called out to the couple as he approached.

No response...

He tried again... he heard nothing.

Hunter stood in the doorway watching closely the older gentleman. He had a half crown of hair that circled his head from temple to temple, his face was pale and wrinkled and on his oval face was several day's growth of silver stubble on his chin. His heart sank when he realized the elder gentleman had the parasite, they were invading his fragile body, were it true he will stay in a coma, dead yet alive, his body in a state of suspended animation until the next full moon.

He cautiously felt his arm. He flinched; it was hot to the touch. He felt for a pulse but he could not find one. No wait… there it was, a beat a few times a minute. Was it a true heartbeat? He edged even closer, there was a faint jolt, like a defibrillator going off forcing the heart to once again beat. The parasite was keeping them alive but just barely. The Hunter knew from experience a weak frail host could not endure the transformation and eventually the brain would atrophy. Just the primal instinct of the brainstem would manage to survive. The only thing that survives is the primitive brain, a wolf's brain, the simple brainstem that the parasite needed to survive with the host until the next full moon when they will wake out of hibernation and breed again. The elderly woman that lay next to the old man was curled up in a ball at his side, as motionless as the man. The Hunter now turned his attention to her. She had the same temperature and pulse as her mate. And they seemed to be in a deep sleep. The Hunter shook them both violently, but to no avail.

He turned his attention on the phone near the bedside picking the receiver up. He had to check in with The God's Light, and report on his progress. The Hunter felt the bed shake, and looked in time to see a wrinkled hand snapping a hold of his shoulder, long nails growing from the finger tips, digging into the Hunter's flesh.

He saw the beast, fury in its animal eyes, a blood lust. Sound was coming from somewhere deep inside a mouth full of teeth as it snarled in delight. The Hunter dropped the phone, reaching down in desperate effort for his gun. Short course hair rippled across the silver-haired man's face as it contorted into a dog-like man beast. Its shoulders drooping, the pajama top ripped open showing sparse silver fur like hairs visible at its ridiculously long stretched sinewy neck. It's impossible! The Full Moon is still a week away, yet more and more he could see with his own eyes the old man had awakened and was going through the transformation.

The beast tossed Hunter across the room with a minimal strain of effort, as it stumbled from the bed onto its feet. Jean slid up the wall, a piercing pain stabbing him in his side as he clambered to his feet. He eyed the gun with longing; it seemed like a million miles away resting on the nightstand between the silver haired beast and the bed. The silver haired wolf man leaned in, his breath putrid and stale, its claws dug into the Hunter's shoulders. It sniffed him up and down his body and then it started a low, guttural snarl. Even though they were in a coma like state, the married couple could still hear and smell the intruder, a rudimentary security system the old man had awakened to protect his mate.

He subscribed to several tabloids like *The National Enquirer, The Star, The Sun, The Eclipse*, and a host of other magazines to keep up with the bizarre, weird, unusual and the supernatural. He had to rifle through myths, bogus sightings, and pure shit… like the sightings of the famous "bat boy" of *The Sun* magazine. Only one or two articles in the tabloids he subscribed to had a fragment of truth to it. For all his investigations, *The Eclipse* Magazine's articles by Amy Anderson were surprisingly factual... all true actually. In his line of work seldom did he find all of the reports were genuine fact. He steadied himself with an elbow on the wall, dizzy and lightheaded from blood loss due to his shoulder wounds. Then a horrible realization came to mind. He stared at the mythic embodiment of death itself and he had been caught off guard. He closed his eyes, preparing for razor sharp teeth rendering his leathery flesh.

Hunter flashed back to where he survived an almost fatal encounter with the beast a long time ago. Before the forest had been an open area now he found himself trapped in the bedroom. He felt the warm wet urine spreading down his legs, saturating his pants. Suddenly he heard a loud wet gasp coming from the bed. The beast heard the sound too. He felt its hands loosen up.

The Wolf Man released the Hunter and jumped toward the bed, the old woman's body lurching as he landed. The old woman's eyes bugged out, mouth open; a pool of saliva darkened the area of the bed. Her heart was beating so fast you could see it through her chest. Her head snapped back and her shoulders arched. She uttered incoherent sounds as fluids spilled over her lips. A purplish red black welt spread throughout her chest as she turned a sick pale gray color.

The old man had a yeti-like appearance with his sprouts of silver fur. Bigfoot-like monstrosity which had him thinking of all those Bigfoot sightings across the United States, no time to dwell on this though as he reached for another weapon. The silver monstrosity with the gray torn, striped PJs had its attention diverted from the Hunter, seemingly more concerned for his wife.

In an almost tearful manner the husband had completely ignored The Hunter to aid his ailing wife. He gently scooped up his dying wife letting out a sorrowful lupine howl. The first time in years Hunter's heart began to ache. The love that he had for her had been obvious even through the lupine haze of instinct and survival. Even with the fast and powerful healing process trying to heal her heart, her heart was too weak to complete the first and critical amalgamation to becoming both human and beast. He hated to kill the lovers, especially since the old woman was dying anyway.

He slowly bent down; his eyes never leaving his target, to retrieve his knife strapped to his calf. He had forgotten what a normal life felt like he had hunted the abominations for so long that only fragments of memory remained. At one time he had had land and a simple home. He had been a farmer once, hadn't he?

Quick as a cobra's strike he restrained the old, but in no means weak, man-beast in a choke hold with his left arm, his knife finding the pulsing artery in the old beast's wrinkled neck. The knife slicing through to the spine breaking bone, his muscle memory from all his work kicking in, until the infected head rolled onto the bed.

The quick hot artery spray warmed his face. He closed his eyes and for a moment he was reminded of his youth back in France and summer time shower and that caught him by surprise before he could run for shelter. He smiled at his misspent, but innocent childhood. While he was lost in this time for a moment, just one moment, everything seemed bright, cheery, and right with the world.

The smell of metallic iron inundated the air; Hunter came to his senses when he tasted the salty copper liquid on his tongue. Gagging, he quickly spit, found his flask in his pocket and unscrewed the lid gulping the medicinal spirits. He gargled and spit then repeating the process again.

Gripping the bloody knife he poised it over the wife's heart but hesitated. The Old woman's heart was in full-blown arrest, He could see the heart struggling, her chest heaving under her sheer nightgown. Animalistic eyes that glinted when they caught the light just right were open wide but they were vacant. She let loose a guttural growl, exhaled once and then went still the heart stopped. Then, like an ode to lovers everywhere, the stricken couple lying in bed, holding hands for the last time.

He knew there was a week before the next full moon, his body had been conditioned to tell the moon's cycles. He had hunted the abominations for so long he had gotten complacent. The old man waking up from their coma to a perceived threat and changing before his eyes had actually frightened him. He had not seen anything like that before. In his experience only through the pack to learn the mysteries of transformation, the ancient, or the powerful could change forms at will. However, apparently the old man in the coma awoke the primeval senses activated an early warning system of sorts; it was a crude survival mechanism spontaneously, instinctively changing the comatose man to protect the love of his life. He felt the heat of embarrassment as it rushed through him. He smelled the urine odor and felt his wet pants. For the first time in all his long years he was surprised, frightened and a little embarrassed.

As he quickly made way hi*s* outside he could not help but think of *The Eclipse* Magazine and articles by Amy Anderson and the tattooed faced missing man. He turned on the engine and rolled down the driveway. The motorcycle only turned down the main road a few feet before he heard close by an explosion, the shockwave threatening to topple the motorcycle on its side if not for the fact of the can-am's three wheel stability, another sign that he had chosen his transportation well! The motorcycle slowly rolled down the main street and into Royal Bay. The town had become a ghost town. Communication towers were torn down and a closer inspection revealed fang and claw marks. Streetlights were down as well, blocking the road.

The auxiliary power station was nothing more than a scrap yard. A ten foot fence was no more. The generators were knocked back from their concrete anchors, only long deep scars remained. The primary power lines, secondary power lines, and ground wires were cut and destroyed, the transformer, circuit breaker, current transformer, lightning arrester, main transformer, and control building all looked like a tornado blew by knocking down the wall and roof on the concrete foundation.

However, the towers that looked like the Eiffel Tower were tilted, and leaning looking more like The Tower of Pisa. The darkness quickly set in, save for the orange incandescent glow of the inferno raging unchecked. He remained armed to the teeth as he was made keenly aware he was completely and utterly alone and helpless when he thought he saw shadows coming from the houses, human figures, coming to the fire, he thought. He throttled the engine, the drivetrain responding in kind. His mind was playing tricks on him; he tried to convince himself, better get on the highway and put the eeriness behind him.

Not for the first time grateful he chose the Spyder, 3-wheel motorcycle as he maneuvered the bike through the downed power line poles safely and was once again on his way to New Roads, to search for Amy Anderson. He had a few ideas where she might be, first the motel, then the libraries, he grunted; it would be a long night.

57

Aticus could barely stand the intoxicating aroma coming from all over the house now, invigorating yet scaring the hell out of him too. Sarah's scent was all over the manor, but it was Alicia's natural aroma as well, wasn't it? Even with her helpers slowly dwindling he could still see with his one good eye how far she had come on fixing up the place.

Aticus braved Sarah's termite rotten deck, his enormous hands resting on the half painted white wash rail. He had snuck in yet again when he knew that everybody had left for the night. He looked out at the moon in wonderment lost in thought. Just a sliver to go and the Moon would be full once again.

"Grandmamma!" Aticus howled.

"Yes, dear?" So-seti asked as she hobbled out of the night, crutches in hand.

"Is everything going to plan on your end?" Aticus questioned. He had a hard time tearing his eye away from the dazzling moon to look at his grandmother.

"Yes, yes my dear, one more month and the perigee full Moon combined with All Hallows Eve are going to be the perfect time to conjure up the Mighty Shade." So-seti comforted Aticus.

"I hope you're right. I hope you're right and she will heal me," he turned swiftly afraid she would see him as a tear began to form in his eye.

So-seti steadied herself on Aticus' solid shoulder, "she is the most powerful of the shaman. A necromancer with the power over life and death… she will be able to heal whatever ails us, my sweet."

For the first time in his long weary life he began to feel hope.

She pressed a shaking hand against his forehead, "head hurts?"

Aticus didn't say anything, only shook his head yes and looked at his grandmother's stumps for legs. Even the mice who made their nest in the second floor deck scurried about on the hard wood floor over toward the shadowy corners of the deck as if frightened by Aticus' mere ominous presence as he bent down to inspect the silver studs through her sheared off bones.

"Don't worry, Aticus, in another month Aisos will rise!"

Everything was going to plan. Montezmu and Tomas, with the help of Maurice, now had a direct pipeline through the drug smuggling operations all over the South Western United States. This new and extremely potent recipe a tweaked out version of the all but forgotten old world formula thanks to the ex-God's Light member, James, and the "street chemist", Michael. They easily synthesized ingredients that once could only be found naturally in the brain then all that was needed was Aticus' blood to complete the mixture. Once the inhaled dark red crystals invaded the brain and bloodstream it filled the users with euphoria they have never felt before. They have a transcendental experience feeling faster, stronger, and completely invincible. The parasites easily bypass the white blood cells, the body's defense system, changing them physiologically and they remain blissfully unaware of changes to come until the next full moon approaches.

Aticus had ordered Viddarr's Wolf's Den Tavern to pick unsuspecting patrons deemed worthy for the chance to taste the elixir called Wolf's Blood. Then he was to give out his flyers to those perspective candidates and the unsuspecting patrons alike for the Blood Moon Festival just over a month away. He smiled ear to ear but in doing so his head began to pound.

"Viddarr's Tavern was a perfect front to pass out the flyers for the Blood Moon Festival, soon your developing pack will be solidified and those that don't make the cut will be fodder for the young changelings." So-seti said confidently.

His visions were increasing with every passing day and he began to get nervous, *I have a surprise for you my dear*, Alicia's apparition softly whispered in his head. He could almost feel her embracing him. He looked around at the land where it all began. Where he lost his eye and he began suffering his ceaseless headaches which tested his sanity.

He peered out over the woods; now this is my den, my region, Aticus thought. The war is coming and he would rule the area with an iron fist. The era of pink fleshy, fragile human beings coming to an end... A lycanthropic rule will change all the human waste and excess which was not the lupine way. He would weed out the weak and infirm and would heal the planet, Aticus reasoned. Humans in their homes with their white washed fences will become just livestock for the wolves while they wait for the slaughter.

Back at the barn in the second floor rafters he could feel the minute heat coming from the fire and the smell of barbecue. He closed his eye and could see a dozen inflicted crowding around the fire. He could hear growling as the inflicted grew stronger, competed for scrap meat.

Finally back where it all began, Aticus on the brink of sanity and madness, sorrow and vengeance, then he saw Alicia. She gave him an expectation of love, acceptance and affection. Aticus told Alicia his most closely guarded secret, born of a Wolf mother he could transform at will... she did not run. For a moment all seemed right with the world, again for a moment Aticus thought that humanity as a whole is not cruel. That not all would try to capture and massacre what they didn't understand. Healing and hopes for a new family, something that he was sorely lacking since he was a child. Until in one night everything changed all that. Left with a horribly scarred face and missing eye and in an instant he lost his love for his troubles. Except for the reincarnation of his love he vowed never to trust a human again.

He searched for her for some time when the mundane injuries of his body and mental scars had healed. He had come close to her about a century ago in the wilds of New York City, she had already given birth to fraternal twins, a boy and girl, but immediately after birth the boy had died. Death gives off a strong scent and he had tracked the dead boy to the family mausoleum. Although really weary with the speedy delivery her family's deep pockets had persuaded The Catholic Church to bring nuns and take away the surviving child and put the baby into a foster home in Canada.

He had tracked Alicia at an open air fare in Lower Manhattan. More interested in Alicia than hiding from the crowds of people all around him he emerged from the shadows, he wore a hood on his head to conceal the twisted visage of his face to the masses. He was almost able to touch her when he caught his reflection in a full-length mirror for sale. Oblivious to his presence and just feet from his love he froze, horrified at his image in the mirror. He cautiously stroked his horribly scarred and permanently injured face. Staring into the mirror the cashier too busy tending to a couple to notice him, he looked first at the permanently lupine ear. The misshapen ear set back further on the skull, lower than a human ear inflicted by silver shards, cut in half from the silver half-Dollars and dotted by sporadically fine short fur. A malformed skull, part permanently lupine, part human, fused together. The scarred part of his forehead through the bridge of his nose enlarged and extended like a massive cancerous tumor. A missing eye and wide high socket seemed to quiver as if wanting to transform but could not. In his mind he would never again be worthy for such an angelic face. His cheeks reddened with humiliation, there would be no homecoming, embarrassment got in the way.

It was the last time he physically saw her. He made preparations to keep track of her and give her everything she needed through the lawyer Richard LeBeau, one of his kin, those sympathetic to the lycanthropes. They had encountered the Wolf's blood but were somehow uninfected. He fell into a deep depression when he could not sense her aroma in the world anymore.

He longingly looked over at Alicia's house. His lucid dreams saved him from certain death and instructed him to the whereabouts of another version of his lost love. The pounding in his brain lessened as excitement coursed through his veins as he thought about smelling her aroma again in the world. So close to the reincarnated version of his love he could taste it. Memories came flooding back to him, some good and some really, really sorrowful. His father, mother, and brother and sister died at the hands of her cruel ancestors but Alicia reminded him of his best friend and sister, Ayaa. Sarah, Sarah reminded him a reincarnated lost love, Alicia, and his long-lost bloodline Ayaa! He would be damned if any, any petty human stood in his way to claim her. He wiped the dripping ooze from his missing eye socket. This time he swore vengeance upon the human race so they couldn't take away his family ever again. He hoped that Aisos could make him whole again then he could have confidence to look upon her beautiful face eye to eye.

"Don't worry my dear," So-seti abandoned her crutches and hugged Aticus partly for love and support, partly for stability, "I will be able to call her forth and she will be able to regenerate my legs and your eye, I swear to you."

Aticus' nerves threatened to get the better of him. After all it was more than 200 years since he felt her touch. He made his way up to her bedroom, running his hand along the wall, and out onto the balcony. He could look into those big doe-like innocent eyes that reminded him of his sister. It had been more than 200 years since he set foot on Raccourci Island. Now looking out from the second floor on acres and acres of land it dawned on him it was the first time ever he looked down from inside the house and it pleased him immensely.

He breathed in a deep breath with his head held high. He yelled out a lupine howl of excitement that could be heard from miles away.

58

Sarah was repeating Alicia's words as a cold chill ran up her spine, ***"Aticus, my love, confessed coolly without any emotion whatsoever, "I stalked you, waiting to end your life… Thank the alligator for moving, for setting off my instincts to give chase."***

"I couldn't believe what I was hearing! He said he was going to annihilate my whole family like my family had murdered his relatives. I should have been sick, thrust into a dreamlike fairytale, horrified and scared for my life."

"Aticus touched my hand, electricity flowing through me once again and I almost swooned, he said softly, "So naïve, so caring, the way that you touched me and the look in your eyes reminded me of simpler, happier days… I cannot kill you, only care for you." The only words I heard are four words… I care for you…"

Sarah stopped reading Alicia's diary for a second, legs outstretched on the sides of the recliner. The sun struggled to peak out from the advancing thick, gray clouds. She heard crackling bacon sizzling, caramelizing on the skillet. The smell of the bacon as it saturated the walls of the motel room made her stomach lurch and twist in knots, reminding her she hadn't eaten. As her friend and practicing alcoholic, AJ, politely declined, and stayed with his preferred "liquid nourishment" going on two days now.

"You have anything for a headache?" Sarah said meekly as if the sound of her own voice pained her.

"No such luck little lady," AJ peeked his body out from where he cooked in the kitchenette, a skillet in one hand and a spatula in the other, "I'm going out for supplies in a little while. It will be on the top of the list."

She smiled in an expectation of this and sat back in her recliner. She always thought about her missing friends and in the back of her mind she reeled at the fact that it was all her fault. She could just hear the one sergeant of the police department and his discouraging words, "adults have a right to disappear" in her head. She drank and she worked tirelessly to renovate her property so that she would not think about her friends too much.

She had no time to obsess over her missing friends despite Capt. Rogers and Detective Jenkins always hitting her up for more information. With no sign of them on the property Capt. Rogers and Detective Jenkins changed gears and restarted at the original arsons with fresh eyes. The two policemen would run over anything with Sarah at the motel room if anything looked suspicious but she could tell by their eyes that they were not telling her everything. When she labored hard at work rehabbing the property sometimes she thought she saw one or both of them spying on her from the outer marker of the property partially concealed by the roadway. Do they think I am a suspect? Really! If she let it, the question infuriated her.

"Here, some of the hair of the dog that bit you!" AJ handed her a glass dark red in color and smelling suspiciously of vodka.

She only hesitated a moment, but with the consistent pounding in her head she would try anything to take away the pain. She sipped her Bloody Mary, cringing with the taste of vodka mixed with a little bit of tomato juice and carrot. Her eyes opened wide and lit up like flashbulbs when she sipped her drink.

She got to thinking about Desiree and Tommy or the lack of their presence the motel. She had to admit she found herself relieved when Tommy's obsessive stalking had come to an end suddenly. Now he looked more mysterious, more sure of himself, and more importantly, disinterested in Sarah's comings and goings. She came to find his company pleasant except for the annoying habit of every once in a while teaming up with Desiree and pestering Sarah about hosting the party. They'd not seen Desiree since the "Wolf's Den Tavern," Too busy chasing her love interest and owner of the Tavern, Viddarr. She would come back once in a while to hound Sarah to use her property for his Festival but she never really stuck around long.

Desiree and Tommy both teamed up against her, convincing her that it was a good idea. And not to mention, Tommy pointed out that the Festival at her house would be a great distraction against the constant worry of her missing friends.

"Thank you, I think my headache is already subsiding." She graciously accepted another drink, "so against my better judgment I am thinking I might host that Blood Moon Festival thing that Desiree was always bugging me about."

She felt the consistently painful pounding in her head slowing down some as she downed the mostly alcoholic remedy down to the last drop.

Sarah handed the empty cup to AJ then flopped back down in the recliner, "That really helped, thanks AJ."

AJ just smiled and nodded in acknowledgment then disappeared around the corner, back to tending to the browning bacon in the kitchen.

"I think we'll skip rehabbing this weekend, okay? I think you deserve it." AJ yelled through the wall, skillets and pots clanking about.

The question did not receive an answer, "okay, okay, a half-day and we'll call it quits, is that alright with you?"

Sarah voiced approval.

After her headache departed and a hearty breakfast had been consumed she coaxed AJ back to the estate. Sarah had enough fuel to bust her ass replacing the termite infested rotten boards in the foyer.

She buffed the floors until her shoulders ached and she couldn't raise her arms anymore but the scorch marks vanished and the floor shone golden like the sun.

Sarah didn't ask any questions when AJ showed up with a water generator to power wash all of the walls since they were caked with grime. She and AJ teamed up and used generators for the electricity to steam clean all the antique furniture that her distant relatives had left behind.

Quick work for a half a day but with a lot of elbow grease, she breathed new life into the dying manor. Hard long day and even harder nights playing had caught up with her so when AJ suggested they were good for the day she was more than happy to go along with it.

"You took the words right out of my mouth." Sarah said with a tired smile. AJ already had the van running.

Sarah shot him a disapproving look, "you know my deal, AJ; I'll drive here and back. You have not consumed a thing except alcohol."

"Well, at least let me make you lunch." AJ said this as he staggered and almost fell into the van head first. A deal was struck and they were on their way with Sarah in the driver's seat.

Sarah could not pay attention to AJ's drunken ramblings as she marked off her checklist of things that she had to do tomorrow. The upstairs bedrooms were almost done and she was finished with the outside. She dreaded the stables and the tool shed. She was staring at the plot of land that used to house a farm. When they were almost ready to go she would walk the property edge to edge lost in thought. For a fleeting moment she could almost hear whispered conversation and commotion. She could even smell the aroma of sweet barbecued meat. In the darkness out of the corner of her eyes, just briefly she thought she saw an ethereal barn.

The closer she walked the eerier the area had gotten, a surreal moment in time that made Sarah's hair on the back of her neck stand on end. She heard wildlife all around her. Crickets chirping, birds singing, she wandered close enough that she could directly see the barn but like a mirage it quickly vanished. She could actually hear the sound of utter silence, unnerving silence encircling her. She could imagine mystical fairies of the forest casting their spells of enchantment hiding them from the material world or the ghost of her ancestors haunting the barn. Either way, via fairies or the restless ghosts of her ancestors, she would go no further, forgoing the last fifty feet. The whole experience had put her on edge.

When she pulled into the motel driveway suddenly arms burst out in her direction, then forearms folded on the open van window distracting her from her train of thought as Tommy leaned in, "Hey, what's up? You guys were gone for a while."

Tommy flashed a smile, grinning from ear to ear. His teeth were somehow whiter and straighter. A leer that looked cunning and sneaky, like he had a secret that no one else was privy to. It filled her with goose bumps and put her on edge.

"You disappeared yourself a time or two now didn't you!" Sarah countered, "Yeah, AJ and I finished up a few things before we could take extended hiatus, how about you?"

"Most definitely!" Tommy's restless eyes were trained AJ who attempted to stagger the fifty feet to Sarah's motel door, he growled, "I'm starving!"

He didn't even glance in Sarah's direction as he hastily made his way towards AJ and the motel room, the overwhelming urge to eat coming over Tommy when he smelled the remnants of the juicy bacon. Tommy helped himself in the refrigerator, and then turned on the stove burners before AJ had even staggered into the kitchen.

"So have you given any more thought about hosting the Tavern's party at your property?" Tommy asked, grabbing several fileted bluegill with his bare hands and dropping them in the pan.

"Tell Viddarr I will host his shindig; just give me the paperwork to fill out." Sarah acknowledged.

AJ hid his shock as he watched Tommy engulf several fish filets in his greedy drooling mouth without even letting them cool, "Oh, thank God! I can tell Desiree. She'll be thrilled and it'll get her off my back!"

The drool mixing with the boiling hot grease instantly blistered Tommy's lips but his expression did not change, it did not faze him. He stared into AJ's eyes, emboldened eyes and a stare that challenged AJ's authority daring him to respond but masquerading as friendship.

AJ tore his eyes away from Tommy's eyes first as he said meekly, "so you and Desiree are awful friendly lately, huh?"

Tommy shook his head no, "Nah, she's too busy with Viddarr but when she sees me she bugs me to death until I promise to ask Sarah for permission again."

AJ turned around for Tommy's response to find him rummaging through the refrigerator crisper drawer to retrieve the half-pound of raw bacon. He tore the vacuum plastic asunder and downed a strip of raw bacon in one gulp.

AJ begrudgingly walked over to the refrigerator getting out tomatoes, mayonnaise and taking the remaining bacon to make B.L.T.s for lunch for Sarah, "Tom, you want more bacon too?" He said sarcastically.

"I hope you get a parasite, you crazy bastard," AJ said under his breath as he dropped several strips of bacon into the hot skillet.

"I'm going to get some fresh air," Tommy said, pieces of chewed up bacon spewing out. He shot AJ an accusing glance as if he had heard everything AJ had said, but he slyly smiled, "AJ I told Viddarr about your singing chops. I think he will be giving you a call pretty soon."

AJ only nodded his recognition. After cooking Sarah lunch he finally passed out on Sarah's bed, the room spinning.

After her delicious lunch Sarah stretched her legs as she scooped up her great-grandmother's diary telling to no one in particular, "I am going to get some fresh air too."

Tommy had once bitched and moaned and pressured Sarah into selling the property, he had wanted to leave Louisiana almost before he had gotten here, Sarah thought. But now he seemed to love the scenic surroundings and he could not get enough of her inherited plantation. If it weren't for the fact she had other things on her mind she would have delved into the mystery more deeply, but as it stood, it had been more of a glancing thought and it was quickly forgotten.

Devon's wolf instinctively crouched down in the shadows immediately beside Amy's cabin. He hid by a cluster of trees. A habit he had gotten used to, while Amy researched the strange and fantastic events, to avoid being seen and captured by Capt. Rogers, Detective Jenkins, or the bizarre Hunter. He saw Tommy come out of the motel room first, followed later by Sarah.

His stomach began to lurch, one in Sarah's group, Tommy, smelled peculiar. He had been infected with the parasite; anxiety went through him as he realized Aticus had infiltrated her group. His mind began to race a mile a minute. What did he want with her specifically? What was his grand scheme?

His body tensed, about to strike; if Tommy tried to attack her he would stop him. But Tommy ignored Sarah as she split off picking a shady tree to flop down beneath and read her diary. He had followed her around like a lost puppy dog until the infection. Now Tommy seemed to ignore Sarah. Maybe Aticus would be a man of his word… The motel would be neutral territory; no harm would come to anybody who remained here.

Of course, Devon had been right; Point Breeze Motel would be a sanctuary and all those that resided there would be safe from harm while there. But he worried that as the Moon cycled around again, bright and full in the sky, 100 miles in diameter from Raccourci Island no parish would be safe as Aticus' plans came to fruition.

59

No human voices around just the sounds of the crickets chirping and bullfrogs croaking relaxing her as she lay on the deck, the full Moon's light reflecting on the water of False River. The motel seemed a quiet, peaceful sanctuary; stark contrast from just miles away in Royal Bay, where insanity ensued.

Royal Bay was an area of serene surroundings and a mere speck on the map that even the GPS could not locate. Royal Bay, blink and you'll miss it, home to just 67 residents. It consisted of only the railroad track and sparsely dotted houses and miles and miles of farmland. A freight train roared past sounding like an F5 tornado whirling by.

David lay in his bed rolled up in the fetal position… restless, turning side to side from a fever that had progressively and steadily gotten worse. He had a skeletal façade, blackened sunken orbs for eyes, and skeletal frame where just yesterday he had a plump, healthy waistline. He was just a shadow of the man that he used to be. He flashed back to that wretched beast that bit him and the first seven days before the full Moon had come upon him.

Side tracking his recollection, he vomited for the fifth time, the nausea growing worse as the moon began to glow brighter in the sky. The sheets were soaked with his sweat and he felt like his head had gotten stuck in a vice and turned until his eyes felt like they were going to burst.

"I knew it was going to be big trouble when I agreed to go out with them!" David cursed, looking at the original wound site, now tender pink and healed; the strange wound from when he got mauled had healed quite rapidly and though severe had no visible infection.

"Every time I go out with those LeBeau boys it leads to nothing but trouble!" David muttered.

Childhood friends for years, the LeBeau brothers consisted of Lennox LeBeau and his little brother Lou LeBeau. Tagging along with the brothers was a group of guys, all workers at Booker A-line: Nathan Bordeaux, and a new person to the group, Alex Seller. Mischief abound when the LeBeau brothers got together. One night the group got wasted and thought that it would be a good idea to move the buoy markers at the end of the Mississippi River's bend. In the morning they awoke to several barges aground and several more in a traffic jam of sorts running into the stranded barges.

David laughed at the memory of this then he remembered Katrina's aftermath. The inebriated brothers and their tag-alongs found an abandoned church. The basement filled up like a swimming pool the group decided to swim the night away, later that week the group all got dysentery. He shuddered at this thought.

Two people were dead, including Lennox, and he hadn't heard from the group since the attack over three months ago. After the initial onset and blacking out he had gotten better and had been back to work, but three times for twenty eight days like clockwork he called in sick, practically at death's door. Now it's happening to him again.

David couldn't help but to think about his ailing body when another round of sharp spastic pains ran through him again. The doctors had given him a round of rabies shots, even an update on his tetanus shot, but it felt like lockjaw had set in anyway. His body felt like it was on fire, the joints hurt everywhere, and if he moved it felt like his bones were going to snap. The fever was getting so bad he couldn't help but imagine taking his hunting rifle and ending it all with one shot to the head. He could get some much needed rest he reasoned if not for the fact of his wife to be and their little kid, Jack. A smile broke out from his pale face and quickly disappeared. Just a week ago he was playing ball with his son now he was an invalid. He looked at the digital clock on his nightstand. Dread came over him, Jill, his wife to be would be getting off soon from work and picking up their son.

"Awwwwwwhwww," He yowled out from a surprising and excruciating pain that centered on his stomach like he had been hit with a sledgehammer in the gut.

The tone of his own voice surprised him the expression of pain sounded almost animal like, canine in nature, "what is happening to me?"

When first bitten he had felt he was at death's door. Apparently sleepwalking, he had arisen outside unclothed and in a daze. His whole body ached from the muscles on down to the nerves, his skeletal system on fire. However, he had refused medical attention once he started to feel better and he would be damned if he sought medical attention again when every medical professional running tests had found no ailment.

Then he started to feel better like he had been strapped into a roller coaster riding out highs and lows every month. When the fog of illness lifted for another month his hearing and eyesight had heightened, was stronger than before. He felt quick, strong, and full of energy as if he had been given a shot of testosterone and adrenaline directly into his bloodstream. He kicked himself for looking on the Internet to see what was wrong with him: apparently he had male menstruation or IMS. Three months had gone by when his doctor's appointment finally arrived. Surprisingly, the doctor agreed with the internet's prognosis much to David's dismay and embarrassment.

Every time his body began to feel recovered again he felt improved, enhanced in some way. In fact he started the habit of jogging every night. Actually, it had become a compulsion. If he wasn't running out in the night sky breathing the fresh air he became antsy and anxiety ridden. But now he had been reduced to an invalid.

David's shaky hands covered his sweating body with a warm blanket as cold chills ran through him again. By the time the sickness overwhelmed him again he had almost forgotten the illness that threatened to end his life in a monthly cycle!

His abdomen clenched rigid, he felt woozy from white-hot pain, making white knuckle fists to take some of the pain away but it didn't help. As soon as the pain subsided and he could take a whole breath again the bones in his forearms snapped like twigs underneath his skin. He looked at his forearms in disbelief then he began to shake uncontrollably.

His eyes rolled back into his head. He started bleeding from his ears his body in the grips of a full blown grand mal seizure. His back violently arched so hard his spine broke. His head swung back and forth blood and froth pooling in his mouth from where he bit his tongue. His whole body thickened, bruises developing on his neck, arms, torso, and legs. As quickly as the seizure started it ended.

His breathing was rapid and shallow, raspy from the blood in his throat. David regained consciousness though foggy and struggling to think right he was re-gaining his senses. He gulped and held his hands to his throat, he was struggling to breathe still and it hurt to touch his neck. Then he noticed his forearms.

"Oh dear God, What is this horror??" He cried out.

Before his seizure he felt the bones shatter in his arms but feeling them now there were only huge ugly purple bruises. That's weird, he thought, his fever had broken. Except for the bite on his tongue and a dull, throbbing in his head he felt a little bit better now. He was feeling so much better that he decided to go to the bathroom, a pilgrimage he dreaded to take when his fever had come upon him.

David staggered into the bathroom and turned the cold water on splashing his face repeatedly. A chill immediately came over him, so he splashed more cold water onto his burning face, enjoying the relief. The water brought him back to his senses and he felt better than ever before.

He turned to the bathroom mirror and what he saw tested the limits of his sanity and filled him with fright. He stumbled backwards towards the wall a monster staring back at him. A horrific image; pointed ears set far apart, a Neanderthal like face, vengeful eyes, and an extended, almost muzzle like nose over a mouth full of canine like fangs.

"What the...?" He quickly closed and rubbed his eyes, sure he was hallucinating. "Is this what I'm becoming?" He desperately tried to remember the beast that assaulted him.

He stumbled to his knees gripping toilet and the tub for stability as he was rocked by a wave of pain the likes of which he hadn't felt before. He tried to get up from the bathroom floor bracing himself on the tub, but was disoriented, his vision cloudy.

For yet another month the parasites tried to fuse wolf and man. With the Moon high up in the night sky his mind exhausted but his body tolerating a conversion to a semi-lupine mutate. He had survived another night's forced transformation. The parasites in his bloodstream were like so many tiny phantoms, invisible shades of the first dire Wolf, trying to invade molecule after molecule finding weak defenses of the white blood cells and delving ever deeper into his system.

He would not remember the pain and agony of the change when he woke up or the lunacy that came upon him with the transformation. Down on all fours now David writhed about, a hybrid-Wolf in every form save for the fact he had sparse short fine hairs on his back instead of thick fur, and a humanoid head. He had a wide black prolonged and mushed snout with thin extended lips. He looked like an ape with wolf's ears.

He heard his family arriving in the driveway. His new skeletal tail a hairless stretch of skin wagged about excitedly.

"We're home, honey!" Jill yelled as the front screen door slammed shut, "the boy actually became a brown belt!"

Jill's brown eyes looked exhausted, the lines on her 32-year-old face more pronounced as she threw Jack's backpack and the night's groceries onto the couch. She adjusted her blue scrunchy to tighten up her blonde ponytail.

"Are you home, honey?" Jill inquired; looking back only once to ensure Jack had gotten out of the car.

"Your son is still outside practicing his stance and footwork, kid's coming off this still high from overloading on ice cream and caffeinated soda." Jill reported loudly, "where are you, baby?"

"I am in the bedroom, come and get me, ha, ha, ha." David answered in a low, hoarse growl.

"Oh, David!" Jill's eyes lit up and her cheeks reddened imagining the prospect of all the lewd things David might do to her, "you know your son is going to be in the house any minute, don't you?"

The screen door opened and closed again. Jill could hear wheels from Jack's skateboard squeaking through the living room toward the kitchen. "I am finally a brown belt, Dad, aren't you proud of me? Man, I am starving!"

"David?"

She didn't wait for David to answer, it had been months since any close physical contact and she would be damned if she missed an opportunity. While he would always be her little boy she knew Jack was growing up, almost 14 years old now. Jill called out that dinner was "make your own" tonight and rationalized that there were plenty of leftovers in the refrigerator if he got hungry. She was relieved when she heard the refrigerator open and the microwave beeping; he could fend for himself tonight.

Entering her bedroom and shutting the door behind her so they would not be interrupted the darkness overwhelmed her. By habit she flipped the light switch to illuminate the ceiling but the light did not respond. Flipping the on and off switch on the wall several times before she gave up. She paused for a moment to let her eyes adjust to the dark. She knew their bedroom by heart. She could close her eyes and virtually see the bedroom. To the extreme right sat the door. Turning left with her back to the wall and squinting she could see the outline in the middle of the room of her bed. The antique wood headboard against the almond colored wall with plain black nightstands on either side and on the left, a table lamp, but no David visible in the gloom.

"David?" Jill whispered.

Putting her left palm to the back wall she cautiously headed toward the nightstand by the bed to try the table lamp, "David?"

"Don't worry I'm here, come and find me," David growled, his voice coming somewhere in the left corner of the room concealed by the bed.

Before she could find the other lamp she heard evil laughter coming from the corner by the bed. She shook off the unsettled feeling and felt around for the lamp. It wasn't there though; it was smashed and lay on the floor in a heap.

Reaching out carefully she followed the cord and pieces of the lamp until she found David's pajama bottoms, excitement stirring in her loins, over taking her uneasiness. Jill kicked herself for not shaving her legs today. A second wind sprang forth, her exhaustion turning into exhilaration and vigor.

"Oh honey, do you have a surprise for me, baby?" She exclaimed her voice giddy with excitement.

The bed frame shook and moved. "Are you hiding from me? Are you on the floor waiting to pounce, you animal?"

Jill climbed onto the bed. She saw the outline of David's pajama shirt torn and tangled up in the sheets. She crawled on her knees until she came to the other side of the mattress. She saw movement on the floor, but could not make out the figure at the side of the bed.

"David?" She said playfully while she took off her silk shirt exposing her numerous faint stretch marks on her hips a proud reminder of the day she gave birth to Jack.

Jill unhooked her bra to reveal her pale breasts. Smiling she licked her lips and touched the figure that lay on the floor. "What the...hell?"

For a moment reality was suspended, when did we get a dog? She wondered. She rubbed the dogs back feeling short soft hairs the length of its body. The tail began to wag excitedly.

"Did we get a dog?" She was slightly annoyed and curious.

Suddenly the animal jumped up onto the bed. All of the "dogs" weight smashing down on Jill's chest. Her equilibrium shaken she fell on the bed the animal lying on top of her. The animal sat up on his haunches four huge lupine legs and paws pressing against her breasts and hips. The animal had small fine hair all over his body, but basically his body felt furless.

She came to her senses and nervously muttered, "We do not have a dog."

He looked down into Jill's hysterical eyes until there was a spark of recognition in her tearful eyes the dog thing managed to mutter, "I love you, honey."

All of David's body except for his head a huge canine form but furless, the face still humanoid but something out of Jill's nightmares. He had the ears of a canine wide and setback an extended forehead bulbous yet oddly compressed nose and wide nostrils. His head almost ape like, but the eyes were wide. His mutated head sniffed Jill's sweet perspiration. Jill stared at the monstrous image. She recognized some of his more striking features as well as her husband's eyes. So in pain were her husband's eyes.

"Honey I am so hungry, starving, can you help me?" The voice of the beast garbled a mouth full of teeth and fangs.

Frozen in with some combination of blind loyalty, fear and disbelief, she muttered just one shaky word, "David?"

His paws tore through her belly, spewing warm lifeblood. They sliced four long strips of flesh making it easy for David's mutated mouth, with its oversized fangs and incisors to bear down and attach to the torn flesh. Jill moaned and gasped as David's altered face buried itself deep into her stomach. After the initial pain and shock only a sharp pressure as David teeth bore down and dug further into her entrails. Jack sat at the kitchen table eating his leftovers trying to ignore his mom's moaning, groaning, and muffled wailing, and sighed.

It wasn't often that his parents were affectionate and he wanted to give them their privacy but he could not contain his excitement staring at his well-deserved Brown belt. He put his skateboard on the kitchen table. The microwave beeped, the rest of his dinner was done. Good, I'm still hungry he thought as he headed toward the microwave ignoring the growls and moans, he grimaced and shut out the sounds, obviously sex sounds.

His belly was full of leftover chicken and reheated stuffing from two nights ago. The moaning had stopped about half an hour ago. He got up and crossed the room putting the dirty plate in the sink. He swore he heard the bedroom door open. He opened the door to the refrigerator to get the pitcher of tea when he heard a rustling and he stopped to listen to an unusual sound coming from the end of the hallway.

A voice sounding not unlike his father could be heard from the hallway, "Come here my son."

He took a mouthful of tea and sputtered "D…da…dad?"

"Come to your father." Jack shrugged, closing the refrigerator.

A form emerged from the hallway on all fours shoulders drooped back as he struggled to talk with his still human voice box, "come here son, come to me, don't be afraid."

Jack's worn-out body stood rigid partly from curiosity and pure exhaustion. The kitchen table shook as the lupine-thing crawled on all fours toward him.

"Don't you recognize your father?" He growled, as he tried to inhale Jack's entire frightened aroma.

David jumped up against Jack's athletic frame. His paws hugging Jack's neck as he fell towards the floor from the sheer weight pressing upon him. His thin long lips and chin dripped with congealing blood, and Jack cringed when he smelled hot putrid breath, the smell of decay on his father's misshapen face.

David's long tongue soaked up the sweat from Jack's neck, as Jack's sanity shattered; such are the things that test humanity's superiority on the planet, the wildly supernatural and paranormal. His mind raced back in time to fairytales and nursery rhymes. His dad reminded him of the Sphinx in Egypt, a man's head with an animal's body and that distracted him until he looked at his father's fangs.

"Please, Dad, don't hurt me!" Jack pleaded squeezing his eyes shut tight as he felt the slobbery scratchy tongue licking his neck.

"Don't worry, I would never hurt you," the man thing said to Jack.

All of a sudden the licking stopped and his fangs bit into Jack's chest breaking the cloth and skin.

"Ouch!" Jack yelled out in shock, wincing in pain and retreating from the thing that used to be his father until the table leg stopped his retreat.

"Don't worry my son," the thing soothed his son instantly licking Jack's wounds; "the pain will subside. I only do this so we can be together."

The beast stopped licking the wounds after it was assured that the wounds had closed up. Jack looked at his wounds that were already healing. Jack looked up at his father his eyes already beginning to glow. The beast could not contain his excitement fangs bared as he smiled from ear to pointed ear.

60

Lunacy

At the other end of Royal Bay a different agony had begun under the bright full moon's light. Over the tracks there stood a different house. A pair of willow trees at either side of the yard. One by one the staggered Willow trees masked a rundown one-story, one bedroom, and tan vinyl-sided home. Where this home sat moans welled up and out into the night sky.

The Fever had returned again. Nathan flashed back to his encounter with the beast that had so seriously wounded him. He writhed in pain as his muscles constricted again, tight and stretching beyond his control. Sweat broke out over his reddened face.

He seemed to have shrunken to half his size and his skin stretched so tightly across his bones that it was almost transparent. He couldn't keep food down, feeling his blood pulsing through his veins, his heartbeat like a bass drum in his head. Tonight when the moon rose the fever dreams would begin. Vivid dreams that quickly turned to nightmares.

Nathan rolled over in the bed unable to open his eyes; even the streetlights that filtered through his eyelids already impaired him. He felt the shooting pain travel up the nerves in his arms, his shoulders and back was sore despite the fact he had been in bed for over 12 hours. The fever hadn't faded and sweat still beaded over his reddened back. He had his girlfriend Tammy turn the thermostat down as she left for work until it felt like the Antarctic but it still seemed too hot.

He cried to himself. Even as a child he never remembered feeling this sick, he kicked off the blankets from the bed and rolled restlessly. In spite of the pain he wriggled from his confining clothing.

His dreams were filled full of visions, the attack... swirling colors of shocking pain. A floating sensation came over him in his feverish state and he could actually see his body stretch violently the skin tearing and bones breaking. His arms and legs and jaw shattered all at once. He could not move, his eyes felt like they were on fire, he rubbed them relentlessly and tried to open them but they still failed to open. A dull, throbbing pain began to build and spread through his bones. His pineal gland began to flood the fatigued and battered body with awakened amoeba and parasites. His failing heart began fluttering like a butterfly with a broken wing, blue faced and struggling for breath about to pass out never to draw a breath again, producing Dimethyltryptamine. Massive amounts of adrenaline started it up again, spine marrow producing stem cells going to work making new genes.

Tammy, Nathan Bordeaux's childhood girlfriend of ten years, couldn't help but worry about Nathan. She was obsessing over his drastically declining health yet again this month. So distracted by him she felt that she had made simple, silly little mistakes, but in a nursing profession silly mistakes could cost lives. So when the head nurse came to her and said she could go early she jumped at the chance. She grabbed her purse and wasted no time heading out the door. Now one by one, the deadbolts unlocked and an exhausted Nurse Tammy headed toward the ailing Nathan's bedroom.

"Oh Nathan!" She exclaimed the gumbo and sandwich that she had gotten for him as a surprise spilling all over the floor.

Tammy stared in horror; He looked minutes from death. She clutched her vanity, blush, mascara and eyeliner spilling all over the bedroom.

Tears moistened her eyes he looked worse today than she had ever seen him before. He was paler in spots, but then at the joints he had purplish black bruises and looked hot to the touch. His ears seemed odd somehow pointed and laid-back on his head. His gums were receded, his fine eyebrows seemed to meet over the bridge of his nose and oddly his index fingers were the same length as the middle one. In fact all his fingers seemed somehow longer than usual.

"Oh Nathan are you sure there isn't anything I can do for you? I love you." She said, her bottom lip trembling as she took in his disfigurement.

Nathan stared at her through sunken eyes, he was calm and quiet. The sound of his own voice scared him so he talked little. It seemed hoarse and deeper than normal. Summing up the courage Tammy held his hand his nails were longer and sharp piercing her delicate skin.

"I love you," he grumbled in a non-human voice.

Nathan's eyes widened, a rush of fire branded his innards his blood boiling and coursing quicker than his pains. His body twitched, muscles seemed to pull free from his bones. He cried out a low growl of rage more animal than man. His eyes bled as the rims darkened and pupils widened, light reflecting from them they seemed to glow.

"I love you," frightened and trembling Tammy whispered under her breath again.

Then Tammy screamed, placing her hands to her mouth falling to her knees before the bed. His hands lengthened and contorted grasping the covers at the foot of the bed to pull himself up onto his knees. Course short brown fur pierced his body like needles emerging from his flesh, his face no longer recognizable; Tammy looked up at him from the floor she screamed but unable to move as he transformed into something nightmarish that until then she had only seen in the horror movies.

"Let me call you an ambulance!" Tammy hysterically screamed and searched around her cluttered purse to find her cell phone.

A sense of relief came over her when she found the cold plastic of her phone in the chaos inside of her bag. Unsteady thumbs dialed 9…1…

"No!!!" Nathan instinctively snatched the cell phone from her hand and smashed it into the wall, the cell phone shattering into pieces.

He was no longer in control of his emotions the beast inside of him taking over his body. He felt strange; his body burned up on the outside but was now cool on the inside. He couldn't take his eyes off Tammy she had a red glow about her, like heat waves ebbing and flowing from her heart out to her fingertips. Nathan zoned in on her fast beating heart.

The unbelievable events began to get a hold of Tammy and her mind began to splinter and crack. What did he whisper to her? Hungry? Looking at Nathan's eyes full of anguish and pain made her heart sink. She would do anything for him to make him feel better.

"Okay, okay, what should I do for you?" Tammy hysterically cried eyeshade and eyeliner running down her face. "I would die to get you better!"

She meant every word of it too! He had rescued her from her painful family life. He protected her until she was able to move out. Then he shielded her from the hospital authorities when she got hooked on OxyContin. Nathan had stayed by her side through the withdrawals taking care of her when she lost her mind until she got back on her feet. Tammy would give her life to make him better.

His hands began to twist and contort. Beads of sweat ran down his face, and utter agony played across his features. The brown hair on the back of his hand rippled and thickened into fur, the sinews shifting. There were little popping noises of cracking bones. The hand gnarled, the knuckles swelled, the flesh turning mottled and thick, the brown fur beginning to spread over his shifting body. His face began to bubble and distort.

He felt his teeth move in his jaws, grinding together in raw, bleeding sockets. He felt broken at the joints, a living rag doll pierced with needles. His pulse was a drummer on crystal meth and Nathan tried to open his mouth to scream but his jaw muscles tensed and scraped like barbed wire. He closed his mouth again as it locked up, he would've thought that the final stages of Tetanus had come upon him but the blinding pain made it hard to rationalize or think straight. He struggled to open his mouth. He felt and heard a pop, the jaw shattering into one million pieces inside of his mouth and chin. A gelatinous mass oozing out and stretching his skin until reforming, twining and attaching to muscle and tendon until it made an extended furry muzzle.

Agony building, ebbing, building again to a new crescendo. He was one moment a furnace and then he was made of ice. He was aware of his body jerking, contorting and bending itself into a new shape. His bones arched and twisted, as if they were the consistency of sugar sticks. He had no control over these contortions; his body had become a strange machine, seemingly intent on self-destruction. Blind, unable to speak or scream as the throat engorged changing orders from new genetic instructions. He could hardly draw a breath for the anguish in his lungs and his pounding heart.

Lupine muscles burrowed under his flesh his whole body sprouting fur. The human muscle began to undulate and untwine. His skin began to itch as bundles of lupine muscles formed on what used to be a humanoid structure. Shoulder bones dislocating as new ligaments began to stitch back together again. The shoulder and hip bones locating ball socket to form a suitable, more human-like arm. The end of another lycanthropic shifting this month! The new and improved beast stood up on human like legs, hip bone expanded and contorted to the biped's requirements. The ankle to the heel functioning as a reverse knee giving him extraordinary jumping power, his head still a lupine visage with long muzzle and curved fangs.

"Oh Nathan!" Tammy cried her heart about to jump out of her chest.

"So hungry, starving, need to feed please!"

She should have run. She should've fought back, but she froze. This is madness she told herself even when the beast pounced on her. "I love you Nathan, anything to get you well!"

The animal Nathan overpowered her knocking her on the ground. Tammy instinctively put her hands up to block the beast's advances but she relented. In her shattered mind she would do anything to save him, even if it cost her life. She closed her eyes and turned her head as Nathan began eviscerating her.

"I love you too!" the beast growled between gulps.

He fed on his beloved until the obsession to feed left him. The animal Nathan collapsed on the floor huddled up to Tammy's corpse. He heard a crash coming from the living room, broken glass falling onto the hard wood floor.

His new lupine ears perked up his blood boiling in rage, "My house!"

"My house!" He roared again, his new lupine construct tensing, drool spilling from his new mouth and teeth. Breathing heavy in a quickly increasing frenzy, preparing to rip the intruder to shreds he tensed ready to strike.

A warning growl issued forth as a figure emerged from the shadowy hallway. Nathan's calves tensed up tight as compressed springs ready to pounce. He heard the click clack of claws on the laminate floor and he instinctively sniffed the air around him.

Glowing yellow eyes pierced the dark hallway. David appeared on all fours, tail wagging behind him, followed by his wild eyed son, Jack, foaming at the mouth. His calves loosened and Nathan's bipedal form arched back his huge lupine head and let out a lovely Aria.

"Arrooo, hoow, arroo..." Nathan paused for a response. David picked up where Nathan left off. Then Jack began to sing along with his blood brothers until they were singing in unison.

61

David and Nathan communicated in tandem yelps and yowls, a secret cypher known only to wolves and lycanthropes. Jack headed off in a furious, bloody delirium all throughout the streets of Royal Bay communicating with strange grunts and growls to his dad.

Nathan, almost a full lupine by look and structure, gave orders to David. David walked on all four paws in a furless lupine form except for his almost human-apelike head. Nathan looked like an absolute monster almost all his top-half a wolf's form. Except for his man-like hands with talon sharp claws his spine thicker and longer than a normal human being, and severely hunched back. Nathan's bone structure in his bipedal hips allowed him to walk erect.

The beast, David, saw headlights approaching and threw himself upon the truck. A thud, the driver didn't know what hit him. A screech of tires and the truck stopped on the road.

"What the…?" Bill, a scraggly gray-haired old man with a beard and overalls exclaimed as he hopped out to see what he had hit, leaving Leon, his drinking buddy, to stay in the truck.

"What did we hit, Bill?" Leon questioned sticking his head out the driver's door window to see what was going on.

"I don't know if it's a dog or a man," Bill exclaimed, "Wait to see what we hit before calling anyone."

The man looked over at the smashed-in bumper and left headlight then whipped his head around to see in the shadows what looked like a homeless, nude man curled up in the fetal position with his injured shoulder gushing blood.

Bill knelt down, knees popping and moaning as he did so. Bill had been right on both fronts. It was a dog and a man. Cold sweat trickled down his forehead as he staggered backward and fell on his buttocks in the dirt.

"Call the police, Leon, or the FBI! We got something alien in our midst!" Bill bellowed in a slurred panic.

Concentrating on the broken mass by the road Bill failed to notice Nathan bursting out from the thickets, his muzzle biting down on Bill's shoulder and rending the overalls strips in half.

"Ahhhhhhhh…" Bill grimaced as the beast's head wiggled from side to side.

"What the fuck?" Leon spilt his 40 ounce liquor all over the floorboard. He saw his good friend as he was thrust up into the air and thrown like a rag doll.

Bill's eyes began to dim as a unique hormone in wolf's blood flooded his blood stream awaking the once hibernating and ossified larvae in Bill's pineal gland. The larvae maturing into parasites merging with invading parasites altered, however slowly, Bill's body from the inside out. The intensive radiance of the Moon saved him from the brink of death, illuminating his eyes until a lunacy came over him.

Leon couldn't help but watch dumb struck as the beast that attacked Bill advanced on the truck. The upright Wolf thing beat the hood, crumpling the flimsy aluminum frame. In his panic Leon reached for the cell phone, instead of Bill's shotgun on the rack in back of the truck which he didn't at first remember. Bill sprang up and marched toward his truck like a man on a mission, still human, but the merged and mutated parasites began swiftly changing him from the inside out. The lunatic with torn overalls and a bloody shoulder growled, frothing at the mouth as he wrenched the driver's side door free.

"Bill!" Leon bellowed as he jumped across the seat, back pressed up against the passenger door.

With nowhere else to go Leon kicked his feet violently wanting to have as much space between himself and his attacker. Leon looked into the eyes of the madman. Instead of a sense of rage and anger in Bill's eyes he saw confusion and hunger…

"I'm sorry, my friend!" Leon grimaced squeezing all the weight of his leg against Bill and the truck seat.

Bill thrashed to be free, growling, spitting, and frothing at the mouth. Leon struggled to confine him stretching to reach for the shotgun on the rack. He could almost reach with his fingertips the cold steel of the gun but he didn't dare take his eyes off of the struggling madman who used to be his friend.

Bill's shotgun teeter tottered back and forth, the long barrel on the peg a precarious balancing act had hovered between the floor and his outstretched hand. Then the shotgun barrel fell into his hand. With one fluid motion he flipped the shotgun around so the business end pointed at Bill, sat up, twisted about and cocked the shotgun.

"I got it!" Leon smiled, revealing his upper missing incisor, chipped and crooked yellowish-brown stained teeth the product from years of poor hygiene, smoking, and drinking coffee.

Leon's legs firmly ensnared Bill's squirming torso and assured he would not escape until the shot was lined up. Concentrating for a perfect shot he had all but forgotten the monster Nathan at the front of the truck as Bill clawed at him and growled and yelled. Unseen Nathan moved to the passenger side window.

An explosion so loud and intense occurred that made Leon drop the gun instinctively covering his ears. He slouched down from a shattering glass and closing his lids to protect his eyes. Nathan entered the passenger window and the beast latched on and bloody fangs gnawed on Leon's head. Leon felt intense pressure then sharp pain as blood flowed like a geyser as he began to get light headed and dizzy.

Leon's legs released their pressure on Bill's torso. He snatched up Leon's broken body and peered at his bloody eyes with curiosity. Nathan's lupine nostrils flared inhaling Leon's aroma as a pale faced Bill watched Leon's eyes as the light dimmed. As parasites traveling through his bloodstream Leon's eyes began to dilate coming to life and illuminating. Nathan threw his head back and howled in triumph.

David, the injured beast, got up off the ground. His bloody shoulder was almost healed already and he galloped over toward the General Store's parking lot. Growling, he slashed the car tires and tore the wires for the phone and electricity from the wall and smashed his way through the plate glass entrance doors.

Lydia, fifty-year resident of Royal Bay and ten-year employee squinted, putting on her glasses the fire's light alerted her to three figures sprinting toward the convenience store parking lot. A display of menthol cigarettes resting on the exhibition shelf fell on the floor. The loyal convenience store employee screamed as she ducked, concealing herself behind the cash register and counter.

Jack jumped through the smashed in door, then jumped over the counter towards Lydia the instinct of separating the weak and the old first over-coming him. The lunatics Bill and Leon, along with David, were down on all fours, all split up taking the three aisles.

"What's happening?" Morgan, a high school dropout and a new clerk to the general store asked Harrison, his assistant manager, as he came out of the walk-in cooler.

"I don't know… you be quiet," urged Harrison.

He peeked out from the double doors in the back room, hands resting on the water heater clasping a cigarette as smoke wafted up toward the nicotine stained ceiling. Harrison quickly shut the cooler door and with frantic gestures moved up Morgan so he would not be seen in the door's window.

Morgan's chest started to pound, confused, he wanted to ask a million questions but like a good employee he kept quiet, he obeyed.

"I think we are getting robbed," Harrison whispered.

From Harrison's vantage point he could see three men, one naked and on all fours running back and forth through the aisles. The lunatics knocking down chips and candy in one row then knickknacks and motor oil in the other row. Two liter soda bottles on the ends fell to the ground as a group, bursting and soaring to the ceiling like rockets blasting off playing havoc about the room, shattering the straight florescent bulbs in a row overhead. He couldn't see Lydia under the counter but he could hear her moans and gasps, her pleas for help and her vicious attacker's growls.

"We need to get out of here," Harrison whispered, after a long inhalation to steady his nerves he smashed his cigarette out in the ashtray.

Morgan nodded in agreement with Harrison and together they ran through the hallway to the emergency exit. The uniformed duo tripped over mops in the dump sink. Packs of toilet paper destined for the customer bathrooms fell, rolling out toward the water heater. The siren wailed as the two opened the emergency door.

Shouting a joyous cry in unison they exclaimed, "We made it!"

Morgan and Harrison both smiled; relieved they made it out alive but their expressions of relief quickly turning to terror. They thought they would be safe from harm once they were outside of the general store; however, they were now staring at an unsavory beast, a fairytale bursting out the pages of fantasy and into real life.

They both stared at a monster that stood erect like a man, but had the upper half of a body that looked just like a wolf. The creature had its hands up to its ears from the piercing sirens, the red light of the emergency exit flashing across its face which held an expression of pain.

"What's going on, Harrison?" Morgan questioned trying not to look away from its horrible façade, urine running down his legs.

"I don't know, Morgan, let's get out of here!" Harrison smacked Morgan on the back, "let's get the fuck out of here!"

The monster hesitated, distracted from the blaring noise causing it excruciating pain, as the two employees took the opportunity to turn and flee. Fast as Morgan and Harrison's instincts were to run from the danger, the monster's lupine instinct to give chase was quicker. The fangs of the monster sinking into Morgan's shoulder stopped him in his tracks; his feet lifting up off the ground. Monster's claws sliced into Harrison's leg, his injured leg giving out beneath him as he stumbled towards the parking lot. Nathan's monster sniffed at the armpits of both of the employees to determine if the Wolf's Blood coursed in their veins before killing them.

The growing pack all but slaughtered the rest of the hiding patrons in the General Store. Bill jumped out of the building and moved onto the parking lot. He let out all his rage on the gas pumps. Bill couldn't help but to grimace, his ears too sensitive to the screech and squeal of metal bending, the gasoline flowing forth hissing like a snake. What once were three lunatics come to town had grown exponentially. Two patrons in the General Store were going through the change, Leon, Nathan, David and Jack made mayhem on Main Street. Now the lunatics made their way along the train tracks leaving a path of death and bloodshed in the unsuspecting town of Royal Bay.

62

A train rocked the rundown trailer on its cinderblocks a few feet from the tracks. The second train to pass by in the last hour. Tired, ready to enjoy her one night without her kids Candy swore she was going to get a good night's sleep, train or no train. She strolled into the kitchen and over to the microwave opening a box and throwing in a frozen burrito and punching the numbers before closing it again. She waited an impatient moment tapping her fingers then "beep" reemerging with her hot burrito. She bit down only to find the hot mixture turning into ice. Dammit, she had told herself she wouldn't get burritos again after the last time it refused to properly heat.

Then an explosion coming from somewhere in the area rocked the trailer's foundation. Candy exclaimed, "What the hell was that?"

No matter, she thought, maybe it's a train wreck. She'll probably see it on the morning news, she mused, her trailer in the back ground. She tried to finish her lukewarm burrito. Too tired to finish it off she drifted to sleep on the couch the plate perched on her lap.

Her eyes wrenched opened, she was startled from sleep by the unusual stillness, not yet used to the kids being gone. The street lamps cast an eerie yellow light through the tattered curtains. The wind had begun increasing, whipping the outside of the trailer, rocking it back and forth like a cradle. The rumbling began again louder than before shaking her reality. Candy grew nauseous from the motion, she stumbled into the bathroom. Another train this late at night, she pushed the curtains aside to peer out the window. No train lights, but the rumbling continued and the trailer shook and groaned like it was ready to fall apart.

She ran to the front door and grasped the door knob. With a quick wrench she had opened the heavy wooden door her eyes were straining to see in the darkness. The shaking suddenly stopped. Candy looked up on the top of her trailer, the hair on the back of her neck rising.

The rumbling started back again, from above her. Headlight-like orbs stared down upon her from the top the trailer; in expectation of a juicy meal strings of black saliva dripped down a long furred nose. With a gasp she scrambled back in and slammed the front door shut.

"Oh my God!" Candy impulsively placed her shaking hands against her rapidly beating heart. Her heart fluttered and stopped for a brief second, "am I dreaming?" She pinched herself, "shit!"

She wasn't dreaming she felt pain she told herself. A crash from a shattering window could be heard coming from the back of the trailer. Another crash from another shattering window closer and coming from the left of the trailer made her jump out of her skin. Another shattering window closer still and to the right made her body spring into action. From the corner of her eye she saw several shadowy individuals coming from the hallway. She tried to run away, swinging open the door and heading toward the rickety steps. Legs turned into pudding beneath her as she tumbled backward down the steps. She landed with a sickening crunch, her head smacking against the concrete.

Candy looked up in horror as the beast jumped from the roof top upon her chest knocking the air from her lungs with a whoosh. She gazed off in a daze, her head pounding from the fall she took. She was dreaming, she convinced herself, it's all a dream. She kept repeating *it's all a dream; it's all a dream…* as things of nightmares rendered her flesh from the bone she could only watch in detached hysteria.

Strange, she laughed, no pain, watching as the beast hungrily devoured her. Her mind slips from reality, she was so tired. Her eyes glazing over, blood dripping from the corner of her lip. She couldn't keep awake any longer, so she drifted off to sleep, as death took her.

Royal Bay began to burn. From the gathering smoke and smoldering debris forty pairs of glowing eyes emerged from the haze. Forty pairs of eyes, including David's son, Jack, minus the countless inhabitants that lay dying, eaten for sustenance for David, Nathan, and the other residents' insatiable hunger.

A figure floated high in the sky above the Earth's troposphere. A normal person would have already passed out and died of oxygen deprivation in the thin air, but not Lucius, the progeny of Caine, the first vampyre, the illegitimate son of תילילִ in the Hebrew, or to the layman, more commonly known as the Succubus called Lilith. He had no need to breathe and he made himself intangible to the fierce winds that blew up here. His preternatural, catlike eyes inspecting, just as a spectator, intently the insignificant speck called Royal Bay, as it burned to the ground. He had to report to Caine, Lucius mused, lowering his body down to the earth again, and then burrowing through the bed rock much, much further fusing to the rocks and minerals and clay before the approaching dawn.

63

The newly infected group honed in on the Seller's house, Asher's place, and Michael's shack, among others that dotted New Roads and Batchelor, circling a large circumference of Louisiana. Residents of Royal Bay awoke to find themselves passed out on the foundation of many burned-out houses. The residents of Royal Bay had heard special instructions, in their lunacy, to wait upon further orders. The homes were strategically placed so that the huddled group had their privacy. No homes in sight, not even a passing car. They laid like feral dogs together in a group basking in the sun.

Smoke curled up into the sky masking the sun, Royal Bay abandoned now, had burned itself out. Amid the smoke and debris Nathan and the others awoke in a daze huddled together, forgetting all of the nightmarish events that they had caused. Then, extreme loss overwhelmed them. They had felt alive and for the first time quite powerful. They recalled an awe inspiring ecstasy that had coursed in their veins that night and they longed for the feeling to come back to them again.

Jack cast his gaze out under an overcast sky, a tear in his eye, eagerly awaiting the moon to rise again, two more to come of three days... the Waxing Gibbous come and gone, soon the glorious full moon will rise then the Waning Gibbous Moon will set as well before this glorious feeling was lost again.

64

New Roads, Louisiana

Kevin, still intoxicated from the raw power he now had in his possession, lingered to get dressed for school. Fragments of memory flashed through his mind, ones of strength and speed. No more a puny weakling, he had filled out nicely. In fact his school uniform pants had become high-water pants as he shot up in the air. He was so enamored by his own Adonis like figure that he arrived at school late with his head still in the clouds.

Mr. Phelps had to make an example out of him ridiculing and riding him all throughout first period. The blood began to boil whenever he thought about the horrible treatment he received from Mr. Phelps. Mr. Phelps couldn't help but stare at the one silver Double 0 gauge piercing in his ear. He couldn't help but stare through Kevin's piercing like he stared out a door's peephole to see the student directly behind.

"No wonder they pick on you, you only have one earring in your ear, you are a sissy," Mr. Phelps teased him mercilessly. He sounded like a recorded conversation on slow motion. He enunciating the syllable at the end of the word, followed by more pirate and faggot jokes.

"You look like a freak!"

Kevin sat quietly stewing in his juices... how dare he, he thought. Kevin had many homosexual friends, even his uncle and cousin. Mr. Phelps had been especially hard on him since he caught him drawing gory artwork on his notebook not paying attention to the lesson. His notebook had quickly made its way to the principal's office where the school's "Catholic values" coupled with occult paranoia synchronized and resulted in the examination and subsequent disposal of his notebook full of art. Since Kevin and Brett's confrontation Phelps had concentrated especially close on his "disruptive" student.

Thinking about every cruel thing Mr. Phelps imposed this semester Kevin's anger grew. He began to get the starting sensation of pins and needles all over his body. He imagined knocking Mr. Phelps' teeth out and erasing his pretentious smile. All his fresh new and fast muscles twitched, engorged as he obsessed on Mr. Phelps insolent and pompous voice.

He had to look at a pleasant face so that his anger would not boil over, something pleasant to distract him, something wonderful, and something he happily stared at every day. He looked around to Tasha's beautiful profile! He breathed in her pleasant perfume, imagining her smiling face like he did a million times a day. His blood pressure began to calm down but he still had a fluttering heart from the proximity of his crush.

Then he thought of Tasha's brother. He felt his blood pressure increase again and the hair in the back of his neck rise as something in him stirred. Thinking about his bully, Brett, and getting revenge made his eyes dilate. He couldn't help but think about all the horrible things Brett perpetrated upon him. All of Kevin's body tensed up thinking about rending him to pieces as well as his teacher. He suddenly knew he had to get out of the classroom before he did something that he would regret.

Kevin sprung up out of his desk knocking his school books, folders, pens, and pencils onto the dusty floor interrupting Mr. Phelps' gut wrenching chicken scratching on the blackboard. Making his way between the aisles he heard hushed whispers from his classmates.

"Look at his eyes." Someone whispered.

"They're so bloodshot." Someone to in the front rasped.

"He looks stoned." Someone else commented.

"Loser," Brett said, smiling as he remembered the vicious beat down he gave Kevin recently.

"Kevin… just where do you think you're going? Sit down and stop interrupting my lecture!" Mr. Phelps said in a stern but annoyed voice, "now march back to that desk."

Kevin threw open the door but paused before walking out, slowly turning his head and glaring at Mr. Phelps, his eyes looking almost homicidal.

A cold chill came over him when he looked into Kevin's vengeful eyes but Mr. Phelps cleared his throat and tried to sound fearless, "did you hear me, Kevin?"

Mr. Phelps strode forward irritated and reached out his hands to stop him from leaving. Kevin impulsively growled a warning originating from his gut. He caught Phelps' wrists and pushed him backwards knocking him against the desk bruising his buttocks and almost throwing his back out.

"Kev…" Mr. Phelps stopped mid-word.

Mr. Phelps saw Kevin's twisted and horrid face so vicious and full of evil. He recoiled and closed his eyes anticipating an inevitable attack but it did not come. Like a dog on its chain he snapped back into reality, logical thinking taking over as a cooler rationale prevailed within him.

When Mr. Phelps thought it was safe to open his eyes again he saw Kevin had vanished. A moment of tense silence passed as Mr. Phelps struggled to steady his heart. He needed to regain his clout with his other students.

"Let's get back to the lesson, shall we?" Mr. Phelps' question sounded more like a command so they quickly obeyed, a backwards glare silencing any whispers.

65

The long walk to his house had not been an effort at all since his altering physiology yesterday. He entered the living room and skipped quickly down into the basement, the stairs groaning under his weight. Unearthly silence surrounded him as nobody was home and eager to greet him.

Kevin cranked up his stereo in the basement as if turning up the volume would distract him from obsessing about Mr. Phelps' cruel treatment and that of his bully, Brett, his anger increasing with every humiliating memory. He flew through the room like a destructive hurricane turning over a couch, the cushions flipping over. The glass coffee table, once solid tempered glass vanished bursting into a shower of pieces. Thinking of every embarrassing offense that Brett and even Mr. Phelps had made against him this semester released a rage. A flood of hormones begot a fever which angered him more. A domino effect until a strange feeling came over him.

"I will kill Mr. Phelps!" Kevin released all his pent-up anger with a massive punch to his 80-lb punching bag.

Thud, Thud, Thud; the chains rattled as Kevin tried to wildly smash his frustrations away. Only stopping when sand spilled out from deep slices that punctured the rawhide bag. He looked at his palms strips of leather and sand spilling onto the floor. A slack-jawed expression came across his face, shock in his eyes when he felt his fingernails spontaneously lengthen further.

Kevin couldn't help but think about Tonya's beautiful songs as the fever progressed, songs sung by the orders of the leader, Aticus, songs that were designed to single out the chosen so those transmissibly comparable, like Kevin, could hear them in their dreams...

Kevin couldn't help himself. He suddenly had the urge to run up the stairs, though still human his knuckles dragged as he ran on all fours tearing outside. Four o'clock and still sunny outside but the Full Moon had risen. As soon as he looked into the dazzling moon light he transmuted; though a young changeling and the parasites were not able to fully infiltrate Kevin's system he changed into a Wolf-type thing seamlessly.

His transformations complete the only rational thoughts in his head were, "Mr. Phelps and Brett are cruel to me, need to punish and consume!"

The fever had lifted all the way. The haze had lifted and flashes of background could be seen and interpreted. The wolf-type thing found itself in the high school parking lot. Driven by instinct and instinct alone Kevin's monstrous lupine form watched from the shadows as Mr. Phelps approached his car.

Mr. Phelps had a headache and was rubbing his temples in a circular motion, staying late to grade test papers always drained him. He was confident that the further he got from this accursed school the sooner his headache went away. He was unaware of the shadowy presence stalking him, waiting for the perfect time to strike. The gray-haired man shifted his glasses on his face fumbling with the keys in his pocket. It had been a long day. He was tired and restless, the sounds of rambunctious youths still played like a broken record over and over again in his mind. Straining his eyes to find the lock he opened the car door. All he wanted to do was return home for a long rest, relaxation, and a little sleep before the horrors of another day.

"You bastard," it whispered through sharp fangs, the words reached Phelps' ears like a blast of air from a furnace causing the hair on the back of his neck to raise.

Not alone, but there was no one there around him to be seen. He peered at the shifting shadows. Something moved just off to the left of him, he could've sworn he saw the glint of savage eyes, like pin lights in the darkening sky. Phelps groaned, keys in hand, he caught the musky aroma coming from the parking lot, like a wet dog smell swirling in the wind. His legs all but turned to putty when the growling began from behind him. He had no time to react as a hulking beast sprang out pinning him to the car. Taking the air from his lungs on impact and leaving a man sized dent, the windshield shattering.

Pinned helplessly between the creature and the car Phelps cried out in agony as rapier sharp fangs tore a savage arc across his throat and chest. The spray of crimson lifeblood coated the gravel around him. The Wolf thing howled out in triumph as Phelps shook uncontrollably and whimpered in pain.

"Please, Oh God," the man pleaded trying to kick free from the beast's grasp.

The beast's eyes reflected Phelps' bloody arterial spray spurting out with every quickening heartbeat. He felt woozy; his vision growing dark. In the last fleeting moments he knew he had to try something. He mustered up his determination and clenched his keys between bloody fingers; he thrashed about trying to hit his target, the exposed eyes of the beast.

The keys found their mark and a yelp escaped through a bloody muzzle as the thing released its captive and stumbled back, claws grasping at its now bloody eye. Phelps fell on trembling knees the last bit of strength slipping as he pulled himself to his feet resting his elbows on the car. Losing blood quickly the earth seemed to spin out of control under his feet. He didn't know how long he could remain conscious but if he stood here much longer he thought he would die one of two ways, being mauled to death or simply from blood loss. He steadied himself, now or never he thought springing into action.

Mr. Phelps' legs popping with arthritis as he pushed off the car and ran for his life. Momentarily stunned the beast had finally turned to chase the injured man. The Wolf thing hurdled over another teacher's car like an Olympic pole-vaulter, closing the gap behind Mr. Phelps.

Snapping at the air as the Wolf thing propelled itself forward, arms and legs working in unison. It hit the man with enough force to break his ribs and pierce his lungs sending him crumbling into a heap of flesh face first into the gravel. Bits of gravel and debris embedded in his bloody arms.

Phelps wearily dragged himself up to his elbows but it was too late, the beast was on him and he could smell its putrid breath, its mangled eye spontaneously healing itself to Phelps' disbelief. The Teacher was lifted from the ground like a rag doll as he cried out for mercy. Staring into large animalistic, vengeful eyes the horrid beast inches from his face he gasped with sudden realization. Mr. Phelps' eyes couldn't help but gravitate towards the pointed Lupine ear, a silver earring through a furless human ear lobe. His heart sank, there would be no mercy found in this thing…in Kevin.

It flung him with such force atop another car the windows shattered as he landed with a sickening thud as his neck broke. As his life faded quickly from his eyes elation came over Kevin the monster. Kevin reveled in his bloodlust, one down, one to go! With Kevin changed into the Wolf thing one word played through its mind "Brett."

66

Kevin tracked Brett by his strong cologne to a Strip Mall off the highway. The full moon sat low on the horizon casting an eerie glow over the town, deepening the shadows and alleyways as the overhead florescent lights systematically shut down in the sleepy shopping plaza. A light breeze made the containers of soda, popcorn and the trash of the day race by through the shadows of the square. The proprietors of the shops in the plaza locked up their doors and one by one slipped into their cars to leave for the night until only one car was left. One car sat alone in the parking lot a young couple together inside. They had parked in the shadows on the side of the building to avoid the watchful eyes of the local security.

Their passionate breathing had already started fogging the windows of Brett's car. They were unaware of the watchful eyes that were glowing yellow through the shadows of darkness, the large muscular figure across the road from the plaza hiding in the bushes by an darkened house. Panting in expectation the preternatural eyes could see clearly through foggy windows the woman and the man locked in passionate embrace.

In his human form he knew them as Leslie and Brett, both seniors in high school, one the twin brother of Tasha and his persistent adversary who hated him with a passion. He knew there was no hope of him getting together with Tasha if Brett had anything to do with it he reasoned and that burned Kevin up inside. In Wolf form however, desperation, longing, and a deep hatred translated to rage as it watched the two love birds, patiently waiting for its moment, its moment to rend human flesh. It would be satisfied that its burning rage would be no more. It saw the opportunity and pounced through the brush running across the street in a blur until it made its way to the shadowy recesses of the plaza.

Leslie looked over the top of Brett's shoulder. Her face flushed red from heat and effort as she straddled Brett's hips her hair glistening with sweat, a noise outside startled her, the sound of rustling trash and a single soda can rolling by the car.

"What's the matter?" Brett questioned, his face contorting in a mixture of pleasure and frustration from Leslie's slow rhythmic grinding stopping suddenly.

"I thought," She was panting, "I thought I heard something." She told Brett, worry taking the place of passion.

The car shifted and rocked violently side to side as the suspension moaned from the weight of the stalker. The sound of metal against metal made Leslie shudder and scream. They saw a flash of fur before the stalker smashed through the rear window. Kevin's snarling muzzle dripped saliva onto the leather upholstery, his ivory fangs bearing large like a death grin. It's large head closing the gap to its helpless captives.

Brett gasped, shaking arms pushing Leslie away toward the invading monster as he reached for the driver's side door handle as a talon paw raked across Leslie's exposed left leg. An arc of crimson gore coated Brett's face and chest as he finally opened the driver's door and fell out onto the pavement, too afraid to even scream.

Leslie moaned as searing pain tore through her body. Through now glassy eyes she searched for the open car door but fell forward on her face on the floorboard. She could barely see Brett as he stumbled to his feet and sprinted away towards safety. Trying to get up she cowered in the corner against the glove compartment wildly waving her hands to ward off the nips from the monster's teeth as it scrambled and maneuvered toward her. The beast lunged for her abdomen, the rest of her breath rushing out of her as the beast hit its mark solid fangs puncturing soft flesh. Leslie reflexively put her arms around the giant beast's shoulders as if she hugged the beast in a loving embrace.

Savage claws tore through her back as she cried out, blood gurgling from her mouth. With a twist of its head and an upward motion Leslie's intestines lifted out of her body like an unraveling rope. Her eyes met the wolf's eyes as darkness threatened to consume her. In her delirium she looked into the beast's eyes and suddenly somehow knew this creature killing her.

"Kevin..." She rasped breathlessly looking into the Wolf's eyes before it splintered her esophagus, and darkness consumed her.

Leslie's arms twitched then they went limp and still. The beast wasted no time it tore through the car door, leaving twisted plastic and metal in its wake. It barreled down the empty parking lot on all fours to catch up to a half-naked Brett. The terrified teen stumbled toward a 24-hour office-supply store with a skeleton crew inside. Frantically checking that the beast was not following him he had not gotten far from his car stumbling a dozen times as he did so.

The Wolf thing was upon him in an instant slamming into him like a sledge hammer knocking him down to the pavement. Brett crawled on his knees and bloody hands, dirt and gravel covered his face and obstructed his eyesight. He kicked out blindly and the Wolf thing took the opportunity to grab Brett's exposed leg and bite down snapping the bones of his ankle. As Brett howled out in pain the Wolf thing's paws found his throat rending it to a bloody pulp.

The Wolf thing looked up for a moment with dominant eyes to see if the late night employee across the parking lot inside took notice of the noise. It saw the worker still oblivious from his headphones that cancelled out the noise of the trains running close by and flickering lights that told the Wolf thing the laptop was on, its confidence increased. The Wolf-thing latched down on Brett's now dead arm and dragged him back toward the car. It lifted Leslie's body out of the car then dragged both the bodies' one by one over to the downward sloped hill. It dragged the corpses over the train tracks running the length of the back of the Plaza into the forest and gathering swampland nearby.

Now, concealed by the trees the monster gazed at Leslie's partially clad body, the bloody shirt concealed her breasts but she was naked below the waist and with victorious eyes he licked the blood from her legs. The Wolf-thing cleaned her off gently before heading to the gaping hole in what once was Leslie's abdomen and consuming her. Powerful endorphins once associated with panic and impending death flooded the wolf thing's blood stream as its swallowed whole her liver and adrenal glands relieving the Wolf-thing's severe hunger. What once was Leslie's body shuddered like a macabre hand puppet as the Wolf thing's head buried itself to the ears and shook from side to side. The Wolf thing's belly full and Leslie's abdomen empty it headed toward her bloody neck lapping up her blood, like a werewolf's imitation of a passionate kiss.

The Wolf-thing dug a hole with its claws and then threw Leslie's body in and covered the dirt hole back up. The Wolf hiked his leg and urinated marking its territory forever then turned to the corpse of Brett. It savagely and systematically tore into the body. All the pent-up rage, all the thoughts of abuse at the hands of its bully dissipated with every limb it tore apart until there was just a pile of flesh indistinguishable from a human corpse. It dug a different hole separate from Leslie's resting place, kicked the pieces in with its hind legs spreading dirt to cover it up, and urinated on it as well.

Now for the car, the Wolf called Kevin thought, the heavy fog that clouded up his brain and made him run on animal instinct alone abated, he was thinking more rationally than last night. With his muzzle he put the car in neutral and with his powerful shoulders he pushed on the vehicle bumper until it rolled forward. He let gravity do the rest as the car picked up speed down the hill stopping on the railroad tracks.

It was perfect the car was positioned so the bushes and slight turn obscured it until the train was unable to stop in time. It wasn't long before he heard a whistle of the train coming. He stayed until he heard the train's warning horn a horrible squeal from the conductor pressing the lever for the brakes then an atrocious crash of metal on metal.

67

John threw down the wrench in frustration and kicked over the dirt bike as he muttered obscenities under his breath. He ran his oily hand through his long, brown, scraggly hair; timing is just not right, he thought. It had taken him all day to fix the bike and he wore his school uniform of Pointe Coupee Central High School the colors Red, Black and White using them as a rag. He notice grime on the back of his hand and promptly wiped the sludge on his white button up uniform shirt.

John strolled back into his shed to turn up the death metal music he was listening to and put his beloved dirt bike back on its kickstand. Four hours and several adjustments later he smiled to himself.

John was crossing his fingers and muttering to himself, "Here goes nothing!"

He jumped on his motorcycle and turned the key; he pressed the start button, a cough and a stutter then silence.

"Dammit!" He muttered.

John was about start the process over again when something big moving through the brush caught his eyes. He moved cautiously to the shed to retrieve his flashlight and turned down his stereo. John listened intently to the sound of movement through the weeds.

Movement ceased as John searched for the source with his flashlight. Glowing eyes out of the darkness startled him making him lose his balance dropping the flashlight and falling backwards on his buttocks. The creature was so close John could smell its breath. He thought it was a huge dog or something but it had no collar and he did not recognize it from any of the dogs that ran around in his neighborhood.

He gently withdrew, John did not want to make any sudden movements that would set a rabid dog off but the flashlight sat peerlessly close to the dog's paws. Against his better judgment he slowly moved for the flashlight.

Almost got it, he thought, just a little further, he could feel the hard plastic on his fingertips when unexpectedly the dog's canines were exposed and it lashed out and bit John on the webbing between his thumb and pointer finger. He screeched out in shock as he went for broke snatching up the flashlight and scrambling back to his dirt bike setting off the motion sensor floodlights in the back of his house.

He could not believe his eyes as the lights filled the darkness, it was not a dog at all but a majestic sinewy flaxen-furred wolf with golden flaked eyes. The Wolf swayed in eerie silence its eyes trying to adjust to the blinding light, looking betrayed, hurt, and confused.

John could not put his finger on it but there was something familiar in the predator's eyes, it was as if he had known those eyes for years. However, he did not have time to ponder this as long as his hand was bleeding profusely he needed to tend to it and get out of danger as the Wolf steadily closed the distance between John and itself.

Looking around John found a flathead screwdriver on the ground by the bike and readied it like a weapon for the inevitability of another attack. John seized his moment as the Wolf-thing closed the distance its body stretched upward its paws resting on the motorcycle seat. He thrust the screwdriver in the wolf's paw so hard it went through its pad and tore into the leather bike seat, only stopping when screwdriver hit metal.

The Wolf-thing jerked back trying to free its impaled paw on the seat. With a violent arcing motion it was free tearing leather and padding as the motorcycle fell on its side. The Wolf whined out in agony its body twirled about in senseless circles as it tried to take out the screwdriver with its teeth.

John hefted up the bike pressed in the clutch; one fluid motion jumped on the punctured seat and desperately pressed start. The engine fired up with one try, the exhaust sounding like a chainsaw. He revved up the throttle and released the clutch as it jerked fiercely and took off leaving a cloud of dust, debris and ruts on the ground in its wake.

Now moving, John's confidence surged and instead of running away he rode around in a circle trapping the injured wolf. Snarling loudly, the wolf-thing feeling trapped, it stood its ground shoulders low to the earth, snapping at the tires every time the dirt bike went around in a dizzying pace. John smiled as the dirt bike circled around to the wolf again; he squeezed hard on the front brake. The back wheel lurching forward and up in the air, the rear of the bike whipping around as the muffler found its target striking the Wolf on the muzzle. Fur and flesh sizzled as the stunned Wolf-thing pulled away from the scorching muffler like removing a slice of cheesy pizza from the whole pizza pie.

The blonde wolf thing's eyes filled with agony and betrayal bounding off with its tail between its legs to the relative safety of the brush. John's confidence growing he stopped the motorcycle to check out his handiwork; he carefully touched the charred meat on the tailpipe.

It was over, John won and he caught his breath, his heart racing a mile a minute as the adrenaline washed through his body. The excitement of it all let out endorphins that had the domino effect on the parasite flooding his mind. He had a light headed and dizzy feeling as his sight left him a calm state of euphoric bliss came over him as he passed out and fell off the bike.

68

John woke up in his bed in his house. Confusion setting in as the last thing he recalled was fighting off a Wolf behind his parent's house. Now he was in his warm fluffy bed wrapped up in blankets and upon closer inspection noticed a bandage on his hand.

"Mom?" Confusion in his voice he rubbed the sleep from out of his eyes, "Mom, what happened last night?"

John looked under the covers with astonishment; he was naked as a jaybird. He called out for his mom again his voice filled with hurried desperation. He urgently wanted to know exactly what had happened that led to him blacking out.

"Yes?" His mom, Linda Wagirde, questioned through the door.

John struggled to hear her shy quivering voice, sounding meek and irresolute. Something was wrong with his mother. Despite his frequent arguments against it she usually burst into his room without knocking first thing in the morning to wake him but now she waited for John outside his bedroom door.

"Mom, come in here please." John said in an urgent and nervous voice.

Linda Wagirde poked her head into John's bedroom but she was leery to come in all the way. She had seen the crazed look in John's eyes last night and she had been trying desperately but failing to hold her naked son down and restrain him as he frothed at the mouth. She made an attempt to concentrate on the homemade cross made of nails on the wall, too frightened to look him in the face. Linda shielded her eyes until she was confident that her son covered his naked body with the bedspread and he seemed calm.

"You don't remember anything?" She said timidly.

"No."

"Your father and I found you scratching on the screen door nude." She said matter-of-factly.

Confident her son was in his right, albeit obnoxious, mind again she sat down on the bed.

"What happened?" John questioned.

"I thought you were out working on your bike. When all of a sudden we heard a scratching on the door, don't you remember anything?" Linda had a comforting motherly tone in her voice now as she patted his back through the comforter.

John noticed the tightness in his shoulders, chest, arms and stomach. He marveled for a moment at his puffed-up biceps, triceps and washboard abs. Before his amnesia he had puny limbs and a belly full of Jell-O. When he touched his gut it jiggled. Many more questions came to mind than answers. First things first, his mom could tell him all that happened last night because he was desperately trying to remember but kept coming up blank.

"I don't remember anything aside from I was fixing my bike..." John said still lying down on the bed staring in the full-length mirror on the wall.

John looked around the room, failing to notice the wisps of fur on the carpet. His mother was too busy straightening up and pacing around now to pay attention to him so he took the opportunity to lift his blanket up and sneak a peek at his new Adonis like physique. Astonished by the transformation he went through overnight John smiled a sly smile. But the smile faded when he looked upon the bandage on his mother's arm.

"What happened to your arm?" John said, concerned.

His mother paused for a moment and then continued to fuss with and fluff the pillows on her son's bed.

"Don't you remember it at all?" she said nervously.

Linda unfurled her bandage then started to cry. It was not the pain that made her cry but the thoughts rolling like images on a movie projector about the bizarre happenings last night. She timidly showed the inflamed and infected bite marks on her forearm.

"You attacked me, bit me several times." Linda balled, tears flowing from her eyes.

He stared at his mom's festering arm with horror; realization hit him like a ton of bricks. Somewhere in the back of his mind he knew he had been responsible for her injury and that made him sick. He reached out with one finger to her wound when he saw his own bandaged hand; suddenly the memory came back to him. He recalled the encounter with the wolf, the injury on his hand and the conflict with the wolf thing. He now unfurled his own bandage and compared them in his head. John's injury had all but healed leaving just a pink scar. Her scar was a different matter entirely though, infected and oozing.

"Are you on drugs?" She was gaining more confidence now as she leaned forward and put her arm on John's shoulder.

A guilty twinge ran through him then John said in a huff, "No mom."

"Well you sure were on something last night." She had a motherly tone to her voice again. All but forgetting the horrors that her son put her through. "Well you were on something last night, PCP or LSD, and frankly it scares the hell out of me."

"No mom, I assure you I'm not doing drugs again." He defended.

John's face reddened when he realized his mom had turned toward his dresser and rummaged his drawers for signs of drug use. If she rummaged further she would have found the marijuana for his recreational use. He had to do something and fast or he would be shipped back to rehab again.

"Mom," he said quivering, his voice cracked. "I assure you that I've not done anything but I don't remember much other than being attacked in our backyard, by a wolf or something."

Linda Wagirde looked in her son's eyes and knew right away he wasn't lying, her heart softened a bit.

"I believe you." She sobbed hugging John tightly, "your father is really furious though, good thing he went to work today. I was afraid he wouldn't, he was a little under the weather today. You really did a number on him, biting his ankles and everything."

Linda went on to tell a strange and frightening story about John's evening.

Linda and Leroy, his father, had finished dinner, the silence getting unbearable. Streetlights had come on, and it was getting late into the night. John had to go to school tomorrow for the first time since his suspension had lifted. Linda had looked for him in the yard, no sign of him just his running motorcycle. Her heart fluttered and she wanted to call the police but Leroy talked her out of it. John was 17 years old so going to the police would be a waste of time.

Leroy explained to his wife that when he was younger he went off with his friends to follow "Phish" touring from city to city. He was gone more than two weeks until the money ran out and he and his friends were forced to come back home and find their angry parents waiting for them. When the fallout cleared from the weeklong fight with Leroy's parents they explained to him that they called the police but the lieutenant in charge told them Leroy was considered a runaway the police would keep an eye out for him but there was nothing else they could do. John on the other hand had been out just a couple of hours. He convinced her to wait it out.

Linda's eyes watered thinking about her boy but she knew Leroy was right so reluctantly she continued sipping on her hot coffee in silence. She stopped her fork halfway between her dessert plate and her mouth; coming from the back door she heard the whining and scratching. Leroy heard the awful noise too; he stopped chewing on his second helping of apple pie to make out the source of the sound.

"What the fuck was that?" Leroy cursed.

Leroy jumped from his seat knocking the chair onto the floor. He motioned for his wife to come open the back door. Linda clutched his shoulders, her hands gripping so tightly on Leroy he grimaced. Leroy slowly opened the door. A gasp filled the kitchen. Linda and Leroy were shocked at what they saw through the screen. They saw their son, his nails bloodied from scratching on the aluminum screen door, naked and covered with filth.

John whipped his head around the lights inside hurting his eyes as he saw two figures standing in the kitchen. His haunches wound up tightly until they suddenly exploded. He launched into the exposed aluminum door. It folded in on itself like a piece of paper. Hinges fractured and exploded from the trim like shrapnel from a grenade. Linda and Leroy were knocked back off their feet. Leroy had been pinned by the mangled screen door and Linda was now pinned beneath Leroy, they were helpless to fend off their out-of-his-mind son.

Leroy tried his best to fight off his berserk son and protect his wife at the same time. He mustered all of his strength to push the broken screen door and his naked son out of the way and get onto his feet. His wife crawled backwards on her buttocks to safety as her husband fought for his life against his own son.

"John, what happened to you!?" He gasped between labored breaths.

John said nothing; Leroy could see the rage in his eyes, the love for his parents he saw so many times was simply gone. He stepped back but it was too late, John filled the gap within an instant and Leroy found himself trapped between the wall and curio cabinet.

"John!" Linda screamed, her hands shielding her face in horror.

John had no idea who Leroy and Linda were, let alone that he loved them. All he knew in his psychosis was that he came home to these strangers that smelled strange and were trespassing in his den. He threw his helpless father against the curio cabinet shattering the glass and wood. The ease with which John threw Leroy with only one hand had Leroy shell shocked. Left breathless, Leroy was a strong strapping 41-year-old man who worked all his life on the assembly line at Booker A-line, he was no weakling but his son was now exceptionally stronger.

Thinking on his feet he yelled to Linda to get blankets and all the belts she could find. He had to find a way to secure his son without hurting him. Linda hurried and did what her husband told her to do even though she was scared out of her mind and worried for her son. Leroy didn't have to say another word being married for 14 years they were on the same wave length. She caught onto the improvised restraints, slowly sneaking behind her son to safely capture him.

Leroy looked at his enraged son and then at Linda with the blankets stretched out over her head. He quickly moved to a better vantage point, a vantage point that left his son blind to his mother who hurriedly came up from behind and trapped her son with a warped loving embrace. John let out an ear splitting roar and Linda trembled as the stress of John's preternatural strength made her arms quiver and shake. Her arms were like twigs finally snapping in the relentless wind giving way to her lunatic son who thrashed about wildly trying to get the blankets off his body. His teeth gnashing and gnawing on the expensive blankets, tearing them to ribbons until John was free.

Untethered, he set his sights on his capture, Linda, sinking his human teeth into her exposed flesh. She cried out in agony. It wasn't the flesh wound itself that hurt, her adrenaline still sky high, but was the betrayal that hurt most of all. She found herself stunned as this maniac went for the kill, his growing nails reaching for her neck.

A brief break in the chaos was all Leroy needed to maneuver around to the side with his belt in hand. He came around on John's blind side and slipped the belt around his neck. He didn't want to hurt his boy but he had to do something. The belt tightened little by little, Leroy afraid to hurt his son, just enough pressure on his neck to take his breath away so he would be too exhausted to put up a fight and release his mother. It worked; John's arms went limp, his vice like grip loosening on Linda's fragile windpipe until she could breathe once again. She gulped precious oxygen to fill her deprived lungs but she didn't miss an opportunity to pick up the fallen blankets and hastily wrap her son back up again.

Assured that his son was safe and secure Leroy unloosed the improvised belt noose. His son dropped so quickly the porcelain kitchen tile cracked underneath his knees. He hastily bound John's ankles together and wrapped the belt around tightly three times. John's sudden restriction to his legs left him teetering on his knees and ultimately with no support from his hands falling on his face on the kitchen floor. John writhed around on the floor loose blankets coming undone as he foamed at the mouth. Leroy moved John's arms enough to wrap around the belt and restrict his wrists but it left his ankles exposed to sudden attack. Leroy winced in pain as John's teeth bore down through Leroy's pants until teeth found flesh. Instinctively Leroy threw up his bloody foot kicking and connecting with John's jaw. Linda cried as she heard the sickening sound of her son's jaw snapping. John stopped struggling, knocked out and peacefully at rest now. They argued about their ill son who peacefully slept, looking like an angel, Linda noted. The silence unnerved Linda who was shocked at the violence instilled by her boy and couldn't contain her hysteria.

She blew up with waves of violent slaps and obscenities towards Leroy, "How dare you! You could have killed him!"

As Linda recalled the horrid night's events back to John, he painstakingly went through the rooms that the events occurred in. The dining room looked like a war zone. He looked at the curio cabinet that had been ripped asunder, glass and china strewn everywhere.

Suddenly he remembered flashes of his actions last night after he had been bitten by the strange animal. John started to cringe then shutter with delight. He thought about the raw power of the monster, a monster not confined to society or its rules, feeling no guilt or remorse.

"I guess if you're feeling better then you should get dressed. You're going to be late for school, it's your first day back and you don't want to get another suspension, you better hurry up, son." Linda's eyes were filled with compassion and love but her nervous façade betrayed her tranquil manner.

"I love you… You know I just worry about you." Linda nervously smiled.

John opened the dresser drawer and found a clean uniform for the day. He hurriedly got dressed, hugged his mother reassuring her that he was healthy. He opened the door to the backyard. John found his BMW Enduro motorcycle where he left it on the ground by the shed last night. Flashes of memory steadily leaking through his cognizance like a fractured dam looking at the web of his hand that seemed to have miraculously healed.

On the way to school John continually thought about the bizarre experience. With the wind whipping through his hair he couldn't help but long for the freedom he'd had. He couldn't remember anything specific, not in great detail, but the sensations and wondrous feelings were seared into his mind. Before he knew it he navigated through the back of the Plaza where the railroad tracks ran. He slowed at the burnt wreckage of a vehicle. One police car sat on top of the hill.

Absorbed by the sheer freedom he experienced last night it would be a crime, going to school when he felt this way. Like a tractor beam his mind on autopilot he found himself at Pointe Coupee Catholic High School. That would be okay, he thought, his friend Kevin attends here and he couldn't help but be excited to share the experience with someone who might actually believe him.

Slipping through security he yelled out in the hall "Hey, Kevin?"

John yelled, looking around the crowded hallway, "Where are you?"

Through a frantic sea of students rushing to get to class John craned his neck to see Kevin until a slower student caught his eye. He wore a baseball hat low, concealing his face. He walked with an air of confidence as if he had a purpose. Crowds of people looking horrified and filled with fear were tripping over their feet to get away from him like he produced a magnetic field, throwing the students back like he had a very powerful, invisible aura. Suddenly, Kevin looked up at John and locked eyes.

"Hey, John!" Kevin exclaimed, smiling at his friend's surprise visit. He walked over to his locker opened it and retrieved school books earmarked for the first period, "what brings you here to my school?"

"I have to talk to you buddy." He said out of breath.

John stared at Kevin's bandaged hand, which held his books. John and Kevin's gaze finally broke, the left side of his face horribly scarred like road rash. It ran the gambit from first to second degree burns. One eye reddened swollen and enclosed. He put two and two together as he remembered the wolf-thing's ear and a 00 gauge stud through it, suddenly it hit him … it was Kevin!

"Oh yes, my friend, you did that to me," Kevin laughed patting John on his cheek with his bandaged hand, "I wasn't going to eat you, you know!"

John gaped.

"Um, thanks? So I guess it's safe to say we can share in the experience… It's amazing…" John whispered pulling Kevin in closely, for the first time they both felt like they belonged to something and wanted to share it with each other, as if they now shared membership to a secret club.

The Full Moon had set but the Waning Gibbous Moon had arisen letting loose the lunatics for another night of horror.

69

The three stages of the moon, which affected the lunatics had come and gone. On the other side of town the fog of amnesia had lifted; Dr. Jacobs pressed both hands against his throbbing skull as if this would help ease the pain. His pants were torn, shirt ripped to shreds. He looked around the room at the shattered mirrors, the headboard of the bed cracked, panic washed over him. He frantically checked the two windows but no cracks, no signs of tampering. He slowly, painfully staggered toward the door which was still locked.

"It's impossible!" Dr. Jacobs beat his fists against his dresser, "I was just scratched, God dammit!"

He had been proactive; a round of antibiotics, tetanus and rabies shots to quell any sickness, it did not work. Every month for three days since the mysterious disappearance of the crazy reanimated ambulance worker the symptoms were getting worse. He could not shake the memory of this horrible figure that had come back to life and attacked him. The figure had to be preternatural in nature. He did his homework, dammit, smiling in disbelief because any mythical creature be it zombie, vampire, or werewolf the infection did not happen through only being scratched!

Dr. Jacobs came to a logical conclusion or as logical as the strange and supernatural could be. He theorized that Cody had died. However, as he learned in medical school and Creole culinary too the cadavers had a lot of fully functioning cells and the cells will be around for weeks to come as they decayed. These cells were attached to dead but otherwise workable machinery… Just like bullfrog legs with a sprinkle of salt forces the amputated legs to do a macabre jig so too the body of Cody… The magnetic pull of the full Moon like salt fools the cells and muscles, especially the heart into movement reviving him.

In time he did not blame the mortally wounded Cody for attacking him. Cody needed a way out; Dr. Jacobs could see it in his cloudy yet frightened eyes. Like a Tasmanian devil caught in a trap, chewing its own arm off to escape so too the frantic and frightened young EMT…

Gears started turning in the rational side of his brain. The mythical creature started to sprout claws and as a result blood began to flow…his eyes widened, it was in the blood, he reasoned.

Exhausted he dropped like a lead weight onto the kitchen chair taking his cell phone out of his pocket. He had tried to contact Capt. Rogers, but he was busy investigating the Royal Bay infernos.

"I need to reach Detective Jenkins, something is happening to me." Jacobs moaned.

After two Alka-Seltzers, three aspirin, and needless destruction to the four kitchen chairs, Dr. Jacobs finally got a hold of Detective Jenkins and now he sat on his front porch steps and waited for him.

"What's wrong with you, Dr. Jacobs?" Detective Jenkins questioned through the truck window before the truck had even stopped.

Jenkins put the truck in Park and opened the door. Almost a month sober now; bathed, clean-shaven, his button-up collared shirt tucked in, ironed and starched, and sporting clean pants. One track mind, a man on a mission, he dragged himself out from the dumps of depression and threw himself into work. Despite his obvious improvement he was still haunted with the vision of his son. His son's ghost vanished out of the cab without having to open the truck door.

"My, oh, my… Dr. Jacobs looks like shit…" The ghost whispered to his father.

Detective Jenkins observed Dr. Jacobs' shaggy hair. He had a real grizzly Adams appearance. Sunken and black and blue eyes, long filthy fingernails turning dark and he wore dirty ripped up dress pants and no shoes on filthy feet.

"The story that you told me when you shot the paramedic... I thought you were crazy but I was loyal, if you told me that you had seen fangs and claws then by damn you saw fangs and claws, even if I hadn't seen it for myself..." Dr. Jacobs explained to Detective Jenkins.

He tried to ignore his son's snarky comments as he produced a stainless steel 38 and checked to see if it was loaded, spun the chamber and handed it to Dr. Jacobs, "I have a revolver for you."

"Capt. Rogers couldn't be here, but he wanted me to check all of the houses destroyed by arson he found in his investigations in Plaucheville, Hessmer, Pollock, Saline, Calvin, Ida, as well as Batchelor and New Roads."

70

"Couldn't you find a more deserted place in Hessmer?" Phillip the ghost scoffed, he threw an incorporeal arm over Jenkins' shoulder.

Detective Jenkins stared at the remains of a two-story house. The ruins now looked like the cross-section of a dollhouse. What used to form the walls in the kitchen was reduced to three kitchen cabinets strewn about on the floor. They were unaware of the four Royal Bay residents on the second floor. They froze, afraid to even breathe lest they be caught.

"I don't even know what we are looking for!" Dr. Jacobs said discouraged.

"There is nobody here and I confess I don't know what we are looking for either." Said Detective Jenkins.

The upstairs residents drew a breath of relief. Confident they were gone. The Royal Bay residents couldn't smell or hear them anymore. Eventually a group consisting of four people drifted back to sleep exhausted from the drastic changes and last night's events.

Dr. Jacobs, Detective Jenkins, and the specter of Phillip rode on to another town with another burned down house. Again they were ignorantly unaware of the infected just feet away, obscured by the burnt up rubble. Yet another village in another burned out home far from society. Detective Jenkins gingerly touched the mysterious sigils written in blood, no signs of life.

With Dr. Jacobs' help to track down any individual involved in the mayhem in their once peaceful parish all clues pointed toward the Asher's house in New Roads. Burnt wood, the coppery gleam of exposed wires, and the smell of urine assaulted their senses. Jenkins caught movement from the corner of the room. Six filthy persons huddled together like a lazy orgy had just happened here. He couldn't believe what he was seeing nude people all sleeping and lying on the floor filled with soot and debris together. One woman while hugging the group sluggishly opened her eyes. Like a deer in headlights she froze, her eyes widening in fright.

Like cockroaches scurrying from the light young filthy nude infected Royal Bay residents ran from Dr. Jacobs and Detective Jenkins. Two strangers, a man and woman obviously a couple, locked eyes on Dr. Jacobs and Detective Jenkins. Their faces obscured by their oily and dirty hair. They were horribly bruised from head to toe. They let out a warning growl. Jenkins whipped his head around to see Col. Miller and the originally double leg amputee Sgt. Adam Alexander, standing before him. Encircling them laid the nude young changelings who had stayed in the house, too exhausted to flee.

A sudden movement gave Detective Jenkins an involuntary flashback to seeing the paramedic's claws. Then the eyes of his shocked son flashed through his mind when he pulled the trigger. Once, twice, the man fell down dead and the dirty woman gasped clutching her wound in her chest as well. Detective Jenkins cautiously advanced on the couple. His finger was still on the trigger and his eye on the target as he gained enough nerve to check the couple's pulse.

Detective Jenkins stared at Col. Miller and Sgt. Adam Alexander closely. Alexander had his boots off and he saw paws where dirty fleshy feet had been and he stood on the balls of his hard pads! His Marine Corps field jacket arms had been torn off and he had fur sprouting out of his right arm with a long talon-like paw.

Col. Miller's once hairy, wrinkly visage and drooping jowls had tightened and his face filled out. He had no need for dentures anymore, emerging with a set of full sharp fangs. Jenkins could not help looking into Col. Miller's eyes and they looked hollow reminding him of a marionette puppet, but who was pulling the strings?

"What are you doing here?" Sgt. Adam Alexander yelled clutching Detective Jenkins' collarbone with his new powerful lupine arm and spinning him around wincing in pain. "You killed my kin now you have to die!"

Dr. Jacobs' eyes widened as he frantically reached for his revolver and fired hitting Sgt. Adam in the chest. Shocked Sgt. Adam stumbled back and fell. Miller growled in fury but instead of attacking Detective Jenkins he came to Sgt. Adam's aid.

Jenkins' incorporeal son whispered into his ear, "Let's get out of here!"

The group stumbled out in unison from the condemned matchbox running toward the truck. They just had time enough to slam the doors shut when from out of the bushes there came two animals one crimson in color the other black as coal on all four legs targeting the truck. Dr. Jacobs craned his neck out the window wiping off dust in a circular motion. He could see through the dust two huge doglike creatures, closer examination revealed two huge hybrid-lupines, running after Detective Jenkins's truck using their tails as rudders for balance and control.

"Shoot them!" Detective Jenkins anxiously ordered Dr. Jacobs.

Dr. Jacobs' gun trained in on one of the two hybrid-wolves, incandescent eyes glinting, and fangs gnashing as they drew closer to the tailgate.

"What are you waiting for? Shoot it!" Detective Jenkins ordered turning the engine on and putting the truck into drive.

He pulled the trigger and the front limb burst with blood. No longer able to support its body the limb gave way; the hybrid-Wolf somersaulted toward the ground before righting itself again and stumbling up on two legs.

Dr. Jacobs shouted, "I thought I shot the monster!"

Dr. Jacobs hit the hybrid-Wolf in the chest but instead of falling down the hybrid-Wolf turned into a monster on two feet. When he was still a boy he believed in the supernatural; picking up his knowledge from books, movies, and television so it did not surprise him that the group of people could not transform under a new moon. But now Dr. Jacobs' mind spun with new questions. Why did one couple die from a simple gunshot while the other seemed to be unstoppable?

He knew he hit the wolf squarely in the chest. He could see the blood but he could also see the wound seal up right before his eyes. Fairytales come to life; the wolves that were chasing them could instantly transform into monsters at will and stood up on two legs, a hybrid of human and lupine. One werewolf was an obvious man with a furry bulge, the other clearly a woman with a petite curvy figure and four pair of teats her uninjured arm gingerly nursing the other injured one. They hurdled toward the truck bed their long claws reaching for the bumper.

Why were the residents of Royal Bay shacking up in four burnt down houses and in human form; unable to change any form at will? Does the cycle of the Moon affect them? The truck was swerving back and forth at breakneck speed but the two wolf-things easily followed.

Dr. Jacobs rolled down the window and with a shaking hand he fired at the male hybrid. He hit the monster again. A slug to the abdomen slowed the male Wolf-thing but did not stop it.

"Impossible!" Dr. Jacobs said, astonished.

The wolves were able to shift with ease; they seemed to have rational conscience thought during this, unlike the doctor. The more that Dr. Jacobs had struggled with his lunacy the fevered transformation had always finished and amnesia hit him and just the powerful emotions remained.

Dr. Jacobs broke out in a cold sweat "Is that what I'm going to be like?"

Dr. Jacobs' logical and inquisitive mind took over; his internal questions had to be put on hold, though. Out the passenger window he aimed for out reached claws and fired. A red fur hybrid-Wolf yelped in pain releasing its hold of the bumper as another hybrid-Wolf howled out in disappointment.

Somewhere concealed by rows and rows of Cyprus trees, Aticus was hugging a huge tree in human form and observed with his one good eye the growing conflict. So-seti emerged from the bushes her crutches giving her stability and her swollen belly looked like a beach ball ready to burst.

"Let them go, my sweet…" So-seti stroked Aticus' gleaming raven black hair.

"First and foremost, two young changelings are dead. Alas I can't help them, they were newly infected and it is too soon for the full moon's influence to do any good. Get them out of our Den before more police find them. However, Adam Alexander will be fine, but he needs rest,"

So-seti consoled him, "We have more important things to attend to, it is almost time to make preparations for the ritual to call upon the mighty shade."

Aticus observed the speeding truck with the werewolves, Lance and Tonya, behind them. He could smell right away that Dr. Jacobs had been infected and they had more important things to do than get in a fight with their own. He shifted into a lupine figure and howled out orders.

"They are stopping!" Dr. Jacobs shouted seeing the beasts abruptly stop, transform into huge wolves again, and vanish into the weeds.

"Good!" Detective Jenkins exclaimed, "What the hell is going on!?"

"I don't know." The specter answered.

"We have to get Rogers, he and I are the only other ones seeing the strange fiends firsthand," Detective Jenkins said never taking his eyes off the road.

Dr. Jacobs stayed silent the apprehension creaking in, and wondered, am I going to become one of those accursed creatures? What is going to happen to me? He knew his body was fighting the infection. When it lost the fight what would happen next?

71

Somewhere high above the Continental Divide

Lucius floated up to the mesosphere, thirty-one miles over North America. Even with his immortality looking out at the dazzling stars in the night sky always amazed him. He saw the brilliant moon, from the Earth, just a sliver more and it will be full. He marveled at the brilliant detail, freed from the ambient light of the city and trappings of civilization.

The jagged peaks of his cheeks had inflated to make gentle hills, his straw-like black hair alive, shining black-blue, full-bodied, and his cat shaped eyes glowing with the world's static energy feeding his leech-like system. But High up in the glacial outer most edges of space where the temperature bottoms out at under -130° F, stalactite ice begins to form on his chin and nose. There begins a thick layer of frost all over his body, but his non-living body shielded him from the mortal consequences of severe cold. But the threat was in early sunrise, he had descended as quickly as he ascended from the shackles of the Earth.

"Caine!" He yelled out in his mind, *"Are you listening?"*

First his big toe touched down in the soft Earth until slowly gravity pulled both of his feet firmly onto the ground. Though he felt no pain, and he had no biological need for oxygen the human trappings of life were just too great as he exhaled his breath and tried rubbing his missing hand. Las Vegas, Nevada, where the casinos operated even at night, was a natural home for the vampyre.

"I am here always, my heir," Lucius heard this clearly but deep in the bowels of the earth. Buried deep in the heart of Mesopotamia, Caine's body had long ago hardened and ossified. Shifting and turning tectonic plates drove him deeper into the earth until he reached the center, gently floating on tectonic rock until finally resting under the Gulf of Mexico region.

"The destruction of the North American Lucem Dei chapter has a European chapter scrambling for answers. The investigation will have them out of operation for months." Caine continued.

No longer satisfied with just stealing vigor from the living to grow strong he had now targeted helpless human prey. His mind getting stronger he purposely led the bride away from her own bachelorette party for some fresh air. The young woman wore a shiny blue dress, beautiful jewels, and a sash that said, "Bride". Clutching the wall for dear life afraid if she let go all balance would go with her as well and she would fall on her ass. He became invisible to any passerby in the street, save for one, the drunken bride to be in the blue dress.

"So-seti has been freed and undoubtedly will find her ancestors. What should I do now?" Lucius thought as he came out of the shadows, mesmerizing the intoxicated woman.

"Nothing, just be patient and wait." Caine ordered, *"We are The Children of the Night, the top of the food chain. I have walked the land with So-seti... I am the one that put in motion these events and I am the one that gave Aticus hope when he dreamed. The lycanthropes are our loyal pets, they are necessary to my plans even if they do not know it!"*

Before the young woman could respond, Lucius pounced on her, ripping into her exposed arm, going for arteries like a guided missile with his razor-sharp teeth. The blood was visceral and warm, sticky, salty, and metallic tasting. Intoxicating, sweet and savory lifeblood flowed out from her arteries in waves, every time her heart fluttered and it flowed into Lucius' throat.

An added benefit to physically drinking human blood, instead of only pulling pure energy from them, he was able to now enjoy actual life fluids. He could even taste the faint hint of alcohol and marijuana, feeling the unmistakable high and dizzying intoxication. When all of the blood had drained from her body Lucius threw her over his shoulder and walked towards the dumpster, throwing her in like she was just an empty shell, a warn and broken husk to be disposed of.

"As you wish master," Lucius rubbed his white and still unclothed stomach, for the first time satisfied and full.

72

Looking out the window Devon divided his time between the stunning scenery of the false River and Sarah's cabin. Anger, jealousy and suspicion growing, Amy made her presence known by stomping through the cabin like a bull in a porcelain shop. She should not be mad, Amy told herself. She wasn't sure what was worse, taking in a stranger that could be a killer or being naive enough to sleep with the stranger as soon as they met. She shouldn't be jealous. She's not in love with Devon! It was only a flurry of spontaneous sex in the heat of the moment. She didn't know what came over her in the first place. In fact, she was in love with a married man, but jealousy reared its ugly head anyway.

"Why are you so interested in her?" Amy angrily asked.

Amy threw back the curtains, finger pointing accusingly toward Sarah leaning on her cabin wall oblivious to the strangers staring at her as she read her diary. The sudden rush of light made Devon howl with pain, flinch, shudder, and shut his eyes tightly from the blinding sun.

Devon's odd disappearances late at night had Amy's stomach all a flutter, second-guessing Devon's presence here, the investigative reporter side taking over, "In one of the vandalized and abandoned houses I saw a sigil that reminded me of your face tattoo, are you responsible for those arsons? Are you in some kind of a murderous cult?"

"Are… are you killing people?" Amy shuddered; she didn't know if she wanted an answer to that or not.

Side stepping the initial question Devon turned apologetic eyes on her, "I swear Amy, I know what you must think but I didn't kill anybody, I wouldn't have done that."

She rolled her eyes and turned up the radio to drown out Devon. Amy had been investigating the arsons on her own. She had seen him in the woods by the murder site then again in the abandoned house. Detective Jenkins and Capt. Rogers investigated the forest murders and arsons and they were there questioning Sarah. Then she had seen Devon stalking Sarah from across the way, although it pained her soul she came to the only conclusion possible. The stranger, Devon, the one she had been most intimate with was a ritual killer.

His gaze too intense, she had to turn away. Amy was unsure whether or not to believe him. She had the overwhelming feeling that she was dreaming, the past several months engulfing her mind with memories and fresh tears. He pressed a gentle hand to her shoulder. Could he really be the killer? She asked herself. Was he the one who had killed so many but left her safe from harm? She should have been horrified and frightened but Instead she felt betrayal. She tensed her body, rigid at his once erotic touch.

She didn't know what to believe anymore, shivering as though a cold wind blew by, reality hit home in her stubborn mind. The residents were getting infected and were taking over the town and he was one of them, maybe the leader, one of the monsters, until now one of legend that she had been writing about.

Devon paced around the room like a trapped animal. To gain trust he had to tell her the full truth... if anybody could understand, he hoped she could. He was preparing to tell her stories of pleasure and pain. Nightmares turned into reality, the power he had over the flesh and where it all began.

"Amy…" Devon's voice quieted and soothed her.

Devon turned from staring out the window at the gray clouds rolling in on an ever increasing overcast sky. Preparing to bare his soul his shoulders had loosened a bit from some heavy secrets that were weighing him down but he didn't dare look at her face. After all, his thoughts and secrets are about to be revealed and he was petrified to look into her eyes. So afraid the innocence and purity in her beautiful trusting pale blue eyes would be gone and replaced by a lifelessness that would cut right through him. Devon's body shook, fists clenched white knuckled at his sides, tension around his forehead beating like a drum, copper taste in his mouth as he ground his teeth. He wanted so badly to slip into a form that could take him away from all the troubles in the world.

"You have to trust me," Devon quietly said in a voice so smooth it soothed her.

He consciously had to stop the fur rippling up his spine and over his shoulders. It took a moment of will. Amy should have run when she first saw him in the woods by the bodies or should have run when she saw him at the abandoned house. Now she should have run when she saw his skin ripple but then Amy looked into his loving eyes.

The fairytales that she wrote about for her rag had come to life and she felt a weird validation. Amy slid closer to him, her fears melting away. He sensed her closeness as she gently ran her fingers on his lips whispering loving words in his ear.

"I'll stand by you… I promise."

"Trust me I didn't kill anyone, I just came to find out what happened to Stefan and I stumbled onto so much more…"

"I trust you." She told him softly, tears stinging her eyes because she did trust him, she didn't know why but it was true.

Still afraid to look Amy in the face he turned away from her and peered outside as it started to rain. "I am extremely ancient, beyond my years and as such, I've learned a lot of things through my blood-brother and mentor, Stefan. And I have been taught our beginnings throughout the centuries…"

"I'll tell you a story, where it all began, and why I am here," Devon cleared his throat and swallowed breathing in deeply trying to remember all the minute details, "it was at the beginning of the end of the Ice Age."

"A Cro-Magnon sorceress, Aisos, set off to find select moss, weeds, flowers, and mystic mushrooms for her monthly rations of ceremonials for necromancy. She had wandered too far into a cave and gotten lost and then an earthquake sealed Aisos in the cave. No trace of sunlight, just impenetrable darkness as she tried to find and dig out of her unexpected tomb."

"Her eyes had adjusted to see a dim gray. She explored every nook of the cave looking for food but to no avail and hunger pangs eventually began to overtake the woman. She found, however, an old, frail and pregnant dire Wolf, which in a struggle with a saber tooth though she won she had been gravely injured and unable to move. Having picked the last of the dead saber tooth's life sustaining meat to the bone she had begun to feel hunger pangs as well." Devon explained.

"Do you want breakfast?" After the bacon and eggs were sizzling on the stove Amy picked up a notebook and readied herself to take notes although her trusty recorder would be running.

"Yes, please," Devon continued, "eventually the sorceress, Aisos, and the she Wolf were both soon out of their minds and reckless in their hunger. Each dared not to look away lest one of them were to attack the other."

"In those days there were giants, werewolves and witches." Amy desperately searched for the particular Bible quote that she sought out loud. Devon paid no attention to the phrase that she mumbled under her breath and continued.

"The sorceress searched in her pouch for herbs and various magical concoctions she had on her person and began mixing them up. She threw part of the concoction to the dire Wolf to give it strength and repress its hunger for just a while longer. Then she ingested one part herself to quell her weakness. The pair of them locked eyes. They mind melded, the dire Wolf and sorceress. The sorceress saw through the dire wolf's eyes and the dire Wolf saw through the sorceress'. They felt each other's pain and hunger and dire need. The sorceress and the she Wolf, half dead of starvation, weak and dizzy, both closed their eyes and listened to the rhythmic patter of raindrops beating down on the cave. Their brains were reduced to a Theta wave, and then a Delta state, the sorceress and the Wolf connecting on a spiritual level. Wolf thought as a sorceress and the weakening sorceress had the instincts of the Wolf. Aisos began to chant, began to pray to powers far more ancient than herself. Then the she Wolf began to howl with her in unison. There came down an eccentric pulsating energy all around the dying pair like a curtain at the end of a show and the eccentric energy covered them like a security blanket.

They struck a bargain, the fatally wounded dire Wolf and the starving sorceress. The pair struck an agreement for both to survive. When one died, the other would consume it and become one body of two, two minds melding together.

"Hey I think I've heard this story," Amy's eyes lit up in recognition.

"It's an old Native American story, right? Only when I heard it was a man and..." Amy abruptly stopped. Devon interrupted her before she could say the rest.

"In all folklore there is some truth behind the fiction, isn't there." Devon closed the curtains and settled down on the floor beside Amy.

"The sorceress kneeled down, arms out, turning her palms up so the dire Wolf would feel at ease. Cautiously, the she Wolf limped toward her until she could stroke her fur. Eventually the dying dire Wolf trusted her enough to rest its head upon her lap and she massaged and comforted her until the she wolf took her last breath."

"Nothing of her corpse went to waste. She made a fur jacket from her pelt with her dwindling supplies she prepared a basic stew from her heart and brain." Devon could see her visibly tense up in disgust as she imagined the vile stew, and couldn't help but laugh, but he shut up just as quickly when she playfully punched his shoulder.

"She survived with the scraps of the spoiling meat. It began to get slimy, blacken, and spoil and I guess that's when the parasites, from nature, magic or a blending of all, were born. But she ate the spoiled meat to survive. She became stronger and more alert, able to see in pitch darkness. She could even smell out the fresh air, which meant she could find freedom."

"A strange amalgamation occurred. She was sleek lined and leaner, a brain more cunning. Fueled by a full belly and particularly heightened new senses the sorceress found a way out of the cave. When she finally freed herself she was no longer a Cro-Magnon woman but also no animal either."

"She made love to the Cro-Magnon men infecting them like a prehistoric Typhoid Mary. The hormones of the dormant amoeba changing the physiology of everything it touched. While her six progeny split off and became outcasts, out-dwellers of the world."

Captivated, Amy had the carafe suspended in midair until she came to her senses, "you want some coffee?"

Devon suspended his story enough to answer timidly but with a sly smile, "yes that would be good, thank you."

"Anyway, feeling odd and unwell on one full Moon howling an aria she ingested the formula that sustained her when trapped in a cave. This woke up the dormant amoeba that grew into parasites and she began the transformation of the once dead dire Wolf. She made it her mission to teach the secrets of the ritual and formula to her progeny. And though there were variations from one to the next it awakened the amoeba that grew into parasites inside of them."

"Just like she promised every full moon she would change into the Wolf, so that the Wolf would live again. True to the bargain with the help of the full moon's light the sorceress transformed into the dire Wolf so she could run on all fours, laze around in the grass. Once she had changed to a Wolf and back again her body had changed as well her genetic structure drastically changing. The parasites, the ghost of the dire Wolf itself, entwined throughout the pineal gland or "third eye". She would be forever genetically changed to be the first carrier of the Wolf's blood parasite. The longer that Aisos survived the Wolf and the sorceress became as one person. An unholy survival instinct mutating, evolving..."

He began to explain to her, "… eventually she could will herself to change when she was furious, or if she was hungry as the wolf blood strengthened inside her, eventually the dire Wolf and the sorceress ceased to exist as two persons. The ghost of the Wolf's lust to survive set in motion a metamorphosis; she was neither human nor Wolf, but a glimpsing of the two. The sorceress could change to a woman or a Wolf at will now quick as a blink of an eye. And every time she changed she improved. It was as if every time she metamorphosed she shed her aging skin, into younger, leaner version, survival of the fittest gone awry."

"The six tribes thrived with Aisos' leadership and legends were told about her. When a brave human called out to her she would give them the wonderful gift of transformation, help, and guidance."

"However, she wandered around the world for millennia aimlessly with each transformation her heart got stronger but her willpower weakened. But by then she had bred more sons and daughters than she could keep track of. And then those sons and daughters had sons and daughters of their own, not knowing they had the gift inside of them." Devon stopped his lecture to breathe in the distinct aroma of coffee percolating again.

"Driven insane from loneliness and depression she threw herself off a cliff into the ocean. She decayed down below the depths of the sea. For years, while she rots, people that drank from the streams were infected by the parasites... Then the rains came. By then it was too late, the genie was released from the bottle and the Wolf shade would not die." Devon couldn't help but pace around the motel room.

Amy stood quietly, patiently listening to his tale.

"The six surviving children: five men and one woman became the original six Wolf covens. They guarded Aisos' secret beginnings, rituals, and potions with their lives. But the human side of the werewolf cults waged war for power and territory. Part lupine they battled fang and claw getting the attention of the Inquisition. Now with all eyes focused on werewolves most cults died out. As the years progressed the Wolf blood diluted. Sons and daughters, grandsons and granddaughters, lived and died not knowing they had the gift inside of them."

"Fighting with the Inquisition had tribes hiding in the shadows, against their nature of a pack mentality they stayed to themselves. A more powerful instinct prevailed in them than a need for a pack, the instinct to stay alive. The surviving werewolves' packs were forced to live in the shadows becoming smarter more cunning. Just like the humans bred domesticated distinct breeds of dogs. Now in the shadows they would meet and breed with each other making new breeds with fresh powers."

"The power of the Wolf shade would find a way to survive, so when a person makes the forbidden potions said the forbidden words did everything right, the Wolf shade would appear. It was a double-edged sword though, sometimes only the young or the strong could survive the change. Their hearts would explode, they had an aneurysm or worst of all, they'd think they've transformed but if the genetics are so deluded or they didn't get the potions and the rituals just right it wouldn't work at all." A pause as Devon caught his breath.

"So why are you here?" Amy couldn't help but question, her inquisitive mind taking over.

"I didn't know it, but I was an ancestor born with wolf's blood. I was no more than a teenager when the change came upon me. The full Moon's position had spontaneously transformed my body but I couldn't control it, I was a mangled version of skin and fur. Without any knowledge and guidance I was helpless to the moon's phases until Stefan, an ancient, took me in under his wing and he became my closest friend. Apparently Aticus has killed my friend, Stefan..." A tear trickled out of Devon's eye. "And he's hunting down and killing the only ancient surviving tribes, a power-play for Alpha. Aticus, though, is diseased and sickened by silver."

Transfixed by the legends Amy realized she wasn't drinking her coffee, the cup pressed to her lips and getting cold. A habit brought about from years of interviewing she frantically looked at the digital recorder assured that it was still recording. It was still on, thank God!

"How do you know all this?" She asked softly.

"I have been around for centuries and have picked up a few things," with just one gulp he emptied his full cup of coffee.

"I can smell the distinct aroma all through the air, I think with his necromancer great grandmother who has the power of life or death, Aticus has been given the knowledge to resurrect the shade Aisos and make her do his bidding. The stench is so powerful now I fear something horrible is going to occur on the perigee Full Moon."

Amy gave Devon a skeptical look, some of her reality had shattered, but she would be damned if she would be naïve enough to believe these monstrosities were directly affected by the moon's phases. After all, she had grown up learning the cycle of the Moon doesn't affect the human brain at all, just a superstitious myth.

"But the super Moon is just a cycle in the orbit of the Moon. It doesn't affect continental plates, the movement of the tides, or much less a human being. It's basically an optical illusion..." Amy tried to explain the science when she was interrupted by Devon.

"I'm going to stop you there," Devon tapping on his forehead explained, "minute, almost infinitesimal gravity shifts affect billions of Wolf blood parasites, they even affected human beings being 80% water and the eyes are a direct route to the brain. Any ER worker, paramedic, or police officer believes wholeheartedly the full Moon affects humans."

"For once in my life, I am afraid," Devon's voice quivered then broke, "I am all alone. Aticus may be sick, but he is a brilliant and a ruthless strategic commander born out of many conflicts. I fear confronting him."

His quiet competence and powerful pheromones that so attracted her to him and responsible for their intimate relations in the first place. For the first time Amy could actually see fear in Devon's eyes.

"I fear Aticus is distracted by something, he only wants the most powerful in his pack and then discards the rest leaving them to fend for themselves. With no direction to guide the infected they're scared and all alone." Devon couldn't help himself; he looked out the bay window again toward Sarah's cabin.

"Changelings need guidance and aid to become full-fledged lycanthropes. The very nature of the werewolf is pack mentality but without guidance, those that were infected go along oblivious until the full Moon changes them into lunatics. The weak and frenzied will do what they're told. But Aticus is diseased." Devon explained to Amy the dangers of a pack-less Army. "The lost lycanthropes are akin to escaped zoo animals, scared and all alone with their backs in a corner, hungry and having no alternative food readily available for them they turn to human beings. Humans are weak and plentiful. It takes a vast amount of energy to transform. When the wayward are done they are hungry. Imagine it, a hungry wolf in a populated city of so many. A balance of power in nature is shifting. The animal doesn't kill for the sheer thrill of it. They kill when they are hungry or cornered just as the lycanthrope. We the lycanthrope are not inherently evil. We're just apex animals driven on hunger and instinct. The humans are plentiful and they're oblivious to any predator that comes their way."

Devon visibly shook at the prospect of the upcoming conflict. Amy slid her hands around Devon's torso. She felt his muscular back. If he is afraid… this massive, unmovable statue of a man with no give at all, Amy thought, then I should be petrified!

"The Wolf is inside of me, but I really am a good guy." Devon explained lycanthropy and Wolf blood, "The blood is neither malevolent nor good, just an extreme and powerful force of nature. An example might be weather, when it storms it gives nourishment to the thirsty crops or it could just as easily destroy houses and lives. The wolf's blood is nonaligned, but I fear Aticus has a black soul."

"I couldn't help Stefan, but maybe I can stop the slaughter that I fear is about to occur. I am moral, ethical, and decent. Aticus is not, he is crazy, evil incarnate, and as Alpha he controls the newly infected to do his evil bidding! Aticus is diseased, he is not thinking clearly, he is ravenous and out for blood. And now for some reason, Aticus has trained his eye on this woman, Sarah." Devon stopped for a moment, Devon and Amy's eyes locked onto each other.

Amy looked back only once at the gorgeous stranger as she paced about the cabin the investigator coming out in her, "so, that is the reason why the midnight strolls occur, huh? You have to keep tabs on her and what's going on around here?"

"Well yes. Aticus and I made an agreement not to touch Sarah or the group here; I go out at night to be sure that the borders are secure. Aticus is a man of his word but as they wander out, they are fair game and I fear the group is dwindling."

"I could help," offered Amy. Electricity encircled the couple as she tenderly touched Devon's shoulder, "I can keep tabs on her so you could check out other suspicious areas. And maybe as a bonus I'll get more information for my growing story."

"That would be lovely!" Using only a plate Devon scarfed down the now cold but generous helping of bacon and eggs.

Amy's heart fluttered as she showered and dressed. She wondered why she was so quick to help. Just for the chance encounter to meet up with Capt. Rogers again? What was wrong with her? She thought. She had gone to bed with Devon at the drop of a hat and now she thought of Rogers. He was married for Christ's sake! It didn't stop her from putting her makeup on and spritzing herself with perfume. With every brushstroke that she applied pleasant but guilt ridden memories flooded through her mind. The memory of the all-night stakeout made her blush.

She ran out the door and began heading toward the motel room, zigzagging as if she could abate the raindrops. She yelled Sarah's name as she dodged for cover from tree to tree, a periodic respite from the deluge. She yelled her name again but she could not hear anything over the noise of the storm.

"Sarah?" She walked over toward the relative safety of the porch. Amy gently touched her hand to get her attention.

"Hi," Sarah looked up from her diary, "what can I do for you?"

Amy's freckled skin and pale blue eyes made her frizzy, fiery red hair entangled with the rain falling down stand out that much more. The mascara that she had carefully applied took just seconds for the rain to smear. Wearing her casual jean shorts and a man's wife beater shirt, countless freckles on her shoulders and thighs were visible. Her cotton tank top started to wear heavy from the rain. Jealousy stirred inside of Amy; from far away Sarah was the epitome of perfection. Close up, a goddess, she thought. She had an exotic look, a perfect blending of races with long silk-like black hair, almond shaped brilliant green eyes and flawless tan skin. Her cheeks reddened as she realized that Sarah looked perfectly dry even amidst the sideways rain. It could not ruin the wool pajamas she wore last night. A flowery perfume smelling of roses and apricot hung in the air even as the rain furiously fell down all around. I think even her flatulence would smell nice, Amy angrily thought, but she suppressed her jealousy with a smile.

"Hi, I am Amy and I work for The Eclipse Magazine, do you mind if I ask you a few questions?"

73

Amy struck up a friendship almost immediately with Sarah, her lonely and scared demeanor working to Amy's advantage. She confessed all of her hopes, dreams and immoralities that stormy night. She also let Amy in on her precious diary that she guarded with her life.

Amy found herself rummaging through the diary on the road headed towards Raccourci Island. She could not believe the preposterous and wild nature of the diary's contents. She began to feel sympathy for Alicia, for her loneliness and progression into madness. She had a remarkable story in her hands.

"We're here!" Roxy enthusiastically shouted as she thoughtlessly threw the gear shift into park.

Roxy opened the driver's side door of the van. The group consisting of Sarah, Amy, and a special appearance by Desiree who graced them with her presence, filed out of the sliding door one by one. Missing was Tommy who took off uncharacteristically early in the morning to hunt and AJ had stayed in the hotel room nursing a severe hangover, a direct result of last night's binging that spilled over into morning.

"Wow, this is amazing!" Amy froze and gasped, slack-jawed staring at the refurbished house.

"Well you can thank AJ! He did a lot of the work." Sarah said smiling, offering up the praise that AJ so rightfully deserved.

"Just in time for the party, don't you think?" Desiree chirped from behind Sarah.

Amy looked over to Desiree then to Roxy, immediately whipping her head back around to do a double take. Desiree looked like death warmed over. She looked wirier, somehow more compact and smaller. However, she was bruised from head to toe which she tried to hide with strategic makeup.

"It is a great idea!" Roxy agreed, remembering Michael Miller's promise.

"You're hounding, aren't you? Sarah sneered, "Yeah."

"Think of it as a housewarming!" Roxy said coyly.

Sarah looked suspiciously at Roxy. She looked like a vampire or a geisha with her white blush pasted all over her face. Her normal blue and heavily black eye-shadowed eyes replaced by a wide-eyed enthusiasm. Her glittery glossy bright blue pouty voluptuous lips were exaggerated in an ear to ear smile.

Reluctance to host the party melted away. She had decided hosting the party would be a good idea, a therapeutic idea as well. Her fears and suspicions had turned into feelings of rage, some friends! Tina and Jac had probably hopped on the next train out of town and back to school. In her heart she did not blame them… Those who stayed were not getting the college experience in the first place.

Desiree had a mysterious new love, Roxy stayed where ever Desiree stayed. AJ found the legendary Bourbon Street and struck up a new band. Tommy come and goes when he pleases. Sometimes he would be missing for days. It was like he was a different person altogether, a confident Tommy, an independent Tommy. He wasn't pestering Sarah and that pleased her immensely.

"You're hosting a party at the house?" Amy questioned.

"Why yes, Desiree, my best friend since junior high has coaxed me into it," Sarah shot a fleeting glance at Roxy and Desiree, "I think she met a friend, a tavern owner and party organizer who was planning a Halloween celebration, but still didn't know where to have it."

Amy left Sarah's side to file into memory the rehabbed manor. The derelict building had come back from the dead with the allowance given to Sarah earmarked for the plantation restoration. Growing up with a professional contractor for a father, AJ flew through what many considered daunting work. He had finished a professional French Creole and Greek style exterior restoration in less than six months.

Clutching Alicia's diary, Amy stepped up on the new deck. The scorched faux Greek columns had been torn out and replaced by shiny, sturdy grand columns. The termite ridden rotten boards on the deck were replaced with 3 x 8 waterproof decking. The rickety damaged screen door had been torn out and replaced with a thick, heavy oak door complete with intricate engravings and decorations. Behind the locked door she could just imagine the living quarters had been refurbished beautifully too.

Amy hopped down from the deck and walked over toward the side of the house towards the field. Amy froze at a bend in the woods concealed by row after row of Cypress trees, Spanish moss with wispy moss straggling down to the ground like several wizards' long white beards.

Amy stopped abruptly gawking at a large square clearing. Circling her in the clearing were Cypress trees like those reminiscent of a Shakespearean theme, *A Midsummer Night's Dream*, When Hermia awoke from a dream to discover a ring of fairies dancing about her. The weeds stopped abruptly in the dirt in long lines and 90° angles almost like a building had been there before. Her skin crawled as she stared at the overgrown bushes and weeds that went all around the parameter and then abruptly stopped at a 12 by 20 foot area of lifeless ground. With the help of a troll born's incantation the barn disappeared from the prying eyes, but the infected could still easily see Amy. She felt uneasy, like invisible eyes were watching her every move.

It was all adding up, Devon's appearance, the incessant stalking of Sarah's dwindling group… houses with esoteric scratches, crazy as it may seem it was not from a cult, but a den… a large human den. The lycanthropes marked their territory in Raccourci Island a long time ago and they were back to reclaim it. The curious nature she had been born with that worked for her so far, she couldn't help but be nosy. It begged the question: what does Sarah have to do with their plans specifically?

The ancestor of the plantation, did they need humans to purchase or pass on the land?

The hairs on her neck stood up as a cold chill washed over her… That's it, she thought, I'm being watched. With all that Devon had confessed to her she'd had to interview Sarah. She fumbled for a business card in her pocket.

"I have to call Captain Rogers." She said to herself checking and memorizing the business card then dialing it on her cell phone.

The anticipation threatened to kill her, the more the phone rang with no answer the more butterflies escaped fluttering about in her stomach. Amy second-guessed herself, was her calling Captain Rogers strictly professional or was there more to it? Out of the hotel room the pheromones that Devon produced started to ebb. Freed of Devon's lustful grasp the school girl crush that she always had for Captain Rogers returned with a vengeance as she heard his voice as he finally picked up.

"Hello, this is Rogers."

"Hi…" awkward silence on the phone. She couldn't help but shake the feeling that she was being watched. Amy shook off her paranoia and gathered her courage to speak, "its Amy, can you talk a minute?"

"Uh, why of course," Captain Rogers heart rate doubled, apparently he had a schoolyard crush too, but tried his best not to show it, "what can I do for you?"

"We need to talk. You won't believe me, but I think I know what is going on around here." Amy whispered looking around; she could swear something dank and dangerous hung in the air, "I have befriended Sarah and I have read inserts in her family's diary."

"I will be over when my shift ends, I need to talk to you and we should compare notes," Captain Rogers regretted his comment before it ever left his mouth, he owed it to his wife to not hurt her again and to be faithful, but he convinced himself it would be only business this time around.

She felt her cheeks redden, imagining forbidden events in her mind, "that would be good, thank you…"

Amy ironed out the plans to meet up with Rogers when she heard a faint rustle coming from behind her. Her heart rate quickened and goose pimples erupted like a wave across her arms. She was being watched, dammit! She spun around dropping Sarah's diary in the process.

Amy dropped her cell phone in surprise. At a glance she saw shoulder length Raven black hair just inches from her. She gasped as she stared up into brilliant green eyes.

"Did I surprise you?!" Sarah got up off her knees, retrieving her diary that Amy had dropped. Laughing, Sarah said, "You need to switch to decaf, come with me and I'll show you around the house!"

In the hidden barn invisible eyes blinked, invisible mouths gave a sigh of relief; Invisible bodies relaxed as Amy and Sarah turned the corner and disappeared from sight.

74

The sun was setting just behind the treetops at the library giving a red hue to the sky. Jack-o'-lanterns, witches, and enormous candy corns littered the sidewalks harkening in the fall season. She arrived at the University of Louisiana, Lafayette, home of the ragin' Cajuns. Amy graduated from this school and as such garnered special privileges in this library that she didn't get in normal libraries. Somewhere in the distance the school bell rang ushering out students that scurried about and hurried home. College students preparing for a weekend of binge drinking that would release them from the hectic day-to-day college life. The students were thinning out now as she reached the library.

The eerie air around Malstros' plantation, sections of Alicia's diary, the gentleman stranger Devon who opened her eyes to the mythical lycanthropes, and lastly the several arsons that she herself reported, compounded her fear. Amy had a long night's conversation with Rogers and it did not soothe her anxiety but she had needed to hear his voice like a crack addict itching for the next fix.

Rogers had given her the green light to investigate further, but he said to stay off the radar of any media sources until she had something concrete to show them. Well I've got Devon and his recorded conversation don't I? She said to herself of course, it would be considered the ravings of a madman. Devon had been gone for several days, though. She had made the long, grueling trip to the library for weeks now with nothing to show for it. There had been no proof that the Malstros plantation ever existed.

She sat hunched over the books in the library with thoughts flooding through her busy mind, the events of the last few weeks hazy like a distant dream. She wasn't sure what she was looking for and nothing she read seemed quite right. Since Devon came into and out of her life nothing had been quite the same. Amy strained her eyes trying to read the last of the first two books, neither one of them were helpful. Too deep in myth, unsuccessfully weeding out more facts than mystery, that was not what she was looking for. Then Amy turned to the census, residence and parishes of Louisiana. No proof of ownership, what had happened to the last residents or even what happened to the mysterious Alicia.

Frustrated, Amy subconsciously nibbled on her pencil, aware the research was amounting to shit. As she wrote in her notebook straining her eyes until she felt a headache coming on. Unaware of piercing eyes watching her from a corner across the room. She threw a pencil and slammed the book as she pulled the chair out from the table and stood up and turned around. Amy jumped; a stranger had emerged from the shadows, taking her breath away. Out of breath she stared at the figure that now stood beside her.

"Don't be afraid…" The stranger assured Amy, "I would like to talk to you, but not here."

James gripped a particularly large branch in the Cyprus tree. The leaves concealed him from occasional passing college students. He stared down into the library window at Amy, drooling. He had tracked her to the library where she had stayed inside researching for hours. He had been given orders by Aticus to record her every movement. James would zealously take any order Aticus gave him. With the guidance and tutelage of So-seti he could shift from one form to the other without the moon's presence. Aticus should respect James as the mate of So-seti whom he had impregnated and by association would be his relative. By all rights Aticus should obey him for his power, but he was repulsed by his very presence.

James stared at her in the window, but he dared not venture much further. He could smell a threat from within the library. He didn't know what to do. With another tall stranger upon her he did not dare to give away his position.

"You are in grave danger," The stranger whispered, pity in his voice as he offered her one hand. "They'll come for you now...." he said as he rested the other hand on her shoulder.

"Come with me." His tone suggested it wasn't a suggestion but a command.

The stranger's gaze too intense, she felt powerless and frightened. She studied his face to avoid looking at his eyes. He had a wide chin, large square face, and thick neck like a professional body builder. He had a rough exaggerated five o'clock shadow, thick wild brown hairs sprouting about his not yet bearded complexion. Her body beyond her control she was following him out the door before she knew it.

"Who are you?" Amy asked pulling her jacket up and across her arms in an unconscious sign of fear.

The huge man turned his back to her. She could see his full form now and felt like a rag doll in his presence. He was a powerful man her head barely even reaching his chin. Dressed in a brown leather duster he had dark, greasy brown hair coming over his shoulders. Until he stopped suddenly she noted a substantial limp when he walked.

"It isn't important who I am, what is important is your safety." He grabbed her wrist cutting off the circulation in her hand.

Amy anxiously looked around for any security or even a helpful stranger. She saw an old woman in the midst of a novel, a college student trying his best moves on a co-ed and a homeless man drooling and asleep on a desk, they would not be helpful though.

Her mind frozen in fear and her body betraying her she did not know what to do. She had actually came face to face with Devon, a self-professed Lupine-noid creation, and now she found herself being forced out the door by a hulking behemoth. Her heart sped up when a uniformed security guard came out of the restroom turned the corner, adjusted his shirt, secured his belt and looked around. She could see the double glass doors of the exit just a few paces away.

"Don't even think about it," Hunter whispered gesturing toward the oblivious security guard and roughly jerking Amy's body to hammer the point home like a nail, "I don't want to kill a human being, but I will if I am discovered. Believe me when I tell you, I'm your friend."

A yawning college security guard with a uniform that looked two sizes too small for him glanced over suspiciously at Amy and the hulking stranger. Her nervous expression managed to change into an insincere smile, and with a flirty bat of her eyelashes the Security guard looked away and leaned on the library wall. Amy could almost hear it groan with the increased weight.

"Good night to you, come back and see us again." Saluting, the security guard mumbled to them with an insincere smile on his face.

Hunter cordially smiled, then dismissed him with a flick of the wrist. The glass doors of the library closed behind him. Hunter glanced around the courtyard nervously like a small rodent in the wild looking out for predators everywhere.

Out of the frying pan and into the fire, Amy thought as the couple walked down the cobblestone sidewalk arm in arm toward the parking lot. Amy glanced at Hunter who sniffed the air around him. Something did not smell right to him and in response Hunter drew Amy closer and a brisk walk turned into an invasive trot.

At his vantage point from the treetops James observed Amy and Hunter coming out of the library. Both Aticus and So-seti had asked him to keep tabs on Amy, but So-seti had plans of her own whispering in secret to him if the opportunity arose he should abduct her for So-seti's own devices. A successful abduction could bolster the respect of the den without Aticus. He breathed in Amy's aroma, Sarah's bouquet all over her body. A split second decision had to be made because though he hadn't been spotted yet he soon would be. He had to act because if somehow the accursed Hunter escaped he surely knew how to cover his tracks. This is it, he told himself, and descended easily from the treetops.

Before Hunter knew what hit him something smashed into him the wind leaving his lungs. He fell headlong into a parked car cracking the fiberglass bumper and falling down on his ass. He came to his senses to see one man… or was it two men? A nasty gash on the back of his head had given him double vision and the Earth spun out of control.

"Help me!" Amy yelled out as James grabbed her and hefted her over his shoulder.

"Stay back. I don't want to hurt you!" with a mouth full of fangs James' warning was garbled.

Hunter crinkled his nose… but that is impossible! Did his nose betray him? He checked the sky for the moons phase then stared at the stranger. The Wolf blood that traveled through his veins smelled fresh, the gravitational influence weak at best. The stranger should not have any control to manipulate his body at will. Yet Hunter stared at hands that transformed into lupine claws. He raised and shook his arm that used to be limp at his side for years, and then pointed a fur covered long, sharp talon pointer finger as a warning to Hunter still lying on the pavement.

Hunter craned his neck to see his van realizing he had left his arms and ammo in a duffel bag. Amy struggled to wriggle in vain. He struggled to find something in his duster, and then frantically stuffed plugs in his ears. He grasped a little black box, a speaker directly in the middle and a red button on the side, a homemade sound grenade. He pressed it and tossed it toward the stranger.

James looked curiously at the foreign device. Hunter was in rescue mode before the alarms squealed into James's ears. The black box vibrated on the concrete. An intermittent amplified shrill like a fire alarm on steroids that violated James's skull forced James down on his knees.

"Now!" Hunter barked. He saw James' claws spontaneously convert back to hands as they shielded him from the harsh sounds.

Amy saw James' hands pressed firmly to his ears, mouth open from immense pain, it was her chance, she thought; now or never, with one firm push of her hands she leapt from James' clutches.

Before she hit the concrete Hunter caught her, then clumsily twirled around metal hitting metal with his brace and ran towards his van. He had started it and was putting it in gear before the sound grenade turned off. James was still covering his ringing and bleeding ears.

Before James came to his senses shaking off the dizzying experience he could see the van's tail lights. It could be a blessing in disguise, James thought to himself as the van disappeared into the distance. He could smell the strong aroma of Sarah and chances were, he thought, they would meet again off neutral territory and he could capture the both of them.

75

Amy looked out at the gathering haze from a seedy motel room on Highway 1, halfway between New Roads and Batchelor. A train could be heard but not seen from the railroad tracks adjacent to the highway. She had become a reluctant prisoner for her own safety for awhile now with a man that called himself Hunter. She was not staying at Point Breeze motel anymore so she could not keep tabs on Sarah and adding insult to injury she almost lost her car. After the close call at the library she was too afraid to go outside, afraid she'd get captured or worse. She had at least coaxed Hunter to pick up the car for her. He did the task with no questions asked hiding the car out of sight so it would not be seen. Only one more night before the full moon's gravitational influences were in full swing, an illusion of fullness in the night sky when she looked up at the dazzling moon.

"Amy!" Hunter yelled out hoarsely.

Amy nervously sat her duffel bag full of reports on the bed and headed toward the kitchenette. Shaking the knobs on the electric burners ensuring they were off then headed over toward the sink turning on and off the water. She had to do something to burn off the nervous energy that put her on edge. Hunter turned immediately to the bathroom searching his pockets for his pills. He was jittery and shaking as he popped the cap off the container.

Amy watched him from the corner of her eye. He was pale and sweating and something about him chilled her to the bone. She watched him several seconds more as he unbuttoned his shirt and took it off. She was taken aback by his horribly scarred neck and shoulder. Beyond the scratches he had a tone, fit body. The beads of cold sweat made him glisten. She was startled when she saw the IV port in his jugular vein.

"Hunter!" Amy sympathetically reached for the IV port in his neck but Hunter quickly pushed her aside, "What is that? What happened?"

Hunter wiped his sweaty face on a bathroom towel and then pushed Amy to the side heading toward the bed. He threw himself down and started to unscrew the metal knee support beneath his pants. He gingerly straightened his bum leg on the bed then went to work unscrewing the long braces also beneath his pants. They fell to the floor with a clang as metal hit metal. He unbuttoned his pants and arching his back pulled them off.

"What the hell happened to you?" Amy looked on horrified at his mangled right leg. His knee was almost nonexistent a chunk of thigh muscle missing. The evidence seemed to point to the bite of a large animal. She could see silver screws that were embedded into his lower thigh and calf. "Who the hell are you? I mean I'm thankful for you saving me but…"

"Does the motel have Wi-Fi?" Hunter asked, avoiding her question as he rubbed his lame leg as if the injuries were new again and he was in pain.

"Yes, why?" Hunter was avoiding the question and Amy got the hint.

"Can you do me a favor? Can you go out to the truck and get my large olive green duffel bag and bring it to me?" Hunter wasn't looking at her but instead concentrating on his half knee intently.

Amy did what he asked without a response, his military style duffel bag made her shoulders slump and the weight slowed her to a snail's pace.

She finally emerged and recklessly threw down the bag. An involuntary sigh came over her, relieved as the weight lifted off her shoulder.

"Why couldn't you get YOUR duffel bag, you know I'm not a...." Her voice trailed off.

She looked on horrified at Hunter's violently shaking leg. His knee literally jumped up and down under his skin. Cold beads of sweat poured down over his entire body his hair matted and wet.

"You trust me?" His voice was raspy and shaky. He knew by her face she was hesitant, "I will tell you who I am… I mean I will tell you who I *really* am, and the whole story and what you're going to do … but first I need you to get into the duffel bag and get out my black leather medicine bag for me and bring it to me."

The pleading expression on his face and the look of an impending seizure developing on his now pasty body prompted her into swift action. She quickly rummaged through the many handguns, rifles, shotguns, an almost futuristic crossbow contraption, and hordes of ammunition until she finally found his medicine.

"Find the plungers that are filled with silver liquid and screw them into the port on my neck please!" His voice a low and deep almost growl; she couldn't help but turn around and see his face.

His eyes glowing red, then rolling back into his head, drool coming out from his lips pooling on the edges of his chin. Amy was horrified; she was almost mauled at the library by monsters now she was shacked up with one!

"Please, just trust me!" His canine teeth were starting to lengthen and several teeth in his jaw started to bud, cracking his jaw.

Amy's body headed toward him on autopilot a surreal moment in time. Like she was looking out from herself as she watched herself move in closer to this now dangerous Hunter. She watched as she unscrewed the caps and fit them into the port on his pale body.

A fur lined, talon claw backhanded her pushing her back toward the wall almost losing her balance on an end table. Hunter plunged the syringe down until the silver liquid went into his veins. He fell back in the bed as if he was pushed, the empty plungers still screwed into his body. He convulsed for a few horrible seconds then he was still. Hunter lifted his shaking human hand toward Amy.

"Pills… please..." He was struggling to speak.

Amy was shaking almost more than Hunter but she managed to find three bottles of pills and walked over to the kitchenette to get a cup and water for Hunter to wash the pills down. She couldn't help but notice the labels. Clozapine, Quetiapine, and finally Risperidone, she noted that all of the drugs were for schizophrenia. He choked them down and his breathing began to slow.

His cold, shrewd eyes began to focus somewhere on the corner of the wall. He began to speak but not to anybody in particular as he remembered the events that that were responsible for bringing him here today.

"In the year of our Lord, 1767, in the village of Ge'vaudan there was a beast terrorizing the land."

Hunter turned to her his eyes focusing and spoke, "I am Andre Clairaux. Jean Chastel, I, and my older brother, Marco, all farmers by trade, were commissioned by the Catholic Church to dispose of the beast of Ge'vaudan. Just a wee lad then and the money would go far to getting my family out of the poor house you see but it will be forever seared into my mind."

Then Hunter placed a sphygmomanometer around his arm and checked both his blood pressure and his heart rate, his pressure visibly coming down, "A strong, young farming man without fear. I thought I would live forever… and now…"

He smirked at the irony of this thought for a second and then continued, "My brother and I went to the church for confession, repentance, and Jean had three silver slugs blessed for luck. Then we were off to capture and kill the beast."

"We were following the beast's tracks before we realized we were far from home and the dark clouds made the sun dim too soon. No time to look for it or set up camp for the first time I felt a sense of my mortality." Hunter said softly, his eyes narrowing, normalizing.

Amy gave more water to Hunter which he greedily sucked down then continued the story, "We cannot sleep lest the beast would sneak up and set upon us. We had to stay alert we were back-to-back with our arms on the ground just within reach. We had each other's back, watching for a fluttering bush trying to distinguish every broken twig or rodent's warning call."

"Hunting for signs of the beast, Jean Chastel had yet to return to our "camp". Just before the dawn apparently Marco, my dear brother, fell asleep and I felt my eyes getting heavy also. I heard a bloodcurdling scream that jolted me awake and to my horror I realized I must have dozed off. When I had thoroughly awoken the beast of Ge'vaudan had latched onto Marco's throat, blood flowing like a collapsed dam Marco's face froze in panic and his body went limp. In the confusion I managed to snatch up my gun and tried to take aim at the beast before I lost track of the monster. The beast doubled back and knocked me to the ground taking my breath away. The beast bit me on the leg, causing my firearm to drop."

"Now woozy from blood loss, adrenaline kicking in I managed to run. Luckily the beast did not give chase. He was too distracted by the aroma of his fresh kill. I managed to take cover in one particularly sturdy oak tree. The beast's head was down and its muzzle hungrily tore through my brother's flesh."

"I saw Jean at the top of the hill. He had already seen the conflict, prepared his gun, got out one silver slug from his pouch, loaded it into his muzzle, and he took aim. He waited until the beast's eyes met his. One shot, one blessed lucky shot... The beast fell down. He returned home to a hero's welcoming with the head of The Beast of Ge'vaudan and paraded it around the village. Meanwhile, I had gotten smuggled off to the healing hands of monks."

"Shortly after this a great fever fell upon me and The Gods Light elders tended to my wounds. They put herbs and roots directly on my wound then placed a light silver mesh around my leg and The Gods Light elders fashioned crude silver braces in which to walk. Then they ordered me into a cave where they chained me to the wall for three days!"

"When the moon was about to crest for three nights the elders drugged me to the point of death. I guess they have dealt with this for millennia, but for three days I was in a stupor, a coma, with two armed guards watching my every move. When I came to my senses the elder told me I survived and no transformations came upon me. I traded my services for a deal that could quell my beastly urges."

"So Jean Chastel got all the credit for killing the beast and I became The Hunter... A loyal asset to the church for all these many years..." Hunter's voice trailed off.

Amy calculated the math in her head, and then spouted, "But that's impossible!"

"Yes, yes. I'm still alive. I have seen the birth of a nation and many wonders in my years but eventually I weakened from age. Desperate to save me the elders would take me to a cave to restrain me for the cycle of the full Moon for three days and I would let loose the beast. They would leave me chained up until the cells in my skin renewed again. The new lupine-human would die out in 90 days. With massive amounts of herbs and medicines to kill any parasites that had escaped were pulled back by massive silver doses to the wound site. Then they were able quell the urge to transform for years until I needed renewing again.

"A partly religious sect they could not ignore the Scriptures. Nobody lives forever, everyone dies. The Gods Light elders frantically searched Scripture after Scripture to give me God's blessing, but my body would die every time I transformed and thus begot a loophole to the rule; I guess I know the Gods Light saw it that way. Having been contracted by the Gods Light to find and destroy lycanthropes and occasionally vampyres as well. I would not get old as I fought the abominations with the blessings of the church…"

"For three days as the moon is about to crest it is as if I have a sports injury sensitive to moisture, my wounded leg would hurt and stiffen," Hunter continued," warning of imminent transformation which I could do something about."

"As the years progressed The God's Light improved the traditional herbs, advancing technology and procedures, operations and medicines. A modern silver ball inserted directly into my missing knee cap, silver shafts embedded directly into my tibia and fibula to quell the beast inside me."

"They have gotten an amazing amount of information from me, from my many blood tests. Apparently the abundance of silver throughout my skin and bones coupled with an immense amount of drugs acts as an electromagnetic field and traps the parasites back into the wound. Only the brightness of the full Moon would awaken the larvae and flood my body turning to parasites in my veins but I have massive amounts of drugs to remedy that. It all started long ago with the Beast of Ge'vaudan."

"So… you travel the around world in search of werewolves to kill… with your blessed bullets?" Amy scoffed.

"Well, not exactly, one particular ghastly night I soon found out that blessing the bullets was useless when I came upon one particularly nasty ancient werewolf. The blessed bullets stopped him, but just for a moment as he healed. In a last ditch effort I set ablaze the fields in a circle where the fire trapped the lycanthrope, but in doing so I was trapped as well. I was lucky enough to survive third degree burns as an inferno that I intentionally set burned the structures all around me."

"I don't know what it is about the silver, be it mystical or basic atoms that have an electrical magnetic charge, but it is death for vampires and apparently werewolves alike. In fact, from my vast scrapes and experiences it's surprising that most of the ways to dispatch a vampire or a werewolf are alike, silver, beheading, burning, or a steak to their heart."

"I don't pretend to comprehend or understand the inner workings of the night dwellers."

Amy tapped her foot on the ground rhythmically; it was a nervous habit she picked up when she was young. But it started to annoy Hunter.

He motioned to her to stop the tapping and spoke, "my colleagues have the great, great, great granddaughter of the first sorceress."

"What?" Her jaw dropped, "you have..." she tried to wrap her head around the fact that she had seen not one but two actual immortal lycanthropes.

"That's why I'm here." He confessed when he felt sturdy enough he got up from the bed and sat down in a chair.

She pressed stop on her digital recorder which she had pulled from her purse at the beginning of the story and stood up wiping her hands on her shorts and after circling a few times collapsed onto the bed.

He produced a syringe and vile of lorazepam and codeine mixture, he tightened the belt against his arm until revealing veins came to the surface. Picking a good plump vein he then stuck a needle in his skin and pressed the plunger down.

The burning dizzying mixture reminded him of his mission, the ancient So-seti, and her escape, "The last time I saw her, So-seti, she was a frail old woman. We had a mixture of silver nitrate solution intravenously injected through her veins so she couldn't transform and because of that she was aging. So-seti and I are not that chemically different. The Gods Light elders thwarted my infliction early before it spread, trapping it in my wounds."

Hunter leaned his body against the chair, shoulders relaxing, his eyelids fluttering and starting to get heavy. Hunter passed out without even taking the syringe out of his veins. Looking at Hunter's drooling face and hearing him snoring Amy pondered her safety.

From muscle memory alone before she knew she found herself dialing Captain Rogers' personal home phone number, "Come on, come on, pickup, please."

"Hello?" A familiar voice questioned. She instinctively hit end before she said anything. Her heart racing, it was the voice of Captain Rogers' wife.

"I've got to get out of here." Amy opened the curtains again and peered out into the night sky.

She had come face-to-face with both men… living, breathing, snarling beasts. Hunter a snoring and drooling shaking mess, no better than a junkie. She doubted her safety staying with Hunter. But the other one, Devon, seemed decent, moral, honorable, strong, and now he was missing.

"I really have to get a hold of Rogers." She told herself as she took her purse, keys and her jacket off from the chair.

She flung open the hotel room door then paused a moment, second thoughts plaguing her mind. Was it a mistake leaving…? Andre Clairaux, the silent partner of Jean Chastel? She looked back, Hunter's head slumped over and drooling.

"Thank you for saving me but I have to go." Amy said shutting the door behind her.

76

Amy cautiously ambled down the deserted highway weary of real life nursery rhymes sinking their teeth into her, the motel room slowly shrinking behind her. It was miles to where Hunter stashed her car and she feared she would never make it. Luckily she thought of the Metro bus system that regularly drove the whirlwind highway.

I wonder what time it is, and if the bus had already finished its route for the night? The answer to her nagging question came in the form of bright headlights rounding a bend in the road. A long, lean white Metro bus with blue LED patterns that read *Lafayette to Baton Rouge* on the top of the windshield barreled down the road. She knew she still had a ways to go to get her car but this was a step in the right direction.

The bus crawled to a stop, over- taxed breaks screeching as the passenger door slid open. She nervously looked around; she couldn't shake the feeling of watchful eyes upon her, before climbing on the bus. She sat down and rummaged through her oversized purse for her notebook and recorder and when she found it turned it on to a transcription of Alicia's diary,

"But time with my love and the bliss that we had with each other did not last… as night after night my Poppa paced the floors ever alert for predators… One night he saw the green eyes close to our homestead. Poppa says this is the last attack on our animals."

Amy clicked the stop button on her recorder then closed her notebook when she neared Baton Rouge, time to take another bus to New Roads. It would be a fantastic story, no doubt, a wonderful page turner and something to get her out of the rut that she had been currently in. But what audience would believe such fantastic tales? She would have to write it in a fictional manner or nobody would believe her.

The bus came to an erratic and rough stop. The brakes moaned almost like they were in pain then the hydraulics hissed as the door opened. Amy debussed and walked up to a dilapidated bench, complete with graffiti and broken glass waiting for her. Two streetlights hissed and buzzed turning on and off like dim strobe lights.

The loud moan from the bus catching gear made Amy shiver. She imagined the taillights of the bus as mad red lupine eyes vanishing into the distance, and her body involuntarily shivered again. She tried to put the bad thoughts behind her. She tried to block out the Booker A-line employees finished with second shift crowding around her. The smell of nickel, copper, acid, and oil on filthy uniform overalls was upsetting her senses and watering her eyes as the group crowded around and sat down with an audible sigh.

She plugged in her ear buds so as not to disturb the exhausted employees then turned her recorder back on again,

"He ran outside, Poppa, I know because I heard the screen door open and close… I hurried to get dressed and strained my ears to hear … Suddenly a bang. I ran downstairs and out to find my Poppa had wounded one of the beasts, Poppa shot him right in the head and it just stood there glaring at him, becoming almost human. My, my Aticus, my love... This thing…. ran off after my father shot it... I'm scared to examine my feelings now. Poppa sends us away into town for the night...I am nauseous and I don't know if... My love will survive… It's like a bad dream. Father promises he'll keep me safe

and that the Wolf thing won't be coming back, but... In my heart I wish that Aticus would come back to find me."

"I couldn't believe it! My Aticus was **a myth come to life, a** ***loup garoux! But he looked so gorgeous, so human. I looked into those caring, brilliant emeralds, forever smitten with him. So loving and forgiving and I couldn't forget he saved my life too. It is funny to think about it now but the first time we made love it was when he told me he had come to kill me."***

The smell of stale cigarette smoke wafting through the open air of the bus stop distracted Amy's train of thought. In fact, she felt herself getting nauseous as she pressed stop.

"Excuse me." She politely smiled as she tried to maneuver from the seated crowd without stumbling.

Clutching her purse a chill came over her, she still could not shake the feeling of eyes upon her, especially since she could look beyond the highway to find miles and miles of corn fields that could conceal a stranger's whereabouts.

In fact, unobstructed she could see the Booker A-line factory lights in the far distance, which told her New Roads wasn't that far away. She broke out her cell phone and dialed Capt. Rogers' cell phone, instead of the house phone that she had previously called on accident.

"Come on, come on!" The sounds of desperation were evident in her voice as it rang and rang and rang.

"Hello…" Capt. Rogers answered and for a moment Amy's heart quickened, her cheeks reddening impulsively, smiling until he continued to speak, "I'm not available right now, please leave me a message after the beep…"

It seemed like forever before the sound that let her know she could talk now, "hey, Cappy, I'm frightened, but I think I figured out what is going on. Meet me at Sarah's motel room when you're off-duty… I really need you."

The headlights of the bus could be seen in the distance when she pressed end. Standing up from the crowd she was first in line when the doors slid open. Amy looked up at the bright white moon, just a sliver from being full. One more night, the full moon would grace the night sky just in time for Halloween.

"How are you tonight?" Amy politely asked as she climbed aboard the bus. She looked up to see the bus driver's cordial but grimacing face.

Something seemed very wrong with the bus driver's demeanor. With a sweating forehead and a pallor complexion, sunken eyes and razor edged cheekbones with a five o'clock shadow he looked like a meth addict or at the very least a weekend drunken binge come to an end. He had an odor about him, a powerful, musky aroma, distinguishable but not entirely unpleasant. She had almost decided to turn around and step off the bus when she looked at his eyes, cunning and intelligent eyes that locked onto her every movement.

"I'm fine," the bus driver, Gene Francis, said looking at her and then looking at the moon, "Will ya look at that moon! It is gonna be a full moon just in time for Halloween, did you know that? That sure is great!"

"Oh, yes…" The gathering crowd bottlenecking in the steps of the entrance gave her an excuse to move further back into the aisles and break off the uneasy conversation.

She instinctively put on the ear buds and looked out of the window until the bus started rolling, ***"Poppa says we will move out of town early in the morning. I went back in the woods today, although Poppa told me in no uncertain terms not to, but I had to see Aticus again, to see if he's all right and to tell him goodbye. Aticus was nowhere to be found."***

"My Poppa did a horrible thing. I hate him and I don't know if I'll ever forgive him … Assaulting and wounding my lover and sending me away from him, away forever."

"Oh God… I fell asleep one night to find myself back at my Poppa's plantation in the morning. I don't know how I got here. It defies all logic; Last thing I remember was going to bed in my new house in Boston. Next thing I know, I'm here in my old room. I know I walked here, I know I am here, I know I walked because of the cuts and bruises on my legs and feet and obvious exhaustion, in fact, my knees hurt me something fierce and the scabs are visible. Is my heart so broken that at night I wander off to the woods, to a place my heart should be, with Aticus? I find myself exposed to the world, naked on the spot where I first met him. Still, open to the elements I found my way to our old house to find my journal, to add in my thoughts. Is the draw to Aticus so strong that it brought me here while I was dreaming? During my waking times I was obsessed by the thoughts of him and his crooked smile, his dazzling eyes, his

hard marble-like body. His ease of talk and his accent that try as I might I couldn't place."

"However, one morning, I began to get sick. Unexpected pains in my abdomen began. I started to really need HIM! Where is my Aticus? Help me, somebody! Help me Poppa!"

She looked up to see a "Welcome to New Roads" sign just passing her window. Couldn't come sooner, Amy thought. An eerie howl pierced the night sky, prompting domestic dogs to howl, whine and pace about. She took out her ear buds and put them back in her purse. Standing out in the aisle and stretching out her legs. From the transcriptions of Alicia's diary apparently the lycanthrope awakening has everything to do with Sarah's property.

"I've got to get to Sarah!" She whispered as she found herself running in the aisles toward the exit.

Amy didn't notice the huge shiny chain and lock used to block the side door as she stumbled toward the driver and the front exit. Almost outside, a clammy hand rested upon Amy's shoulder, stopping her in her tracks.

"What the…?" Amy twirled around to see the bus driver Gene's eyes staring back at her.

Gene leaned in much too close to Amy's body invading her personal bubble as he breathed in her aroma then sniffed the air around him. Amy's body reflexively stiffened up and she was about to protest when Gene let go of her shoulder. Amy shrunk down into a sniveling helpless baby when she looked into Gene's eyes. The eyes had changed into some kind of horrible animal's eyes. There was something sinister in his hungry lupine eyes glowing red from the moonlight.

"Have a good night, Miss… Have yourself a happy Halloween too!" Gene pushed Amy out the door and out of the bus with one hand giving a salute with the other. Gene pressed the lever to slide the door closed when a worker from Booker A-line noticing the lock on the door tried to get Gene's attention.

She shook with fear when she said, "Excuse me, but I need to get off here please…"

Gene leaned in towards the factory employee. Gene sniffed in her oily scent and cringed. Bloody talons sprang out from his fingers. In a flash claws swiped through her exposed neck before she could respond. Her legs crumbled and slumped over the railing. Most of the Booker

A-line employees were still oblivious, still seated and unconcerned. One employee smiled as he gained a level and high score from a game on his tablet. One employee asleep on the bench and three employees were engaged in a conversation in the middle benches unaware of what had just transpired.

Gene doubled over in pain, a pain that he had gradually gotten used to. Seams in his shirt began to rip as his spine grew visible protruding from under his skin. A sharp pain surprised him as the bottom of his spine shattered. Then a dull, throbbing pain as new stem cells programmed with the wolf's blood flooded his veins. Gradually a tingling, numbness ran through him. His ears began to lengthen as his skull cracked and reformed to accommodate a more lupine feature. The involuntary growls gradually grabbed the A-line employee's attention.

Gene's new lupine head swayed back and forth tracking its prey any signs of movement would kick in its instinct to attack. Gene had a human-like torso and arms but the lower half was all lupine, including a tail. A subtle movement towards the door is all that it took to set in motion the bloodbath. His Lupine legs and feet were excellent tools to weave back and forth among the seats selectively finding candidates with their distinct smell and biting them, and slaughtering the rest.

A pile of bodies were strewn about in the aisles blocking the way out the front door. A temp worker, just a week on the job, thought he found a way out from the side door, but soon his heart sank as he yanked at the chains. The rear emergency door of the bus burst open, freezing the trapped passengers in the aisles. What appeared in the darkness set every passenger into a mad frenzy. The interloper had a lupine head and body for from head to toe, but he had bipedal legs. The beast leapt onto the bus sniffing the panicky passengers' bodies one by one. The fear that wafted up from the bus exhilarated the beast. He had blocked a number of slower or oblivious Booker A-line employees still in their seats. The monster massacred each passenger that the monster deemed unworthy.

The bipedal beast and monstrous bus driver drew closer sniffing the other's aroma. Even though they had distorted and monstrous faces, the scents were unmistakable. Gene and Chance, father and son united. The wounded but not dead started to stir and stood up drool spilling out from their mouths as they growled, their eyes glowing full of lunacy. The unfortunate souls were now still forever.

Amy had walked several yards before she realized the bus hadn't moved an inch yet and the screams of trapped passengers got her attention. The bus rocked back and forth, a sure sign of a struggle. Her curiosity got the better of her and instead of fleeing she concealed herself in a nearby bush and watched for her ongoing article. Suddenly the bloody crowd with glowing eyes jumped off the bus, sprinting off in either direction onto Highway 1.

"Oh God, I have to get a hold of Rogers." Amy tried to quietly dial on the cell phone while the infected ran by her sounding like stampeding bulls, "Cappy, its Amy, I need you, come quickly if you can… something horrible is happening. I REALLY need you!"

The moaning lunatics rambled by, their combined growls loud enough Amy found herself stumbling backwards. Retreating further onto the shoulder and from the gutter into the bushes entwining in branches until she splashed into a deep puddle, her new shoes were now soaked with mud and grime. She breathed a sigh of relief until she heard growling close by. Her body instinctively stiffened and she held her breath the only saving grace was her concealment in the bushes. The animalistic duo emerged from a bright streetlight filling Amy with dread. Pumping fear pheromones all throughout the air, the father and son stopped to breathe the air around them.

"Oh God!" Amy put her hands to her mouth. Do not move! If she moved she would be safe, she thought.

Both beasts' heads turned straight at her hiding place, slowly trailing her, sniffing the air. Something in the air displeased the beasts. A powerful aroma, something more ancient, powerful stopped them in their tracks. Even in the darkness and concealed by thick leaves turning a brilliant auburn Amy swore the beasts saw her, but they turned and ran off towards the other infected leaving her unscathed.

77

Spreading Lunacy

When Susan came down from the sales office to the factory floor, which she did every week, it was like she had stepped into a different world, the well-maintained, up-to-date million-dollar office, fit for a Fortune 500 company. The upstairs floor had climate controlled heating

& air-conditioning with state-of-the-art communications which was silent save for the rhythmic typing and the occasional fax machine noise. The ground floor was the extreme opposite; it looked forsaken, two shakes from bankruptcy. Hot in the summer due to the working presses and freezing in the winter due to the loading and unloading of trailer trucks. The deafening racket of a dozen working presses competed with the loud Rock 'n Roll music piped into the intercom installed in the 70s. She was at her station by the machine running at full steam. It was hard for her to hear and she had a coil of steel running through the press so she had an obstructed view but it was hard not to notice something eerie happening. Managers and supervisors with concerned faces would run past sporadically every so often, rushing to an unknown location.

She had to concentrate on her husband, a state police officer, and her daughter, Hannah, or she would cower in fear on the 300-ton press pounding away right next to her. The familiar ting, ting, ting from the finished product hitting the basket soothed her a little. Nevertheless, traveling at 3400 revolutions a minute all it would take is one poorly maintained die punch to overheat and it would shatter into pieces. The entire world couldn't stop a runaway projectile coming straight for her head. She used a shaky hand for the computer that slowed down the feed from a 14-inch coil and the piston press itself so she could write down monthly numbers. When the bay doors would open for the forklifts even with earplugs she could hear the sound of a Wolf wailing in the distance. She did not give it another thought until the paramedics arrived rolling a gurney with them leaving oil tracks in its wake. Susan was curious for a moment but she went back to work, it was rare but in this profession horrible accidents occurred from time to time. Was it that horrible, she thought, when she came down from the upstairs sales floor and an accident occurred she was relieved that it hadn't happened to her. There was always the risk of being impaled by a runaway forklift or a lacerated finger or even losing a hand from a slip on the oily floor. The paramedics finally got around to her station again and rounded the corner.

She just got finished with the diagnostics of the press when she remembered the paramedics. Half-hour went by with no sign of them. It may have been her imagination but she thought she heard faint screaming from more than one person. At her isolated workstation she longed for any interaction that could explain what was happening. When a coworker and good friend Leroy appeared out of thin air, finally, she thought someone could tell her what was going on.

"Hey!" She yelled over the roar of the presses, "Hey, Leroy, what's going….."

Susan stopped short when she looked into her coworker's eyes, empty of all human emotion, eyes full of frenzy. He was frothing at the mouth and mumbling. Her good friend, Leroy, the one who made it his personal mission to visit the hospital when she had been sick and made sure that Hannah had a babysitter when her husband visited her now growled at her, foaming at the mouth.

"Leroy!"

Susan closed her eyes and crinkled her nose; Leroy was close enough to feel the heat and smell of his pungent breath.

"Leroy!" She pleaded, her eyes still closed.

In the long concrete hallway she could hear several dozen footfalls scampering about resonating in the distance. She heard a commotion like a pack of starving, savage dogs fighting for scraps. As if she had been transported to an animal shelter she could hear growling, yelping, howling, whining and occasional human screaming.

He creased his nose as well trying to absorb her scent then he growled, "Sssssusan!"

Leroy sniffed Susan again, then grabbed and squeezed her by the waist. He hoisted her off the ground, the breath leaving her. She found herself flying through the air stopping only when she hit the hulking machinery. She tripped over the control panel for the lethal 300-ton press. Her palm rested on the hard oily shiny surface of the bottom half of a massive die.

Susan gasped as she looked up to see the top half of the die swiftly falling in a collision course toward her palm. The punches were like hardened ice picks able to blow out 0.1644 inch galvanized steel with ease and would surely impale her hand. The top half of the die would rest on the bottom like a well-fitting jigsaw puzzle before opening again revealing her bloody stump. Her feet were moving in the slippery oil, but her body remained still like a ludicrous cartoon character she forgot all about Leroy, but thankfully he did not attack her, choosing to move on to the shipping department.

"Shit, shit, shit!" Susan swore bracing for the inevitable.

Susan heard the sound of brakes from the 300 pound press squealing as it halted just before it smashed her hand like a pancake the safety sensors doing what they were designed for.

"That's it!" She thought to herself out loud, "I have got to get out of here!"

Susan rubbed her hands together, if it were not for the safety sensors working as they should she would have one less appendage. At the babysitters house for Halloween her daughter Hannah had plans to go out with her friends to trick-or-treat. With all that happened to her and the strange things going on Susan wanted her daughter by her side.

With shaking hands Susan retrieved her cell phone and dialed her husband, Capt. Rogers, "Honey, I'm taking off early. I'm going to take Hannah and I'm really kind of scared, there is some weird shit going on, if you get this please come home!"

Susan had to get through the employee parking lot, but in doing so she had to run through the sales room where all the noise and commotion had come from.

Luckily she had made it through the Booker A-line labyrinth unscathed. She ran toward the parking lot and to her car. As she sat in the driver seat she lit a stale cigarette from an old pack of cigarettes that she had hoarded away in her glove box. She looked in her rear view mirror. Relief washed through her as she inhaled the caustic smoke for the first time since she had been sick. She left through the chain link gate.

Escaping from the frenzy at A-line and driving on down the road a bizarre event caught her eye over at a wedding in the park. The bizarre makeup and tattered clothing suggested a zombie themed wedding which wasn't so outlandish being Halloween but what transpired made her cringe. It all started when the howling began. The bride-to-be stopped in the middle of her vows staring vacantly into space until she fell to the ground having a grand mal seizure and foaming at the mouth. Suddenly, she sat up, her animalistic eyes aglow delivering a savage bite to the neck of first bridesmaid to come to her aid. A groomsman had to pull the bride away getting bit too, prompting action from the stunned guests. The audience taking out their cell phones in unison to call 911. Susan put her foot to the accelerator speeding off unable to watch the rest of strange scene, too worried about the safety of Hannah.

She turned into a subdivision that did not skimp on the Halloween décor. House after house, she saw decorated. Houses had gravestones and animatronic slashers as seen on the silver screen, even a huge spider web from sidewalk to roof top. Spotlighting the spider web a blacklight and strobe light flashed incessantly lending an eerie glow to the scene.

Miles away from the factory and the park's madness it started to feel like it had been just a dream. When Susan turned into the parking lot of the babysitter's house she saw Hannah anxiously watching her through a dirty window and all fears began melting away.

"Mama!" Hannah excitedly shouted. The storm door slamming closed behind her.

"Hannah!" Susan's eyes brightened seeing her daughter safe from harm.

Dressed as little red riding hood for Halloween this year, Hannah's face all elaborately done with bright red lips and her hair all done up, she wore a silk white ruffled shirt and an old pleated skirt, holding a basket empty for now but after a nights worth of trick or treating it would be suitable for grandmother's house. Susan had to take a picture with her cell phone, the cuteness too much to stand.

"Say cheese!" Susan smiled.

"Cheese!" Hannah's dimples deepened as she smiled and posed proudly.

A dark shadow appeared from the edges of the house. When Susan's eyes come to focus she saw thick brown fur and long black nails coming toward Hannah. Instincts to protect her child taking over she lunged forward.

"Roar!" The small werewolf grabbed and squeezed Hannah before her mom got to her.

She could smell the makeup and latex as soon as the Wolf-man playfully grabbed for her neck. She squealed saying "Stop it, Terrell!"

Susan breathed a sigh of relief, "it's time to go, Hannah."

"Awwww, mom!" Hannah protested. "But we were going to meet Tasha by the library to trick-or-treat for a while, she promised to go with me."

Susan looked at the big bad Wolf and the little red riding hood so cute in their costumes then looked over at the streetlights. Dusk was quickly approaching but the brilliance of the Moon suspended the lights for a good while longer. About a dozen trick-or-treaters walked the sidewalks filling her with a sense of calm.

"Okay, I guess you can go trick-or-treating with Tasha for a while after I call your father and tell him where we are at." Susan relented, knowing Hannah loved spending time with her favorite babysitter.

Hannah and Terrell in unison squealed with delight.

78

The costumed residents on the streets of New Roads, Batchelor, and the other surrounding towns soon were dwindling and any persons foolish enough to venture out for trick-or-treating soon found their costumes soaked in the blood of the innocent. The schools had no children frolicking about and the swing sets sat empty with just the gentle wind to push the empty seats. The playground with its overgrown yard was just perfect for an ambush, hybrid wolves waiting patiently for unsuspecting prey. The roads were desolate along with the various fuelling stations dotted around town. Those needing gas pulling into numerous Gas & Go stations in the area were quickly ambushed.

The full moon had changed some of them to their Wolf like state, each one different from the other depending on their physiological anomalies and how long the parasite had progressed in their body. The people that were infected walked around in the day in a dreamlike state feverishly dreaming about howling wolves, oblivious to their sickness but with the moon's gravitational influence they were raving lunatics. The infected that had fully changed shadowed the oblivious costumed groups. With savage intelligence, groups of lunatics all in a variety of forms, from ape-like to hybrid Wolves stalked children before encircling them.

In the middle of the street two four-legged hybrid wolves sprinted toward the group in a collision course with one another. Four more lunatics emerged from the murky twilight between the houses. The lunatics who were infected just one month were ridiculously taller than normal so much so that the outfits looked like high-water pants with tight belly shirts with disheveled hair and pointed ears. Though they still had a humanoid form their animalistic eyes were trained on the group. The two legged Wolf-men emerged from both sides of the street the circle getting smaller, the lunatics effectively tightening the noose. The ape-like lunatics who were just shy of nude with fur all over their exposed bodies and only wearing torn rags for clothing watched from the treetops. Unseen by the group were furry legs hugging the high branches long, strong, furry arms and outstretched paws gripping the bark deeply. Extended muzzles all around were exposing drooling sharp fangs. They had varying forms, but they made a cohesive pack with Aticus commanding the groups behind the scenes by yelps and howls.

A ragtag costumed group of adolescents were oblivious to the danger threatening them. They were caught up in conversation. The group comprised of a cheap dime store hooded ninja outfitted with plastic swords and completing the ensemble with a plastic throwing star, a faux fat clown with a red afro and a bulbous red nose, ironically manning this hilarious ensemble was an extremely tall and thin boy, a Superman complete with red cape and a padded shirt imitating the striations in the muscles, and making up the rear a painted up zombie with dirty, torn up shirt and pants, representing his climb up from the grave and a mask of Jason the antihero of Friday the 13th franchise, complete with foam chain on his neck and a hockey mask. They were arguing over which comic book franchise was better, Marvel or DC.

"What was that?" The ninja broke from the group and stared at the trees.

"What is it?" The painted clown asked, looking around the neighborhood side to side.

The clown saw a surreal scene playing out in front of him. They were all dressed up as extremely hairy men like The Wolf Man of 1941 or they were all stricken with Congenital Hypertrichosis. He could see a variance of wolf-men and wolf-like creatures running through the deserted streets. Closer inspections, however, those were not costumed men, not costumes at all, and they were wreaking havoc in the streets.

"I heard something." The ninja wasn't looking at the fat clown but instead he stared up at the branches of trees.

A windless evening, the treetops should not be moving at all, much less shaking so violently. One particularly large Wolf stopped in the middle of the road and yelped a sequence of orders and suddenly an ape-like lunatic dropped from the trees.

The kid dressed up like the classic zombie didn't know what hit him as long claws swiped his neck. A crimson spray re-painted his blue and green rigor mortis face. Unfortunately the kid dressed up as Jason saw the whole thing.

"What the fuck, man!?" Jason bellowed.

The hockey masked boy could hear the surprised gasp and screams of his friends nearby. He madly twirled around trying to adjust his disguise with the obstructed view of his full head mask. He could hear something huge drop down into the gravel behind him.

The clown tripped on his ludicrously long feet. Two biped lunatics and one quadruped Wolf-thing pounced on the helpless clown sniffing him but the ninja did not stop to help instead he ran for his life. Jason Voorhees froze. He could not see anything but he could hear the slobbering chomping feast from his dying friend as he moaned in pain for another moment, then silence.

The costumed Jason turned around to the sound of growling, but with his mask he did not see a thing. A powerful hand smacked him in the face and the force had twirled his foam latex mask around. Suddenly he could see. It was then he realized that he had been cut up. The hockey mask and the foam appliance had been cut in four parts but he was unscathed.

Jason Voorhees took full advantage of his luck and wound up for one good swing his long plastic ax as if he was in a championship Little League game. The apelike Wolf gave out a howl of pain as the center of the ax smacked into the center of its skull.

The apelike Wolf staggered back in pain the adolescent Voorhees ran to catch up with the ninja, "hey, wait up!"

Voorhees ran for several blocks before catching up with the ninja. He finally stopped with his hands on his thighs and out breath, comfortable enough to look back at his fallen friends. The two hybrid wolves and the furry apelike wolves were feasting on their catch. The four lunatics left the uncomfortable glare of the bright streetlights for the murky shadows between the houses. Somehow the fat clown had escaped.

"We have to get to get the fuck outta here!" The older kid dressed as a ninja ordered his scared friend.

The young boy agreed, clutching his plastic axe like a bat in one hand and finally took his ruined mask off his face with the other, "but what about Brian?" referring to the costumed clown.

"I'm sorry, but I saw him fall and those things were all over him!" The ninja rasped hysterically looking around for pursuers.

Disembodied howls nearby made the boys instinctively drop their play weapons and cover their injured and bleeding ears. The deafening howl had a beacon affect to the lunatics for finding the remaining surviving costumed couple.

Jason and the ninja saw a dozen madmen burst out from the nearby bushes from either side of the street. They had no time to react before the men were upon them. Men with ragged, torn and bloody clothing restrained their wrists. Save for glowing animalistic hungry eyes that were staring directly into the terrified kids' eyes they looked human. Rough tongues licked exposed flesh.

"Wait!" A stranger growled. Jason and the ninja did not recognize the low and deep scratchy voice.

A tall ragged clown with a bitten and torn fat suit on emerged from the concealment from the crowd. Ninja and Jason stared at the dirty red twisted and out of placed Afro his extended and furrowed brow. A purple and blue bruised visage was visible from beneath his cream-white face paint. He had a smashed in and extended black nose instead of the traditional red nose. The ninja felt steam coming out of his extra-large nostrils.

"Brian!" Jason exclaimed.

The restrained boys saw ludicrously long shoes scuttle forward. The pair could see several bites on his forearms in the rips of his costume that were trying to heal. The clown's small feet had lengthened to fit his shoes. Brian grinned, revealing his lips that were stretched out, revealing a vicious smile and bleeding gums.

"Brian, no!" The pair both pleaded for their lives.

The chaos went unnoticed by the squad car's squealing sirens and lights. Capt. Rogers too preoccupied by the task at hand. He had checked his missed messages from his cell phone. The first missed message was from his wife.

He listened to the first message from his wife and waited for the next to play, "Please help me! Please, something is going on here and I think they are following me! I'm sorry, it's Amy and I am trying to get back to my room at the Point Breeze motel..." She hesitated a moment, then began again, "I know you don't owe me anything but I think I bit off more than I can chew, please help me..." a moment of silence then she said silently, "I love you, please... hurry."

He waited for the obligatory set of choices then, next message... "Honey...um, I left work early; I'm taking Hannah and Terrell out trick-or-treating just around the neighborhood. Meet us at Upper Pointe Coupee Elementary."

"Dammit!" Capt. Rogers swore; he had heard worry and concern in both women's voices. He slowed the car as A-line factory could be seen in the distance.

Capt. Rogers' stomach rolled when he realized the coroner, Dr. Jacobs, had been called there. The paramedics were taking their sweet time to load the stretcher with the dead into the ambulance. Apparently his wife had gotten off early; she probably left before the strange events could affect her and he of course worried about her but his mind was on Amy's frantic call now.

Dr. Jacobs saw the captain before the captain realized it and now he sped for his car before Rogers could do a U-turn, "Boy I'm glad you're here that factory scares me to death, except for the occasional body it is completely deserted..."

Rogers glowered looking at the doctor's visage so ashen his eyes sunken in and looking dead. He swore he could even feel the extreme heat that radiated off of the doctor's body.

The doctor placed a palm on his forehead; his head was killing him like his skull was splitting apart at the sutures. He tried to brush it off but Rogers noticed it and cringed. He could swear that the doctor's skin on his forehead intermittently rippled.

"Are you alright?" Rogers asked.

Some concern in his voice, but it wasn't so much concern for him as it was for all the unsuspecting people. His heart beat quickly and goose pimples rose all over his body. Looking up at the full moon he feared the cycle had begun again.

"Oh yes..." As he said this he coughed and gagged then wiped his bloody mouth with a handkerchief.

Years of medical study fell by the wayside. The doctor determined he could not cure what ails him. No biological source could be determined but something far worse, something preternatural was at play. Goose pimples arose on his arms as he heard a haunting howl. It had been obvious to the doctor that Rogers hadn't heard the ongoing battle cry.

"I have an eerie feeling about tonight, a Halloween coupled with a full moon." He worried aloud. The doctor was right, Rogers thought about all those innocent kids trick-or-treating.

Rogers reached for his cell phone and dialed the detective, "Jenkins, I need a favor."

"Would you go and pick up my wife and daughter? I have important things to attend to." The captain watched as the double doors swung open paramedics coming out with yet another body on the stretcher.

"Okay, Will d…" An abrupt silence… Rogers looked down at his dead cell phone… no service.

Miles away two shadowy wolves, a crimson wolf and one dreadlocked wolf emerge from a shack at the last cell phone tower smoke billowing out before bursting into flames. It effectively quieted a good chunk of the Louisiana area, Internet and cell phones now fell in a circle of silence.

79

Tasha had just gotten off of a grueling 12 hour shift at the diner where she worked. Her body exhausted, it took all her willpower to keep from closing her eyes and falling asleep where she sat in the car. She rolled down the windows letting the cold air stimulate her body and then she turned up the radio until she couldn't stand the noise, hoping that it would keep her awake. The colossal amount of homework, coupled by her long shifts at the diner had started to catch up with her.

She thought about Kevin and the horrible treatment and injuries befalling him by her twin brother, Brett. Nasty as he could be he was still her brother and she loved him and she couldn't shake the horrifying feeling that something terrible had happened to him. She thought about Kevin a lot while she carefully navigated the sharp twists and turns from the horribly maintained but shorter back road to Bachelor. He seemed different lately. She closed her eyes for just one moment on one of the hairier s-curved roads but she awoke and righted the wheel before almost crashing. She breathed a sigh of relief, on the home stretch to her house now.

"Yesterday… was a million years ago…" Tasha drummed her hands on the steering wheel as she hummed to the song by Marilyn Manson, "I know it's the last day on Earth, we'll never say good bye."

"I'm still empty here without you…" For the moment the singing had stopped and something grabbed her attention on the left side of the road, "what the…?"

She could swear she could see in between the trees a huge animal, a blonde blur following her. She could swear a dog on the left side of its face a horribly fresh shiny, pink scar. Instinctively she pressed on the accelerator and shook off the feeling of easiness. It was probably just a costume, it is Halloween she told herself, a time to be scared.

Through regularly babysitting, Hannah had been a regular fixture around the house. Tasha began to think about Hannah like her own sister and she would do anything for her. Terrell, Tasha's next-door neighbor, just barely old enough to babysit had been watching Hannah tonight until she got off work. In exchange she had promised to take Terrell and Hannah out trick-or-treating before the night's end. Although Hannah's mom Susan ended up getting off early so there would be no need for her anymore but Tasha would be damned if she did not make good on her promise. Tasha had gotten directions before she had lost signal. She smiled when she saw the big bad Wolf and little red riding hood, with Susan under the bright street lights of Upper Pointe Coupee Elementary.

"Tasha!" Hannah exclaimed.

"You're here!" Terrell shouted.

"Hey guys," Tasha opened her car door, "you look good in your costumes!"

"Hey!" Tasha was surprised to see Susan there at the school, "Susan, what are you doing off work so soon?"

Susan hesitated a moment trying to choose her words carefully so as to not frighten her daughter, "I just got off early to celebrate Halloween with my baby, nothing more, let's go get some candy!"

Susan stalled, walking at a snail's pace waiting for her husband, obviously frightened from the creepy events around them. The howling was almost too much for Susan as she looked up and down the eerily quiet street. Suddenly she swore she could see the glowing eyes of wolves darting back and forth across the street. The Wolf-men's tails would straighten up like an arrow as if pointing the way to certain houses. The half-wolves moved as if they were common burglars. The wolves on the street smelled the area of every house; wolf-men were taking their cue from a particularly big and strong, four-legged hybrid-Wolf with silver studs dotting his lupine skull the bipedal Wolf-men would sneak into the unlocked windows of houses.

"What's happening?" Tasha said inquisitively craning her neck to see what Susan was gaping at.

"Please let my husband come soon." Susan whispered resting a shaking hand on her useless phone.

Screams coming from the Gas & Go nearby had Tasha and Susan ill at ease. Hannah's curiosity got the better of her as she slipped from her mother's protective hand. She tore away from the group and wandered into the vicinity of commotion without being noticed to investigate a large teddy bear like creature still as a statue surveying the scene.

It reminded Hannah of an old brown grizzly bear she once saw at the zoo. She smiled as she remembered the frisky bear playing with a ball, oblivious to the crowd around him. As she got closer Hannah realized that it wasn't a bear at all but some form of a huge furry dog!

It was Viddarr, the last of the Úlfhéðnar, who sat on his haunches with his long forelimbs straight and huge paws sunken into the gravel. Close up the form was unmistakable. He looked like an enormous prehistoric dire Wolf save for his tattooed muscular forearms and just shorter than normal muzzle and wide human-like eyes.

The memory of the bear and the wolf's appearance intrigued Hannah, who bravely rushed forward and stuck her hand out, "Doggie!"

Hannah placed a small gentle hand on Viddarr's back stroking his soft fur. The distracted wolf howled out in surprise. His Nictitating membrane, or third eyelid, blinked rapidly, his fangs snapping a snarling warning as he twirled around to face Hannah.

Hannah stood her ground and stretching out her other hand to pat his muzzle she said with a giggle, "silly doggie!"

She did not flee so he did not feel the need to instinctively give chase; she wasn't frightened so she did not give off the distress pheromones which might lead him to instinctively attack like she was a wounded and panicked deer. Viddarr looked into her pure and innocent eyes and his heart melted.

Susan noticed a car stopped at the Gas & Go for fuel. An oblivious individual dressed up like a classic vampire got out of his car. He reached into his wallet for a credit card from his cheap black faux tuxedo and quickly swiped it through the scanner; already late for the costume party he kicked himself for his constant procrastination.

"I'm going to miss the party!" he cursed, his fake fangs almost falling out as he violently thrust the nozzle into his gas tank like he was stabbing his economy vehicle.

Suddenly he heard a loud thump feeling the car rock back and forth prompting him to turn around and glance up at the roof of his car. He stared face to face, eye to eye, with a furless hybrid Wolf with a thick neck and claws scratching his roof like nails on a chalkboard.

"What the fuc…!" The vampire instinctively whipped the nozzle from his gas tank and holding the nozzle like a gun he sprayed 91 octane super unleaded gasoline into the beast's eyes.

The beast howled in agony, mechanically protecting its lupine face from the gasoline that already seared its eyes. The Classic vampire dropped the nozzle on the pavement, now the flammable liquid steadily inched its way toward the Gas & Go. Classic vampire quickly spun around preparing to flee to the safety of the streets from the horrible monster on top of his car. He reached for his cell phone to call 911.

He dialed several times with no result until he looked down at the screen of his cell phone, no bars, no service, "shit!"

He turned his head to see the beast jump down to the pavement. He turned to run but in doing so tripped on his own cheap plastic cape. The furless beast seized the opportunity to prolong the torture of its prey. It slowly loped toward the falling vampire soaking up the sweet stench of his fear. The wolf's pads splashing about in gasoline.

"Shit, shit, shit, shit!" The cheap vampire went for his pockets. He wasn't looking for his cigarettes, but for his butane torch. He scurried backwards trying to avoid the slowly advancing monstrosity.

He found his novelty brass torch, cast as a hand with the middle finger sticking out. Shrinking away from the advancing puddle he stuck the middle finger to the puddle of gasoline and pressed the button.

"Fuck you!" a mechanical voice in the novelty lighter exclaimed and there was a whoosh, heat and bright light flooded out.

"Yaahhh!" The beast howled in pain and agony. Engulfed in flames and blind the beast ran about in a frantic and futile circle before collapsing in a flaming heap.

He breathed a sigh of relief, but it was short lived. The fire was encroaching not only toward the pumps but his car as well. He struggled to get off the ground and dusted the grime off his shiny black costume and turned around and started to run.

The vampire's heart skipped a beat as he realized while he was distracted another lunatic had made his way toward him. This one furred from head to toe, extremely long limbed but otherwise human just barely clawed his outfit but it was torn to ribbons. He blocked his way of escape and grabbed him by the shoulders. He tried to flee, but he was just too strong as another lunatic, seemingly human as well, burst out of the store exit running on all four limbs.

"Nooooo!" He protested but the pair's bloody teeth bore down through his cheap suit.

Susan gasped her hands clawing her cheeks as the a horrible realization came over her, "Hannah!"

Distracted by the chaotic scene she didn't realize that Hannah had strayed away from her and now she frantically looked around for a trace of her, "Hannah, Hannah!"

When she finally found her daughter her blood ran cold from the frightening sight… she stood face-to-face with a brown beast. If she tried to rescue Hannah the beast would strike out before she could reach her precious daughter.

Viddarr cautiously skulked closer sniffing in all of her bouquet, no anxiety or panic. He licked her small outstretched hand; absolutely no trace of the fear pheromone.

"You silly doggie!" Hannah laughed and squealed as she prompted a spontaneous hug.

Hannah rubbed the Brown wolf's abdomen. Instead of attacking her Viddarr flopped over on his back in the middle of the street short tail turning in whirls with his belly exposed. Hannah flopped down on her knees to knead the wolf's furry belly with her delicate small hands. The wolf's tail wagged uncontrollably.

Susan stood still as a statue. When she saw both of them, Hannah dressed up as little red riding hood and here was the big bad wolf, entangled together, her voice broke in dread as she exclaimed, "Hannaaaaaaaah!!!"

Hannah jumped out of her skin, looking around for her mother. She stopped patting Viddarr, "mommy?"

Viddarr whirled around to his feet. Unscented pheromones emerging in the air made him apprehensive and nervous his fangs exposed and growling a warning.

"Hannah, come over here now!" Susan screamed waving and motioning with her hands.

Detective Jenkins turned into the subdivision where, according to the directions from Capt. Rogers he could find Rogers' wife and child. At the edge of the subdivision in the cul-de-sac a flag waved by the library and he could see smoke billowing out from sparse treetops where the Gas & Go went up in flames.

Panicked movement by a black SUV by the library parking lot caught his eye. Tasha, Terrell, and Susan were staring at something, their expressions one of fear. He turned to see a little girl on her knees dressed up like red riding Hood with a huge fearsome Wolf.

The panicked cries of the group told him it was Hannah, Rogers' daughter, in danger. He had to act quickly and switching on the sirens, alarms, and flashing headlights from his unmarked police car detective Jenkins yelled out, "hey!"

The Wolf Viddarr stopped what he was doing to cover his lupine ears from the piercing sirens. He suddenly stood up on his hind legs his femur balls rotating as a familiar pop could be heard coming from his hips. His paws lengthened and spread like claws preparing to walk on two legs. Now he stood upright and sturdy as he angrily howled out.

Hysteria straining through in her voice as she held out her shaking hands, "Hannah, honey, come here please. I love you!"

"My God, what is that?" Phillip the ghost exclaimed.

"I don't know!" Jenkins answered the ghost, but in the dark recesses of Jenkins' memory he did know or at least he had run into this one time before as he stopped the car and got out his shotgun.

He simultaneously pumped the shotgun with one hand got down on one knee swung it around and took aim at the beast and with the car door shielding him, fired. The Wolf staggered back close enough that the 10 gauge pellets did not even have time enough to spread and it was a perfect shot center mass missing Hannah altogether.

"Get in!" Jenkins ordered as he prepared to fire his last shot.

Hannah obeyed, running away from the bipedal beast and into Jenkins car out of harm's way. No longer in the line of fire Jenkins fired the remaining shot. Another perfect shot that made Viddarr stagger back.

Assured Hannah had been strapped in and safe from harm Jenkins jumped into the car. He put the car in drive and looked at Viddarr. Two direct hits to the chest not even a mark upon him. It was like Jenkins just hit him with two nonlethal beanbags and nothing more. He didn't have time to think about the consequences as he pressed his foot on the gas.

The 10gauge shots did him no real physical harm but it was enough to shock him and the sirens pierced his skull making it hard to think. With the car barreling down upon him he jumped out of the way and out of sight.

Susan gasped with relief when she saw the headlights and Hannah safe in the back of the seat, "oh, Hannah, baby, oh I'm glad you're safe!"

The screeching sirens were enough to keep the lunatics at bay as Jenkins skidded to a stop "get in!"

The shell shocked group obeyed. Phillip the ghost moved over toward his dad as they all piled in. He wasted no time to get to the relative safety of Tasha's house. Susan beamed and finally looked over at what she thought would be her husband's face. Until she realized it wasn't her husband at all.

"Hey, I am detective Jenkins. I think you have met me a time or two before. Thompson Rogers wanted me to pick you up, he was hung up," Detective Jenkins exclaimed, not even taking his eyes off the road.

"Oh," Susan hugged her daughter tightly. She grimaced with pain in her eyes, "thank you, for saving us."

"It's no problem ma'am," he replied, turning into the driveway at Tasha's house.

80

"A midwife guided me through the agonizing experience of labor pains. I literally felt my heart stop and restart several times before I had given birth to my beautiful son. He had a stout body. His eyes were shut but he had a head full of black hair and a full set of teeth. He latched onto me and surprisingly opened his eyes, brilliant green eyes! What strength in his eyes! And for the moment, the loneliness faded before he turned a horrible shade of purple…

My baby boy struggled to breathe, struggled for each breath, his body wriggling in my arms before relenting, motionless… My baby boy was dead… He had a strong frame but a weak heart… My heart shattered and I couldn't help but be brought back to the horrible night that Aticus disappeared from my life… My poor dead baby boy, I would name him Aticus, for his father… he had left me too!"

The diary excerpt jolted fragmented memories from the murky depths of Sarah's unconsciousness to the surface. She crumpled pages of the diary as she remembered over hearing faceless adoption workers talking about her,

"Yeah, she actually said the first time she tried to breast-feed she bit the hell out of her! Baby had been born with a full set of teeth and long, long nails... She actually said the baby had scratched her inside and out ... She said she can't deal with her...I guess she is better off here... I heard her mother went insane...I heard that after she gave the baby up for adoption she committed suicide." Sarah trapped a stray tear on her cheek with a forearm. The painful memory threatened to consume her until she bottled it up again and symbolically threw it in the ocean of her mind, the dark waves swirling around it.

Sarah slammed down her diary the painful memories coupled with incessant wailing too much for her to bear. Tommy's whining had worked; he had gotten her undivided attention.

"You know AJ is going to be there, right? He weaseled his way to the top entertainment after all." Tommy actually resorted to using the on-again, off-again relationship that AJ and Sarah had as leverage.

"The party is being held in your house for God's sakes, come on let's go, let's have a little fun, its Halloween, let loose...." Tommy stopped staring at the brilliant moon and looked her in the eye as he smiled one of pity towards her, openly pouting.

"I don't know..." Sarah put her head down and kicked at the dirty shag carpet, mumbling in no one in particular, "but it was just a smart business venture. The Wolf's Den Tavern is going to reward me handsomely for the venue and Viddarr assured me that everything would be okay."

She started to pick up her diary again to read where she left off, "I was just going to lie down and read. Amy is going to come over and keep me company."

"Oh no! That's okay because didn't you hear Amy is going to be at the party too! Something about she had to cover it for her paper." Tommy commented with a sly smile.

Skepticism in her voice, "Really?"

"Oh yeah! So come with me." Tommy held out his inviting hand.

"Okay," she shook her head in defeat, "I will go for a little while." Relenting, Sarah accepted his hand as she thrust her diary into her purse, and slung the purse over her shoulder, she mumbled under her breath again, "just for a little while."

After Sarah locked the cabin door the pair went off into the night, the quiet and serene cabin area made Sarah oblivious to the chaos that had stricken several of the nearby villages. A hybrid Wolf sprung into attention with glowing eyes peering at the taillights of Sarah's van as it faded from view. A white wolf with Crimson tattoos marking his visage and its lower half loosely dressed with a gray toga style configuration leaped forth from in between the cabins toward the parking lot.

Almost to the road when he felt a sudden sharp searing pain through his wolf's shoulder and into his chest. His left limb crumpled out from underneath him crudely propelling him toward the rocks head first. Shot in the back, Devon thought, and searing pain told him that it was silver.

"Bull's-eye!" Hunter shouted with triumph.

Hunter had come out of hiding between the cabins and scored a direct hit with his harpoon gun. He had modified it, lightweight and portable, but instead of hunting whales he hunted lycanthropes. He finally had the white furred and red tattooed magnificent specimen on the line. He would be damned if he let it out of his sight.

The beautiful white Wolf instantly and involuntarily changed form into the human, Devon, save for the left limb still a lupine's upper limb and paw. The silver barbed harpoon with silver laced steel rope impaled Devon's upper body disrupting a complete conversion back to man. The bright red blood saturated once soft white fur then began trickling down his impaled and limp extremity.

"I got you now!" Hunter had been watching Devon for weeks until he made a move and now, though groggy with massive amounts of narcotics running through his veins, a sense of pride and relief could be heard in Hunter's voice.

Devon tried to grip the barbed harpoon where it came out from his shoulder. The warm blood running off the shaft made it slip from his fingertips. When he did get a hold of the harpoon to yank from the front the silver rope only went into his body further. Hunter started to reel in his captured prey just like he had been fishing for swordfish on the open sea. Devon tried to resist, leaving track marks in the dirt, but Hunter managed to wind in the rope until Devon was only feet from him.

Devon stopped his resistance and whipped around to the hunter and growled, "I am not the bad guy you were looking for. I am here to help you, let me go!"

His pleas fell on deaf ears however as Hunter dropped the harpoon gun and pulled out from his backpack a massive shotgun.

"I don't believe you!" Hunter pumped his shotgun and aimed, "I have been deceived too many times in my good works to believe you!"

Dr. Jacobs and Rogers had just exited the office. The attendant said that Amy Anderson had just paid to stay here another month, but he hadn't seen neither hide nor hair of her since his shift and that worried the Captain. He had ordered Dr. Jacobs to walk over toward the cabin that Amy was staying in while he took a look around the place when he came upon this strange conflict. All of Hunter's attention focused on his capture he had failed to notice a man sneaking up to get the drop on him.

His gun was trained on Hunter who was the obvious aggressor in the situation the limp lupine limb hidden from view. Capt. Rogers ordered, "Stop, Police! Drop your weapon!"

Capt. Rogers found himself in a field by the lake next to the parking lot brandishing a weapon. His back straight as a board, his feet shoulder width apart and firmly planted on the ground, both hands planted on the handle his spare finger on the trigger staring down a strange man in bizarre antique apparel a 1800s blue wool duster overcoat. This strange man held a shotgun to an almost naked man that look like he had just been ripped out of the pages of anime. The man with the tattoo on his face had obviously been injured and now he sat bleeding on the ground.

"I said Police! Drop your weapon now or I will be forced to shoot you!" His gun still trained on the crazy haired, bearded man brandishing the shotgun.

The man with white hair stood to the side in profile to Capt. Rogers so he couldn't see the white lupine limb and paw as it shook involuntarily now. The Captain's attention was focused completely on his aggressor he took the opportunity to violently pull the harpoon through his chest so as to not do any more damage from the extremely sharp and curved edges. He grunted in frustration, when he pulled from the front the silver cord which had been fixed in between the top of harpoon and the shaft went in deeper tethering him to Hunter.

"You are making a big mistake!" He turned around and slowly raised his hands in the air but he did not drop the shotgun, "I am Hunter, a *bounty* hunter, charged to bring this man in!"

"I don't care what you are; I want the weapon down, now!" Capt. Rogers said with authority.

Devon dreaded to pull the harpoon out in reverse. The hooks and curved barbs would tear his chest and deltoid muscles to shreds. However he assessed the situation, he had no choice to be free from Hunter. He reached with his one long arm gritted his teeth and with one good jerk the harpoon and the silver cord fell to the ground with a splatter of gore.

Now free, Devon wasted no time to transform back into a Wolf and on all four legs, though his left limb considerably weaker and bleeding, the now free Wolf ran off into the seclusion of the forest.

"No!" Hunter cursed as he realized his tether now lay on the ground and the white Wolf was escaping from his clutches. Without thinking he pointed the shotgun at the detective in protest.

Without blinking the Captain fired one, two, and the final shot into Hunter's chest. Hunter dropped the shotgun at his feet. He fell on his back with a sickening thud.

Of course Rogers saw the unbelievable sight straight out of fairytales. He wouldn't have believed it if he hadn't already seen it before at Michael's shack. What the hell is going on here? He asked himself as he got down on one knee to inspect the stranger, what's so hard to believe, just some… shape shifters?

Rogers bent down to the stranger's motionless body. He stumbled back startled when the stranger started to stir and cough. The stranger impulsively tore his white dress shirt open to reveal a Kevlar vest. The tight grouping of bullets made a shape over his heart where they were stopped only by the vest.

Out of fear Dr. Jacobs rushed out of Amy's empty cabin, "I heard gunshots, are you all right?"

"Yeah, I'm all right." the Captain said almost to himself, almost in a daze.

"Yes," he reached for a pair of handcuffs and gave them to the doctor, "cuff him."

The Doctor complied cuffing the prisoner on his wrists effectively subduing him. The Captain nodded his head in approval. The cuffs loose and in the front, but it would do until such time as a more thorough search could be done. Dr. Jacobs was about to stand up when a familiar aroma caught his attention on the crisp fall breeze. A familiar smell emanating from the Hunter and he knew this odor because it radiated from him as well. He could not help but look Hunter in his eyes, an addict's eyes, glossy and dilated.

"Do YOU know what you've done?" Hunter winced as he sat up still clutching his chest and coughing.

Static then a squawk coming from the walkie-talkie clipped to his belt got Capt. Rogers' attention, "Hello? Hello? Anybody read me? All of the phone lines are out, even the cell phones; over."

"I read you, come in, who is this speaking? This is Capt. Rogers, over." Rogers kicked the shotgun from the strangers reach and motioned for him to remain still.

Now he faced a barrage of questions coming from all sides as he listened on his walkie-talkie, "this is Capt. Rogers, and is this Jenkins? Did… did you find my family? Over."

"Yes it is and yes I did. They are safe at the moment, over."

Failing to get the captain's attention Hunter turned his sights to the Doctor as he vented his frustration, "you let that monster go! I have been stalking the white beast for months and he finally made his move and you fools blew it!"

The Doctor could not get in a word edgewise as Hunter continued on his rant, "I fear the fiends are multiplying, I could smell it in the air, I fear a war with humanity is inevitable!" He swore, uncontrollably shaking his head and fists rattling the cuffs.

Strangely the Doctor could sense the faint odor as well. He could actually feel a change in his bones and it hurt him. He tried his best to quell it but could essentially feel the beast fighting to get out. The Doctor couldn't help but taking in the Hunter's strange aroma. The familiar aroma that they both shared but something smelled different in the strange handcuffed man. Something that quelled the beast raging inside he reasoned.

Rogers was obviously distracted, his tone changing, as he turned back to question the Doctor, "Did you find her, did you find Amy?"

"No, no sign of her, I went to her cabin to search but…there is no sign of her," the doctor responded to the Captain but his eyes did not stray away from Hunter.

Worry and disappointment fluttered briefly across his face as the Captain acknowledged the doctor with a nod as he heard the pleas from the walkie-talkie, "Captain, I found your wife and daughter, but we have a situation. Your wife and daughter, the babysitter, their friends, and I are holed up in the house; I need backup to come quickly. Do you copy?"

The strange incident with Cody, the conflict at Michael's shack made it clear they were going to need all the help that they could get, "I copy, I'll be there ASAP!"

He went over to Hunter and then un-cuffed his wrists, "I don't know what is going on, but the more help the better."

Hunter rubbed his wrists and picked up his shotgun carefully so as not to alarm Rogers, "We'll take my van."

81

"No, I say we take my cruiser, it will be faster with the lights and sirens," the Capt. had already pulled out his keys.

There were no objections as the motley crew filed into the police car one by one. The Captain had a sickening feeling coming over him now that he had gotten into the car. His mistress, Amy Anderson, had gone missing and his family might be in trouble.

"Dammit!" He slapped the dashboard in frustration, even the GPS did not respond to his commands.

Rogers had to rely on his memory of the one-time visit to the babysitter to come to their rescue. Luckily, his adrenaline kicked in and he was able to recall all the minute details as they left Point Breeze Motel and Lakeside Kitchenette Apartments heading out on Highway 1. All seemed normal on the road to Batchelor. The Captain's guard had come down a little bit breathing normally now as he drove on the tranquil road but looks could be deceiving. The further away from the motel and the self-imposed neutral zones the creepier the scene had become.

The group could see carefree lazy movements of families in the alternating luminous homes and light of the lampposts as they drove on down the highway. They came to another tiny village the type that if you didn't know it was there you would miss it. Suddenly contrast uneasy darkness coming up before the group. They struggled to see shapes in shadows before them until they got used to the murk.

Hunter took off his backpack to see what ammunition and rations he had left. Dr. Jacobs stared out the window. He had a sickening feeling as well but it wasn't the same as the Captain's as he looked at the full moon's presence in the sky. He felt a force that needed to come out. The more he thought about it, the sicker he became.

The Doctor could see a pack of sinister four-legged figures moving from the shadows stalking the police car. Glowing red penlight orbs coming from a throng of angry eyes caught the Hunter's attention as well. They only saw a blurred mass as it jumped toward the back window.

The trio exclaimed in unison, "What the..."

The car stalled and bounced as if all four shock absorbers blew out all at once. The car rocked back and forth mimicking rough seas. Suddenly lunatics emerged from the darkness and beat their fists against the side windows.

Capt. Rogers looked over at the humanoid lunatic. Staring at Rogers with vicious glowing eyes through the safety of the glass the lunatic scored the whole of the roof with his claws. He clung to the side of the car hitting the driver's side window with his fist until it burst. Seemingly out of nowhere the Doctor saw another lunatic, sprinting in out of the yard into the streets. Yet another lunatic came from the side street this one naked as a jaybird with extremely long arms, legs and elongated bare feet heading straight toward the police car. Hunchback, he had a bulging spine, his palms on the pavement jumping up and down like a bullfrog on all fours. He jumped and landed on the hood of the car making Rogers stomp on the brake.

The Hunter reached for the Captain's shotgun in the middle of the patrol car and quickly opened the bullet proof window barrier and threw it over to the Doctor then rummaged through his own pack to get out his shiny .44 magnum desert eagle, and a handgun for the Captain beside him.

"Shoot the normal looking ones with regular bullets but leave the monsters to me; I know how to handle them!" Hunter yelled staring directly at the fiend who was coming to rest on the windshield.

Rogers looked around and shouted, "But... they all look like monsters!"

The Hunter cocked the .44 Magnum and shouted commands at both Roger and the Doctor, "Just shoot!"

Through the driver's side window without the glass the lunatic clutched Rogers' arm as he pulled the trigger. The bullet hit with a sickening thud. The lunatic yelped then fell on the concrete rolling over toward the ditch. The Doctor closed his eyes; mirroring Rogers he fired the shotgun at the fiend through the back window, shattering glass in the process. The lunatic in the rear yelped as well as he fell backward falling headfirst onto the pavement.

Hunter sat face-to-face with the lunatic crouched on the middle of the hood. Eye to eye with an eerily human visage save for short fine furs sprouted up on his cheeks and forehead. The lunatic thrust his hard head against the windshield to get at Hunter. He flinched as the glass burst into pieces. No barrier between the lunatic his prolonged crown sliced and bloody. The Hunter could smell his revolting breath and feel his spittle as he hungrily growled. He stuck the desert eagle up to the aggressor's rib cage and without hesitation fired.

"Go, go, go!" Hunter ordered as he dug for another weapon.

Rogers obeyed his commands and almost stomped on the gas when another form of the beast emerged, two ape-like lupines in appearance with an extremely short muzzles, but, bipedal with no tail catching his attention. They flanked the patrol-car before leaping onto the sides of the car doors. They bent the feeble doors with ease. Tearing the drivers and back passenger side door hinges from the car before Rogers could react. Rogers instinctively whipped around to target the invader, but Hunter grabbed the gun with one hand and forcefully wrenched it from him.

"No! It won't help, it's about as effective as a CO2 pellet gun." A homemade compact repeating 90 pound crossbow emerged from Hunter's backpack, "you just concentrate on getting us to safety!"

Meanwhile the back passenger door having broken free from its hinges now swung back and forth in the ditch as the beast clawed its way onto the seat, long arms and claws greedily reaching for the Doctor. Now the Doctor squirmed backwards until he was inevitably stopped at the other side.

Its muzzle opened up to reveal sharp ivory fangs. The doctor cringed at the inevitable bite until it breathed in the Doctor's unusual but familiar scent as it paused. The fiend crooked its neck hesitating for a moment.

The Doctor had more than enough time to swing the shotgun up toward its head and fire.

The strange amalgamation of animal yelped in pain. Hot blood painted the partition and the back window as it showered onto his face. The Doctor wiped the blood from his eyes and saw just a meaty pulp where once its head had been. It's hybrid lupine head looking like shredded pulverized meat. Its claws searching futilely for blown out eyes, its nose was a hollow shell. The monster now blind and unable to smell searching around for its prey ears ringing from the loud blast it's cracked fangs still lethal, however. Its arms flailed about unable to catch the Doctor. The doctor praised the shotgun for its effectiveness but at that close of range the shotgun should have blown its skull clean off but it only managed to virtually skin the fiend. He could already see healing taking place! He pumped the shotgun again spent shell falling towards to floor board. He put the barrel in-between its missing eyes and fired. He pumped again ejected the shell and fired until it fell backward out of the car, rolling down the street. Exsanguination made the abomination spontaneously transform back into a human being.

Rogers and Hunter had their own set of problems on the driver's side of the partition. With the driver's door compromised the apelike beast straddled the detective. The beast's hot and rank breath assaulted his senses trying his best to fend him off. Hunter revealed his dog whistle hidden around his neck clicked the magazine full of silver bolts into his repeating crossbow and bore down on the beast.

"Drive, drive, get out of here! Don't worry about the abomination, I have him," the Hunter placed the whistle to his mouth and pursed his lips to get the beast's attention.

Rogers and Hunter couldn't hear anything as the whistle blew, but the fiend heard the shrill sound it gave off even the Doctor heard the high octave sound waves through the partition. The beast stopped the assault on Rogers turning to Hunter, who immediately pulled the trigger to his bow. Rogers didn't even give it another thought as he put both hands on the wheel and stepped on the gas.

Bull's eye, a silver bolt right between the fiend's eyes, Rogers glanced at the homemade contraption and said, "What's with the crossbow?"

Hunter waited as the mechanized gears whirred, automatically restraining 90 pound draw on his bow while another silver bolt slid back into its position, "silver bullets are naturally soft and they stray when they are shot out of a gun thus the arrow. Jean Chastel got lucky with one shot, one kill; it is funny that it started my career."

Hunter shot the beast in the heart then mused, "Or it helped that the bullets were blessed!"

Rogers swung around to see the ape-like beast motionless on the highway as they pressed on convert into a man again. He saw the silver bolt in its fur lined forehead.

"How can you tell these monsters apart!?"

"I have been stalking the abominations for almost all my life now, I can actually smell the abominations, and I can tell how far the curse has progressed in their eyes. Look out!" Hunter pointed at the rearview mirror.

The calming reprieve from the madness did not last. Rogers looked into the mirror to see large four legged hybrid wolves running to catch the patrol car the bright moon sending them into a lunacy. These fiends were cunning as they split up to catch the car from both sides. For a split second Rogers and Hunter caught sight of their glowing predatory eyes in the windows as they caught up to the car.

"Impossible!" Rogers exclaimed, "How did they catch up to us?" He pressed on the gas.

They didn't have time to hear the answer as the Wolf on the driver side jumped onto the car like it had caught a deer. Sharp claws tore through the front bumper. Its fangs finding the tire as if were a deer's neck. A bang and vibration spooked the hybrid Wolf. Its limbs faltered its lupine head falling on the pavement. A sudden rush of air released from the tire as the left front tire went flat.

"Switch on the lights and sirens, for the new changelings and lunatics, it will drive them mad," Hunter screamed as he went for his dog whistle and blew.

As the lights and sirens wailed the wolves and lunatics stopped, howling out in pain. Rogers spit in surprise, "I think it is working!"

The Doctor wiped away the blood from the rear windshield to get a better view. The wolves circled in the middle of the street whining and snapping at the air though they dare not go any further like an invisible barrier had crashed down.

The patrol car limped on down the road riding on the rim with sirens blaring, keeping them safe from harm for the moment. Rogers began to see a burning and deserted "Gas n Go" station under the burnt out streetlamps. Relief came when he saw the "Welcome to Batchelor, Louisiana" sign ahead. He was anxious to get to his daughter, Hannah.

82

Raccourci Island, LA
Sarah's inherited property

Tommy coaxed Sarah into going to Viddarr's party even though she was not in the mood for celebrating. As soon as they arrived Tommy had wandered off into the woods where he could participate in the festivities. Sarah shut herself off from the outside world cozied up on the chaise lounge and opened the diary as she read Alicia's addictive words.

"I had no time to dwell on my loss, however; my labor pains were upon me again." She paused for a moment when a horrible cheer went up from the woods, then read on.

"Drenched with sweat, my precious child Aticus dead in my arms, I gave birth to a second child, my head dizzy and racked with exhaustion I delivered my second baby, a baby girl who I named Sara. A weak puny little thing with a lock of blonde hair, full set of teeth and then her eyes opened early. I saw her eyes looking up lovingly at me. Her left eye looked blue as the sea. I looked into her right eye the color of shimmering emeralds. The midwife cut the umbilical cord and offered Sara to me. So tiny but every time she breathed in life I could feel her warm heart beating and a calm sensation came over me until Sara was snatched from my arms!"

She paused reading Alicia's diary to walk over to the back of the house venturing out onto the screened porch to peer out into the night. A raging bonfire made her wonder suddenly if the water had even been turned on yet. Cursing her curious nature she found herself on autopilot wandering in the night toward the party. She had a flashlight in her lips to see the pages in front of her.

"In an open air fare once I thought I felt his presence, my heart raced as I turned around. Realization hit me like a new-fangled steam locomotive because he wasn't there. I had lost my beautiful, mysterious Aticus to my Poppa, lost my neonatal son in childbirth, and I lost my new born baby girl to an unscrupulous boarding school because apparently the sight of Sara's fragile face reminded

him of that horrible night, and my Poppa could not stand the sight of her. A great shame I have brought upon my family all because I had disobeyed the rules and gone into the forest...but I found the love of my life there."

She stopped for a moment when a particularly memorable song caught her ears. The sound of AJ's band's playing a particularly haunting melody, "The October moon" one of AJ's catchier songs appropriate for the night.

"It is a full Moon out tonight and Aticus' aroma permeates my body, I fear I will turn in and then wake up tomorrow in the place of my sorrows ... oh Aticus why did you forsake me? I need help, I Need you to guide me... my body and my soul!"

"Looking out at the Louisiana sunrise I am thankful for my Poppa's foresight, even though he felt shamed with the pregnancy and insanely early birth of my bastard child he entrusted a friend and lawyer, Thomas LeBeau. So she had been adopted he would procure the family land and to keep tabs on my precious child, Sara, too support her in every way ..."

"I find myself in my bedroom after the sun came up the following morn... I have to come to my senses quickly... I slept walked my way across the land with no memory when I woke up... Just fragments of a lucid dream that I was a powerful she Wolf strutting across the land, on a direct route to my home and place of birth."

"Hey Sarah," Tommy exclaimed. He put his hand on her shoulder and squeezed, I'm glad you decided to socialize!"

Sarah grimaced, dropping her flashlight from her mouth and her open diary, saving her page number with her fingers, "Hey Tommy."

Tommy had stopped short of the clearing with the bonfire and crowd of people deliberately concealing the main mystery event shrouded with a tarp. Amongst the brilliant glare and dancing shadows from the bonfire she could make out a shadowy form of an impressive man his back turned away from her.

"The master will be pleased!" Tommy grinned drooling from a mouth full of fangs, "He wanted you. Here where it all began to replay what he lost long ago."

"What?" She saw glowing light in his animalistic eyes.

"I used to pine for you, but no more... I used to feel inferior to your mere presence, but no more, the power that courses inside of me replaces it," Tommy put two claws on her shoulders, I love the experience and I would do anything for my master."

She was too stunned to move as the DJ took over as AJ who had just played his last set now packed up to leave. AJ saw Tommy, his arms around Sarah at the empty edge of the clearing and waved as Aticus stepped up on the stage. Sarah could not see as Lance shut down the PA system.

Already fuming from Viddarr's refusal to partake in the blood unity ceremony he would've killed Viddarr for spiriting away his soulmate Desiree before the chaos and bloodshed began. But he needed Viddarr's raw power and subterfuge. With the help from the spells from an ugly troll born Rune caster masking the decrepit barn so the young changelings were safely hidden away and had shelter. Viddarr's idea of sound waves prevented the infected from changing until a crowd formed and it worked like a charm. The PA had been putting out low frequency waves.

Aticus had no need for a microphone his voice echoing into the night, he raised his hand and made a fist "Your quaint dwellings will become your kennels; your manicured yards your cells and your white picket fences will become bars as they wait for the slaughter!"

A thousand pairs of vacant eyes glowing in the darkness exhilarated Aticus. Thick black fur spontaneously began sprouting as some of the partygoers involuntarily transformed into monstrous forms. An orgy of transforming flesh began to transpire, a twisted writhing mass of skin. Soon mayhem and chaos would come upon unsuspecting partygoers.

Sarah looked down at the open pages of Alicia's diary and read them,

"I dream about Aticus and his horribly scarred body. He had the features of a man and a Wolf. I cannot deny it any longer. I am a lycanthrope, a she wolf... You left me all alone Aticus, to navigate my infliction without any guidance!"

Then Sarah looked up at the moving tarp as a shrouded woman with no legs braced herself on her crutches and pulled all the sheets down, releasing the main oversized sheet. She gasped in shock. Amy had indeed attended the party after all! Her expression was one of horror as she saw terror in her eyes as she struggled, all tied up and gagged, to the post.

"It's almost time to begin," the shrouded woman So-seti whispered, the crutches firmly in her armpits a ceremonial dagger clutched in her left hand clasping Amy's cheeks with her right, "don't worry honey. You'll die for a good cause… the mighty shade Aisos will appear to us and bring back the glory of the wolves den, the necromancer's healing properties will grow back my legs and with her saving grace bring back my grandson's eyesight and hopefully regain his sanity."

"See, what did I tell you?" Tommy said with a sinister grin with large white fangs he seemed even more terrifying, "Amy is here at the party just like I said she would be!"

She put her open diary to her ears in the midst of a sensory overload. She couldn't help but overhear a symphony of screams and cries and begging that were drowned out amidst the wolves' howls. Sarah's knees began to knock and quiver threatening to buckle. She found herself running with no regard to Tommy. She didn't know how she had gotten away from him, but she headed back to the plantation. Her mind already began to betray her rationalizing and denying the malicious scene as she burst through the clearing. The foggy delirium that all humans get was setting in, assuring the ghost of the Wolf shade survives.

Tommy howled to her, "That is right. Run, sweetie run, run. Back toward your plantation back where it all began, Aticus will be waiting for you."

83

Batchelor, Louisiana

Susan timidly peeked out the curtains careful not to let any light out to draw attention to herself, Hannah, Tasha, Terrell and Jenkins. One hybrid Wolf had made short work of Susan's car. Glass shattered, tires flattened, rims resting on the driveway, fiberglass fenders and plastic bumpers looked like paper that had gone through the shredder.

"I'm glad everybody is safe," Jenkins said, glancing over at his ghost son then wandering over and putting his arm around Susan's shoulder to comfort her.

Jenkins looked over at his son glaring at the front door. His ghost son stared out through the closed door as if it had been open and he could see everything. The ghost could see the glowing eyes crisscrossing the subdivision and in the distance could hear the terrified screams of the helpless victims.

"I hope my husband gets here soon. There is still no response on the house or cell phones and the Internet is out," she clung to her daughter Hannah for dear life.

Terrell had been afraid to go home until his mom arrived, so instead they had brought his older brother and his girlfriend next door to Tasha's; his parents were working at A-line on second shift. He had expected to see them arrive home before trick-or-treating ended but they were still not home. He had to make conversation with Tasha in the kitchen to keep his mind off of them. His brother and his girlfriend sat in the other room watching TV.

"So you went as a waitress, then?" Terrell nervously laughs.

Tasha chuckled, "yeah, you ass!"

Terrell's dad, a black machinist, and his mother, a Latin nurse, found each other when Terrell's dad received a grievous injury while trying to repair a stalled engine on his press by himself. They locked eyes and they were never separated again, 20 years and counting. Terrell had an exotic mix of Nubian and Latino in him. He had black shiny curly hair and he was tall and toned with caramel skin. Tasha thought that he would surely make the girls swoon when he developed a little more but still barely 13 years old he had a lot of growing up to do.

Barring pregnancy when she bore children, his parents did not deviate from their routine for 20 years. They were a pillar of consistency for his brothers and sisters. When work ended they were home at 10:15 without fail. Even when his parents got a flat tire they got a cab so they wouldn't be late. Now it was 10:40 and they were still not home and that worried him. He could feel his stomach clench. He involuntarily shook like a Chihuahua. She noticed his prideful and defiant pale eyes looked frightened and scared.

Tasha could see the worry in his eyes and tried to console him, "maybe your parents went out to dinner after work to see everybody, all dressed up, this being Halloween and all."

Sirens began to wail quietly in the distance at first, then louder and louder as a car turned into the subdivision, a sudden squawk on the walkie-talkie, "Come in, come in, this is Rogers, can anybody hear me? Over."

Jenkins saw Susan's eyes light up when she heard her husband's voice as he responded, "This is Jenkins. We are at Tasha's house; everything is okay, what is your E.T.A.?"

"Just a few blocks away, we will be there soon, over." The walkie-talkie squawked.

"Did you find the reporter that you were looking for?" Jenkins asked unknowingly.

Only static and silence come from the walkie-talkie in Jenkins' hand. Jenkins could cut the tension with a knife when Rogers meekly spoke, "there was no sign of her…"

Rogers' voice broke from the unconscious guilt, "but we did acquire a stranger that can tell us more about what is going on."

If jealousy and anger could kill, Jenkins would've been dead when he looked at Susan's betrayed and angry eyes. He was kicking himself for not realizing. Jenkins wanted so much to comfort her and tell her how sorry he was but he didn't know what to say. He felt a sigh of relief when he heard the squealing's siren then the warning howls of a dozen animals close by.

"They're here!" Phillip exclaimed, looking at his father and pointing at the closed door.

The wail of sirens and shouting could be heard coming from outside. They could hear footsteps and then a loud banging on the door, "this is Rogers, let me in!"

Susan rushed toward the door and let her husband in. She threw the door open and threw herself into Rogers' arms. Hunter and Dr. Jacobs filed in around them. As Detective Jenkins saw a dozen lunatics some lurching but upright, others on all fours. They looked human in the shadows save for their eyes all aglow. The shadows in the middle of the street were held at bay by the incessant blare of the sirens. He saw lupine like beasts leaping in and out of the shadows. Some beasts had long muzzles and long, pointed ears and long tails while some beasts sported short muzzles without tails to speak of.

The wind had picked up through the subdivision the last leaves on the trees falling to the ground and gusting into the living room. Closing the door, Dr. Jacobs could smell the strong stench of the gathering aroma of the infected. Hunter sat down at the kitchen table. Hunter motioned Terrell, Tasha, and Rogers' wife to come as he had a story to tell.

84

Sarah's inherited property

Sarah fled up to her front porch without incident, closing and locking the door behind her once inside. The conflict had quieted down just a sickening slurp and crunch of the bones could be heard. The rest of the unlucky party members whimpered and cried surrounded by claw and fang. They were hunched over as they waited to be picked off by the hungry lunatics and changelings who used to be their friends.

Aticus drew in a long deep breath of the blood and carnage as it excited his sensitive senses when an unusual smell, something foreign yet so familiar, stirred up in the air. James emerged from the barn. He looked at James with distain. Something rubbed him the wrong way about him and didn't know why; he had been a remarkable asset thus far. This is the chance to prove his loyalty once and for all he thought.

"I smell Devon; he is now out of the safety zone on his way to my island!" Aticus was beside himself shaking from rage, time for James to prove his loyalty. Maybe if he caught Devon after all it would change how he felt about him and the peculiar essence all about him, "James, find him!"

James shifted form into a hybrid-wolf as he sped off on all fours to intercept Devon. He could not see him but he could smell him, a wild musky aroma. He flew through the foliage as he had use of all fours limbs, an experience that he had yet to get used to, euphoric his mind and body were one now in symbiosis of wolf and man.

James tore through the thicket like a silver bullet. The fully functional Wolf almost forgot he had a job to do his heart racing as excitement coursed through him, he was running! The Wolf James was sprinting through the grass at breakneck speeds.

James had tried to catch and lock onto the interloper, Devon's aroma, about a mile away from the plantation. The Wolf James tilted his head and sniffed the air. The wind had suddenly changed coming from behind him now, his heart skipped a beat. The wolf suddenly stopped, skidding on his belly in the dirt and leaves. Downwind from Devon, the scent had gone away. Invisible hands pushed the leaves up into the air; leaves floating away like sailboats on a clear ocean drifting past James's head, teasing his watchful eyes. A gust of crisp wind blew back the fur on his hackles between his shoulder blades. Large triangular ears strained to hear just a minute signal that would betray Devon's position. His ears listened a few seconds longer, all he heard was Brown Pelicans somewhere miles away singing their mating song.

His huge strapping neck turned frantically this way and that to see past the rows and rows of bald Cypress trees. Suddenly a thick, fibrous, red-brown scaly, large branch hit him over the head dropping him onto his belly. Long thick talons able to clasp onto the branches clung from the treetops the white wolf with red sigils had been patiently waiting until James traversed below. From seemingly nowhere the branches gave way as he dropped down to the ground. He hesitated wincing in pain the wounds from earlier still evident, the hesitation more than enough time for the Wolf James to get up on his limbs.

The brown hybrid-wolf saw the white wolf standing upright. He had a severe wound, minute silver shavings interfering with the healing process bleeding into his fur matching the red sigils on his muzzle. James shook off the dizziness and lunged toward the wounded Wolf. Devon transformed with blinding speed to accommodate his fighting style thwarting James' meager nips and strikes. The powerful yet wounded white wolf threw the inexperienced wolf like a rag doll. The brunt of the wolf's body came to rest at the base of a large Cypress.

He bore down on the wolf's neck only thick furs coming between skin and fang when a strange aroma emanating from the wolf made him hesitate. Devon decided not to kill James, just incapacitate him; his large paw clasped the base of his forehead. He smashed the backside of the skull into the trunk of the tree until the wolf went limp. Devon only waited until making sure if the wolf woke up he would heal normally before he then staggered and limped onward.

85

Batchelor, Louisiana

"What's going on?" Terrell's brother, Tyson, questioned coming in on the middle of the conversation. He sat on a chair near the kitchen table, "I don't understand."

Hunter told him the Cliff Notes version walking him through the improbable events again. The sirens and strobe lights keeping them safe in the house, "the car battery won't last very much longer."

Hunter rummaged through his backpack emerging with a handful of portable powerful lights, "newer, weaker lycanthropes will be discouraged and be feeling pain from the bright intense lights we will be safe until we are rested a moment, then shore up our defenses. Who is going out there?"

Susan's vengeful eyes were cutting holes into her husband. She very well knew Capt. Rogers handed off the job of rescuing her and Hannah to Detective Jenkins because he had to search for his ex-girlfriend. Detective Jenkins tried to distract and defuse the situation. Neither one were paying attention to Hunter.

She was too jittery from thinking about Hannah's safety she paced about the room. Tasha's protective nature over Hannah took over, "I will do it."

"You will?" Hunter questioned more rhetorical in nature as he was taken by Tasha's bravery.

"Yes..." Tasha meekly responded.

"I will give you instructions for placing them and I will protect you, but you should be fine with the sirens keeping them at bay," Hunter handed off the lights and pumped his shotgun.

Tasha headed out the door and down the steps. She looked around for hidden predators, not finding anything she got on with the work at hand. She stuck in the lights, with Hunter's precise instructions. She wired up the last of the floodlights to the house then stepped back to survey her work. Six lights crisscrossed the front and back of the house, four lights were on the sides. She patted the sweat from her forehead the rest of the job was up to those inside wiring the lights to the main electrical system.

"Okay, it's done, it's all on your end in the house," Tasha yelled, the loud sirens were driving her nuts.

The darkening sky held no stars to speak of from the gathering low, heavy black clouds on the horizon the wind whipping up in the air. She awoke from a daze with a start from the sound of footfalls approaching cautiously; Tasha peered through the gathering darkness to find what she perceived as a dog... It was no dog, however! A large blonde hybrid Wolf with a large burn on its cheek, its muzzle twitching as it sniffed the air, approached, disregarding the pain in its ears from the sirens. It snarled as she scrambled away in fear towards the house screaming.

She was half way between the blonde wolf and the back door. She backed up as the wolf clambered towards her. The wolf came closer and closer still…enough so she could smell its putrid breath and feel the heat that it exuded. She could feel its soft fur brush against her body. This is it; she cursed herself for letting her guard down. She closed her eyes expecting to be mauled any second, she wondered if it would hurt or would she go numb before she died. Please be merciful to me! She thought in her head.

Hunter glanced out the door after directing Jacobs to his job to find a horrible sight. Tasha and a monstrous blonde wolf were practically intertwined with one another. He drew up his shotgun and tried to get a bead on the wolf. He cursed in frustration; he couldn't get a good shot without a chance of wounding the girl. He pointed his shotgun to the sky and fired a warning shot. She protected her ears as the report that rang off made her ears ring, but it was loud enough to spook the blonde wolf who jumped away from Tasha and ran toward the alleyway.

"Get in here!" Hunter hoarsely yelled, ordering her to the house by waving his hands frantically.

"Come inside!" The second figure this time Tyson yelled, though he was clutching Hunter's waist for protection.

She got up on her knees from the grass running toward the back door. They wrenched the screen door open and before she went in she turned her head to see the blonde wolf pacing back and forth in the alleyway.

"We've got a problem here!" Susan yelled, staring out another window.

She peeked through the curtains to see three bipedal lupine creatures at the end of the street staring directly at the patrol car. Their long pointed ears visibly hurting from the shrill siren sounds. They were communicating orders in rumbles, snarls, growls and yaps to another shirtless lunatic, human in feature save for his glowing eyes, fangs and talon-like claws.

The shirtless lunatic lurched forward leaping on all four limbs and running across the street. He tore the rack of revolving lights off the car. The lights fell onto the windshield cracking the glass, bolts and washers falling on the grass. He growled in satisfaction heading toward the hood ripping through the flimsy sheet metal like a can opener.

"He is trying to destroy the sirens!" Someone in the house warned Hunter.

The lunatic was successful and the sound of the sirens stopped suddenly as he cut the wires to the battery. He shook off the painful dizziness in his head a big sigh of relief came from the lunatic his ears needing a rest from the loud whining. He leaped onto the porch and beat on the front door with his fists.

"Once the sirens are out he is going to get in here!" Hannah yelled. Her arms wrapped tight around Terrell in fear.

The relentless loud knocking had stopped but a form appeared in the bay window cast in shadow by the draperies. A loud crash startled the group as jagged glass fell to the floor. The curtains whipped wildly back and forth in the wind. Kids screamed and Hannah began sobbing.

The lunatic burst inside the house. The balls of his feet were firmly planted on the shag carpet; they were enlarging, filthy and barefoot. The lunatic snarled as he lunged grabbing for the small girl dressed in a red riding hood outfit first. Hunter knew from the lunatic's eyes that he didn't have to waste a silver bolt to put him down. Hunter lowered his shotgun cursing because now Hannah was blocking his shot.

"He is still partially human! He could be stopped with regular bullets! Anyone with a clear shot, take it!" Hunter yelled advancing.

Capt. Rogers and Detective Jenkins both fired their guns; one bullet hit him in the chest and one in the head. For a moment the lunatic still stood upright and both were prepared to shoot the lunatic again until he staggered and fell to the ground. Susan had scooped up Hannah who cowered in a ball.

"The new ones can be killed with ordinary bullets," Hunter said to no one in particular more for the information purposes, "modern embalming practices are a good way to stop any regeneration that may occur."

Hunter went into action. He cut his head off with a survival knife then sprinkled white phosphorus all over his body. The white phosphorus looked like it exploded blazing up in the living room.

Hunter turned to the group and said, "Of course, cutting their heads off and burning the hell out of them works too, better safe than sorry!"

The Wolf-things could smell the burning flesh of their pack mate. With the bay window broken and the sirens turned off the hairy beasts cautiously entered Tasha's yard. Their skin had stretched thin to accommodate the growth in skeletal and cartilage tissue in their mouth and cheeks; they had enlarged nostrils and flattened noses. Their skin had become almost transparent revealing engorged muscles the jaw swollen becoming slack-jawed, tight skin curled up even further revealing bleeding gums that accommodated a mouth full of fangs when they snarled.

The Wolf-things were stopped at the threshold of the house, as a corpse consumed in fire was tossed into the yard, the only thing keeping them out was the flames but it was all but a skeleton now and it was smoldering.

"I almost got it!" Dr. Jacobs' excitedly exclaimed from the utility room at the end of the hallway. Per Hunter's instructions he had just one more wire to connect and he was done.

The world brightened as floodlights and mirrors positioned so they magnified the light 5000 lumen came to life, enough light that with her eyes still closed Tasha could still see it. The motley crew heard a pitiful yelp from the Wolf-things. They shook their lupine-human heads in unison and closed their eyes while backing off of the house from the intense lights.

"I can't believe it! I can't believe my eyes! The crazy old tales of Halloween are true!" Tasha exclaimed.

"No, no the date, this is just coincidental... though the beings are supernatural straight out of myth and folklore." Hunter had Tasha's undivided attention, "...They are the lycanthropes; werewolves are coming out of the shadows and blatantly attacking humanity."

Tasha's head swam from all the unbelievable information in her head, cottonmouth setting in she needed a drink. A sickening feeling came over her and unbelievable as it seemed now she worried something awful had befallen her brother. She imagined her brother getting mauled by a monster. Was he attacked by these creatures too? Tasha thought as she turned on the kitchen faucet for a drink.

"What the...?" from the corner of her eye Tasha thought she saw out the window the blonde Wolf staring at her from the alleyway.

The blonde Wolf visibly hurt by the sudden and powerful light rubbed its eyes with its paws, a human like reaction Tasha thought, then bolted behind the garage casting protective shadows for the Wolf whose cunning familiar eyes squinted at the dazzling house with an almost humanlike contemplation, as if thinking what to do next.

Latoya, Tyson's girlfriend had her back against the wall. Her eyes were wide and she clutched her useless cell phone in her sweaty hands. Terrell peeked out the back door, his arm still around Hannah for comfort. The blonde Wolf was still there looking intently up at the electric pole.

Tyson popped his head out for a look, "That fucker! It's looking at the line that comes into the house." Tyson had a sickening feeling in the pit of his stomach. "It's like he's thinking!"

Tyson motioned for the Tasha to look out the window as he dug around in the pockets of his baggy pants to retrieve something. Tasha pulled the curtains back even further to get a closer view of the scene in the brilliant circle of absolute light that protected the house.

"Tyson, what are you doing?" Latoya cried.

Tasha was horrified when she realized Tyson pulled out a silver automatic handgun. He slid the magazine out of the 9 mm assured it had a full clip then he slid the magazine back in again with a snap.

The gun looked menacing, weighing heavily in his hand. In truth he hadn't shot a gun in his life the gun felt foreign to him. He just felt at ease having it on him when he was managing a show, or during a crisis, for protection.

"There's something in its eyes, something's just not right! It's thinking… I know it, it's up to something, and I know it's crazy but I feel it!" Tyson shouted. With the bright lights protecting Tyson he headed out the back storm door with the gun in hand, pushing past his little brother.

The howls of the blonde wolf began; an eerie symphony of higher then deep octaves, an unnerving sound, and a sound of foreboding. Stopping and then starting again like an animal version of Morse code, until his howls were answered. Three wolves were talking now in a language foreign to man.

Bobby and Terry mindlessly came running; two burn-out high school drop outs, now lunatics as the parasite transforming them almost completely into two hybrid wolf-things. Long bipedal forms with shredded clothing, long pointed ears, full of fur head to paws, and they had heard the blonde wolf's calls. Though the two wolf-things were bigger Kevin exuded eccentric pheromones that the wolf-things' absorbed in their olfactory system mimicking strength and leadership that the weaker willed have to obey. The blonde wolf pushed at the electrical pole, it didn't budge. The blonde wolf hung his head down seemingly in defeat. Then the blonde wolf barked out orders to the others.

Bobby, a wolf-thing with vacant eyes, and Terry's wolf-thing with its slobbering fangs, and the original blonde wolf, all dug feverishly at the ground next to the electric pole. Blonde fur turned brown as they dug into the Earth. A dirt cloud dusted over the relentless hybrid-wolves. It took just five minutes to reveal the moist dark brown underbelly of the submerged pole. A few minutes more and the electric pole quivered, unsteady now with no support from the earth.

Tyson could hear the conversational yelps and growls from the three wolves in the relative safety of the lighted backyard but curiosity got the better of him and with an unsteady hand he closed in on the wolves.

"What are you doing?" Tasha yelled at him from the safety of the kitchen. She was losing her mind.

Tasha laughed hysterically, only hours ago all she had to worry about was the freshness of the coffee and now she had to keep Hannah and her friends safe from supernatural rabid wolves! She then crouched down by the table, hidden beside the kitchen island that acted as a shield between her and the world outside. She tried desperately not to hyperventilate as her helplessness over whelmed her.

Tyson put a finger to his lips as he looked back at everybody in the house watching, the universal sign to be quiet, then looked on in horror as the blonde wolf stopped digging, turned from the pole pacing as if measuring the distance then turned to face the pole again. Tyson glanced at the pole, the house wires, and then the pole again. He cursed because he knew; it's cutting off the power from the house!

The red and brown wolves stood back as the blonde wolf dug in its paws and sprinted toward the now precariously perched electrical pole. The wolf ran at the pole going full speed. The wolf didn't stop until its shoulder impacted in the low center with a Wham! The Wolf shook his head dazed from the impact and then ran toward the pole again, Wham! Now the pole was at a 60° angle and the electrical wires to the house now taunt connections groaned as if any minute they would snap.

"They're trying to cut off the lights to the house! Everybody try all the phones again, landline and cell phone!" His voice was audibly quivering.

"If the power goes out we have to leave or we are sitting ducks." Hunter said.

Both Detective Jenkins and Capt. Rogers agreed.

"I think I know a place." Hunter said matter-of-factly.

"We have to get everyone ready in case we need to move quickly!"

Tasha hesitantly got up from her hiding place and realizing Latoya was not in the room sprinted toward the hallway looking for her. She turned in to her brother's bedroom to her right but she was nowhere to be found. She then preceded left to her room all the while the thumbs working frantically on the buttons on her cell phone, but it was empty as well.

"Dammit Latoya, where are you?" Her voice was a mixture of trepidation and frustration with two doors left, her parent's bedroom and the bathroom, she headed toward the open bathroom door where she saw Latoya clutching the toilet, the stress and excitement had gotten the better of her. She prayed to the porcelain god, about to pass out on her knees, dry heaves wracking her body.

The blonde wolf, Kevin, was pleased by the progress he and Bobby and Terry, the Wolf-things, had made with the electrical pole. The utility pole now leaned down just enough that he could walk on it with four legs. The wires stretched to the breaking point so that if he stressed the pole just a little bit more something will have to give way. Breaking the circuits and with that the accursed circle of blinding light so he can get into the house. A little further and sparks began to light up the night sky.

Ear splitting crackle and crash could be heard in the house that sounded like lightning striking a huge Oak tree as it fell hitting the forest floor so violently it scared the wildlife miles away. The power went out. Now they were blind, forced into sudden darkness.

"You fuckers!" Tyson cursed blindly taking potshots at the Wolf-things until one of them howled out in pain, "Ha-ha I got one!"

Terry the Wolf thing had been wounded gravely in the chest and abdomen. He spontaneously and involuntarily began transforming into a pale and bloody adolescent again, then immediately collapsed. Bobby gingerly scooped his wounded friend up and belted out a sorrowful howl as he left in the cover of darkness, leaving Kevin alone.

More glowing animalistic eyes had materialized in the darkness. Some figures were on all fours, figures that lurched, hunchbacked, knuckles dragging to the ground and figures looking like men but their glowing eyes gave them away. Those who had tails wagged them in anticipation. Tyson immediately retreated back inside. It seemed like eerie howls of victory could be heard from those that circled the house effectively trapping them in. Hunter could see several glowing eyes slowly lumbering closer to the house. Think quickly, he told himself, or all would be lost. The Devils would overrun the house. Then suddenly a light bulb went on in his head.

"I have a helicopter at False River airport if we can make it over there," Hunter explained shooing them all into the claustrophobic hallway toward the garage door.

They heard the back door shatter and scuttling large paws in the kitchen, the Wolf-things almost upon them. The group consisting of Tasha, Terrell, Tyson, Latoya, Hannah, who was in the protective arms of her mother Susan, Detective Jenkins, Capt. Rogers and Dr. Jacobs all funneled into the hallway ahead of Hunter. They could see several glowing yellow, green and red eyes in the murky darkness as Hunter turned around to face the horde as Tasha turned on the light to her useless cell phone and hurriedly opened the garage door.

Hunter searched through a burlap sack and took out a fist full of copper coins flinging them in the air in an arc. Their time to flee started to count down when the coins hit the ground. The Wolf-men were forced to stop their twisted lupine heads turning away from the group and down to the shiny coins where they sniffed and counted them one by one.

Hunter turned around to see Tyson staring at him, he shrugged and said, "Yeah don't waste the shots or silver bullets on the young changelings, if you throw out copper coins they will feel a compelling force to acknowledge and count each and every one of them."

With shaking hands, she searched using her smart phone for a flashlight for the keys to the minivan in her purse while she opened the adjoining garage door. She had never been so relieved to see the trusted minivan in the garage.

"I think I can make it out!" Tasha exclaimed as she peeked outside from the garage door window.

The torn up vehicle in the driveway and the torn up patrol car in the grass did not give Tasha much room to maneuver out to the street, but she was confident that she could make it. Everybody piled into the van and it was a tight fit but everybody made it. Tasha turned around one last time to see if everybody made it in.

"Hold on everyone!" Tasha warned as she dropped it into gear and stepped on the gas.

Tasha didn't even bother to wait for the garage door to finish going up, the van busted out the garage door, bending the aluminum frame and splintering the siding in its wake as the van headlights pierced the night sky. She barely missed scraping the front left fender of Susan's car then cut the wheel almost hitting the squad car head on before she maneuvered safely onto the street with a bump and a screech of tires.

The wind started blowing and the rains fell down gently at first, then an onslaught as rain like pebbles fell down onto the pavement and bouncing up again as if it looked like the rain came from in both directions at once.

"Oh shit!" Tyson cursed, He couldn't be sure because of the sudden downpour but he thought he saw glowing eyes following them.

The group heard a loud rumbling sound like a freight train coming straight for them and a violent shaking forced Tasha to press on the brakes, she asked quivering, "Was that an earthquake?"

"Why yes, yes, it was! In fact I think we're experiencing aftershocks!" Hunter immediately turned on the radio but was rewarded with static, "Damn! Something is messing up the radio signal!"

Static then a chorus of howling, "St. Louis…" Incessant howling again, then, "New Madrid fault line…" Another bout of static then rhythmic howling, "The National Guard has been alerted but they are slow to deploy due to the unexpected hurricane in the Gulf Coast region… Meteorological phenomenon that has the community…" Then static again as Hunter turned the knobs trying to get a better signal.

"I think I see it!" Hannah blurted out loudly pointing past the perimeter fence to the tower in the distance.

"Thank God," Susan prayed, "we can get out of here!"

Tasha smiled relief her hand reached over to Susan's hand to comfort her. Her color had drained from her face and her nervous smile was frozen on her face. Tasha could barely see the road with the power outage and onslaught of rain she didn't see the padlocked chain link gate until it was too late.

"Shit, look out!" Tasha warned as she stomped on the gas.

The chain link fence gave way with only a little resistance. Detective Jenkins patted her on the back and complemented her, "way to go, that's some impressive driving!"

"I have a chopper in Hangar three; it is just a little ways past the tower. We can get out of here." Hunter offered, trying to see through the fog.

The group collectively sighed in relief; turning onto a street called "Tower Road" and on to the hangars where the helicopter had been stowed away.

They headed toward False River Airport, a small airport with only three hangars that housed around twenty aircrafts, most of which were Cessna's and other private mid-sized to small crafts. With the storm moving in there would be minimal personnel let alone with the chaos going on to deal with the headache of explaining the unbelievable situation they found themselves in needing to flee.

An aftershock had the van veering off the road as fissures appeared in the asphalt. The front left tire exploded as it dropped into the sudden open crack leaving only the rim.

"Shit!" Tasha cursed; she stepped on the gas, a lurch from the van but no forward movement.

"That's okay, the hangars are just the length of a football field or so away and we can walk from here as long as you all don't mind the rain!" Latoya pointed out.

"She's right." Susan and Tasha answered in unison to each other.

One by one they all filed out of the van and out into the torrent. Dr. Jacobs stopped legs halfway between the asphalt and the van to look out at the horizon. He could smell the pack quickly advancing toward them. What was worse is he felt a stirring in his gut. He almost passed out from the increasing pressure in his jaw. The terrible hunger threatened to twist his body in knots, an urge he couldn't explain.

"Hey, uh Hunter, isn't it? I don't think we can make it all the way to the chopper!" Detective Jenkins pointed toward Hangar three.

Hunter peered out into the rain to see murky shadows of an extremely large Wolf pack guarding the hangar. He reached to retrieve a pair of binoculars from his inside jacket pocket. He adjusted the binoculars until he could see the wolves clearly. One particularly large wolf with a large deep gash in the front limbs where he had escaped from the barbed wire fence had stood up. The Wolf, an alpha by the other wolves' actions watched them in earnest.

"Quick, we have to do something, the loup-garoux, I smell them and they are really close!" Dr. Jacobs warned Hunter.

Hunter pressed Dr. Jacobs' cheeks with his callused hands. He forced Jacobs' head around to get a good look at his eyes. His eyes were bloodshot and dilated; Hunter proceeded to inspect his teeth. Dr. Jacobs' gums were profusely bleeding, down to his hands where his fingernails were thicker, growing and bleeding too.

"You're infected..." Hunter looked into the doctors eyes, shocked.

"I know..." The Dr. acknowledged quietly, clenching his jaw.

"Well, that is rather impressive. You have to be struggling to hide the infection. You have a strong mind but you'll eventually be hungry as the parasite progresses through you and needs sustenance," Hunter matter-of-factly explained, "you need to eat or the hunger is going to overtake you... that's why the lycanthropes attack man, it's the easy prey, they are plentiful and unsuspecting and ignorant... When the hunger comes upon you, your rational, logical mind is hazy." he reached into his pocket for what looked like an energy bar.

"Listen, I can tell from your eyes, you're not an evil person, this will help with the hunger so you can think straight," Hunter unwrapped and offered the energy bar to Dr. Jacobs knowing it was loaded with protein and iron, "and for the time being this will keep the beast satisfied." Hunter adjusted his binoculars to physically count the wolves guarding his hangar.

"With the Wolf pack guarding the hangar I'm afraid we're not getting to the chopper any time soon. We have to get to the tower before the werewolves are upon us," Hunter shook his head in frustration.

Dr. Jacobs could see clearly through the rain with his new sight. There were more werewolves coming and he could smell the leader of it all, he was close, "I'm afraid I might be losing the battle for sanity, I can help you before...in case I change, stall some of the werewolves so the group can make it to the tower and maybe kill the alpha that's responsible for all of this before I lose my fight for my soul."

Hunter protested until he thought about his situation in life. He had been bitten and the curse or blessing however you may perceive it had turned his life around. From a little-known farmer he had become the fevered Hunter, the slayer of the children of the night.

"You then," Hunter stuck a knife, gun, and finally two grenades into the palms of his hands. "Make them bleed! The grenades are white phosphorus so use them as a last resort if you get close to the alpha. I will be protecting the group and getting them to safety."

The doctor nodded, accepted the gifts, and then ran off to intercept the oncoming beasts before they caught the group. Running as a tight group they made it safely to the tower. Capt. Rogers got there first but found it locked. An electronic lock pick in well-trained hands Capt. Rogers unlocked the door in record time. Several drenched rats that escaped from the rising waters of the underground sewer system just to become trapped in the tower fled at the first sign of light. Glowing red eyes could be seen their bodies twitching the bloody rain saturating their fur as they disappeared into the tall grass.

Tasha, Susan, Hannah and Latoya stopped before they got to the stairwell as if the darkness blocked them from progressing any further.

"The power is out in the tower as well!" Terrell shrieked.

"Don't worry little brother; I saw a generator just outside. We will have power in no time." Tyson said with a nervous smile.

"There is still nothing coming, I think we are safe for the time being," Detective Jenkins said, but the ghost of his son shook his head glancing in and out.

"Okay, okay," Hunter comforted the group, "head upstairs, all of us stay together, I'll lead us to higher ground. Maybe we will be able to assess the situation better."

Tyson walked back outside and pressed the binoculars that he borrowed from Hunter up to his eyes. He saw two nude gravely injured forms just on the other side from the chain link fence.

"Will shit, I think the Doc actually got the fuckers!" It was the Doc against several beasts, but it looked as though he killed them, he thought.

There wasn't any more interest from the wolves at Hangar three, either. He put his hands on the wall as if the tower was a lifeboat and he'd be lost at sea without it, and circled the tower until he found the generator.

Tyson dropped to one knee and pulled the drawstring to the 10,000 Watt, 4-Cycle gas powered portable Generator. It started and then sputtered out. He pulled the drawstring again. It sputtered then steadily roared to life. He looked up at the dark windows and still silent sound sirens.

"Dammit! The lights still don't work, must be the breakers somewhere in the basement!" Tyson cursed turning around.

He heard a roar then suddenly was thrown off his feet and onto the ground the wind knocked from his lungs. A man-beast had broken off from the struggle with Dr. Jacobs and the others and ran off when he caught the smell of Tyson, an easy meal.

Tyson could have seen the human features in its face but he was too busy staring at his enormous fangs. After he caught his breath he struggled to pull up his knees against his chest and pushed with all his might.

"Get off me!" With an audible oomph the beast was hoisted up off the ground with his feet. He pulled out his gun and began to fire blindly while he scrambled a retreat back to the tower.

He stopped shooting when the beast fell he held his breath for several moments intently watching the fallen beast. Tyson swore to himself if the beast even flinched, he would unload the whole clip until it was on its ass! Several moments went by, however, without a movement building up his confidence enough to let his eyes off of the monster and walk back to the tower's doors.

He trolled around the basement in search of an electrical box until he came upon a door with a sign saying "Maintenance". Tyson swung his fist in the air, his other hand still clutching his warm 9 mm, "That's more like it!"

Searching for what felt like an eternity in the dark Tyson finally found the electrical box, putting his gun in his jeans and opened it.

"Shit!" His hopes were dashed for an easy fix. When he realized that instead of circuit breakers which he could have easily tripped the airport still used fuses, "You gotta be kidding me! I thought it was a violation of some kind of code to have these ancient things still in there."

Tyson would not be deterred though, searching for fuses in drawer after drawer feeling his way around. Boxes of washers, screws and nails hit the floor as Tyson rummaged through to find fuses, like looking for a needle in the proverbial haystack, Tyson scoffed. He had an idea hit him and stopped rummaging through the boxes and ran outside into the rain. He had fired three or four shots at the monster before it went down. Brass casings are conductors and he could use the casings to connect broken fuses!

Tyson groaned as he bent down to pick up the shells his mind racing with a plan. The floor had a familiar balance to it with many years of maintenance in his belt he knew that there was an ergonomic rubber mat. The mat could be used as a natural resistor in electrical flow. Confident with his well-thought-out plan he stood up when a cold chill ran through him. Tyson's head whipped around back and forth in search for a body that apparently had got up and walked away.

"Oh fuck!" Instantly he was filled with worry and stress for his little brother's safety. He had to stick the fuses in and get up to the top of the tower to protect him in case the monster was to return.

He ran for the safety of the tower every inch feeling like an eternity and flung open the door running back downstairs to the maintenance room. He flipped open his pocket knife and cut a 4 x 4 piece of rubber, just big enough to protect his hand while trying to put the shells into the fuse box. He positioned the rubber slice with three brass casings still holding the pocket knife and opened the box.

The wounded beast burst through the basement maintenance door, leaving only splinters in its wake. It startled Tyson, prompting him to drop the knife from his hand. It still had monstrous features, but he recognized the torn clothing and two bullet holes yet to heal oozing blackened blood. It no longer had a humanoid face. It no longer had a human head at all as the infection rapidly progressed in the body. It looked like an amalgamated Wolf form with an extended muzzle, exaggerated fangs, and with a long thick neck and true lupine head.

"No! That's impossible. I shot you, you bastard!" And with that he fired on the beast several more times.

The wounded Wolf-thing howled in pain, but it did not stop it from tackling Tyson to the ground. It looked down at its wounded body in surprise, but the beast did not stop from swiping Tyson's thigh with its enormous claws severing important nerves to his legs.

"Impossible..."

The rubber strip and casings slipped from Tyson's bloody hand but he managed to pick up two of the shell casings on the ground in the darkness, "I beat you before, I will beat you again! You are not gonna get your filthy claws on my little brother!"

Tyson managed to drag himself to the fuse box despite his paralyzed leg just as fangs bore down on his exposed neck. He stuck the brass casings into the empty hole like they were a square peg in a round hole, forcing in to the fuse box with his sweaty palm. Broken circuits connecting the lights began to flicker at first, and then a steady hum as the lights brightened all over the tower.

The last sound Tyson heard was the emergency sirens start up and he could smell burnt fur and cooking flesh. He smiled as his heart went into arrest. At least his brother would be safe. The sirens blared from the airport tower keeping the beasts at bay for a while longer. It began to rain down blood. The blood was the color of crimson. In stained the cars, houses, trailers, and shacks of Louisiana.

86

Sarah's inherited property

Aticus went around rounding up mauled and long dead bodies of partygoers shooing off the occasional beast still gnawing the bones of the dead. He filleted the torn skin to the bone then dropped the freshly skinned bones into his backpack.

Lance strolled out of the veiled barn when some of the lunatics sped off into the night, looking around at the carnage and slyly smiling. He couldn't help himself mimicking a reference to the A-team series and movie, giving his best Hannibal impression, "I love it when a plan comes together!"

"It's time!" Aticus blurted out.

Aticus smirked at Lance's corny reference but in truth though, his excitement had been building up, butterflies in his stomach fluttering about threatening to burst out of his skin. If So-seti actually conjured up the mother of all werewolves, the necromancer Aisos, she could heal his infection.

"My dear Aticus make a circle!" So-seti commanded. "Find rocks to mark the elements."

Amy struggled, bound by the wrists and gagged. Lance and Aticus drew in the dirt with their feet until a large 8 foot circle was made.

So-seti instructed the men where the rocks should go all while keeping an eye on the captive.

"Earth." So-seti pointed at the circle and instructed the men to find five rocks so they could place them in the circle breaking off into five sections. The men made short work of their tasks as Lance lay down the last rock completing the pentagram.

So-seti made esoteric hand movements as she said, "Air."

"Fire, water, and spirit," So-seti shouted completing the incantation.

So-seti braced herself and motioned an esoteric hand signal murmuring something ritualistic then spat orders, her excitement growing, "Now for the bones!"

Aticus put down his backpack and proceeded to carefully take out several bones. Some fresh human bones that he scooped up from the night's party and some lycanthropic regurgitated from Oung's mouth and positioned them atomically just outside the circle. Confident that the skeleton, minus the head, was in place he stood up. He cautiously brought out the masterpiece of perfectly fossilized prehistoric dire Wolf skull ascertained from Tonya who obtained it materializing in the La Brea tar pits after-hours then disappearing without a trace.

Lance held the captive tightly by the shoulders as So-seti spat in the dirt and mixed the saliva around until it was the consistency of ink then began arcane writing on the rocks.

Aticus left So-seti, Lance, and the hostage and ventured into the woods. When he reemerged again he carried with just one hand a 10-foot log which he procured somewhere near the barn. If she wasn't so frightened Amy would have been impressed by Aticus' raw strength but his deformed face with a huge round shiny emerald in his missing eye socket had her cringing in fear. He hefted the post up and proceeded to pound it into the ground like a human posthole digger by the mish mass of bones on the ground.

"Please don't hurt me." Amy pleaded, her feet had been bound as well and when she tried to move she looked like a waddling penguin.

Aticus stopped what he was doing a look of hurt in his eye. He slowly approached Amy and tenderly stroked her cheek. The touch of her captor made her cringe. She so desperately needed Devon right now to save her.

"My dear don't worry. I'm not the one that is going to harm you." Aticus said matter-of-factly as he looked at her and stroked her cheek.

Aticus nodded at Lance the orders clear; he grabbed a hold of Amy her feet marking the grass as he began dragging her to the new post. Her back to the post he began lashing her up snugly.

"No, please… I don't want to die!" She pleaded as Lance finished binding her to the sturdy log, "Please, you can still let me go!"

So-seti hobbled over to Amy pointing at her with her homemade crutch, "I wish I could, precious, but you are an intricate part of this ritual."

Amy was mesmerized by So-seti's appearance. She seemed to age backwards right before her eyes. The silver nitrate poison running through her veins had run its course. Her neck and body looked like a young 30 year old, somehow more elastic, tighter and glowing. Her baby soft skin had no visible imperfections whatsoever. Her hair was brilliant, glowing, full-bodied, black as night. Even her eyes reflecting the full Moon's light when the dark rain clouds gave way for an extremely brief moment seemed young and alive. She started a spark that quickly became a bonfire in the middle of the circle. Her breasts were fuller; Amy's eyes were mesmerized as she realized So-seti had six pair of small additional nipples. Her belly swollen, Amy could see unborn fetuses' moved actively in her womb. So-seti was very pregnant.

"Human blood has to be shed to bring Aisos back to life," So-seti said as she picked up a golden dagger she had successfully smuggled from The God's Light compound before it burnt to the ground and handed it to Aticus, "to heal the alpha, to unify the fractured pack, and to strengthen the Wolf blood that too long has been diluted to almost nonexistence in the pathetic human population! We will be powerful again and unstoppable. With Aisos' help the pack will avenge my shame and embarrassment, and destroy the entire God's Light *disease* that exists throughout the world, one already down, and five more chapters to go. Amy, dear, we need you. Aisos cannot return without you, a fresh human sacrifice."

So-seti thrust one hand into the dirt and with the other hand carefully picked up ash from the smoldering branches mixing them all together with both hands and blew the mixture between the bones of the ribs, like she was blowing a kiss into the air.

Aticus checked the blade with his thumb, sliding his thumb from the point to the hilt. He slowly circled around the makeshift pentagram stopping to look at Amy bound to the post.

"Wait..." Amy screamed out but her voice broke as she stared at the bones at her feet.

Aticus gave the blade to So-seti who proceeded to cut her own wrists horizontally to forearm slicing arteries painting the bones red. The grievous wounds would have been fatal if not for her healing factor. After the wounds had healed So-seti did not hesitate to slice Amy's neck from ear to ear cleanly. Bubbles began to form as she tried to breath.

Rising up through the smoke and fire, a form began to materialize. Supported by her crutches the witch's fingers and hands laced together as she slithered and danced to her unholy spell. She danced clumsily her stumps making an impression in the mud as she circled. Amy's blood pooled and ran into So-seti's blood and almost immediately the blood began to boil and spew out like a volcano as a chain reaction occurred.

A torrent of life blood began to stir like a mini tornado building upon itself until the plasma whirlwind orbited the skeleton the broken pieces levitating taller than a full grown man. The larvae and parasites in So-seti's spittle fueled on by the close gravity field of the perigee full Moon and So-seti's incantations began to animate and multiply. The larvae a microscopic roly-poly of sorts rolled up it looked like the moon itself. The parasites began to uncurl from their ball looking like a centipede in nature, an exoskeleton with plates. Trillions upon trillions began to manifest their selves and layer after layer began to adhere to human and lycanthropic bones. The intangible form started to darken and materialize. Microscopic parasite appendages interlaced working together acting as one unit to make the unholy dire Wolf shade.

Suddenly the earth quaked and the wind began to blow even harder. The trees once visible in the distance disappeared as the ghost like specter where indistinguishable shadows had once been were now replaced by hairs that glowed silver in the moonlight. Empty eye sockets began to glow red over the orange light of the fire. Embers arced and hit the ground as the specter's feet began to form.

Crutches supported under her shoulders, arms rose up toward the sky as So-seti continued the unholy incantation. The Wolf shade stood upright its translucent paw shown through disarticulated bones. Her phantom feet firmly planted on the ground the long arch and heel up in the air mimicking the hock of the Wolf shade. Aisos picked up the cauldron with translucent paws; The Wolf shade's tongue lapped up the Virgin Wolf cult's mixtures of blood. She let out a loud deep howl that frightened and scared away the small animals and birds from miles around. The reverberations shook the Earth. The shade's snarling and howling was spewing out loose parasites like droplets into the air.

Aticus took the emerald from his wounded eye. It had been scored by So-seti in runic incantations to bring solid what once had been incorporeal. Placed in Aisos' translucent chest it began to materialize before he had his hand out from the body.

"Yes, my child?" Aisos questioned her now physical paw brushed So-seti's cheek as her fiery gaze turned upon her and Aticus.

So-seti hobbled over to the great mother of all werewolves anxious to be cured from the amputations but Aticus pushed her aside. Unsteady, she faltered on her crutches and fell to the ground.

"I'm first!" Aticus yelled. "You must heal me!"

He forced Aisos' hand onto his face. He closed his one good eye and kneeled down before Aisos. The pain was excruciating as solid silver embedded in his brain and body began to liquefy. From his useless eye came silver tears. His body was quivering, he had been waiting for this for a long time, the silver ran out of his body, no more a mishmash of human and lupine, able to see clearly again.

"Urg!" Labor pains which started in the base of So-seti's pelvis and continued to the base of her skull had her lunging over in pain and clutching her swollen belly, "Aticus… James, where are you? Help me..."

Aticus ignored her pleas for help as he touched his forehead gingerly it first, then he lifted up his eye lid poked at his new brilliant emerald eye, whole again. No longer a mixture of lupine skull and human face he could feel his tendons, cartilage in his ears and nose, his very skull altering, his headache abating for the first time in a Century.

He looked toward the two-story farmhouse the foundation raised up encased in concrete in case of flood. Flickering candle light could be seen in the two story bedroom where it all began. Alicia had been leading him there in his dream, and that is when he saw Sarah. Since then he had been spying on Sarah, watching her every movement a spitting image of his love Alicia she had her eyes, no longer baby blue but emerald in color and her blonde hair now a raven black. Now he had the opportunity to come face-to-face with Sarah trapped in Alicia's farmhouse. With his deformed visage he had been embarrassed to be seen by her until now, he was whole again, emboldened. He turned away from the materialized mother of all lycanthropes and his grandmother in need of help and sprinted toward the porch. Aticus opened the storm door stopping ever so briefly to look back towards Amy, who gasped for breath, dying, So-seti in the midst of the labor pains and the powerful Aisos wakened from the dead before disappearing into the house.

"Aticus!" she winced in pain again as another labor pang rocked her, "Where are you going? Come back here! Where is James? I need to finish the ritual."

So-seti lay on her back, trying to heal her stumps had been suspended as she tried to finish the ritual in-between labor pains. Aisos threw her head back and howled spewing a flood of a trillion invisible larvae out of the sorceresses' lycanthrope muzzle. Trillions spherical full moons the surface pot-holed and cratered until they uncurled into the adult parasites. The head of the parasites look like a lupine skull unfurling with a whip like tail with tendril like appendages looking like a basic spinal column. Trillions of larvae and adult parasites flew up into the gray clouds eventually red droplets raining down upon the earth.

Devon burst out of the thickets. Blood, fear, brimstone and fur surrounding all five senses disorienting him. The materialized mother of all werewolves and Devon still wounded and bleeding stared at one another sizing each other up. Is it friend or foe that had burst out of the bushes? Determining the trespasser harmless she turned her back lifted her head and howled out again spewing parasitic saliva into the cloudy sky.

Devon in the form of a bipedal beast turned toward Amy's limp form, bleeding and bound at the stake. Through his long and pointed lupine ears he heard So-seti spinning out her secret ritual to materialize and maintain the dead between gasps and moans from labor pangs. The sorceress ordered Aisos to spew out into the world the wolf's blood through Amy's dying gasps.

"Amy!" Devon tried to speak but lupine vocal chords wouldn't allow it coming out in a growl.

Devon lurched forward converting to a hybrid-wolf with all fours paws on the ground so he could reach Amy before she exsanguinated but he had to get past Aisos and So-seti to do that. The mother of all werewolves stopped her howling and hunched forward as well dragging her knuckles on the ground to intercept the white wolf. The powerful shade with her long reach caught him lifting the wolf up off the ground. She pressed Devon's lupine body against her like a morbid embrace stealing the breath from his lungs. Compressing his ribs as she hyperextended her long spine twisted around and drove his head into the ground. A skull jarring reverberation resulting in a concussion had forced his involuntary change to human again. Large claws tore through Devon's bare shoulders as he was hoisted off the ground.

"Rrrrrrrruuuuuuuuu," Devon howled in pain, agony, and sadness. He howled out an aria of defeat as he looked upon Amy with sad eyes.

Amy felt herself getting weaker and weaker as the lifeblood drained from her neck. A low humming sound started in her ears. Fainter now but she heard the melee behind her a life or death struggle between Devon and the materialized spirit Wolf. She could not tell for sure but thought the spirit wolf was winning from the sound of things.... She'd seen before her So-seti writhing on the ground. Howling out her arcane song until in the midst of full on labor pains gave her pause but just for a moment the pains gone singing again her attention elsewhere. She was all alone now the opportunities of escape flirting through her mind but now arms were limp and useless.

She thought of the Captain and although she ended the affair her professional and personal life were down crapper. Even though Devon had no responsibility to her, he probably would die trying to save her. She wondered where Rogers was at that moment. She thought of her award-winning story or novel that now she wouldn't be able to bring to fruition. She looked up in the grey cloud covered sky instantly knowing that was a mistake as the gaping wound in her neck opened further like a second mouth spewing forth more blood.

Devon came to his senses in enough time to narrowly miss having his throat torn out by the Shade's deadly fangs. Somehow he found his second wind and escaped her claws penetrating his shoulder again. Converting back into paws with talons-like claws he swiped in her direction, bull's-eye! Blood began to flow from five lengthy scratches parting her fur. He could faintly hear So-seti rumbling her verse and his heart sank when he saw the deep scratches immediately seal up and heal.

87

The battle waged on for what seemed like hours but it had only been mere minutes. Devon got in several direct hits but even a seemingly mortal wound healed up in seconds. Aisos' fangs clamped down on Devon's torso like a vice. Her huge head twisted back and forth tossing him around like a cat playing with a mouse until her jaws released him and he crumpled like a limp rag doll on the dirt. He clawed into the dirt, trying to gain space for a hastily retreat. He had to re-strategize his whole plan. Aisos leapt upon his crumpled body before he could escape into the woods. Her enormous claws began disemboweling his abdomen. He squirmed to get away trapped on his back while Aisos' haunches squeezed his thighs. He twisted his spine around until his chest submerged in wet mud while simultaneously transfiguring his upper body to a white Wolf again. The conversion had barely sealed the gaping hole in his belly like a broken zipper with missing teeth. Weakened by the blood loss he remained trapped with the woods so tantalizingly close yet so far away.

"Help… me… please…" Amy's pleas were pitifully soft and trailed off into the raging storm, no human could have heard her cries but Devon did, it came in loud and clear, and he desperately wanted to rescue her.

Amy felt herself getting weaker and weaker as the lifeblood drained from her neck. The melee before her a life or death struggle between Devon and the materialized spirit Wolf had grown fainter and she heard a low humming in her ears. She could not tell for sure but thought the spirit Wolf was still winning. She'd seen before her sight betrayed her So-seti still writhing on the ground howling out her arcane song until the labor pains made her pause but just for a moment the pains gone she sang again.

Through blurry eyes she saw a break in the dark clouds for just one moment, just enough that the enormous moon could be seen in her rapidly dimming eyes. A magnificent sight so close to the Earth, a good thing that she felt herself floating off almost free from the restraints of earth because the moon was going to smash into the planet anyway, she mused. In the back of her mind she heard the wounded howls of Devon again.

She suddenly could translate his yaps and pleas and it was an order to transform. DMT hormones which would lessen her fears of death were coupled with the fluids that the awakened larvae spewed out which flooded her body. In her softening pineal gland the preternatural mixture began to boil, freeing trapped larvae to flood her bloodstream. A perfect storm of happenstance, the straw that broke the camel's back, like a line of dominoes perfectly balanced until a flick of the thumb then they began falling one by one. The new invaders and the larvae that unknowingly made residence inside her were melding and metamorphosing into parasites.

As the blood flowed out of her she thought of Devon when he had revealed the secrets of lycanthropy to her, "There are 100 trillion microbes living inside of us and only 10 trillion with our human DNA… We live with parasites… we are living with a beast within ourselves… when the full moon is powerful enough to awaken the wolf's blood…"

Amy's heart fluttered and skipped a beat, and stopped. She found her body slipping in and out of reality; she began to feel as light as air.

As she lay dying she thought about the way she had felt after their coupling, she'd felt odd. She felt manic in some respects, like she had boundless amounts of energy to spare. Unable to sleep at night, anxiety ridden as she lay in bed with him she had an insatiable hunger. She even thought she had maybe a tape worm… "100 trillion microbes" he'd said, and she realized now…she had been infected…

"The sorcerer Aisos and the original dire Wolf produced The Wolf's Blood parasite...a symbiotic relationship together, the spirit and the host as they got stronger…All the venerable, gravely sick she-Wolf had wanted was to survive…" Devon's words echoed in her mind.

Suddenly her heart started again, faster and stronger than before as the mixture flooded her pleasure centers. Her eyes began to glow, dilating and growing a second lid in her eyes. The delicate skin and wound across her neck began to seal up, replaced with something thick and leathery sprouting coarse red fur.

Microscopic eyes would have seen parasites awakened from their hibernation. Little glowing moons with writhing appendages that attached onto the specific ladders of her DNA structure like Velcro. Dainty hands began to sprout paws with claws as she started scratching the rope that bound her.

"No! No! This is impossible!" So-seti barked, looking at the torn rope scratched away and the now empty post.

So-seti gasped as she looked up and saw the sacrifice victim standing before her. Her feet busted out of her high heels the moment that she transformed but she was used to balancing on the balls of her feet and they turned into pads. Her muzzle had not yet lengthened and was looking like a pug's face but her human ears had changed and lengthened like lupine ears.

Amy's spine lurched as her fangs instinctively found So-seti's exposed neck. If So-seti had not been on the ground in the midst of labor pangs she could easily fended off the fledgling wolf-woman, even killed her within the blink of an eye but Amy got to her in the middle of a contraction and rendered her neck to shreds before she could defend herself or she could yell out. Bright red blood spurted out hitting Amy's soft red fur. The fledgling wolf-woman took out her anger out on a dying So-seti, tearing her spine from her body. The spurting blood was concealed by the thick red fur as the rest of her clothing ripped apart and fell away.

Devon saw Aisos turning toward Amy, he waved his arms around to get her attention warning weakly, "Go! Go! Get out of here!"

The fiery red Wolf-woman obeyed her alpha, running off into the night on four new legs. Without So-seti's spells to bind her and the human sacrifice no longer human and alive, Aisos began to weaken. Fur fell off in patches fluttering away leaving exposed skin. Her elastic skin started to get brittle now and began cracking. Her vision had clouded but her eyes were no longer hollow simply following the spell's will, and now her faculties were fully functional and under her own control again but her body was fraying before Devon's eyes. The shade Aisos staggered dying she fell down onto her haunches and paws. Though he had lost a significant amount of blood he saw Aisos' translucent form, the mishmash of bones and a green jewel where her heart should be and sprang into action.

"Goodbye mother!" Devon grunted and with a tear in his eye he ripped through brittle skin with sharp's claws and came out with the jewel. A pile of bones fell to the blood and rain covered ground and Devon immediately collapsed with them.

88

The window wipers were working overtime as Dr. Jacobs stuck his hand out the driver's side window franticly wiping the bloody rain from sticking onto the windshield. The destination was foreign to him but the steering wheel had a mind of its own, every time he breathed in, the scent pointed to Raccourci Island. He could not tolerate the aching pain all over his body, fever, hallucinations, the dreams of fur and fangs, the nightmares that reminded him of demons and he feared he would become one of them. He knew he could not resist what was happening to him any longer, but now armed with his new found senses by damn maybe he could do something about it!

He could feel himself changing from within and he was powerless to stop it now! Envisioning he was on the autopsy table. He was envisioning his cold body riddled with bullets until awakening with fangs and nails when the beast came out. Surely he was going to hell unless he could do something about it. Maybe something good will come out of this horrible situation he thought, he could smell a group of lunatics including the leader.

The Doc drove excruciatingly slow through ever increasing flash flood waters. Some turns he had to squint to see the road better the river and the highway threatening to merge with each other. He shuddered at the thought with this accursed power coursing through his veins maybe he'll take out some of the lunatics and beast-men before he himself gets ripped apart, remembering the fangs and claws that threatened slice him up in the morgue as well. Yes, he could stop a lot of them before they made any more havoc and threatened to infect all of Louisiana. His body hair from his neck to his forearms curled up goose flesh began to rise as he turned onto a horribly rundown gravel road.

He could scarcely see the fire in the middle of the field, which in its intensity was able to withstand the deluge but now the logs were water soaked and the fire barely flickered. He parked the truck at the end of the driveway and glanced at the empty post and house that sat caddy-corner, bright candlelight flickering in the upstairs window.

The Doc looked around his hand stuck to the side of the truck as if the truck grounded him as if the truck were magnetized. He saw a pile of bones, a mixture of Wolf and human, heaped upon the ground. He swiveled his head around to see a mortally wounded man lying on the ground just on the edge of the safety of the woods and a dead, pregnant paraplegic making up an invisible triangle. He had to work fast opening the minivan door he proceeded to pull out a plastic gas can.

Although Devon's glowing eyes were dimming now they still had enough life in them to motion toward the swollen pregnant body with her spine torn out and decapitated. The Doc reasoned he would set fire to the bones and the body first, and then even though the white haired stranger was a werewolf and seemingly wanted to help him he would be dead soon and there would be plenty of time to set his body ablaze as well. He looked at the mishmash of bones and the dead body again then poured a healthy amount of gasoline on both of them.

Like a macabre snail Devon left a bloody trail behind him inching longingly closer to the woods, they were so tantalizingly close. He tried to transform to heal some of his wounds but all that he managed was a furless, fleshy indistinguishable and quivering blob. He was now a form neither lupine nor human, severe blood loss momentarily preventing him from reverting back to a wounded shivering man again.

A sudden whoosh, flash and a loud crackle came from behind Devon who knelt on his hands and knees. He felt the heat on his back in welcomed relief warming up in his shivering body. He couldn't help but look upon the light and heat warming up his clammy face.

Doc found himself off his feet and on the ground. The Doctor struggled for breath as the lunatics smashed into him like a quarterback during the blitz crushing his sternum. Dizzy, his vision faded, he thought he saw an outline of a barn. His vision clearing he strained his eyes to see something bizarre. Blood rain falling casting shrouded shadows upon an otherwise invisible barn. A light suddenly appeared in the middle of the clearing like an invisible door had just been opened.

Devon wanted to help the stranger his heart eager but the body grudging.

89

Aticus smashed through the locked entrance with ease as if Sarah forgot to lock the door behind her. The doorframe splintering as he stepped inside the living room then gingerly sealed the damaged door the best he could. He quickly rummaged through his leather pouch to obtain the stolen runic pendant mystically scribed, as Viddarr told him, from the trollborn Rune caster. The incantation had been expressly purposed to enlighten the reincarnated soulmate of Viddarr's first and only love.

Aticus drew in a deep breath as he slid out his now antique flintlock double-barreled pistol and blunderbuss from his belt. Not Gerome's blunderbuss made in France that wounded him but an almost exact duplicate intricately inscribed made in Germany and a fist full of silver coins stuffed in the barrel to remind him of the horrible night. He had lost his love and he had lost his eye. He laid the weapons down on a chaise lounge as he surveyed the living room. Mesmerized by the oil painting on the wall his heart quickened and skipped a beat as he saw Alicia staring at him from across the room. He looked up to see Gerome Malstros, ancestor to the eradicators of his family, and once a God's Light member himself, in all his glory and hideousness staring at him also as his blood pressure began rising as anger overtaking him talons formed in his hands instantly like he had pressed the button of multiple switchblades swiping the face of the head of the household, Gerome's features were no longer recognizable. He grew a fully functional muzzle two lupine ears and two canine eyes longing to be a mammoth true wolf again pouncing on all four paws but he had to suppress a complete transformation, he had to find Alicia.

Aticus clutched the railing leading upstairs howling out longingly her name, softly murmuring "Alicia…"

Sarah didn't know why she hid inside the house instead of running but now she kneeled down trying to be as small as possible looking out the French doors to the porch outside, the curtains pulled back far enough that she could peer outside. The three figures, two nude lunatics and a salt-and-pepper haired older man with a grungy lab coat wrestled on the ground in a life or death struggle.

The low rough but gentle voice startling her coming from inside the house she was caught by surprise, eyes locked at the outside, she muttered to herself "No one by that name lives here now..."

Aticus cringed with every sound that he made trying to be silent but the hallway creaked as he tiptoed ever closer to her room. Weary not to spook her he opened the door ever so slowly and crept into the room. He looked into the mirror mesmerized by his new look. Two Emerald eyes were staring back at him.

"Alicia, I have a gift for you," He grinned.

Sarah started to protest.

"Alicia…"

Sarah stood still like a deer in headlights petrified by the stranger standing in the doorway. She looked for a way out, but the French doors to the outside porch had been blocked for safety while AJ replaced some of the termite ridden boards and across the room her way was blocked by the enormous stranger. For all of Alicia's descriptions Sarah felt as if she knew the tall gentleman standing before her. His long thin face had healed and black hair framed a quite regal nose and brilliant green eyes, as if he had been ripped out of the pages of the diary, Alicia's long lost love, Aticus.

Aticus stopped for a moment to look at his reflection in the intricately carved and gilded vanity's mirror. His features had become whole now where before he had been utterly defaced and ashamed. The moment he longed for so long in his dreams had come true as his breathing quickened, heart rate quickened and his cheeks warmed.

Aticus couldn't help but eye Alicia's diary, his fingers couldn't resist touching some of Alicia's precious written pages. Mesmerized by his eyes her delicate hands shook as impulsively she dropped the book into his grasp. Aticus thumbed through several pages until coming to an interesting section then read the page out loud.

"Out in the forest just shy of my poppa's house we stopped to rest at a clearing in the woods, trees encircling us he took a knife to a particularly hard oak inscribing our names then stepped back so I could see the heart around these letters. He had stepped behind me, but so agonizingly close to me still. Suddenly he wrapped a beautiful necklace around my neck and he spoke..."

Sarah tried to slip past the imposing figure to pass by the vanity and the bed but Aticus grabbed her twirling her around to face the mirror his huge protective arm around her hips. Catching his breath and steadying his nerves he quietly quoted directly out of the diary pages, "I have a gift for you."

"No, don't!" Sarah protested.

Aticus ignored her pleas. He unclasped her family heirloom which Aticus himself had given to Alicia many years ago and slid it safely in his bag. Sarah's protests quieted as he clasped the Onyx amulet round her neck then stood back to look at her reflection, "oh Alicia, I have missed you so..."

Sarah looked at her reflection as well. She looked at the magic necklace that had been clasped to her delicate neck. She imagined that Aticus had given her the Onyx heirloom instead of her reflection; however Alicia's visage stared back at her. In her mind the green eyes and black hair had merged with blue eyes and silky golden hair as she looked at her reflection.

She looked into the mirror with Aticus standing behind her, "Do you remember?"

Silence, the walls melted away and she saw a circling of Cyprus trees. There standing tall in the middle of the clearing a Weeping Willow tree. In her mind she saw the scratches that had been made on the Willow tree.

Remembering long ago events she clutched the amulet as she tenderly whispered, "I have a gift for you, my sweet Alicia."

"Do you remember now, Alicia?"

"Yes," Sarah spun the pendant hitting the candlelight and shining, "I remember Aticus... How could you just leave me?"

Looking at her reflection in the mirror he remembered his sister, "Oh Ayaa..."

He tried to choke back tears starting in his eyes, "My Alicia..." For the first time in centuries tears flowed down both cheeks.

An explosion rocked the upstairs windows. The reincarnated face with Alicia's features softened within a look of horror as she stared out the window at a fire spreading like water to several of the dense tree trunks, a pile of bones and So-seti's charred, smoldering body on the ground. Lastly she saw Devon bloody and down on his knees just before the curtain of trees.

Aticus grabbed the diary before heading downstairs Alicia watching from the window upstairs. Without looking Aticus reached for his trusty flintlock and the blunderbuss and smashed through the already broken front door.

Fearful to move into the downpour and puddles that spread the fire Alicia stood at the bottom of the steps, "Devon!"

Devon! Aticus ran out on the slick porch and out into the rain clutching at her diary. Devon! He quickly read the paragraphs to himself the pages quickly getting soaked in the rain. ***"I met a stranger that told me the secrets of what I have become but he could not fill the loneliness in my heart... Now that I know what I am becoming, I am horrified, I need a place to be on my own and think so I left the helpful stranger... Though Pregnant again..."***

"It can't be!" Shaking his head in disbelief he had to read more.

"I dreamt that I howled at the top of my lungs an aria owed to the night sky and what was lost and never found... I should be used to this now, every month awakening in Louisiana in my childhood home... An old woman now"

"This is going to be my last entry I am so tired physically and mentally. The loss of my love, Aticus, hurts me so and missing memories every three days, once a month… no more. Even the tryst with the gorgeous, wild, and mysterious young man with fiery red sigils tattooed on the whole of his face, Devon, who had been a thoughtful and caring individual, cannot fill the hole in my heart that my sweet Aticus has left behind."

Devon knelt in the wet grass. The onslaught of crimson rain mixed with the red sigils on his face. His own blood oozed out from his white hair. However, as he closed his eyes and smiled tuning out the world around him, he was assured his lineage will go on after his death.

His head awash, Aticus reeled from all the missed opportunities, betrayal and regret. He envisioned Devon and Alicia ***his*** love in a passionate embrace. Although his silver sickness had been cured by the mighty shade he felt a splitting headache coming on again. His headache worsening until his vision blurred. Even his daily throbs when he still had 100 silver shards embedded into his brain did not compare to this moment, like a pounding jackhammer in his skull. Without thinking he found himself reaching toward his antique dual flintlock which he quickly aimed and fired, though he aimed for Devon's head, the softness of the silver made the silver stray off the mark two slugs finding their way into his chest.

The prone Doctor was still struggling to stave off the nude fiends and managed to throw two phosphorous grenades at the gathering crowd that emerged from the invisible barn. A flickering brilliant warm orange lit the ominous gloomy clouds that hung in the air and the ferocity of the fire would not be quenched by the strong gale and torrent. Dr. Jacobs howled out as his blood began to boil mucus streaming down his thickening snout as his jaws began to ache new teeth began to emerge and grow. The Doc began to frantically grind his teeth until they were filed down to manageable fangs. As the spine began to crack and expand to accommodate a lupine form he managed to get the upper hand on one of the lunatics twirling him around and pinning him down in the mud. The nude fiend caked in mud yelped in pain as swollen jaws crushed his clavicle in an audible crunch.

A strange odor permeated the air and he now knew the aroma. Out of the dark canopy of trees and into the bright light of the fires there appeared the ancestor of Alicia and Devon's forbidden coupling, James. A hybrid wolf still weak from his scrap with Devon his head still dizzy but on all four limbs firmly planted on the ground. He had fully functional human arms with coarse Brown fur and hands, though, his palms had thickened like the starting of pads and extremely elongated feet. Aticus somehow knew from James' pungent odor there was something odd, something just not quite right with him. His hatred for James had been justified.

Although his silver sickness had been cured by the mighty shade the splitting headache would now not subside, so without a second thought he found James' hybrid Wolf by smell, zeroed in on his form and pulled the trigger… nothing… He had spent both of the shots in the gun.

Howls of pain echoed through the night as the Doc proceeded to chew through the lunatic's ribcage until his arm had almost severed from his body. However, the other lunatic sliced through the lab coat with his claws grabbing onto Jacobs' shoulders and forcing his jaws back, freeing the now mangled cavernous chest. Warm blood spewed out like a fountain in his face while powerful human teeth latched onto the Doc's exposed neck.

His frustration heightened, Aticus reached for his antique blunderbuss, the replica of the gun that started his decline into psychosis, and fired blindly. The Doc managed to get a grasp on the last phosphorus grenade, removed the pin and closed his eyes. At least he could take two of them out before he died, the Doc thought, this way instead of a monster he would be a martyr, surely a fast-track into Heaven. The thought comforted Doc as he dropped to the ground between the two lunatics, one of which lies dying. Through the darkness he heard the sickening sounds of crunching and felt a pressure on his back, but he felt no pain at all as his extremities went limp, lastly he heard the explosion.

James yelped hitting the ground hard, Aticus smiled marching over to Devon and whispered, "I'm sorry my friend but you violated my love, Alicia, and you won't stop my dreams!"

Aticus grabbed a fist full of Devon's hair and forced Devon to look him in the eyes, cold hardened merciless and vengeful emerald eyes. Aticus looked smug and confident and Devon couldn't stand his toothy smile.

"You killed my mentor, my friend, Stefan! You deserve to die!" Devon hoarsely said foaming up blood from his mouth.

Devon's face and broken body began undulating like waves in the sea trying to fix the damage the shade had done. Somehow he summoned the energy to manifest claws and swiped at Aticus' healed face. Surprised he faltered feeling white hot pain and warm blood spill out.

"Fuck you, you sneaking whore!" Aticus roared a pounding in his brain back like a knife stabbing him in the head over and over again, a dizzying pressure in his head now at a feverish pitch.

Once again horribly disfigured and blinded by blood running down his eye he grasped for Devon's bloody white hair flipped open the silver garrote on his flintlock and buried the blade deep into his exposed neck. Aticus blacked out his body on autopilot with a twisting motion and a hard yank he tore off Devon's head and dropped it, it bounced like a basketball coming to rest against Aticus' well-worn boots.

Aticus dropped both empty guns and hastily kneeled down. The sound of bones cracking as Aticus plunged both hands into Devon's body and decapitated head. He emerged with glands in one hand and Devon's heart in the other. He chewed Devon's heart and glands vigorously until Devon's organs were the consistency of Mash. The Pulp easily made its way down Aticus' gullet and the pounding migraine instantly went away.

"Aticus!" He heard the unmistakable voice of his lost love, the reincarnated form of Alicia.

She had heard the shot, a familiar sound flashing a lost memory of a horrible night spurred her out of her house and running up just in time to see her ancestor, James, lying prone and still just outside the forest and then she saw Aticus. She hesitated, looking back and forth between James and Aticus, the agony of her decision so heavy upon her face.

"Oh, Aticus!" Alicia almost floated to Aticus' side and gingerly touched his injured face.

An embarrassed and skittish Aticus jumped back but Alicia insisted putting in a gentle palm on his mangled cheek, "oh, love, let me care for you."

Instead of running away in fear and shame like he did so long ago he stood his ground and let Alicia's gentle hands caress his face. He began to tear up in his one good functional eye as he wrapped his hands around hers, trembling at her touch.

The bright Inferno of light was obstructing James view he didn't even know what hit him. Aticus had targeted the hybrid wolf and in profile and on all four limbs trying to hit his head but the silver strayed from the mark. Several silver coins hit the wolf in the upper hip and thigh. The coins spread out in a circle in the body in the legs slicing into the wolf's body lodging into his bones. For the second time James had passed out from the excruciating pain, but now he had stirred.

Aticus clung onto Alicia for dear life as if he accidentally let go again she would be lost forever. Peering around at the fires to see James' Wolf form stagger up on his broad hands and elongated feet. Though he had been filled with silver coins in his hip the Wolf instantly transformed and stood on two feet.

"That's impossible!" Aticus shook his head in disbelief. Though still bleeding profusely Aticus looked upon James' human legs with confusion and jealousy.

"Oh Aticus, he is hurt," the piteousness of her voice and her doe like eyes melted the vengeance in his cold heart.

With malice and bile in his voice he begrudgingly barked, "Go, and care for him, quickly."

90

False river- Airport tower

Arriving upstairs to find a well-dressed man with dark slacks and a white button up dress shirt surprised the group and he turned around face hung in a state of annoyance. One Man stood guard in the tower, a lone survivor maybe. Upon closer inspection, however, Hunter saw blood on his dress shirt, cuffs, caked up blood on his chin and the unmistakable eyes of an animal. That is when he saw the bodies on the floor, opening his eyes to the carnage around him.

The air traffic controller remained perfectly still as if sizing up the situation, then he exploded forward in a fit of rage drool spewing out from his fangs and oversized mouth. Without a moment's hesitation Jenkins and Capt. Rogers pulled out their service revolvers and opened fire.

The well-dressed man stumbled falling on his back coming to rest on the control panel and Hunter sprang into action.

"Check the control room, we have to barricade the door," Hunter barked out orders to Terrell then motioned for the two men.

Hunter checked his pulse, "you guys got lucky! This abominable beast is newly infected so normal bullets brought him down… let's hope these slugs stay put until the full Moon's cycle is over…"

"Fuck it!" concealed from small of his back Hunter pulled out a machete and made quick work of the dead man's neck slicing his head clean off, looked over at the group, and smiled, "just to be sure."

Terrell opened the break room door, "Hey, I found a table that we can use to block the door, can anybody help me?"

Hunter systematically began to lob off all the dead attendants' heads. He separated the heads from their bodies and put them in a neat, organized pile. Capt. Rogers upended the table until it rested flush along the door. His usually healthy pink face turned green sickness over taking him as he saw the morbid scene taking place. Suddenly struck with the familiarity of the position of the corpses the hairs on his neck stood erect, the pieces were all fitting together now. He and Detective Jenkins saw the monster responsible for the arson and vandalism now standing before them all coated with blood, he was undoubtedly the man responsible for the decapitations.

The villains had been systematically infecting tiny towns and neighborhoods. Hunter had been pursuing them but by the time he had a good lead the group had vanished. Although he found newly infected stragglers who stayed behind and chopped off their heads, hoping to stave off an outbreak before it began but he had failed.

Hunter had paused mid-swing to look over at Capt. Rogers. They silently stared at one another for several seconds, but it seemed like an eternity until Capt. Rogers nodded in grim approval. Hunter nodded as well, as if to say, I know what I'm doing is wrong, but it is a necessary evil, before he broke Rogers' stare and carried on.

Jenkins' checked the time on his watch, quarter to four, the onslaught of red rain beat down upon the windows, they were safe in the tower for now... A silent war raged on, no shots or explosions, tooth and claw dominating where only fifty feet below him no one was safe. Those that walked about under the full moon's powerful spell no longer human, a hybrid form of man and beast, humanity all but drained from them. They were under full control of Aticus' bloodline, the alpha. Looking down below Tasha could see three airport employees' bodies. They were dead sprawled out in the open a constant reminder of the terrifying and hopeless situation the group had been placed in.

They were safe for now, Jenkins told himself once more. The door was made of steel, there was a table up righted with several chairs against it blocking the stairway to the tower itself. They huddled in a corner together. Susan, Terrell, Tasha, Latoya and Hannah huddled close together under the control systems panels. Captain Thompson (named for the surname of his great-grandfather a great source of ridicule when he was growing up) Rogers, Detective Jenkins and the stranger called Hunter stood back-to-back. They could only survive there for the time being without food but another day was coming upon them which meant new hope, possibly new beginnings. Rogers watched Susan sob her face buried into her hands, shaking uncontrollably as her body not used to the unusual conditions and psychological trauma at hand. Tasha and Hannah watched as the blood rain fell while Terrell worried over his brother's absence, fearing the worst, denying in his heart what he knew was probably true.

"Well at least the boy succeeded in getting the generators working." Hunter shook his head, fearing Tyson had surely died. He adjusted his binoculars to see the building about 150 yards from the tower itself, "we can probably make it to the chopper if anyone wants to give it a try."

No one seemed overly enthusiastic about that proposition.

"They run a hell of a lot faster than any of you can!" Jenkins' ghost snapped "you'd have no chance."

Rogers nudged Jenkins' chest to get his attention, "look at this!"

Rogers pointed out beyond the tower Jenkins looked to see one shadowy lunatic on all fours more beast than man leading the procession of three humanoids, the lunatics standing upright following behind. They were naked, filthy, all coated with caked up blood and on the path to the tower. Out from the overgrown thickets before the eight-foot chain link fence that circled the entire airport emerged two more shadowy figures and one dragging his knuckles like an ape, they were attracted by the faint but unique smell of life holed up in the tower.

Hunter turned his binoculars to see the encroachers, his face crumpling with distain. He thought all may be lost until he turned and saw the speaker system. His eyes lit up, wheels turning in his brain as he looked over at the emergency broadcast system.

"Can anybody use this?" Hunter impatiently thumbed his fingers on the controls. A slow rhythmic tapping of first, culminating in a fast chaotic beat.

Jenkins felt a cold chill as Philip repeatedly poked him in the back as he whispered, "you know how to work this dad, when I died you spent time in the 911 control center riding the desk while they were investigating you…"

"Yes…" Jenkins said meekly sliding over.

The detective inspected the electrical board briefly before pressing one of the buttons. There came a click which resonated through the speakers then buzzing all about the room. Rogers watched the advancing lunatics and noted they were gaining more to their group as they shuffled closer.

Hunter impatiently intertwined his fingers and ringed his hands as his heart quickened watching the detective flip the switch of the speakers from *internal* to *external* as he found the switch that turned the sirens on. A harsh wailing resonated from the tower immediately stalling the drooling maniacs but just for a moment before they advanced forward again.

"Shit! How do you increase the volume on the speakers?" Hunter hit the control center with his fists.

"Here!" Jenkins impatiently yelled sliding the dial up to *maximum*.

"I don't think it's working the fangs are still coming!" Rogers yelled as he counted more than ten of them until they passed beneath the tower windows where he lost sight of them.

Hunter studied the controls intently until he had gained the confidence to take over the controls, "I got this!"

Hunter pushed past Rogers and Jenkins who freely relented, taking control of the situation. He thought for a moment, then went over to *Tempo* control and slid the lever all the way up to maximum. The slow intermittent and persisted whine became a continuous ear-splitting cry as sirens wailed on without a break.

The group scurried back upon their feet when they heard a loud boom, boom, boom a pounding on the metal door. Terrell clung to Tasha who clung to Hannah and Latoya with Susan protectively hugging them all. Hannah stared wide eyed at the door, tears still wet on her face.

"They're trying to get in!" shouted Latoya and Terrell at once.

Hunter grunted in frustration trying the last knobs and buttons that he could find, "Aha!"

He found the lever for the frequency and slowly turned it up. The siren's higher pitch made the wolves waiting near the Hangar and the lunatics at the tower impulsively howl out and the banging on the door stopped. This pleased Hunter immensely as he turned the frequency dial to an even higher pitch. Domestic dogs in the adjacent neighborhoods began to cry out as he turned the dial as far as it will go. The warning sounds of the tower horn still persisted to wail out outside assaulting human ears but canines could hear it also, house pets and feral dogs alike could feel the frequency in their bones. Lunatics and beasts close to the tower were physically injured, eardrums bursting blood spurting from ears.

"Look!" Susan pointed out the window a nervous smile began to creep onto her cracked lips, "I don't know who they are but they are going away!"

Hunter turned to survey the scene. Susan had been right. His gamble paid off instead of frying the system when he turned up the frequency he succeeded in stopping the fiends in their tracks. Three lunatics were in full view of the window. Their inner ears had ruptured and bled. Dizzy even the fur covered powerful beast on four limbs now a naked puny man on two legs stumbling about retreating for shelter as an invisible wall of sound circled and enveloped the tower. Susan, Jenkins, Rogers, Terrell, Tasha, Latoya, Hannah, and lastly Hunter all offered a well-deserved collective sigh of relief.

Amy reluctantly awakened from some sort of a lucid dream-like state from the consistently resonating sirens somewhere in the distance to find herself lost in the middle of the woods. Feeling numb and pausing for a second in the middle of an incredibly close cropping of Cyprus trees she stretched her extremities. She began to feel odd, like covered with pins and needles. Every muscle in her body sore yet oddly refreshed, as if they were clay or silly putty moldable, bendable and stretchy like she had just been through a workout. She knew she had been asleep yet her mind rejuvenated swimming in some sort of orgasmic bliss enough that she so badly wanted to repeat the experience like she needed a drag on a cigarette, she wished she had a cigarette when a sudden awareness came over her. She didn't have anywhere to keep cigarettes! She was completely nude from head toe. Her cheeks flushed with this thought and she found herself moving toward the source of the dreadful noise.

She began to feel cold now her wet red hair pasted to her forehead but the thick canopy of trees filtered out the rain. She tried to stay modest keeping an arm near to her exposed breasts to conceal them while navigating the treacherous terrain. She began remembering the events that had gotten her here, remembering as if her lucid memories were an out of body experience. She remembered everything but instead of using rational thought and blinding her powerful body she released control to pure instinct.

Amy couldn't help but think she could learn how to control her powerful new form if Devon instructed her in the ways of the wolf, Devon! Where was Devon?

She could remember suddenly, being tied up, having her throat slit from ear to ear… lifeblood spilling from the gaping wound and almost dying then hearing Devon's desperate call to action. She heeded her sire's orders, a powerful urge to survive coming up over her, breaking her bonds and letting loose her rage and vengeance upon the woman that so grievously injured her.

She remembered killing her captor before running off to the woods obeying Devon's frantic pleas to flee.

"De…" The pain in her throat had forced her to stop for moment.

Her fingers inspecting her tender but healed throat she fell down on her knees with a splash. She squinted at murky mud the hazy reflection revealing the gaping hole in her neck had sealed just a pink scar remained.

The coarseness in her voice surprised her when she continued with a shriek, "Devon!"

She staggered up and continued propelling herself forward toward the source of the sound. Eventually her ears began to hurt, her equilibrium faltering she had to stop to steady herself. Her legs however, feeling weaker with every step she took as the sirens blared louder and louder. One agonizing step more and her legs collapsed in the mud. The tears welled from her eyes, her hands cupping her ears she cried in pain as blood ran out from her ears.

AJ had also escaped from Viddarr's bloody Moon party before the bloodshed had begun. He had wandered through the woods, trying to shield himself from the torrent of rain until he discovered the nude stranger, Amy, down on her knees visibly in pain. He had watched her concealed in the bushes until he had confidence no harm would come to him and approached her.

"Hey!" AJ yelled, "Are you hurt?" He timidly placed a palm on her bloody backside.

She whipped her head around physically tensing up eyes widened with fear as he questioned again, this time softly in a more comforting tone, "are… are you hurt?"

She paused for a moment checking her body for marks or abrasions, cheeks reddening acutely aware of her nakedness as she replied, "no, it's not my blood…"

Her red hair had camouflaged the dripping blood soaked into her scalp AJ's cheeks began to flush as well his eyes tried to deliberately avoid her bloody, but firm breasts, nipples standing firm from the damp cold.

"Are you cold?" AJ did not give her time to respond taking off his jacket so he could remove his T-shirt and giving it to the beautiful red haired stranger.

Amy stayed silent just shaking her head yes, gratefully accepting his gift, his concert t-shirt enveloping her like a dress. It radiated heat from his body still, and she sighed as she felt it. Shrugging on his thin jacket he tried using his smartphone again; hoping to get a connection but nothing, still no signal. Listening very closely, he could hear only a faint, strange howling. AJ offered his hand and gratefully accepting it she got up on her bare feet.

"I am going toward the source of the sirens; would you like to go with me and get out of the woods to shelter?" AJ asked.

She simply responded with only one word, "yes."

AJ treaded ever onward avoiding several nude human lunatics that were now in the fetal position hands protecting their heads until Amy could not take it anymore suddenly stopping clenching his hand with a death grip, "what is wrong?"

AJ saw fresh blood dripping from her ears as she answered, "I can't go any further, it hurts!"

AJ moved wet red luscious locks so he could see her injured ears more closely. Just then a thought crossed through his mind like a hand smacking him in the face. Being in a music band he had procured his fair share of earplugs and his fist delved deep into his jacket pocket emerging with several plugs the consistency of putty.

"There you go, sweetie." AJ fit the putty-like substance into her ears molding it with his thumbs until the substance made an airtight seal, silence enveloping her.

AJ gently cupped his hands to her ears and coaxed her hesitant and trembling body forward until she started to walk on her own power. AJ embraced Amy's limp body to gain foot by grueling foot onward toward the siren sounds.

The hazy light of the full moon between gray clouds had almost set over the tree line when the couple finally burst forth from the thicket. Amy's bare feet finally stepped onto the cold pavement leading toward the highway as AJ peered toward the airport tower in the distance. The rain had suddenly stopped the eye of the storm now upon the whole False River Airport, the source of the ungodly noise, like a beacon for survivors.

"We made it!"

AJ looked into Amy's eyes full of agony, however AJ's eyes were filled with hope and opportunity as he knocked on the tower door with his knee; he did not remove his hands protecting her ears, knocking on the door with his knees again.

"We made it!"

Hunter had lost himself deep in thought of whether or not the intercom to the outside world could be fixed five claw symmetrical marks gouged deep in the metal and wiring didn't hear the banging on the door, but the others did startling them and spurring Detective Jenkins and Capt. Rogers up and into action.

"They must have broken through your defenses!" Philip whispered in his dad's ear while he and Rogers ran halfway down the stairs their guns in hand.

Capt. Rogers' heart began to race, "When they breech the door, don't hesitate to fire!"

Detective Jenkins nodded his knees locked both arms extended both hands braced the cold steel with trigger fingers firmly on the trigger and braced himself for the inevitable. Capt. Rogers had flanked him, an invincible barrier guarding the steps up to the control tower.

"Hello? Is anyone in there? Please let us in!" AJ shouted his voice breaking and hoarse as a consequence.

"Should we help them?"

"If they were lunatics they would growl not ask for help!" Philip whispered, a cold chill coming over Jenkins.

A clanking squeaking sound echoed through the halls as the door burst open AJ thrust his hand in first, "don't shoot!"

The commotion had gathered a crowd as Susan stood at the edge of the stairs clutching Hannah who held Terrell's hand, "What's going on?"

Susan answered her own question peering at AJ who was shirtless with only his suede jacket on and unbuttoned, now ruined by the rain. Her eyes squinting in jealousy as she noticed the woman that almost wrecked her marriage, Amy, though she feigned obliviousness so their marriage would continue she couldn't hide her feelings of envy, jealousy and rage at seeing her here suddenly at the bottom of the stairs.

Capt. Rogers inspected AJ then the disheveled woman who wore a shirt as a make shift dress. He quickly recognized the red haired stranger. He had found Amy and he carefully inspected her for injuries seeing she was covered in crusted blood until he realized it had apparently run from her scabbed up inner ears, and he sighed with relief that she was virtually unscathed until the uneasy realization came over him whipping his head around to see his wife standing on the stairs.

A cold chill ran through his body as he whipped his head back and forth between Amy and his wife locking eyes on them both. The information he had been force-fed by Hunter coupled with actually seeing the Doctor go through the accursed change he quickly deduced that Amy had been infected.

"They're all dead!" AJ mumbled to himself, "All my friends are missing or dead!"

Capt. Rogers trained his gun upon Amy's redhead.

"Don't let him shoot her!" Philip gestured to Capt. Rogers' gun, "you have seen the Dr. and his infliction, they are not all mindless beasts bent on evil… He is just getting rid of a personal problem!"

Phillip turned to face his father, locking eyes, "Please Dad, do it for me, you have to stop him!"

All the familiar and painful images went through his mind of the night he shot his son and he found his hands involuntarily gripping Rogers' gun before his mind had registered his movement.

"Dad?"

A Shot echoed throughout the antechamber missing Amy's head by just a quarter inch the stray shot ricocheting off the wall.

Detective Jenkins shook his head at Capt. Rogers, who lowered his head sulking. He holstered his gun and stepped aside so AJ and Amy could go upstairs to the control room.

"Thank you," AJ gently acknowledged as he nudged Amy upstairs so she could rest, "thank you again."

Susan's sobs intensified at a higher pitch than everything else as she looked at her husband and Amy. It seemed so final now she thought they were trapped. The power cords ran underground so the werewolves had no way to disable them but getting out there was the trick that seemed a daunting task.

Hunter watched in nervous anticipation as the sun peeked out from the horizon. He looked over at Hangar 3; the white furred werewolf, Montezu, who had been calling all the shots, was gone now. Several wolves strolled about standing sentry to the doors and he noticed one particularly sinewy grizzled wolf with nasty cuts on its forelimbs.

The dance had begun; the line had been drawn in the sand. He had tried to get a hold of Dr. Atkins and check in but was unable. He knew in his heart it was not the end, far from it, the bloodshed had only begun. He looked around and counted the people in the tower. The line had been drawn and they either needed to escape or make a final stand.

Epilogue

I

High enough that the hurricane winds would not affect Lucius, one palm stroked his forehead, the other hadn't grown back, but he started having phantom feelings, a good sign indeed! He peered out into the calm eye of the storm, the unexpected hurricane that took the residents by surprise and ravaged the coastline before weakening to a tropical storm, and watched as it continued further North.

So-seti has died...

Caine and Lucius had no problem hearing over the furious deafening winds as they struck up a conversation in their minds. Thrashing about was so much power, like a cracking whip powerful forces moved around him, but Lucius was steadfast and concentrated with his ethereal body.

That is a shame; I have known her for a long time. She was stubborn, but I considered her my friend, she will be missed... Caine stopped for a moment reflecting as a particularly fierce gust like an angry wailing poltergeist blew past. Though Lucius had been ethereal his luscious black hair whipped back and forth like slithering snakes, *but the American branch of the accursed Gods Light is burnt to the ground...*

Lucius descended lost in the clouds as several of the aftershocks made the Earth quake yet again under Louisiana. Caine softly spoke in Lucius' head as he let out a hearty laugh, *So-seti's spell was a powerful one indeed, the five elements of earth stirred after her incantations!*

Lucius informed his master, *Alas Aisos has died ...*

No worries, Aisos' Wolfshade is a spirit; energy and such will never truly die only the corporal form is destroyed. She managed to saturate much of the South with her blood.

I don't understand, what should I do now master? Lucius loyally questioned as the full moon had finally descended over the horizon.

You will make your move, all in good time, until then do nothing, watch and be patient my son, just watch as all events develop ... These new turn of events are interesting; don't you think?

Yes, master, bowing his head and agreeing *thy will be done,* though it confused him. He did not dare question his sire. Lucius bent his elbow and looked at the stump where once his hand and fingers had been. In the early dawn's refracting mists if he squinted just right he could see the glowing reflection of his once detached hand, which meant his phantom hand was regenerating even earlier than he expected.

As Lucius sank down into the cold Earth a thought ran through that comforted him as he closed his eyes before dawn. Chuckling he remembered that Dr. Atkins' mangled hand will never regenerate as he thought about the broken Doctor and how he inevitably had to report his failure and the destruction of the compound to the other Gods Light superior commanders.

II

Dr. Atkins shuddered as the continuous turbulence jarred him awake, and finally aware of his surroundings on his nonstop flight to Rome. Hospitalized by his severe injuries and slipping into a coma, he had just recently awakened but was severely anemic taking five transfusions before he could be taken off the critical list. In a severely jaundiced state it took sitting him in natural sunlight before healthy color came back to his face and he was healthy enough to eventually be released from the hospital. He angrily gripped his mangled hand like a rotten husk dialed the numbers to God's Light's minion, Hunter, but no response.

Dr. Atkins beat his fist on the armrest spilling his expensive brandy, cursing loudly, "Damn! I still can't get Hunter on the line!"

The steward immediately cleaned the spill uncorking more brandy and promptly topping off his empty glass comforting him, "If you can't get Hunter on the line you shouldn't worry so much about it Sir, stormy skies all through the Southwest the Captain had to go up and over just to skirt the edge of the enormous storm."

"Right, Right," Atkins forced smile as he looked out his private jet as the US landscape turned to sea.

Dr. Atkins began to visibly shake as he remembered the savage beating he sustained courtesy of Lucius. His complexion turned ashen drained of all color as he looked at his horribly crushed and inoperable hand. He nervously drank another glass full of brandy.

III

An emerald eye, Aticus' eye emerged from the smoke with his prize, the reincarnated Alicia, in hand. The fires were not burning anymore but still smoldered. Spewing thick smoke becoming low hanging fog as Aticus took in a deep breath and surveyed the scene. Only a short time ago a gravely wounded James transformed before feeling weakened extremely dizzy he eventually stumbled and fell in the mud and lost consciousness. With the chaos all around he didn't know where the shot had come from and it didn't matter his thigh hemorrhaging his wasted life passing before his eyes.

It is happening all over again, history repeating itself, remembering the horrid events that led to her son's death, and the murder of her alpha, Stefan. Not this time, tears flooded her eyes as she rushed to his aid. She placed her healing hands on his thigh and began to work her magic. Aticus' jaw dropped filled with absolute rage, jealousy, and confusion he looked on in amazement as Tonya pulled out of his body several of the life threatening silver shards, destroyed when the coins hit muscle, sinew and bone and tried to stop the bleeding.

"That's impossible!" his thoughts vengeful as the wheels in his head began turning, "the bastard could not have transformed with silver in his veins."

He clutched at his freshly wounded and missing eye reminding him again of that horrid night as his mangled face bared the resemblance of human and lupine features unable to transform until it heals again. Aisos melted the silver free and he could shift his beautiful façade between human or Wolf with ease before getting his face torn off again by Devon. But how could that bastard James possibly even change freely with silver in his body!? His thoughts shifted when something cooed and rustled in the grass nearby.

"I hear survivors! They are just babies," Tonya yelled in surprise.

There were charred wolf fetuses dead in the blood pool. Something near the rocks stirred. The swollen belly of a charred woman's corpse fluttered and kicked. Something moved beneath her thighs. A human baby… two human babies… they were small and frail but otherwise in good health. The stronger one, the boy, chewed through the flesh to get at the baby girl. Girl and a boy both had a full head of hair and sharp teeth.

Although James' body was still weak and in shock he limped towards his offspring scooping them up in a loving embrace. He overlooked the pain; he forgot the pain in his hip and ignored the crushing sadness of So-seti's loss as he closed his eyes and breathed in the twin's sweet and innocent scent.

"My babies!" James shouted," they survive!"

All around Raccourci Island a faint distant chorus of wolf howls could be heard. Lou's Wolf with its silver spikes, drilled into its lupine head distinguished itself among all the rest, Lou howled a series of grunts and growls that instructing the pack where to go. David's Wolf emerged from the haze. Its Limbs soaked from the swim. If scrutinized only minor differences between the hybrid-Wolf versus a natural one. Nathan's wolf closely followed Steve's Wolf. Chance had almost truly transformed down on four limbs his huge lupine head turned back to see Gene closely behind still up on two legs hunched over his long arms dragging the ground. Following closely behind the group Tracy made to be a breeder.

Not far behind followed Col. Miller abruptly turning to watch the pack, ever vigilant, his canine eyes aglow. The Colonel still dressed as always in his dress military uniform although the sleeves shredded to accommodate his unusually elongated arms. His long gray beard now rust colored and had receded Sgt. Adam's lupine limb and paw replacing his missing arm and two furry sinewy limbs with reverse knee and large paws. Kevin with his amalgamated human and lupine head muzzle burnt from cheek to 0gauge stud in ear, John, Christopher, Bobby and Terry from two different high schools. Next in tight succession emerged several humanoid lunatics wet to their knees from the flooded road their radiant eyes illumination in the darkness.

There the pack stood in all its glory, with a gambit of forms, from the different times they were infected. There stood true Wolves, hybrid-wolves on all fours, hybrid wolves on two legs, wolf men with lupine faces with a long muzzle but the body of a man, wolf-men with human faces but their body lupine, complete with long tail and reverse knee. Down to men that didn't change physically, true lunatics with only their feverish minds lupine. Recent lycanthropes, weak willed and a slave to the moon and Aticus' will, the infection flowing through tonight or just a couple of months. Still others that were infected several months ago or the strong-willed who could change form at will, regardless of the cycle of the Moon the spirit of the Wolf fully flowing through their veins and last but not least the ancient lycanthropes altering their very chemistry.

Aticus peered at his inner circle with Lance his best friend, Tonya, whose powers consisted of manipulating the dreams of others, Tomas with the manipulation of true wolves at his fingertips. Oung, and O-kami who killed all that opposed his rule and Montezmu found a pipeline for the dark-age formula which had been updated and synthesized to illicit pink crystals. Viddarr had gone but he considered him and his the actual workhorses of his army.

The two-story plantation house was still there though some of the woods around it blackened and burning even in the hurricane conditions. It worked out to his advantage the roads to the island were flooded and God's Light wouldn't look for them here on Sarah's plantation, as he stroked Sarah's hair. Sure there were losses and the unexpected appearance of Devon, he put a hand to his horribly scarred face and missing eye, but Devon was ultimately dealt with. As far as the double cross of and the switching allegiance, Viddarr was a different matter. They were just annoyances and his growing army would deal with them if needed. James wrapped his hands around his baby son and daughter as Aticus squinted at James with distaste, growing jealousy and looking on his infants with suspiciousness.

Aticus stopped before he shut the barn door a smile permeating his crooked lips. The world had been silenced now from the eye of the storm. All in all Aticus mused as far as he was concerned his campaign of terror was a resounding success. Although the nightshade was defeated the hurricane that ravaged most of the Southeast of the United States and the San Andreas earthquake that rocked the central states and Aisos' wolf blood rain only saturated the southeast the wolf's blood crystals were in circulation in the Northwest and everywhere society will be in a state of disorder. He felt as if it just took a month and in the blink of an eye for the whole campaign to come to this. It was time to take a well-deserved break to rest and reflect. They could watch now from in the protection of the Malstros' plantation as the whole of the nation slowly squeezed together like a vice according to Aticus' will.

"Aticus?" Alicia said softly, "shut the door before the storm comes upon us again."

Sarah's heart raced at the sight of Aticus something in her heart told her she was destined to be at his side. She was reincarnation of Alicia; she just knew it as she rested her head on Aticus' chest.

"Yes my dear." Aticus said as he slid the door shut.

Aticus smiled his famous long fanged toothy and crooked smile looking back at the plantation for a moment to collect his thoughts. With just one or two hiccups things were going according to his plans extremely well. One dream had come to fruition which pleased him immensely. It would be the first time in a long time he would have a good night's sleep, he would not dream the nightmare anymore.

He couldn't see the sun coming up from the massive clouds and downpour that beat down on the island. After the rain had passed, the pack would move into the manor. Until then, though, Aticus lay down in the damp hay in the invisible barn. He curled up into the fetal position. His arms around Sarah or "Alicia" to keep warm reminding him of... His sister? His lover? Or his prodigy? It didn't matter. He had finally found her and he'd be damned if he would let her go. A poison green eye peered out through the hurricane. A half sneer on Aticus' thin lips revealing fangs, it is not the end it is only the beginning!

Next

The blood rain had stopped long-ago and there was now a reprieve from the hurricane, in the eye of the storm. The rats took advantage of the reprieve to find higher ground and to get dried off from the red sticky rain that fell down. Small grey rats in groups ran into the deserted streets, a pair of medium sized brown rats licking the droplets dry from one another and drenched, black rats with cunning eyes all trying to get dry. The drenched rats tried to shake off the sticky, wet substance. The wolf's blood parasite invaded the rat's circulatory systems. Absent of a human host the parasites mutated in the bodies of the rats, confused and ravenous they were scurrying back-and-forth toward dry land and into abandoned businesses and boarded up homes. The families that wanted to weather out the storm were held hostage by the floodwaters until they receded. Frightened and confused rats were lashing out, snapping and biting at everything that moved and infecting them with the mutated parasite, releasing poisons which ran through their bloodstream making them violently ill before succumbing to them and ultimately dying...

Coming soon

Wolves' blood: the plague

CPSIA information can be obtained at www.ICGtesting.com
Printed in the USA
BVOW03*0134171214

379709BV00008B/39/P